Spies Among Us

Spies Among Us

INCLUDING

THEY CAME TO BAGHDAD

N OR M?

MURDER IN MESOPOTAMIA

By Agatha Christie

DODD, MEAD & COMPANY
New York

Contents

They Came to Baghdad

I

CAPTAIN CROSBIE CAME out of the bank with the pleased air of one who has cashed a cheque and has discovered that there is just a little more in his account than he thought there was.

Captain Crosbie often looked pleased with himself. He was that kind of man. In figure he was short and stocky, with rather a red face and a bristling military moustache. He strutted a little when he walked. His clothes were, perhaps, just a trifle loud, and he was fond of a good story. He was popular among other men. A cheerful man, commonplace but kindly, unmarried. Nothing remarkable about him. There are heaps of Crosbies in the East.

The street into which Captain Crosbie emerged was called Bank Street for the excellent reason that most of the banks in the city were situated in it. Inside the bank it was cool and dark and rather musty. The predominant sound was of large quantities of typewriters clicking in the background.

Outside in Bank Street it was sunny and full of swirling dust, and the noises were terrific and varied. There were the persistent honking of motor horns, the cries of vendors of various wares. There were hot disputes between small groups of people who seemed ready to murder each other but were really fast friends; men, boys and children were selling every type of tree, sweetmeats, oranges and bananas, bath towels, combs, razor blades and other assorted merchandise carried rapidly through the streets on trays. There was also a perpetual and ever renewed sound of throat clearing and spitting, and above it the thin melancholy wail of men conducting donkeys and horses among the stream of motors and pedestrians shouting *"Balek-Balek!"*

It was eleven o'clock in the morning in the city of Baghdad.

Captain Crosbie stopped a rapidly running boy with an armful of newspapers and bought one. He turned the corner of Bank Street and came into Rashid Street which is the main street of Baghdad, running through it for about four miles, parallel with the river Tigris.

Captain Crosbie glanced at the headlines in the paper, tucked it under his arm, walked for about two hundred yards and then turned down a small alleyway and into a large Khan or Court. At the further side of this he pushed open a door with a brass plate and found himself in an office.

A neat young Iraqi clerk left his typewriter and came forward smiling a welcome.

"Good morning, Captain Crosbie. What can I do for you?"

"Mr. Dakin in his room? Good, I'll go through."

He passed through a door, up some very steep stairs and along a rather dirty passage. He knocked at the end door and a voice said "Come in."

It was a high rather bare room. There were an oil stove with a saucer of water on top of it, a long low cushioned seat with a little coffee table in front of it and a large rather shabby desk. The electric light was on and the daylight was carefully excluded. Behind the shabby desk was a rather shabby man, with a tired and indecisive face—the face of one who has not got on in the world and knows it and has ceased to care.

The two men, the cheerful self-confident Crosbie, and the melancholy fatigued Dakin, looked at each other.

Dakin said, "Hullo, Crosbie. Just in from Kirkuk?"

The other nodded. He shut the door carefully behind him. It was a shabby looking door, badly painted, but it had one rather unexpected quality; it fitted well, with no crevices and no space at the bottom.

It was, in fact, soundproof.

With the closing of the door, the personalities of both men changed ever so slightly. Captain Crosbie became less aggressive and cocksure. Mr. Dakin's shoulders drooped less, his manner was less hesitating. If anyone had been in the room listening they would have been surprised to find that Dakin was the man in authority.

"Any news, sir?" asked Crosbie.

"Yes." Dakin sighed. He had before him a paper which he had just been busy decoding. He dotted down two more letters and said:

"It's to be held in Baghdad."

Then he struck a match, set light to the paper and watched it burn. When it had smouldered to ashes, he blew gently. The ashes flew up and scattered.

"Yes," he said. "They've settled on Baghdad. Twentieth of next month. We're to 'preserve all secrecy.'"

"They've been talking about it in the Suq—for three days," said Crosbie drily.

The tall man smiled his weary smile.

"Top secret! No top secrets in the East, are there, Crosbie?"

"No, sir. If you ask me, there aren't any top secrets anywhere. During the war I often noticed a barber in London knew more than the High Command."

"It doesn't matter much in this case. If the meeting is arranged for Baghdad it will soon have to be made public. And then the fun—our particular fun—starts."

"Do you think it ever will take place, sir?" asked Crosbie sceptically. "Does the great Dictator" (thus disrespectfully did Captain Crosbie refer to the head of a Great European Power) "really mean to come?"

"I think he does this time, Crosbie," said Dakin thoughtfully. "Yes, I think so. And if the meeting comes off—comes off without a hitch—well, it might be the saving of—everything. If some kind of understanding could only be reached—" he broke off.

Crosbie still looked slightly sceptical. "Is—forgive me, sir—is understanding of any kind possible?"

"In the sense you mean, Crosbie, probably not! If it were just a bringing together of two men representing totally different ideologies, probably the whole thing would end as usual—in increased suspicion and misunderstanding. But there's the third element. If that fantastic story of Carmichael's is true—"

He broke off.

"But surely, sir, it can't be true. It's too fantastic!"

The other was silent for a few moments. He was seeing, very vividly, an earnest troubled face, hearing a quiet nondescript voice saying fantastic and unbelievable things. He was saying to himself, as he had said then, "Either my best, my most reliable man has gone mad; or else—this thing is true. . . ."

He said in the same thin melancholy voice:

"Carmichael believed it. Everything he could find out confirmed his hypothesis. He wanted to go there to find out more—to get proof . . . Whether I was wise to let him or not, I don't know. If he doesn't get back, it's only my story of what Carmichael told me, which again is a story of what someone told him. Is that enough? I don't think so. It is, as you say, such a fantastic story . . . But if the man himself is here, in Baghdad, on the twentieth, to tell his own story, the story of an eyewitness and to produce proof—"

"Proof?" said Crosbie sharply.

The other nodded.

"Yes, he's got proof."

"How do you know?"

"The agreed formula. The message came through Salah Hassan." He quoted carefully: *"A white camel with a load of oats is coming over the Pass."*

He paused and then went on:

"So Carmichael has got what he went to get, but he didn't get away unsuspected. They're on his trail. Whatever route he takes will be watched, and what is far more dangerous, they'll be waiting for him—here. First on the frontier. And if he succeeds in passing the frontier, there will be a cordon drawn round the Embassies and the Consulates. Look at this."

He shuffled amongst the papers on his desk and read out:

"An Englishman travelling in his car from Persia to Iraq shot dead—Supposedly by bandits. A Kurdish merchant travelling down from the hills ambushed and killed. Another Kurd, Abdul Hassan, suspected of being a cigarette smuggler, shot by the police. Body of a man, afterwards identified as an Armenian lorry driver, found on the Rowanduz road. All of them, mark you, of roughly the same description. Height, weight, hair, build, it corresponds with a description of Carmichael. They're taking no chances. They're out to get him. Once he's in Iraq the danger will be greater still. A gardener at the Embassy, a servant at the Consulate, an official at the Airport, in the Customs, at the Railway Stations . . . all hotels watched . . . A cordon, stretched tight."

Crosbie raised his eyebrows.

"You think it's as widespread as all that, sir?"

"I've no doubt of it. Even in our show there have been leakages. That's the worst of all. How am I to be sure that the measures we're adopting to get Carmichael safely into Baghdad aren't known already to the other side? It's one of the elementary moves of the game, as you know, to have someone in the pay of the other camp."

"Is there anyone you—suspect?"

Slowly Dakin shook his head.

Crosbie sighed.

"In the meantime," he said, "we carry on?"

"Yes."

"What about Crofton Lee?"

"He's agreed to come to Baghdad."

"Everyone's coming to Baghdad," said Crosbie. "Even the great Dictator, according to you, sir. But if anything should happen to the President—while he's here—the balloon will go up with a vengeance."

"Nothing must happen," said Dakin. "That's our business. To see it doesn't."

When Crosbie had gone Dakin sat bent over his desk. He murmured under his breath,

"They came to Baghdad. . . ."

On the blotting pad he drew a circle and wrote under it *Baghdad* —Then, dotted round it, he sketched a camel, an aeroplane, a steamer, a small puffing train—all converging on the circle. Then on the corner of the pad he drew a spider's web. In the middle of the spider's web he wrote a name: *Anna Scheele*. Underneath that he put a big query mark.

Then he took his hat, and left the office. As he walked along Rashid Street some man asked another who that was.

"That? Oh, that's Dakin. In one of the oil companies. Nice fellow, but never gets on. Too lethargic. They say he drinks. He'll never get anywhere. You've got to have drive to get on in this part of the world."

II

"Have you got the reports on the Krugenhorf property, Miss Scheele?"

"Yes, Mr. Morganthal."

Miss Scheele, cool and efficient, slipped the papers in front of her employer.

He grunted as he read.

"Satisfactory, I think."

"I certainly think so, Mr. Morganthal."

"Is Schwartz here?"

"He's waiting in the outer office."

"Have him sent right in now."

Miss Scheele pressed a buzzer—one of six.

"Will you require me, Mr. Morganthal?"

"No, I don't think so, Miss Scheele."

Anna Scheele glided noiselessly from the room.

She was a platinum blonde—but not a glamorous blonde. Her pale flaxen hair was pulled straight back from her forehead into a neat roll at the neck. Her pale blue intelligent eyes looked out on the world from behind strong glasses. Her face had neat small features, but was quite expressionless. She had made her way in the world not by her charm but by sheer efficiency. She could memorize anything, however complicated, and produce names, dates and times without having to refer to notes. She could organize the staff of a big office in such a way that it ran as by well oiled machinery. She was discretion itself and her energy, though controlled and disciplined, never flagged.

Otto Morganthal, head of the New York firm of Morganthal, Brown and Shipperke, international bankers, was well aware that to Anna Scheele he owed more than mere money could repay. He trusted her completely. Her memory, her experience, her judgment, her cool level head were invaluable. He paid her a large salary and would have made it a larger one, had she asked for it.

She knew not only the details of his business but the details of his private life. When he had consulted her in the matter of the second Mrs. Morganthal, she had advised divorce and suggested the exact amount of alimony. She had not expressed sympathy or curiosity. She was not, he would have said, that kind of woman. He didn't think she had any feelings, and it had never occurred to him to wonder what she thought about. He would indeed have been astonished if he had been told that she had any thoughts—other that is, than thoughts connected with Morganthal, Brown and Shipperke, and with the problems of Otto Morganthal.

So it was with complete surprise that he heard her say as she prepared to leave his office,

"I should like three weeks' absence from New York if I might have it, Mr. Morganthal. Starting from Tuesday next."

Staring at her, he said uneasily: "It will be awkward—very awkward."

"I don't think it will be too difficult, Mr. Morganthal. Miss Wygate is fully competent to deal with things. I shall leave her my notes and full instructions. Mr. Cornwall can attend to the Ascher Merger."

Still uneasily he asked:

"You're not ill, or anything?"

He couldn't imagine Miss Scheele being ill. Even germs respected Anna Scheele and kept out of her way.

"Oh no, Mr. Morganthal. I want to go to London to see my sister there."

"Your sister?" He didn't know she had a sister. He had never conceived of Miss Scheele as having any family or relations. She had never mentioned having any. And here she was, casually referring to a sister in London. She had been over in London with him last fall but she had never mentioned having a sister then.

With a sense of injury he said,

"I never knew you had a sister in England?"

Miss Scheele smiled very faintly.

"Oh yes, Mr. Morganthal. She is married to an Englishman connected with the British Museum. It is necessary for her to undergo a very serious operation. She wants me to be with her. I should like to go."

In other words, Otto Morganthal saw, she had made up her mind to go.

He said grumblingly, "All right, all right . . . Get back as soon as you can. I've never seen the market so jumpy. All this damned communism. War may break out at any moment. It's the only solution, I sometimes think. The whole country's riddled with it—riddled with it. And now the President's determined to go to this fool conference at Baghdad. It's a put-up job in my opinion. They're out to get him. Baghdad! Of all the outlandish places!"

"Oh I'm sure he'll be very well guarded," Miss Scheele said soothingly.

"They got the Shah of Persia last year, didn't they? They got Bernadotte in Palestine. It's madness—that's what it is—madness."

"But then," added Mr. Morganthal heavily, "all the world is mad."

II

VICTORIA JONES WAS sitting moodily on a seat in FitzJames Gardens. She was wholly given up to reflections—or one might almost say moralizations—on the disadvantages inherent in employing one's particular talents at the wrong moment.

Victoria was, like most of us, a girl with both qualities and defects. On the credit side she was generous, warm hearted and courageous. Her natural leaning towards adventure may be regarded as either meritorious or the reverse in this modern age which places the value of security high. Her principal defect was a tendency to tell lies at both opportune and inopportune moments. The superior fascination of fiction to fact was always irresistible to Victoria. She lied with fluency, ease and artistic fervour. If Victoria was late for an appointment (which was often the case) it was not sufficient for her to murmur an excuse of her watch having stopped (which actually was quite often the case) or of an unaccountably delayed bus. It would appear preferable to Victoria to tender the mendacious explanation that she had been hindered by an escaped elephant lying across a main bus route, or by a thrilling smash and grab raid in which she herself had played a part to aid the police. To Victoria an agreeable world would be one where tigers lurked in the Strand and dangerous bandits infested Tooting.

A slender girl, with an agreeable figure and first class legs, Victoria's features might actually have been described as plain. They were small and neat. But there was a piquancy about her, for "little indiarubber face," as one of her admirers had named her, could twist those immobile features into a startling mimicry of almost anybody.

It was this last named talent that had led to her present predicament. Employed as a typist by Mr. Greenholtz of Greenholtz, Simmon and Lederbetter, of Graysholme Street, London, W.C.2, Victoria had been whiling away a dull morning by entertaining the three other typists and the office boy with a vivid performance of Mrs. Greenholtz paying a visit to her husband's office. Secure in the knowledge that Mr. Greenholtz had gone round to his solicitors, Victoria let herself go.

"Why do you say we not have that Knole settee, daddee?" she demanded in a high whining voice. "Mrs. Dievtakis she have one in electric blue satin. You say it is money that is tight? But then why you take that blonde girl out dining and dancing—Ah! you think I do not know—and if you take that girl—then I have a settee and all done plum coloured and gold cushions. And when you say it is a business dinner you are a damn fool—yes—and come back with lipstick on your shirt. So I have the Knole settee and I order a fur cape—very nice—all like mink but not really mink and I get him very cheap and it is good business—"

The sudden failure of her audience—at first entranced, but now suddenly resuming work with spontaneous agreement caused Victoria to break off and swing round to where Mr. Greenholtz was standing in the doorway, observing her.

Victoria, unable to think of anything relevant to say, merely said "Oh!"

Mr. Greenholtz grunted.

Flinging off his overcoat Mr. Greenholtz proceeded to his private office and banged the door. Almost immediately his buzzer sounded, two shorts and a long. That was a summons for Victoria.

"It's for you, Jonesey," a colleague remarked unnecessarily, her eyes alight with the pleasure occasioned by the misfortunes of others. The other typists collaborated in this sentiment by ejaculating: "You're for it, Jones" and "On the mat, Jonesey." The office boy, an unpleasant child, contented himself with drawing a forefinger across his throat and uttering a sinister noise.

Victoria picked up her notebook and pencil and sailed into Mr. Greenholtz's office with such assurance as she could muster.

"You want me, Mr. Greenholtz?" she murmured, fixing a limpid gaze on him.

Mr. Greenholtz was rustling three pound notes and searching his pockets for coin of the realm.

"So there you are," he observed. "I've had about enough of you, young lady. Do you see any particular reason why I shouldn't pay you a week's salary in lieu of notice and pack you off here and now?"

Victoria (an orphan) had just opened her mouth to explain how the plight of a mother at this moment suffering a major operation had so demoralized her that she had become completely light headed, and how her small salary was all the aforesaid mother had to depend upon, when, taking an opening glance at Mr. Greenholtz's unwholesome face, she shut her mouth and changed her mind.

"I couldn't agree with you more," she said heartily and pleasantly. "I think you're absolutely right, if you know what I mean."

Mr. Greenholtz appeared slightly taken aback. He was not used to having his dismissals treated in this approving and congratulatory spirit. To conceal a slight discomfiture he sorted through the pile of coins on the desk in front of him. He then sought once more in his pockets.

"Ninepence short," he murmured gloomily.

"Never mind," said Victoria kindly. "Take yourself to the pictures or spend it on sweets."

"Don't seem to have any stamps, either."

"It doesn't matter. I never write letters."

"I could send it after you," said Mr. Greenholtz but without much conviction.

"Don't bother. What about a reference?" said Victoria.

Mr. Greenholtz's choler returned.

"Why the Hell should I give you a reference?" he demanded wrathfully.

"It's usual," said Victoria.

Mr. Greenholtz drew a piece of paper towards him and scrawled a few lines. He shoved it towards her.

"That do for you?"

Miss Jones has been with me two months as a shorthand typist. Her shorthand is inaccurate and she cannot spell. She is leaving owing to wasting time in office hours.

Victoria made a grimace.

"Hardly a recommendation," she observed.

"It wasn't meant to be," said Mr. Greenholtz.

"I think," said Victoria, "that you ought at least to say I'm honest, sober and respectable. I am, you know. And perhaps you might add that I'm discreet."

"Discreet?" barked Mr. Greenholtz.

Victoria met his gaze with an innocent stare.

"Discreet," she said gently.

Remembering sundry letters taken down and typed by Victoria, Mr. Greenholtz decided that prudence was the better part of rancour.

He snatched back the paper, tore it up and indited a fresh one.

"Miss Jones has been with me for two months as a shorthand typist. She is leaving owing to redundancy of office staff."

"How about that?"

"It could be better," said Victoria, "but it will do."

So it was that with a week's salary (less ninepence) in her bag Victoria was sitting in meditation upon a bench in FitzJames Gardens which are a triangular plantation of rather sad shrubs flanking a church and overlooked by a tall warehouse.

It was Victoria's habit on any day when it was not actually raining to purchase one cheese, and one lettuce and tomato sandwich at a Milk Bar and eat this simple lunch in these pseudo rural surroundings.

Today, as she munched meditatively, she was telling herself, not for the first time, that there was a time and place for everything—and that the office was definitely not the place for imitations of the boss's wife. She must, in future, curb the natural exuberance that led her to brighten up the performance of a dull job. In the meantime, she was free of Greenholtz, Simmon and Lederbetter, and the prospect of obtaining a situation elsewhere filled her with pleasurable anticipation. Victoria was always delighted when she was about to take up a new job. One never knew, she always felt, what might happen.

She had just distributed the last crumb of bread to three attentive sparrows who immediately fought each other with fury for it, when she became aware of a young man sitting at the other end of the seat. Victoria had noticed him vaguely already, but her mind full of good resolutions for the future, she had not observed him closely until now. What she now saw (out of the corner of her eye) she liked very much. He was a good looking young man, cherubically fair, but with a firm chin and extremely blue eyes which had been, she rather imagined, examining her with covert admiration for some time.

Victoria had no inhibitions about making friends with strange young men in public places. She considered herself an excellent judge of character and well able to check any manifestations of freshness on the part of unattached males.

She proceeded to smile frankly at him and the young man responded like a marionette when you pull the string.

"Hullo," said the young man. "Nice place, this. Do you often come here?"

"Nearly every day."

"Just my luck that I never came here before. Was that your lunch you were eating?"

"Yes."

"I don't think you eat enough. I'd be starving if I only had two sandwiches. What about coming along and having a sausage at the S.P.O. in Tottenham Court Road?"

"No, thanks. I'm quite all right. I couldn't eat any more now."

She rather expected that he would say: "Another day" but he did not. He merely sighed—then he said:

"My name's Edward, what's yours?"

"Victoria."

"Why did your people want to call you after a railway station?"

"Victoria isn't only a railway station," Miss Jones pointed out. "There's Queen Victoria as well."

"Mm, yes. What's your other name?"

"Jones."

"Victoria Jones," said Edward trying it over on his tongue. He shook his head. "They don't go together."

"You're quite right," said Victoria with feeling. "If I were Jenny it would be rather nice—Jenny Jones. But Victoria needs something with a bit more class to it. Victoria Sackville-West for instance. That's the kind of thing one needs. Something to roll round the mouth."

"You could tack something on to the Jones," said Edward with sympathetic interest.

"Bedford Jones."

"Carisbrooke Jones."

"St. Clair Jones."

"Lonsdale Jones."

This agreeable game was interrupted by Edward's glancing at his watch and uttering a horrified ejaculation.

"I must tear back to my blinking boss—er—what about you?"

"I'm out of a job. I was sacked this morning."

"Oh I say, I am sorry," said Edward with real concern.

"Well, don't waste sympathy, because I'm not sorry at all. For one thing, I'll easily get another job, and besides that, it was really rather fun."

And delaying Edward's return to duty still further, she gave him a spirited rendering of this morning's scene, reenacting her impersonation of Mrs. Greenholtz to Edward's immense enjoyment.

"You really are marvellous, Victoria," he said. "You ought to be on the stage."

Victoria accepted this tribute with a gratified smile and remarked that Edward had better be running along if he didn't want to get the sack himself.

"Yes—and I shouldn't get another job as easily as you will. It must be wonderful to be a good shorthand typist," said Edward with envy in his voice.

"Well actually I'm not a good shorthand typist," Victoria admitted frankly, "but fortunately even the lousiest of shorthand typists can get some sort of a job nowadays—at any rate an educational or charitable one—they can't afford to pay much and so they get people like me. I prefer the learned type of job best. These scientific names and places and terms are so frightful anyway that if you can't spell them properly it doesn't really shame you because nobody could. What's your job? I suppose you're out of one of the services. R.A.F.?"

"Good guess."

"Fighter pilot?"

"Right again. They're awfully decent about getting us jobs and all that, but you see, the trouble is, that we're not particularly brainy. I mean one didn't need to be brainy in the R.A.F. They put me in an office with a lot of files and figures and some thinking to do and I just folded up. The whole thing seemed utterly purposeless anyway. But there it is. It gets you down a bit to know that you're absolutely no good."

Victoria nodded sympathetically—Edward went on bitterly:

"Out of touch. Not in the picture any more. It was all right during the war—one could keep one's end up all right—I got the D.F.C. for instance—but now—well, I might as well write myself off the map."

"But there ought to be—"

Victoria broke off. She felt unable to put into words her conviction that those qualities that brought a D.F.C. to their owner should somewhere have their appointed place in the world of 1950.

"It's got me down, rather," said Edward. "Being no good at anything, I mean. Well—I'd better be pushing off—I say—would you mind —would it be most awful cheek—if I only could—"

As Victoria opened surprised eyes, stammering and blushing, Edward produced a small camera.

"I would like so awfully to have a snapshot of you. You see, I'm going to Baghdad tomorrow."

"To Baghdad?" exclaimed Victoria with lively disappointment.

"Yes. I mean I wish I wasn't—now. Earlier this morning I was quite bucked about it—it's why I took this job really—to get out of this country."

"What sort of job is it?"

"Pretty awful. Culture—poetry, all that sort of thing. A Dr. Rathbone's my boss. Strings of letters after his name, peers at you soulfully through pince-nez. He's terrifically keen on uplift and spreading it far and wide. He opens bookshops in remote places—he's starting one in Baghdad. He gets Shakespeare's and Milton's works translated into Arabic and Kurdish and Persian and Armenian and has them all on tap. Silly, I think, because you've got the British Council doing much the same thing all over the place. Still, there it is. It gives me a job so I oughtn't to complain."

"What do you actually do?" asked Victoria.

"Well, really it boils down to being the old boy's personal Yes-man and Dogsbody. Buy the tickets, make the reservations, fill up the passport forms, check the packing of all the horrid little poetic manuals, run round here, there, and everywhere. Then, when we get out there I'm supposed to fraternise—kind of glorified youth movement—all nations together in a united drive for uplift." Edward's tone became more and more melancholy. "Frankly, it's pretty ghastly, isn't it?"

Victoria was unable to administer much comfort.

"So you see," said Edward, "if you wouldn't mind awfully—one sideways and one looking right at me—oh I say, that's wonderful—"

The camera clicked twice and Victoria showed that purring complacence displayed by young women who know they have made an impression on an attractive member of the opposite sex.

"But it's pretty foul really, having to go off just when I've met you," said Edward. "I've half a mind to chuck it—but I suppose I couldn't do that at the last moment—not after all those ghastly forms and visas and everything. Wouldn't be a very good show, what?"

"It mayn't turn out as bad as you think," said Victoria consolingly.

"N-no," said Edward doubtfully. "The funny thing is," he added, "that I've got a feeling there's something fishy somewhere."

"Fishy?"

"Yes. Bogus. Don't ask me why. I haven't any reason. Sort of feeling one gets sometimes. Had it once about my port oil. Began fussing about the damned thing and sure enough there was a washer wedged in the spur-gear pump."

The technical terms in which this was couched made it quite unintelligible to Victoria, but she got the main idea.

"You think he's bogus—Rathbone?"

"Don't see how he can be. I mean he's frightfully respectable and learned and belongs to all these societies—and sort of hob-nobs with Archbishops and Principals of Colleges. No, it's just a feeling—Well, time will show. So long. I wish you were coming, too."

"So do I," said Victoria.

"What are you going to do?"

"Go round to St. Guildric's Agency in Gower Street and look for another job," said Victoria gloomily.

"Goodbye, Victoria. Partir, say mourir un peu," added Edward with a very British accent. "These French johnnies know their stuff. Our English chaps just maunder on about parting being a sweet sorrow— silly asses."

"Goodbye, Edward, good luck."

"I don't suppose you'll ever think about me again."

"Yes, I shall."

"You're absolutely different from any girl I've ever seen before—I only wish—" The clock chimed a quarter, and Edward said, "Oh Hell —I must fly—"

Retreating rapidly, he was swallowed up by the great maw of London. Victoria, remaining behind on her seat absorbed in medita- tion, was conscious of two distinct streams of thought.

One dealt with the theme of Romeo and Juliet. She and Edward, she felt, were somewhat in the position of that unhappy couple, al- though perhaps Romeo and Juliet had expressed their feelings in rather more high class language. But the position, Victoria thought, was the same. Meeting, instant attraction—frustration—two fond hearts thrust asunder. A remembrance of a rhyme once frequently recited by her old nurse came to her mind.

> *Jumbo said to Alice, "I love you."*
> *Alice said to Jumbo, "I don't believe you do;*
> *If you really loved me, as you say you do,*
> *You wouldn't go to America and leave me in the Zoo."*

Substitute Baghdad for America and there you were!

Victoria rose at last, dusting crumbs from her lap, and walked briskly out of FitzJames Gardens in the direction of Gower Street. Victoria had come to two decisions: the first was that (like Juliet) she loved this young man, and meant to have him.

The second decision that Victoria had come to was that as Edward would shortly be in Baghdad, the only thing to do was for her to go to Baghdad also. What was now occupying her mind was how this could be accomplished. That it could be accomplished somehow or other, Vic- toria did not doubt. She was a young woman of optimism and force of character.

Parting is such sweet sorrow appealed to her as a sentiment no more than it did to Edward.

"Somehow," said Victoria to herself, "I've got to get to Baghdad!"

III

THE SAVOY HOTEL welcomed Miss Anna Scheele with the *empressement* due to an old and valued client—they inquired after the health of Mr. Morganthal—and assured her that if her suite was not to her liking she had only to say so—for Anna Scheele represented *Dollars*.

Miss Scheele bathed, dressed, made a telephone call to a Kensington number and then went down in the lift. She passed through the revolving doors and asked for a taxi. It drew up and she got in and directed it to Cartier's in Bond Street.

As the taxi turned out of the Savoy approach into the Strand a little dark man who had been standing looking into a shop window suddenly glanced at his watch and hailed a taxi that was conveniently cruising past and which had been singularly blind to the hails of an agitated woman with parcels a moment or two previously.

The taxi followed along the Strand keeping the first taxi in sight. As they were both held up by the lights in going round Trafalgar Square, the man in the second taxi looked out of the left hand window and made a slight gesture with his hand. A private car, which had been standing in the side street by the Admiralty Arch started its engine and swung into the stream of traffic behind the second taxi.

The traffic had started on again. As Anna Scheele's taxi followed the stream of traffic going to the left into Pall Mall, the taxi containing the little dark man swung away to the right continuing round Trafalgar Square. The private car, a grey Standard, was now close behind Anna Scheele. It contained two passengers, a fair, rather vacant-looking young man at the wheel and a smartly dressed young woman beside him. The Standard followed Anna Scheele's taxi along Piccadilly and up Bond Street. Here for a moment it paused by the curb and the young woman got out.

She called brightly and conventionally,

"Thanks so much."

The car went on. The young woman walked along glancing every now and again into a window. A block held up the traffic. The young woman passed both the Standard and Anna Scheele's taxi. She arrived at Cartier's and went inside.

Anna Scheele paid off her taxi and went into the jeweller's. She spent some time looking at various pieces of jewellery. In the end she selected a sapphire and diamond ring. She wrote a cheque for it on a London bank. At the sight of the name on it, a little extra *empressement* came into the assistant's manner.

"Glad to see you in London again, Miss Scheele. Is Mr. Morganthal over?"

"No."

"I wondered. We have a very fine star sapphire here—I know he is interested in star sapphires. If you would care to see it?"

Miss Scheele expressed her willingness to see it, duly admired it, and promised to mention it to Mr. Morganthal.

She went out again into Bond Street, and the young woman who had been looking at clip earrings expressed herself as unable to make up her mind and emerged also.

The grey Standard car, having turned to the left in Grafton Street and gone down to Piccadilly, was just coming up Bond Street again. The young woman showed no signs of recognition.

Anna Scheele had turned into the Arcade. She entered a florist's. She ordered three dozen long stemmed roses, a bowl full of sweet big purple violets, a dozen sprays of white lilac, and a jar full of mimosa. She gave an address for them to be sent.

"That will be twelve pounds, eighteen shillings, madam."

Anna Scheele paid and went out. The young woman who had just come in asked the price of a bunch of primroses but did not buy them.

Anna Scheele crossed Bond Street and went along Burlington Street and turned into Savile Row. Here she entered the establishment of one of those tailors who, while catering essentially for men, occasionally condescend to cut a suit for certain favoured members of the feminine sex.

Mr. Bolford received Miss Scheele with the greeting accorded to a valued client, and the materials for a suit were considered.

"Fortunately, I can give you our export quality. When will you be returning to New York, Miss Scheele?"

"On the twenty-third."

"We can manage that nicely. By the clipper, I presume?"

"Yes."

"And how are things in America? They are very sadly here—very sadly indeed." Mr. Bolford shook his head like a doctor describing a patient. "No heart in things, if you know what I mean. And no one coming along who takes any pride in a good job of work. D'you know who will cut your suit, Miss Scheele? Mr. Lantwick—seventy-two years of age he is, and he's the only man I've got I can really trust to cut for our best people. All the others—"

Mr. Bolford's plump hands waved them away.

"Quality," he said. "That's what this country used to be renowned for. Quality! Nothing cheap, nothing flashy. When we try mass production we're no good at it, and that's a fact. That's your country's speciality, Miss Scheele. What we ought to stand for, and I say it again, is quality. Take time over things, and trouble, and turn out an article that no one in the world can beat. Now what day shall we say for the first fitting. This day week? At 11.30? Thank you very much."

Making her way through the archaic gloom round bales of material, Anna Scheele emerged into daylight again. She hailed a taxi and returned to the Savoy. A taxi that was drawn up on the opposite side of the street and which contained a little dark man, took the same route but did not turn into the Savoy. It drove round to the Embankment and there picked up a short plump woman who had recently emerged from the service entrance of the Savoy.

"What about it, Louisa? Been through her room?"

"Yes. Nothing."

Anna Scheele had lunch in the restaurant. A table had been kept for her by the window. The Maitre d'Hôtel inquired affectionately after the health of Otto Morganthal.

After lunch Anna Scheele took her key and went up to her suite. The bed had been made, fresh towels were in the bathroom and everything was spick and span. Anna crossed to the two light air cases that constituted her luggage, one was open, the other locked. She cast an eye over the contents of the unlocked one, than taking her keys from her purse she unlocked the other. All was neat, folded, as she had folded things, nothing had apparently been touched or disturbed. A brief case of leather lay on top. A small Leica camera and two rolls of films were in one corner. The films were still sealed and unopened. Anna ran her nail across the flap and pulled it up. Then she smiled, very gently. The single almost invisible blonde hair that had been there was there no longer. Deftly she scattered a little powder over the shiny leather of the brief case and blew it off. The brief case remained clear and shiny. There were no fingerprints. But that morning after patting a little brilliantine onto the smooth flaxen cap of her hair, she had handled the brief case. There should have been fingerprints on it, her own.

She smiled again.

"Good work," she said to herself. "But not quite good enough. . . ."

Deftly, she packed a small overnight case and went downstairs again. A taxi was called and she directed the driver to 17 Elmsleigh Gardens.

Elmsleigh Gardens was a quiet, rather dingy Kensington Square. Anna paid off the taxi and ran up the steps to the peeling front door. She pressed the bell. After a few minutes an elderly woman opened the door with a suspicious face which immediately changed to a beam of welcome.

"Won't Miss Elsie be pleased to see you! She's in the study at the back. It's only the thought of your coming that's been keeping her spirits up."

Anna went quickly along the dark hallway and opened the door at the far end. It was a small shabby, comfortable room with large worn leather armchairs. The woman sitting in one of them, jumped up.

"Anna, darling."

"Elsie."

The two women kissed each other affectionately.

"It's all arranged," said Elsie. "I go in tonight. I do hope—"

"Cheer up," said Anna. "Everything is going to be quite all right."

II

The small dark man in the raincoat entered a public call box at High Street Kensington Station, and dialled a number.

"Valhalla Gramophone Company?"

"Yes."

"Sanders here."

"Sanders of the River? What river?"

"River Tigris. Reporting on A.S. arrived this morning from New York. Went to Cartier's. Bought sapphire and diamond ring costing one hundred and twenty pounds. Went to florist's, Jane Kent—twelve pounds eighteen shillings' worth of flowers to be delivered at a nursing home in Portland Place. Ordered coat and skirt at Bolford and Avory's.

None of these firms known to have any suspicious contacts, but particular attention will be paid to them in future. A.S.'s room at Savoy gone through. Nothing suspicious found. Brief case in suitcase containing papers relating to Paper Merger with Wolfensteins. All aboveboard. Camera and two rolls of apparently unexposed films. Possibility of films being photostatic records, substituted other films for them, but original films reported upon as being straightforward unexposed films. A.S. took small overnight case and went to sister at 17 Elmsleigh Gardens. Sister entering nursing home in Portland Place this evening for internal operation. This confirmed from nursing home and also appointment book of surgeon. Visit of A.S. seems perfectly aboveboard. Showed no uneasiness or consciousness of being followed. Understand she is spending tonight at nursing home. Has kept on her room at the Savoy. Return passage to New York by clipper booked for twenty-third."

The man who called himself Sanders of the River paused and added a postscript off the record as it were.

"And if you ask what I think, it's all a mare's nest! Throwing money about, that's all she's doing. Twelve pounds eighteen on flowers! I ask you!"

IV

IT SAYS A good deal for the buoyancy of Victoria's temperament that the possibility of failing to attain her objective did not for a moment occur to her. Not for her the lines about ships that pass in the night. It was certainly unfortunate, when she had—well—frankly—fallen for an attractive young man, that that young man should prove to be just on the verge of departure to a place distant some three thousand miles. He might so easily have been going to Aberdeen or Brussels or even Birmingham.

That it should be Baghdad, thought Victoria, was just her luck! Never the less, difficult though it might be, she intended to get to Baghdad somehow or other. Victoria walked purposefully along Tottenham Court Road, revolving ways and means. Baghdad. What went on in Baghdad? According to Edward: "Culture." Could she, in some way, play up culture? Unesco? Unesco was always sending people here, there and everywhere, sometimes to the most delectable places. But these were usually, Victoria reflected, superior young women with university degrees who had got into the racket early on.

Victoria, deciding that first things came first, finally bent her steps to a travel agency, and there made her inquiries. There was no difficulty, it seemed, in travelling to Baghdad. You could go by air, by long sea to Basrah, by train to Marseilles and by boat to Beirut and across the desert by car. You could go via Egypt. You could go all the way by train if you were determined to do so, but visas were at present difficult and uncertain and were apt to have actually expired by the time you received them. Baghdad was in the sterling area and money therefore presented no difficulties. Not, that is to say, in the clerk's meaning of the word. What it all boiled down to was that there was no difficulty whatsoever in getting to Baghdad, so long as you had between sixty and a hundred pounds in cash.

As Victoria had at this moment three pounds ten (less ninepence), an extra twelve shillings, and five pounds in the P.O. Savings Bank, the simple and straightforward way was out of the question.

She made tentative queries as to a job as Air Hostess or stewardess, but these, she gathered, were highly coveted posts for which there was a waiting list.

Victoria next visited St. Guildric's Agency where Miss Spenser, sitting behind her efficient desk, welcomed her as one of those who were destined to pass through the office with reasonable frequency.

"Dear me, Miss Jones, not out of a post again. I really hoped this last one—"

"Quite impossible," said Victoria firmly. "I really couldn't begin to tell you what I had to put up with."

A pleasurable flush rose in Miss Spenser's pallid cheek.

"Not—" she began—"I do hope not—He didn't seem to me really that sort of a man—but of course he is a trifle gross—I do hope—"

"It's quite all right," said Victoria. She conjured up a pale brave smile. "I can take care of myself."

"Oh, of course, but it's the unpleasantness."

"Yes," said Victoria. "It is unpleasant. However—" she smiled bravely again.

Miss Spenser consulted her books.

"The St. Leonard's Assistance to Unmarried Mothers want a typist," said Miss Spenser. "Of course, they don't pay very much—"

"Is there any chance," asked Victoria brusquely, "of a post in Baghdad?"

"In Baghdad?" said Miss Spenser in lively astonishment.

Victoria saw she might as well have said in Kamskatka or at the South Pole.

"I should very much like to get to Baghdad," said Victoria.

"I hardly think—in a secretary's post you mean?"

"Anyhow," said Victoria. "As a nurse or a cook, or looking after a lunatic. Anyway at all."

Miss Spenser shook her head.

"I'm afraid I can't hold out much hope. There was a lady in yesterday with two little girls who was offering a passage to Australia."

Victoria waved away Australia.

She rose. "If you did hear of anything. Just the fare out—that's all I need." She met the curiosity in the other woman's eye by explaining —"I've got—er—relations out there. And I understand there are plenty of well paid jobs. But of course, one has to get there first."

"Yes," repeated Victoria to herself as she walked away from St. Guildric's Bureau. "One has to get there."

It was an added annoyance to Victoria that, as is customary, when one has had one's attention suddenly focussed on a particular name or subject, everything seemed to have suddenly conspired to force the thought of Baghdad on to her attention.

A brief paragraph in the evening paper she bought stated that Dr. Pauncefoot Jones, the well known archaeologist, had started excavation on the ancient city of Murik, situated a hundred and twenty miles from Baghdad. An advertisement mentioned Shipping Lines to Basrah (and thence by train to Baghdad, Mosul etc.). In the newspaper that lined her stocking drawer, a few lines of print about students in Baghdad leapt to her eyes. *The Thief of Baghdad* was on at the local cinema, and in the high class highbrow bookshop into whose window she always gazed, a New Biography of Haroun al Rashid, Caliph of Baghdad, was prominently displayed.

The whole world, it seemed to her, had suddenly become Baghdad conscious. And until that afternoon at approximately 1.45 she had, for all intents and purposes, never heard of Baghdad, and certainly never thought about it.

The prospects of getting there were unsatisfactory, but Victoria had no idea of giving up. She had a fertile brain and the optimistic outlook that if you want to do a thing there is always some way of doing it.

She employed the evening in drawing up a list of possible approaches. It ran:

Insert advertisement?
Try Foreign Office?
Try Iraq Legation?
What about Date firms?
Ditto Shipping firms?
British Council?
Selfridge's Information Bureau?
Citizen's Advice Bureau?

None of them, she was forced to admit, seemed very promising. She added to the list:

Somehow or other, get hold of a hundred pounds?

II

The intense mental efforts of concentration that Victoria had made overnight, and possibly the subconscious satisfaction at no longer having to be punctually in the office at nine a.m., made Victoria oversleep herself.

She awoke at five minutes past ten, and immediately jumped out of bed and began to dress. She was just passing a final comb through her rebellious dark hair when the telephone rang.

Victoria reached for the receiver.

A positively agitated Miss Spenser was at the other end.

"So glad to have caught you, my dear. Really the most amazing coincidence."

"Yes?" cried Victoria.

"As I say, really a startling coincidence. A Mrs. Hamilton Clipp—travelling to Baghdad in three days' time—has broken her arm—needs someone to assist her on journey—I rang you up at once. Of course I don't know if she has also applied to any other agencies—"

"I'm on my way," said Victoria. "Where is she?"

"The Savoy."

"And what's her silly name? Tripp?"

"Clipp, dear. Like a paper clip, but with two P's—I can't think why, but she's an American," ended Miss Spenser as if that explained everything.

"Mrs. Clipp at the Savoy."

"Mr. and Mrs. Hamilton Clipp. It was actually the husband who rang up."

"You're an angel," said Victoria. "Goodbye."

She hurriedly brushed her suit and wished it were slightly less shabby, recombed her hair so as to make it seem less exuberant and more in keeping with the role of ministering angel and experienced traveller. Then she took out Mr. Greenholtz's recommendation and shook her head over it.

We must do better than that, said Victoria.

From a 19 bus, Victoria alighted at Green Park, and entered the Ritz Hotel. A quick glance over the shoulder of a woman reading in the bus had proved rewarding. Entering the writing room Victoria wrote herself some generous lines of praise from Lady Cynthia Bradbury who had been announced as having just left England for East Africa . . . "*excellent in illness*," wrote Victoria, "*and most capable in every way. . . .*"

Leaving the Ritz she crossed the road and walked a short way up Albemarle Street until she came to Balderton's Hotel, renowned as the haunt of the higher clergy and of old fashioned dowagers up from the country.

In less dashing handwriting, and making neat small Greek e's she wrote a recommendation from the Bishop of Llangow.

Thus equipped, Victoria caught a No. 9 bus and proceeded to the Savoy.

At the reception desk she asked for Mrs. Hamilton Clipp and gave her name as coming from St. Guildric's Agency. The clerk was just about to pull the telephone towards him when he paused, looked across, and said,

"That is Mr. Hamilton Clipp now."

Mr. Hamilton Clipp was an immensely tall and very thin grey haired American of kindly aspect and slow deliberate speech.

Victoria told him her name and mentioned the Agency.

"Why now, Miss Jones, you'd better come right up and see Mrs. Clipp. She's still in our suite. I fancy she's interviewing some other young lady, but she may have gone by now."

Cold panic clutched at Victoria's heart.

Was it to be so near and yet so far?

They went up in the lift to the third floor.

As they walked along the deep carpeted corridor, a young woman came out of a door at the far end and came towards them. Victoria had a kind of hallucination that it was herself who was approaching. Possibly, she thought, because the young woman's tailor made suit was so exactly what she would have liked to be wearing herself. "And it would fit me too. I'm just her size. How I'd like to tear it off her," thought Victoria with a reversion to primitive female savagery.

The young woman passed them. A small velvet hat perched on the side of her fair hair partially hid her face, but Mr. Hamilton Clipp turned to look after her with an air of surprise.

"Well now," he said to himself. "Who'd have thought of that? Anna Scheele."

He added in an explanatory way,

"Excuse me, Miss Jones. I was surprised to recognise a young lady whom I saw in New York only a week ago, secretary to one of our big International bankers—"

He stopped as he spoke at a door in the corridor. The key was hanging in the lock and with a brief tap, Mr. Hamilton Clipp opened the door and stood aside for Victoria to precede him into the room.

Mrs. Hamilton Clipp was sitting on a high backed chair near the window and jumped up as they came in. She was a short bird-like sharp-eyed little woman. Her right arm was encased in plaster.

Her husband introduced Victoria.

"Why, it's all been most unfortunate," exclaimed Mrs. Clipp breathlessly. "Here we were, with a full itinerary, and enjoying London and all our plans made and my passage booked. I'm going out to pay a visit to my married daughter in Iraq, Miss Jones. I've not seen her for nearly two years. And then what do I do but take a crash—as a matter of fact, it was actually in Westminster Abbey—down some stone steps—and there I was. They rushed me to Hospital and they've set it, and all things considered it's not too uncomfortable—but there it is, I'm kind of helpless, and however I'd manage travelling, I don't know. And George here, is just tied up with business, and simply can't get away for at least another three weeks. He suggested that I should take a nurse along with me—but after all, once I'm out there I don't need a nurse hanging around, Sadie can do all that's necessary—and it means paying her fare back as well, and so I thought I'd ring up the Agencies and see if I couldn't find someone who'd be willing to come along just for the fare out."

"I'm not exactly a nurse," said Victoria managing to imply that that was practically what she was. "But I've had a good deal of experience of nursing." She produced the first testimonial. "I was with Lady

Cynthia Bradbury for over a year. And if you should want any correspondence or secretarial work done, I acted as my uncle's secretary
for some months. My uncle," said Victoria modestly, "is the Bishop of
Llangow."

"So your uncle's a Bishop. Dear me, how interesting."

Both the Hamilton Clipps were, Victoria thought, decidedly impressed. And so they should be after the trouble she had taken!

Mrs. Hamilton Clipp handed the two testimonials to her husband.
"It really seems quite wonderful," she said reverently. "Quite Provi-
dential. It's an answer to prayer."

Which, indeed, was exactly what it was, thought Victoria.

"You're taking up a position of some kind out there? Or joining a
relative?" asked Mrs. Hamilton Clipp.

In the flurry of manufacturing testimonials, Victoria had quite forgotten that she might have to account for her reasons for travelling
to Baghdad. Caught unprepared, she had to improvise rapidly. The
paragraph she had read yesterday came to her mind.

"I'm joining my uncle out there. Dr. Pauncefoot Jones," she
explained.

"Indeed? The archaeologist?"

"Yes." For one moment Victoria wondered whether she were perhaps endowing herself with too many distinguished uncles. "I'm terribly interested in his work, but of course I've no special qualifications
so it was out of the question for the Expedition to pay my fare out.
They're not too well off for funds. But if I can get out on my own, I
can join them and make myself useful."

"It must be very very interesting work," said Mr. Hamilton Clipp,
"and Mesopotamia is certainly a great field for archaeology."

"I'm afraid," said Victoria turning to Mrs. Clipp, "that my uncle the
Bishop is up in Scotland this moment. But I can give you his secretary's
telephone number. She is staying in London at the moment. Pimlico
87693—one of the Fulham Palace extensions. She'll be there any time
from (Victoria's eyes slid to the clock on the mantelpiece) 11.30 on-
wards if you would like to ring her up and ask about me."

"Why, I'm sure—" Mrs. Clipp began, but her husband interrupted.

"Time's very short, you know. This plane leaves day after tomorrow.
Now have you got a passport, Miss Jones?"

"Yes." Victoria felt thankful that owing to a short holiday trip to
France last year, her passport was up to date. "I brought it with me
in case," she added.

"Now that's what I call businesslike," said Mr. Clipp approvingly. If any other candidate had been in the running, she had obviously dropped out now. Victoria with her good recommendations, and her uncles, and her passport on the spot had successfully made the grade.

"You'll want the necessary visas," said Mr. Clipp, taking the passport. "I'll run round to our friend Mr. Burgeon in American Express, and he'll get everything fixed up. Perhaps you'd better call round this afternoon, so you can sign whatever's necessary."

This Victoria agreed to do.

As the door of the apartment closed behind her, she heard Mrs. Hamilton Clipp say to Mr. Hamilton Clipp—

"Such a nice straightforward girl. We really are in luck."

Victoria had the grace to blush.

She hurried back to her flat and sat glued to the telephone prepared to assume the gracious refined accents of a Bishop's secretary in case Mrs. Clipp should seek confirmation of her capability. But Mrs. Clipp had obviously been so impressed by Victoria's straightforward personality that she was not going to bother with these technicalities. After all, the engagement was only for a few days as a travelling companion.

In due course, papers were filled up and signed, the necessary visas were obtained and Victoria was bidden to spend the final night at the Savoy so as to be on hand to help Mrs. Clipp get off at 7 a.m. on the following morning for Airways House and Heathrow Aerodrome.

V

THE BOAT THAT had left the marshes two days before paddled gently along the Shatt el Arab. The stream was swift and the old man who was propelling the boat needed to do very little. His movements were gentle and rhythmic. His eyes were half closed. Almost under his breath he sang very softly, a sad unending Arab chant

ASRI BI LEL YA YAMALI
HADHI ALEK YA IBN ALI

Thus, on innumerable other occasions, had Abdul Suleiman of the Marsh Arabs come down the river to Basrah. There was another man in the boat, a figure often seen nowadays, with a pathetic mingling of West and East in his clothing. Over his long robe of striped cotton he wore a discarded khaki tunic, old and stained and torn. A faded red knitted scarf was tucked into the ragged coat. His head showed again the dignity of the Arab dress, the inevitable keffiyah of black and white held in place by the black silk *agal*. His eyes, unfocussed in a wide stare, looked out blearily over the river bund. Presently he, too, began to hum in the same key and tone. He was a figure like thousands of other figures in the Mesopotamia landscape. There was nothing to show that he was an Englishman, and that he carried with him a secret that influential men in almost every country in the world were striving to intercept and to destroy, along with the man who carried it.

His mind went hazily back over the last weeks. The ambush in the mountains. The ice cold of the snow coming over the Pass. The caravan of camels. The four days spent trudging on foot over bare desert in company with two men carrying a portable "cinema." The days in the black tent and the journeying with the Aneizeh tribe, old friends of his. All difficult, all fraught with danger—slipping again and again through the cordon spread out to look for him and intercept him.

"Henry Carmichael. British agent. Age about thirty. Brown hair, dark eyes, five foot ten. Speaks Arabic, Kurdish, Persian, Armenian, Hindustani, Turkish and many mountain dialects. Befriended by the tribesmen. Dangerous."

Carmichael had been born in Kashgar where his father was a Government official. His childish tongue had lisped various dialects and patois—his nurses, and later his bearers, had been natives of many different races. In nearly all the wild places of the Middle East he had friends.

Only in the cities and the towns did his contacts fail him. Now, approaching Basrah, he knew that the critical moment of his mission had come. Sooner or later, he had got to re-enter the civilised zone. Though Baghdad was his ultimate destination, he had judged it wise not to approach it direct. In every town in Iraq facilities were awaiting him, carefully discussed and arranged many months beforehand. It had had to be left to his own judgment where he should, so to speak, make his landing ground. He had sent no word to his superiors, even through the indirect channels where he could have done so. It was safer thus. The easy plan, the aeroplane waiting at the appointed rendezvous—had failed, as he had suspected it would fail. That rendezvous had been known to his enemies. Leakage! Always that deadly, that incomprehensible, leakage.

And so it was that his apprehensions of danger were heightened. Here in Basrah, in sight of safety, he felt instinctively sure that the danger would be greater than during the wild hazards of his journey. And to fail at the last lap—that would hardly bear thinking about.

Rhythmically pulling at his oars, the old Arab murmured without turning his head.

"The moment approaches, my son. May Allah prosper you."

"Do not tarry long in the city, my father. Return to the marshes. I would not have harm befall you."

"That is as Allah decrees. It is in his hands."

"In shâ Allâh," the other repeated.

For a moment he longed intensely to be a man of Eastern and not of Western blood. Not to worry over the chances of success or of failure, not to calculate again and again the hazards, repeatedly asking himself if he had planned wisely and with forethought. To throw responsibility on the All Merciful, the All Wise. In shâ Allâh, I shall succeed!

Even saying the words over to himself he felt the calmness and the fatalism of the country overwhelming him and he welcomed it. Now, in a few moments, he must step from the haven of the boat, walk the streets of the city, run the gauntlet of keen eyes. Only by feeling as well as looking like an Arab could he succeed.

The boat turned gently into the water-way that ran at right angles to the river. Here all kinds of river craft were tied up, and other boats were coming in before and after them. It was a lovely, almost Venetian scene; the boats with their high scrolled prows and the soft faded colours of their paintwork. There were hundreds of them tied up close alongside each other.

The old man asked softly,

"The moment has come. There are preparations made for you?"

"Yes, indeed, my plans are set. The hour has come for me to leave."

"May God make your path straight, and may he lengthen the years of your life."

Carmichael gathered his striped skirts about him and went up the slippery stone steps to the wharf above.

All about him were the usual waterside figures. Small boys, orange sellers squatting down by their trays of merchandise. Sticky squares of cakes and sweetmeats, trays of bootlaces and cheap combs and pieces of elastic. Contemplative strollers, spitting raucously from time to time, wandering along with their beads clicking in their hands. On the opposite side of the street where the shops were and the banks, busy young *effendis* walked briskly in European suits of a slightly purplish tinge. There were Europeans, too, English and foreigners. And nowhere was there interest shown, or curiosity, because one amongst fifty or so Arabs had just climbed onto the wharf from a boat.

Carmichael strolled along very quietly, his eyes taking in the scene with just the right touch of childlike pleasure in his surroundings. Every now and then he hawked and spat, not too violently, just to be in the picture. Twice he blew his nose with his fingers.

And so, the stranger come to town, he reached the bridge at the top of the canal, and turned over it and passed into the Suq.

Here all was noise and movement. Energetic tribesmen strode along, pushing others out of their way—laden donkeys made their way along, their drivers calling out raucously. *Balek-balek* . . . Children quarrelled and squealed and ran after Europeans calling hopefully, Baksheesh, madame. Baksheesh. Meskin-meskin . . .

Here the produce of the west and the east were equally for sale, side by side. Aluminum saucepans, cups and saucers and teapots, hammered copper ware, silverwork from Amara, cheap watches, enamel mugs, embroideries and gay patterned rugs from Persia. Brass bound chests from Kuwait, secondhand coats and trousers and children's woolly cardigans. Local quilted bedcovers, painted glass lamps, stacks of clay water jars and pots. All the cheap merchandise of civilisation together with the native products.

All as normal and as usual. After his long sojourn in the wilder spaces, the bustle and confusion seemed strange to Carmichael, but it was all as it should be, he could detect no jarring note, no sign of interest in his presence. And yet, with the instinct of one who has for long years known what it is to be a hunted man, he felt a growing uneasiness—a vague sense of menace. He could detect nothing amiss. No one had looked at him. No one, he was almost sure, was following him or keeping him under observation. Yet he had that indefinable certainty of danger.

He moved up a narrow dark turning, again to the right, then to the left. Here, among the small booths, he came to the opening of a khan, and stepped through the doorway into the court. Various shops were all round it. Carmichael went to one where *ferwahs* were hanging—the sheepskin coats of the North. He stood there handling them tentatively. The owner of the store was offering coffee to a customer, a tall bearded man of fine presence, who wore green round his fez, showing him to be a Hajji who had been to Mecca.

Carmichael stood there fingering the *ferwah.*

"Besh hadha?" he asked.

"Seven dinars."

"Too much."

The Hajji said, "You will deliver the carpets at my Khan?"

"Without fail," said the merchant. "You start tomorrow?"

"At dawn for Kerbela."

"It is my city, Kerbela," said Carmichael. "It is fifteen years now since I have seen the Tomb of the Hussein."

"It is a holy city," said the Hajji.

The shopkeeper said over his shoulder to Carmichael,

"There are cheaper *ferwahs* in the inner room."

"A white *ferwah* from the north is what I need."

"I have such a one in the farther room."

The merchant indicated the door set back in the inner wall.

The ritual had gone according to pattern—a conversation such as might be heard any day in any Suq—but the sequence was exact—the keywords all there—Kerbela—white *ferwah.*

Only, as Carmichael passed to cross the room and enter the inner enclosure, he raised his eyes to the merchant's face—and knew instantly that the face was not the one he expected to see. Though he had seen this particular man only once before, his keen memory was not at fault. There was a resemblance, a very close resemblance, but it was not the same man.

He stopped. He said, his tone one of mild surprise,

"Where, then, is Salah Hassan?"

"He was my brother. He died three days ago. His affairs are in my hands."

Yes, this was probably a brother. The resemblance was very close. And it was possible that the brother was also employed by the department. Certainly the responses had been correct. Yet it was with an increased awareness that Carmichael passed through into the dim inner chamber. Here again was merchandise piled on shelves, coffee pots and sugar hammers of brass and copper, old Persian silver, heaps of embroideries, folded abas, enamelled Damascus trays and coffee sets.

A white *ferwah* lay carefully folded by itself on a small coffee table.

Carmichael went to it and picked it up. Underneath it was a set of European clothes, a worn, slightly flashy business suit. The pocket book with money and credentials was already in the breast pocket. An unknown Arab had entered the store; Mr. Walter Williams of Messrs. Cross and Co. Importers and Shipping agents would emerge and would keep certain appointments made for him in advance. There was, of course, a real Mr. Walter Williams—it was as careful as that— a man with a respectable open business past. All according to plan. With a sigh of relief Carmichael started to unbutton his ragged Army jacket. All was well.

If a revolver had been chosen as the weapon, Carmichael's mission would have failed then and there. But there are advantages in a knife— noticeably noiselessness.

On the shelf in front of Carmichael was a big copper coffee pot and that coffee pot had been recently polished to the order of an American tourist who was coming in to collect it. The gleam of the knife was reflected in that shining rounded surface—a whole picture, distorted but apparent, was reflected there. The man slipping through the hangings behind Carmichael, the long curved knife he had just pulled from beneath his garments. In another moment that knife would have been buried in Carmichael's back.

Like a flash Carmichael wheeled round. With a low flying tackle he brought the other to the ground. The knife flew across the room. Carmichael disentangled himself quickly, leaped over the other's body, rushed through the outer room where he caught a glimpse of the merchant's startled malevolent face and the placid surprise of the fat Hajji. Then he was out, across the Khan, back into the crowded Suq, turning first one way, then another, strolling again now, showing no signs of haste in a country where to hurry is to appear unusual.

And walking thus, almost aimlessly, stopping to examine a piece of stuff, to feel a texture, his brain was working with furious activity. The machinery had broken down! Once more, he was on his own, in hostile country. And he was disagreeably aware of the significance of what had just happened.

It was not only the enemies on his trail he had to fear. Nor was it the enemies guarding the approaches to civilisation. There were enemies to fear within the system. For the passwords had been known, the responses had come pat and correct. The attack had been timed for exactly the moment when he had been lulled into security. Not surprising, perhaps, that there was treachery from within. It must have always been the aim of the enemy to introduce one or more of their own number into the system. Or, perhaps, to buy the man that they needed. Buying a man was easier than one might think—one could buy with other things than money.

Well, no matter how it had come about, there it was. He was on the run—back on his own resources. Without money, without the help of a new personality, and his appearance known. Perhaps at this very moment he was being quietly followed.

He did not turn his head. Of what use would that be? Those who followed were not novices at the game.

Quietly, aimlessly, he continued to stroll. Behind his listless manner he was reviewing various possibilities. He came out of the Suq at last and crossed the little bridge over the canal. He walked on until he saw the big painted hatchment over the doorway and the legend: British Consulate.

He looked up the street and down. No one seemed to be paying the least attention to him. Nothing, it appeared, was easier than just to step into the British Consulate.

He thought, for a moment, of a mousetrap, an open mousetrap with its enticing piece of cheese. That, too, was easy and simple for the mouse . . .

Well, the risk had to be taken. He didn't see what else he could do. He went through the doorway.

VI

RICHARD BAKER SAT in the outer office of the British Consulate waiting until the Consul was disengaged.

He had come ashore from the *Indian Queen* that morning and seen his baggage through the customs. It consisted almost entirely of books. Pyjamas and shirts were strewed among them, rather as an afterthought.

The *Indian Queen* had arrived on time and Richard, who had allowed a margin of two days, since small cargo boats such as the *Indian Queen* were frequently delayed, had now two days in hand before he need proceed, via Baghdad, to his ultimate destination, Tell Aswad, the site of the ancient city of Murik.

His plans were already made as to what to do with these two days. A certain reputed mound containing ancient remains at a spot near the sea shore in Kuwait had long excited his curiosity. This was a heaven sent opportunity to investigate same.

He drove to the Airport Hotel and inquired as to the methods of getting to Kuwait. A plane left at ten o'clock the following morning, he was told, and he could return the next day. Everything therefore was plain sailing. There were, of course, the inevitable formalities, exit visa and visa for Kuwait. For these he would have to repair to the British Consulate. The Consul General at Basrah, Mr. Clayton, Richard had met some years previously in Persia. It would be pleasant, Richard thought, to meet him again.

The Consulate had several entrances. A main gate for cars. Another small gate leading out from the garden to the road that lay alongside the Shatt el Arab. The business entrance to the Consulate was in the main street. Richard went in, gave his card to the man on duty, was told the Consul General was engaged at the moment but would soon be free, and was shown into a small waiting room to the left of the passage which ran straight through from the entrance to the garden beyond.

There were several people already in the waiting room. Richard hardly glanced at them. He was, in any case, seldom interested by members of the human race. A fragment of antique pottery was always more exciting to him than a mere human being born somewhere in the twentieth century A.D.

He allowed his thoughts to dwell pleasantly on some aspects of the Mari letters and the movements of the Benjaminite tribes in 1750 B.C.

It would be hard to say exactly what awoke him to a vivid sense of the present and of his fellow human beings. It was, first, an uneasiness, a sense of tension. It came to him, he thought, though he could not be sure, through his nose. Nothing you could diagnose in concrete terms—but it was there, unmistakable, taking him back to days in the late war. One occasion in particular when he, and two others, had been parachuted from a plane, and had waited in the small cold hours of dawn for the moment to do their stuff. A moment when morale was low, when the full hazards of the undertaking were clearly perceived, a moment of dread lest one might not be adequate, a shrinking of the flesh. The same acrid, almost imperceptible tang in the air.

The smell of fear . . .

For some moments, this registered only subconsciously. Half of his mind still obstinately strove to focus itself B.C. But the pull of the present was too strong.

Someone in this small room was in deadly fear . . .

He looked round. An Arab in a ragged khaki tunic, his fingers idly slipping over the amber beads he held. A stoutish Englishman with a grey moustache—the commercial traveller type—who was jotting down figures in a small notebook and looking absorbed and important. A tired looking man, very dark skinned, who was leaning back in a reposeful attitude, his face placid and uninterested. A man who looked like an Iraqi clerk. An elderly Persian in flowing snowy robes. They all seemed quite unconcerned.

The clicking of the amber beads fell into a definite rhythm. It seemed, in an odd way, familiar. Richard jerked himself to attention. He had been nearly asleep. Short long—long—short—that was Morse—definite Morse signalling. He was familiar with Morse; part of his job during the war had dealt with signalling. He could read it easily enough. *OWL. F.L.O.R.E.A.T. E.T.O.N.A.* What the devil! Yes, that was it. It was being repeated *Floreat Etona*. Tapped out (or rather clicked out) by a ragged Arab. Hullo, what was this? "Owl. Eton. Owl."

His own nickname at Eton—where he had been sent with an unusually large and solid pair of spectacles.

He looked across the room at the Arab, noting every detail of his appearance—the striped robe—the old khaki tunic—the ragged hand-knitted red scarf full of dropped stitches. A figure such as you saw hundreds of on the waterfront. The eyes met his vacantly with no sign of recognition. But the beads continued to click.

Fakir here. Stand by. Trouble.

Fakir? *Fakir?* Of course! Fakir Carmichael! A boy who had been born or who had lived in some outlandish part of the world—Turkestan, Afghanistan?—

Richard took out his pipe. He took an exploratory pull at it—peered into the bowl and then tapped it on an adjacent ashtray: *Message received.*

After that, things happened very fast. Later, Richard was at pains to sort them out.

The Arab in the torn army jacket got up and crossed towards the door. He stumbled as he was passing Richard, his hand went out and clutched Richard to steady himself. Then he righted himself, apologised and moved towards the door.

It was so surprising and happened so quickly that it seemed to Richard like a cinema scene rather than real life. The stout commercial traveller dropped his notebook and tugged at something in his coat pocket. Because of his plumpness and the tight fit of the coat, he was a second or two in getting it out and in that second or two Richard acted. As the man brought the revolver up, Richard struck it out of his hand. It went off and a bullet buried itself in the floor.

The Arab had passed through the doorway and had turned towards the Consul's office, but he paused suddenly, and turning he ran swiftly the other way to the door by which he had entered and into the busy street.

The kavass ran to Richard's side where he stood holding the stout man's arm. Of the other occupants of the room, the Iraqi clerk was dancing excitedly on his feet, the dark thin man was staring and the elderly Persian gazed into space unmoved.

Richard said:

"What the devil are you doing, brandishing a revolver like that?"

There was just a moment's pause, and then the stout man said in a plaintive cockney voice,

"Sorry, old man. Absolute accident. Just clumsy."

"Nonsense. You were going to shoot at that Arab fellow who's just run out."

"No, no, old man, not shoot him. Just give him a fright. Recognised him suddenly as a fellow who swindled me over some antikas. Just a bit of fun."

Richard Baker was a fastidious soul who disliked publicity of any kind. His instincts were to accept the explanation at its face value. After all, what could he prove? And would old Fakir Carmichael thank him for making a song and dance about the matter? Presumably if he were on some hush-hush, cloak and dagger business he would not.

Richard relaxed his grasp on the man's arm. The fellow was sweating, he noticed.

The kavass was talking excitedly. It was very wrong, he was saying, to bring firearms into the British Consulate. It was not allowed. The Consul would be very angry.

"I apologise," said the fat man. "Little accident—that's all." He thrust some money into the kavass's hand who pushed it back again indignantly.

"I'd better get out of this," said the stout man. "I won't wait to see the Consul." He thrust a card suddenly on Richard. "That's me and I'm at the Airport Hotel if there's any fuss, but actually it was a pure accident. Just a joke if you know what I mean."

Reluctantly, Richard watched him walk with an uneasy swagger out of the room and turn towards the street.

He hoped he had done right, but it was a difficult thing to know what to do when one was as much in the dark as he was.

"Mr. Clayton, he is disengaged now," said the kavass.

Richard followed the man along the corridor. The open circle of sunlight at the end grew larger. The Consul's room was on the right at the extreme end of the passage.

Mr. Clayton was sitting behind his desk. He was a quiet grey haired man with a thoughtful face.

"I don't know whether you remember me?" said Richard. "I met you in Teheran two years ago."

"Of course. You were with Dr. Pauncefoot Jones, weren't you? Are you joining him again this year?"

"Yes. I'm on my way there now, but I've got a few days to spare, and I rather wanted to run down to Kuwait. There's no difficulty, I suppose?"

"Oh no. There's a plane tomorrow morning. It's only about an hour and a half. I'll wire to Archie Gaunt—he's the President there. He'll put you up. And we can put you up here for the night."

Richard protested slightly.

"Really—I don't want to bother you and Mrs. Clayton. I can go to the hotel."

"The Airport Hotel's very full. We'd be delighted to have you here. I know my wife would like to meet you again. At the moment—let me see—we've got Crosbie of the Oil Company and some young sprig of Dr. Rathbone's who's down here clearing some cases of books through the customs. Come upstairs and see Rosa—"

He got up and escorted Richard out through the door and into the sunlit garden. A flight of steps led up to the living quarters of the Consulate.

Gerald Clayton pushed open the wire door at the top of the steps and ushered his guest into a long dim hallway with attractive rugs on the floor and choice examples of furniture on either side. It was pleasant coming into the cold dimness after the glare outside.

Clayton called, "Rosa, Rosa," and Mrs. Clayton whom Richard remembered as a buoyant personality with abounding vitality came out of an end room.

"You remember Richard Baker, dear? He came to see us with Dr. Pauncefoot Jones in Teheran."

"Of course," said Mrs. Clayton shaking hands. "We went to the bazaars together and you bought some lovely rugs."

It was Mrs. Clayton's delight when not buying things herself to urge on her friends and acquaintances to seek for bargains in the local Suqs. She always had a wonderful knowledge of values and was an excellent bargainer.

"One of the best purchases I've ever made," said Richard. "And entirely owing to your good offices."

"Baker wants to fly to Kuwait tomorrow," said Gerald Clayton. "I've said that we can put him up here for tonight."

"But if it's any trouble," began Richard.

"Of course, it's no trouble," said Mrs. Clayton. "You can't have the best spare room, because Captain Crosbie has got it, but we can make you quite comfortable. You don't want to buy a nice Kuwait chest, do you? Because they've got some lovely ones in the Suq just now. Gerald won't let me buy another one for here, though it would be quite useful to keep extra blankets in."

"You've got three already, dear," said Clayton mildly. "Now, if you'll excuse me, Baker. I must get back to the office. There seems to have been a spot of trouble in the outer office. Somebody let off a revolver, I understand."

"One of the local sheikhs, I suppose," said Mrs. Clayton. "They are so excitable and they do so love firearms."

"On the contrary," said Richard. "It was an Englishman. His intention seemed to be to take a pot shot at an Arab." He added gently, "I knocked his arm up."

"So you were in it all," said Clayton. "I didn't realise that." He fished a card out of his pocket. "Robert Hall. Achilles Works, Enfield seems to be his name. I don't know what he wanted to see me about. He wasn't drunk, was he?"

"He said it was a joke," said Richard drily, "and that the gun went off by accident."

Clayton raised his eyebrows.

"Commercial travellers don't usually carry loaded guns in their pockets," he said.

Clayton, Richard thought, was no fool.

"Perhaps I ought to have stopped him going away."

"It's difficult to know what one should do when these things happen. The man he fired at wasn't hurt."

"No."

"Probably was better to let the thing slide, then."

"I wonder what was behind it?"

"Yes, yes . . . I wonder too."

Clayton looked a little distrait.

"Well, I must be getting back," he said and hurried away.

Mrs. Clayton took Richard into the drawing room, a large inside room, with green cushions and curtains, and offered him a choice of coffee or beer. He chose beer and it came deliciously iced.

She asked him why he was going to Kuwait and he told her.

She asked him why he hadn't got married yet, and Richard said he didn't think he was the marrying kind, to which Mrs. Clayton said briskly: "Nonsense." Archaeologists, she said, made splendid husbands, —and were there any young women coming out to the Dig this season? One or two, Richard said, and Mrs. Pauncefoot Jones of course.

Mrs. Clayton asked hopefully if they were nice girls who were coming out, and Richard said he didn't know because he hadn't met them yet. They were very inexperienced, he said.

For some reason this made Mrs. Clayton laugh.

Then a short stocky man with an abrupt manner came in and was introduced as Captain Crosbie. Mr. Baker, said Mrs. Clayton, was an archaeologist and dug up the most wildly interesting things thousands of years old. Captain Crosbie said he never could understand how archaeologists were able to say so definitely how old these things were. Always used to think they must be the most awful liars, ha ha, said Captain Crosbie. Richard looked at him in a rather tired kind of way. No, said Captain Crosbie, but how did an archaeologist know how old a thing was? Richard said that that would take a long time to explain, and Mrs. Clayton quickly took him away to see his room.

"He's very nice," said Mrs. Clayton, "but not quite quite, you know. Hasn't got any idea of culture."

Richard found his room exceedingly comfortable, and his appreciation of Mrs. Clayton as a hostess rose still higher.

Feeling in the pocket of his coat, he drew out a folded up piece of dirty paper. He looked at it with surprise, for he knew quite well that it had not been there earlier in the morning.

He remembered how the Arab had clutched him when he stumbled. A man with deft fingers might have slipped this into his pocket without his being aware of it.

He unfolded the paper. It was dirty and seemed to have been folded and refolded many times.

In six lines of rather crabbed handwriting Major John Wilberforce recommended one Ahmed Mohammed as an industrious and willing worker, able to drive a lorry and do minor repairs and strictly honest— It was, in fact, the usual type of "chit" or recommendation given in the East. It was dated eighteen months back, which again is not unusual, as these chits are hoarded carefully by their possessors.

Frowning to himself, Richard went over the events of the morning in his precise orderly fashion.

Fakir Carmichael, he was now well assured, had been in fear of his life. He was a hunted man and he had bolted into the Consulate. Why? To find security? But instead of that he had found a more instant menace. The enemy, or a representative of the enemy, had been waiting for him. This commercial traveller chap must have had very definite orders—to be willing to risk shooting Carmichael in the Consulate in the presence of witnesses. It must, therefore, have been very urgent. And Carmichael had appealed to his old school friend for help, and had managed to pass this seemingly innocent document into his possession. It must, therefore, be very important, and if Carmichael's enemies caught up with him, and found that he no longer possessed this document, they would doubtless put two and two together and look for any person or persons to whom Carmichael might conceivably have passed it on.

What then was Richard Baker to do with it?

He could pass it on to Clayton, as His Britannic Majesty's representative.

Or he could keep it in his own possession until such time as Carmichael claimed it?

After a few minutes' reflection he decided to do the latter.

But first he took certain precautions.

Tearing a blank half sheet of paper off an old letter, he sat down to compose a reference for a lorry driver in much the same terms, but using different wording—if this message was a code that took care of that—though it was possible, of course, that there was a message written in some kind of invisible ink.

Then he smeared his own composition with dust from his shoes—rubbed it in his hands, folded and refolded it—until it gave a reasonable appearance of age and dirt.

Then he crumpled it up and put it into his pocket. The original he stared at for some time whilst he considered and rejected various possibilities.

Finally, with a slight smile, he folded and refolded it until he had a small oblong. Taking a stick of plasticine (without which he never travelled) out of his bag, he first wrapped his packet in oilsilk cut from his spongebag, then encased it in plasticine. This done he rolled and patted out the plasticine till he had a smooth surface. On this he rolled out an impression from a cylinder seal that he had with him.

He studied the result with grim appreciation.

It showed a beautifully carved design of the Sun God Shamash, armed with the Sword of Justice.

"Let's hope that's a good omen," he said to himself.

That evening, when he looked in the pocket of the coat he had worn in the morning, the screwed up paper had gone.

VII

LIFE, THOUGHT VICTORIA, life at last! Sitting in her seat at Airways Terminal there had come the magic moment when the words "Passengers for Cairo, Baghdad and Teheran, take your places in the bus, please," had been uttered.

Magic names, magic words. Devoid of glamour to Mrs. Hamilton Clipp who, as far as Victoria could make out, had spent a large portion of her life jumping from boats into aeroplanes and from aeroplanes into trains, with brief intervals at expensive hotels in between. But to Victoria they were a marvellous change from the oft repeated phrases "Take this down, please, Miss Jones." "This letter's full of mistakes. You'll have to type it again, Miss Jones." "The kettle's boiling, ducks, just make the tea, will you." "I know where you can get the most marvellous perm." Trivial boring everyday happenings! And now: Cairo, Baghdad, Teheran—all the romance of the glorious East (and Edward at the end of it).

Victoria returned to earth to hear her employer whom she had already diagnosed as a non-stop talker, concluding a series of remarks by saying:

"—and nothing really clean if you know what I mean. I'm always very very careful what I eat. The filth of the streets and the bazaars you wouldn't believe. And the unhygienic rags the people wear. And some of the toilets—why, you just couldn't call them toilets at all!"

Victoria listened dutifully to these depressing remarks, but her own sense of glamour remained undimmed. Dirt and germs meant nothing in her young life. They arrived at Heathrow and she assisted Mrs. Clipp to alight from the bus. She was already in charge of passports, tickets, money, etc.

"My," said that lady, "it certainly is a comfort to have you with me, Miss Jones. I just don't know what I'd have done if I'd had to travel alone."

Travelling by air, Victoria thought, was rather like being taken on a school treat. Brisk teachers, kind but firm, were at hand to shepherd you at every turn. Air hostesses, in trim uniform with the authority of nursery governesses dealing with feeble minded children, explained kindly just what you were to do. Victoria almost expected them to preface their remarks with: "Now, children."

Tired looking young gentlemen behind desks extended weary hands to check passports, to enquire intimately of money and jewellery. They managed to induce a sense of guilt in those questioned. Victoria, suggestible by nature, knew a sudden longing to describe her one meagre brooch as a diamond tiara value ten thousand pounds, just to see the expression on the bored young man's face. Thoughts of Edward restrained her.

The various barriers passed, they sat down to wait once more in a large room giving directly on the aerodrome. Outside the roar of a plane being revved up gave the proper background. Mrs. Hamilton Clipp was now happily engaged in making a running commentary on their fellow travellers.

"Aren't those two little children just too cute for words? But what an ordeal to travel alone with a couple of children. British, I guess they are. That's a well-cut suit the mother has on. She looks kind of tired, though. That's a good looking man—rather Latin looking, I'd say.

What a loud check that man has on—I'd call it very bad taste. Business, I guess. That man over there's a Dutchman; he was just ahead of us at the controls. That family over there is either Turkish or Persian, I should say. There don't seem to be any Americans. I guess they go mostly Pan American. I'd say those three men talking together are Oil, wouldn't you? I just love looking at people and wondering about them. Mr. Clipp says to me I've got a real yen for human nature. It seems to me just natural to take an interest in your fellow creatures. Wouldn't you say that mink coat over there cost every bit of three thousand dollars?"

Mrs. Clipp sighed. Having duly appraised her fellow travellers, she became restless.

"I'd like to know what we are waiting for like this. That plane's revved up four times. We're all here. Why can't they get on with things? They're certainly not keeping to schedule."

"Would you like a cup of coffee, Mrs. Clipp? I see there is a buffet at the end of the room?"

"Why, no, thank you, Miss Jones. I had coffee before I started, and my stomach feels too unsettled right now to take anything more. What are we waiting for, I'd like to know?"

Her question seemed to be answered almost before the words were out of her mouth.

The door leading from the corridor out of the Customs and Passport department swung open with a rush and a tall man came through with the effect of a gust of wind. Air officials of the line hovered around him. Two large canvas sacks sealed were carried by an officer of B.O.A.C.

Mrs. Clipp sat up with alacrity.

"He's certainly some big noise," she remarked.

"And knows it," thought Victoria.

There was something of calculated sensationalism about the late traveller. He wore a kind of dark grey travelling cloak with a capacious hood at the back. On his head was what was in essence a wide sombrero, but in light grey. He had silver grey curling hair, worn rather long, and a beautiful silver grey moustache curling up at the ends. The effect was that of a handsome stage bandit. Victoria, who disliked theatrical men who posed, looked at him with disapproval.

The Air Officials were, she noted with displeasure, all over him.

"Yes, Sir Rupert." "Of course, Sir Rupert." "The plane is leaving immediately, Sir Rupert."

With a swirl of his voluminous cloak, Sir Rupert passed out through the door leading to the aerodrome. The door swung to behind him with vehemence.

"Sir Rupert," murmured Mrs. Clipp. "Now who would he be, I wonder?"

Victoria shook her head, though she had a vague feeling that the face and general appearance were not unknown to her.

"Somebody important in your Government," suggested Mrs. Clipp. "I shouldn't think so," said Victoria.

The few members of the Government she had ever seen had impressed her as men anxious to apologise for being alive. Only on platforms did they spring into pompous and didactic life.

"Now then, please," said the smart Nursery Governess Air Hostess. "Take your seats in the plane. This way. As quickly as you can, please."

Her attitude implied that a lot of dawdling children had been keeping the patient grown-ups waiting.

Everybody filed out onto the aerodrome.

The great plane was waiting, its engine ticking over like the satisfied purring of a gigantic lion.

Victoria and a steward helped Mrs. Clipp on board and settled her in her seat. Victoria sat next to her on the aisle. Not until Mrs. Clipp was comfortably ensconced, and Victoria had fastened her safety belt, did the girl have leisure to observe that in front of them was sitting the great man.

The doors closed. A few seconds later, the plane began to move slowly along the ground.

"We're really going," thought Victoria in ecstasy. "Oh, isn't it frightening. Suppose it never gets up off the ground? Really I don't see how it can!"

During what seemed an age the plane taxied along the aerodrome, then it turned slowly round and stopped. The engines rose to a ferocious roar. Chewing gum, barley sugar and cotton wool were handed round.

Louder and louder, fiercer and fiercer. Then, once more, the aeroplane moved forward. Mincingly at first, then faster—faster still—they were rushing along the ground.

"It will never go up," thought Victoria, "we'll be killed."

Faster—more smoothly—no jars—no bumps—they were off the ground skimming along, up, round, back over the car park and the main road, up, higher—a silly little train puffing below—dolls' houses—toy cars on roads . . . Higher still—and suddenly the earth below lost interest, was no longer human or alive—just a large flat map with lines and circles and dots.

Inside the plane people undid their safety belts, lit cigarettes, opened magazines. Victoria was in a new world—a world so many feet long and a very few feet wide, inhabited by twenty to thirty people. Nothing else existed.

She peered out of the small window again. Below her were clouds, a fluffy pavement of clouds. The plane was in the sun. Below the clouds somewhere was the world she had known heretofore.

Victoria pulled herself together. Mrs. Hamilton Clipp was talking. Victoria removed cotton wool from her ear and bent attentively towards her.

In the seat in front of her, Sir Rupert rose, tossed his wide brimmed grey felt hat to the rack, drew up his hood over his head and relaxed into his seat.

"Pompous ass," thought Victoria, unreasonably prejudiced.

Mrs. Clipp was established with a magazine open in front of her. At intervals, she nudged Victoria when on trying to turn the page with one hand, the magazine slipped.

Victoria looked round her. She decided that air travel was really rather boring. She opened a magazine, found herself faced with an advertisement that said "Do you want to increase your efficiency as a shorthand typist?" shuddered, shut the magazine, leant back, and began to think of Edward.

They came down at Castel Benito Aerodrome in a storm of rain. Victoria was by now feeling slightly sick, and it took all her energies to accomplish her duties vis-à-vis with her employer. They were driven through scurrying rain to the rest house. The magnificent Sir Rupert, Victoria noted, had been met by an officer in uniform with red tabs, and hurried off in a staff car to some dwelling of the mighty in Tripolitania.

They were allotted rooms; Victoria helped Mrs. Clipp with her toilet and left her to rest on her bed in a dressing gown until it was time for the evening meal. Victoria retired to her own room, lay down and closed her eyes, grateful to be spared the sight of the heaving and sinking floor.

She awakened an hour later in good health and spirits and went to help Mrs. Clipp. Presently a rather more peremptory Air Hostess instructed them that cars were ready to convey them to the evening meal. After dinner, Mrs. Clipp got into conversation with some of her fellow travellers. The man in the loud check coat seemed to have taken a fancy to Victoria and told her at some length all about the manufacture of lead pencils.

Later, they were conveyed back to their sleeping quarters and told curtly that they must be ready to depart at 5.30 a.m. the following morning.

"We haven't seen much of Tripolitania, have we," said Victoria rather sadly. "Is Air Travel always like this?"

"Why, yes, I'd say so. It's just positively sadistic the way they get you up in the mornings. After that, often they keep you hanging round the aerodrome for an hour or two. Why, in Rome, I remember they called us at 3.30. Breakfast in the restaurant at 4 o'clock. And then actually at the Airport we didn't leave until eight. Still the great thing is they get you to your destination right away with no fooling about on the way."

Victoria sighed. She could have done with a good deal of fooling about. She wanted to see the world.

"And what do you know, my dear," continued Mrs. Clipp excitedly, "you know that interesting looking man? The Britisher? The one that there's all the fuss about. I've found out who he is. That's Sir Rupert Crofton Lee, the great traveller. You've heard of him, of course."

Yes, Victoria remembered now. She had seen several pictures in the press about six months ago. Sir Rupert was a great authority upon the interior of China. He was one of the few people who had been to Tibet and visited Lhasa. He had travelled through the unknown parts of Kurdistan and Asia Minor. His books had had a wide sale, for they had been racily and wittily written. If Sir Rupert was just noticeably a self advertiser, it was with good reason. He made no claims that were not fully justified. The cloak with the hood and the wide brimmed hat were, Victoria remembered now, a deliberate fashion of his own choosing.

"Isn't that thrilling, now?" demanded Mrs. Clipp with all a lion hunter's enthusiasm as Victoria adjusted the bedclothes over her recumbent form.

Victoria agreed that it was very thrilling, but she said to herself that she preferred Sir Rupert's books to his personality. He was, she considered, what children call "a show off!"

A start was made in good order the next morning. The weather had cleared and the sun was shining. Victoria still felt disappointed to have

seen so little of Tripolitania. Still the plane was due to arrive at Cairo
by lunch time and the departure to Baghdad did not take place until
the following morning, so she would at least be able to see a little of
Egypt in the afternoon.

They were flying over the sea, but clouds soon blocked out the blue
water below them and Victoria settled back in her seat with a yawn.
In front of her Sir Rupert was already asleep. The hood had fallen
back from his head which was hanging forwards, nodding at intervals.
Victoria observed with a faint malicious pleasure that he had a small
boil starting on the back of his neck. Why she should have been pleased
at this fact was hard to say—perhaps it made the great man seem more
human and vulnerable. He was as other men, after all—prone to the
small annoyances of the flesh. It may be said that Sir Rupert had kept
up his Olympian manner and had taken no notice whatever of his
fellow travellers.

"Who does he think he is, I wonder?" thought Victoria to herself.
The answer was obvious. He was Sir Rupert Crofton Lee, a celebrity,
and she was Victoria Jones, an indifferent shorthand typist, and of no
account whatever.

On arrival at Cairo, Victoria and Mrs. Hamilton Clipp had lunch
together. The latter then announced that she was going to nap until
six o'clock, and suggested that Victoria might like to go and see the
Pyramids.

"I've arranged for a car for you, Miss Jones, because I know that
owing to your Treasury regulations, you won't be able to cash any
money here."

Victoria who had in any case no money to cash, was duly grateful,
and said so with some effusion.

"Why, that's nothing at all. You've been very very kind to me. And,
travelling with dollars, everything is easy for us. Mrs. Kitchin—the
lady with the two cute children—is very anxious to go, also, so I suggested you'd join up with her—if that suits you?"

So long as she saw the world, anything suited Victoria.

"That's fine. Then you'd better get off right now."

The afternoon at the Pyramids was duly enjoyed. Victoria, though
reasonably fond of children, might have enjoyed it more without Mrs.
Kitchin's offspring. Children when sight seeing is in progress are apt to
be somewhat of a handicap. The youngest child became so fretful that
the two women returned earlier from the expedition than they had
meant to do.

Victoria threw herself on her bed with a yawn. She wished very much that she could stay a week in Cairo—perhaps go up the Nile. "And what would you use for money, my girl?" she asked herself witheringly. It was already a miracle that she was being transported to Baghdad free of charge.

And what, enquired a cold inward voice, are you going to do, once you are landed in Baghdad with only a few pounds in your pocket? Victoria waved that query aside. Edward must find her a job. Or failing that, she would find herself a job. Why worry?

Her eyes, dazzled with strong sunlight, closed gently.

A knock on the door, as she thought, roused her. She called "Come in"; then as there was no response, she got off the bed, crossed to the door and opened it.

But the knock had not been at her door, but at the next door down the passage. Another of the inevitable Air Hostesses, dark haired and trim in her uniform, was knocking at Sir Rupert Crofton Lee's door. He opened it just as Victoria looked out.

"What's the matter now?"

He sounded annoyed and sleepy.

"I'm so sorry to disturb you, Sir Rupert," cooed the Air Hostess, "but would you mind coming to the B.O.A.C. office. It's just three doors down the passage here. Just a small detail about the flight to Baghdad tomorrow."

"Oh, very well."

Victoria withdrew into her room. She was less sleepy now. She glanced at her watch. Only half past four. An hour and a half until Mrs. Clipp would be requiring her. She decided to go out and walk about Heliopolis. Walking, at least, required no money.

She powdered her nose and resumed her shoes. They felt rather full of feet. The visit to the Pyramids had been hard on feet.

She came out of her room and walked along the corridor towards the main hall of the Hotel. Three doors down she passed the B.O.A.C. office. It had a card announcing the fact nailed to the door. Just as she passed it, the door opened and Sir Rupert came out. He was walking fast and he overtook her in a couple of strides. He went on ahead of her, his cloak swinging, and Victoria fancied that he was annoyed about something.

Mrs. Clipp was in a somewhat petulant mood when Victoria reported for duty at six o'clock.

"I'm worried about the excess on my baggage, Miss Jones. I took it that I'd paid for that right through, but it seems that it's only paid until Cairo. We go on tomorrow by Iraqi Airways. My ticket is a through ticket, but not the excess baggage. Perhaps you'd go and find out if that is really so? Because maybe I ought to change another traveller's cheque."

Victoria agreed to make enquiries. She could not find the B.O.A.C. office at first, and finally located it in the far corridor—the other side of the hall—quite a big office. The other, she supposed, had been a small office only used during the afternoon siesta hours. Mrs. Clipp's fears about the excess baggage were found to be justified which annoyed that lady very much.

VIII

On the fifth floor of a block of offices in the City of London are situated the offices of the Valhalla Gramophone Company. The man who sat behind the desk in that office was reading a book on economics. The telephone rang and he picked up the receiver. He said in a quiet unemotional voice:

"Valhalla Gramophone Company."

"Sanders here."

"Sanders of the River? What River?"

"River Tigris. Reporting as to A.S. We've lost her."

There was a moment's silence. Then the quiet voice spoke again, with a steely note in it.

"Did I hear what you said correctly?"

"We've lost Anna Scheele."

"No names. This is a very serious error on your part. How did it come about?"

"She went into that nursing home. I told you before. Her sister was having an operation."

"Well?"

"The operation went off all right. We expected A.S. to return to the Savoy. She had kept on her suite. She didn't return. Watch had been kept on the nursing home and we were quite sure she hadn't left it. We assumed she was still there."

"And she isn't?"

"We've just found out. She left there, in an ambulance, the day after the operation."

"She deliberately fooled you?"

"Looks like it. I'd swear she didn't know she was being followed. We took every precaution. There were three of us and—"

"Never mind the excuses. Where did the ambulance take her?"

"To University College Hospital."

"What have you learnt from the Hospital?"

"That a patient was brought in accompanied by a Hospital Nurse. The Hospital Nurse must have been Anna Scheele. They've no idea where she went after she brought the patient in."

"And the patient?"

"The patient knows nothing. She was under morphia."

"So Anna Scheele walked out of University College Hospital dressed as a nurse and may now be anywhere?"

"Yes. If she goes back to the Savoy—"

The other interrupted.

"She won't go back to the Savoy."

"Shall we check up on other hotels?"

"Yes, but I doubt if you'll get any result. That's what she'd expect you to do."

"What instructions otherwise?"

"Check on the ports—Dover, Folkestone, etc. Check with Air Lines. In particular check all bookings to Baghdad by plane for the next fortnight. The passage won't be booked in her own name. Check up on all passengers of suitable age."

"Her baggage is still at the Savoy. Perhaps she'll claim."

"She won't do anything of the sort. You may be a fool—she isn't! Does the sister know anything?"

"We're in contact with her special nurse at the Home. Apparently the sister thinks A.S. is in Paris doing business for Morganthal and staying at Ritz Hotel. She believes A.S. is flying home to States on 23rd."

"In other words A.S. has told her nothing. She wouldn't. Check up on those air passages. It's the only hope. She's got to get to Baghdad—and Air is the only way she can do it in time, and, Sanders—"

"Yes?"

"No more failures. This is your last chance."

IX

Young Mr. Shrivenham of the British Embassy shifted from one foot to the other and gazed upwards as the plane zoomed over Baghdad aerodrome. There was a considerable dust-storm in progress. Palm trees, houses, human beings were all shrouded in a thick brown haze. It had come on quite suddenly.

Lionel Shrivenham observed in a tone of deep distress:

"Ten to one they can't come down here."

"What will they do?" asked his friend Harold.

"Go on to Basrah, I imagine. It's clear there, I hear."

"You're meeting some kind of a V.I.P., aren't you?"

Young Mr. Shrivenham groaned again.

"Just my luck. The new Ambassador has been delayed coming out. Lansdowne, the Counsellor, is in England. Rice, the Oriental Counsellor, is ill in bed with gastric flu, dangerously high temperature. Best is in Teheran, and here am I, left with the whole bag of tricks. No end of a flap about this fellow. I don't know why. Even the hush hush boys are in a flap. He's one of these world travellers, always off somewhere inaccessible on a camel. Don't see why he's so important, but apparently he's absolutely the cat's whiskers, and I'm to conform to his slightest wish. If he gets carried on to Basrah he'll probably be wild. Don't know what arrangements I'd better lay on. Train up tonight? Or get the R.A.F. to fly him up tomorrow?"

Mr. Shrivenham sighed again, as his sense of injury and responsibility deepened. Since his arrival three months ago in Baghdad he had been consistently unlucky. One more raspberry, he felt, would finally blight what might have been a promising career.

The plane swooped overhead once more.

"Evidently thinks he can't make it," said Shrivenham, then added excitedly: "Hullo—I believe he's coming down."

A few moments later and the plane had taxied sedately to its place and Shrivenham stood ready to greet the V.I.P.

His unprofessional eye noted "rather a pretty girl . . ." before he sprang forward to greet the buccaneer-like figure in the swirling cloak.

"Practically fancy dress," he thought to himself disapprovingly as he said aloud:

"Sir Rupert Crofton Lee? I'm Shrivenham of the Embassy."

Sir Rupert, he thought, was slightly curt in manner—perhaps understandable after the strain of circling round the city uncertain whether a landing could be effected or not.

"Nasty day," continued Shrivenham. "Had a lot of this sort of thing this year. Ah, you've got the bags. Then, if you'll follow me, sir, it's all laid on . . ."

As they left the aerodrome in the car, Shrivenham said:

"I thought for a bit that you were going to be carried on to some other airport, sir. Didn't look as though the pilot could make a landing. Came up suddenly, this dust-storm."

Sir Rupert blew out his cheeks importantly as he remarked:

"That would have been disastrous—quite disastrous. Had my schedule been jeopardised, young man, I can tell you that the results would have been grave and far-reaching in the extreme."

"Lot of cock," thought Shrivenham disrespectfully. "These V.I.P's think their potty affairs are what makes the world go round."

Aloud he said respectfully:

"I expect that's so, sir."

"Have you any idea when the Ambassador will reach Baghdad?"

"Nothing definite as yet, sir."

"I shall be sorry to miss him. Haven't seen him since—let me see, yes, India in 1938."

Shrivenham preserved a respectful silence.

"Let me see, Rice is here, isn't he?"

"Yes, sir, he's Oriental Counsellor."

"Capable fellow. Knows a lot. I'll be glad to meet him again."

Shrivenham coughed.

"As a matter of fact, sir, Rice is on the sick list. They've taken him to hospital for observation. Violent type of gastro enteritis. Something a bit worse than the usual Baghdad tummy, apparently."

"What's that?" Sir Rupert turned his head sharply. "Bad gastro enteritis—hm. Came on suddenly, did it?"

"Day before yesterday, sir."

Sir Rupert was frowning. The rather affected grandiloquence of manner had dropped from him. He was a simpler man—and somewhat of a worried one.

"I wonder," he said. "Yes, I wonder."

Shrivenham looked politely enquiring.

"I'm wondering," said Sir Rupert, "if it might be a case of Scheele's Green. . . ."

Baffled, Shrivenham remained silent.

They were just approaching the Feisal Bridge, and the car swung off to the left towards the British Embassy.

Suddenly Sir Rupert leant forward.

"Just stop a minute, will you?" he said sharply. "Yes, right hand side. Where all those pots are."

The car glided in to the right hand curb and stopped. It was a small native shop piled high with crude white clay pots and water jars.

A short stocky European who had been standing talking to the proprietor moved away towards the bridge as the car drew up. Shrivenham thought it was Crosbie of the I and P whom he had met once or twice.

Sir Rupert sprang from the car and strode up to the small booth. Picking up one of the pots, he started a rapid conversation in Arabic with the proprietor. The flow of speech was too fast for Shrivenham whose Arabic was as yet slow and painstaking and distinctly limited in vocabulary.

The proprietor was beaming, his hands flew wide, he gesticulated, he explained at length. Sir Rupert handled different pots, apparently asking questions about them. Finally he selected a narrow mouthed water jar, tossed the man some coins and went back to the car.

"Interesting technique," said Sir Rupert. "Been making them like this for thousands of years, same shape as in one of the hill districts in Armenia."

His finger slipped down through the narrow aperture, twisting round and round.

"It's very crude stuff," said Shrivenham unimpressed.

"Oh, no artistic merit! But interesting historically. See these indications of lugs here? You pick up many a historical tip from observation of the simple things in daily use. I've got a collection of them."

The car turned in through the gates of the British Embassy.

Sir Rupert demanded to be taken straight to his room. Shrivenham was amused to note that, his lecture on the clay pot ended, Sir Rupert had left it nonchalantly in the car. Shrivenham made a point of carrying it upstairs and placing it meticulously upon Sir Rupert's bedside table.

"Your pot, sir."

"Eh? Oh, thank you, my boy."

Sir Rupert appeared distrait. Shrivenham left him after repeating that luncheon would be ready shortly and drinks awaited his choice.

When the young man had left the room, Sir Rupert went to the window and unfolded the small slip of paper that had been tucked into the mouth of the pot. He smoothed it out. There were two lines of writing on it. He read them over carefully, then set light to the paper with a match.

Then he summoned a servant.

"Yes, sir? I unpack for you, sir?"

"Not yet. I want to see Mr. Shrivenham—up here."

Shrivenham arrived with a slight apprehensive expression.

"Anything I can do, sir? Anything wrong?"

"Mr. Shrivenham, a drastic change has occurred in my plans. I can count upon your discretion, of course?"

"Oh absolutely, sir."

"It is some time since I was in Baghdad; actually I have not been here since the war. The hotels lie mainly on the other bank, do they not?"

"Yes, sir. In Rashid Street."

"Backing on the Tigris?"

"Yes. Babylonian Palace is the biggest of them. That's the more or less official hotel."

"What do you know about a hotel called the Tio?"

"Oh, a lot of people go there. Food's rather good and it's run by a terrific character called Marcus Tio. He's quite an institution in Baghdad."

"I want you to book me a room there, Mr. Shrivenham."

"You mean—you're not going to stay at the Embassy?" Shrivenham looked nervously apprehensive. "But—but—it's all laid on, sir."

"What is laid on can be laid off," barked Sir Rupert.

"Oh, of course, sir. I didn't mean. . . ."

Shrivenham broke off. He had a feeling that in the future someone was going to blame him.

"I have certain somewhat delicate negotiations to carry out. I learn that they cannot be carried out from the Embassy. I want you to book me a room tonight at the Tio Hotel and I wish to leave the Embassy in a reasonably unobtrusive manner. That is to say I do not want

to drive up to the Tio in an Embassy car. I also require a seat booked
on the plane leaving for Cairo the day after tomorrow."

Shrivenham looked more dismayed still.

"But I understood you were staying five days—"

"That is no longer the case. It is imperative that I reach Cairo as soon
as my business here is terminated. It would not be safe for me to remain
longer."

"Safe?"

A sudden grim smile transformed Sir Rupert's face. The manner
which Shrivenham had been likening to that of a Prussian drill sergeant was laid aside. The man's charm became suddenly apparent.

"Safety hasn't usually been one of my preoccupations, I agree," he
said. "But in this case it isn't only my own safety I have to consider—my
safety includes the safety of a lot of other people as well. So make those
arrangements for me. If the air passage is difficult, apply for priority.
Until I leave here tonight, I shall remain in my room." He added, as
Shrivenham's mouth opened in surprise, "Officially, I'm sick. Touch
of malaria." The other nodded. "So I shan't need food."

"But surely we can send you up—"

"Twenty-four hours' fast is nothing to me. I've gone hungrier longer
than that on some of my journeys. You just do as I tell you."

Downstairs, Shrivenham was greeted by his colleagues and groaned
in answer to their enquiries.

"Cloak and dagger stuff in a big way," he said. "Can't quite make
his grandiloquence Sir Rupert Crofton Lee out. Whether it's genuine
or playacting. That swirling cloak and bandit's hat and all the rest of
it. Fellow who'd read one of his books told me that although he's a bit
of a self advertiser, he really has done all these things and been to
these places—but I don't know . . . Wish Thomas Rice was up and
about to cope. That reminds me, what's Scheele's Green?"

"Scheele's Green?" said his friend, frowning. "Something to do with
wallpaper, isn't it? Poisonous. It's a form of arsenic, I think."

"Cripes!" said Shrivenham, staring, "I thought it was a disease. Something like amoebic dysentery."

"Oh no, it's something in the chemical line. What wives do their
husbands in with, or vice versa."

Shrivenham had relapsed into startled silence. Certain disagreeable
facts were becoming clear to him. Crofton Lee had suggested, in effect,
that Thomas Rice, Oriental Counsellor to the Embassy was suffering,
not from gastro enteritis, but from arsenical poisoning. Added to

that Sir Rupert had suggested that his own life was in danger, and his
decision not to eat food and drink prepared in the kitchens of the
British Embassy shook Shrivenham's decorous British soul to the core.
He couldn't imagine what to make of it all.

X

VICTORIA, BREATHING IN hot choking yellow dust, was unfavourably
impressed by Baghdad. From the Airport to the Tio Hotel, her ears
had been assailed by continuous and incessant noise. Horns of cars
blaring with maddening persistence, voices shouting, whistles blowing, then more deafening senseless blaring of motor horns. Added
to the loud incessant noises of the street was a small thin trickle of
continuous sound which was Mrs. Hamilton Clipp talking.

Victoria arrived at the Tio Hotel in a dazed condition.

A small alleyway led back from the fanfare of Rashid Street towards the Tigris. A short flight of steps to go up and there at the
entrance of the Hotel, they were greeted by a very stout young man
with a beaming smile who, metaphorically at least, gathered them to
his heart. This, Victoria gathered was Marcus—or more correctly Mr.
Tio, the owner of the Tio Hotel.

His words of welcome were interrupted by shouted orders to various
underlings regarding the disposal of their baggage.

"And here you are, once more, Mrs. Clipp—but your arm—why
is it in that funny stuff?—(You fools, do not carry that with the strap!
Imbeciles! Don't trail that coat!)—But, my dear—what a day to arrive
—never, I thought, would the plane land. It went round and round
and round. Marcus, I said to myself—it is not you that will travel by
planes—all this hurry, what does it matter?—And you have brought
a young lady with you—it is nice always to see a new young lady in
Baghdad—why did not Mr. Harrison come down to meet you—I expected him yesterday—but, my dear, you must have a drink at once—"

Now, somewhat dazed, Victoria, her head reeling slightly under the
effect of a double whisky authoritatively pressed upon her by Marcus,
was standing in a high whitewashed room containing a large brass

bedstead, a very sophisticated dressing table of newest French design, an aged Victorian wardrobe, and two vivid plush chairs. Her modest baggage reposed at her feet and a very old man with a yellow face and white whiskers had grinned and nodded at her as he placed towels in the bathroom and asked her if she would like the water made hot for a bath.

"How long would it take?"

"Twenty minutes, half an hour. I go and do it now."

With a fatherly smile he withdrew. Victoria sat down on the bed and passed an experimental hand over her hair. It felt clogged with dust and her face was sore and gritty. She looked at herself in the glass. The dust had changed her hair from black to a strange reddish brown. She pulled aside a corner of the curtain and looked out onto a wide balcony which gave on the river. But there was nothing to be seen of the Tigris except a thick yellow haze. A prey to deep depression, Victoria said to herself: "What a hateful place."

Then rousing herself, she stepped across the landing and tapped on Mrs. Clipp's door. Prolonged and active ministrations would be required of her here before she could attend to her own cleansing and rehabilitation.

After a bath, lunch and a prolonged nap, Victoria stepped out from her bedroom onto the balcony and gazed with approval across the Tigris. The dust-storm had subsided. Instead of a yellow haze, a pale clear light was appearing. Across the river was a delicate silhouette of palm trees and irregularly placed houses.

Voices came up to Victoria from the garden below. She stepped to the edge of the balcony and looked over.

Mrs. Hamilton Clipp, that indefatigable talker and friendly soul, had struck up an acquaintanceship with an Englishwoman—one of those weatherbeaten Englishwomen of indeterminate age who can always be found in any foreign city.

"—and whatever I'd have done without her, I really don't know," Mrs. Clipp was saying. "She's just the sweetest girl you can imagine. And very well connected. A niece of the Bishop of Llangow."

"Bishop of who?"

"Why, Llangow, I think it was."

"Nonsense, there's no such person," said the other.

Victoria frowned. She recognized the type of County Englishwoman who is unlikely to be taken in by the mention of spurious Bishops.

"Why, then, perhaps I got the name wrong," Mrs. Clipp said doubtfully.

"But," she resumed, "she certainly is a very charming and competent girl."

The other said "Ha!" in a noncommittal manner.

Victoria resolved to give this lady as wide a berth as possible. Something told her that inventing stories to satisfy that kind of woman was no easy job.

Victoria went back into her room, sat on the bed, and gave herself up to speculation on her present position.

She was staying at the Tio Hotel which was, she was fairly sure, not at all inexpensive. She had four pounds seventeen shillings in her possession. She had eaten a hearty lunch for which she had not yet paid and for which Mrs. Hamilton Clipp was under no obligation to pay. Travelling expenses to Baghdad were what Mrs. Clipp had offered. The bargain was completed. Victoria had got to Baghdad. Mrs. Clipp had received the skilled attention of a Bishop's niece, an ex-hospital nurse and competent secretary. All that was over, to the mutual satisfaction of both parties. Mrs. Hamilton Clipp would depart on the evening train to Kirkuk—and that was that. Victoria toyed hopefully with the idea that Mrs. Clipp might press upon her a parting present in the form of hard cash, but abandoned it reluctantly as unlikely. Mrs. Clipp could have no idea that Victoria was in really dire financial straits.

What then must Victoria do? The answer came immediately. Find Edward, of course.

With a sense of annoyance she realised that she was quite unaware of Edward's last name. Edward—Baghdad. Very much, Victoria reflected, like the Saracen maid who arrived in England, knowing only the name of her lover "Gilbert" and "England". A romantic story—but certainly inconvenient. True that in England at the time of the Crusades, nobody, Victoria thought, had had any surname at all. On the other hand England was larger than Baghdad. Still, England was sparsely populated then—

Victoria wrenched her thoughts away from these interesting speculations and returned to hard facts. She must find Edward immediately and Edward must find her a job. Also immediately.

She did not know Edward's last name, but he had come to Baghdad as the secretary of a Dr. Rathbone and presumably Dr. Rathbone was a man of importance.

Victoria powdered her nose, patted her hair and started down stairs in search of information.

The beaming Marcus, passing through the hall of his establishment, hailed her with delight.

"Ah, it is Miss Jones, you will come with me and have a drink, will you not, my dear? I like very much English ladies. All the English ladies in Baghdad, they are my friends. Everyone is very happy in my Hotel. Come, we will go into the bar."

Victoria, not at all averse to free hospitality, consented gladly.

Sitting on a stool and drinking gin, she began her search for information.

"Do you know a Dr. Rathbone who has just come to Baghdad?" she asked.

"I know everyone in Baghdad," said Marcus Tio joyfully. "And everybody knows Marcus. That is true, what I am telling you. Oh! I have many many friends."

"I'm sure you have," said Victoria. "Do you know Dr. Rathbone?"

"Last week I have the Air Marshal commanding all Middle East passing through. He says to me, 'Marcus, you villain, I haven't seen you since '46. You haven't grown any thinner.' Oh, he is very nice man. I like him very much."

"What about Dr. Rathbone? Is he a nice man?"

"I like, you know, people who can enjoy themselves. I do not like sour faces. I like people to be gay and young and charming—like you. He says to me, that Air Marshal, 'Marcus, you like too much the women.' But I say to him: 'No, my trouble is I like too much Marcus . . .'"

Marcus roared with laughter, breaking off to call out, "Jesus—Jesus!"

Victoria looked startled, but it appeared that Jesus was the barman's Christian name. Victoria felt again that the East was an odd place.

"Another gin and orange, and whisky," Marcus commanded.

"I don't think I—"

"Yes, yes, you will—they are very very weak."

"About Dr. Rathbone," persisted Victoria.

"That Mrs. Hamilton Clipp—what an odd name—with whom you arrive, she is American—is she not? I like also American people but I like English best. American peoples, they look always very worried. But sometimes, yes, they are good sports. Mr. Summers—you know him? —he drink so much when he come to Baghdad, he go to sleep for three days and not wake up. It is too much, that. It is not nice."

"Please, do help me," said Victoria.

Marcus looked surprised.

"But of course I help you. I always help my friends. You tell me what you want—and at once it shall be done. Special steak—or turkey cooked very nice with rice and raisins and herbs—or little baby chickens."

"I don't want baby chickens," said Victoria. "At least not now," she added prudently. "I want to find this Dr. Rathbone. Dr. Rathbone. He's just arrived in Baghdad. With a—with a—secretary."

"I do not know," said Marcus. "He does not stay at the Tio."

The implication was clearly that anyone who did not stay at the Tio did not exist for Marcus.

"But there are other hotels," persisted Victoria, "or perhaps he has a house?"

"Oh, yes, there are other hotels. Babylonian Palace, Senacherib, Zobeide Hotel. They are good hotels, yes, but they are not like the Tio."

"I'm sure they're not," Victoria assured him. "But you don't know if Dr. Rathbone is staying at one of them? There is some kind of society he runs—something to do with culture—and books."

Marcus became quite serious at the mention of culture.

"It is what we need," he said. "There must be much culture. Art and music, it is very nice, very nice indeed. I like violin sonatas myself if it is not very long."

While thoroughly agreeing with him, especially in regard to the end of the speech, Victoria realised that she was not getting any nearer to her objective. Conversation with Marcus was, she thought, most entertaining, and Marcus was a charming person in his childlike enthusiasm for life, but conversation with him reminded her of Alice in Wonderland's endeavours to find a path that led to the hill. Every topic found them returning to the point of departure—Marcus!

She refused another drink and rose sadly to her feet. She felt slightly giddy. The cocktails had been anything but weak. She went out from the bar onto the terrace outside and stood by the railing looking across the river, when somebody spoke from behind her.

"Excuse me, but you'd better go and put a coat on. Daresay it seems like summer to you coming out from England, but it gets very cold about sundown."

It was the Englishwoman who had been talking to Mrs. Clipp earlier. She had the hoarse voice of one who is in the habit of training and calling to sporting dogs. She wore a fur coat, had a rug over her knees and was sipping a whisky and soda.

"Oh, thank you," said Victoria and was about to escape hurriedly when her intentions were defeated.

"I must introduce myself. I'm Mrs. Cardew Trench." (The implication was clearly: one of the Cardew Trenches.) "I believe you arrived with Mrs.—what's her name—Hamilton Clipp."

"Yes," said Victoria, "I did."

"She told me you were the niece of the Bishop of Llangow."

Victoria rallied.

"Did she really?" she inquired with the correct trace of light amusement.

"Got it wrong, I suppose?"

Victoria smiled.

"Americans are bound to get some of our names wrong. It does sound a little like Llangow. My uncle," said Victoria improvising rapidly, "is the Bishop of Languao."

"Languao?"

"Yes—in the Pacific Archipelago. He's a Colonial bishop, of course."

"Oh, a Colonial bishop," said Mrs. Cardew Trench, her voice falling at least three semitones.

As Victoria had anticipated: Mrs. Cardew Trench was magnificently unaware of Colonial bishops.

"That explains it," she added.

Victoria thought with pride that it explained it very well for a spur of the moment plunge!

"And what are you doing out here?" asked Mrs. Cardew Trench with that inexorable geniality that conceals natural curiosity of disposition.

"Looking for a young man I talked to for a few moments in a public square in London," was hardly an answer that Victoria could give. She said, remembering the newspaper paragraph she had read, and her statement to Mrs. Clipp.

"I'm joining my uncle, Dr. Pauncefoot Jones."

"Oh, so that's who you are." Mrs. Cardew Trench was clearly delighted at having "placed" Victoria. "He's a charming little man, though a bit absent-minded—still I suppose that's only to be expected. Heard him lecture last year in London—excellent delivery—couldn't understand a word of what it was all about, though. Yes, he passed through Baghdad about a fortnight ago. I think he mentioned some girls were coming out later in the season."

Hurriedly, having established her status, Victoria chipped in with a question.

"Do you know if Dr. Rathbone's out here?" she asked.

"Just come out," said Mrs. Cardew Trench. "I believe they've asked him to give a lecture at the Institute next Thursday. On World Relationships and Brotherhood—or something like that. All nonsense if you ask me. The more you try to get people together, the more suspicious they get of each other. All this poetry and music and translating Shakespeare and Wordsworth into Arabic and Chinese and Hindustani. 'A primrose by the river's brim, etc.' . . . what's the good of that to people who've never seen a primrose?"

"Where is he staying, do you know?"

"At the Babylonian Palace Hotel, I believe. But his headquarters are up near the Museum. The Olive Branch—ridiculous name. Full of young women in slacks with unwashed necks and spectacles."

"I know his secretary slightly," said Victoria.

"Oh yes, whatshisname Edward Thingummy—nice boy—too good for that long haired racket—did well in the war, I hear. Still a job's a job, I suppose. Nice looking boy—those earnest young women are quite fluttered by him, I fancy."

A pang of devastating jealousy pierced Victoria.

"The Olive Branch," she said. "Where did you say it was?"

"Up past the turning to the second bridge. One of the turnings off Rashid Street—tucked away rather. Not far from the copper bazaar."

"And how's Mrs. Pauncefoot Jones?" continued Mrs. Cardew Trench. "Coming out soon? I hear she's been in poor health?"

But having got the information she wanted, Victoria was taking no more risks in invention. She glanced at her wristwatch and uttered an exclamation.

"Oh dear—I promised to wake Mrs. Clipp at half past six and help her to prepare for the journey. I must fly."

The excuse was true enough, though Victoria had substituted half past six for seven o'clock. She hurried upstairs feeling quite exhilarated. Tomorrow she would get in touch with Edward at the Olive Branch. Earnest young women with unwashed necks, indeed! They sounded most unattractive . . . Still, Victoria reflected uneasily that men are less critical of dingy necks than middle-aged hygienic Englishwomen are—especially if the owners of the said necks are gazing with large eyes of admiration and adoration at the male subject in question.

The evening passed rapidly. Victoria had an early meal in the dining room with Mrs. Hamilton Clipp, the latter talking nineteen to the dozen on every subject under the sun. She urged Victoria to come and pay a visit later—and Victoria noted down the address carefully, because, after all, one never knew . . . She accompanied Mrs. Clipp to Baghdad North station, saw her safely ensconced in her compartment and was introduced to an acquaintance also travelling to Kirkuk who would assist Mrs. Clipp with her toilet on the following morning.

The engine uttered loud melancholy screams, like a soul in distress, Mrs. Clipp thrust a thick envelope into Victoria's hand, said: "Just a little remembrance, Miss Jones, of our very pleasant companionship which I hope you will accept with my most grateful thanks." Victoria said: "But it's really too kind of you, Mrs. Clipp," in a delighted voice, the engine gave forth a final supreme banshee wail of anguish, and the train pulled slowly out of the station.

Victoria took a taxi from the station back to the hotel since she had not the faintest idea how to get back to it any other way and there did not seem anyone about whom she could ask.

On her return to the Tio, she ran up to her room and eagerly opened the envelope. Inside were a couple of pairs of nylon stockings.

Victoria at any other moment would have been enchanted—nylon stockings having been usually beyond the reach of her purse. At the moment, however, hard cash was what she had been hoping for. Mrs. Clipp, however, had been far too delicate to think of giving her a five dinar note. Victoria wished heartily that she had not been quite so delicate.

However, tomorrow there would be Edward. Victoria undressed, got into bed and in five minutes was fast asleep, dreaming that she was waiting at an aerodrome for Edward, but that he was held back from joining her by a spectacled girl who clasped him firmly round the neck while the aeroplane began slowly to move away . . .

XI

Victoria awoke to a morning of vivid sunshine. Having dressed, she went out onto the wide balcony outside her window. Sitting in a chair a little way along with his back to her was a man with curling grey hair growing down onto a muscular red brown neck. When

the man turned his head sideways Victoria recognised, with a distinct
feeling of surprise, Sir Rupert Crofton Lee. Why she should be so
surprised she could hardly have said. Perhaps because she had assumed
as a matter of course that a V.I.P. such as Sir Rupert would have been
staying at the Embassy and not at a hotel. Nevertheless, there he was,
staring at the Tigris with a kind of concentrated intensity. She noticed,
even, that he had a pair of field glasses slung over the side of his chair.
Possibly, she thought, he studied birds.

A young man whom Victoria had at one time thought attractive,
had been a bird enthusiast, and she had accompanied him on several
week-end tramps, to be made to stand as though paralysed in wet weeds
and icy winds, for what seemed like hours, to be at last told in tones
of ecstasy to look through the glasses at some drab looking bird on a
remote twig which in appearance, as far as Victoria could see, compared unfavourably in bird appeal with a common robin or chaffinch.

Victoria made her way downstairs, encountering Marcus Tio on
the terrace between the two buildings of the hotel.

"I see you've got Sir Rupert Crofton Lee staying here," she said.

"Oh, yes," said Marcus, beaming, "he is a nice man—a very nice
man."

"Do you know him well?"

"No, this is the first time I see him. Mr. Shrivenham of the British
Embassy bring him here last night. Mr. Shrivenham, he is very nice
man, too. I know him very well."

Proceeding into breakfast, Victoria wondered if there was anyone
whom Marcus would not consider a very nice man. He appeared to
exercise a wide charity.

After breakfast, Victoria started forth in search of the Olive Branch.

A London bred Cockney, she had no idea of the difficulties involved
in finding any particular place in a city such as Baghdad, until she
had started on her quest.

Coming across Marcus again on her way out, she asked him to direct
her to the Museum.

"It is a very nice Museum," said Marcus, beaming. "Yes. Full of interesting, very very old things. Not that I have been there myself. But
I have friends, archaeological friends, who stay here always when they
come through Baghdad. Mr. Baker—Mr. Richard Baker, you know
him? And Professor Kalzman? And Dr. Pauncefoot Jones—and Mr.
and Mrs. McIntyre—they all come to the Tio. They are my friends.

And they tell me about what is in the Museum. Very very interesting."

"Where is it, and how do I get there?"

"You go straight along Rashid Street—a long way—past the turn to the Feisal Bridge and past Bank Street—you know Bank Street?"

"I don't know anything," said Victoria.

"And then there is another street—also going down to a bridge and it is along there on the right. You ask for Mr. Betoun Evans, he is English Adviser there—very nice man. And his wife, she is very nice, too, she came here as Transport Sergeant during the war. Oh, she is very very nice."

"I don't really want to go actually to the Museum," said Victoria. "I want to find a place—a Society—a kind of club called the Olive Branch."

"If you want olives," said Marcus, "I give you beautiful olives—very fine quality. They keep them especially for me—for the Tio Hotel. You see, I send you some to your table tonight."

"That's very kind of you," said Victoria and escaped towards Rashid Street.

"To the left," Marcus shouted after her, "not to the right. But it is a long way to the Museum. You had better take a taxi."

"Would a taxi know where the Olive Branch was?"

"No, they do not know where anything is! You say to the driver left, right, stop, straight on—just where you want to go."

"In that case, I might as well walk," said Victoria.

She reached Rashid Street and turned to the left.

Baghdad was entirely unlike her idea of it. A crowded main thoroughfare thronged with people, cars hooting violently, people shouting, European goods for sale in the shop windows, hearty spitting all round her with prodigious throat clearing as a preliminary. No mysterious Eastern figures, most of the people wore tattered or shabby Western clothes, old army and air force tunics, the occasional shuffling black robed and veiled figures were almost inconspicuous amongst the hybrid European styles of dress. Whining beggars came up to her— women with dirty babies in their arms. The pavement under her feet was uneven with occasional gaping holes.

She pursued her way, feeling suddenly strange and lost and far from home. Here was no glamour of travel, only confusion.

She came at last to the Feisal Bridge, passed it and went on. In spite of herself she was intrigued by the curious mixtures of things in the shop windows. Here were babies' shoes and woollies, toothpaste and cosmetics, electric torches and china cups and saucers—all shown together. Slowly a kind of fascination came over her, the fascination of assorted merchandise coming from all over the world to meet the strange assorted and varied wants of a mixed population.

She found the Museum, but not the Olive Branch. To one accustomed to finding her way about London it seemed incredible that here was no one she could ask. She knew no Arabic. Those shopkeepers who spoke to her in English as she passed, pressing their wares, presented blank faces when she asked for direction to the Olive Branch.

If one could only "ask a policeman," but gazing at the policemen actively waving their arms, and blowing their whistles, she realised that here that would be no solution.

She went into a bookshop with English books in the window, but a mention of the Olive Branch drew only a courteous shrug and shake of the head. Regrettably they had no idea at all.

And then, as she walked along the street, a prodigious hammering and clanging came to her ears and peering down a long dim alley, she remembered that Mrs. Cardew Trench had said the Olive Branch was near the Copper Bazaar. Here, at least, was the Copper Bazaar.

Victoria plunged in, and for the next three quarters of an hour she forgot the Olive Branch completely. The Copper Bazaar fascinated her. The blowlamps, the melting metal, the whole business of craftsmanship came like a revelation to the little Cockney used only to finished products stacked up for sale. She wandered at random through the Suq, passed out of the Copper Bazaar, came to the gay striped horse blankets, and the cotton quilted bed covers. Here European merchandise took on a totally different guise, in the arched cool darkness it had the exotic quality of something come from overseas, something strange and rare. Bales of cheap printed cottons in gay colours made a feast for the eyes.

Occasionally with a shout of *Balek, Balek,* a donkey or laden mule pushed past her, or men bearing great loads balanced on their backs. Little boys rushed up to her with trays slung round their necks.

"See, lady, elastic, good elastic, English elastic. Comb, English comb?"

The wares were thrust at her, close to her nose, with vehement urgings to buy. Victoria walked in a happy dream. This was really seeing the world. At every turn of the vast arched cool world of alleyways you came to something totally unexpected—an alley of tailors, sitting stitching, with smart pictures of European men's tailoring, a line of watches and cheap jewellery. Bales of velvets and rich metal embroidered brocades, then a chance turn and you were walking down an alley of cheap and shoddy second-hand European clothes, quaint pathetic little faded jumpers and long straggly vests.

Then every now and then there were glimpses into vast quiet courtyards open to the sky.

She came to a vast vista of men's trouserings, with cross-legged dignified merchants in turbans sitting in the middle of their little square recesses.

"*Balek!*"

A heavily-laden donkey coming up behind her made Victoria turn aside into a narrow alleyway open to the sky that twisted through tall houses. Walking along it she came, quite by chance, to the object of her search. Through an opening she looked into a small square courtyard and at the farther side of it an open doorway with THE OLIVE BRANCH on a huge sign and a rather impossible-looking plaster bird holding an unrecognisable twig in its beak.

Joyously Victoria sped across the courtyard and in at the open door. She found herself in a dimly lit room with tables covered with books and periodicals and more books ranged round on shelves. It looked a little like a book shop, except that there were little groups of chairs arranged together here and there.

Out of the dimness a young woman came up to Victoria and said in careful English,

"What can I do for you, yes, please?"

Victoria looked at her. She wore corduroy trousers and an orange flannel shirt and had black dank hair cut in a kind of depressed bob. So far she would have looked more suited to Bloomsbury, but her face was not Bloomsbury. It was a melancholy face with great sad dark eyes and a heavy nose.

"This is—is this—is—is Dr. Rathbone here?"

Maddening still not to know Edward's surname! Even Mrs. Cardew Trench had called him Edward Thingummy.

"Yes. Dr. Rathbone. The Olive Branch. You wish to join us? Yes? That will be very nice."

"Well, perhaps. I'd—can I see Dr. Rathbone, please?"

The young woman smiled in a tired way.

"We do not disturb. I have a form. I tell you all about everything. Then you sign your name. It is two dinars, please."

"I'm not sure yet that I want to join," said Victoria, alarmed at the mention of two dinars. "I'd like to see Dr. Rathbone—or his secretary. His secretary would do."

"I explain. I explain to you everything. We all are friends here, friends together, friends for the future—reading very fine educational books—reciting poems each to other."

"Dr. Rathbone's secretary," said Victoria loudly and clearly. "He particularly told me to ask for him."

A kind of mulish sullenness came into the young woman's face. "Not today," she said. "I explain—"

"Why not today? Isn't he here? Isn't Dr. Rathbone here?"

"Yais, Dr. Rathbone is here. He is upstairs. We do not disturb."

A kind of Anglo-Saxon intolerance of foreigners swept over Victoria. Regrettably, instead of the Olive Branch creating friendly international feelings, it seemed to be having the opposite effect as far as she was concerned.

"I have just arrived from England," she said—and her accents were almost those of Mrs. Cardew Trench herself—"and I have a very important message for Dr. Rathbone which I must deliver to him personally. Please take me to him at once! I am sorry to disturb him, but I have got to see him.

"At once!" she added, to clinch matters.

Before an imperious Briton who means to get his or her own way, barriers nearly always fall. The young woman turned at once and led the way to the back of the room and up a staircase and along a gallery overlooking the courtyard. Here she stopped before a door and knocked. A man's voice said, Come in.

Victoria's guide opened the door and motioned to Victoria to pass in. "It is a lady from England for you."

Victoria walked in.

From behind a large desk covered with papers, a man got up to greet her.

He was an imposing-looking elderly man of about sixty with a high domed forehead and white hair. Benevolence, kindliness and charm were the most apparent qualities of his personality. A producer of plays would have cast him without hesitation for the rôle of the great philanthropist.

He greeted Victoria with a warm smile and an outstretched hand. "So you've just come out from England," he said. "First visit East, eh?"

"Yes."

"I wonder what you think of it all . . . You must tell me sometime. Now, let me see, have I met you before or not? I'm so short-sighted and you didn't give your name."

"You don't know me," said Victoria, "but I'm a friend of Edward's."

"A friend of Edward's," said Dr. Rathbone. "Why, that's splendid. Does Edward know you're in Baghdad?"

"Not yet," said Victoria.

"Well, that will be a pleasant surprise for him when he gets back."

"Back?" said Victoria, her voice falling.

"Yes, Edward's in Basrah at the moment. I had to send him down there to see about some crates of books that have come out for us. There have been most vexatious delays in the Customs—we simply have not been able to get them cleared. The personal touch is the only thing, and Edward's good at that sort of thing. He knows just when to charm and when to bully, and he won't rest till he's got the thing through. He's a sticker. A very fine quality in a young man. I think a lot of Edward."

His eyes twinkled.

"But I don't suppose I need to sing Edward's praises to you, young lady."

"When—when will Edward be back from Basrah?" asked Victoria faintly.

"Well—now that I couldn't say. He won't come back till he's finished the job—and you can't hurry things too much in this country. Tell me where you are staying and I'll make sure he gets in touch with you as soon as he gets back."

"I was wondering—" Victoria spoke desperately, aware of her financial plight. "I was wondering if—if I could do some work here?"

"Now that I do appreciate," said Dr. Rathbone warmly. "Yes, of course you can. We need all the workers, all the help we can get. And especially English girls. Our work is going splendidly—quite splendidly—but there's lots more to be done. Still, people are keen. I've got thirty voluntary helpers already—thirty—all of 'em keen as mustard! If you're really in earnest, you can be most valuable."

The word voluntary struck unpleasantly on Victoria's ear.

"I really wanted a paid position," she said.

"Oh dear!" Dr. Rathbone's face fell. "That's rather more difficult. Our paid staff is very small—and for the moment, with the voluntary help, it's quite adequate."

"I can't afford not to take a job," explained Victoria. "I'm a competent shorthand typist," she added without a blush.

"I'm sure you're competent, my dear young lady, you radiate competence, if I may say so. But with us it's a question of L.S.D. But even if you take a job elsewhere, I hope you'll help us in your spare time. Most of our workers have their own regular jobs. I'm sure you'll find helping us really inspiring. There must be an end of all the savagery in the world, the wars, the misunderstandings, the suspicions. A common meeting ground, that's what we all need. Drama, art, poetry—the great things of the spirit—no room there for petty jealousies or hatreds."

"N-no," said Victoria doubtfully, recalling friends of hers who were actresses and artists and whose lives seemed to be obsessed by jealousy of the most trivial kind, and by hatreds of a peculiarly virulent intensity.

"I've had the 'Midsummer Night's Dream' translated into forty different languages," said Dr. Rathbone. "Forty different sets of young people all reacting to the same wonderful piece of literature. Young people—that's the secret. I've no use for anybody but the young. Once the mind and spirit are muscle-bound, it's too late. No, it's the young who must get together. Take that girl downstairs, Catherine, the one who showed you up here. She's a Syrian from Damascus. You and she are probably about the same age. Normally you'd never come together, you'd have nothing in common. But at the Olive Branch you and she and many many others, Russians, Jewesses, Iraqis, Turkish girls, Armenians, Egyptians, Persians, all meet and like each other and read the same books and discuss pictures and music (we have excellent lecturers who come out) all of you finding out and being excited by encountering a different point of view—why, that's what the world is meant to be."

Victoria could not help thinking that Dr. Rathbone was slightly overoptimistic in assuming that all those divergent elements who were coming together would necessarily like each other. She and Catherine, for instance, had not liked each other at all. And Victoria strongly suspected that the more they saw of each other the greater their dislike would grow.

"Edward's splendid," said Dr. Rathbone. "Gets on with everybody. Better, perhaps, with the girls than with the young men. The men students out here are apt to be difficult at first—suspicious—almost hostile. But the girls adore Edward, they'll do anything for him. He and Catherine get on particularly well."

"Indeed," said Victoria coldly. Her dislike of Catherine grew even more intense.

"Well," said Dr. Rathbone, smiling, "come and help us if you can." It was a dismissal. He pressed her hand warmly. Victoria went out of the room and down the stairs. Catherine was standing near the door talking to a girl who had just come in with a small suitcase in her hand. She was a good-looking dark girl, and just for a moment Victoria fancied that she had seen her before somewhere. But the girl looked at her without any sign of recognition. The two young women had been talking eagerly together in some language Victoria did not know. They stopped when she appeared and remained silent, staring at her. She walked past them to the door, forcing herself to say "Goodbye" politely to Catherine as she went out.

She found her way out from the winding alley into Rashid Street and slowly back to the Hotel, her eyes unseeing of the throngs around her. She tried to keep her mind from dwelling on her own predicament (penniless in Baghdad) by fixing her mind on Dr. Rathbone and the general setup of the Olive Branch. Edward had had an idea in London that there was something "fishy" about his job. What was fishy? Dr. Rathbone? Or the Olive Branch itself?

Victoria could hardly believe that there was anything fishy about Dr. Rathbone. He appeared to her to be one of those misguided enthusiasts who insist on seeing the world in their own idealistic manner, regardless of realities.

What had Edward meant by fishy? He'd been very vague. Perhaps he didn't really know himself.

Could Dr. Rathbone be some kind of colossal fraud?

Victoria, fresh from the soothing charm of his manner, shook her head. His manner had certainly changed, ever so slightly, at the idea of paying her a salary. He clearly preferred people to work for nothing.

But that, thought Victoria, was a sign of common sense.

Mr. Greenholtz, for instance, would have felt just the same.

XII

Victoria arrived back at the Tio, rather footsore, to be hailed enthusiastically by Marcus who was sitting out on the grass terrace overlooking the river and talking to a thin rather shabby middle-aged man.

"Come and have a drink with us, Miss Jones. Martini—sidecar? This is Mr. Dakin. Miss Jones from England. Now then, my dear, what will you have?"

Victoria said she would have a sidecar "and some of those lovely nuts?" she suggested hopefully, remembering that nuts were nutritious.

"You like nuts. Jesus!" He gave the order in rapid Arabic. Mr. Dakin said in a sad voice that he would have a lemonade.

"Ah," cried Marcus, "but that is ridiculous. Ah, here is Mrs. Cardew Trench. You know Mr. Dakin? What will you have?"

"Gin and lime," said Mrs. Cardew Trench, nodding to Dakin in an offhand manner. "You look hot," she added to Victoria.

"I've been walking round seeing the sights."

When the drinks came, Victoria ate a large plateful of pistachio nuts and also some potato chips.

Presently, a short thickset man came up the steps and the hospitable Marcus hailed him in his turn. He was introduced to Victoria as Captain Crosbie; and by the way his slightly protuberant eyes goggled at her, Victoria gathered that he was susceptible to feminine charm.

"Just come out?" he asked her.

"Yesterday."

"Thought I hadn't seen you around."

"She is very nice and beautiful, is she not?" said Marcus joyfully. "Oh, yes, it is very nice to have Miss Victoria. I will give a party for her—a very nice party."

"With baby chickens?" said Victoria hopefully.

"Yes, yes—and foie gras—Strasburg foie gras—and perhaps caviare—and then we have a dish with fish—very nice—a fish from the Tigris, but all with sauce and mushrooms. And then there is a turkey stuffed in the way we have it at my home—with rice and raisins and spice—

and all cooked so! Oh, it is very good—but you must eat very much of it—not just a tiny spoonful. Or if you like it better you shall have a steak—a really big steak and tender—I see to it. We will have a long dinner that goes on for hours. It will be very nice. I do not eat myself— I only drink."

"That will be lovely," said Victoria in a faint voice. The description of these viands made her feel quite giddy with hunger. She wondered if Marcus really meant to give this party and if so, how soon it could possibly happen.

"Thought you'd gone to Basrah," said Mrs. Cardew Trench to Crosbie.

"Got back yesterday," said Crosbie.

He looked up at the balcony.

"Who's the bandit?" he asked. "Feller in fancy dress in the big hat."

"That, my dear, is Sir Rupert Crofton Lee," said Marcus. "Mr. Shrivenham brought him here from the Embassy last night. He is very nice man, very distinguished traveller. He rides on camels over the Sahara, and climbs up mountains. It is very uncomfortable and dangerous, that kind of life. I should not like it myself."

"Oh, he's that chap, is he?" said Crosbie. "I've read his book."

"I came over on the plane with him," said Victoria.

Both men, or so it seemed to her, looked at her with interest.

"He's frightfully stuck up and pleased with himself," said Victoria with disparagement.

"Knew his aunt in Simla," said Mrs. Cardew Trench. "The whole family is like that. Clever as they make them, but can't help boasting of it."

"He's been sitting out there doing nothing all the morning," said Victoria with slight disapproval.

"It is his stomach," explained Marcus. "Today he cannot eat anything. It is sad."

"I can't think," said Mrs. Cardew Trench, "why you're the size you are, Marcus, when you never eat anything."

"It is the drink," said Marcus. He sighed deeply. "I drink far too much. Tonight my sister and her husband come. I will drink and drink almost until morning." He sighed again, then uttered his usual sudden roar. "Jesus! Jesus! Bring the same again."

"Not for me," said Victoria hastily, and Mr. Dakin refused also, finishing up his lemonade, and ambling gently away while Crosbie went up to his room.

Mrs. Cardew Trench flicked Dakin's glass with her finger-nail, "Lemonade as usual?" she said. "Bad sign, that."

Victoria asked why it was a bad sign.

"When a man only drinks when he's alone."

"Yes, my dear," said Marcus. "That is so."

"Does he really drink, then?" asked Victoria.

"That's why he's never got on," said Mrs. Cardew Trench. "Just manages to keep his job and that's all."

"But he is a very nice man," said the charitable Marcus.

"Pah," said Mrs. Cardew Trench. "He's a wet fish. Potters and dilly dallies about—no stamina—no grip on life. Just one more Englishman who's come out East and gone to seed."

Thanking Marcus for the drink and refusing a second, Victoria went up to her room, removed her shoes, and lay down on her bed to do some serious thinking. The three pounds odd to which her capital had dwindled was, she fancied, already due to Marcus for board and lodging. Owing to his generous disposition, and if she could sustain life mainly on alcoholic liquor assisted by nuts, olives and chip potatoes, she might solve the purely alimentary problem of the next few days. How long would it be before Marcus presented her with her bill, and how long would he allow it to run unpaid? She had no idea. He was not really, she thought, careless in business matters. She ought, of course, to find somewhere cheaper to live. But how would she find out where to go? She ought to find herself a job—quickly. But where did one apply for jobs? What kind of a job? Who could she ask about looking for one? How terribly handicapping to one's style it was to be dumped down practically penniless in a foreign city where one didn't know the ropes. With just a little knowledge of the terrain, Victoria felt confident (as always) that she could hold her own. When would Edward get back from Basrah? Perhaps (horror) Edward would have forgotten all about her. Why on earth had she come rushing out to Baghdad in this asinine way? Who and what was Edward after all? Just another young man with an engaging grin and an attractive way of saying things. And what—what—what was his surname? If she knew that, she might wire him—no good, she didn't even know where he was staying. She didn't know anything—that was the trouble—that was what was cramping her style.

And there was no one to whom she could go for advice. Not Marcus who was kind but never listened. Not Mrs. Cardew Trench (who had

had suspicions from the first). Not Mrs. Hamilton Clipp who had vanished to Kirkuk. Not Dr. Rathbone—

She must get some money—or get a job—any job. Look after children,
stick stamps on in an office, serve in a restaurant . . . Otherwise they
would send her to a Consul and she would be repatriated to England
and never see Edward again . . .

At this point, worn out with emotion, Victoria fell asleep.

She woke some hours later and deciding that she might as well
be hanged for a sheep as a lamb, went down to the restaurant and
worked her way solidly through the entire menu—a generous one.
When she had finished, she felt slightly like a boa constrictor, but
definitely heartened.

"It's no good worrying any more," thought Victoria. "I'll leave it all
till tomorrow. Something may turn up, or I may think of something,
or Edward may come back."

Before going to bed she strolled out onto the terrace by the river.
Since in the feelings of those living in Baghdad it was arctic winter,
nobody else was out there except one of the waiters who was leaning
over a railing staring down into the water, and he sprang away guiltily
when Victoria appeared and hurried back into the hotel by the service
door.

Victoria to whom, coming from England, it appeared to be an ordinary summer night with a slight nip in the air, was enchanted by the
Tigris seen in the moonlight with the further bank looking mysterious
and Eastern with its fringes of palms.

"Well, anyway, I've got here," said Victoria, cheering up a good deal,
"and I'll manage somehow. Something is bound to turn up."

With this Micawber-like pronouncement, she went up to bed, and
the waiter slipped quietly out again and resumed his task of attaching
a knotted rope so that it hung down to the river's edge.

Presently another figure came out of the shadows and joined him.
Mr. Dakin said in a low voice,

"All in order?"

"Yes, sir, nothing suspicious to report."

Having completed the task to his satisfaction, Mr. Dakin retreated
into the shadows, exchanged his waiter's white coat for his own nondescript blue pinstripe and ambled gently along the terrace until he
stood outlined against the water's edge, just where the steps led up from
the street below.

"Getting pretty chilly in the evenings now," said Crosbie strolling out from the bar and down to join him. "Suppose you don't feel it so much, coming from Teheran."

They stood there for a moment or two smoking. Unless they raised their voices, nobody could overhear them. Crosbie said quietly,

"Who's the girl?"

"Niece apparently of the archaeologist, Pauncefoot Jones."

"Oh well—that should be all right. But coming on the same plane as Crofton Lee—"

"It's certainly as well," said Dakin, "to take nothing for granted."

The men smoked in silence for a few moments.

Crosbie said: "You really think it's advisable to shift the thing from the Embassy to here?"

"I think so, yes."

"In spite of the whole thing being taped down to the smallest detail."

"It was taped down to the smallest detail in Basrah—and that went wrong."

"Oh, I know. Mohammed Salah Hassan was poisoned, by the way."

"Yes—he would be. Was there any signs of an approach to the Consulate?"

"I suspect there may have been. Bit of a shindy there. Chap drew a revolver." He paused and added, "Richard Baker grabbed him and disarmed him."

"Richard Baker," said Dakin thoughtfully.

"Know him? He's—"

"Yes, I know him."

There was a pause and then Dakin said,

"Improvisation. That's what I'm banking on. If we have, as you say, got everything taped—and our plans are known, then it's easy for the other side to have got us taped, too. I very much doubt if Carmichael would even so much as get near the Embassy—and even if he reached it—" He shook his head.

"Here, only you and I and Crofton Lee are wise to what's going on."

"They'll know Crofton Lee moved here from the Embassy."

"Oh, of course. That was inevitable. But don't you see, Crosbie, that whatever show they put up against our improvisation has got to be improvised, too. It's got to be hastily thought of and hastily arranged. It's got to come, so to speak, from the outside. There's no question here of someone established in the Tio six months ago waiting. The Tio's never been in the picture until now. There's never been any idea or suggestion of using the Tio as the rendezvous."

He looked at his watch. "I'll go up now and see Crofton Lee."

Dakin's raised hand had no need to tap on Sir Rupert's door. It opened silently to let him in.

The traveller had only one small reading lamp alight and had placed his chair beside it. As he sat down again, he gently slipped a small automatic pistol onto the table within reach of his hand.

He said: "What about it, Dakin? Do you think he'll come?"

"I think so, yes, Sir Rupert." Then he said, "You've never met him, have you?"

The other shook his head.

"No. I'm looking forward to meeting him tonight. That young man, Dakin, must have got guts."

"Oh yes," said Mr. Dakin in his flat voice. "He's got guts."

He sounded a little surprised at the fact needing to be stated.

"I don't mean only courage," said the other. "Lots of courage in the war—magnificent. I mean—"

"Imagination?" suggested Dakin.

"Yes. To have the guts to believe something that isn't in the least degree probable. To risk your life finding out that a ridiculous story isn't ridiculous at all. That takes something that the modern young man usually hasn't got. I hope he'll come."

"I think he'll come," said Mr. Dakin.

Sir Rupert glanced at him sharply.

"You've got it all sewn up?"

"Crosbie's on the balcony, and I shall be watching the stairs. When Carmichael reaches you, tap on the wall and I'll come in."

Crofton Lee nodded.

Dakin went softly out of the room. He went to the left and onto the balcony and walked to the extreme corner. Here, too, a knotted rope dropped over the edge and came to earth in the shade of a eucalyptus tree and some Judas bushes.

Mr. Dakin went back past Crofton Lee's door and into his own room beyond. His room had a second door in it, leading onto the passage behind the rooms, and it opened within a few feet of the head of the stairs. With this door unobtrusively ajar, Mr. Dakin settled down to his vigil.

It was about four hours later that a *gufa*, that primitive craft of the Tigris, dropped gently downstream and came to shore on the mud flat beneath the Tio Hotel. A few moments later a slim figure swarmed up the rope and crouched amongst the Judas trees.

XIII

IT HAD BEEN Victoria's intention to go to bed and to sleep and to leave all problems until the morning; but having already slept most of the afternoon, she found herself devastatingly wide awake.

In the end she switched on the light, finished a magazine story she had been reading in the plane, darned her stockings, tried on her new nylons, wrote out several different advertisements requiring employment—(she could ask tomorrow where these should be inserted) wrote three or four tentative letters to Mrs. Hamilton Clipp, each setting out a different and more ingenious set of unforeseen circumstances which had resulted in her being "stranded" in Baghdad, sketched out one or two telegrams appealing for help to her sole surviving relative, a very old, crusty, and unpleasant gentleman in the North of England who had never helped anybody in his life, tried out a new style of hairdo, and finally with a sudden yawn decided that at last she really was desperately sleepy and ready for bed and repose.

It was at this moment that without any warning her bedroom door swung open, a man slipped in, turned the key in the lock behind him and said to her urgently,

"For God's sake hide me somewhere—quickly . . ."

Victoria's reactions were never slow. In the twinkling of an eye she had noted the laboured breathing, the fading voice, the way the man held an old red knitted scarf bunched on his breast with a desperate clutching hand. And she rose immediately in response to the adventure.

The room did not lend itself to many hiding places. There was the wardrobe, a chest of drawers, a table and the rather pretentious dressing table. The bed was a large one—almost a double bed and memories of childish hide-and-seek made Victoria's reaction prompt.

"Quick," she said. She swept off pillows, and raised sheet and blanket.

The man lay across the top of the bed. Victoria pulled sheet and blanket over him, dumped the pillows on top and sat down herself on the side of the bed.

Almost immediately there came a low insistent knocking on the door. Victoria called out, "Who is it?" in a faint alarmed voice.

"Please," said a man's voice outside. "Open, please. It is the police."

Victoria crossed the room, pulling her dressing gown round her. As she did so, she noticed the man's red knitted scarf was lying on the floor and she caught it up and swept it into a drawer, then she turned the key and opened the door of her room a small way, peering out with an expression of alarm.

A dark-haired young man in a mauve pinstripe suit was standing outside and behind him was a man in police officer's uniform.

"What's the matter?" Victoria asked, letting a quaver creep into her voice.

The young man smiled brilliantly and spoke in very passable English.

"I am so sorry, miss, to disturb you at this hour," he said, "but we have a criminal escaped. He has run into this hotel. We must look in every room. He is a very dangerous man."

"Oh dear!" Victoria fell back, opening the door wide. "Do come in, please, and look. How very frightening. Look in the bathroom, please. Oh! and the wardrobe—and, I wonder, would you mind looking under the bed? He might have been there all the evening."

The search was very rapid.

"No, he is not here."

"You're sure he's not under the bed? No, how silly of me. He couldn't be in here at all. I locked the door when I went to bed."

"Thank you, miss, and good evening."

The young man bowed and withdrew with his uniformed assistant. Victoria, following him to the door, said,

"I'd better lock it again, hadn't I? To be safe."

"Yes, that will be best, certainly. Thank you."

Victoria relocked the door and stood by it for some few minutes. She heard the police officers knock in the same way on the door the other side of the passage, heard the door open, an exchange of remarks and the indignant hoarse voice of Mrs. Cardew Trench, and then the door closing. It reopened a few minutes later, and the sound of their footsteps moved down the passage. The next knock came from much further away.

Victoria turned and walked across the room to the bed. It was borne in upon her that she had probably been excessively foolish. Led away by the romantic spirit, and by the sound of her own language, she had impulsively lent aid to what was probably an extremely dangerous criminal. A disposition to be on the side of the hunted against the hunter sometimes brings unpleasant consequences. Oh, well, thought Victoria, I'm in for it now, anyway!

Standing beside the bed she said curtly,

"Get up."

There was no movement, and Victoria said sharply, though without raising her voice,

"They've gone. You can get up now."

But still there was no sign of movement from under the slightly raised hump of pillows. Impatiently, Victoria threw them all off.

The young man lay just as she had left him. But now his face was a queer greyish colour and his eyes were closed.

Then with a sharp catch in her breath, Victoria noticed something else—a bright red stain seeping through onto the blanket.

"Oh no," said Victoria, almost as though pleading with someone. "Oh, no—no!"

And as though in recognition of that plea the wounded man opened his eyes. He stared at her, stared as though from very far away at some object he was not quite certain of seeing.

His lips parted—the sound was so faint that Victoria scarcely heard.

She bent down.

"What?"

She heard this time. With difficulty, great difficulty, the young man said two words. Whether she heard them correctly or not Victoria did not know. They seemed to her quite nonsensical and without meaning. What he said was, "Lucifer—Basrah . . ."

The eyelids drooped and flickered over the wide anxious eyes. He said one word more—a name. Then his head jerked back a little and he lay still.

Victoria stood quite still, her heart beating violently. She was filled now with an intense pity and anger. What to do next she had no idea. She must call someone—get someone to come—She was alone here with a dead man and sooner or later the police would want an explanation.

While her brain worked rapidly on the situation, a small sound made her turn her head. The key had fallen out of her bedroom door, and as she stared at it, she heard the sound of the lock turning. The door opened and Mr. Dakin came in, carefully closing the door behind him.

He walked across to her, saying quietly,

"Nice work, my dear. You think quickly. How is he?"

With a catch in her voice Victoria said:

"I think he's—he's dead."

She saw the other's face alter, caught just a flash of intense anger, then his face was just as she had seen it the day before—only now it seemed to her that the indecision and flabbiness of the man had vanished, giving place to something quite different.

He bent down—and gently loosened the ragged tunic.

"Very neatly stabbed through the heart," said Dakin as he straightened up. "He was a brave lad—and a clever one."

Victoria found her voice.

"The police came. They said he was a criminal. Was he a criminal?"

"No. He wasn't a criminal."

"Were they—were they the police?"

"I don't know," said Dakin. "They may have been. It's all the same."

Then he asked her:

"Did he say anything—before he died?"

"Yes."

"What was it?"

"He said Lucifer—and then Basrah. And then after a pause he said a name—a French name it sounded like—but I mayn't have got it right."

"What did it sound like to you?"

"I think it was Lefarge."

"Lefarge," said Dakin thoughtfully.

"What does it all mean?" said Victoria, and added with some dismay, "And what am I to do?"

"We must get you out of it as far as we can," said Dakin. "As for what it's all about, I'll come back and talk to you later. The first thing to do is to get hold of Marcus. It's his hotel and Marcus has a great deal of sense, though one doesn't always realise it in talking to him. I'll get hold of him. He won't have gone to bed. It's only half past one. He seldom goes to bed before two o'clock. Just attend to your appearance before I bring him in. Marcus is very susceptible to beauty in distress."

He left the room. As though in a dream she moved over to the dressing table, combed back her hair, made up her face to a becoming pallor and collapsed onto a chair as she heard footsteps approaching.

Dakin came in without knocking. Behind him loomed the bulk of Marcus Tio. This time Marcus was serious. There was not the usual smile on his face.

"Now, Marcus," said Mr. Dakin, "you must do what you can about this. It's been a terrible shock to this poor girl. The fellow burst in, collapsed—she's got a very kind heart and she hid him from the police. And now he's dead. She oughtn't to have done it, perhaps, but girls are soft-hearted."

"Of course she did not like the police," said Marcus. "Nobody likes the police. I do not like the police. But I have to stand well with them because of my hotel. You want me to square them with money?"

"We just want to get the body away quietly."

"That is very nice, my dear. And I, too, I do not want a body in my hotel. But it is, as you say, not so easy to do?"

"I think it could be managed," said Dakin. "You've got a doctor in your family, haven't you?"

"Yes, Paul, my sister's husband, is a doctor. He is a very nice boy. But I do not want him to get into trouble."

"He won't," said Dakin. "Listen, Marcus. We move the body from Miss Jones' room across into my room. That lets her out of it. Then I use your telephone. In ten minutes' time a young man reels into the hotel from the street. He is very drunk, he clutches his side. He demands me at the top of his voice. He staggers into my room and collapses. I come out and call you and ask for a doctor. You produce your brother-in-law. He sends for an ambulance and he goes in it with this drunken friend of mine. Before they get to the hospital my friend is dead. He has been stabbed. That is all right for you. He has been stabbed in the street before coming into your hotel."

"My brother-in-law takes away the body—and the young man who plays the part of the drunkard, he goes away quietly in the morning perhaps?"

"That's the idea."

"And there is no body found in my hotel? And Miss Jones she does not get any worry or annoyance? I think, my dear, that that is all a very good idea."

"Good, then if you'll make sure the coast is clear, I'll get the body across to my room. Those servants of yours potter round the corridors half the night. Go along to your room and raise a shindy. Get them all running to fetch you things."

Marcus nodded and left the room.

"You're a strong girl," said Dakin. "Can you manage to help me to carry him across the corridor to my room?"

Victoria nodded. Between them they lifted the limp body, carried it across the deserted corridor (in the distance Marcus' voice could be heard upraised in furious anger) and laid it on Dakin's bed.

Dakin said:

"Got a pair of scissors? Then cut off top of your underblanket where it's stained. I don't think the stain's gone through to the mattress. The tunic soaked up most of it. I'll come along to you in about an hour. Here, wait a minute, take a pull from this flask of mine."

Victoria obeyed.

"Good girl," said Dakin. "Now go back to your room. Turn out the light. As I said, I'll be along in about an hour."

"And you'll tell me what it all means?"

He gave her a long rather peculiar stare but did not answer her question.

XIV

VICTORIA LAY IN bed with her light out, listening through the darkness. She heard sounds of loud drunken altercation. Heard a voice declaring: "Felt I got to look you up, ole man. Had a row with a fellow outside." She heard bells ring. Heard other voices. Heard a good deal of commotion. Then came a stretch of comparative silence—except for the far off playing of Arab music on a gramophone in somebody's room. When it seemed to her as though hours had passed, she heard the gentle opening of her door, sat up in bed and switched on the bedside lamp.

"That's right," said Dakin approvingly.

He brought a chair up to the bedside and sat down in it. He sat there, staring at her in the considering manner of a physician making a diagnosis.

"Tell me what it's all about?" demanded Victoria.

"Suppose," said Dakin, "that you tell me all about yourself first. What are you doing here? Why did you come to Baghdad?"

Whether it was the events of the night, or whether it was something in Dakin's personality (Victoria thought afterwards that it was the latter) Victoria for once did not launch out on an inspired and meretricious account of her presence in Baghdad. Quite simply and straightforwardly she told him everything. Her meeting with Edward, her determination to get to Baghdad, the miracle of Mrs. Hamilton Clipp, and her own financial destitution.

"I see," said Dakin when she'd finished.

He was silent for a moment before he spoke.

"Perhaps I'd like to keep you out of this. I'm not sure. But the point is, you can't be kept out of it! You're in it, whether I like it or not. And as you're in it, you might as well work for me."

"You've got a job for me?" Victoria sat up in bed, her cheeks bright with anticipation.

"Perhaps. But not the kind of job you're thinking of. This is a serious job, Victoria. And it's dangerous."

"Oh, that's all right," said Victoria cheerfully. She added doubtfully, "It's not dishonest, is it? Because though I know I tell an awful lot of lies, I wouldn't really like to do anything that was dishonest."

Dakin smiled a little.

"Strangely enough, your capacity to think up a convincing lie quickly is one of your qualifications for the job. No, it's not dishonest. On the contrary, you are enlisted in the cause of law and order. I'm going to put you in the picture—only in a general kind of way, but so that you can understand fully what it is you are doing and exactly what the dangers are. You seem to be a sensible young woman and I don't suppose you've thought much about world politics which is just as well, because as Hamlet very wisely remarked, 'There is nothing either good or bad, but thinking makes it so'."

"I know everybody says there's going to be another war sooner or later," said Victoria.

"Exactly," said Mr. Dakin. "Why does everybody say so, Victoria?"

She frowned. "Why, because Russia—the Communists—America—" she stopped.

"You see," said Dakin. "Those aren't your own opinions or words. They're picked up from newspapers, and casual talk, and the wireless. There are two divergent points of view dominating different parts of the world; that is true enough. And they are represented loosely in the public mind as 'Russia and the Communists' and 'America'. Now the only hope for the future, Victoria, lies in peace, in production, in constructive activities and not destructive ones. Therefore, everything depends on those who hold those two divergent viewpoints, either agreeing to differ and each contenting themselves with their respective spheres of activity, or else finding a mutual basis for agreement or at least toleration. Instead of that, the opposite is happening, a wedge is being driven in the whole time to force two mutually suspicious groups further and further apart. Certain things led one or two people to believe that this activity comes from a third party or group working under cover and so far absolutely unsuspected by the world at large. Whenever there is a chance of agreement being reached or any sign of dispersal of suspicion, some incident occurs to plunge one side back in distrust, or the other side into definite hysterical fear. These things are not accidents, Victoria, they are deliberately produced for a calculated effect."

"But why do you think so and who's doing it?"

"One of the reasons we think so is because of money. The money, you see, is coming from the wrong sources. Money, Victoria, is always the great clue to what is happening in the world. As a physician feels your pulse, to get a clue to your state of health, so money is the life blood that feeds any great movement or cause. Without it, the movement can't make headway. Now here, there are very large sums of money involved and although very cleverly and artfully camouflaged, there is definitely something wrong about where the money comes from and where it is going. A great many unofficial strikes, various threats to Governments in Europe who show signs of recovery, are staged and brought into being by Communists, zealots for their cause—but the funds for these measures do not come from Communist sources, and traced back, they come from very strange and unlikely quarters. It is not Capitalist money, though it naturally passes through Capitalist hands. Another point, enormous sums of money seem to be going completely out of circulation. As much as though—to put it simply—you spent your salary every week on things—bracelets or tables or chairs—and those things then disappeared or passed out of ordinary circulation and sight. All over the world a great demand for diamonds and other precious stones has arisen. They change hands a dozen or more times until finally they disappear and cannot be traced.

"This, of course, is only a vague sketch. The upshot is that somewhere a third group of people whose aim is as yet obscure, are fomenting strife and misunderstanding and are engaging in cleverly camouflaged money and jewel transactions for their own ends. We have reason to believe that in every country there are agents of this

group, some established there many years ago. Some are in very high
and responsible positions, others are playing humble parts, but all
are working with one unknown end in view. In substance, it is exactly
like the Fifth Column activities at the beginning of the last war, only
this time it is on a world wide scale."

"But who are these people?" Victoria demanded.

"They are not, we think, of any special nationality. What they
want is, I fear, the betterment of the world! The delusion that by
force you can impose the Millennium on the human race is one of
the most dangerous delusions in existence. Those who are out only to
line their own pockets can do little harm—mere greed defeats its own
ends. But the belief in a superstratum of human beings—in Supermen to
rule the rest of the decadent world—that, Victoria, is the most evil of all
beliefs. For when you say, 'I am not as other men'—you have lost the
two most valuable qualities we have ever tried to attain:—humility
and brotherhood."

He coughed. "Well, I mustn't preach a sermon. Let me just explain
to you what we do know. There are various centers of activity. One in
the Argentine, one in Canada—certainly one or more in the United
States of America, and I should imagine, though we can't tell, one in
Russia. And now we come to a very interesting phenomenon.

"In the past two years, twenty-eight promising young scientists of
various nationalities have quietly faded out of their background. The
same thing has happened with constructional engineers, with aviators,
with electricians and many other skilled trades. These disappearances
have this in common: those concerned are all young, all ambitious, and
all without close ties. Besides those we know of, there must be many
many more, and we are beginning to guess at something of what they
may be accomplishing."

Victoria listened, her brows drawn together.

"You might say it was impossible in these days for anything to go on
in any country, unknown to the rest of the world. I do not, of course,
mean undercover activities; those may go on anywhere. But anything
on a large scale of up-to-date production. And yet there are still obscure
parts of the world, remote from trade routes, cut off by mountains and
deserts, in the midst of peoples who still have the power to bar out
strangers and which are never known or visited except by a solitary
and exceptional traveller. Things could go on there the news of which
would never penetrate to the outside world, or only as a dim and
ridiculous rumour.

"I won't particularize the spot. It can be reached from China—and nobody knows what goes on in the interior of China. It can be reached from the Himalayas, but the journey there, save to the initiated, is hard and long to travel. Machinery and personnel dispatched from all over the globe reaches it, after being diverted from its ostensible destination. The mechanics of it all need not be gone into.

"But one man got interested in following up a certain trail. He was an unusual man, a man who has friends and contacts throughout the East. He was born in Kashgar and he knows a score of local dialects and languages. He suspected and he followed up the trail. What he heard was so incredible that when he got back to civilization and reported it, he was not believed. He admitted that he had had fever and he was treated as a man who had had delirium.

"Only two people believed his story. One was myself. I never object to believing impossible things—they're so often true. The other—" he hesitated.

"Yes?" said Victoria.

"The other was Sir Rupert Crofton Lee, a great traveller, and a man who had himself travelled through these remote regions and who knew something about their possibilities.

"The upshot of it all was that Carmichael, that's my man, decided to go and find out for himself. It was a desperate and hazardous journey, but he was as well equipped as any man to carry it through. That was nine months back. We heard nothing until a few weeks ago and then news came through. He was alive and he'd got what he went to get. Definite proof.

"But the other side were on to him. It was vital to them that he should never get back with his proofs. And we've had ample evidence of how the whole system is penetrated and infiltrated with their agents. Even in my own department there are leaks. And some of those leaks, Heaven help us, are at a very high level.

"Every frontier has been watched for him. Innocent lives have been sacrificed in mistake for his—they don't set much store by human life. But somehow or other he got through unscathed—until tonight."

"Then that was who—he was?"

"Yes, my dear. A very brave and indomitable young man."

"But what about the proofs? Did they get those?"

A very slow smile showed on Dakin's tired face.

"I don't think they did. No, knowing Carmichael, I'm pretty sure

they didn't. But he died without being able to tell us where those
proofs are and how to get hold of them. I think he probably tried to
say something when he was dying that should give us the clue." He
repeated slowly, "Lucifer—Basrah—Lefarge. He'd been in Basrah—
tried to report at the Consulate and narrowly missed being shot. It's
possible that he left the proofs somewhere in Basrah. What I want
you to do, Victoria, is to go there and try to find out."

"Me?"

"Yes. You've no experience. You don't know what you're looking for.
But you heard Carmichael's last words and they may suggest something to you when you get there. Who knows—you may have beginner's
luck?"

"I'd love to go to Basrah," said Victoria eagerly.

Dakin smiled.

"Suits you because your young man is there, eh? That's all right.
Good camouflage, too. Nothing like a genuine love affair for
camouflage. You go to Basrah, keep your eyes and ears open and look
about you. I can't give you any instructions on how to set about things
—in fact, I'd much rather not. You seem a young woman with plenty
of ingenuity of your own. What the words Lucifer and Lefarge
mean—assuming that you heard correctly—I don't know. I'm inclined
to agree with you that Lefarge must be a name. Look out for that name."

"How do I get to Basrah?" said Victoria in a businesslike way. "And
what do I use for money?"

Dakin took out his pocketbook and handed her a wad of paper money.

"That's what you use for money. As for how you get to Basrah, fall
into conversation with that old trout Mrs. Cardew Trench tomorrow
morning, say you're anxious to visit Basrah before you go off to this
dig you're pretending to work at. Ask her about a hotel. She'll tell you
at once you must stay at the Consulate and will send a telegram to
Mrs. Clayton. You'll probably find your Edward there. The Claytons
keep open house—everyone who passes through stays with them. Beyond that, I can't give you any tips except one. If—er—anything unpleasant happens, if you're asked what you know and who put you up
to what you're doing—don't try and be heroic. Spill the beans at once."

"Thank you very much," said Victoria gratefully. "I'm an awful
coward about pain, and if anyone were to torture me I'm afraid I
shouldn't hold out."

"They won't bother to torture you," said Mr. Dakin. "Unless some
sadistic element enters in. Torture's very old fashioned. A little prick

with a needle and you answer every question truthfully without realising you're doing it. We live in a scientific age. That's why I didn't want you to get grand ideas of secrecy. You won't be telling them anything they don't know already. They'll be wise to me after this evening—bound to be. And to Rupert Crofton Lee."

"What about Edward? Do I tell him?"

"That I must leave to you. Theoretically, you're to hold your tongue about what you're doing to everybody. Practically!" His eyebrows went up quizzically. "You put him in danger, too. There's that aspect of it. Still, I gather he had a good record in the Air Force. I don't suppose danger will worry him. Two heads are often better than one. So he thinks there's something fishy about this 'Olive Branch' he's working for? That's interesting—very interesting."

"Why?"

"Because we think so, too," said Dakin.

Then he added:

"Just two parting tips. First, if you don't mind my saying so, don't tell too many different kind of lies. It's harder to remember and live up to. I know you're a bit of a virtuoso, but keep it simple, is my advice."

"I'll remember," said Victoria with becoming humility. "And the other tip?"

"Just keep your ears strained for any mention of a young woman called Anna Scheele."

"Who is she?"

"We don't know much about her. We could do with knowing a little more."

XV

"Of course you must stay at the Consulate," said Mrs. Cardew Trench. "Nonsense, my dear—you can't stay at the Airport Hotel. The Claytons will be delighted. I've known them for years. We'll send a wire and you can go down on tonight's train. They know Dr. Pauncefoot Jones quite well."

Victoria had the grace to blush. The Bishop of Llangow, alias the Bishop of Languao was one thing; a real flesh and blood Dr. Pauncefoot Jones was quite another.

"I suppose," thought Victoria guiltily, "I could be sent to prison for that—false pretences or something."

Then she cheered herself up by reflecting that it was only if you attempted to obtain money by false statements that the rigours of the law were set in motion. Whether this was really so or not, Victoria did not know, being as ignorant of the law as most average people, but it had a cheering sound.

The train journey had all the fascination of novelty—to Victoria's idea the train was hardly an express—but she had begun to feel conscious of her Western impatience.

A Consular car met her at the station and she was driven to the Consulate. The car drove in through big gates into a delightful garden and drew up before a flight of steps leading up to a balcony surrounding the house. Mrs. Clayton, a smiling energetic woman, came through the swinging wire mesh door to meet her.

"We're so pleased to see you," she said. "Basrah's really delightful this time of year, and you oughtn't to leave Iraq without seeing it. Luckily there's no one much here just at the moment—sometimes we just don't know where to turn so as to fit people in, but there's no one here now except Dr. Rathbone's young man who's quite charming. You've just missed Richard Baker, by the way. He left before I got Mrs. Cardew Trench's telegram."

Victoria had no idea who Richard Baker was—but it seemed fortunate that he had left when he did.

"He had been down to Kuwait for a couple of days," continued Mrs. Clayton. "Now that's a place you ought to see—before it's spoilt. I daresay it soon will be. Every place gets ruined sooner or later. What would you like first—a bath or some coffee?"

"A bath, please," said Victoria gratefully.

"How's Mrs. Cardew Trench? This is your room and the bathroom's along here. Is she an old friend of yours?"

"Oh no," said Victoria truthfully. "I've only just met her."

"And I suppose she turned you inside out in the first quarter of an hour? She's a terrific gossip as I expect you've gathered. Got quite a mania for knowing all about everybody. But she's quite good company and a really first class bridge player. Now are you sure you wouldn't like some coffee or something first?"

"No, really."

"Good—then I'll see you later. Have you got everything you want?"

Mrs. Clayton buzzed away like a cheerful bee, and Victoria took a bath, and attended to her face and her hair with the meticulous care of a young woman who is shortly going to be reunited to a young man who has taken her fancy.

If possible, Victoria hoped to meet Edward alone. She did not think that he would make any tactless remarks—fortunately he knew her as Jones and the additional Pauncefoot would probably cause him no surprise. The surprise would be that she was in Iraq at all, and for that Victoria hoped that she could catch him alone even for a bare second or two.

With this end in view, when she had put on a summer frock (for to her the climate of Basrah recalled a June day in London) she slipped out quietly through the wire door and took up her position on the balcony where she could intercept Edward when he arrived back from whatever he was doing—wrestling with the Customs officials, she presumed.

The first arrival was a tall thin man with a thoughtful face, and as he came up the steps Victoria slipped round the corner of the balcony. As she did so, she actually saw Edward entering through a garden door that gave on to the river bend.

Faithful to the tradition of Juliet, Victoria leaned over the balcony and gave a prolonged hiss.

Edward (who was looking, Victoria thought, more attractive than ever) turned his head sharply, looking about him.

"Hist! Up here," called Victoria in a low voice.

Edward raised his head, and an expression of utter astonishment appeared on his face.

"Good Lord," he exclaimed. "It's Charing Cross!"

"Hush. Wait for me. I'm coming down."

Victoria sped round the balcony, down the steps and along round the corner of the house to where Edward had remained obediently standing, the expression of bewilderment still on his face.

"I can't be drunk so early in the day," said Edward. "It is you?"

"Yes, it's me," said Victoria happily and ungrammatically.

"But what are you doing here? How did you get here? I thought I was never going to see you again."

"I thought so too."

"It's really just like a miracle. How did you get here?"

"I flew."

"Naturally you flew. You couldn't have got here in the time, otherwise. But I mean what blessed and wonderful chance brought you to Basrah?"

"The train," said Victoria.

"You're doing it on purpose, you little brute. God, I'm pleased to see you. But how did you get here—really?"

"I came out with a woman who'd broken her arm—a Mrs. Clipp. An American. I was offered the job the day after I met you, and you'd talked about Baghdad, and I was a bit fed up with London, so I thought, well, why not see the world?"

"You really are awfully sporting, Victoria. Where's this Clipp woman, here?"

"No, she's gone to a daughter near Kirkuk. It was only a journey out job."

"Then what are you doing now?"

"I'm still seeing the world," said Victoria. "But it has required a few subterfuges. That's why I wanted to get at you before we met in public, I mean, I don't want any tactless references to my being a shorthand typist out of a job when you last saw me."

"As far as I'm concerned, you're anything you say you are. I'm ready for briefing."

"The idea is," said Victoria, "that I am Miss Pauncefoot Jones. My uncle is an eminent archaeologist who is excavating in some more or less inaccessible place out here, and I am joining him there shortly."

"And none of that is true?"

"Naturally not. But it makes quite a good story."

"Oh, yes, excellent. But suppose you and old Pussyfoot Jones come face to face?"

"Pauncefoot. I don't think that is likely. As far as I can make out once archaeologists start to dig, they go on digging like mad, and don't stop."

"Rather like terriers. I say, there's a lot in what you say. Has he got a real niece?"

"How should I know?" said Victoria.

"Oh, then you're not impersonating anybody in particular. That makes it easier."

"Yes, after all, a man can have lots of nieces. Or, at a pinch, I could say I'm only a cousin but that I always call him uncle."

"You think of everything," said Edward admiringly. "You really are an amazing girl, Victoria. I've never met anyone like you. I thought I wouldn't see you again for years, and when I did see you, you'd have forgotten all about me. And now here you are."

The admiring and humble glance which Edward cast on her caused Victoria intense satisfaction. If she had been a cat she would have purred.

"But you'll want a job, won't you?" said Edward. "I mean, you haven't come into a fortune or anything?"

"Far from it! Yes," said Victoria slowly, "I shall want a job. I went into your Olive Branch place, as a matter of fact, and saw Dr. Rathbone and asked him for a job, but he wasn't very responsive—not to a salaried job, that is."

"The old beggar's fairly tight with his money," said Edward. "His idea is that everybody comes and works for the love of the thing."

"Do you think he's a phoney, Edward?"

"N—o. I don't know exactly what I do think. I don't see how he can be anything but on the square—he doesn't make any money out of the show. So far as I can see all that terrific enthusiasm must be genuine. And yet, you know, I don't really feel he's a fool."

"We'd better go in," said Victoria. "We can talk later."

"I'd no idea you and Edward knew each other," exclaimed Mrs. Clayton.

"Oh, we're old friends," laughed Victoria. "Only, as a matter of fact, we'd lost sight of each other. I'd no idea Edward was in this country."

Mr. Clayton, who was the quiet thoughtful-looking man Victoria had seen coming up the steps, asked:

"How did you get on this morning, Edward? Any progress?"

"It seems very uphill work, sir. The cases of books are there, all present and correct, but the formalities needed to clear them seem unending."

Clayton smiled.

"You're new to the delaying tactics of the East."

"The particular official who's wanted always seems to be away that day," complained Edward. "Everyone is very pleasant and willing—only nothing seems to happen."

Everyone laughed and Mrs. Clayton said consolingly:

"You'll get them through in the end. Very wise of Dr. Rathbone to send someone down personally. Otherwise they'd probably stay here for months."

"They are very suspicious about bombs. Also subversive literature. They suspect everything."

"Dr. Rathbone isn't shipping out bombs here disguised as books, I hope," said Mrs. Clayton laughing.

Victoria thought she caught a sudden flicker in Edward's eye, as though Mrs. Clayton's remark had opened up a new line of thought.

Clayton said, with a hint of reproof: "Dr. Rathbone's a very learned and well-known man, my dear. He's a Fellow of various important Societies and is known and respected all over Europe."

"That would make it all the easier for him to smuggle in bombs," Mrs. Clayton pointed out with irrepressible spirits.

Victoria could see that Gerald Clayton did not quite like this light-hearted suggestion.

He frowned at his wife.

Business being at a standstill during the midday hours, Edward and Victoria went out together after lunch to stroll about and see the sights. Victoria was delighted with the river, the Shatt el Arab, with its bordering of date palm groves. She adored the Venetian look of the high-prowed Arab boats tied up in the canal in the town. Then they wandered into the Suq and looked at Kuwait bride chests studded with patterned brass and other attractive merchandise.

It was not until they turned towards the Consulate and Edward was preparing himself to assail the Customs department once more that Victoria said suddenly,

"Edward, what's your name?"

Edward stared at her.

"What on earth do you mean, Victoria?"

"Your last name. Don't you realise that I don't know it."

"Don't you? No, I suppose you don't. It's Goring."

"Edward Goring. You've no idea what a fool I felt going into that Olive Branch place and wanting to ask for you and not knowing anything but Edward."

"Was there a dark girl there? Rather long bobbed hair?"

"Yes."

"That's Catherine. She's awfully nice. If you'd said Edward she'd have known at once."

"I daresay she would," said Victoria with reserve.

"She's a frightfully nice girl. Didn't you think so?"

"Oh quite . . ."

"Not actually good looking—in fact nothing much to look at, but she's frightfully sympathetic."

"Is she?" Victoria's voice was now quite glacial—but Edward apparently noticed nothing.

"I don't really know what I should have done without her. She put me in the picture and helped me out when I might have made a fool of myself. I'm sure you and she will be great friends."

"I don't suppose we shall have the opportunity."

"Oh yes, you will. I'm going to get you a job in the show."

"How are you going to manage that?"

"I don't know but I shall manage it somehow. Tell old Rattlebones what a wonderful typist et cetera you are."

"He'll soon find out I'm not," said Victoria.

"Anyway, I shall get you into the Olive Branch somehow. I'm not going to have you beetling round on your own. Next thing I know, you'd be heading for Burma or darkest Africa. No, young Victoria, I'm going to have you right under my eye. I'm not going to take any chances on your running out on me. I don't trust you an inch. You're too fond of seeing the world."

"You sweet idiot," thought Victoria, "don't you know wild horses wouldn't drive me away from Baghdad!"

Aloud she said: "Well, it would be quite fun to have a job at the Olive Branch."

"I wouldn't describe it as fun. It's all terribly earnest. As well as being absolutely goofy."

"And you still think there's something wrong about it?"

"Oh, that was only a wild idea of mine."

"No," said Victoria thoughtfully, "I don't think it was only a wild idea. I think it's true."

Edward turned on her sharply.

"What makes you say that?"

"Something I heard—from a friend of mine."

"Who was it?"

"Just a friend."

"Girls like you have too many friends," grumbled Edward. "You are a devil, Victoria. I love you madly and you don't care a bit."

"Oh, yes, I do," said Victoria. "Just a little bit."

Then, concealing her delighted satisfaction, she asked:

"Edward, is there anyone called Lefarge connected with the Olive Branch or with anything else?"

"Lefarge?" Edward looked puzzled. "No, I don't think so. Who is he?"

Victoria pursued her inquiries.

"Or anyone called Anna Scheele?"

This time Edward's reaction was very different. He turned on her abruptly, caught her by the arm and said:

"What do you know about Anna Scheele?"

"Ow! Edward, let go! I don't know anything about her. I just wanted to know if you did."

"Where did you hear about her? Mrs. Clipp?"

"No—not Mrs. Clipp—at least I don't think so, but actually she talked so fast and so unendingly about everyone and everything that I probably wouldn't remember if she had mentioned her."

"But what made you think this Anna Scheele had anything to do with the Olive Branch?"

"Has she?"

Edward said slowly, "I don't know . . . It's all so—so vague."

They were standing outside the garden door to the Consulate. Edward glanced at his watch. "I must go and do my stuff," he said. "Wish I knew some Arabic. But we've got to get together, Victoria. There's a lot I want to know."

"There's a lot I want to tell you," said Victoria.

Some tender heroine of a more sentimental age might have sought to keep her man out of danger. Not so, Victoria. Men, in Victoria's opinion were born to danger as the sparks fly upwards. Edward wouldn't thank her for keeping him out of things. And, on reflection, she was quite certain that Mr. Dakin hadn't intended her to keep him out of things.

II

At sunset that evening Edward and Victoria walked together in the Consulate garden. In deference to Mrs. Clayton's insistence that the weather was wintry Victoria wore a woollen coat over her summer frock. The sunset was magnificent but neither of the young people noticed it. They were discussing more important things.

"It began quite simply," said Victoria, "with a man coming into my room at the Tio Hotel and getting stabbed."

It was not, perhaps, most people's idea of a simple beginning. Edward stared at her and said: "Getting what?"

"Stabbed," said Victoria. "At least I think it was stabbed, but it might have been shot, only I don't think so because then I would have heard the noise of the shot. Anyway," she added, "he was dead."

"How could he come into your room if he was dead?"

"Oh, Edward, don't be stupid."

Alternately baldly and vaguely, Victoria told her story. For some mysterious reason Victoria could never tell of truthful occurrences in a dramatic fashion. Her narrative was halting and incomplete and she told it with the air of one offering a palpable fabrication.

When she had come to the end, Edward looked at her doubtfully and said, "You do feel all right, Victoria, don't you? I mean you haven't had a touch of the sun or—a dream, or anything?"

"Of course not."

"Because, I mean, it seems such an absolutely impossible thing to have happened."

"Well, it did happen," said Victoria touchily.

"And all that melodramatic stuff about world forces and mysterious secret installations in the heart of Tibet or Baluchistan. I mean, all that simply couldn't be true. Things like that don't happen."

"That's what people always say before they've happened."

"Honest to God, Charing Cross—are you making all this up?"

"No!" cried Victoria exasperated.

"And you've come down here looking for someone called Lefarge and someone called Anna Scheele—"

"Whom you've heard of yourself," Victoria put in. "You had heard of her, hadn't you?"

"I'd heard the name—yes."

"How? Where? At the Olive Branch?"

Edward was silent for some moments, then he said:

"I don't know if it means anything. It was just—odd—"

"Go on. Tell me."

"You see, Victoria, I'm so different from you; I'm not as sharp as you are. I just feel, in a queer kind of way, that things are wrong somehow—I don't know why I think so. You spot things as you go along and deduce things from them. I'm not clever enough for that. I just feel vaguely that things are—well—wrong—but I don't know why."

"I feel like that sometimes, too," said Victoria. "Like Sir Rupert on the balcony of the Tio."

"Who's Sir Rupert?"

"Sir Rupert Crofton Lee. He was on the plane coming out. Very haughty and showing off. A V.I.P. You know. And when I saw him sitting out on the balcony at the Tio in the sun, I had that queer feeling you've just said of something being wrong, but not knowing what it was."

"Rathbone asked him to lecture to the Olive Branch, I believe, but he couldn't make it. Flew back to Cairo or Damascus or somewhere yesterday morning."

"Well, go on about Anna Scheele."

"Oh, Anna Scheele. It was nothing really. It was just one of the girls."

"Catherine?" said Victoria instantly.

"I believe it was Catherine now I think of it."

"Of course, it was Catherine. That's why you don't want to tell me about it."

"Nonsense, that's quite absurd."

"Well, what was it?"

"Catherine said to one of the other girls, 'When Anna Scheele comes, we can go forward. Then we take our orders from her—and from her alone'."

"That's frightfully important, Edward."

"Remember, I'm not even sure that that was the name," Edward warned her.

"Didn't you think it queer at the time?"

"No, of course I didn't. I thought it was just some female who was coming out to boss things. A kind of Queen Bee. Are you sure you're not imagining all this, Victoria?"

Immediately he quailed slightly before the glance his young friend gave him.

"All right, all right," he said hastily. "Only you'll admit the whole story does sound queer. So like a thriller—a young man coming in and gasping out one word that doesn't mean anything—and then dying —It just doesn't seem real."

"You didn't see the blood," said Victoria and shivered slightly.

"It must have given you a terrible shock," said Edward sympathetically.

"It did," said Victoria. "And then on top of it, you come along and ask me if I'm making it all up."

"I'm sorry. But you are rather good at making things up. The Bishop of Llangow and all that!"

"Oh, that was just girlish *joie de vivre*," said Victoria. "This is serious, Edward, really serious."

"This man, Dakin—is that his name?—impressed you as knowing what he was talking about?"

"Yes, he was very convincing. But, look here, Edward, how do you know—"

A hail from the balcony interrupted her.

"Come in—you two—drinks waiting."

"Coming," called Victoria.

Mrs. Clayton, watching them coming towards the steps, said to her husband:

"There's something in the wind there! Nice couple of children—probably haven't got a bean between them. Shall I tell you what I think, Gerald?"

"Certainly, dear. I'm always interested to hear your ideas."

"I think that girl has come out here to join her uncle on his Dig simply and solely because of that young man."

"I hardly think so, Rosa. They were quite astonished to see each other."

"Poosh!" said Mrs. Clayton. "That's nothing. He was astonished, I daresay."

Gerald Clayton shook his head at her and smiled.

"She's not an archaeological type," said Mrs. Clayton. "They're usually earnest girls with spectacles—and very often damp hands."

"My dear, you can't generalize in that way."

"—And intellectual and all that. This girl is an amiable nitwit with a lot of common sense. Quite different. He's a nice boy. A pity he's tied up with all this silly Olive Branch stuff—but I suppose jobs are hard to get. They should find jobs for these boys."

"It's not so easy, dear, they do try. But you see, they've no training, no experience and usually not much habit of concentration."

Victoria went to bed that night in a turmoil of mixed feelings.

The object of her quest was attained, Edward was found! She suffered from the inevitable reaction. Do what she might a feeling of anticlimax persisted.

It was partly Edward's disbelief that made everything that had happened seem stagey and unreal. She, Victoria Jones, a little London typist, had arrived in Baghdad, had seen a man murdered almost before her eyes, had become a secret agent or something equally melodramatic, and had finally met the man she loved in a tropical garden with palms waving overhead, and in all probability not far from the spot where the original Garden of Eden was said to be situated.

A fragment of a nursery rhyme floated through her head.

> How many miles to Babylon?
> Threescore and ten:
> Can I get there by candlelight?
> Yes, and back again.

But she wasn't back again—she was still in Babylon.

Perhaps she would never get back—she and Edward in Babylon.

Something she had meant to ask Edward—there in the garden. Garden of Eden—she and Edward—Ask Edward—but Mrs. Clayton had called—and it had gone out of her head—But she must remember—because it was important—It didn't make sense—Palms—garden—Edward—Saracen Maiden—Anna Scheele—Rupert Crofton Lee—All wrong somehow—And if only she could remember—

A woman coming towards her along a hotel corridor—a woman in a tailored suit—it was herself—but when the woman got near she saw the face was Catherine's. Edward and Catherine—absurd! "Come with me," she said to Edward, "we will find M. Lefarge—" And suddenly there he was, wearing lemon yellow kid gloves and a little pointed black beard.

Edward had gone now and she was alone. She must get back from Babylon before the candles went out.

And we are for the dark.

Who had said that? Violence, terror—evil—blood on a ragged khaki tunic. She was running—running—down a hotel corridor. And they were coming after her.

Victoria woke up with a gasp.

III

"Coffee?" said Mrs. Clayton. "How do you like your eggs? Scrambled?"

"Lovely."

"You look rather washed out. Not feeling ill?"

"No, I didn't sleep very well last night. I don't know why. It's a very comfortable bed."

"Turn the wireless on, will you, Gerald? It's time for the news."

Edward came in just as the pips were sounding.

"In the House of Commons last night, the Prime Minister gave fresh details of the cuts in dollar imports.

"A report from Cairo announces that the body of Sir Rupert Crofton Lee has been taken from the Nile. Victoria put down her coffee cup sharply and Mrs. Clayton uttered an ejaculation. *Sir Rupert left his Hotel yesterday afternoon, after arriving by plane from Baghdad, and did not return to it that night. He had been missing for twenty-four hours when his body was recovered. Death was due to a stab wound in the heart and not to drowning. Sir Rupert was a renowned traveller, was famous for his travels through China and Baluchistan and was the author of several books."*

"Murdered!" exclaimed Mrs. Clayton. "I think Cairo is worse than any place now. Did you know anything about all this, Gerry?"

"I knew he was missing," said Mr. Clayton. "It appears he got a note, brought by hand, and left the Hotel in a great hurry on foot without saying where he was going."

"You see," said Victoria to Edward after breakfast when they were alone together. "It is all true. First this man Carmichael and now Sir Rupert Crofton Lee. I feel sorry now I called him a show off. It seems unkind. All the people who know or guess about this queer business are being got out of the way. Edward, do you think it will be me next?"

"For Heaven's sake don't look so pleased by the idea, Victoria! Your sense of drama is much too strong. I don't see why anyone should eliminate you because you don't really know anything—but do, please, do, be awfully careful."

"We'll both be careful. I've dragged you into it."

"Ah. That's all right. Relieves the monotony."

"Yes, but take care of yourself."

She gave a sudden shiver.

"It's rather awful. He was so very much alive—Crofton Lee, I mean—and now he's dead too. It's frightening, really frightening."

XVI

"FIND YOUR YOUNG man?" asked Mr. Dakin.

Victoria nodded.

"Find anything else?"

Rather mournfully, Victoria shook her head.

"Well, cheer up," said Mr. Dakin. "Remember in this game, results are few and far between. You might have picked up something there —one never knows, but I wasn't in any way counting on it."

"Can I still go on trying?" asked Victoria.

"Do you want to?"

"Yes, I do. Edward thinks he can get me a job at the Olive Branch. If I keep my ears and eyes open, I might find out something, mightn't I? They know something about Anna Scheele there."

"Now that's very interesting, Victoria. How did you learn that?"

Victoria repeated what Edward had told her—about Catherine's remark that when "Anna Scheele came" they would take their orders from her.

"Very interesting," said Mr. Dakin.

"Who is Anna Scheele?" asked Victoria. "I mean, you must know something about her—or is she just a name?"

"She's more than a name. She's confidential secretary to an American banker—head of an international banking firm. She left New York and came to London about ten days ago. Since then she's disappeared."

"Disappeared? She's not dead?"

"If so, her dead body hasn't been found."

"But she may be dead?"

"Oh yes, she may be dead."

"Was she—coming to Baghdad?"

"I've no idea. It would seem from the remarks of this young woman

Catherine, that she was. Or shall we say—is—since as yet there's no reason to believe she isn't still alive."

"Perhaps I can find out more at the Olive Branch."

"Perhaps you can—but I must warn you once more to be very careful, Victoria. The organization you are up against are quite ruthless. I would much rather not have your dead body found floating down the Tigris."

Victoria gave a little shiver and murmured:

"Like Sir Rupert Crofton Lee. You know that morning he was at the Hotel here there was something odd about him—something that surprised me. I wish I could remember what it was . . ."

"In what way—odd?"

"Well—different." Then in response to the inquiring look, she shook her head vexedly. "It will come back to me, perhaps. Anyway I don't suppose it really matters."

"Anything might matter."

"If Edward gets me a job, he thinks I ought to get a room like the other girls in a sort of boarding house or paying guest place, not stay on here."

"It would create less surmise. Baghdad hotels are very expensive. Your young man seems to have his head screwed on the right way."

"Do you want to see him?"

Dakin shook his head emphatically.

"No, tell him to keep right away from me. You, unfortunately, owing to the circumstances on the night of Carmichael's death, are bound to be suspect. But Edward is not linked with that occurrence or with me in any way—and that's valuable."

"I've been meaning to ask you," said Victoria. "Who actually did stab Carmichael? Was it someone who followed him here?"

"No," said Dakin slowly. "That couldn't have been so."

"Couldn't?"

"He came in a *gufa*—one of those native boats—and he wasn't followed. We know that because I had someone watching the river."

"Then it was someone—in the Hotel?"

"Yes, Victoria. And what is more someone in one particular wing of the Hotel—for I myself was watching the stairs and no one came up them."

He watched her rather puzzled face and said quietly:

"That doesn't really give us very many names. You and I and Mrs. Cardew Trench, and Marcus and his sisters. A couple of elderly serv-

ants who have been here for years. A man called Harrison from Kirkuk
against whom nothing is known. A nurse who works at the Jewish
Hospital . . . It might be any of them—yet all of them are unlikely
for one very good reason."

"What is that?"

"Carmichael was on his guard. He knew that the peak moment of
his mssion was approaching. He was a man with a very keen instinct
for danger. How did that instinct let him down?"

"Those police that came—" began Victoria.

"Ah, they came after—up from the street. They'd had a signal, I
suppose. But they didn't do the stabbing. That must have been done
by someone Carmichael knew well, whom he trusted . . . or alternatively whom he judged negligible. If I only knew . . ."

II

Achievement brings with it its own anticlimax. To get to Baghdad,
to find Edward, to penetrate the secrets of the Olive Branch: all this
had appeared as an entrancing program. Now, her objective attained,
Victoria, in a rare moment of self questioning, sometimes wondered
what on earth she was doing! The rapture of reunion with Edward
had come and gone. She loved Edward, Edward loved her. They were,
on most days, working under the same roof—but thinking about it dis-
passionately, what on earth were they doing?

By some means or other, sheer force of determination, or ingenious
persuasion, Edward had been instrumental in Victoria's being offered
a meagrely paid job at the Olive Branch. She spent most of her time
in a small dark room with the electric light on, typing on a very faulty
machine various notices and letters and manifestos of the milk and
water program of the Olive Branch activities. Edward had had a hunch
there was something wrong about the Olive Branch. Mr. Dakin had
seemed to agree with that view. She, Victoria, was here to find out what
she could, but as far as she could see, there was nothing to find out!
The Olive Branch activities dripped with the honey of international
peace. Various gatherings were held with orangeade to drink and depressing edibles to go with it, and at these Victoria was supposed to act
as quasi hostess; to mix, to introduce, to promote general good feeling
among various foreign nationals, who were inclined to stare with
animosity at one another, and wolf refreshments hungrily.

As far as Victoria could see, there were no undercurrents, no conspiracies, no inner rings. All was aboveboard, mild as milk and water, and desperately dull. Various dark-skinned young men made tentative love to her, others lent her books to read which she skimmed through and found tedious. She had, by now, left the Tio Hotel and had taken up her quarters with some other young women workers of various nationalities in a house on the West Bank of the river. Amongst these young women was Catherine, and it seemed to Victoria that Catherine watched her with a suspicious eye; but whether this was because Catherine suspected her of being a spy on the activities of the Olive Branch or whether it was the more delicate matter of Edward's affections, Victoria was unable to make up her mind. She rather fancied the latter. It was known that Edward had secured Victoria her job and several pairs of jealous dark eyes looked at her without undue affection.

The fact was, Victoria thought moodily, that Edward was far too attractive. All these girls had fallen for him, and Edward's engaging friendly manner to one and all did nothing to help. By agreement between them, Victoria and Edward were to show no signs of special intimacy. If they were to find out anything worth finding out, they must not be suspected of working together. Edward's manner to her was the same as to any of the other young women, with an added shade of coldness.

Though the Olive Branch itself seemed so innocuous, Victoria had a distinct feeling that its head and founder was in a different category. Once or twice she was aware of Dr. Rathbone's dark thoughtful gaze resting upon her, and though she countered it with her most innocent and kitten-like expression, she felt a sudden throb of something like fear.

Once, when she had been summoned to his presence (for explanation of a typing error), the matter went further than a glance.

"You are happy working with us, I hope?" he asked.

"Oh, yes, indeed, sir," said Victoria, and added: "I'm sorry I make so many mistakes."

"We don't mind mistakes. A soulless machine would be no use to us. We need youth, generosity of spirit, broadness of outlook."

Victoria endeavoured to look eager and generous.

"You must love the work . . . love the object for which you are working . . . look forward to the glorious future. Are you truly feeling all that, dear child?"

"It's all so new to me," said Victoria. "I really don't feel I have taken it all in yet."

"Get together—get together—young people everywhere must get together. That is the main thing. You enjoy our evenings of free discussion and comradeship?"

"Oh! yes," said Victoria who loathed them.

"Agreement, not dissension—brotherhood, not hatred. Slowly and surely it is growing—you do feel that, don't you?"

Victoria thought of the endless petty jealousies, the violent dislikes, the endless quarrels, hurt feelings, apologies demanded; and hardly knew what she was expected to say.

"Sometimes," she said cautiously, "people are difficult."

"I know . . . I know . . ." Dr. Rathbone sighed. His noble domed forehead furrowed itself in perplexity. "What is this I hear of Michael Rakounian striking Isaac Nahoum and cutting his lip open?"

"They were just having a little argument," said Victoria.

Dr. Rathbone brooded mournfully.

"Patience and faith," he murmured. "Patience and faith."

Victoria murmured a dutiful assent and turned to leave. Then, remembering she had left her typescript, she came back again. The glance she caught in Dr. Rathbone's eye startled her a little. It was a keen suspicious glance, and she wondered uneasily just how closely she was being watched, and what Dr. Rathbone really thought about her.

Her instructions from Mr. Dakin were very precise. She was to obey certain rules for communicating with him if she had anything to report. He had given her an old faded pink handkerchief. If she had anything to report she was to walk, as she often did when the sun was setting, along the river bank, near her hostel. There was a narrow path in front of the houses there for perhaps a quarter of a mile. In one place a big flight of steps led down to the water's edge and boats were constantly being tied up there. There was a rusty nail in one of the wooden posts at the top. Here she was to affix a small piece of the pink handkerchief if she wanted to get into communication with Dakin. So far, Victoria reflected bitterly, there had been no need for anything of the sort. She was merely doing an ill-paid job in a slovenly fashion. Edward she saw at rare intervals, since he was always being sent to far off places by Dr. Rathbone. At the moment, he had just come back from Persia. During his absence, she had had one short and somewhat unsatisfactory interview with Dakin. Her instructions had been to go to the Tio Hotel and ask if she had left a cardigan behind. The answer having been in the negative, Marcus appeared and immediately swept her out onto the river bank for a drink. During the process Dakin had shambled in from the street and had been hailed by Marcus to join them and presently, as Dakin supped lemonade, Marcus had been called away and the two of them sat there on opposite sides of the small painted table.

Rather apprehensively Victoria confessed her utter lack of success, but Dakin was indulgently reassuring.

"My dear child, you don't even know what you are looking for or even if there is anything to find. Taken by and large, what is your considered opinion of the Olive Branch?"

"It's a thoroughly dim show," said Victoria slowly.

"Dim, yes. But not bogus?"

"I don't know," said Victoria slowly. "People are so sold on the idea of culture if you know what I mean?"

"You mean that where anything cultured is concerned, nobody examines *bona fides* in the way they would if it were a charitable or a financial proposition? That's true. And you'll find genuine enthusiasts there, I've no doubt. But is the organization being used?"

"I think there's a lot of Communist activity going on," said Victoria doubtfully. "Edward thinks so, too—he's making me read Karl Marx and leave it about just to see what reactions there will be."

Dakin nodded.

"Interesting. Any response so far?"

"No, not yet."

"What about Rathbone? Is he genuine?"

"I think really that he is—" Victoria sounded doubtful.

"He's the one I worry about, you see," said Dakin. "Because he's a big noise. Suppose there is Communist plotting going on—students and young revolutionaries have very little chance of coming in contact with the President. Police measures will look after bombs thrown from the street. But Rathbone's different. He's one of the high ups, a distinguished man with a fine record of public beneficence. He could come in close contact with the distinguished visitors. He probably will. I'd like to know about Rathbone."

Yes, Victoria thought to herself, it all revolved round Rathbone. On that first meeting in London, weeks ago, Edward's vague remarks about the "fishiness" of the show had had their origin in his employer. And there must, Victoria decided suddenly, have been some incident, some word, that had awakened Edward's uneasiness. For that, in Victoria's belief, was how minds worked. Your vague doubt or distrust was never just a hunch—it was really always due to a cause. If Edward, now, could be made to think back, to remember; between them they might hit upon the fact or incident that had aroused his suspicions. In the same way, Victoria thought, she herself must try to think back to what it was that had so surprised her when she came out upon the balcony at the Tio and found Sir Rupert Croften Lee sitting there in the sun. It was true that she had expected him to be at the Embassy and not at the Tio Hotel but that was not enough to account for the strong feeling she had had that his sitting there was quite impossible! She would go over and over the events of that morning, and Edward must be urged to go over and over his early association with Dr. Rathbone. She would tell him so when next she got him alone. But to get Edward alone was not easy. To begin with, he had been away in Persia and now that he was back, private communications at the Olive Branch were out of the question where the slogan of the last war (*Les oreilles enemis nous écoutent*) might have been written up all over the walls. In the Armenian household where she was a paying guest, privacy was equally impossible. Really, thought Victoria to herself, for all I see of Edward, I might as well have stayed in England!

That this was not quite true, was proved very shortly afterwards.

Edward came to her with some sheets of manuscript and said:

"Dr. Rathbone would like this typed out at once, please, Victoria. Be especially careful of the second page, there are some rather tricky Arab names on it."

Victoria, with a sigh, inserted a sheet of paper in her typewriter and started off in her usual dashing style. Dr. Rathbone's handwriting was not particularly difficult to read and Victoria was just congratulating herself that she had made fewer mistakes than usual. She laid the top sheet aside and proceeded to the next—and at once realised the meaning of Edward's injunction to be careful of the second page. A tiny note in Edward's handwriting was pinned to the top of it.

Go for a walk along the Tigris bank past the Beit Melik Ali tomorrow morning about eleven.

The following day was Friday, the weekly holiday. Victoria's spirits rose mercurially. She would wear her jade green pullover. She ought really to get her hair shampooed. The amenities of the house where she lived made it difficult to wash it herself. "And it really needs it," she murmured aloud.

"What did you say?" Catherine, at work on a pile of circulars and envelopes, raised her head suspiciously from the next table.

Victoria quickly crumpled up Edward's note in her hand as she said lightly:

"My hair wants washing. Most of these hairdressing places look so frightfully dirty, I don't know where to go."

"Yes, they are dirty and expensive, too. But I know a girl who washes hair very well and the towels are clean. I will take you there."

"That's very kind of you, Catherine," said Victoria.

"We will go tomorrow. It is holiday."

"Not tomorrow," said Victoria.

"Why not tomorrow?"

A suspicious stare was bent upon her. Victoria felt her usual annoyance and dislike of Catherine rising.

"I'd rather go for a walk—get some air. One is so cooped up here."

"Where can you walk? There is nowhere to walk in Baghdad."

"I shall find somewhere," said Victoria.

"It would be better to go to the Cinema. Or there is an interesting lecture."

"No, I want to get out. In England we like going for walks."

"Because you are English, you are so proud and stuck up. What does it mean to be English? Next than nothing. Here we spit upon the English."

"If you start spitting on me you may get a surprise," said Victoria, wondering as usual at the ease with which angry passions seemed to rise at the Olive Branch.

"What would you do?"

"Try and see."

"Why do you read Karl Marx? You cannot understand it. You are much too stupid. Do you think they would ever accept you as a member of the Communist party? You are not well enough educated politically."

"Why shouldn't I read it? It was meant for people like me—workers."

"You are not a worker. You are a bourgeoise. You cannot even type properly. Look at the mistakes you make."

"Some of the cleverest people can't spell," said Victoria with dignity. "And how can I work when you keep talking to me?"

She rattled off a line at breakneck speed—and was then somewhat chagrined to find that as a result of unwittingly depressing the shift key, she had written a line of exclamation marks, figures and brackets. Removing the sheet from the machine she replaced it with another and applied herself diligently until, her task finished, she took the result in to Dr. Rathbone.

Glancing over it and murmuring, "Shiraz is in Iran not Iraq—and anyway you don't spell Iraq with a K . . . Wasit—not Wuzle—er—thank you, Victoria."

Then, as she was leaving the room, he called her back.

"Victoria, are you happy here?"

"Oh yes, Dr. Rathbone."

The dark eyes under the massive brows were very searching. She felt uneasiness rising.

"I'm afraid we do not pay you very much."

"That doesn't matter," said Victoria. "I like the work."

"Do you really?"

"Oh, yes," said Victoria. "One feels," she added, "that this sort of thing is really worth while."

Her limpid gaze met the dark searching eyes and did not falter.

"And you manage—to live?"

"Oh yes—I've found quite a good cheap place—with some Armenians. I'm quite all right."

"There is a shortage at present of shorthand typists in Baghdad," said Dr. Rathbone. "I think, you know, that I could get you a better position than the one you have here."

"But I don't want any other position."

"You might be wise to take one."

"Wise?" Victoria faltered a little.

"That is what I said. Just a word of warning—of advice."

There was something faintly menacing now in his tone.

Victoria opened her eyes still wider.

"I really don't understand, Dr. Rathbone," she said.

"Sometimes it is wiser not to mix oneself up in things one does not understand."

She felt quite sure of the menace this time, but she continued to stare in kitten-eyed innocence.

"Why did you come and work here, Victoria? Because of Edward?"

Victoria flushed angrily.

"Of course not," she said indignantly. She was much annoyed.

Dr. Rathbone nodded his head.

"Edward has his way to make. It will be many many years before he is in a position to be of any use to you. I should give up thinking of Edward if I were you. And, as I say, there are good positions to be obtained at present, with a good salary and prospects—and which will bring you among your own kind."

He was still watching her, Victoria thought, very closely. Was this a test? She said with an affectation of eagerness,

"But I really am very keen on the Olive Branch, Dr. Rathbone."

He shrugged his shoulders then and she left him, but she could feel his eyes in the centre of her spine as she left the room.

She was somewhat disturbed by the interview. Had something occurred to arouse his suspicions? Did he guess that she might be a spy placed in the Olive Branch to find out its secrets? His voice and manner had made her feel unpleasantly afraid. His suggestion that she had come there to be near Edward had made her angry at the time and she had vigorously denied it, but she realised now that it was infinitely safer that Dr. Rathbone should suppose her to have come to the Olive Branch for Edward's sake, then to have even an inkling that Mr. Dakin had been instrumental in the matter. Anyway, owing to her idiotic blush, Rathbone probably did think that it was Edward—so that all had really turned out for the best.

Nevertheless, she went to sleep that night with an unpleasant little clutch of fear at her heart.

XVII

It PROVED FAIRLY simple on the following morning for Victoria to go out by herself with few explanations. She had inquired about the Beit Melek Ali and had learnt it was a big house built right out on the river some way down the west bank.

So far, Victoria had had very little time to explore her surroundings and she was agreeably surprised when she came to the end of the narrow street and found herself actually on the river bank. She turned to her right and made her way slowly along the edge of the high bank. Sometimes the going was precarious—the bank had been eaten away and had not always been repaired or built up again. One house had steps in front of it which, if you took one more, would land you in the river on a dark night. Victoria looked down at the water below and edged her way round. Then, for a while, the way was wide and paved. The houses on her right hand had an agreeable air of secrecy. They offered no hint as to their occupancy. Occasionally the central door stood open, and peering inside Victoria was fascinated by the contrasts. On one such occasion she looked into a courtyard with a fountain playing and cushioned seats and deck chairs round it, with tall palms growing up and a garden beyond, that looked like the backcloth of a stage set. The next house, looking much the same outside, opened on a litter of confusion and dark passages, with five or six dirty children playing in rags. Then she came to palm gardens in thick groves. On her left she had passed uneven steps leading down to the river and an Arab boatman seated in a primitive rowing boat gesticulated and called, asking evidently if she wanted to be taken across to the other side. She must by now, Victoria judged, be just about opposite the Tio Hotel, though it was hard to distinguish difference in the architecture viewed from this side, and the hotel buildings looked more or less alike. She came now to a road leading down through the palms and then to two tall houses with balconies. Beyond was a big house built right out onto the river with a garden and balustrade. The path on the bank passed on the inside of what must be the Beit Melek Ali or the House of King Ali.

In a few minutes more Victoria had passed its entrance and had come to a more squalid part; the river was hidden from her by palm plantations fenced off with rusty barbed wire. On the right were tumbledown houses inside rough mudbrick walls, and small shanties with children playing in the dirt and clouds of flies hanging over garbage heaps. A road led away from the river and a car was standing there—a somewhat battered and archaic car. By the car, Edward was standing.

"Good," said Edward, "you've got here. Get in."

"Where are we going?" asked Victoria, entering the battered automobile with delight. The driver, who appeared to be an animate bundle of rags, turned round and grinned happily at her.

"We're going to Babylon," said Edward. "It's about time we had a day out."

The car started with a terrific jerk and bumped madly over the rude paving stones.

"To Babylon?" cried Victoria. "How lovely it sounds. Really to Babylon?"

The car swerved to the left and they were bowling upon a well paved road of imposing width.

"Yes, but don't expect too much. Babylon—if you know what I mean—isn't quite what it was."

Victoria hummed:

"*How many miles to Babylon?*
Three score and ten:
Can I get there by candlelight?
Yes, and back again.

I used to sing that when I was a small child. It always fascinated me. And now we're really going there!"

"And we'll get back by candlelight. Or we should. Actually you never know in this country."

"This car looks very much as though it might break down."

"It probably will. There's sure to be simply everything wrong with it. But these Iraqis are frightfully good at tying it up with string and saying Inshallah, and then it goes again."

"It's always Inshallah, isn't it?"

"Yes, nothing like laying the responsibility upon the Almighty."

"The road isn't very good, is it?" gasped Victoria, bouncing in her seat. The deceptively well-paved and wide road had not lived up to its promise. The road was still wide but was now corrugated with ruts.

"It gets worse later on," shouted Edward.

They bounced and bumped happily. The dust rose in clouds round them. Large lorries covered with Arabs tore along in the middle of the track and were deaf to all intimations of the horn.

They passed walled-in gardens, and parties of women and children and donkeys, and to Victoria it was all new and part of the enchantment of going to Babylon with Edward beside her.

They reached Babylon bruised and shaken in a couple of hours. The meaningless pile of ruined mud and burnt brick was somewhat of a disappointment to Victoria who expected something in the way of columns and arches, looking like pictures she had seen of Baalbek.

But little by little her disappointment ebbed as they scrambled over mounds and lumps of burnt brick, led by the Guide. She listened with only half an ear to his profuse explanations, but as they went along the Processional Way to the Ishtar Gate, with the faint reliefs of unbelievable animals high on the walls, a sudden sense of the grandeur

of the past came to her and a wish to know something about this
vast proud city that now lay dead and abandoned. Presently their duty
to Antiquity accomplished, they sat down by the Babylonian Lion to
eat the picnic lunch that Edward had brought with him. The Guide
moved away, smiling indulgently and telling them firmly that they
must see the Museum later.

"Must we?" said Victoria dreamily. "Things all labeled and put into
cases don't seem a bit real somehow. I went to the British Museum
once. It was awful, and dreadfully tiring on the feet."

"The past is always boring," said Edward. "The future's much more
important."

"This isn't boring," said Victoria waving a sandwich towards the
panorama of tumbled brick. "There's a feeling of—of greatness here.
What's the poem

> *When you were a King in Babylon*
> *And I was a Christian Slave?*

Perhaps we were. You and I, I mean."

"I don't think there were any Kings in Babylon by the time there
were Christians," said Edward. "I think Babylon stopped functioning
somewhere about five or six hundred B.C. Some archaeologist or other
is always turning up to give lectures about these things—but I really
never grasp any of the dates—I mean not until proper Greek and
Roman ones."

"Would you have liked being a King in Babylon, Edward?"

Edward drew a deep breath.

"Yes, I should."

"Then we'll say you were. You're in a new incarnation now."

"They understood how to be Kings in those days!" said Edward.
"That's why they could rule the world and bring it into shape."

"I don't know that I should have liked being a slave much," said Victoria meditatively, "Christian or otherwise."

"Milton was quite right," said Edward. "Better to reign in Hell
than serve in Heaven. I always admired Milton's Satan."

"I never quite got around to Milton," said Victoria apologetically.
"But I did go and see Comus at Sadler's Wells and it was lovely, and
Margot Fonteyn danced like a kind of frozen angel."

"If you were a slave, Victoria," said Edward, "I should free you and
take you into my harem—over there," he added gesticulating vaguely
at a pile of debris.

A glint came into Victoria's eye.

"Talking of harems—" she began.

"How are you getting on with Catherine?" asked Edward hastily.

"How did you know I was thinking about Catherine?"

"Well, you were, weren't you? Honestly, Viccy, I do want you to become friends with Catherine."

"Don't call me Viccy."

"All right, Charing Cross. I want you to become friends with Catherine."

"How fatuous men are! Always wanting their girl friends to like each other."

Edward sat up energetically. He had been reclining with his hands behind his head.

"You've got it all wrong, Charing Cross. Anyway, your references to harems are simply silly—"

"No, they're not. The way all those girls glower intensely at you and yearn at you! It makes me mad."

"Splendid," said Edward. "I love you to be mad. But to return to Catherine. The reason I want you to be friends with Catherine is that I'm fairly sure she's the best way of approach to all the things we want to find out. She knows something."

"You really think so?"

"Remember what I heard her say about Anna Scheele."

"I'd forgotten that."

"How have you been getting on with Karl Marx? Any results?"

"Nobody's made a bee-line at me and invited me into the fold. In fact, Catherine told me yesterday the Party wouldn't accept me, because I'm not sufficiently politically educated. And to have to read all that dreary stuff—honestly, Edward, I haven't the brains for it."

"You're not politically aware, are you?" Edward laughed. "Poor Charing Cross. Well, well, Catherine may be frantic with brains and intensity and political awareness, my fancy is still a little cockney typist who can't spell any words of three syllables."

Victoria frowned suddenly. Edward's words brought back to her mind the curious interview she had had with Dr. Rathbone. She told Edward about it. He seemed much more upset than she would have expected him to be.

"This is serious, Victoria, really serious. Try and tell me exactly what he said."

Victoria tried her best to recall the exact words Rathbone had used.

"But I don't see," she said, "why it upsets you so."

"Eh?" Edward seemed abstracted. "You don't see—But my dear girl, don't you realise that this shows that they've got wise to you. They're warning you off. I don't like it, Victoria—I don't like it at all."

He paused and then said gravely,

"Communists, you know, are very ruthless. It's part of their creed to stick at nothing. I don't want you knocked on the head and thrown into the Tigris, darling."

How odd, thought Victoria, to be sitting amid the ruins of Babylon debating whether or not she was likely in the near future to be knocked on the head and thrown into the Tigris. Half closing her eyes, she thought dreamily, "I shall wake up soon and find I'm in London dreaming a wonderful melodramatic dream about dangerous Babylon. Perhaps," she thought, closing her eyes altogether, "I am in London . . . and the alarm clock will go off very soon, and I shall get up and go to Mr. Greenholtz's office—and there won't be any Edward—"

And at that last thought she opened her eyes again hastily to make sure that Edward was indeed really there (and what was it I was going to ask him at Basrah and they interrupted us and I forgot?) and it was not a dream. The sun was glaring down in a dazzling and most unLondonlike way, and the ruins of Babylon were pale and shimmering with a background of dark palms, and sitting up with his back a little towards her was Edward. How extraordinarily nicely his hair grew down with a little twirl into his neck—and what a nice neck—bronzed red brown from the sun—with no blemishes on it—so many men had necks with cysts or pimples where their collars had rubbed—a neck like Sir Rupert's, for instance, with a boil just starting—

Suddenly with a stifled exclamation Victoria sat bolt upright and her daydreams were a thing of the past. She was wildly excited.

Edward turned an inquiring head.

"What's the matter, Charing Cross?"

"I've just remembered," said Victoria, "about Sir Rupert Crofton Lee—"

As Edward still turned a blank inquiring look upon her Victoria proceeded to elucidate her meaning which, truth to tell, she did not do very clearly.

"It was a boil," she said, "on his neck."

"A boil on his neck?" Edward was puzzled.

"Yes, in the aeroplane. He sat in front of me, you know, and that hood thing he wore fell back and I saw it—the boil."

"Why shouldn't he have a boil? Painful, but lots of people get them."

"Yes, yes, of course they do. But the point is that that morning on the balcony he hadn't."

"Hadn't what?"

"Hadn't got a boil. Oh Edward, do try and take it in. In the aeroplane he had a boil and on the balcony at the Tio he hadn't got a boil. His neck was quite smooth and unscarred—like yours now."

"Well, I suppose it had gone away."

"Oh no, Edward, it couldn't have. It was only a day later, and it was just coming up. It couldn't have gone away—not completely without a trace. So you see it means—yes, it must mean—the man at the Tio wasn't Sir Rupert at all."

She nodded her head with vehemence. Edward stared at her.

"You're crazy, Victoria. It must have been Sir Rupert. You didn't see any other difference in him."

"But don't you see, Edward, I'd never really looked at him properly—only at his—well, you might call it general effect. The hat—and the cape—and the swashbuckling attitude. He'd be a very easy man to impersonate."

"But they'd have known at the Embassy—"

"He didn't stay at the Embassy, did he? He came to the Tio. It was one of the minor secretaries or people who met him. The Ambassador's in England. Besides, he's travelled and been away from England so much."

"But why—"

"Because of Carmichael, of course. Carmichael was coming to Baghdad to meet him—to tell him what he'd found out. Only they'd never met before. So Carmichael wouldn't know he wasn't the right man—and he wouldn't be on his guard. Of course—it was Rupert Crofton Lee (the false one) who stabbed Carmichael! Oh, Edward, it all fits in."

"I don't believe a word of it. It's crazy. Don't forget Sir Rupert was killed afterwards in Cairo."

"That's where it all happened. I know now. Oh Edward, how awful. I saw it happen."

"You saw it happen—Victoria, are you quite mad?"

"No, I'm not in the least mad. Just listen, Edward. There was a knock on my door—in the Hotel in Heliopolis—at least I thought it was on my door and I looked out, but it wasn't—it was one door down, Sir Rupert Crofton Lee's. It was one of the stewardesses or Air Hostesses or whatever they call them. She asked him if he would mind coming to B.O.A.C. office—just along the corridor. I came out of my room just afterwards. I passed a door which had a notice with B.O.A.C. on it, and the door opened and he came out. I thought then that he had had some news that made him walk quite differently. Do you see, Edward? It was a trap, the substitute was waiting, all ready, and as soon as he came in, they just conked him on the head and the other one came out and took up the part. I think they probably kept him somewhere in Cairo, perhaps in the Hotel as an invalid, kept him drugged and then killed him just at the right moment when the wrong one had come back to Cairo."

"It's a magnificent story," said Edward. "But you know, Victoria, quite frankly you are making the whole thing up. There's no corroboration of it."

"There's the boil—"

"Oh, damn the boil!"

"And there are one or two other things."

"What?"

"That B.O.A.C. notice on the door. It wasn't there later. I remember being puzzled when I found the B.O.A.C. office was the other side of the entrance hall. That's one thing. And there's another. That Air stewardess, the one who knocked at his door. I've seen her since —here in Baghdad—and what's more, at the Olive Branch. The first day I went there. She came in and spoke to Catherine. I thought then I'd seen her before."

After a moment's silence, Victoria said:

"So you must admit, Edward, that it isn't all my fancy."

Edward said slowly:

"It all comes back to the Olive Branch—and to Catherine. Victoria, all ragging apart, you've got to get closer to Catherine. Flatter her, butter her up, talk Bolshie ideas to her. Somehow or other get sufficiently intimate with her to know who her friends are and where she goes and who she's in touch with outside the Olive Branch."

"It won't be easy," said Victoria, "but I'll try. What about Mr. Dakin? Ought I to tell him about this?"

"Yes, of course. But wait a day or two. We may have more to go on," Edward sighed. "I shall take Catherine to Le Select to hear the Cabaret one night."

And this time Victoria felt no pang of jealousy. Edward had spoken with a grim determination that ruled out any anticipation of pleasure in the commission he had undertaken.

II

Exhilarated by her discoveries, Victoria found it no effort to greet Catherine on the following day with an effusion of friendliness. It was so kind of Catherine, she said, to have told her of a place to have her hair washed. It needed washing terribly badly. (This was undeniable; Victoria had returned from Babylon with her dark hair the color of red rust from the clogging sand.)

"It is looking terrible, yes," said Catherine, eyeing it with a certain malicious satisfaction. "You went out then in that dust storm yesterday afternoon?"

"I hired a car and went to see Babylon," said Victoria. "It was very interesting, but on the way back, the dust storm got up and I was nearly choked and blinded."

"It is interesting, Babylon," said Catherine, "but you should go with someone who understands it and can tell you about it properly. As for your hair, I will take you to this Armenian girl tonight. She will give you a cream shampoo. It is the best."

"I don't know how you keep your hair looking so wonderful," said Victoria, looking with what appeared to be admiring eyes at Catherine's heavy erections of greasy sausage-like curls.

A smile appeared on Catherine's usually sour face, and Victoria thought how right Edward had been about flattery.

When they left the Olive Branch that evening, the two girls were on the friendliest of terms. Catherine wove in and out of narrow passages and alleys and finally tapped on an unpromising door which gave no sign of hairdressing operations being conducted on the other side of it. They were, however, received by a plain but competent looking young woman who spoke careful slow English and who led Victoria to a spotlessly clean basin with shining taps and various bottles and lotions ranged round it. Catherine departed and Victoria surrendered her mop of hair into Miss Ankoumian's deft hands. Soon her hair was a mass of creamy lather.

"And now if you please—"

Victoria bent forward over the basin. Water streamed over her hair and gurgled down the waste pipe.

Suddenly her nose was assailed by a sweet rather sickly smell that she associated vaguely with hospitals. A wet saturated pad was clasped firmly over her nose and mouth. She struggled wildly, twisting and turning, but an iron grip kept the pad in place. She began to suffocate, her head reeled dizzily, a roaring sound came in her ears . . .

And after that, blackness, deep and profound.

XVIII

WHEN VICTORIA REGAINED consciousness, it was with a sense of an immense passage of time. Confused memories stirred in her—jolting in a car—high jabbering and quarrelling in Arabic—lights that flashed into her eyes—a horrible attack of nausea—then vaguely she remembered lying on a bed and someone lifting her arm—the sharp agonizing prick of a needle—then more confused dreams and darkness and behind it a mounting sense of urgency . . .

Now at last, dimly, she was herself—Victoria Jones . . . And something had happened to Victoria Jones—a long time ago—months—perhaps years . . . after all, perhaps only days.

Babylon—sunshine—dust—hair—Catherine—Catherine, of course, smiling, her eyes sly under the sausage curls—Catherine had taken her to have her hair shampooed and then—what had happened? That horrible smell—she could still smell it—nauseating—chloroform, of course. They had chloroformed her and taken her—where?

Cautiously Victoria tried to sit up. She seemed to be lying on a bed—a very hard bed—her head ached and felt dizzy—she was still drowsy, horribly drowsy . . . that prick, the prick of a hypodermic, they had been drugging her . . . she was still half drugged.

Well, anyway they hadn't killed her (why not?). So that was all right. The best thing, thought the still half-drugged Victoria, is to go to sleep. And promptly did so.

When next she awakened she felt much more clearheaded. It was daylight now and she could see more clearly where she was.

She was in a small but very high room, distempered a depressing pale bluish grey. The floor was of beaten earth. The only furniture in the room seemed to be the bed on which she was lying, with a dirty rug thrown over her, and a rickety table with a cracked enamel basin on it and a zinc bucket underneath it. There was a window with a kind of wooden lattice work outside it. Victoria got gingerly off the bed, feeling distinctly headachy and queer, and approached the window. She could see through the lattice work quite plainly, and what she saw was a garden with palm trees beyond it. The garden was quite a pleasant one by Eastern standards, though it would have been looked down on by an English suburban householder. It had a lot of bright orange marigolds in it, and some dusty eucalyptus trees and some rather wispy tamarisks.

A small child with a face tattooed in blue and a lot of bangles on, was tumbling about with a ball and singing in a high nasal whine rather like distant bagpipes.

Victoria next turned her attention to the door which was large and massive. Without much hope she went to it and tried it. The door was locked. Victoria went back and sat on the side of the bed.

Where was she? Not in Baghdad, that was certain. And what was she going to do next?

It struck her after a minute or two that the last question did not really apply. What was more to the point was what was someone else going to do to her? With an uneasy feeling in the pit of the stomach she remembered Mr. Dakin's admonition to tell all she knew. But perhaps they had already got all that out of her while she was under the drug.

Still—Victoria returned to this one point with determined cheerfulness—she was alive. If she could manage to keep alive until Edward found her—what would Edward do when he found she had vanished? Would he go to Mr. Dakin? Would he play a lone hand? Would he put the fear of the Lord into Catherine and force her to tell—Would he suspect Catherine at all? The more Victoria tried to conjure up a reassuring picture of Edward in action, the more the image of Edward faded and became a kind of faceless abstraction. How clever was Edward? That was really what it amounted to. Edward was adorable. Edward had glamour. But had Edward got brains? Because clearly, in her present predicament, brains were going to be needed.

Mr. Dakin, now, would have the necessary brains. But would he have the impetus? Or would he merely cross off her name from a mental ledger, scoring it through, and writing after it a neat R.I.P. After all, to Mr. Dakin she was merely one of a crowd. They took their chance, and if luck failed, it was just too bad. No, she didn't see Mr. Dakin staging a rescue. After all, he had warned her. And Dr. Rathbone had warned her. (Warned her or threatened her?) And on her refusing to be threatened, there had not been much delay in carrying out the threat . . .

But I'm still alive, repeated Victoria, determined to look upon the bright side of things.

Footsteps approached outside and there was the grinding of a key in a rusty lock. The door staggered on its hinges and flew open. In the aperture appeared an Arab. He carried an old tin tray on which were dishes.

He appeared to be in good spirits, grinned broadly, uttered some incomprehensible remarks in Arabic, finally deposited the tray, opened his mouth and pointed down his throat and departed, re-locking the door behind him.

Victoria approached the tray with interest. There was a large bowl of rice, something that looked like rolled up cabbage leaves and a large flap of Arab bread. Also a jug of water and a glass.

Victoria started by drinking a large glass of water and then fell to on the rice, the bread, and the cabbage leaves which were full of rather peculiar tasting chopped meat. When she had finished everything on the tray she felt a good deal better.

She tried her best to think things out clearly. She had been chloroformed and kidnapped. How long ago? As to that, she had only the foggiest idea. From drowsy memories of sleeping and waking she judged that it was some days ago. She had been taken out of Baghdad —where? There again, she had no means of knowing. Owing to her ignorance of Arabic, it was not even possible to ask questions. She could not find out a place, or a name, or a date.

Several hours of acute boredom followed.

That evening her gaoler reappeared with another tray of food. With him this time came a couple of women. They were in rusty black with their faces hidden. They did not come into the room but stood just outside the door. One had a baby in her arms. They stood there and giggled. Through the thinness of the veil their eyes, she felt, were appraising her. It was exciting to them and highly humorous to have a European woman imprisoned here.

Victoria spoke to them in English and in French, but got only giggles in reply. It was queer, she thought, to be unable to communicate with her own sex. She said slowly and with difficulty one of the few phrases she had picked up,

"El hamdu lillah."

Its utterance was rewarded by a delighted spate of Arabic. They nodded their heads vigorously. Victoria moved towards them, but quickly the Arab servant or whatever he was, stepped back and barred her way. He motioned the two women back and went out himself, closing and locking the door again. Before he did so, he uttered one word several times over.

"*Bukra—Bukra . . .*"

It was a word Victoria had heard before. It meant tomorrow.

Victoria sat down on her bed to think things over. Tomorrow? Tomorrow, someone was coming or something was going to happen. Tomorrow her imprisonment would end (or wouldn't it?)—or if it did end, she herself might end too! Taking all things together, Victoria didn't much care for the idea of tomorrow. She felt instinctively that it would be much better if by tomorrow she was somewhere else.

But was that possible? For the first time, she gave this problem full attention. She went first to the door and examined it. Certainly nothing doing there. This wasn't the kind of lock you picked with a hairpin—if indeed she would have been capable of picking any lock with a hairpin, which she very much doubted.

There remained the window. The window, she soon found, was a much more hopeful proposition. The wooden lattice work that screened it was in the final stages of decrepitude. Granted she could break away sufficient of the rotten woodwork to force herself through, she could hardly do so without a good deal of noise which could not fail to attract attention. Moreover since the room in which she was confined was on an upper floor, it meant either fashioning a rope of some kind or else jumping with every likelihood of a sprained ankle or other injury. In books, thought Victoria, you make a rope of strips of bedclothes. She looked doubtfully at the thick cotton quilt and ragged blanket. Neither of them seemed at all suitable to her purpose. She had nothing with which to cut the quilt in strips, and though she could probably tear the blanket, its condition of rottenness would preclude any possibility of trusting her weight to it.

"Damn," said Victoria aloud.

She was more and more enamoured of the idea of escape. As far as she could judge, her gaolers were people of very simple mentality to whom the mere fact that she was locked in a room spelt finality. They would not be expecting her to escape for the simple reason that she was a prisoner and could not. Whoever had used the hypodermic on her and presumably brought her here was not now on the premises—of that she was sure. He or she or they were expected "bukra." They had left her in some remote spot in the guardianship of simple folk who would obey instructions but who would not appreciate subtleties, and who were not, presumably, alive to the inventive faculties of a European young woman in imminent fear of extinction.

"I'm getting out of here somehow," said Victoria to herself.

She approached the table and helped herself to the new supply of food. She might as well keep her strength up. There was rice again and some oranges, and some bits of meat in a bright orange sauce.

Victoria ate everything and then had a drink of water. As she replaced the jug on the table, the table tilted slightly and some of the water went on the floor. The floor in that particular spot at once became a small puddle of liquid mud. Looking at it, an idea stirred in Miss Victoria Jones' always fertile brain.

The question was, had the key been left in the lock on the outside of the door?

The sun was setting now. Very soon it would be dark. Victoria went over to the door, knelt down and peered into the immense keyhole. She could see no light. Now what she needed was something to prod with —a pencil or the end of a fountain pen. How tiresome that her handbag had been taken away. She looked round the room frowning. The only article of cutlery on the table was a large spoon. That was no good for her immediate need, though it might come in handy later. Victoria sat down to puzzle and contrive. Presently she uttered an exclamation, took off her shoe and managed to pull out the inner leather sole. She rolled this up tightly. It was reasonably stiff. She went back to the door, squatted down and poked vigorously through the keyhole. Fortunately the immense key fitted loosely into the lock. After three or four minutes it responded to the efforts and fell out of the door on the outside. It made little noise falling on the earthen floor.

Now, Victoria thought, I must hurry, before the light goes altogether. She fetched the jug of water and poured a little carefully on a spot at the bottom of the door frame as near as possible to where she judged the key had fallen. Then, with the spoon and her fingers she scooped and scrabbled in the muddy patch that resulted. Little by little, with fresh applications of water from the jug, she scooped out a low trough under the door. Lying down she tried to peer through it but it wasn't easy to see anything. Rolling up her sleeves, she found she could get her hand and part of her arm under the door. She felt about with exploratory fingers and finally the tip of one finger touched something metallic. She had located the key, but she was unable to get her arm far enough to claw it nearer. Her next procedure was to secure the safety pin which was holding up a torn shoulder strap. Bending it into a hook, she embedded it in a wedge of Arab bread and lay down again to fish. Just as she was ready to cry with vexation the hooked safety pin caught in the key and she was able to draw it within reach of her fingers and then to pull it through the muddy trough to her side of the door.

Victoria sat back on her heels full of admiration for her own in-genuity. Grasping the key in her muddy hand, she got up and fitted it into the lock. She waited for a moment when there was a good chorus of pi-dogs barking in the near neighbourhood, and turned it. The door yielded to her push and swung open a little way. Victoria peered cautiously through the aperture. The door gave onto another small room with an open door at the end of it. Victoria waited a moment, then tiptoed out and across. This outside room had large gaping holes in the roof and one or two in the floor. The door at the end gave on the top of a flight of rough mudbrick stairs affixed to the side of the house, and which led down to the garden.

That was all Victoria wanted to see. She tiptoed back to her own place of imprisonment. There was little likelihood that anyone would come near her again tonight. She would wait until it was dark and the village or town more or less settled down to sleep and then she would go.

One other thing she had noted. A torn shapeless bit of black material lay in a heap near the outside door. It was, she thought, an old *Aba* and would come in useful to cover her Western clothes.

How long she waited Victoria did not know. It seemed to her inter-minable hours. Yet at last the various noises of local human kind died down. The far off blaring of a gramophone or phonograph stopped its Arab songs, the raucous voices and the spitting ceased, and there was no more far off women's high-pitched squealing laughter; no chil-dren's crying.

At last she heard only a far off howling noise which she took to be jackals, and the intermittent bursts of dog barking, which she knew would continue all through the night.

"Well, here goes!" said Victoria and stood up.

After a moment's cogitation she locked the door of her prison on the outside and left the key in the lock. Then she felt her way across the outer room, picked up the black heap of material and came out at the top of the mud stairs. There was a moon, but it was still low in the sky. It gave sufficient light for Victoria to see her way. She crept down the stairs, then paused about four stairs from the bottom. She was level here with the mudwall that enclosed the garden. If she continued down the stairs she would have to pass along the side of the house. She could hear snoring from the downstairs rooms. If she went along the top of the wall it might be better. The wall was sufficiently thick to walk along.

She chose the latter course and went swiftly and somewhat precariously to where the wall turned at right angles. Here, outside, was what seemed to be a palm garden, and at one point the wall was crumbling away. Victoria found her way there, partly jumped and partly slithered down and a few moments later was threading her way through palm trees towards a gap in the far wall. She came out upon a narrow street of a primitive nature, too small for the passage of a car, but suitable for donkeys. It ran between mudbrick walls. Victoria sped along it as fast as she could.

Now dogs began to bark furiously. Two fawn coloured pi-dogs came snarlingly out of a doorway at her. Victoria picked up a handful of rubble and brick and shied a piece at them. They yelped and ran away. Victoria sped on. She rounded a corner and came into what was evidently the main street. Narrow and heavily rutted, it ran through a village of mudbrick houses, uniformly pale in the moonlight. Palms peeped over walls, dogs snarled and barked. Victoria took a deep breath and ran. Dogs continued to bark, but no human being took any interest in this possible night marauder. Soon she came out on a wide space with a muddy stream and a decrepit humpbacked bridge over it. Beyond the road or track lay heading towards what seemed infinite space. Victoria continued to run until she was out of breath.

The village was well behind her now. The moon was high in the sky. To the left and the right and in front of her was bare stony ground, uncultivated and without a sign of human habitation. It looked flat but was really faintly contoured. It had, as far as Victoria could see, no landmarks, and she had no idea in what direction the track led. She was not learned enough in the stars to know even towards what point of the compass she was heading. There was something subtly terrifying in this large empty waste, but it was impossible to turn back. She could only go on.

Pausing a few moments to get her breath back, and assuring herself by looking back over her shoulder, that her flight had not been discovered, she set forth, walking a steady three and a half miles an hour towards the unknown.

Dawn came at last to find Victoria weary, footsore and almost on the verge of hysteria. By noting the light in the sky she ascertained that she was heading roughly southwest, but since she did not know where she was, that knowledge was of little use to her.

A little to the side of the road ahead of her was a kind of small compact hill or knob. Victoria left the track and made her way to the knob, the sides of which were quite steep, and climbed up to the top of it.

Here she was able to take a survey of the country all around and her feeling of meaningless panic returned. For everywhere there was nothing . . . The scene was beautiful in the early morning light. The ground and horizon shimmered with faint pastel shades of apricot and cream and pink on which were patterns of shadows. It was beautiful but frightening. "I know what it means now," thought Victoria, "when anyone says they are alone in the world . . ."

There was a little faint scrubby grass in dark patches here and there and some dry thorn. But otherwise there was no cultivation, and no signs of life. There was only Victoria Jones.

Of the village from which she had fled there were no signs either. The road along which she had come stretched back apparently into an infinity of waste. It seemed incredible to Victoria that she could have walked so far as to have lost the village altogether from view. For a moment she had a panic-stricken yearning to go back. Somehow or other to regain touch with human kind . . .

Then she took herself in hand. She had meant to escape, and had escaped, but her troubles were not likely to be at an end simply because she had placed several miles between her and her gaolers. A car, however old and rickety, would make short work of those miles. As soon as her escape was discovered, someone would come in search of her. And how on earth was she going to take cover or hide. There simply wasn't anywhere to hide. She still carried the ragged black *Aba* she had snatched up. Now tentatively she wrapped herself in its folds, pulling it down over her face. She had no idea what she looked like because she had no mirror with her. If she took off her European

shoes and stockings and shuffled along with bare feet, she might possibly evade detection. A virtuously veiled Arab woman, however ragged
and poor, had, she knew, all possible immunity. It would be the height
of bad manners for any man to address her. But would that disguise
fool Western eyes who might be out in a car looking for her. At any
rate, it was the only chance.

She was much too tired to go on at present. She was terribly
thirsty, too, but it was impossible to do anything about that. The best
thing, she decided, was to lie down on the side of this hillock. She
could hear a car coming and if she kept herself flattened into a little
ravine which had eroded down the side of the hillock, she could get
some idea of who was in the car.

She could take cover by moving round the back of the hillock so as
to keep out of sight of the road.

On the other hand, what she badly needed was to get back to civilization, and the only means, as far as she could see, was to stop a car
with Europeans in it and ask for a lift.

But she must be sure that the Europeans were the right Europeans.
And how on earth was she to make sure of that?

Worrying over this point, Victoria quite unexpectedly fell asleep,
worn out by her long trudge and her general exhaustion.

When she awoke the sun was directly overhead. She felt hot and
stiff and dizzy, and her thirst was now a raging torment. Victoria gave
a groan, but as the groan issued from her dry sore lips, she suddenly
stiffened and listened. She heard faintly but distinctly the sound of a
car. Very cautiously she raised her head. The car was not coming from
the direction of the village but towards it. That meant that it was not
in pursuit. It was as yet a small black dot far off on the track. Still lying
as much concealed as she could, Victoria watched it come nearer. How
she wished she had field glasses with her.

It disappeared for a few minutes in a depression of the landscape,
then reappeared surmounting a rise not very far away. There was an
Arab driver and beside him was a man in European dress.

"Now," thought Victoria, "I've got to decide." Was this her chance?
Should she run down to the road and hail the car to stop?

Just as she was getting ready to do so, a sudden qualm stopped her.
Suppose, just suppose, that this was the Enemy?

After all, how could she tell? The track was certainly a very deserted one. No other car had passed. No lorry. Not even a train of

donkeys. This car was making, perhaps, for the village she had left last night . . .

What should she do? It was a horrible decision to have to make at a moment's notice. If it was the Enemy, it was the end. But if it wasn't the Enemy, it might be her only hope of survival. Because if she went on wandering about, she would probably die of thirst and exposure. What should she do?

And as she crouched paralysed with indecision, the note of the approaching car changed. It slackened speed, then, swerving, it came off the road and across the stony ground towards the mound on which she squatted.

It had seen her! It was looking for her!

Victoria slithered down the gully and crawled round the back of the mound away from the approaching car. She heard it come to a stop and the bang of the door as someone got out.

Then somebody said something in Arabic. After that, nothing happened. Suddenly, without any warning, a man came into view. He was walking round the mound, about half way up it. His eyes were bent on the ground and from time to time he stooped and picked something up. Whatever he was looking for, it did not seem to be a girl called Victoria Jones. Moreover, he was unmistakably an Englishman.

With an exclamation of relief Victoria struggled to her feet and came towards him. He lifted his head and stared in surprise.

"Oh please," said Victoria. "I'm so glad you've come."

He still stared.

"Who on earth," he began. "Are you English? But—"

With a spurt of laughter, Victoria cast away the enveloping *Aba*.

"Of course I'm English," she said. "And please, can you take me back to Baghdad?"

"I'm not going to Baghdad. I've just come from it. But what on earth are you doing all alone out here in the middle of the desert?"

"I was kidnapped," said Victoria breathlessly. "I went to have my hair shampooed and they gave me chloroform. And when I woke up I was in an Arab house in a village over there."

She gesticulated towards the horizon:

"In Mandali?"

"I don't know its name. I escaped last night. I walked all through the night and then I hid behind this hill in case you were an Enemy."

Her rescuer was staring at her with a very odd expression on his face. He was a man of about thirty-five, fair-haired, with a somewhat supercilious expression. His speech was academic and precise. He now put on a pair of pince-nez and stared at her through them with an expression of distaste. Victoria realised that this man did not believe a word of what she was saying.

She was immediately moved to furious indignation.

"It's perfectly true," she said. "Every word of it!"

The stranger looked more disbelieving than ever.

"Very remarkable," he said in a cold tone.

Despair seized Victoria. How unfair it was that while she could always make a lie sound plausible, in recitals of stark truth she lacked the power to make herself believed. Actual facts she told baldly and without conviction.

"And if you haven't got anything to drink with you, I shall die of thirst," she said. "I shall die of thirst anyway, if you leave me here and go on without me."

"Naturally I shouldn't dream of doing that," said the stranger stiffly. "It is most unsuitable for an Englishwoman to be wandering about alone in the wilds. Dear me, your lips are quite cracked . . . Abdul."

"Sahib?"

The driver appeared round the side of the mound.

On receiving instructions in Arabic he ran off towards the car, to return shortly with a large Thermos flask and a bakelite cup.

Victoria drank water avidly.

"Oo!" she said. "That's better."

"My name's Richard Baker," said the Englishman.

Victoria responded.

"I'm Victoria Jones," she said. And then, in an effort to recover lost ground and to replace the disbelief she saw by a respectful attention, she added:

"Pauncefoot Jones. I'm joining my uncle, Dr. Pauncefoot Jones, on his excavation."

"What an extraordinary coincidence," said Baker, staring at her surprisedly. "I'm on my way to the Dig myself. It's only about fifteen miles from here. I'm just the right person to have rescued you, aren't I?"

To say that Victoria was taken aback is to put it mildly. She was completely flabbergasted. So much so, that she was quite incapable of saying a word of any kind. Meekly and in silence she followed Richard to the car and got in.

"I suppose you're the anthropologist," said Richard, as he settled her in the back seat and removed various impedimenta. "I heard you were coming out, but I didn't expect you so early in the season."

He stood for a moment sorting through various potsherds which he removed from his pockets and which, Victoria now realised, were what he had been picking up from the surface of the mound.

"Likely looking little *Tell*," he said, gesturing towards the mound. "But nothing out of the way on it, so far as I can see. Late Assyrian ware mostly—a little Parthian, some quite good ring bases of the Kassite period." He smiled as he added, "I'm glad to see that in spite of your troubles your archaeological instincts led you to examine a *Tell*."

Victoria opened her mouth and then shut it again. The driver let in the clutch and they started off.

What, after all, could she say? True, she would be unmasked as soon as they reached the Expedition House—but it would be infinitely better to be unmasked there and confess penitence for her inventions, than it would be to confess all to Mr. Richard Baker in the middle of nowhere. The worst they could do to her would be to send her into Baghdad. And anyway, thought Victoria, incorrigible as ever, perhaps before I get there I shall have thought of something. Her busy imagination got to work forthwith. A lapse of memory? She had travelled out with a girl who had asked her to—no really, as far as she could see, she would have to make a complete breast of it. But she infinitely preferred making a clean breast of it to Dr. Pauncefoot Jones, whatever kind of man he was, than to Mr. Richard Baker, with his supercilious way of lifting his eyebrows and his obvious disbelief of the exact and true story she had told him.

"We don't go right into Mandali," said Mr. Baker, turning in the front seat. "We branch off from the road into the desert about a mile further on. A bit difficult to hit the exact spot sometimes with no particular landmarks."

Presently he said something to Abdul and the car turned sharply off the track and made straight for the desert. With no particular landmarks to guide him, as far as Victoria could see, Richard Baker directed Abdul with gestures—he bent now to the right—now to the left. Presently Richard gave an exclamation of satisfaction.

"On the right track now," he said.

Victoria could not see any track at all. But presently she did catch sight every now and again of faintly marked tyre marks.

Once they crossed a slightly more clearly marked track and when they did so, Richard made an exclamation and ordered Abdul to stop.

"Here's an interesting sight for you," he said to Victoria. "Since you're new to this country you won't have seen it before."

Two men were advancing towards the car along the cross track. One man carried a short wooden bench on his back, the other a big wooden object about the size of an upright piano.

Richard hailed them; they greeted him with every sign of pleasure. Richard produced cigarettes and a thoroughly party spirit seemed to be developing.

Then Richard turned to her.

"Fond of the Cinema? Then you shall see a performance."

He spoke to the two men and they smiled with pleasure. They set up the bench and motioned to Victoria and Richard to sit on it. Then they set up the round contrivance on a stand of some kind. It had two eyeholes in it and as she looked at it, Victoria cried,

"It's like things on piers. *What the butler saw.*"

"That's it," said Richard. "It's a primitive form of same."

Victoria applied her eyes to the glass-fronted peephole, one man began slowly to turn a crank or handle, and the other began a monotonous kind of chant.

"What is he saying?" Victoria asked.

Richard translated as the sing-song chant continued,

"Draw near and prepare yourself for much wonder and delight. Prepare to behold the wonders of antiquity."

A crudely coloured picture of negroes reaping wheat swam into Victoria's gaze.

"Fellahin in America," announced Richard, translating.

Then came:

"The wife of the great Shah of the Western world," and the Empress Eugenie simpered and fingered a long ringlet. A picture of the King's Palace in Montenegro, another of the Great Exhibition.

An odd and varied collection of pictures followed each other, all completely unrelated and sometimes announced in the strangest terms.

The Prince Consort, Disraeli, Norwegian Fjords and Skaters in Switzerland completed this strange glimpse of olden far off days.

The showman ended his exposition with the following words,

"And so we bring to you the wonders and marvels of antiquity in other lands and far off places. Let your donation be generous to match the marvels you have seen, for all these things are true."

It was over. Victoria beamed with delight.

"That really was marvellous!" she said. "I wouldn't have believed it."

The proprietors of the travelling Cinema were smiling proudly. Victoria got up from the bench and Richard who was sitting on the other end of it was thrown to the ground in a somewhat undignified posture. Victoria apologised but was not ill pleased. Richard rewarded the Cinema men and with courteous farewells and expressions of concern for each other's welfare, and invoking the blessing of God on each other, they parted company. Richard and Victoria got into the car again and the men trudged away into the desert.

"Where are they going?" asked Victoria.

"They travel all over the country. I met them first in Trans-Jordan coming up the road from the Dead Sea to Ammaan. Actually they're bound now for Kerbela, going of course by unfrequented routes so as to give shows in remote villages."

"Perhaps someone will give them a lift?"

Richard laughed.

"They probably wouldn't take it. I offered an old man a lift once who was walking from Basrah to Baghdad. I asked him how long he expected to be and he said a couple of months. I told him to get in and he would be there late that evening, but he thanked me and said no. Two months ahead would suit him just as well. Time doesn't mean anything out here. Once one gets that into one's head, one finds a curious satisfaction in it."

"Yes. I can imagine that."

"Arabs find our Western impatience for doing things quickly extraordinarily hard to understand, and our habit of coming straight to the point in conversation strikes them as extremely ill-mannered. You should always sit round and offer general observations for about an hour—or if you prefer, you need not speak at all."

"Rather odd if we did that in offices in London. One would waste a lot of time."

"Yes, but we're back again at the question: What is time? And what is waste?"

Victoria meditated on these points. The car still appeared to be proceeding to nowhere with the utmost confidence.

"Where is this place?" she said at last.

"Tell Aswad? Well out in the middle of the desert. You'll see the Zigcurat very shortly now. In the meantime, look over to your left. There—where I'm pointing."

"Are they clouds?" asked Victoria. "They can't be mountains."

"Yes, they are. The snow-capped mountains of Kurdistan. You can only see them when it's very clear."

A dream-like feeling of contentment came over Victoria. If only she could drive on like this for ever. If only she wasn't such a miserable liar. She shrank like a child at the thought of the unpleasant denouement ahead of her. What would Dr. Pauncefoot Jones be like? Tall, with a long grey beard, and a fierce frown. Never mind, however annoyed Dr. Pauncefoot Jones might be, she had circumvented Catherine and the Olive Branch and Dr. Rathbone.

"There you are," said Richard.

He pointed ahead. Victoria made out a kind of pimple on the far horizon.

"It looks miles away."

"Oh no, it's only a few miles now. You'll see."

And, indeed, the pimple developed with astonishing rapidity into first a blob and then a hill and finally into a large and impressive *Tell*. On one side of it was a long sprawling building of mud brick.

"The Expedition House," said Richard.

They drew up with a flourish amid the barking of dogs. White robed servants rushed out to greet them, beaming with smiles.

After an interchange of greetings, Richard said:

"Apparently they weren't expecting you so soon. But they'll get your bed made. And they'll take you in hot water at once. I expect you'd like to have a wash and a rest? Dr. Pauncefoot Jones is up on the *Tell*. I'm going up to him. Ibrahim will look after you."

He strode away and Victoria followed the smiling Ibrahim into the house. It seemed dark inside at first after coming in out of the sun. They passed through a living room with some big tables and a few battered armchairs and she was then led round a courtyard and into a small room with one tiny window. It held a bed, a rough chest of drawers, a chair and a table with a jug and basin on it. Ibrahim smiled and nodded and brought her a large jug of rather muddy-looking hot water and a rough towel. Then, with an apologetic smile, he returned with a small looking glass which he carefully affixed upon a nail on the wall.

Victoria was thankful to have the chance of a wash. She was just beginning to realise how utterly weary and worn out she was and how very much encrusted with grime.

"I suppose I look simply frightful," she said to herself and approached the looking glass.

For some moments she stared at her reflection uncomprehendingly. This wasn't her—this wasn't Victoria Jones.

And then she realised that, though the features were the small neat features of Victoria Jones, her hair was now platinum blonde!

XIX

RICHARD FOUND Dr. Pauncefoot Jones in the excavations, squatting by the side of his foreman and tapping gently with a small pick at a section of wall.

Dr. Pauncefoot Jones greeted his colleague in a matter of fact manner.

"Hullo, Richard my boy, so you've turned up. I had an idea you were arriving on Tuesday, I don't know why."

"This is Tuesday," said Richard.

"Is it really now?" said Dr. Pauncefoot Jones without interest. "Just come down here and see what you think of this. Perfectly good walls coming out already and we're only down three feet. Seems to me there are a few traces of paint here. Come and see what you think. It looks very promising to me."

Richard leaped down into the trench and the two archaeologists enjoyed themselves in a highly technical manner for about a quarter of an hour.

"By the way," said Richard. "I've brought a girl."

"Oh, have you? What sort of a girl?"

"She says she's your niece."

"My niece?" Dr. Pauncefoot Jones brought his mind back with a struggle from his contemplation of mudbrick walls. "I don't think I have a niece," he said doubtfully, as though he might have had one and forgotten about her.

"She's coming to work with you here, I gathered."

"Oh." Dr. Pauncefoot Jones' face cleared. "Of course. That will be Veronica."

"Victoria, I think she said."

"Yes, yes, Victoria. Emerson wrote to me about her from Cambridge. A very able girl, I understand. An anthropologist. Can't think why anyone wants to be an anthropologist, can you?"

"I heard you had some anthropologist girl coming out."

"There's nothing in her line so far. Of course we're only just beginning. Actually I understood she wasn't coming out for another fortnight or so, but I didn't read her letter very carefully, and then I mislaid it, so I didn't really remember what she said. My wife arrives next week—or the week after—now what have I done with her letter?—and I rather thought Venetia was coming out with her—but of course I may have got it all wrong. Well, well, I daresay we can make her useful. There's a lot of pottery coming up."

"There's nothing odd about her, is there?"

"Odd?" Dr. Pauncefoot Jones peered at him. "In what way?"

"Well, she hasn't had a nervous breakdown or anything?"

"Emerson did say, I remember, that she had been working very hard. Diploma or degree or something, but I don't think he said anything about a breakdown. Why?"

"Well, I picked her up at the side of the road, wandering about all by herself. It was on that little *Tell*, as a matter of fact, that you come to about a mile before you turn off the road—"

"I remember," said Dr. Pauncefoot Jones. "You know, I once picked up a bit of Nuzu ware on that *Tell*. Extraordinary really, to find it so far South."

Richard refused to be diverted to archaeological topics and went on firmly.

"She told me the most extraordinary story. Said she'd gone to have her hair shampooed, and they chloroformed her and kidnapped her and carried her off to Mandali and imprisoned her in a house, and she'd escaped in the middle of the night—the most preposterous rigmarole you ever heard."

Dr. Pauncefoot Jones shook his head.

"Doesn't sound at all probable," he said. "Country's perfectly quiet and well policed. It's never been safer."

"Exactly. She'd obviously made the whole thing up. That's why I asked if she'd had a breakdown. She must be one of those hysterical girls who say curates are in love with them, or that doctors assault them. She may give us a lot of trouble."

"Oh I expect she'll calm down," said Dr. Pauncefoot Jones optimistically. "Where is she now?"

"I left her to have a wash and brush up." He hesitated. "She hasn't got any luggage of any kind with her."

"Hasn't she? That really is awkward. You don't think she'll expect me to lend her pyjamas? I've only got two pairs and one of them is badly torn."

"She'll have to do the best she can until the lorry goes in next week. I must say I wonder what she can have been up to—all alone and out in the blue."

"Girls are amazing nowadays," said Dr. Pauncefoot Jones vaguely. "Turn up all over the place. Great nuisance when you want to get on with things. This place is far enough out, you'd think, to be free of visitors, but you'd be surprised how cars and people turn up when you can least do with them. Dear me, the men have stopped work. It must be lunch time. We'd better go back to the house."

II

Victoria, waiting in some trepidation, found Dr. Pauncefoot Jones wildly far from her imaginings. He was a small rotund man with a semi-bald head and a twinkling eye. To her utter amazement he came towards her with outstretched hands.

"Well, well, Venetia—I mean Victoria," he said. "This is quite a surprise. Got it into my head you weren't arriving until next month. But I'm delighted to see you. Delighted. How's Emerson? Not troubled too much by asthma, I hope?"

Victoria rallied her scattered senses and said cautiously that the asthma hadn't been too bad.

"Wraps his throat up too much," said Dr. Pauncefoot Jones. "Great mistake. I told him so. All these Academic fellows who stick around universities get far too absorbed in their health. Shouldn't think about it—that's the way to keep fit. Well, I hope you'll settle down—my wife will be out next week—or the week after—she's been seedy, you know. I really must find her letter. Richard tells me your luggage has gone astray. How are you going to manage? Can't very well send the lorry in before next week?"

"I expect I can manage until then," said Victoria. "In fact, I shall have to."

Dr. Pauncefoot Jones chuckled.

"Richard and I can't lend you much. Toothbrush will be all right.

There are a dozen of them in our stores—and cotton wool if that's any good to you and—let me see—talcum powder—and some spare socks and handkerchiefs. Not much else, I'm afraid."

"I shall be all right," said Victoria and smiled happily.

"No signs of a cemetery for you," Dr. Pauncefoot Jones warned her. "Some nice walls coming up—and quantities of potsherds from the far trenches. Might get some joins. We'll keep you busy somehow or other. I forget if you do photography?"

"I know something about it," said Victoria cautiously, relieved by a mention of something that she did actually have a working knowledge of.

"Good, good. You can develop negatives? I'm old fashioned—use plates still. The dark room is rather primitive. You young people who are used to all the gadgets, often find these primitive conditions rather upsetting."

"I shan't mind," said Victoria.

From the Expedition's stores, she selected a toothbrush, toothpaste, a sponge and some talcum powder.

Her head was still in a whirl as she tried to understand exactly what her position was. Clearly she was being mistaken for a girl called Venetia Something who was coming out to join the Expedition and who was an Anthropologist. Victoria didn't even know what an anthropologist was. If there was a dictionary somewhere about, she must look it up. The other girl was presumably not arriving for at least another week. Very well then, for a week—or until such time as the car or the lorry went into Baghdad, Victoria would be Venetia Thingummy, keeping her end up as best she could. She had no fears for Dr. Pauncefoot Jones who seemed delightfully vague, but she was nervous of Richard Baker. She disliked the speculative way he looked at her, and she had an idea that unless she was careful he would soon see through her pretences. Fortunately she had been, for a brief period, a secretary typist at the Archaeological Institute in London, and she had a smattering of phrases and odds and ends that would be useful now. But she would have to be very careful not to make any real slip. Luckily, thought Victoria, men were always so superior about women that any slip she did make would be treated less as a suspicious circumstance than as a proof of how ridiculously addlepated all women were!

This interval would give her a respite which, she felt, she badly needed. For, from the point of view of the Olive Branch, her complete disappearance would be very disconcerting. She had escaped from her prison, but what had happened to her afterwards would be very hard to trace. Richard's car had not passed through Mandali so that nobody could guess she was now at Tell Aswad. No, from their point of view, Victoria would seem to have vanished into thin air. They might conclude, very possibly they would conclude, that she was dead. That she had strayed into the desert and died of exhaustion.

Well, let them think so. Regrettably, of course, Edward would think so, too! Very well, Edward must lump it. In any case he would not have to lump it long. Just when he was torturing himself with remorse for having told her to cultivate Catherine's society—there she would be—suddenly restored to him—back from the dead—only a blonde instead of a brunette.

That brought her back to the mystery of why They (whoever they were) had dyed her hair. There must, Victoria thought, be some reason—but she could not for the life of her understand what the reason could be. As it was, she was soon going to look very peculiar when her hair started growing out black at the roots. A phoney platinum blonde, with no face powder and no lipstick! Could any girl be more unfortunately placed? Never mind, thought Victoria, I'm alive, aren't I? And I don't see at all why I shouldn't enjoy myself a good deal—at any rate for a week. It was really great fun to be on an Archaeological Expediton and see what it was like. If only she could keep her end up and not give herself away.

She did not find her role altogether easy. Reference to people, to publications, to styles of architecture and categories of pottery had to be dealt with cautiously. Fortunately a good listener is always appreciated. Victoria was an excellent listener to the two men, and warily feeling her way, she began to pick up the jargon fairly easily.

Surreptitiously, she read furiously when she was alone in the house. There was a good library of Archaeological publications. Victoria was quick to pick up a smattering of the subject. Unexpectedly, she found the life quite enchanting. Tea brought to her in the early morning, then out on the Dig. Helping Richard with camera work. Piecing together and sticking up pottery. Watching the men at work, appreciating the skill and delicacy of the pickmen—enjoying the songs and laughter of the little boys who ran to empty their baskets of earth on the dump. She mastered the periods, realised the various levels where digging was going on, and familiarised herself with the work of the previous season. The only thing she dreaded was that burials might turn up. Nothing that she read gave her any idea of what would be expected of her as a working anthropologist! "If we do get bones or a grave," said Victoria to herself, "I shall have to have a frightful cold—no, a severe bilious attack—and take to my bed."

But no graves did appear. Instead, the walls of a palace were slowly excavated. Victoria was fascinated and had no occasion to show any aptitude or special skill.

Richard Baker still looked at her quizzically sometimes and she sensed his unspoken criticism, but his manner was pleasant and friendly, and he was genuinely amused by her enthusiasm.

"It's all new to you coming out from England," he said one day. "I remember how thrilled I was my first season."

"How long ago was that?"

He smiled.

"Rather a long time. Fifteen—no, sixteen years ago."

"You must know this country very well."

"Oh, it's not only been here. Syria—and Persia as well."

"You talk Arabic very well, don't you. If you were dressed as one could you pass as an Arab?"

He shook his head.

"Oh no—that takes some doing. I doubt if any Englishman has ever been able to pass as an Arab—for any length of time, that is."

"Lawrence?"

"I don't think Lawrence ever passed as an Arab. No, the only man I know who is practically indistinguishable from the native product is a fellow who was actually born out in these parts. His father was Consul at Kashgar and other wild spots. He talked all kinds of outlandish dialects as a child and, I believe, kept them up later."

"What happened to him?"

"I lost sight of him after we left school. We were at school together. Fakir, we used to call him, because he could sit perfectly still and go into a queer sort of trance. I don't know what he's doing now—though actually I could make a pretty good guess."

"You never saw him after school?"

"Strangely enough, I ran into him only the other day—at Basrah, it was. Rather a queer business altogether."

"Queer?"

"Yes. I didn't recognise him. He was got up as an Arab, keffiyah and striped robe and an old Army coat. He had a string of those amber beads they carry sometimes and he was clicking it through his fingers in the orthodox way—only, you see, he was actually using Army code. Morse. He was clicking out a message—to me!"

"What did it say?"

"My name—or nickname, rather—and his, and then a signal to stand by, expecting trouble."

"And was there trouble?"

"Yes. As he got up and started out of the door, a quiet inconspicuous commercial traveller sort of fellow tugged out a revolver. I knocked his arm up—and Carmichael got away."

"Carmichael?"

He switched his head round quickly at her tone.

"That was his real name. Why—do you know him?"

Victoria thought to herself—How odd it would sound if I said "He died in my bed."

"Yes," she said slowly. "I knew him."

"Knew him? Why—is he—"

Victoria nodded.

"Yes," she said. "He's dead."

"When did he die?"

"In Baghdad. In the Tio Hotel." She added quickly "It was—hushed up. Nobody knows."

He nodded his head slowly.

"I see. It was that kind of business. But you—" he looked at her. "How do you know?"

"I got mixed up in it—by accident."

He gave her a long considering look.

Victoria asked suddenly,

"Your nickname at school wasn't Lucifer, was it?"

He looked surprised.

"Lucifer? no. I was called Owl—because I always had to wear shiny glasses."

"You don't know anyone who is called Lucifer—in Basrah?"

Richard shook his head.

"Lucifer, Son of the Morning—the fallen Angel."

He added "Or an old-fashioned wax match. Its merit, if I remember rightly, was that it didn't go out in a wind."

He watched her closely as he spoke, but Victoria was frowning abstractedly.

"I wish you'd tell me," she said presently, "exactly what happened at Basrah."

"I have told you."

"No. I mean where were you when all this occurred?"

"Oh I see. Actually it was in the waiting room of the Consulate. I was waiting to see Clayton, the Consul."

"And who else was there? This commercial traveller person, and Carmichael? Anyone else?"

"There were a couple of others, a thin dark Frenchman or Syrian, and an old man—a Persian, I should say."

"And the commercial traveller got the revolver out and you stopped him, and Carmichael got out—how—?"

"He turned first towards the Consul's office. It's at the other end of a passage with a garden—"

She interrupted.

"I know. I stayed there for a day or two. As a matter of fact, it was just after you left."

"It was, was it?" Once again he watched her narrowly—but Victoria was unaware of it. She was seeing the long passage at the Consulate, but with the door open at the other end—opening onto green trees and sunlight.

"Well, as I was saying, Carmichael headed that way first. Then he wheeled round and dashed the other way into the street. That's the last I saw of him."

"What about the commercial traveller?"

Richard shrugged his shoulders.

"I understand he told some garbled story about having been attacked and robbed by a man the night before and fancying he had recognised his assailant in the Arab in the Consulate. I didn't hear much more about it because I flew on to Kuwait."

"Who was staying at the Consulate just then?" Victoria asked.

"A fellow called Crosbie—one of the oil people. Nobody else. Oh yes, I believe there was someone else down from Baghdad, but I didn't meet him. Can't remember his name."

"Crosbie," thought Victoria. She remembered Captain Crosbie, his short stocky figure, his staccato conversation. A very ordinary person. A decent soul without much finesse about him. And Crosbie had been back in Baghdad the night when Carmichael came to the Tio. Could it be because he had seen Crosbie at the other end of the passage, silhouetted against the sunlight, that Carmichael had turned so suddenly and made for the street instead of attempting to reach the Consul General's office?

She had been thinking this out in some absorption. She started rather guiltily when she looked up to find Richard Baker watching her with close attention.

"Why do you want to know all this?" he asked.

"I'm just interested."

"Any more questions?"

Victoria asked:

"Do you know anybody called Lefarge?"

"No—can't say I do. Man or woman?"

"I don't know."

She was wondering again about Crosbie. Crosbie? Lucifer? Did Lucifer equal Crosbie?

That evening, when Victoria had said good night to the two men and gone to bed, Richard said to Dr. Pauncefoot Jones,

"I wonder if I might have a look at that letter from Emerson. I'd like to see just exactly what he said about this girl."

"Of course, my dear fellow, of course. It's somewhere lying around. I made some notes on the back of it, I remember. He spoke very highly of Veronica, if I remember rightly—said she was terrifically keen. She seems to me a charming girl—quite charming. Very plucky the way she's made so little fuss about the loss of her luggage. Most girls would have insisted on being motored into Baghdad the very next day to buy a new outfit. She's what I call a sporting girl. By the way, how was it that she came to lose her luggage?"

"She was chloroformed, kidnapped, and imprisoned in a native house," said Richard impassively.

"Dear, dear, yes, so you told me. I remember now. All most improbable. Reminds me—now what does it remind me of?—ah! yes, Elizabeth Canning, of course. You remember she turned up with a most impossible story after being missing a fortnight. Very interesting conflict of evidence—about some gypsies, if it's the right case I'm thinking of. And she was such a plain girl, it didn't seem likely there could be a man in the case. Now little Victoria—Veronica—I never *can* get her name right—she's a remarkably pretty little thing. Quite likely there is a man in her case."

"She'd be better looking if she didn't dye her hair," said Richard drily.

"Does she dye it? In-deed. How knowledgeable you are in these matters."

"About Emerson's letter, sir—"

"Of course—of course—I've no idea where I put it. But look any-where you choose—I'm anxious to find it anyway because of those notes I made on the back—and a sketch of that coiled wire bead."

XX

ON THE FOLLOWING afternoon Dr. Pauncefoot Jones uttered a dis-gusted exclamation as the sound of a car came faintly to his ears. Pres-ently he located it, winding across the desert towards the *Tell.*

"Visitors," he said with venom. "At the worst possible moment, too. I want to superintend the cellulosing of that painted rosette on the North East corner. Sure to be some idiots come out from Baghdad with a lot of social chatter and expecting to get shown all over the excavations."

"This is where Victoria comes in useful," said Richard. "You hear, Victoria? It's up to you to do a personally conducted tour."

"I shall probably say all the wrong things," said Victoria. "I'm really very inexperienced, you know."

"I think you're doing very well indeed," said Richard pleasantly. "Those remarks you made this morning about plano convex bricks might have come straight out of Delougaz's book."

Victoria changed colour slightly, and resolved to paraphrase her erudition more carefully. Sometimes the quizzical glance through the thick lenses made her uncomfortable.

"I'll do my best," she said meekly.

"We push all the odd jobs on to you," said Richard.

Victoria smiled.

Indeed, her activities during the last five days surprised her not a little. She had developed plates with water filtered through cotton wool and by the light of a primitive dark lantern containing a candle which always went out at the most crucial moment. The dark-room table was a packing case and to work she had to crouch or kneel—the darkroom itself being, as Richard remarked, a modern model of the fa-mous mediaeval Little Ease. There would be more amenities in the seasons to come, Dr. Pauncefoot Jones assured her—but at the moment every penny was needed to pay workmen and get results.

The baskets of broken potsherds had at first excited her astonished derision (though this she had been careful not to display). All these broken bits of coarse stuff—what was the good of them?

Then as she found joins, stuck them and propped them up in boxes of sand, she began to take an interest. She learned to recognise shapes and even periods. And she came finally to try and reconstruct in her own mind just how and for what these vessels had been used some three thousand odd years ago. In the small area where some poor quality private houses had been dug, she pictured the houses as they had originally stood and the people who had lived in them with their wants and possessions and occupations, their hopes and their fears. Since Victoria had a lively imagination, a picture rose up easily enough in her mind. On a day when a small clay pot was found encased in a wall with a half dozen gold earrings in it, she was enthralled. Probably dowry of a daughter, Richard Baker had said smiling.

Dishes filled with grain, gold earrings saved up for a dowry, bone needles, querns and mortars, little figurines and amulets. All the everyday life and fears and hopes of a community of unimportant simple people.

"That's what I find so fascinating," said Victoria to Richard. "You see I always used to think that archaeology was just Royal Graves and Palaces.

"Kings in Babylon," she added, with a strange little smile. "But what I like so much about all this is that it's the ordinary everyday people—people like me. My St. Anthony who finds things for me when I lose them—and a lucky china pig I've got—and an awfully nice mixing bowl, blue inside and white out, that I used to make cakes in. It got broken and the new one I bought wasn't a bit the same. I can understand why these people mended up their favourite bowls or dishes so carefully with bitumen. Life's all the same really, isn't it—then or now?"

She was thinking of these things as she watched the visitors ascending the side of the Tell. Richard went to greet them, Victoria following behind him.

They were two Frenchmen, interested in Archaeology, who were making a tour through Syria and Iraq. After civil greetings, Victoria took them round the excavations, reciting parrot wise what was going on, but being unable to resist, being Victoria, adding sundry embellishments of her own, just, as she put it to herself, to make it more exciting.

She noticed that the second man was a very bad colour, and that he dragged himself along without much interest. Presently he said, if Mademoiselle would excuse him, he would retire to the house. He had not felt well since early that morning—and the sun was making him worse.

He departed in the direction of the Expedition House, and the other, in suitably lowered tones explained that, unfortunately, it was his estomac. The Baghdad Tummy they called it, did they not? He should not really have come out today.

The tour was completed, the Frenchman remained talking to Victoria, finally Fidos was called and Dr. Pauncefoot Jones, with a determined air of hospitality, suggested the guests should have tea before departing.

To this, however, the Frenchman demurred. They must not delay their departure until it was dark or they would never find the way. Richard Baker said immediately that this was quite right. The sick friend was retrieved from the house and the car rushed off at top speed.

"I suppose that's just the beginning," grunted Dr. Pauncefoot Jones. "We shall have visitors every day now."

He took a large flap of Arab bread and covered it thickly with apricot jam.

Richard went to his room after tea. He had letters to answer, and others to write in preparation for going into Baghdad on the following day.

Suddenly he frowned. Not a man of particular neatness to the outward view, he yet had a way of arranging his clothes and his papers that never varied. Now he saw at once that every drawer had been disturbed. It was not the servants, of that he was sure. It must be, then, that the sick visitor who had made a pretext to go down to the house, had coolly ransacked through his belongings. Nothing was missing, he assured himself of that. His money was untouched. What, then, had they been looking for? His face grew grave as he considered the implications.

He went into the Antika Room and looked into the drawer which held the seals and seal impressions. He gave a grim smile—nothing had been touched or removed. He went into the living room. Dr. Pauncefoot Jones was out in the courtyard with the foremen. Only Victoria was there, curled up with a book.

Richard said, without preamble, "Somebody's been searching my room."

Victoria looked up, astonished.

"But why? And who?"

"It wasn't you?"

"Me?" Victoria was indignant. "Of course not. Why should I want to pry among your things?"

He gave her a hard stare. Then he said:

"It must have been that damned stranger—the one who shammed sick and came down to the house."

"Did he steal something?"

"No," said Richard. "Nothing was taken."

"But why on earth should anyone—"

Richard cut in to say:

"I thought you might know that."

"Me?"

"Well, by your own account, rather odd things have happened to you."

"Oh that—yes." Victoria looked rather startled. She said slowly, "But I don't see why they should search your room. You've nothing to do with—"

"With what?"

Victoria did not answer for a moment or two. She seemed lost in thought.

"I'm sorry," she said at last. "What did you say? I wasn't listening."

Richard did not repeat his question. Instead he asked:

"What are you reading?"

Victoria made a slight grimace.

"You don't have much choice of light fiction here. 'Tale of Two Cities,' 'Pride and Prejudice' and 'The Mill on the Floss.' I'm reading the 'Tale of Two Cities.' "

"Never read it before?"

"Never. I always thought Dickens would be stuffy."

"What an idea!"

"I'm finding it most exciting."

"Where have you got to?" He looked over her shoulder and read out " 'And the knitting women count One.' "

"I think she's awfully frightening," said Victoria.

"Madame Defarge? Yes, a good character. Though whether you could keep a register of names in knitting has always seemed to me rather doubtful. But then, of course, I'm not a knitter."

"Oh I think you could," said Victoria, considering the point. "Plain and purl—and fancy stitches—and the wrong stitch at intervals and dropped stitches. Yes—it could be done . . . Camouflaged, of course, so that it just looked like someone who was rather bad at knitting and made mistakes . . ."

Suddenly, with a vividness like a flash of lightning, two things came together in her mind and affected her with the force of an explosion. A name—and a visual memory. The man with the ragged handknitted red scarf clasped in his hands—the scarf she had hurriedly picked up later and flung into a drawer. And together with that a name. *Defarge* —not Lefarge—*Defarge,* Madame Defarge.

She was recalled to herself by Richard saying to her courteously, "Is anything the matter?"

"No—no, that is, I just thought of something."

"I see." Richard raised his eyebrows in his most supercilious way.

Tomorrow, thought Victoria, they would all go in to Baghdad. To-morrow her respite would be over. For over a week she had had safety, peace, time to pull herself together. And she had enjoyed that time—enjoyed it enormously. Perhaps I'm a coward, thought Victoria, perhaps that's it. She had talked gaily about adventure, but she hadn't liked it very much when it really came. She had hated that struggle against chloroform and the slow suffocation, and she had been fright-ened, horribly frightened, in that upper room when the ragged Arab had said "Bukra."

And now she'd got to go back to it all. Because she was employed by Mr. Dakin and paid by Mr. Dakin and she had to earn her pay and show a brave front! She might even have to go back to the Olive Branch. She shivered a little when she remembered Dr. Rathbone and that searching dark glance of his. He'd warned her . . .

But perhaps she wouldn't have to go back. Perhaps Mr. Dakin would say it was better not—now that they knew about her. But she would have to go back to her lodgings and get her things because thrust carelessly into her suitcase was the red knitted scarf . . . She had bundled everything into suitcases when she left for Basrah. Once she had put that scarf into Mr. Dakin's hands, perhaps her task would be done. He would say to her, perhaps, like on the pictures "Oh! Good show, Victoria."

She looked up to find Richard Baker watching her.

"By the way," he said, "will you be able to get hold of your passport tomorrow?"

"My passport?"

Victoria considered the position. It was characteristic of her that she had not as yet defined her plan of action as regarded the Expedition. Since the real Veronica (or Venetia) would shortly be arriving from England, a retreat in good order was necessary. But whether she would merely fade away, or confess her deception with suitable penitence, or indeed what she intended to do, had not yet presented itself as a problem to be solved. Victoria was always prone to adopt the Micawber-like attitude that Something would Turn Up.

"Well," she said temporising, "I'm not sure."

"It's needed, you see, for the police of this district," explained Richard. "They enter its number and your name and age and special distinguishing marks, etc., all the whole caboodle. As we haven't got the passport, I think we ought at any rate to send your name and description to them. By the way, what is your last name? I've always called you 'Victoria'."

Victoria rallied gallantly.

"Come now," she said. "You know my last name as well as I do."

"That's not quite true," said Richard. His smile curved upwards with a hint of cruelty. "I do know your last name. It's you, I think, who don't know it."

Through the glasses the eyes watched her.

"Of course I know my own name," snapped Victoria.

"Then I'll challenge you to tell it to me—now."

His voice was suddenly hard and curt.

"It's no good lying," he said. "The game's up. You've been very clever about it all. You've read up your subject, you've brought out very telling bits of knowledge—but it's the kind of imposture you can't keep up all the time. I've laid traps for you and you've fallen into them. I've quoted bits of sheer rubbish to you and you've accepted them." He paused. "You're not Venetia Savile. Who are you?"

"I told you who I was the first time I met you," said Victoria. "I'm Victoria Jones."

"Dr. Pauncefoot Jones' niece?"

"I'm not his niece—but my name is Jones."

"You told me a lot of other things."

"Yes, I did. And they were all true! But I could see you didn't believe me. And that made me mad, because though I do tell lies sometimes—in fact quite often—what I'd just told you wasn't a lie. And so, just to make myself more convincing, I said my name was Pauncefoot

Jones—I've said that before out here, and it's always gone down frightfully well. How could I tell you were actually coming to this place?"

"It must have been a slight shock to you," said Richard grimly. "You
carried it off very well—cool as a cucumber."

"Not inside," said Victoria. "I was absolutely shaking. But I felt that
if I waited to explain until I got here—well at any rate I should be
safe."

"Safe?" he considered the word. "Look here, Victoria, was that incredible rigmarole you told me about being chloroformed really true?"

"Of course it was true! Don't you see, if I wanted to make up a
story I could make up a much better one than that, and tell it better!"

"Knowing you a little more closely now, I can see the force of
that! But you must admit that, on first hearing, the story was wildly
improbable."

"But you are willing to think it's possible now. Why?"

Richard said slowly,

"Because if, as you say, you were mixed up in Carmichael's death—
well, then it might be true."

"That's what it all began with," said Victoria.

"You'd better tell me about it."

Victoria stared at him very hard.

"I'm wondering," she said, "if I can trust you."

"The boot is on the other leg! Do you realise that I've had grave
suspicions that you'd planted yourself here under a false name in order
to get information out of me? And perhaps that is what you are doing."

"Meaning that you know something about Carmichael that They
would like to know?"

"Who exactly are They?"

"I shall have to tell you all about it," said Victoria. "There isn't any
other way—and if you are one of Them you know it already, so it
doesn't matter."

She told him of the night of Carmichael's death, of her interview
with Mr. Dakin, of her journey to Basrah, her employment in the
Olive Branch, of Catherine's hostility, of Dr. Rathbone and his warning and of the final denouement, including this time the enigma of the
dyed hair. The only things she left out were the red scarf and Madame
Defarge.

"Dr. Rathbone?" Richard seized on that point. "You think he's mixed
up in this? Behind it? But my dear girl, he's a very important man. He's

known all over the world. Subscriptions pour in from all over the globe for his schemes."

"Wouldn't he have to be all those things?" asked Victoria.

"I've always regarded him as a pompous ass," said Richard meditatively.

"And that's a very good camouflage, too."

"Yes—yes, I suppose it is. Who was Lefarge that you asked me about?"

"Just another name," said Victoria. "There's Anna Scheele, too," she said.

"Anna Scheele? No, I've never heard of her."

"She's important," said Victoria. "But I don't know exactly how or why? It's all so mixed up."

"Just tell me again," said Richard. "Who's the man who started you on to all this?"

"Edwar—Oh, you mean Mr. Dakin. He's in Oil, I think."

"Is he a tired, stooping, rather vacant-looking chap?"

"Yes—but he's not really. Vacant, I mean."

"Doesn't he drink?"

"People say so, but I don't think he does."

Richard sat back and looked at her.

"Phillips Oppenheim, William Le Queux and several distinguished imitators since? Is this real? Are you real? And are you the persecuted heroine, or the wicked adventuress?"

Victoria said in a practical manner,

"The real point is, what are we going to say to Dr. Pauncefoot Jones about me?"

"Nothing," said Richard. "It really won't be necessary."

XXI

THEY STARTED IN to Baghdad early. Victoria's spirits felt curiously low. She had almost a lump in her throat as she looked back on the Expedition House. However, the acute discomfort entailed in the mad bumping of the lorry effectively distracted her mind from anything but the torture of the moment. It seemed strange to be driving along a so-called road again, passing donkeys and meeting dusty lorries. It took nearly three hours to reach the outskirts of Baghdad. The lorry decanted them at the Tio Hotel and then went off with the cook and the driver to do all necessary shopping. A large bundle of mail was awaiting Dr. Pauncefoot Jones and Richard. Marcus appeared suddenly, massive and beaming, and welcomed Victoria with his usual friendly radiance.

"Ah," he said, "it is a long time since I have seen you. You do not come to my Hotel. Not for a week—two weeks. Why is that? You lunch here today, you have everything you want? The baby chickens? The big steak? Only not the turkey stuffed very special with flavouring and rice, because for that you must let me know the day before."

It seemed clear that as far as the Tio Hotel was concerned, the kidnapping of Victoria had not been noticed. Possibly Edward, on the advice of Mr. Dakin, had not been to the police.

"Is Mr. Dakin in Baghdad, do you know, Marcus?" she asked.

"Mr. Dakin—ah yes, very nice man—of course, he is friend of yours. He was here yesterday—no, day before. And Captain Crosbie, you know him? A friend of Mr. Dakin's. He arrives today from Kermanshah."

"You know where Mr. Dakin's office is?"

"Sure I know. Everybody knows the Iraqi Iranian Oil Co."

"Well, I want to go there now. In a taxi. But I want to be sure the taxi knows where to take me."

"I tell him myself," said Marcus obligingly.

He escorted her to the head of the alleyway and yelled in his usual violent fashion. A startled minion arrived at a run. Marcus commanded him to procure a taxi. Then Victoria was escorted to the taxi and Marcus addressed the driver. Then he stepped back and waved a hand.

"And I want a room," said Victoria. "Can I have one?"

"Yes, yes. I give you a beautiful room and I order you the big steak and tonight I have—very special—some caviare. And before that we have a little drink."

"Lovely," said Victoria. "Oh Marcus, can you lend me some money?"

"Of course, my dear. Here you are. Take all you want."

The taxi started off with a violent honk and Victoria fell back onto the seat clutching an assortment of coins and notes.

Five minutes later Victoria entered the offices of the Iraqi Iranian Oil Co. and asked for Mr. Dakin.

Mr. Dakin looked up from the desk where he was writing when

Victoria was shown in. He rose and shook hands with her in a formal manner.

"Miss—er—Miss Jones, isn't it? Bring coffee, Abdullah."

As the sound-proof door closed behind the clerk, he said quietly, "You shouldn't really come here, you know."

"I had to this time," said Victoria. "There's something I've got to tell you at once—before anything more happens to me."

"Happens to you? Has anything happened to you?"

"Don't you know?" asked Victoria. "Hasn't Edward told you?"

"As far as I know, you are still working at the Olive Branch. Nobody has told me anything."

"Catherine," exclaimed Victoria.

"I beg your pardon."

"That cat Catherine! I bet she's stuffed Edward up with some tale or other and the goop has believed her."

"Well, let's hear about it," said Mr. Dakin. "Er—if I may say so," his eye went discreetly to Victoria's blonde head, "I prefer you as a brunette."

"That's only part of it," said Victoria.

There was a tap at the door and the messenger entered with two little cups of sweet coffee. When he had gone, Dakin said,

"Now take your time and tell me all about it. We can't be overheard here."

Victoria plunged into the story of her adventures. As always when she was talking to Dakin, she managed to be both coherent and concise. She finished her story with an account of the red scarf Carmichael had dropped and her association of it with Madame Defarge.

Then she looked anxiously at Dakin.

He had seemed to her when she came in, to be even more bowed and tired looking. Now she saw a new glint come into his eye.

"I should read my Dickens more often," he said.

"Then you do think I'm right? You think it was Defarge he said—and you think some message is knitted into the scarf?"

"I think," said Dakin, "that this is the first real break we've had—and we've got you to thank for it. But the important thing is the scarf. Where is it?"

"With all the rest of my things. I shoved it into a drawer that night —and when I packed I remember bundling everything in without sorting or anything."

"And you've never happened to mention to anyone—to anyone *at all*—that that scarf belonged to Carmichael?"

"No, because I'd forgotten all about it. I bundled it into a suitcase with some other things when I went to Basrah and I've never even opened the case since."

"Then it ought to be all right. Even if they've been through your things, they won't have attached any importance to an old dirty woollen scarf—unless they were tipped off to it which as far as I can see, is impossible. All we've got to do now is to have all your things collected and sent to you at—have you got anywhere to stay, by the way?"

"I've booked a room at the Tio."

Dakin nodded.

"Best place for you."

"Have I—do you want me—to go back to the Olive Branch?"

Dakin looked at her keenly.

"Scared?"

Victoria stuck her chin out.

"No," she said with defiance. "I'll go if you like."

"I don't think it's necessary—or even wise. However they learned it, I presume that someone there got wise to your activities. That being so, you wouldn't be able to find out anything more, so you'd better stay clear."

He smiled.

"Otherwise you may be a red head next time I see you."

"That's what I want to know most of all," cried Victoria. "Why did they dye my hair? I've thought and I've thought and I can't see any point in it. Can you?"

"Only the somewhat unpleasant one that your dead body might be less easy to identify."

"But if they wanted me to be a dead body, why didn't they kill me straight away?"

"That's a very interesting question, Victoria. It's the question I want answered most of all."

"And you haven't any idea?"

"I haven't got a clue," said Mr. Dakin with a faint smile.

"Talking of clues," said Victoria, "do you remember my saying that there was something about Sir Rupert Crofton Lee that didn't seem right, that morning at the Tio?"

"Yes."

"You didn't know him personally, did you?"

"I hadn't met him before, no."

"I thought not. Because, you see, he wasn't Sir Rupert Crofton Lee."

And she plunged once more into animated narrative, starting with the incipient boil on the back of Sir Rupert's neck.

"So that was how it was done," said Dakin. "I didn't see how Carmichael could have been sufficiently off his guard to be killed that night. He got safely to Crofton Lee—and Crofton Lee stabbed him, but he managed to get away and burst into your room before he collapsed. And he hung on to the scarf—literally like grim death."

"Do you think it was because I was coming to tell you this that they kidnapped me? But nobody knew except Edward."

"I think they felt they had to get you out of the picture quickly. You were tumbling to too much that was going on at the Olive Branch."

"Dr. Rathbone warned me," said Victoria. "It was—more of a threat than a warning. I think he realised that I wasn't what I pretended to be."

"Rathbone," said Dakin drily, "is no fool."

"I'm glad I haven't got to go back there," said Victoria. "I pretended to be brave just now—but really I'm scared stiff. Only if I don't go to the Olive Branch, how can I get hold of Edward?"

Dakin smiled.

"If Mohammed won't come to the mountain, the mountain must come to Mohammed. Write him a note now. Just say you're at the Tio and ask him to get your clothes and luggage and bring them along there. I'm going to consult Dr. Rathbone this morning about one of his Club Soirées. It will be easy for me to slip a note to his secretary—so there will be no danger of your enemy Catherine causing it to go astray. As for you, go back to the Tio and stay there—and, Victoria—"

"Yes?"

"If you're in a jam—of any kind—do the best you can for yourself. As far as possible you'll be watched over, but your adversaries are rather formidable, and unfortunately you know rather a lot. Once your luggage is in the Tio Hotel, your obligations to me are over. Understand that."

"I'll go straight back to the Tio now," said Victoria. "At least I shall just buy some face powder and lipstick and vanishing cream on the way. After all—"

"After all," said Mr. Dakin, "one cannot meet one's young man completely unarmoured."

"It didn't matter so much with Richard Baker, though I'd like him to know I can look quite nice if I try," said Victoria. "But Edward—"

XXII

HER BLONDE HAIR carefully arranged, her nose powdered and her lips freshly painted, Victoria sat upon the balcony of the Tio, once more in the rôle of a modern Juliet, waiting for Romeo.

And in due course Romeo came. He appeared on the grass sward, looking this way and that.

"Edward," said Victoria.

Edward looked up.

"Oh, there you are. Victoria—"

"Come up here."

"Right."

A moment later he came out upon the balcony which was deserted.

"It's more peaceful up here," said Victoria. "We'll go down and let Marcus give us drinks presently."

Edward was staring at her in perplexity.

"I say, Victoria, haven't you done something to your hair?"

Victoria gave an exasperated sigh.

"If anybody mentions hair to me, I really think I shall bat them over the head."

"I think I liked it better as it was," said Edward.

"Tell Catherine so!"

"Catherine? What has she got to do with it?"

"Everything," said Victoria. "You told me to chum up to her, and I did, and I don't suppose you've any idea what it let me in for!"

"Where've you been all this time, Victoria? I've been getting quite worried."

"Oh you have, have you? Where did you think I'd been?"

"Well, Catherine gave me your message. Said you'd told her to tell me that you'd had to go off to Mosul suddenly. It was something very important and good news, and I'd hear from you in due course."

"And you believed that?" asked Victoria in an almost pitying voice.

"I thought you'd got on the track of something. Naturally, you couldn't say much to Catherine—"

"It didn't occur to you that Catherine was lying, and that I'd been knocked on the head."

"What?" Edward stared.

"Drugged, chloroformed—starved . . ."

Edward cast a sharp glance round.

"Good Lord! I never dreamed—look here, I don't like talking out here. All these windows. Can't we go to your room?"

"All right. Did you bring my luggage?"

"Yes, I dumped it all with the porter."

"Because when one hasn't had a change of clothes for a fortnight—"

"Victoria, what has been happening? I know—I've got the car here. Let's go out to Devonshire. You've never been there, have you?"

"Devonshire?" Victoria stared in surprise.

"Oh, it's just a name for a place not far out of Baghdad. It's rather lovely this time of year. Come on. I haven't had you to myself for years."

"Not since Babylon. But what will Dr. Rathbone and the Olive Branch say?"

"Blast Dr. Rathbone. I'm fed up with the old ass anyway."

They ran down the stairs and out to where Edward's car was parked. Edward drove southwards through Baghdad, along a wide avenue. Then he turned off from there; they jolted and twisted through palm groves and over irrigation bridges. Finally, with a strange unexpectedness they came to a small wooded copse surrounded and pierced by irrigation streams. The trees of the copse, mostly almond and apricot, were just coming into blossom. It was an idyllic spot. Beyond the copse, at a little distance, was the Tigris.

They got out of the car and walked together through the blossoming trees.

"This is lovely," said Victoria, sighing deeply. "It's like being back in England in Spring."

The air was soft and warm. Presently they sat down on a fallen tree trunk with pink blossom hanging down over their heads.

"Now, darling," said Edward. "Tell me what's been happening to you. I've been so dreadfully miserable."

"Have you?" she smiled dreamily.

Then she told him. Of the girl hairdresser. Of the smell of chloroform and her struggle. Of waking up drugged and sick. Of how she had escaped and of her fortuitous meeting with Richard Baker, and of how she had claimed to be Victoria Pauncefoot Jones on her way to the Excavations, and of how she had almost miraculously sustained the part of an archaeological student arriving from England.

At this point Edward shouted with laughter.

"You are marvellous, Victoria! The things you think of—and invent."

"I know," said Victoria. "My uncles. Dr. Pauncefoot Jones and before him—the Bishop."

And at that she suddenly remembered what it was she had been going to ask Edward at Basrah when Mrs. Clayton had interrupted by calling them in for drinks.

"I meant to ask you before," she said. "How did you know about the Bishop?"

She felt the hand that held hers stiffen suddenly. He said quickly, too quickly:

"Why, you told me, didn't you?"

Victoria looked at him. It was odd, she thought afterwards, that that one silly childish slip should have accomplished what it did.

For he was taken completely by surprise. He had no story ready—his face was suddenly defenceless and unmasked.

And as she looked at him, everything shifted and settled itself into a pattern, exactly as a kaleidoscope does, and she saw the truth. Perhaps it was not really sudden. Perhaps in her subconscious mind that question: How did Edward know about the Bishop? had been teasing and worrying, and she had been slowly arriving at the one, the inevitable, answer . . . Edward had not learned about the Bishop of Llangow from her, and the only other persons he could have learned it from, would have been Mr. or Mrs. Hamilton Clipp. But they could not possibly have seen Edward since her arrival in Baghdad, for Edward had been in Basrah then, so he must have learned it from them before he himself left England. He must have known all along, then, that Victoria was coming out with them—and the whole wonderful coincidence was not, after all, a coincidence. It was planned and intended . . .

And as she stared at Edward's unmasked face, she knew, suddenly, what Carmichael had meant by Lucifer. She knew what he had seen that day as he looked along the passage to the Consulate Garden. He had seen that young beautiful face that she was looking at now—for it was a beautiful face—

Lucifer, Son of the Morning, how art thou fallen?

Not Dr. Rathbone—Edward! Edward, playing a minor part, the part of the secretary, but controlling and planning and directing, using Rathbone as a figurehead—and Rathbone, warning her to go while she could . . .

As she looked at that beautiful evil face, all her silly adolescent calf love faded away, and she knew that what she felt for Edward had never been love. It had been the same feeling that she had experienced some years earlier for Humphrey Bogart, and later for the Duke of Edinburgh. It had been glamour. And Edward had never loved her. He had exerted his charm and his glamour deliberately. He had picked her up that day, using his charm so easily, so naturally, that she had fallen for it without a struggle. She'd been a sucker.

It was extraordinary how much could flash through your mind in just a few seconds. You didn't have to think it out. It just came. Full and instant knowledge. Perhaps because really, underneath, you'd known it all along. . . .

And at the same time some instinct of self preservation, quick as all Victoria's mental processes were quick, kept her face in an expression of foolish unthinking wonder. For she knew, instinctively, that she was in great danger. There was only one thing that could save her, only one card she could play. She made haste to play it.

"You knew all along!" she said. "You knew I was coming out here. You must have arranged it. Oh Edward, you are wonderful!"

Her face, that plastic impressionable face, showed one emotion only—an almost cloying adoration. And she saw the response—the faintly scornful smile, the relief. She could almost feel Edward saying to himself, "The little fool! She'll swallow anything! I can do what I like with her."

"But how did you arrange it?" she said. "You must be very powerful. You must be quite different from what you pretend to be. You're—it's like what you said the other day—you're a King in Babylon."

She saw the pride that lit up his face. She saw the power and strength and beauty and cruelty that had been disguised behind the façade of a modest likeable young man.

"And I'm only a Christian slave," thought Victoria. She said quickly and anxiously, as a final artistic touch (and what its cost was to her pride no one will ever know), "But you do love me, don't you?"

His scorn was hardly to be hidden now. This little fool—all these fools of women! So easy to make them think you loved them and that was all they cared about! They'd no conception of greatness of construction, of a new world, they just whined for love! They were slaves and you used them as slaves to further your ends.

"Of course I love you," he said.

"But what is it all about? Tell me, Edward? Make me understand."

"It's a new world, Victoria. A new world that will rise out of the muck and ashes of the old."

"Tell me."

He told her, and in spite of herself she was almost carried away, carried into the dream. The old bad things must destroy each other. There must be total war—total destruction. And then—the new Heaven and the new Earth. The small chosen band of higher beings, the scientists, the agricultural experts, the administrators—The young men like Edward—the young Siegfrieds of the New World. All young, all believing in their destiny as Supermen. When destruction had run its course, they would step in and take over.

It was madness—but it was constructive madness. It was the sort of thing that in a world, shattered and disintegrating, could happen.

"But think," said Victoria, "of all the people who will be killed first."

"You don't understand," said Edward. "That doesn't matter."

It doesn't matter—that was Edward's creed. And suddenly, for no reason, a remembrance of that three thousand years' old coarse pottery bowl mended with bitumen flashed across Victoria's mind. Surely those were the things that mattered—the little everyday things, the family to be cooked for, the four walls that enclosed the home, the one or two cherished possessions. All the thousands of ordinary people on the earth, minding their own business, and tilling that earth, and making pots and bringing up families and laughing and crying, and getting up in the morning and going to bed at night. They were the people who mattered, not these Angels with wicked faces who wanted to make a new world and who didn't care who they hurt to do it.

And carefully, feeling her way, for here in Devonshire she knew that death might be very near, she said:

"You are wonderful, Edward. But what about me? What can I do?"

"You want to—help? You believe in it?"

But she was prudent. Not sudden conversion. That would be too much.

"I think I just believe in you!" she said. "Anything you tell me to do, Edward, I'll do."

"Good girl," he said.

"Why did you arrange for me to come out here to begin with? There must have been some reason?"

"Of course there was. Do you remember I took a snap of you that day?"

"I remember," said Victoria.

(You fool, how flattered you were, how you simpered! she thought to herself.)

"I'd been struck by your profile—by your resemblance to someone. I took that snap to make sure."

"Who do I resemble?"

"A woman who's been causing us a good deal of trouble—Anna Scheele."

"Anna Scheele," Victoria stared at him in blank surprise. Whatever she had expected, it was not this. "You mean—she looks like me?"

"Quite remarkably so, side-view. The features in profile, are almost exactly the same. And there's one most extraordinary thing, you've got a tiny mark of a scar on your upper lip, left side—"

"I know. It's where I fell on a tin horse when I was a child. It had a sharp ear sticking up and it cut quite deep in. It doesn't show much —not with powder on."

"Anna Scheele has a mark in just the same place. That was a most valuable point. You're alike in height and build—she's about four or five years older than you. The real difference is the hair, you're a brunette and she's a blonde. And your style of hairdressing is quite different. Your eyes are a darker blue, but that wouldn't matter with tinted glasses."

"And that's why you wanted me to come to Baghdad? Because I looked like her."

"Yes, I thought the resemblance might—come in useful."

"So you arranged the whole thing . . . The Clipps—who are the Clipps?"

"They're not important—they just do as they're told."

Something in Edward's tone sent a faint shiver down Victoria's spine. It was as though he had said with inhuman detachment, "They are under Obedience."

There was a religious flavour about this mad project. "Edward," she thought, "is his own God. That's what's so frightening."

Aloud she said:

"You told me that Anna Scheele was the boss, the Queen Bee, in your show?"

"I had to tell you something to put you off the scent. You had already learnt too much."

"And if I hadn't happened to look like Anna Scheele that would have been the end of me," thought Victoria.

She said:

"Who is she really?"

"She's confidential secretary to Otto Morganthal, the American and international banker. But that isn't all she is. She has the most remarkable financial brain. We've reason to believe she's traced out a lot of our financial operations. Three people have been dangerous to us—Rupert Crofton Lee, Carmichael—well, they're both wiped out. There remains Anna Scheele. She's due in Baghdad in three days' time. In the meantime, she's disappeared."

"Disappeared? Where?"

"In London. Vanished, apparently, off the face of the earth."

"And does no one know where she is?"

"Dakin may know."

But Dakin didn't know. Victoria knew that, though Edward didn't—so where was Anna Scheele?

She asked:

"You really haven't the least idea?"

"We've an idea," said Edward slowly.

"Well?"

"It's vital that Anna Scheele should be here in Baghdad for the Conference. That, as you know, is in five days' time."

"As soon as that? I'd no idea."

"We've got every entry into this country taped. She's certainly not coming here under her own name. And she's not coming in on a Government service plane. We've our means of checking that. So we've investigated all the private bookings. There's a passage booked by B.O.A.C. in the name of Grete Harden. We've traced Grete Harden back and there's no such person. It's an assumed name. The address given is a phony one. It's our idea that Grete Harden is Anna Scheele."

He added:

"Her plane will touch down at Damascus the day after tomorrow."

"And then?"

Edward's eyes looked suddenly into hers.

"That's up to you, Victoria."

"To me?"

"You'll take her place."

Victoria said slowly:

"Like Rupert Crofton Lee?"

It was almost a whisper. In the course of that substitution Rupert Crofton Lee had died. And when Victoria took her place, presumably Anna Scheele, or Grete Harden, would die . . . But even if she didn't agree, Anna Scheele would still die.

And Edward was waiting—and if for one moment Edward doubted her loyalty, then she, Victoria, would die—and die without the possibility of warning anyone.

No, she must agree and seize a chance to report to Mr. Dakin.

She drew a deep breath and said:

"I—I—oh, but Edward, I couldn't do it. I'd be found out. I can't do an American voice."

"Anna Scheele has practically no accent. In any case, you will be suffering from laryngitis. One of the best doctors in this part of the world will say so."

"They've got people everywhere," thought Victoria.

"What would I have to do?" she asked.

"Fly from Damascus to Baghdad as Grete Harden. Take to your bed immediately. Be allowed up by our reputable doctor just in time to go to the Conference. There you will lay before them the documents which you have brought with you."

Victoria asked: "The real documents?"

"Of course not. We shall substitute our version."

"What will the documents show?"

Edward smiled.

"Convincing details of the most stupendous plot in America."

Victoria thought: "How well they've got it planned."

Aloud she said:

"Do you really think I can get away with it, Edward?"

Now that she was playing a part, it was quite easy for Victoria to ask it with every appearance of anxious sincerity.

"I'm sure you can. I've noticed that your playing of a part affords you such enjoyment that it's practically impossible to disbelieve you."

Victoria said meditatively:

"I still feel an awful fool when I think of the Hamilton Clipps."

He laughed in a superior way.

Victoria, her face still a mask of adoration, thought to herself viciously, "But you were an awful fool, too, to let slip that about the Bishop at Basrah. If you hadn't I'd never have seen through you."

She said suddenly: "What about Dr. Rathbone?"

"What do you mean 'What about him?'"

"Is he just a figurehead?"

Edward's lips curved in cruel amusement.

"Rathbone has got to toe the line. Do you know what he's been doing all these years? Cleverly appropriating about three quarters of the subscriptions which pour in from all over the world to his own use. It's the cleverest swindle since the time of Horatio Bottomley. Oh yes, Rathbone's completely in our hands—we can expose him at any time and he knows it."

Victoria felt a sudden gratitude to the old man with the noble domed head, and the mean acquisitive soul. He might be a swindler—but he had known pity—he had tried to get her to escape in time.

"All things work towards our new order," said Edward.

She thought to herself, "Edward, who looks so sane, is really mad! You get mad, perhaps, if you try and act the part of God. They always say humility is a Christian virtue—now I see why. Humility is what keeps you sane and a human being. . . ."

Edward got up.

"Time to be moving," he said. "We've got to get you to Damascus and our plans there worked out by the day after tomorrow."

Victoria rose with alacrity. Once she was away from Devonshire, back in Baghdad with its crowds, in the Tio Hotel with Marcus shouting and beaming and offering her a drink, the near persistent menace of Edward would be removed. Her part was to play a double game—continue to fool Edward by a sickly doglike devotion, and counter his plans secretly.

She said: "You think that Mr. Dakin knows where Anna Scheele is? Perhaps I could find that out. He might drop some hint."

"Unlikely—and in any case, you won't be seeing Dakin."

"He told me to come and see him this evening," said Victoria mendaciously, a slightly chilly feeling attacking her spine. "He'll think it odd if I don't turn up."

"It doesn't matter at this stage what he thinks," said Edward. "Our plans are made." He added, "You won't be seen in Baghdad again."

"But Edward, all my things are at the Tio! I've booked a room."

The scarf. The precious scarf.

"You won't need your things for some time to come. I've got a rig-out waiting for you. Come on."

They got in the car again. Victoria thought, "I ought to have known that Edward would never be such a fool as to let me get in touch with Mr. Dakin after I'd found him out. He believes I'm besotted about him—yes, I think he's sure of that—but all the same he isn't going to take any chances."

She said: "Won't there be a search for me if I—don't turn up?"

"We'll attend to that. Officially you'll say goodbye to me at the bridge and go off to see some friends on the West Bank."

"And actually?"

"Wait and see."

Victoria sat silent as they bumped over the rough track and twisted round palm gardens and over the little irrigation bridges.

"Lefarge," murmured Edward. "I wish we knew what Carmichael meant by that."

Victoria's heart gave a leap of anxiety.

"Oh," she said. "I forgot to tell you. I don't know if it means anything. A M. Lefarge came to the Excavations one day at Tell Aswad."

"What?" Edward almost stalled the car in his excitement. "When was this?"

"Oh! About a week ago. He said he came from some Dig in Syria. M. Parrot's, would it be?"

"Did two men called André and Juvet come while you were there?"

"Oh yes," said Victoria. "One of them had a sick stomach. He went to the house and lay down."

"They were two of our people," said Edward.

"Why did they come there? To look for me?"

"No—I'd no idea where you were. But Richard Baker was in Basrah at the same time as Carmichael. We had an idea Carmichael might have passed something on to Baker."

"He said his things had been searched. Did they find anything?"

"No—now think carefully, Victoria. Did this man Lefarge come before the other two or afterwards?"

Victoria reflected in a convincing manner, as she decided what movements to impute to the mythical M. Lefarge.

"It was—yes, the day before the other two came," she said.

"What did he do?"

"Well," said Victoria, "he went over the Dig—with Dr. Pauncefoot

Jones. And then Richard Baker took him down to the house to see
some of the things in the Antika Room there."

"He went to the house with Richard Baker. They talked together?"

"I suppose so," said Victoria. "I mean, you wouldn't look at things
in absolute silence, would you?"

"Lefarge," murmured Edward. "Who is Lefarge? Why have we got
no line on him?"

Victoria longed to say, "He's brother to Mrs. Harris," but refrained.
She was pleased with her invention of M. Lefarge. She could see him
quite clearly now in her mind's eye—a thin rather consumptive-looking
young man with dark hair and a little moustache. Presently, when
Edward asked her, she described him carefully and accurately.

They were driving now through the suburbs of Baghdad. Edward
turned off down a side street of modern villas built in a pseudo European style, with balconies and gardens round them. In front of one
house a big touring car was standing. Edward drew up behind it and
he and Victoria got out, and went up the steps to the front door.

A thin dark woman came out to meet them and Edward spoke
to her rapidly in French. Victoria's French was not sufficiently good
to understand fully what was said, but it seemed to be to the effect
that this was the young lady and that the change must be effected
at once.

The woman turned to her and said politely in French:

"Come with me, please."

She led Victoria into a bedroom where, spread out on a bed, was
the habit of a nun. The woman motioned to her, and Victoria undressed and put on the stiff wool undergarment and the voluminous
mediaeval folds of dark stuff. The Frenchwoman adjusted the headdress. Victoria caught a glimpse of herself in the glass. Her small pale
face under the gigantic (was it wimple?) with the white folds under
her chin, looked strangely pure and unearthly. The Frenchwoman
threw a Rosary of wooden beads over her head. Then, shuffling in the
over-large coarse shoes, Victoria was led out to rejoin Edward.

"You look all right," he said approvingly. "Keep your eyes down,
particularly when there are men about."

The Frenchwoman rejoined them a moment or two later similarly
apparelled. The two nuns went out of the house and got into the
touring car which now had a tall dark man in European dress in the
driver's seat.

"It's up to you now, Victoria," said Edward. "Do exactly as you are told."

There was a slight steely menace behind the words.

"Aren't you coming, Edward?" Victoria sounded plaintive.

He smiled at her.

"You'll see me in three days' time," he said. And then, with a resumption of his persuasive manner, he murmured, "Don't fail me, darling. Only you could do this—I love you, Victoria. I daren't be seen kissing a nun—but I'd like to."

Victoria dropped her eyes in approved nunlike fashion, but actually to conceal the fury that showed for a moment.

"Horrible Judas," she thought.

Instead she said with an assumption of her usual manner:

"Well, I seem to be a Christian Slave all right."

"That's the girl!" said Edward. He added, "Don't worry. Your papers are in perfect order—you'll have no difficulty at the Syrian frontier. Your name in religion, by the way, is Sister Marie des Anges. Sister Thérèse who accompanies you has all the documents and is in full charge, and for God's sake obey orders—or I warn you frankly, you're for it."

He stepped back, waved his hand cheerfully, and the touring car started off.

Victoria leaned back against the upholstery and gave herself up to contemplation of possible alternatives. She could, as they were passing through Baghdad, or when they got to the frontier control, make an agitation, scream for help, explain that she was being carried off against her will—in fact, adopt one or other variants of immediate protest.

What would that accomplish? In all probability it would mean the end of Victoria Jones. She had noticed that Sister Thérèse had slipped into her sleeve a small and businesslike automatic pistol. She would be given no chance of talking.

Or she could wait until she got to Damascus? Make her protest there? Possibly the same fate would be meted out, or her statements might be overborne by the evidence of the driver and her fellow nun. They might be able to produce papers saying that she was mentally afflicted.

The best alternative was to go through with things—to acquiesce in the plan. To come to Baghdad as Anna Scheele and to play Anna Scheele's part. For, after all, if she did so, there would come a moment, at the final climax, when Edward could no longer control her tongue or her actions. If she could continue to convince Edward that she would do anything he told her, then the moment would come when she was standing with her forged documents before the Conference—and Edward would not be there.

And no one could stop her then from saying, "I am not Anna Scheele and these papers are forged and untrue."

She wondered that Edward did not fear her doing just that. But she reflected that vanity was a strangely blinding quality. Vanity was the Achilles heel. And there was also the fact to be considered that Edward and his crowd had more or less got to have an Anna Scheele if their scheme was to succeed. To find a girl who sufficiently resembled Anna Scheele—even to the point of having a scar in the right place was extremely difficult. In the Lyons Mail, Victoria remembered, Dubosc and Lesurque had the extraordinary coincidence of both having a scar above one eyebrow and also of having a distortion, one by birth and one by accident, of the little finger of one hand. These coincidences must be very rare. No, the Supermen needed Victoria Jones, typist—and to that extent Victoria Jones had them in her power—not the other way round.

The car sped across the bridge. Victoria watched the Tigris with a nostalgic longing. Then they were speeding along a wide dusty highway. Victoria let the beads of her Rosary pass through her fingers. Their click was comforting.

"After all," thought Victoria with sudden comfort. "I am a Christian. And if you're a Christian, I suppose it's a hundred times better to be a Christian Martyr than a King in Babylon—and I must say, there seems to me a great possibility that I am going to be a Martyr. Oh! well, anyway, it won't be lions. I should have hated lions!"

XXIII

THE BIG SKYMASTER swooped down from the air and made a perfect landing. It taxied gently along the runway and presently came to a stop at the appointed place. The passengers were invited to descend.

Those going on to Basrah were separated from those who were catching a connecting plane to Baghdad.

Of the latter there were four. A prosperous looking Iraqi business man, a young English doctor and two women. They all passed through the various controls and questioning.

A dark woman with untidy hair imperfectly bound in a scarf and a tired face came first.

"Mrs. Pauncefoot Jones? British. Yes. To join your husband. Your address in Baghdad, please? What money have you? . . ."

It went on. Then the second woman took the first one's place.

"Grete Harden. Yes. Nationality? Danish. From London. Purpose of visit? Masseuse at hospital? Address in Baghdad? What money have you?"

Grete Harden was a thin fair-haired young woman wearing dark glasses. She wore neat but slightly shabby clothes.

Her French was halting—occasionally she had to have the question repeated.

Then the four passengers were told that the Baghdad plane took off that afternoon. They would be driven now to the Abbassid Hotel for a rest and lunch.

Grete Harden was sitting on her bed when a tap came on the door. She opened it and found a tall dark young woman wearing B.O.A.C. uniform.

"I'm so sorry, Miss Harden. Would you come with me to the B.O.A.C. office? A little difficulty has arisen about your ticket. This way, please."

Grete Harden followed her guide down the passage. On a door was a large board lettered in gold B.O.A.C. Office.

The Air Hostess opened the door and motioned the other inside. Then, as Grete Harden passed through, she closed the door from outside and quickly unhooked the board.

As Grete Harden came through the door, two men who had been standing behind it passed a cloth over her head. They stuffed a gag into her mouth. One of them rolled her sleeve up, and bringing out a hypodermic syringe gave her an injection.

In a few minutes her body sagged and went limp.

The young doctor said cheerfully, "That ought to take care of her for about six hours, anyway. Now then, you two, get on with it."

He nodded towards two other occupants of the room. They were nuns who were sitting immobile by the window. The men went out of the room. The elder of the two nuns went to Grete Harden and began to take the clothes off her inert body. The younger nun, trembling a little, started taking off her habit. Presently Grete Harden, dressed in a nun's habit, lay reposefully on the bed. The younger nun was now dressed in Grete Harden's clothes.

The older nun turned her attention to her companion's flaxen hair. Looking at a photograph which she propped up against the mirror, she combed and dressed the hair, bringing it back from the forehead and coiling it low on the neck.

She stepped back and said in French:

"Astonishing how it changes you. Put on the dark spectacles. Your eyes are too deep a blue. Yes—that is admirable."

There was a slight tap on the door and the two men came in again. They were grinning.

"Grete Harden is Anna Scheele all right," one said. "She'd got the papers in her luggage, carefully camouflaged between the leaves of a Danish publication on Hospital Massage. Now then, Miss Harden," he bowed with mock ceremony to Victoria, "you will do me the honour to have lunch with me."

Victoria followed him out of the room and along to the hall. The other woman passenger was trying to send off a telegram at the desk.

"No," she was saying, "P.A.U.N.C.E foot. Dr. Pauncefoot Jones. Arriving today Tio Hotel. Good journey—"

Victoria looked at her with sudden interest. This must be Dr. Pauncefoot Jones' wife, coming out to join him. That she was a week earlier than expected did not seem to Victoria at all extraordinary since Dr. Pauncefoot Jones had several times lamented that he had lost her letter giving the date of arrival but that he was almost certain it was the 26th!

If only she could somehow or other send a message through Mrs. Pauncefoot Jones to Richard Baker. . . .

Almost as though he read her thoughts, the man accompanying her steered her by the elbow away from the desk.

"No conversations with fellow travellers, Miss Harden," he said. "We don't want that good woman to notice that you're a different person from the one she came out from England with."

He took her out of the Hotel to a restaurant for lunch. As they came back, Mrs. Pauncefoot Jones was coming down the steps of the Hotel. She nodded without suspicion at Victoria.

"Been sightseeing?" she called. "I'm just going to the Bazaars."

"If I could slip something into her luggage—" thought Victoria.

But she was not left alone for a moment.

The Baghdad plane left at three o'clock.

Mrs. Pauncefoot Jones' seat was right up in front. Victoria's was in the tail, near the door, and across the aisle sat the fair young man who was her gaoler. Victoria had no chance of reaching the other woman or of introducing a message into any of her belongings.

The flight was not a long one. For the second time, Victoria looked down from the air and saw the city outlined below her, the Tigris dividing it like a streak of gold.

So she had seen it less than a month ago. How much had happened since then.

In two days' time the men who represented the two predominant ideologies of the world would meet here to discuss the future—

And she, Victoria Jones, would have a part to play.

II

"You know," said Richard Baker, "I'm worried about that girl."

Dr. Pauncefoot Jones said vaguely,

"What girl?"

"Victoria."

"Victoria?" Dr. Pauncefoot Jones peered about. "Where is—why, God bless me, we came back without her yesterday."

"I wondered if you'd noticed it," said Richard.

"Very remiss of me. I was so interested by that report of the Excavations at Tell Yameni. Completely unsound stratification. Didn't she know where to find the lorry?"

"There was no question of her coming back here," said Richard. "As a matter of fact, she isn't Venetia Savile."

"Not Venetia Savile? How very odd. But I thought you said her Christian name was Victoria."

"It is. But she's not an anthropologist. And she doesn't know Emerson. As a matter of fact, the whole thing has been a—well—a misunderstanding."

"Dear me. That seems very odd." Dr. Pauncefoot Jones reflected for some moments. "Very odd. I do hope—am I to blame? I know I am somewhat absent-minded. The wrong letter, perhaps?"

"I can't understand it," said Richard Baker frowning and paying no attention to Dr. Pauncefoot Jones' speculations. "She went off in a car with a young man, it seems, and she didn't come back. What's more, her baggage was there and she hadn't bothered to open it. That seems to me very strange—considering the mess she was in. I'd have thought she'd be sure to doll herself up. And we agreed to meet for lunch . . . No, I can't understand it. I hope nothing's happened to her."

"Oh, I shouldn't think so for a moment," said Dr. Pauncefoot Jones comfortably. "I shall start going down in H. tomorrow. From the general plan I should say that would be the best chance of getting a record office. That fragment of tablet was very promising."

"They've kidnapped her once," said Richard. "What's to prevent their having kidnapped her again?"

"Very improbable—very improbable," said Dr. Pauncefoot Jones. "The country's really very settled nowadays. You said so yourself."

"If I could only remember the name of that man in some oil company. Was it Deacon? Deacon, Dakin? Something like that."

"Never heard of him," said Dr. Pauncefoot Jones. "I think I shall change over Mustafa and his gang to the North East corner. Then we might extend Trench J—"

"Would you mind awfully, sir, if I went in to Baghdad again tomorrow?"

Dr. Pauncefoot Jones, suddenly giving his colleague his full attention, stared at him.

"Tomorrow? But we were there yesterday."

"I'm worried about that girl. I really am."

"Dear me, Richard, I had no idea there was anything of that kind."

"What kind?"

"That you'd formed an attachment. That's the worst of having women on a Dig—especially good looking ones. I really did think we were safe with Sybil Muirfield the year before last, a really distressingly plain girl—and see what came of it! I ought to have listened to Claude in London—these Frenchmen always hit the nail on the head. He commented on her legs at the time—was most enthusiastic about them. Of course this girl, Victoria Venetia, whatever her name is—most attractive and such a nice little thing. You've got good taste, Richard, I will admit that. Funny thing, she's the first girl I've ever known you take any interest in."

"There's nothing of that kind," said Richard, blushing and looking even more supercilious than usual. "I'm just—er—worried about her. I must go to Baghdad."

"Well, if you are going tomorrow," said Dr. Pauncefoot Jones, "you might bring back those extra picks. That fool of a driver forgot them."

Richard started into Baghdad at early dawn and went straight to the Tio Hotel. Here he learnt that Victoria had not returned.

"And it was all arranged that she was to have special dinner with me," said Marcus. "And I kept her a very nice room. It is odd, is it not?"

"Have you been to the Police?"

"Ah no, my dear, it would not be nice, that. She might not like it. And I certainly would not like it."

After a little inquiry, Richard tracked down Mr. Dakin and called upon him in his office.

His memory of the man had not played him false. He looked at the stooping figure, the indecisive face and the slight tremor of the hands. This man was no good! He apologised to Mr. Dakin if he was wasting his time, but had he seen Miss Victoria Jones.

"She called on me the day before yesterday."

"Can you give me her present address?"

"She's at the Tio Hotel, I believe."

"Her luggage is there, but she isn't."

Mr. Dakin raised his eyebrows slightly.

"She has been working with us on the Excavations at Tell Aswad," explained Richard.

"Oh I see. Well—I'm afraid I don't know anything that can help you. She has several friends in Baghdad, I believe—but I don't know her well enough to say who they are."

"Would she be at this Olive Branch?"

"I don't think so. You could ask."

Richard said: "Look here. I'm not leaving Baghdad until I find her." He frowned angrily at Mr. Dakin and strode out of the room.

Mr. Dakin, as the door closed behind Richard, smiled and shook his head.

"Oh Victoria," he murmured reproachfully.

Fuming into the Tio Hotel, Richard was met by a beaming Marcus.

"She's come back," cried Richard eagerly.

"No, no, it is Mrs. Pauncefoot Jones. She has just arrived by plane. Dr. Pauncefoot Jones, he told me she was coming next week."

"He always gets dates wrong. What about Victoria Jones?"

Marcus's face went grave again.

"No, I have heard nothing of her. And I do not like it, Mr. Baker. It is not nice. She is so young a girl. And so pretty. And so gay and charming."

"Yes, yes," said Richard flinching. "I'd better go up and see Mrs. Pauncefoot Jones. What's her number?"

"She is in 19."

With a heavy tread, Richard went up the stairs.

III

"You!" said Victoria with undisguised hostility.

Ushered up to her room in the Babylonian Palace Hotel, the first person she saw was Catherine.

Catherine nodded her head with equal venom.

"Yes," she said. "It is I. And now please go to bed. The doctor will soon arrive."

Catherine was dressed as a hospital nurse and she took her duties seriously, being obviously quite determined never to leave Victoria's side. Victoria, lying disconsolately in bed, murmured:

"If I could get hold of Edward—"

"Edward—Edward!" said Catherine scornfully. "Edward has never cared for you, you stupid English girl. It is me whom Edward loves!"

Victoria looked at Catherine's stubborn fanatical face without enthusiasm.

Catherine went on:

"Always I have hated you from that first morning you came in and demanded to see Dr. Rathbone with such rudeness."

Searching about for an irritant, Victoria said:

"At any rate I'm much more indispensable than you are. Anybody could do your hospital nurse act. But the whole thing depends on me doing mine."

Catherine said with prim smugness:

"Nobody is indispensable. We are taught that."

"Well, I am. For goodness' sake order up a substantial meal. If I don't get something to eat, how do you expect me to give a good performance of an American banker's secretary when the time comes?"

"I suppose you might as well eat while you can," said Catherine grudgingly.

Victoria took no notice of the sinister implication.

IV

Captain Crosbie said:
"I understand you've got a Miss Harden just arrived."
The suave gentleman in the office of the Babylonian Palace inclined his head.
"Yes, sir. From England."
"She's a friend of my sister's. Will you take my card up to her."
He pencilled a few words on the card and sent it up in an envelope. Presently the boy who had taken it returned.
"The lady is not well, sir. Very bad throat. Doctor coming soon. She has hospital nurse with her."
Crosbie turned away. He went along to the Tio where he was accosted by Marcus.
"Ah, my dear, let us have a drink. This evening my Hotel is quite full. It is for the Conference. But what a pity, Dr. Pauncefoot Jones went back to his Expedition the day before yesterday and now here is his wife who arrives and expects that he will be here to meet her. And she is not pleased, no! She says she told him she was coming on this plane. But you know what he is like, that one. Every date, every time—he always gets it wrong. But he is a very nice man," finished Marcus with his usual charity. "And I have had to squeeze her in somehow—I turn out a very important man from UNO—"
"Baghdad seems quite mad."
"All the police they have drafted in—they are taking great precautions—they say—have you heard?—there is a plot to assassinate the President. They have arrested sixty-five students! They are very suspicious of everybody. But all this is very good for trade—very good indeed."

V

The telephone bell rang and was promptly answered.
"American Embassy."
"This is the Babylonian Palace Hotel. Miss Anna Scheele is staying here."

Anna Scheele? Presently one of the Attachés was speaking. Could Miss Scheele come to the phone?

"Miss Scheele is ill in bed with laryngitis. This is Dr. Smallbrook. I am attending Miss Scheele. She has some important papers with her and would like some responsible person from the Embassy to come and fetch them. Immediately? Thank you. I will be waiting for you."

VI

Victoria turned from the mirror. She was wearing a well-cut tailored suit. Every blonde hair was in place. She felt nervous but exhilarated.

As she turned, she caught the exultant gleam in Catherine's eye and was suddenly on her guard. Why was Catherine exultant?

What was going on?

"What are you so pleased about?" she asked.

"Soon you will see."

The malice was quite unconcealed now.

"You think you are so clever," said Catherine scornfully. "You think everything depends on you. Pah, you are just a fool."

With a bound Victoria was upon her! She caught her by the shoulder and dug her fingers in.

"Tell me what you mean, you horrible girl."

"Ach—you hurt me."

"Tell me—"

A knock came on the door. A knock twice repeated and then, after a pause, a single one.

"Now you will see!" cried Catherine.

The door opened and a man slipped in. He was a tall man, dressed in the uniform of the International Police. He locked the door behind him and removed the key. Then he advanced to Catherine.

"Quickly," he said.

He took a length of thin cord from his pocket and, with Catherine's full cooperation, bound her swiftly to a chair. Then he produced a scarf and tied it over her mouth. He stood back and nodded appreciatively.

"So—that will do nicely."

Then he turned towards Victoria. She saw the heavy truncheon he was brandishing and in a moment it flashed across her brain what the real plan was. They had never intended that she should play the part of Anna Scheele at the Conference. How could they risk such a thing? Victoria was too well known in Baghdad. No, the plan was, had always been, that Anna Scheele should be attacked and killed at the last moment—killed in such a way that her features would not be too recognisable . . . Only the papers she had brought with her—those carefully forged papers—would remain.

Victoria turned away to the window—she screamed. And with a smile the man came at her—

Then several things happened—there was a crash of broken glass—a heavy hand sent her headlong down—she saw stars—and blackness . . . Then out of the blackness a voice spoke, a reassuring English voice.

"Are you all right, Miss?" it asked.

Victoria murmured something.

"What did she say?" asked a second voice.

The first man scratched his head.

"Said it was better to serve in Heaven than reign in Hell," he said doubtfully.

"That's a quotation," said the other. "But she's got it wrong," he added.

"No, I haven't," said Victoria and fainted.

VII

The telephone rang and Dakin picked up the receiver. A voice said: "Operation Victoria successfully concluded."

"Good," said Dakin.

"We've got Catherine Serakis and the medico. The other fellow threw himself off the balcony. He's fatally injured."

"The girl's not hurt?"

"She fainted—but she's O.K."

"No news still of the real A.S.?"

"No news whatever."

Dakin laid down the receiver.

At any rate Victoria was all right—Anna herself, he thought, must be dead . . . She had insisted on playing a lone hand, had reiterated that she would be in Baghdad without fail on the 19th. Today was the 19th and there was no Anna Scheele. Perhaps she had been right not to trust the official setup—he didn't know. Certainly there had been leakages—betrayals. But apparently her own native wits had served her no better. . . .

And without Anna Scheele, the evidence was incomplete.

A messenger came in with a piece of paper on which was written Mr. Richard Baker and Mrs. Pauncefoot Jones.

"I can't see anybody now," said Dakin. "Tell them I am very sorry. I am engaged."

The messenger withdrew, but presently returned. He handed Dakin a note.

Dakin tore open the envelope and read:

"I want to see you about Henry Carmichael. R.B."

"Show him in," said Dakin.

Presently Richard Baker and Mrs. Pauncefoot Jones came in. Richard Baker said:

"I don't want to take up your time, but I was at school with a man called Henry Carmichael. We lost sight of each other for many years, but when I was at Basrah a few weeks ago I encountered him in the Consulate waiting room. He was dressed as an Arab, and without giving any overt sign of recognition, he managed to communicate with me. Does this interest you?"

"It interests me very much," said Dakin.

"I formed the idea that Carmichael believed himself to be in danger. This was very soon verified. He was attacked by a man with a revolver which I managed to knock up. Carmichael took to his heels but before he went, he slipped something into my pocket which I found later—It didn't appear to be important—it seems to be just a 'chit'—a reference for one Ahmed Mohammed. But I acted on the assumption that to Carmichael it was important.

"Since he gave me no instructions, I kept it carefully, believing that he would one day reclaim it. The other day I learnt from Victoria Jones that he was dead. From other things that she told me, I have come to the conclusion that the right person to deliver this object to is you."

He got up and placed a dirty sheet of paper with writing on it on Dakin's desk.

"Does this mean anything to you?"

Dakin drew a deep sigh.

"Yes," he said. "It means more than you can possibly imagine."

He got up.

"I'm deeply obliged to you, Baker," he said. "Forgive my cutting this interview short, but there is a lot that I have to see to without wasting a minute." He shook hands with Mrs. Pauncefoot Jones, saying, "I suppose you are joining your husband on his Dig. I hope you have a good season."

"It's a good thing Pauncefoot Jones didn't come into Baghdad with me this morning," said Richard. "Dear old John Pauncefoot Jones doesn't notice much that goes on, but he'd probably notice the difference between his wife and his wife's sister."

Dakin looked with slight surprise at Mrs. Pauncefoot Jones. She said in a low pleasant voice.

"My sister Elsie is still in England. I dyed my hair black and came out on her passport. My sister's maiden name was Elsie Scheele. *My name, Mr. Dakin, is Anna Scheele.*"

XXIV

BAGHDAD WAS TRANSFORMED. Police lined the streets—police drafted in from outside, the International Police. At last the historic Conference had begun.

In a small anteroom certain events were taking place which might well alter the course of history. Like most momentous happenings, the proceedings were not at all dramatic.

Doctor Alan Breck of the Harwell Atomic Institute contributed his quota of information in a small precise voice.

Certain specimens had been left with him for analysis by the late Sir Rupert Crofton Lee. They had been acquired in the course of one of Sir Rupert's journeys through China and Turkestan through Kurdistan to Iraq. Dr. Breck's evidence then became severely technical. Metallic ores . . . high uranium content . . . Source of deposit not known exactly, since Sir Rupert's notes and diaries had been destroyed during the war by enemy action.

Then Mr. Dakin took up the tale. In a gentle tired voice he told the saga of Henry Carmichael, of his belief in certain rumours and wild tales of vast installations and underground laboratories functioning in a remote valley beyond the bounds of civilization. Of his search —and of the success of his search. Of how that great traveller, Sir Rupert Crofton Lee, the man who had believed Carmichael because of his own knowledge of those regions, had agreed to come to Baghdad, and of how he had died. And of how Carmichael had met his own death at the hands of Sir Rupert's impersonator.

"Sir Rupert is dead, and Henry Carmichael is dead. But there is a third witness who is alive and who is here today. I will call upon Miss Anna Scheele to give us her testimony."

Anna Scheele, as calm and composed as if she were in Mr. Morgan-thal's office, gave lists of names and figures. From the depths of that remarkable financial brain of hers, she outlined the vast financial network that had drained money from circulation, and poured it into the financing of activities that should tend to split the civilized world into two opposing factions. It was no mere assertion. She produced facts and figures to support her contention. To those who listened she carried a conviction that was not as yet fully accorded to Carmichael's wild tale.

Dakin spoke again.

"Henry Carmichael is dead," he said. "But he brought back with him from that hazardous journey tangible and definite proofs. He did not dare to keep those proofs on him—his enemies were too close on his track. But he was a man of many friends. By the hands of two of those friends, he sent the proofs to the safekeeping of another friend—a man whom all Iraq reveres and respects. He has courteously consented to come here today. I refer to Sheikh Hussein el Ziyara of Kerbela."

Sheikh Hussein el Ziyara was renowned, as Dakin had said, throughout the Moslem world, both as a Holy Man and a poet. He was considered by many to be a Saint. He stood up now, an imposing figure with his deep brown hennaed beard. His grey jacket edged with gold braid was covered by a flowing brown cloak of gossamer fineness. Round his head he wore a green cloth headdress which was bound with many strands of heavy gold *agal* and which gave him a patriarchal appearance. He spoke in a deep sonorous voice.

"Henry Carmichael was my friend," he said. "I knew him as a boy and he studied with me the verses of our great poets. Two men came to Kerbela, men who travel the country with a picture show. They are simple men, but good followers of the Prophet. They brought me a packet which they said they had been told to deliver into my hands from my friend the Englishman Carmichael. I was to keep this in secrecy and security and to deliver it only to Carmichael himself, or to a messenger who should repeat certain words."

Dakin said, "Sayyid, the Arabic poet Mutanabbi, called some times the Pretender to Prophecy, who lived just one thousand years ago, wrote an Ode to Prince Sayfu 'l-Dawla at Aleppo in which these words occur: *Zid hashshi bashshi tafaddal adni surrar sili.*"*

With a smile Sheikh Hussein el Ziyara held out a packet to Dakin. "I say, as Prince Sayfu 'l-Dawla said: 'You shall have your desire' . . ."

"Gentlemen," said Dakin. "These are the microfilms brought back by Henry Carmichael in proof of his story . . ."

One more witness spoke—a tragic broken figure: an old man with a fine domed head who had once been universally admired and respected.

He spoke with a tragic dignity.

"Gentlemen," he said. "I shall shortly be arraigned as a common swindler. But there are some things that even I cannot countenance. There is a band of men, mostly young men, so evil in their hearts and aims that the truth would hardly be believed."

He lifted up his head and roared out:

"Antichrist! I say this thing must be stopped! We have got to have peace—peace to lick our wounds and make a new world—and to do that we must try to understand each other. I started a racket to make money—but, by God, I've ended in believing in what I preach—though I don't advocate the methods I've used. For God's sake, gentlemen, let's start again and try to pull together . . ."

There was a moment's silence, and then a thin official voice, with the bloodless impersonality of bureaucracy, said:

"These facts will be put forthwith before the Powers Assembled. . . ."

*Add, laugh, rejoice, bring nigh, gladden, show favour, give!

XXV

"WHAT BOTHERS ME," said Victoria, "is that poor Danish woman who got killed by mistake in Damascus."

"Oh! she's all right," said Mr. Dakin cheerfully. "As soon as your plane had taken off, we arrested the French woman and took Grete Harden to hospital. She came round all right. They were going to keep her drugged for a bit until they were sure the Baghdad business went off all right. She was one of our people, of course."

"Was she?"

"Yes, when Anna Scheele disappeared, we thought it might be as well to give the other side something to think about. So we booked a passage for Grete Harden and carefully didn't give her a background. They fell for it—jumped to the conclusion that Grete Harden must be Anna Scheele. We gave her a nice little set of faked papers to prove it."

"While the real Anna Scheele remained quietly in the nursing home till it was time for Mrs. Pauncefoot Jones to join her husband out here."

"Yes. Simple—but effective. Acting on the assumption that in times of stress the only people you can really trust are your own family. She's an exceedingly clever young woman."

"I really thought I was for it," said Victoria. "Were your people really keeping tabs on me?"

"All the time. Your Edward wasn't really quite so clever as he thought himself, you know. Actually we'd been investigating the activities of young Edward Goring for some time. When you told me your story, the night Carmichael was killed, I was frankly very worried about you.

"The best thing I could think of was to send you deliberately into the setup as a spy. If your Edward knew that you were in touch with me, you'd be reasonably safe, because he'd learn through you what we were up to. You'd be too valuable to kill. And he could also pass on false information to us through you. You were a link. But then you spotted the Rupert Croften Lee impersonation, and Edward decided you'd better be kept out of it until you were needed (if you should be needed) for the impersonation of Anna Scheele. Yes, Victoria, you're very lucky to be sitting where you are now, eating all those pistachio nuts."

"I know I am."

Mr. Dakin said:

"How much do you mind—about Edward?"

Victoria looked at him steadily.

"Not at all. I was just a silly little fool. I let Edward pick me up and do his glamour act. I just had a thoroughly schoolgirl crush on him—fancying myself Juliet and all sorts of silly things."

"You needn't blame yourself too much. Edward had a wonderful natural gift for attracting women."

"Yes, and he used it."

"He certainly used it."

"Next time I fall in love," said Victoria, "it won't be looks that attract me, or glamour. I'd like a real man—not one who says pretty things to you. I shan't mind if he's bald or wears spectacles or anything like that. I'd like him to be interesting—and know about interesting things."

"About thirty-five or fifty-five?" asked Mr. Dakin.

Victoria stared.

"Oh thirty-five," she said.

"I am relieved. I thought for a moment you were proposing to me."

Victoria laughed.

"And—I know I mustn't ask questions—but was there really a message knitted into the scarf?"

"There was a name. The *tricoteuses* of whom Madame Defarge was one, knitted a register of names. The scarf and the 'chit' were the two halves of the clue. One gave us the name of Sheikh Hussein el Ziyara of Kerbela. The other when treated with iodine vapour gave us the words to induce the Sheikh to part with his trust. There couldn't have been a safer place to hide the thing, you know, than in the sacred City of Kerbela."

"And it was carried through the country by those two wandering cinema men—the ones we actually met?"

"Yes. Simple well known figures. Nothing political about them. Just Carmichael's personal friends. He had a lot of friends."

"He must have been very nice. I'm sorry he's dead."

"We've all got to die sometime," said Mr. Dakin. "And if there's another life after this which I myself fully believe, he'll have the satisfaction of knowing that his faith and his courage have done more to save this sorry old world from a fresh attack of bloodletting and misery than almost anyone that one can think of."

"It's odd, isn't it," said Victoria meditatively, "that Richard should have had one half of the secret and I should have had the other. It almost seems as though—"

"As though it were meant to be," finished Mr. Dakin with a twinkle. "And what are you going to do next, may I ask?"

"I shall have to find a job," said Victoria. "I must start looking about."

"Don't look too hard," said Mr. Dakin. "I rather think a job is coming towards you."

He ambled gently away to give place to Richard Baker.

"Look here, Victoria," said Richard. "Venetia Savile can't come out after all. Apparently she's got mumps. You were quite useful on the Dig. Would you like to come back? Only your keep, I'm afraid. And probably your passage back to England—but we'll talk about that later. Mrs. Pauncefoot Jones is coming out next week. Well, what do you say?"

"Oh, do you really want me?" cried Victoria.

For some reason Richard Baker became very pink in the face. He coughed and polished his pince-nez.

"I think," he said, "we could find you—er—quite useful."

"I'd love it," said Victoria.

"In that case," said Richard, "you'd better collect your luggage and come along back to the Dig now. You don't want to hang about Baghdad, do you?"

"Not in the least," said Victoria.

"So there you are, my dear Veronica," said Dr. Pauncefoot Jones. "Richard went off in a great state about you. Well, well—I hope you'll both be very happy."

"What does he mean?" asked Victoria bewildered, as Dr. Pauncefoot Jones pottered away.

"Nothing," said Richard. "You know what he's like. He's being— just a little—premature."

N or M?

I

TOMMY BERESFORD REMOVED his overcoat in the hall of the flat. He hung it up with some care, taking time over it. His hat went carefully on the next peg.

He squared his shoulders, affixed a resolute smile to his face and walked into the sitting room where his wife sat knitting a Balaclava helmet in khaki wool.

Mrs. Beresford gave him a quick glance and then busied herself by knitting at a furious rate. She said after a minute or two:

"Any news in the evening paper?"

Tommy said:

"The Blitzkrieg is coming, hurray, hurray! Things look bad in France."

Tuppence said:

"It's a depressing world at the moment."

There was a pause and then Tommy said:

"Well, why don't you ask? No need to be so damned tactful."

"I know," admitted Tuppence. "There is something about conscious tact that is very irritating. But then it irritates you if I do ask. And anyway I don't *need* to ask. It's written all over you."

"I wasn't conscious of looking a Dismal Desmond."

"No, darling," said Tuppence. "You had a kind of nailed to the mast smile which was one of the most heart-rending things I have ever seen."

Tommy said with a grin:

"No, was it really as bad as all that?"

"And more! Well, come on, out with it. Nothing doing?"

"Nothing doing. They don't want me in any capacity. I tell you, Tuppence, it's pretty thick when a man of forty-six is made to feel like a doddering grandfather. Army, Navy, Air Force, Foreign Office, one and all say the same thing—I'm too old. I *may* be required later."

Tuppence said:

"Well, it's the same for me. They don't want people of my age for nursing—no, thank you. Nor for anything else. They'd rather have a fluffy chit who's never seen a wound, or sterilized a dressing, than they would have me who worked for three years, 1915 to 1918, in various capacities, nurse in the surgical ward and operating theatre, driver of a trade delivery van and later of a General. This, that and the other—all, I assert firmly, with conspicious success. And now I'm a poor, pushing, tiresome, middle-aged woman who won't sit at home quietly and knit as she ought to do."

Tommy said gloomily:

"This War is Hell."

"It's bad enough having a war," said Tuppence, "but not being allowed to do anything in it just puts the lid on."

Tommy said consolingly:

"Well, at any rate Deborah has got a job."

Deborah's mother said:

"Oh, she's all right. I expect she's good at it, too. But I still think, Tommy, that I could hold my own with Deborah."

Tommy grinned.

"She wouldn't think so."

Tuppence said:

"Daughters can be very trying. Especially when they *will* be so kind to you."

Tommy murmured:

"The way young Derek makes allowances for me is sometimes rather hard to bear. That 'poor old Dad' look in his eye."

"In fact," said Tuppence, "our children, although quite adorable, are also quite maddening."

But at the mention of the twins, Derek and Deborah, her eyes were very tender.

"I suppose," said Tommy thoughtfully, "that it's always hard for people themselves to realize that they're getting middle-aged and past doing things."

Tuppence gave a snort of rage, tossed her glossy dark head and sent her ball of khaki wool spinning from her lap.

"Are we past doing things? *Are* we? Or is it only that everyone keeps insinuating that we are. Sometimes I feel that we never were any use."

"Quite likely," said Tommy.

"Perhaps so. But at any rate we did once feel important. And now I'm beginning to feel that all that never really happened. Did it happen, Tommy? Is it true that you were once crashed on the head and kidnapped by German agents? Is it true that we once tracked down a dangerous criminal—and got him? Is it true that we rescued a girl and got hold of important secret papers, and were practically thanked by a grateful country? Us! You and me! Despised, unwanted Mr. and Mrs. Beresford."

"Now, dry up, darling. All this does no good."

"All the same," said Tuppence, blinking back a tear. "I'm disappointed in our Mr. Carter."

"He wrote us a very nice letter."

"He didn't *do* anything—he didn't even hold out any hope."

"Well, he's out of it all nowadays. Like us. He's quite old. Lives in Scotland and fishes."

Tuppence said wistfully:

"They might have let us do *something* in the Intelligence."

"Perhaps we couldn't," said Tommy. "Perhaps, nowadays, we wouldn't have the nerve."

"I wonder," said Tuppence. "One feels just the same. But perhaps, as you say, when it came to the point—"

She sighed. She said:

"I wish we could find a job of some kind. It's so rotten when one has so much time to think."

Her eyes rested just for a minute on the photograph of the very young man in Air Force uniform, with the wide grinning smile so like Tommy's.

Tommy said:

"It's worse for a man. Women can knit, after all—and do up parcels and help at canteens."

Tuppence said:

"I can do all that twenty years from now. I'm not old enough to be content with that. I'm neither one thing nor the other."

The front door bell rang. Tuppence got up. The flat was a small service one.

She opened the door to find a broad-shouldered man with a big fair moustache and a cheerful red face, standing on the mat.

His glance, a quick one, took her in as he asked in a pleasant voice: "Are you Mrs. Beresford?"

"Yes."

"My name's Grant. I'm a friend of Lord Easthampton's. He suggested I should look you and your husband up."

"Oh, how nice, do come in."

She preceded him into the sitting room.

"My husband, er—Captain—"

"Mr."

"Mr. Grant. He's a friend of Mr. Car—of Lord Easthampton's."

The old *nom de guerre* of the former Chief of the Intelligence, "Mr. Carter," always came more easily to her lips than their old friend's proper title.

For a few minutes the three talked happily together. Grant was an attractive person with an easy manner.

Presently Tuppence left the room. She returned a few minutes later with the sherry and some glasses.

After a few minutes, when a pause came, Mr. Grant said to Tommy:

"I hear you're looking for a job, Beresford?"

An eager light came into Tommy's eye.

"Yes, indeed. You don't mean—"

Grant laughed, and shook his head.

"Oh, nothing of that kind. No, I'm afraid that has to be left to the young active men—or to those who've been at it for years. The only things I can suggest are rather stodgy, I'm afraid. Office work. Filing papers. Tying them up in red tape and pigeon-holing them. That sort of thing."

Tommy's face fell.

"Oh, I see!"

Grant said encouragingly:

"Oh, well, it's better than nothing. Anyway, come and see me at my office one day. Ministry of Requirements. Room 22. We'll fix you up with something."

The telephone rang. Tuppence picked up the receiver.

"Hullo—yes—*what?*" A squeaky voice spoke agitatedly from the other end. Tuppence's face changed. "When? Oh, my dear—of course—I'll come over right away. . . ."

She put back the receiver.

She said to Tommy:

"That was Maureen."

"I thought so—I recognized her voice from here."

Tuppence explained breathlessly:

"I'm so sorry, Mr. Grant. But I must go round to this friend of mine. She's fallen and twisted her ankle and there's no one with her but her little girl, so I must go round and fix up things for her and get hold of someone to come in and look after her. Do forgive me."

"Of course, Mrs. Beresford, I quite understand."

Tuppence smiled at him, picked up a coat which had been lying over the sofa, slipped her arms into it and hurried out. The flat door banged.

Tommy poured out another glass of sherry for his guest.

"Don't go yet," he said.

"Thank you." The other accepted the glass. He sipped it for a moment in silence. Then he said: "In a way, you know, your wife's being called away is a fortunate occurrence. It will save time."

Tommy stared.

"I don't understand."

Grant said deliberately:

"You see, Beresford, if you had come to see me at the Ministry, I was empowered to put a certain proposition before you."

The colour came slowly up in Tommy's freckled face. He said:

"You don't mean—"

Grant nodded.

"Easthampton suggested you," he said. "He told us you were the man for the job."

Tommy gave a deep sigh.

"Tell me," he said.

"This is strictly confidential, of course."

Tommy nodded.

"Not even your wife must know. You understand?"

"Very well—if you say so. But we worked together before."

"Yes, I know. But this proposition is solely for you."

"I see. All right."

"Ostensibly you will be offered work—as I said just now—office work —in a branch of the Ministry functioning in Scotland—in a prohibited area where your wife cannot accompany you. Actually you will be somewhere very different."

Tommy merely waited.

Grant said:

"You've read in the newspapers of the Fifth Column? You know, roughly at any rate, just what that term implies."

Tommy murmured:

"The enemy within."

"Exactly. This war, Beresford, started in an optimistic spirit. Oh, I don't mean the people who really knew—we've known all along what we were up against—the efficiency of the enemy, his aerial strength, his deadly determination, and the co-ordination of his well-planned war machine. I mean the people as a whole. The good-hearted, muddle-headed democratic fellow who believes what he wants to believe—that Germany will crack up, that she's on the verge of revolution, that her weapons of war are made of tin and that her men are so underfed that they'll fall down if they try to march—all that sort of stuff. Wishful thinking, as the saying goes.

"Well, the war didn't go that way. It started badly and it went on worse. The men were all right—the men on the battleships and in the planes and in the dugouts. But there was mismanagement and unpreparedness—the defects, perhaps, of our qualities. We don't want war, haven't considered it seriously, weren't good at preparing for it.

"The worst of that is over. We've corrected our mistakes, we're slowly getting the right men in the right places. We're beginning to run the war as it should be run—and we can win the war—make no mistake about that—but only if we don't lose it first. And the danger of losing it comes, not from outside—not from the might of Germany's bombers, not from her seizure of neutral countries and fresh vantage points from which to attack—but from within. Our danger is the danger of Troy—the wooden horse within our walls. Call it the Fifth Column if you like. It is here, among us. Men and women, some of them highly placed, some of them obscure, but all believing genuinely in the Nazi aims and the Nazi creed and desiring to substitute that sternly efficient creed for the muddled easy-going liberty of our democratic institutions."

Grant leaned forward. He said, still in that same pleasant unemotional voice:

"*And we don't know who they are. . . .*"

Tommy said: "But surely—"

Grant said, with a touch of impatience:

"Oh, we can round up the small fry. That's easy enough. But it's the others. We know about them. We know that there are at least two highly placed in the Admiralty—that one must be a member of General G——'s staff—that there are three or more in the Air Force, and that two, at least, are members of the Intelligence, know Cabinet secrets. We know that because it must be so from the way things have happened. The leakage—a leakage from the top—of information to the enemy, shows us that."

Tommy said helplessly, his pleasant face perplexed:

"But what good should I be to you? I don't know any of these people."

Grant nodded.

"Exactly. You don't know any of them—*and they don't know you.*"

He paused to let it sink in and then went on.

"These people, these high up people, know most of our lot. Information can't be very well refused to them. I was at my wits' end. I went to Easthampton. He's out of it all now—a sick man—but his brain's the best I've ever known. He thought of you. Nearly twenty years since you worked for the Department. Name quite unconnected with it. Your face not known. What do you say—will you take it on?"

Tommy's face was almost split in two by the magnitude of his ecstatic grin.

"Take it on? You bet I'll take it on. Though I can't see how I can be of any use. I'm just a blasted amateur."

"My dear Beresford, amateur status is just what is needed. The professional is handicapped here. You'll take on in place of the best man we had or are likely to have."

Tommy looked a question. Grant nodded.

"Yes. Died in St. Bridget's Hospital last Tuesday. Run down by a lorry—only lived a few hours. Accident case—but it wasn't an accident."

Tommy said slowly: "I see."

Grant said quietly:

"And that's why we have reason to believe that Farquhar was on to something—that he was getting somewhere at last. By his death that wasn't an accident."

Tommy looked a question.

Grant went on:

"Unfortunately we know next to nothing of what he had discovered. Farquhar had been methodically following up one line after another. Most of them led nowhere."

Grant paused and then went on:

"Farquhar was unconscious until a few minutes before he died. Then he tried to say something. What he said was this: *N or M Song Susie.*"

"That," said Tommy, "doesn't seem very illuminating."

Grant smiled.

"A little more so than you might think. N or M, you see, is a term we have heard before. It refers to two of the most important and trusted German agents. We have come across their activities in other countries and we know just a little about them. It is their mission to organize a Fifth Column in foreign countries and to act as liaison officer between the country in question and Germany. N, we know, is a man. M is a woman. All we know about them is that these two are Hitler's most highly trusted agents and that in a code message we managed to decipher towards the beginning of the war there occurred this phrase—*Suggest N or M for England. Full powers—*"

"I see. And Farquhar—"

"As I see it, Farquhar must have got on the track of one or other of them. Unfortunately we don't know *which*. Song Susie sounds very cryptic—but Farquhar hadn't a high class French accent! There was a return ticket to Leahampton in his pocket which is suggestive. Leahampton is on the South coast—a budding Bournemouth or Torquay. Lots of private hotels and guest houses. Amongst them is one called *Sans Souci*—"

Tommy said again:

"Song Susie—Sans Souci—I see."

Grant said:

"Do you?"

"The idea is," Tommy said, "that I should go there and—well—ferret round."

"That *is* the idea."

Tommy's smile broke out again.

"A bit vague, isn't it?" he asked. "I don't even know what I'm looking for."

"And I can't tell you. I don't know. It's up to you."

Tommy sighed. He squared his shoulders.

"I can have a shot at it. But I'm not a very brainy sort of chap."

"You did pretty well in the old days, so I've heard."

"Oh, that was pure luck," said Tommy hastily.

"Well, luck is rather what we need."

Tommy considered a minute or two. Then he said:

"About this place, Sans Souci—"

Grant shrugged his shoulders.

"May be all a mare's nest. I can't tell. Farquhar may have been thinking of 'Sister Susie's sewing shirts for soldiers.' It's all guesswork."

"And Leahampton itself?"

"Just like any other of these places. There are rows of them. Old ladies, old Colonels, unimpeachable spinsters, dubious customers, fishy customers, a foreigner or two. In fact, a mixed bag."

Tommy said doubtfully:

"And N or M amongst them?"

"Not necessarily. Somebody, perhaps, who's in touch with N or M. But it's quite likely to be N or M themselves. It's an inconspicuous sort of place, a boarding-house at a seaside resort."

"You've no idea whether it's a man or a woman I've to look for?"

Grant shook his head.

Tommy said: "Well, I can but try."

"Good luck to your trying, Beresford. Now—to details—"

II

Half an hour later, when Tuppence broke in, panting and eager with curiosity, Tommy was alone, whistling in an armchair with a doubtful expression on his face.

"*Well?*" demanded Tuppence, throwing an infinity of feeling into the word.

"A job—of kinds."

"What kind?"

Tommy made a suitable grimace.

"Office work in the wilds of Scotland. Hush-hush and all that, but doesn't sound very thrilling."

"Both of us, or only you?"

"Only me, I'm afraid."

"Blast and curse you. How *could* our Mr. Carter be so mean?"

"I imagine they segregate the sexes in these jobs. Otherwise, too distracting for the mind."

"Is it coding—or code breaking? Is it like Deborah's job? Do be careful, Tommy; people go queer doing that and can't sleep; walk about all night groaning and repeating 978345286 or something like that and finally have nervous breakdowns and go into homes."

"Not me."

Tuppence said gloomily:

"I expect you will sooner or later. Can I come, too—not to work but just as a wife? Slippers in front of the fire and a hot meal at the end of the day?"

Tommy looked uncomfortable.

"Sorry, old thing. I *am* sorry. I hate leaving you—"

"But you feel you ought to go," murmured Tuppence reminiscently.

"After all," said Tommy feebly, "you can knit, you know."

"Knit?" said Tuppence. "*Knit?*"

Seizing her Balaclava helmet, she flung it on the ground.

"I hate khaki wool," said Tuppence, "*and* Navy wool *and* Air Force blue. I should like to knit something *magenta!*"

"It has a fine military sound," said Tommy. "Almost a suggestion of Blitzkrieg."

He felt definitely very unhappy. Tuppence, however, was a Spartan and played up well, admitting freely that of course he had to take the job and that it didn't *really* matter about her. She added that she had heard they wanted someone to scrub down the First Aid Post floors. She might possibly be found fit to do that.

Tommy departed for Aberdeen three days later. Tuppence saw him off at the station. Her eyes were bright and she blinked once or twice, but she kept resolutely cheerful.

Only as the train drew out of the station and Tommy saw the forlorn little figure walking away down the platform did he feel a lump in his own throat. War or no War he felt he was deserting Tuppence. . . .

He pulled himself together with an effort. Orders were orders.

Having duly arrived in Scotland, he took a train the next day to Manchester. On the third day a train deposited him at Leahampton. Here he went to the principal Hotel and on the following day made a tour of various private hotels and guest houses, seeing rooms and inquiring terms for a long stay.

Sans Souci was a dark red Victorian villa, set on the side of a hill with a good view over the sea from its upper windows. There was a slight smell of dust and cooking in the hall and the carpet was worn, but it compared quite favourably with some of the other establishments Tommy had seen. He interviewed the proprietress, Mrs. Perenna, in her office, a small untidy room with a large desk covered with loose papers.

Mrs. Perenna herself was rather untidy looking, a woman of middle-age with a large mop of fiercely curling black hair, some vaguely applied makeup and a determined smile showing a lot of very white teeth.

Tommy murmured a mention of his elderly cousin, Miss Meadowes, who had stayed at Sans Souci two years ago. Mrs. Perenna remembered

Miss Meadowes quite well—such a dear old lady—at least perhaps not really old—very active and such a sense of humour.

Tommy agreed cautiously. There was, he knew, a real Miss Meadowes—the Department was careful about these points.

And how was dear Miss Meadowes?

Tommy explained sadly that Miss Meadowes was no more and Mrs. Perenna clicked her teeth sympathetically and made the proper noises and put on a correct mourning face.

She was soon talking volubly again. She had, she was sure, just the room that would suit Mr. Meadowes. A lovely sea view. She thought Mr. Meadowes was so right to want to get out of London. Very depressing nowadays, so she understood, and of course, after such a bad go of influenza—

Still talking, Mrs. Perenna led Tommy upstairs and showed him various bedrooms. She mentioned a weekly sum. Tommy displayed dismay. Mrs. Perenna explained that prices had risen so appallingly. Tommy explained that his income had unfortunately decreased and what with taxation and one thing and another—

Mrs. Perenna groaned and said:

"This terrible War—"

Tommy agreed and said that in his opinion that fellow Hitler ought to be hanged. A madman, that's what he was, a madman.

Mrs. Perenna agreed and said that what with rations and the difficulty the butchers had in getting the meat they wanted—and sometimes too much—and sweetbreads and liver practically disappeared, it all made housekeeping very difficult, but as Mr. Meadowes was a relation of Miss Meadowes, she would make it half a guinea less.

Tommy then beat a retreat with the promise to think it over and Mrs. Perenna pursued him to the gate, talking more volubly than ever and displaying an archness that Tommy found most alarming. She was, he admitted, quite a handsome woman in her way. He found himself wondering what her nationality was. Surely not quite English? The name was Spanish or Portuguese, but that would be her husband's nationality, not hers. She might, he thought, be Irish, though she had no brogue. But it would account for the vitality and the exuberance.

It was finally settled that Mr. Meadowes should move in the following day.

Tommy timed his arrival for six o'clock. Mrs. Perenna came out into the hall to greet him, threw a series of instructions about his luggage to an almost imbecile-looking maid, who goggled at Tommy with her mouth open, and then led him into what she called the lounge.

"I always introduce my guests," said Mrs. Perenna, beaming determinedly at the suspicious glares of five people. "This is our new arrival, Mr. Meadowes—Mrs. O'Rourke." A terrifying mountain of a woman with beady eyes and a moustache gave him a beaming smile. "Major Bletchley." Major Bletchley eyed Tommy appraisingly and made a stiff inclination of the head. "Mr. von Deinim." A young man, very stiff, fair-haired and blue-eyed, got up and bowed. "Miss Minton." An elderly woman with a lot of beads, knitting with khaki wool, smiled and tittered. "And Mrs. Blenkensop." More knitting—an untidy dark head which lifted from an absorbed contemplation of a Balaclava helmet.

Tommy held his breath; the room spun round.

Mrs. Blenkensop! Tuppence! By all that was impossible and unbelievable—Tuppence, calmly knitting in the lounge of Sans Souci.

Her eyes met his—polite uninterested stranger's eyes.

His admiration rose.

Tuppence!

II

How TOMMY GOT through that evening he never quite knew. He dared not let his eyes stray too often in the direction of Mrs. Blenkensop. At dinner three more habitués of Sans Souci appeared—a middle-aged couple—Mr. and Mrs. Cayley and a young mother, Mrs. Sprot, who had come down with her baby girl from London and was clearly much bored by her enforced stay at Leahampton. She was placed next to Tommy and at intervals fixed him with a pair of pale gooseberry eyes and in a slightly adenoidal voice asked: "Don't you think it's really quite safe now? Everybody's going back, aren't they?"

Before Tommy could reply to these artless queries, his neighbour on the other side, the beaded lady, struck in: "What I say is one mustn't risk anything with children. Your sweet little Betty. You'd never forgive yourself and you know that Hitler has said the Blitz-krieg on England is coming quite soon now—and quite a new kind of gas, I believe."

Major Bletchley cut in sharply:

"Lot of nonsense talked about gas. The fellows won't waste time fiddling round with gas. High explosive and incendiary bombs. That's what was done in Spain."

The whole table plunged into the argument with gusto. Tuppence's voice, high pitched and slightly fatuous, piped out:

"My son Douglas says—"

"Douglas, indeed," thought Tommy. "Why Douglas, I should like to know."

After dinner, a pretentious meal of several meagre courses, all of which were equally tasteless, everyone drifted into the lounge. Knit-ting was resumed and Tommy was compelled to hear a long and ex-tremely boring account of Major Bletchley's experiences on the North West Frontier.

The fair young man with the bright blue eyes went out, executing a little bow on the threshold of the room.

Major Bletchley broke off his narrative and administered a kind of dig in the ribs to Tommy.

"That fellow who's just gone out. He's a refugee. Got out of Germany about a month before the war."

"He's a German?"

"Yes. Not a Jew, either. His father got into trouble for criticizing the Nazi régime. Two of his brothers are in a concentration camp over there. This fellow got out just in time."

At this moment Tommy was taken possession of by Mrs. Cayley, who told him at interminable length all about her health. So absorb-ing was the subject to the narrator that it was close upon bedtime be-fore Tommy could escape.

On the following morning Tommy rose early and strolled down to the front. He walked briskly to the pier and was returning along the esplanade when he spied a familiar figure coming in the other direc-tion. Tommy raised his hat.

"Good morning," he said pleasantly. "Er—Mrs. Blenkensop, isn't it?"

There was no one within earshot. Tuppence replied:

"Dr. Livingstone to you."

"How on earth did you get here, Tuppence?" murmured Tommy. "It's a miracle—an absolute miracle."

"It's not a miracle at all—just brains."

"Your brains, I suppose?"

"You suppose rightly. You and your uppish Mr. Grant. I hope this will teach him a lesson."

"It certainly ought to," said Tommy. "Come on, Tuppence, tell me how you managed it. I'm simply devoured with curiosity."

"It was quite simple. The moment Grant talked of our Mr. Carter I guessed what was up. I knew it wouldn't be just some miserable office job. But his saying so showed me that I wasn't going to be allowed in on this. So I resolved to go one better. I went to fetch some sherry and, when I did, I nipped down to the Browns' flat and rang up Maureen. Told her to ring me up and what to say. She played up loyally—nice high squeaky voice—you could hear what she was saying all over the room. I did my stuff, registered annoyance, compulsion, distressed friend, and rushed off with every sign of vexation. Banged the hall door, carefully remaining inside it, and slipped into the bedroom and eased open the communicating door that's hidden by the tallboy."

"And you heard everything?"

"Everything," said Tuppence complacently.

Tommy said reproachfully:

"And you never let on."

"Certainly not. I wished to teach you a lesson. You and your Mr. Grant."

"He's not exactly my Mr. Grant and I should say you have taught him a lesson."

"Mr. Carter wouldn't have treated me so shabbily," said Tuppence. "I don't think the Intelligence is anything like what it was in our day."

Tommy said gravely:

"It will attain its former brilliance now we're back in it. But why Blenkensop?"

"Why not?"

"It seems such an odd name to choose."

"It was the first one I thought of and it's handy for underclothes."

"What do you mean, Tuppence?"

"B, you idiot. B for Beresford, B for Blenkensop. Embroidered on my cami-knickers. Patricia Blenkensop. Prudence Beresford. Why did you choose Meadowes? It's a silly name."

"To begin with," said Tommy, "I don't have large B's embroidered on my pants. And to continue, I didn't choose it. I was told to call myself Meadowes. Mr. Meadowes is a gentleman with a respectable past —all of which I've learned by heart."

"Very nice," said Tuppence. "Are you married or single?"

"I'm a widower," said Tommy with dignity. "My wife died ten years ago at Singapore."

"Why at Singapore?"

"We've all got to die somewhere. What's wrong with Singapore?"

"Oh, nothing. It's probably a most suitable place to die. I'm a widow."

"Where did your husband die?"

"Does it matter? Probably in a nursing home. I rather fancy he died of cirrhosis of the liver."

"I see. A painful subject. And what about your son Douglas?"

"Douglas is in the Navy."

"So I heard last night."

"And I've got two other sons. Raymond is in the Air Force and Cyril, my baby, is in the Territorials."

"And suppose someone takes the trouble to check up on these imaginary Blenkensops?"

"They're not Blenkensops. Blenkensop was my second husband. My first husband's name was Hill. There are three pages of Hills in the telephone book. You couldn't check up on all the Hills if you tried."

Tommy sighed.

"It's the old trouble with you, Tuppence. You *will* overdo things. Two husbands and three sons. It's too much. You'll contradict yourself over the details."

"No, I shan't. And I rather fancy the sons may come in useful. I'm not under orders, remember. I'm a free-lance. I'm in this to enjoy myself and I'm going to enjoy myself."

"So it seems," said Tommy. He added gloomily: "If you ask me, the whole thing's a farce."

"Why do you say that?"

"Well, you've been at Sans Souci longer than I have. Can you honestly say you think any one of those people who were there last night could be a dangerous enemy agent?"

Tuppence said thoughtfully:

"It does seem a little incredible. There's the young man, of course."

"Carl von Deinim? The police check up on refugees, don't they?"

"I suppose so. Still, it might be managed. He's an attractive young man, you know."

"Meaning the girls will tell him things? But what girls? No Generals' or Admirals' daughters floating around here. Perhaps he walks out with a Company Commander in the A.T.S."

"Be quiet, Tommy. We ought to be taking this seriously."

"I am taking it seriously. It's just that I feel we're on a wild goose chase."

Tuppence said seriously:

"It's too early to say that. After all, nothing's going to be obvious about this business. What about Mrs. Perenna?"

"Yes," said Tommy thoughtfully, "there's Mrs. Perenna, I admit—she does want explaining."

Tuppence said in a business-like tone:

"What about us? I mean, how are we going to co-operate?"

Tommy said thoughtfully:

"We mustn't be seen about too much together."

"No, it would be fatal to suggest we know each other better than we appear to do. What we want to decide is the attitude. I think—yes, I think—pursuit is the best angle."

"Pursuit?"

"Exactly. I pursue you. You do your best to escape, but being a mere chivalrous male doesn't always succeed. I've had two husbands and I'm on the look-out for a third. You act the part of the hunted widower. Every now and then I pin you down somewhere, pen you in a café, catch you walking on the front. Everyone sniggers and thinks it very funny."

"Sounds feasible," agreed Tommy.

Tuppence said: "There's a kind of age-long humour about the chased male. That ought to stand us in good stead. If we are seen together, all anyone will do is to snigger and say, 'Look at poor old Meadowes.' "

Tommy gripped her arm suddenly.

"Look," he said. "Look ahead of you."

By the corner of one of the shelters a young man stood talking to a girl. They were both very earnest, very wrapped up in what they were saying.

Tuppence said softly:

"Carl von Deinim. Who's the girl, I wonder?"

"She's remarkably good looking, whoever she is."

Tuppence nodded. Her eyes dwelt thoughtfully on the dark passionate face, and on the tight-fitting pullover that revealed the lines of the girl's figure. She was talking earnestly, with emphasis. Carl von Deinim was listening to her.

Tuppence murmured:

"I think this is where you leave me."

"Right," agreed Tommy.

He turned and strolled in the opposite direction.

At the end of the promenade he encountered Major Bletchley. The latter peered at him suspiciously and then grunted out, "Good morning."

"Good morning."

"See you're like me, an early riser," remarked Bletchley.

Tommy said:

"One gets in the habit of it out East. Of course, that's many years ago now, but I still wake early."

"Quite right, too," said Major Bletchley with approval. "God, these young fellows nowadays make me sick. Hot baths—coming down to breakfast at ten o'clock or later. No wonder the Germans have been putting it over on us. No stamina. Soft lot of young pups. Army's not what it was, anyway. Coddle 'em, that's what they do nowadays. Tuck 'em up at night with hot water bottles. Faugh! Makes me sick!"

Tommy shook his head in a melancholy fashion and Major Bletchley, thus encouraged, went on.

"Discipline, that's what we need. Discipline. How are we going to win the War without discipline? Do you know, sir, some of these fellows come on parade in slacks—so I've been told. Can't expect to win a War that way. Slacks! My God!"

Mr. Meadowes hazarded the opinion that things were very different from what they had been.

"It's all this democracy," said Major Bletchley gloomily. "You can overdo anything. In my opinion they're overdoing the democracy business. Mixing up the officers and the men, feeding together in restaurants—Paugh!—the men don't like it, Meadowes. The troops know. The troops always know."

"Of course," said Mr. Meadowes, "I have no real knowledge of Army matters myself—"

The Major interrupted him, shooting a quick sideways glance.

"In the show in the last War?"

"Oh, yes."

"Thought so. Saw you'd been drilled. Shoulders. What regiment?"

"Fifth Corfeshires." Tommy remembered to produce Meadowes' military record.

"Ah, yes, Salonica!"

"Yes."

"I was in Mespot."

Bletchley plunged into reminiscences. Tommy listened politely. Bletchley ended up wrathfully.

"And will they make use of me now? No, they will not. Too old. Too old be damned. I could teach one or two of these young cubs something about war."

"Even if it's only what not to do?" suggested Tommy with a smile.

"Eh, what's that?"

A sense of humour was clearly not Major Bletchley's strong suit. He peered suspiciously at his companion. Tommy hastened to change the conversation.

"Know anything about that Mrs.—Blenkensop, I think her name is?"

"That's right. Blenkensop. Not a bad looking woman—bit long in the tooth—talks too much. Nice woman, but foolish. No, I don't know her. She's only been at Sans Souci a couple of days." He added: "Why do you ask?"

Tommy explained.

"Happened to meet her just now. Wondered if she was always out as early as this?"

"Don't know, I'm sure. Women aren't usually given to walking before breakfast—thank God," he added.

"Amen," said Tommy. He went on: "I'm not much good at making polite conversation before breakfast. Hope I wasn't rude to the woman, but I wanted my exercise."

Major Bletchley displayed instant sympathy.

"I'm with you, Meadowes. I'm with you. Women are all very well in their place, but not before breakfast." He chuckled a little. "Better be careful, old man. She's a widow, you know."

"Is she?"

The Major dug him cheerfully in the ribs.

"We know what widows are. She's buried two husbands and if you ask me, she's on the look-out for number three. Keep a very wary eye open, Meadowes. A wary eye. That's my advice."

And in high good humour Major Bletchley wheeled about at the end of the parade and set the pace for a smart walk back to breakfast at Sans Souci.

In the meantime, Tuppence had gently continued her walk along the esplanade, passing quite close to the shelter and the young couple talking there. As she passed she caught a few words. It was the girl speaking.

"But you must be careful, Carl. The very least suspicion—"

Tuppence was out of earshot. Suggestive words? Yes, but capable of any number of harmless interpretations. Unobtrusively she turned and again passed the two. Again words floated to her.

"Smug, detestable English . . ."

The eyebrows of Mrs. Blenkensop rose ever so slightly.

Hardly, she thought, a very wise conversation. Carl von Deinim was a refugee from Nazi persecution, given asylum and shelter by England. Neither wise nor grateful to listen assentingly to such words.

Again Tuppence turned. But this time, before she reached the shelter, the couple had parted abruptly, the girl to cross the road leaving the sea front, Carl von Deinim to come along in Tuppence's direction.

He would not, perhaps, have recognized her but for her own pause and hesitation. Then quickly, he brought his heels together and bowed.

Tuppence twittered at him.

"Good morning, Mr. von Deinim, isn't it? Such a lovely morning."

"Ah, yes. The weather is fine."

Tuppence ran on.

"It quite tempted me. I don't often come out before breakfast. But this morning, what with not sleeping very well—one often doesn't sleep well in a strange place, I find. It takes a day or two to accustom oneself, I always say."

"Oh, yes, no doubt that is so."

"And really this little walk has quite given me an appetite for breakfast."

"You go back to Sans Souci now? If you permit I will walk with you." He walked gravely by her side.

Tuppence said:

"You also are out to get an appetite?"

Gravely he shook his head.

"Oh, no. My breakfast I have already had it. I am on my way to work."

"Work?"

"I am a research chemist."

So that's what you are, thought Tuppence, stealing a quick glance at him.

Carl von Deinim went on, his voice stiff.

"I came to this country to escape Nazi persecution. I had very little money—no friends. I do now what useful work I can."

He stared straight ahead of him. Tuppence was conscious of some undercurrent of strong feeling moving him powerfully.

She murmured vaguely:

"Oh, yes, I see. I see. Very creditable, I am sure."

Carl von Deinim said:

"My two brothers are in concentration camps. My father died in one. My mother died of sorrow and fear."

Tuppence thought:

"The way he says that—as though he had learned it by heart."

Again she stole a quick glance at him. He was still staring ahead of him, his face impassive.

They walked in silence for some moments. Two men passed them. One of them shot a quick glance at Carl. She heard him mutter to his companion:

"Bet you that fellow is a German."

Tuppence saw the colour rise in Carl von Deinim's cheeks.

Suddenly he lost command of himself. That tide of hidden emotion came to the surface. He stammered:

"You heard—you heard—that is what they say—I—"

"My dear boy!" Tuppence reverted suddenly to her real self. Her voice was crisp and compelling. "Don't be an idiot. You can't have it both ways."

He turned his head and stared at her.

"What do you mean?"

"You're a refugee. You have to take the rough with the smooth. You're alive, that's the main thing. Alive and free. For the other—realize that it's inevitable. This country's at War. You're a German." She smiled suddenly. "You can't expect the mere man in the street—literally the man in the street—to distinguish between bad Germans and good Germans, if I may put it so crudely."

He still stared at her. His eyes, so very blue, were poignant with suppressed feeling. Then, suddenly, he too smiled. He said:

"They said of Red Indians, did they not, that a good Indian was a dead Indian?" He laughed. "To be a good German I must be on time at my work. Please. Good morning."

Again that stiff bow. Tuppence stared after his retreating figure. She said to herself:

"Mrs. Blenkensop, you had a lapse then. Strict attention to business in future. Now for breakfast at Sans Souci."

The hall door of Sans Souci was open. Inside, Mrs. Perenna was conducting a vigorous conversation with someone.

"And you'll tell him what I think of that last lot of margarine. Get the cooked ham at Quiller's—it was twopence cheaper last time there, and be careful about the cabbages—"

She broke off as Tuppence entered.

"Oh, good morning, Mrs. Blenkensop, you are an early bird. You haven't had breakfast yet. It's all ready in the dining room." She added, indicating her companion: "My daughter, Sheila. You haven't met her. She's been away and only came home last night."

Tuppence looked with interest at the vivid, handsome face. No longer full of tragic energy, bored now, and resentful. "My daughter Sheila. Sheila Perenna."

Tuppence murmured a few pleasant words and went into the dining room. There were three people breakfasting—Mrs. Sprot and her baby girl, and big Mrs. O'Rourke. Tuppence said, "Good morning" and Mrs. O'Rourke replied with a hearty, "The top of the morning to you" that quite drowned Mrs. Sprot's more anaemic salutation.

The old woman stared at Tuppence with a kind of devouring interest.

"'Tis a fine thing to be out walking before breakfast," she observed. "A grand appetite it gives you."

Mrs. Sprot said to her offspring:

"Nice bread and milk, darling," and endeavoured to insinuate a spoonful into Miss Betty Sprot's mouth.

The latter cleverly circumvented this endeavour by an adroit movement of her head, and continued to stare at Tuppence with large round eyes.

She pointed a milky finger at the newcomer, gave her a dazzling smile and observed in gurgling tones: "Ga—Ga Bouch."

"She likes you," cried Mrs. Sprot, beaming on Tuppence as on one marked out for favour. "Sometimes she's so shy with strangers."

"Bouch," said Betty Sprot. "Ah pooth ah bag," she added with emphasis.

"And what would she be meaning by that?" demanded Mrs. O'Rourke, with interest.

"She doesn't speak awfully clearly yet," confessed Mrs. Sprot. "She's only just over two, you know. I'm afraid most of what she says is just Bosh. She can say Mama, though, can't you, darling?"

Betty looked thoughtfully at her mother and remarked with an air of finality:

"Guggle bick."

" 'Tis a language of their own they have, the little angels," boomed out Mrs. O'Rourke. "Betty darling, say Mama now."

Betty looked hard at Mrs. O'Rourke, frowned and observed with terrific emphasis: "Nazer—"

"There now, if she isn't doing her best! And a lovely sweet girl she is."

Mrs. O'Rourke rose, beamed in a ferocious manner at Betty, and waddled heavily out of the room.

"Ga, ga ga," said Betty with enormous satisfaction, and beat with a spoon on the table.

Tuppence said with a twinkle:

"What does Na-zer really mean?"

Mrs. Sprot said with a flush: "I'm afraid, you know, it's what Betty says when she doesn't like anyone or anything."

"I rather thought so," said Tuppence.

Both women laughed.

"After all," said Mrs. Sprot, "Mrs. O'Rourke means to be kind but she is rather alarming—with that deep voice and the beard and—and everything."

With her head on one side Betty made a cooing noise at Tuppence.

"She has taken to you, Mrs. Blenkensop," said Mrs. Sprot.

There was a slight jealous chill, Tuppence fancied, in her voice. Tuppence hastened to adjust matters.

"They always like a new face, don't they?" she said easily.

The door opened and Major Bletchley and Tommy appeared. Tuppence became arch.

"Ah, Mr. Meadowes," she called out. "I've beaten you, you see. First past the post. But I've left you just a *little* breakfast!"

She indicated with the faintest of gestures the seat beside her.

Tommy, muttering vaguely: "Oh, er—rather—thanks," and hurriedly sat down at the other end of the table.

Betty Sprot said *"Putch!"* with a fine splutter of milk at Major

Bletchley, whose face instantly assumed a sheepish but delighted expression.

"And how's little Miss Bo Peep this morning?" he asked fatuously.

"Bo Peep!" He enacted the play with a newspaper.

Betty crowed with delight.

Serious misgivings shook Tuppence. She thought: "There *must* be some mistake. There *can't* be anything going on here. There simply can't!"

To believe in Sans Souci as a headquarters of the Fifth Column needed the mental equipment of the White Queen in *Alice*.

III

ON THE SHELTERED terrace outside, Miss Minton was knitting.

Miss Minton was thin and angular, her neck was stringy. She wore pale sky-blue jumpers, and chains or bead necklaces. Her skirts were tweedy and had a depressed droop at the back. She greeted Tuppence with alacrity.

"Good morning, Mrs. Blenkensop. I do hope you slept well."

Mrs. Blenkensop confessed that she never slept very well the first night or two in a strange bed. Miss Minton said, "Now, wasn't that curious? It was exactly the same with *me*."

Mrs. Blenkensop said, "What a coincidence, and what a very pretty stitch that was." Miss Minton, flushing with pleasure, displayed it. "Yes, it was rather uncommon, and really quite simple. She could easily show it to Mrs. Blenkensop if Mrs. Blenkensop liked." "Oh, that was very kind of Miss Minton, but Mrs. Blenkensop was so stupid, she wasn't really very good at knitting, not at following patterns, that was to say. She could only do simple things like Balaclava helmets, and even now she was afraid she had gone wrong somewhere. It didn't look *right*, somehow, did it?"

Miss Minton cast an expert eye over the khaki mass. Gently she pointed out just what had gone wrong. Thankfully, Tuppence handed the faulty helmet over. Miss Minton exuded kindness and patronage. "Oh, no, it wasn't a trouble at all. She had knitted for so many years."

"I'm afraid I've never done any before this dreadful War," confessed Tuppence. "But one feels so terribly, doesn't one, that one must do *something*."

"Oh, yes, indeed. And you actually have a boy in the Navy, I think I heard you say last night?"

"Yes, my eldest boy. Such a splendid boy he is—though I suppose a mother shouldn't say so. Then I have a boy in the Air Force and Cyril, my baby, is out in France."

"Oh, dear, dear, how terribly anxious you must be."

Tuppence thought:

"Oh, Derek, my darling Derek. . . . Out in the hell and mess—and here I am playing the fool—acting the thing I'm really feeling . . ."

She said in her most righteous voice:

"We must all be brave, mustn't we? Let's hope it will all be over soon. I was told the other day on very high authority indeed that the Germans can't possibly last out more than another two months."

Miss Minton nodded with so much vigour that all her bead chains rattled and shook.

"Yes, indeed, and I believe"—her voice lowered mysteriously—"that Hitler is suffering from a *disease*—absolutely fatal—he'll be raving mad by August."

Tuppence replied briskly:

"All this Blitzkrieg is just the Germans' last effort. I believe the shortage is something frightful in Germany. The men in the factories are very dissatisfied. The whole thing will crack up."

"What's this? What's all this?"

Mr. and Mrs. Cayley came out on the terrace, Mr. Cayley putting his questions fretfully. He settled himself in a chair and his wife put a rug over his knees. He repeated fretfully:

"What's that you are saying?"

"We're saying," said Miss Minton, "that it will all be over by the Autumn."

"Nonsense," said Mr. Cayley. "This War is going to last at least six years."

"Oh, Mr. Cayley," protested Tuppence. "You don't really think so?"

Mr. Cayley was peering about him suspiciously.

"Now I wonder," he murmured. "Is there a draught? Perhaps it would be better if I moved my chair back into the corner."

The resettlement of Mr. Cayley took place. His wife, an anxious-faced woman who seemed to have no other aim in life than to minister to Mr. Cayley's wants, manipulating cushions and rugs, asking from time to time: "Now, how is that, Alfred? Do you think that will be all right? Ought you, perhaps, to have your sun glasses? There is rather a glare this morning."

Mr. Cayley said irritably:

"No, no. Don't fuss, Elisabeth. Have you got my muffler? No, no, my silk muffler. Oh, well, it doesn't matter. I daresay this will do—for once. But I don't want to get my throat overheated, and wool—in this sunlight—well, perhaps you *had* better fetch the other." He turned his attention back to matters of public interest. "Yes," he said. "I give it six years."

He listened with pleasure to the protests of the two women.

"You dear ladies are just indulging in what we call wishful thinking. Now I know Germany. I may say I know Germany extremely well. In the course of my business before I retired I used to be constantly to and fro. Berlin, Hamburg, Munich, I know them all. I can assure you that Germany can hold out practically indefinitely. With Russia behind her—"

Mr. Cayley plunged triumphantly on, his voice rising and falling in pleasurably melancholy cadences, only interrupted when he paused to receive the silk muffler his wife brought him and wind it round his throat.

Mrs. Sprot brought out Betty and plumped her down with a small woollen dog that lacked an ear and a woolly doll's jacket.

"There, Betty," she said. "You dress up Bonzo ready for his walk while Mummy gets ready to go out."

Mr. Cayley's voice droned on, reciting statistics and figures, all of a depressing character. The monologue was punctuated by a cheerful twittering from Betty talking busily to Bonzo in her own language.

"Truckle—truckly—pah bat," said Betty. Then, as a bird alighted near her, she stretched out loving hands to it and gurgled. The bird flew away and Betty glanced round the assembled company and remarked clearly:

"Dicky," and nodded her head with great satisfaction.

"That child is learning to talk in the most wonderful way," said Miss Minton. "Say Ta ta, Betty. Ta ta."

Betty looked at her coldly and remarked:

"Gluck!"

Then she forced Bonzo's one arm into his woolly coat and, toddling over to a chair, picked up the cushion and pushed Bonzo behind it. Chuckling gleefully, she said with terrific pains:

"Hide! Bow wow. Hide."

Miss Minton, acting as a kind of interpreter, said with vicarious pride:

"She loves hide and seek. She's always hiding things." She cried out with exaggerated surprise:

"*Where* is Bonzo? Where *is* Bonzo? Where *can* Bonzo have gone?"

Betty flung herself down and went into ecstasies of mirth.

Mr. Cayley, finding attention diverted from his explanation of Germany's methods of substitution of raw materials, looked put out and coughed aggressively.

Mrs. Sprot came out with her hat on and picked up Betty.

Attention returned to Mr. Cayley.

"You were saying, Mr. Cayley?" said Tuppence.

But Mr. Cayley was affronted. He said coldly:

"That woman is always plumping that child down and expecting people to look after it. I think I'll have the woollen muffler after all, dear. The sun is going in."

"Oh, but, Mr. Cayley, do go on with what you were telling us. It was so interesting," Miss Minton begged.

Mollified, Mr. Cayley weightily resumed his discourse, drawing the folds of the woolly muffler closer round his stringy neck.

"As I was saying, Germany has so perfected her system of—"

Tuppence turned to Mrs. Cayley, and asked:

"What do you think about the war, Mrs. Cayley?"

Mrs. Cayley jumped.

"Oh, what do I think? What—what do you mean?"

"Do you think it will last as long as six years?"

Mrs. Cayley said doubtfully:

"Oh, I hope not. It's a very long time, isn't it?"

"Yes, a long time. What do you really think?"

Mrs. Cayley seemed quite alarmed by the question. She said:

"Oh, I—I don't know. I don't know at all. Alfred says it will."

"But you don't think so?"

"Oh, I don't know. It's difficult to say, isn't it?"

Tuppence felt a wave of exasperation. The chirruping Miss Minton, the dictatorial Mr. Cayley, the nitwitted Mrs. Cayley—were these people really typical of her fellow countrymen? Was Mrs. Sprot any better with her slightly vacant face and boiled gooseberry eyes? What could she, Tuppence, ever find out here? Not one of these people, surely— Her thought was checked. She was aware of a shadow. Someone behind her who stood between her and the sun. She turned her head. Mrs. Perenna, standing on the terrace, her eyes on the group. And something in those eyes—scorn, was it? A kind of withering contempt.

Tuppence thought:

I must find out more about Mrs. Perenna.

II

Tommy was establishing the happiest of relationships with Major Bletchley.

"Brought down some golf clubs with you, didn't you, Meadowes?"

Tommy pleaded guilty.

"Ha! I can tell you, *my* eyes don't miss much. Splendid! We must have a game together. Ever played on the links here?"

Tommy replied in the negative.

"They're not bad—not bad at all. Bit on the short side, perhaps, but lovely view over the sea and all that. And never very crowded. Look here, what about coming along with me this morning? We might have a game."

"Thanks very much. I'd like it."

"Must say I'm glad you've arrived," remarked Bletchley as they were trudging up the hill. "Too many women in that place. Gets on one's nerves. Glad I've got another fellow to keep me in countenance. You can't count Cayley—the man's a kind of walking chemist's shop. Talks of nothing but his health and the treatments he's tried and the drugs he's taking. If he threw away all his little pill boxes and went out for a good ten mile walk every day he'd be a different man. The only other male in the place is von Deinim, and to tell you the truth, Meadowes, I'm not too easy in my mind about him."

"No?" said Tommy.

"No. You take my word for it, this refugee business is dangerous. If I had my way I'd intern the lot of them. Safety first."

"A bit drastic, perhaps."

"Not at all. War's War. And I've got my suspicions of Master Carl. For one thing, he's clearly not a Jew. Then he came over here just a month—only a month, mind you—before War broke out. That's a bit suspicious."

Tommy said invitingly:

"Then you think—"

"*Spying*—that's his little game!"

"But surely there's nothing of great military or naval importance hereabouts?"

"Ah, old man, that's where the artfulness comes in! If he were anywhere near Plymouth or Portsmouth he'd be under supervision. In a sleepy place like this, nobody bothers. But it's on the coast, isn't it? The truth of it is the Government is a great deal too easy with these enemy aliens. Anyone who cared could come over here and pull a long face and talk about their brothers in concentration camps. Look at that young man—arrogance in every line of him. He's a Nazi—that's what he is—a Nazi."

"What we really need in this country is a witch doctor or two," said Tommy pleasantly.

"Eh, what's that?"

"To smell out the spies," Tommy explained gravely.

"Ha, very good that—very good. Smell 'em out—yes, of course."

Further conversation was brought to an end, for they had arrived at the clubhouse.

Tommy's name was put down as a temporary member, he was introduced to the secretary, a vacant looking elderly man, and with the subscription duly paid, Tommy and the Major started on their round.

Tommy was a mediocre golfer. He was glad to find that his standard of play was just about right for his new friend. The Major won by two up and one to play, a very happy state of events.

"Good match, Meadowes, very good match—you had bad luck with that mashie shot, just turned off at the last minute. We must have a game fairly often. Come along and I'll introduce you to some of the fellows. Nice lot on the whole; some of them inclined to be rather old women, if you know what I mean? Ah, here's Haydock—you'll like Haydock. Retired naval wallah. Has that house on the cliff next door to us. He's our local A.R.P. warden."

Commander Haydock was a big hearty man with a weatherbeaten face, intensely blue eyes, and a habit of shouting most of his remarks. He greeted Tommy with friendliness.

"So you're going to keep Bletchley countenance at Sans Souci? He'll be glad of another man. Rather swamped by female society, eh, Bletchley?"

"I'm not much of a ladies' man," said Major Bletchley.

"Nonsense," said Haydock. "Not your type of lady, my boy, that's it. Old boarding house pussies. Nothing to do but gossip and knit."

"You're forgetting Miss Perenna," said Bletchley.

"Ah, Sheila—she's an attractive girl all right. Regular beauty if you ask me."

"I'm a bit worried about her," said Bletchley.

"What do you mean? Have a drink, Meadowes? What's yours, Major?"

The drinks ordered and the men settled on the verandah of the clubhouse, Haydock repeated his question.

Major Bletchley said with some violence:

"That German chap. She's seeing too much of him."

"Getting sweet on him, you mean? H'm, that's bad. Of course he's a good looking young chap in his way. But it won't do. It won't do, Bletchley. We can't have that sort of thing. Trading with the enemy, that's what it amounts to. These girls—where's their proper spirit? Plenty of decent young English fellows about."

Bletchley said:

"Sheila's a queer girl—she gets odd sullen fits when she will hardly speak to anyone."

"Spanish blood," said the Commander. "Her father was half Spanish, wasn't he?"

"Don't know. It's a Spanish name, I should think."

The Commander glanced at his watch.

"About time for the news. We'd better go in and listen to it."

The news was meagre that day, little more in it than had been already in the morning papers. After commenting with approval on the latest exploits of the Air Force—first-rate chaps, brave as lions—the Commander went on to develop his own pet theory—that sooner or later the Germans would attempt a landing at Leahampton itself—his argument being that it was such an unimportant spot.

Not even an anti-aircraft gun in the place! Disgraceful!"

The argument was not developed, for Tommy and the Major had to hurry back to lunch at Sans Souci. Haydock extended a cordial invitation to Tommy to come and see his little place, "Smugglers' Rest." "Marvellous view—my own beach—every kind of handy gadget in the house. Bring him along, Bletchley."

It was settled that Tommy and Major Bletchley should come in for drinks on the evening of the following day.

III

After lunch was a peaceful time at Sans Souci. Mr. Cayley went to have his "rest" with the devoted Mrs. Cayley in attendance. Mrs. Blenkensop was conducted by Miss Minton to a depot to pack and address parcels for the Front.

Mr. Meadows strolled gently out into Leahampton and along the front. He bought a few cigarettes, stopped at Smith's to purchase the latest number of *Punch*, then after a few minutes of apparent irresolution, he entered a bus bearing the legend OLD PIER.

The old pier was at the extreme end of the promenade. That part of Leahampton was known to house agents as the least desirable end. It was West Leahampton and poorly thought of. Tommy paid twopence and strolled up the pier. It was a flimsy and weather-worn affair with a few moribund penny-in-the-slot machines placed at far distant intervals. There was no one on it but some children running up and down and screaming in voices that matched quite accurately the screaming of the gulls, and one solitary man sitting on the end fishing.

Mr. Meadowes strolled up to the end and gazed down into the water. Then he asked gently:

"Caught anything?"

The fisherman shook his head.

"Don't often get a bite." Mr. Grant reeled in his line a bit. He said without turning his head:

"What about you, Meadowes?"

Tommy said:

"Nothing much to report as yet, sir. I'm digging myself in."

"Good. Tell me."

Tommy sat on an adjacent post, so placed that he commanded the length of the pier. Then he began.

"I've gone down quite all right, I think. I gather you've already got a list of the people there?" Grant nodded. "There's nothing to report as yet. I've struck up a friendship with Major Bletchley. We played golf this morning. He seems the ordinary type of retired officer. If anything, a shade too typical. Cayley seems a genuine hypochondriacal invalid. That, again, would be an easy part to act. He has, by his own admission, been a good deal in Germany during the last few years."

"A point," said Grant, laconically.

"Then there's von Deinim."

"Yes. I don't need to tell you, Meadowes, that von Deinim's the one I'm most interested in."

"You think he's N?"

Grant shook his head.

"No, I don't. As I see it, N couldn't afford to be a German."

"Not a refugee from Nazi persecution, even?"

"Not even that. We watch, and they know we watch, all the enemy aliens in this country. Moreover—this is in confidence, Beresford—very shortly all enemy aliens between 16 and 60 will be interned. Whether our adversaries are aware of that fact or not, they can at any rate anticipate that such a thing might happen. They would never risk the head of their organization being interned. N, therefore, must be either a neutral—or else he is (apparently) an Englishman. The same, of course, applies to M. No, my meaning about von Deinim is this: He may be a link in the chain. N or M may not be at Sans Souci, it may be Carl von Deinim who is there and through him we may be led to our objective. That does seem to be highly possible. The more so as I cannot very well see that any of the other inmates of Sans Souci are likely to be the person we are seeking."

"You've had them more or less investigated, I suppose, sir?"

Grant sighed—a sharp quick sigh of vexation.

"No, that's just what it's impossible for me to do. I could have them looked up by the department easily enough—*but I can't risk it, Beresford*. For, you see, the rot is in the department itself. Onc hint that I've got my eye on Sans Souci for any reason—and the organization may be put wise. That's where *you* come in, the outsider. That's why you've got to work in the dark, without help from us. It's our only chance—and I daren't risk alarming them. There's only one person I've been able to check up on."

"Who's that, sir?"

Grant smiled.

"Carl von Deinim himself. That's easy enough. Routine. I can have him looked up—not from the Sans Souci angle, but from the enemy alien angle."

Tommy asked curiously:

"And the result?"

A curious smile came over the other's face.

"Master Carl is exactly what he says he is. His father was indiscreet, was arrested and died in a concentration camp. Carl's elder brothers are in camps. His mother died in great distress of mind a year ago. He escaped to England a month before war broke out. Von Deinim has professed himself anxious to help this country. His work in a chemical research laboratory has been excellent and most helpful on the problem of immunizing certain gases and in general decontamination experiments."

Tommy said:

"Then he's all right?"

"Not necessarily. Our German friends are notorious for their thoroughness. If von Deinim was sent as an agent to England special care would be taken that his record should be consistent with his own account of himself. There are two possibilities. The whole von Deinim family may be parties to the arrangement—not improbable under the painstaking Nazi régime. Or else this is not really Carl von Deinim but *a man playing the part of Carl von Deinim.*"

Tommy said slowly: "I see." He added inconsequently:

"He seems an awfully nice young fellow."

Sighing, Grant said: "They are—they nearly always are. It's an odd life this service of ours. We respect our adversaries and they respect us. You usually like your opposite number, you know—even when you're doing your best to down him."

There was a silence as Tommy thought over the strange anomaly of war. Grant's voice broke into his musings.

"But there are those for whom we've neither respect nor liking—and those are the traitors within our own ranks—the men who are willing to betray their country and accept office and promotion from the foreigner who has conquered it."

Tommy said with feeling:

"My God, I'm with you, sir. That's a skunk's trick."

"And deserves a skunk's end."

Tommy said incredulously:

"And there really are these—these swine?"

"Everywhere. As I told you. In our service. In the fighting forces. On Parliamentary benches. High up in the Ministries. We've got to comb them out—we've *got* to! And we must do it quickly. It can't be done from the bottom—the small fry, the people who speak in the Parks, who sell their wretched little news-sheets, they don't know who the big bugs are. It's the big bugs we want, they're the people who can do untold damage—and will do it unless we're in time."

Tommy said confidently:

"We shall be in time, sir."

Grant asked:

"What makes you say that?"

Tommy said:

"You've just said it—we've *got* to be!"

The man with the fishing line turned and looked full at his subordinate for a minute or two, taking in anew the quiet resolute line of the jaw. He had a new liking and appreciation of what he saw. He said quietly:

"Good man."

He went on:

"What about the women in this place? Anything strike you as suspicious there?"

"I think there's something odd about the woman who runs it."

"Mrs. Perenna?"

"Yes. You don't—know anything about her?"

Grant said slowly:

"I might see what I could do about checking her antecedents, but as I told you, it's risky."

"Yes, better not take any chances. She's the only one who strikes me as suspicious in any way. There's a young mother, a fussy spinster, the hypochondriac's brainless wife, and a rather fearsome looking old Irishwoman. All seem harmless enough on the face of it."

"That's the lot, is it?"

"No. There's a Mrs. Blenkensop—arrived three days ago."

"Well?"

Tommy said:

"Mrs. Blenkensop is my wife."

"*What?*"

In the surprise of the announcement Grant's voice was raised. He spun around, sharp anger in his gaze. "I thought I told you, Beresford, not to breathe a word to your wife!"

"Quite right, sir, and I didn't. If you'll just listen—"

Succinctly, Tommy narrated what had occurred. He did not dare look at the other. He carefully kept out of his voice the pride that he secretly felt.

There was a silence when he brought the story to an end. Then a queer noise escaped from the other. Grant was laughing. He laughed for some minutes.

He said:

"I take my hat off to the woman! She's one in a thousand!"

"I agree," said Tommy.

"Easthampton will laugh when I tell him this. He warned me not to leave her out. Said she'd get the better of me if I did. I wouldn't listen to him. It shows you, though, how damned careful you've got to be. I thought I'd taken every precaution against being overheard. I'd satisfied myself beforehand that you and your wife were alone in the flat. I actually heard the voice in the telephone asking your wife to come round at once, and so—and so I was tricked by the old simple device of the banged door. Yes, she's a smart woman, your wife."

He was silent for a minute, then he said:

"Tell her from me, will you, that I eat dirt?"

"And I suppose, now, she's in on this?"

Mr. Grant made an expressive grimace.

"She's in on it whether we like it or not. Tell her the department will esteem it an honour if she will condescend to work with us over the matter."

"I'll tell her," said Tommy with a faint grin.

Grant said seriously:

"You couldn't persuade her, I suppose, to go home and stay home?"

Tommy shook his head.

"You don't know Tuppence."

"I think I am beginning to. I said that because—well, it's a very dangerous business. If they get wise to you or to her—"

He left the sentence unfinished.

Tommy said gravely:

"I do understand that, sir."

"But I suppose even you couldn't persuade your wife to keep out of danger."

Tommy said slowly:

"I don't know that I really would want to do that . . . Tuppence and I, you see, aren't on those terms. We go into things—together!"

In his mind was that phrase, uttered years ago, at the close of an earlier war. A *joint venture*. . . .

That was what his life with Tuppence had been and would always be—a Joint Venture. . . .

IV

WHEN TUPPENCE ENTERED the lounge at Sans Souci just before dinner,
the only occupant of the room was the monumental Mrs. O'Rourke, who
was sitting by the window looking like some gigantic Buddha.

She greeted Tuppence with a lot of geniality and verve.

"Ah, now, if it isn't Mrs. Blenkensop! You're like myself, it pleases
you to be down on time and get a quiet minute or two here before
going into the dining room, and a pleasant room this is in good weather
with the windows open in the way that you'll not be noticing the
smell of cooking. Terrible that is, in all of these places, and more
especially if it's onion or cabbage that's on the fire. Sit here now,
Mrs. Blenkensop, and tell me what you've been doing with yourself
this fine day and how you like Leahampton."

There was something about Mrs. O'Rourke that had an unholy
fascination for Tuppence. She was rather like an ogress dimly remembered from early fairy tales. With her bulk, her deep voice, her unabashed beard and moustache, her deep twinkling eyes and the
impression she gave of being more than life-size, she was indeed not
unlike some childhood fantasy.

Tuppence replied that she thought she was going to like Leahampton
very much, and be happy there.

"That is," she added in a melancholy voice, "as happy as I can be
anywhere with this terrible anxiety weighing on me all the time."

"Ah, now, don't you be worrying yourself," Mrs. O'Rourke advised
comfortably. "Those fine boys of yours will come back to you safe and
sound. Not a doubt of it. One of them's in the Air Force, so I think
you said?"

"Yes, Raymond."

"And is he in France now, or in England?"

"He's in Egypt at the moment, but from what he said in his last
letter—not exactly *said*—but we have a little private code if you know
what I mean?—certain sentences mean certain things. I think that's
quite justified, don't you?"

Mrs. O'Rourke replied promptly:

"Indeed and I do. 'Tis a mother's privilege."

"Yes, you see I feel I must know just where he is."

Mrs. O'Rourke nodded the Buddha-like head.

"I feel for you entirely, so I do. If I had a boy out there I'd be deceiving the censor the very same way, so I would. And your other boy,
the one in the Navy?"

Tuppence entered obligingly upon a saga of Douglas.

"You see," she ended. "I feel so lost without my three boys. They've
never been all away together from me before. They're all so sweet
to me. I really do think they treat me more as a *friend* than a mother."
She laughed self-consciously. "I have to scold them sometimes and
make them go out without me."

("What a pestilential woman I sound," thought Tuppence to herself.)
She went on aloud.

"And really I didn't know quite *what* to do or *where* to go. The
lease of my house in London was up and it seemed so foolish to re-
new it and I thought if I came somewhere quiet, and yet with a good
train service—" She broke off.

Again the Buddha nodded.

"I agree with you entirely. London is no place at the present. Ah!
the gloom of it! I've lived there myself for many a year now. I'm by
way of being an antique dealer, you know. You may know my shop
in Cornaby Street, Chelsea? Kate Kelly's the name over the door. Lovely
stuff I had there, too—oh, lovely stuff—mostly glass—Waterford, Cork—
beautiful. Chandeliers and lustres and punchbowls and all the rest
of it. Foreign glass, too. And small furniture—nothing large—just small
period pieces—mostly walnut and oak. Oh, lovely stuff—and I had some
good customers. But there, when there's a War on, all that goes west.
I'm lucky to be out of it with as little loss as I've had."

A faint memory flickered through Tuppence's mind. A shop filled
with glass, through which it was difficult to move, a rich persuasive
voice, a compelling massive woman. Yes, surely, she had been into that
shop.

Mrs. O'Rourke went on.

"I'm not one of those that like to be always complaining—not like
some that's in this house. Mr. Cayley for one, with his muffler and
his shawls and his moans about his business going to pieces. Of course
it's to pieces, there's a War on—and his wife with never Boo to say to a
goose. Then there's that little Mrs. Sprot, always fussing about her
husband."

"Is he out at the front?"

"Not he. He's a tuppenny-halfpenny clerk in an insurance office, that's all, and so terrified of air raids he's had his wife down here since the beginning of the War. Mind you, I think that's right where the child's concerned—and a nice wee mite she is—but Mrs. Sprot, she frets, for all that her husband comes down when he can. . . . Keeps saying Arthur must miss her so. But if you ask me Arthur's not missing her overmuch—maybe he's got other fish to fry."

Tuppence murmured:

"I'm terribly sorry for all these mothers. If you let your children go away without you, you never stop worrying. And if you go with them it's hard on the husbands being left."

"Ah! yes, and it comes expensive running two establishments."

"This place seems quite reasonable," said Tuppence.

"Yes, I'd say you get your money's worth. Mrs. Perenna's a good manager. There's a queer woman for you now."

"In what way?" asked Tuppence.

Mrs. O'Rourke said with a twinkle:

"You'll be thinking I'm a terrible talker. It's true. I'm interested in all my fellow creatures, that's why I sit in this chair as often as I can. You see who goes in and who goes out and who's on the verandah and what goes on in the garden. What were we talking of now—ah, yes, Mrs. Perenna, and the queerness of her. There's been a grand drama in that woman's life or I'm much mistaken."

"Do you really think so?"

"I do now. And the mystery she makes of herself! 'And where might you come from in Ireland?' I asked her. And would you believe it, she held out on me, declaring she was not from Ireland at all."

"You think she is Irish?"

"Of course she's Irish. I know my own countrywomen. I could name you the county she comes from. But there! 'I'm English,' she says, 'and my husband was a Spaniard'—"

Mrs. O'Rourke broke off abruptly as Mrs. Sprot came in, closely followed by Tommy.

Tuppence immediately assumed a sprightly manner.

"Good evening, Mr. Meadowes. You look very brisk this evening."

Tommy said:

"Plenty of exercise, that's the secret. A round of golf this morning and a walk along the front this afternoon."

Millicent Sprot said:

"I took Baby down to the beach this afternoon. She wanted to paddle but I really thought it was rather cold. I was helping her build a castle and a dog ran off with my knitting and pulled out yards of it. So annoying, and so difficult picking up all the stitches again. I'm such a bad knitter."

"You're getting along fine with that helmet, Mrs. Blenkensop," said Mrs. O'Rourke, suddenly turning her attention to Tuppence. "You've been just racing along. I thought Miss Minton said that you were an inexperienced knitter."

Tuppence flushed faintly. Mrs. O'Rourke's eyes were sharp. With a slightly vexed air, Tuppence said:

"I have really done quite a lot of knitting. I told Miss Minton so. But I think she likes teaching people."

Everybody laughed in agreement, and a few minutes later the rest of the party came in and the gong was sounded.

The conversation during the meal turned on the absorbing subject of spies. Well-known hoary chestnuts were retold. The nun with the muscular arm; the clergyman descending from his parachute and using unclergymanlike language as he landed with a bump; the Austrian cook who secreted a wireless in her bedroom chimney; and all the things that had happened or nearly happened to aunts and second cousins of those present. That led easily to Fifth Column activities. To denunciations of the British Fascists, of the Communists, of the Peace Party, of conscientious objectors. It was a very normal conversation, of the kind that may be heard almost every day, nevertheless Tuppence watched keenly the faces and demeanour of the people as they talked, striving to catch some tell-tale expression or word. But there was nothing. Sheila Perenna alone took no part in the conversation, but that might be put down to her habitual taciturnity. She sat there, her dark rebellious face sullen and brooding.

Carl von Deinim was out tonight, so tongues could be quite unrestrained.

Sheila only spoke once towards the end of dinner.

Mrs. Sprot had just said in her thin fluting voice:

"Where I do think the Germans made such a mistake in the last war was to shoot Nurse Cavell. It turned everybody against them."

It was then that Sheila, flinging back her head, demanded in her fierce young voice: "Why shouldn't they shoot her? She was a spy, wasn't she?"

"Oh, no, not a spy."

"She helped English people to escape—in an enemy country. That's the same thing. Why shouldn't she be shot?"

"Oh, but shooting a woman—and a nurse."

Sheila got up.

"I think the Germans were quite right," she said.

She went out of the window into the garden.

Dessert, consisting of some under-ripe bananas and some tired oranges, had been on the table some time. Everyone rose and adjourned to the lounge for coffee.

Only Tommy unobtrusively betook himself to the garden. He found Sheila Perenna leaning over the terrace wall staring out at the sea. He came and stood beside her.

By her hurried, quick breathing he knew that something had upset her badly. He offered her a cigarette, which she accepted.

He said:

"Lovely night."

In a low intense voice the girl answered:

"It could be. . . ."

Tommy looked at her doubtfully. He felt, suddenly, the attraction and the vitality of this girl. There was a tumultuous life in her, a kind of compelling power. She was the kind of girl, he thought, that a man might easily lose his head over.

"If it weren't for the War, you mean?" he said.

"I don't mean that at all. I hate the War."

"So do we all."

"Not in the way I mean. I hate the cant about it, the smugness—the horrible, horrible patriotism."

"Patriotism?" Tommy was startled.

"Yes, I hate patriotism, do you understand? All this *country, country, country!* Betraying your country—dying for your country—serving your country. Why should one's country mean anything at all?"

Tommy said simply: "I don't know. It just does."

"Not to me! Oh, it would to you—you go abroad and buy and sell in the British Empire and come back bronzed and full of clichés, talking about the natives and calling for Chota Pegs and all that sort of thing."

Tommy said gently:

"I'm not quite as bad as that, I hope, my dear."

"I'm exaggerating a little—but you know what I mean. You believe in the British Empire—and—and—the stupidity of dying for one's country."

"My country," said Tommy drily, "doesn't seem particularly anxious to allow me to die for it."

"Yes, but you *want* to. And it's so stupid! *Nothing's* worth dying for. It's all an *idea*—talk—froth—high-flown idiocy. My country doesn't mean anything to me at all."

"Some day," said Tommy, "you'll be surprised to find that it does."

"No. Never. I've suffered—I've seen—"

She broke off—then turned suddenly and impetuously upon him.

"Do you know who my father was?"

"No." Tommy's interest quickened.

"His name was Patrick Maguire. He—he was a follower of Casement in the last War. He was shot as a traitor! All for nothing! For an idea—he worked himself up with those other Irishmen. Why couldn't he just stay at home quietly and mind his own business? He's a martyr to some people and a traitor to others. I think he was just—*stupid!*"

Tommy could hear the note of pent-up rebellion coming out into the open. He said:

"So that's the shadow you've grown up with?"

"Shadow's right. Mother changed her name. We lived in Spain for some years. She always says that my father was half a Spaniard. We always tell lies wherever we go. We've been all over the Continent. Finally we came here and started this place. I think this is quite the most hateful thing we've done yet."

Tommy asked:

"How does your mother feel about—things?"

"You mean—about my father's death." Sheila was silent a moment frowning, puzzled. She said slowly: "I've never really known . . . she never talks about it. It's not easy to know what mother feels or thinks."

Tommy nodded his head thoughtfully.

Sheila said abruptly:

"I—I don't know why I've been telling you this. I got worked up. Where did it all start?"

"A discussion on Edith Cavell."

"Oh, yes—patriotism. I said I hated it."

"Aren't you forgetting Nurse Cavell's own words?"

"What words?"

"Before she died. Don't you know what she said?"

He repeated the words:

"*Patriotism is not enough . . . I must have no hatred in my heart.*"

"Oh." She stood there stricken for a moment.

Then, turning quickly, she wheeled away into the shadow of the garden.

II

"So you see, Tuppence, it would all fit in."

Tuppence nodded thoughtfully. The beach around them was empty. She herself leaned against a breakwater, Tommy sat above her, on the breakwater itself, from which post he could see anyone who approached along the esplanade. Not that he expected to see anyone, having ascertained with a fair amount of accuracy where people would be this morning. In any case his rendezvous with Tuppence had borne all the signs of a casual meeting, pleasurable to the lady and slightly alarming to himself.

Tuppence said:

"Mrs. Perenna?"

"Yes. M, not N. She satisfies the requirements."

Tuppence nodded thoughtfully again.

"Yes. She's Irish—as spotted by Mrs. O'Rourke—won't admit the fact. Has done a good deal of coming and going on the continent. Changed her name to Perenna, came here and started this boarding house. A splendid bit of camouflage, full of innocuous bores. Her husband was shot as a traitor—she's got every incentive for running a Fifth Column show in this country. Yes, it fits. Is the girl in it, too, do you think?"

Tommy said finally:

"Definitely not. She'd never have told me all this otherwise. I—I feel a bit of a cad, you know."

Tuppence nodded with complete understanding.

"Yes, one does. In a way it's a foul job, this."

"But very necessary."

"Oh, of course."

Tommy said, flushing slightly:

"I don't like lying any better than you do—"

Tuppence interrupted him.

"I don't mind lying in the least. To be quite honest I get a lot of artistic pleasure out of my lies. What gets me down is those moments when one forgets to lie—the times when one is just oneself—and gets results that way that you couldn't have got any other." She paused and went on: "That's what happened to you last night—with the girl. She responded to the *real* you—that's why you feel badly about it."

"I believe you're right, Tuppence."

"I know. Because I did the same thing myself—with the German boy."

Tommy said:

"What do you think about him?"

Tuppence said quickly:

"If you ask me, I don't think he's got anything to do with it."

"Grant thinks he has."

"Your Mr. Grant!" Tuppence's mood changed. She chuckled. "How I'd like to have seen his face when you told him about me."

"At any rate, he's made the *amende honorable*. You're definitely on the job."

Tuppence nodded, but she looked a trifle abstracted.

She said:

"Do you remember after the last War—when we were hunting down Mr. Brown? Do you remember what fun it was? How excited we were?"

Tommy agreed, his face lighting up.

"Rather!"

"Tommy—why isn't it the same now?"

He considered the question, his quiet ugly face grave. Then he said:

"I suppose it's really—a question of age."

Tuppence said sharply:

"You don't think—we're too old?"

"No, I'm sure we're not. It's only that—this time—it won't be *fun*. It's the same in other ways. This is the second War we've been in—and we feel quite different about this one."

"I know—we see the pity of it and the waste—and the horror. All the things we were too young to think about before."

"That's it. In the last war I was scared every now and then—and had some pretty close shaves, and went through hell once or twice, but there were good times, too."

Tuppence said:

"I suppose Derek feels like that?"

"Better not think about him, old thing," Tommy advised.

"You're right." Tuppence set her teeth. "We've got a job. We're going to *do* that job. Let's get on with it. Have we found what we're looking for in Mrs. Perenna?"

"We can at least say that she's strongly indicated. There's no one else, is there, Tuppence, that you've got your eye on?"

Tuppence considered.

"No, there isn't. The first thing I did when I arrived, of course, was to size them all up and assess, as it were, possibilities. Some of them seem quite impossible."

"Such as?"

"Well, Miss Minton, for instance, the 'compleat' British spinster, and Mrs. Sprot and her Betty, and the vacuous Mrs. Cayley."

"Yes, but nitwittishness can be assumed."

"Oh, quite, but the fussy spinster and the absorbed young mothers are parts that would be fatally easy to overdo—and these people are quite natural. Then, where Mrs. Sprot is concerned, there's the child."

"I suppose," said Tommy, "that even a secret agent might have a child."

"Not with her on the job," said Tuppence. "It's not the kind of thing you'd bring a child into. I'm quite sure about that, Tommy. I *know*. You'd keep a child out of it."

"I withdraw," said Tommy. "I'll give you Mrs. Sprot and Miss Minton, but I'm not so sure about Mrs. Cayley."

"No, she might be a possibility. Because she really does overdo it. I mean there can't be many women *quite* as idiotic as she seems."

"I have often noticed that being a devoted wife saps the intellect," murmured Tommy.

"And where have you noticed that?" demanded Tuppence.

"Not from you, Tuppence. Your devotion has never reached those lengths."

"For a man," said Tuppence kindly, "you don't really make an undue fuss when you are ill."

Tommy reverted to a survey of possibilities.

"Cayley," said Tommy thoughtfully. "There might be something fishy about Cayley."

"Yes, there might. Then there's Mrs. O'Rourke."

"What do you feel about her?"

"I don't quite know. She's disturbing. Rather *fee fo fum*, if you know what I mean."

"Yes, I think I know. But I rather fancy that's just the predatory note. She's that kind of woman."

Tuppence said slowly:

"She—notices things."

She was remembering the remark about knitting.

"Then there's Bletchley," said Tommy.

"I've hardly spoken to him. He's definitely your chicken."

"I *think* he's just the ordinary pukka old school type. I *think* so."

"That's just it," said Tuppence, answering a stress rather than actual words. "The worst of this sort of show is that you look at quite ordinary everyday people and twist them to suit your morbid requirements."

"I've tried a few experiments on Bletchley," said Tommy.

"What sort of thing? I've got some experiments in mind myself."

"Well—just gentle ordinary little traps—about dates and places— all that sort of thing."

"Could you condescend from the general to the particular?"

"Well, say we're talking of duck shooting. He mentions the Fayum —good sport there such and such a year, such and such a month. Some other time I mention Egypt in quite a different connection. Mummies, Tutankhamen, something like that—has he seen that stuff? When was he there? Check up on the answers. Or P. & O. boats—I mention the names of one or two, say So-and-so was a comfortable boat. He mentions some trip or other, later I check that. Nothing important, or anything that puts him on his guard—just a check up on accuracy."

"And so far he hasn't slipped up in any way?"

"Not once. And that's a pretty good test, let me tell you, Tuppence."

"Yes, but I suppose *if* he was N, he *would* have his story quite pat."

"Oh, yes—the main outlines of it. But it's not so easy not to trip up on unimportant details. And then occasionally you remember too much —more, that is, than a bona fide person would do. An ordinary person doesn't usually remember offhand whether they took a certain shooting trip in 1926 or 1927. They have to think a bit and search their memory."

"But so far you haven't caught Bletchley out?"

"So far he's responded in a perfectly normal manner."

"Result—negative."

"Exactly."

"Now," said Tuppence. "I'll tell you some of my ideas."

And she proceeded to do so.

III

On her way home, Mrs. Blenkensop stopped at the post office. She bought stamps and on her way out, went into one of the public call boxes. There she rang up a certain number, asked for "Mr. Faraday," and held a short conversation with him. She came out smiling and walked slowly homewards, stopping on the way to purchase some knitting wool.

It was a pleasant afternoon with a light breeze. Tuppence curbed the natural energy of her own brisk trot to that leisurely pace that accorded with her conception of the part of Mrs. Blenkensop. Mrs. Blenkensop had nothing on earth to do with herself except knit (not too well) and write letters to her boys. She was always writing letters to her boys—sometimes she left them about half finished.

Tuppence came slowly up the hill towards Sans Souci. Since it was not a through road (it ended at Smugglers' Rest, Commander Haydock's house) there was never much traffic—a few tradesmen's vans in the morning. Tuppence passed house after house, amusing herself by noting their names. Bella Vista (inaccurately named, since the merest glimpse of the sea was to be obtained, and the main view was the vast Victorian bulk of Edenholme on the other side of the road). Karachi was the next house. After that came Shirley Tower. Then Sea View (appropriate this time), Castle Clare (somewhat grandiloquent, since it was a small house), Trelawny, a rival establishment to that of Mrs. Perenna, and finally the vast maroon bulk of Sans Souci.

It was just as she came near to it that Tuppence became aware of a woman standing by the gate peering inside. There was something tense and vigilant about the figure.

Almost unconsciously, Tuppence softened the sound of her own footsteps, stepping cautiously upon her toes.

It was not until she was close behind her, that the woman heard her and turned. Turned with a start.

She was a tall woman, poorly, even meanly dressed, but her face was unusual. She was not young—probably between forty and fifty—but there was a contrast between her face and the way she was dressed. She was fair-haired, with wide cheekbones and had been—indeed still was—beautiful. Just for a minute Tuppence had a feeling that the woman's face was somehow familiar to her, but the feeling faded. It was not, she thought, a face easily forgotten.

The woman was obviously startled, and the flash of alarm that flitted across her face was not lost on Tuppence. (Something odd here?)

Tuppence said:

"Excuse me, are you looking for someone?"

The woman spoke in a slow foreign voice, pronouncing the words carefully as though she had learned them by heart.

"This 'ouse is Sans Souci?"

"Yes. I live here. Did you want someone?"

There was an infinitesimal pause, then the woman said:

"You can tell me, please. There is a Mr. Rosenstein there, no?"

"Mr. Rosenstein?" Tuppence shook her head. "No. I'm afraid not. Perhaps he has been there and left. Shall I ask for you?"

But the strange woman made a quick gesture of refusal. She said: "No—no. I make mistake. Excuse, please."

Then, quickly, she turned and walked rapidly down the hill again.

Tuppence stood staring after her. For some reason, her suspicions were aroused. There was a contrast between the woman's manner and her words. Tuppence had an idea that "Mr. Rosenstein" was a fiction, that the woman had seized at the first name that came into her head.

Tuppence hesitated a minute, then she started down the hill after the other. What she could only describe as a "hunch" made her want to follow the woman.

Presently, however, she stopped. To follow would be to draw attention to herself in a rather marked manner. She had clearly been on the point of entering Sans Souci when she spoke to the woman; to reappear on her trail would be to arouse suspicion that Mrs. Blenkensop was something other than appeared on the surface—that is to say if this strange woman was indeed a member of the enemy plot.

No, at all costs Mrs. Blenkensop must remain what she seemed.

Tuppence turned and retraced her steps up the hill. She entered Sans Souci and paused in the hall. The house seemed deserted, as was usual early in the afternoon. Betty was having her nap, the elder members were either resting or had gone out.

Then, as Tuppence stood in the dim hall thinking over her recent encounter, a faint sound came to her ears. It was a sound she knew quite well—the faint echo of a ting.

The telephone at Sans Souci was in the hall. The sound that Tuppence had just heard was the sound made when the receiver of an extension is taken off or replaced. There was one extension in the house—in Mrs. Perenna's bedroom.

Tommy might have hesitated. Tuppence did not hesitate for a minute. Very gently and carefully she lifted off the receiver and put it to her ear.

Someone was using the extension. It was a man's voice. Tuppence heard:

"—everything going well. On the fourth, then, as arranged."

A woman's voice said:

"Yes, carry on."

There was a click as the receiver was replaced.

Tuppence stood there frowning. Was that Mrs. Perenna's voice? Difficult to say with only those three words to go upon. If there had been only a little more to the conversation. It might, of course, be quite an ordinary conversation—certainly there was nothing in the words she had overheard to indicate otherwise.

A shadow obscured the light from the door. Tuppence jumped and replaced the receiver as Mrs. Perenna spoke.

"Such a pleasant afternoon. Are you going out, Mrs. Blenkensop, or have you just come in?"

So it was not Mrs. Perenna who had been speaking from Mrs. Perenna's room. Tuppence murmured something about having had a pleasant walk and moved to the staircase.

Mrs. Perenna moved along the hall after her. She seemed bigger than usual. Tuppence was conscious of her as a strong athletic woman.

She said:

"I must get my things off," and hurried up the stairs. As she turned the corner of the landing she collided with Mrs. O'Rourke, whose vast bulk barred the top of the stairs.

"Dear, dear, now, Mrs. Blenkensop, it's a great hurry you seem to be in."

She did not move aside, just stood there smiling down at Tuppence just below her. There was, as always, a frightening quality about Mrs. O'Rourke's smile.

And suddenly, for no reason, Tuppence felt afraid.

The big smiling Irishwoman, with her deep voice, barring her way and below Mrs. Perenna closing in at the foot of the stairs.

Tuppence glanced over her shoulder. Was it her fancy that there was something definitely meancing in Mrs. Perenna's upturned face? Absurd, she told herself, absurd. In broad daylight—in a commonplace seaside boarding house. But the house was so very quiet. Not a sound. And she herself here on the stairs between the two of them. Surely there *was* something a little queer in Mrs. O'Rourke's smile—some fixed ferocious quality about it. Tuppence thought wildly, "Like a cat with a mouse."

And then suddenly the tension broke. A little figure darted along the top landing uttering shrill squeals of mirth. Little Betty Sprot in vest and knickers, darting past Mrs. O'Rourke, shouting happily "Peek Bo," as she flung herself on Tuppence.

The atmosphere had changed. Mrs. O'Rourke, a big genial figure, was crying out:

"Ah, the darlin'. It's a great girl she's getting."

Below, Mrs. Perenna had turned away to the door that led into the kitchen. Tuppence, Betty's hand clasped in hers, passed Mrs. O'Rourke and ran along the passage to where Mrs. Sprot was waiting to scold the truant.

Tuppence went in with the child.

She felt a queer sense of relief at the domestic atmosphere—the child's clothes lying about, the woolly toys, the painted crib, the sheeplike and somewhat unattractive face of Mr. Sprot in its frame on the dressing table, the burble of Mrs. Sprot's denunciation of laundry prices and really she thought Mrs. Perenna was a little unfair in refusing to sanction guests having their own electric irons—

All so normal, so reassuring, so everyday.

And yet—just now—on the stairs.

"Nerves," said Tuppence to herself. "Just nerves!"

But had it been nerves? Someone *had* been telephoning from Mrs. Perenna's room. Mrs. O'Rourke? Surely a very odd thing to do. It ensured, of course, that you would not be overheard by the household.

It must have been, Tuppence thought, a very short conversation. The merest brief exchange of words.

Everything going well. On the fourth as arranged.

It might mean nothing—or a good deal.

The fourth. Was that a date? The fourth, say, of a month?

Or it might mean the fourth seat, or the fourth lamp-post, or the fourth breakwater—impossible to know.

It might just conceivably mean the Forth Bridge. There had been an attempt to blow that up in the last War.

Did it mean anything at all?

It might quite easily have been the confirmation of some perfectly ordinary appointment. Mrs. Perenna might have told Mrs. O'Rourke she could use the telephone in her bedroom any time she wanted to do so.

And the atmosphere on the stairs, that tense moment, might have been just her own overwrought nerves . . .

The quiet house—the feeling that there was something sinister—something evil . . .

"Stick to facts, Mrs. Blenkensop," said Tuppence sternly. "And get on with your job."

V

COMMANDER HAYDOCK TURNED out to be a most genial host. He welcomed Mr. Meadowes and Major Bletchley with enthusiasm and insisted on showing the former "all over my little place."

Smugglers' Rest had been originally a couple of coastguards' cottages standing on the cliff overlooking the sea. There was a small cove below, but the access to it was perilous, only to be attempted by adventurous boys.

Then the cottages had been bought by a London business man who had thrown them into one and attempted half-heartedly to make a garden. He had come down occasionally for short periods in summer.

After that the cottages had remained empty for some years, being let with a modicum of furniture to summer visitors.

"Then in 1926," explained Haydock, "it was sold to a man called Hahn. He was a German, and if you ask me, he was neither more nor less than a spy."

Tommy's ears quickened.

"That's interesting," he said, putting down the glass from which he had been sipping sherry.

"Damned thorough fellows they are," said Haydock. "Getting ready even then for this show—at least that is my opinion. Look at the situation of this place. Perfect for signalling out to sea. Cove below where you could land a motor-boat. Completely isolated, owing to the contour of the cliff. Oh, yes, don't tell me that fellow Hahn wasn't a German agent."

Major Bletchley said:

"Of course he was."

"What happened to him?" asked Tommy.

"Ah!" said Haydock, "thereby hangs a tale. Hahn spent a lot of money on this place. He had a way cut down to the beach for one thing—concrete steps—expensive business. Then he had the whole of the house done over—bathrooms, every expensive gadget you can imagine. And who did he set to do all this? Not local men. No, a firm from London, so it was said—but a lot of the men who came down were foreigners. Some of them *didn't speak a word of English*. Don't you agree with me that that sounds extremely fishy?"

"A little odd, certainly," agreed Tommy.

"I was in the neighbourhood myself at the time, living in a bungalow, and I got interested in what this fellow was up to. I used to hang about to watch the workmen. Now I'll tell you this—they didn't like it— they didn't like it at all. Once or twice they were quite threatening about it. Why should they be if everything was all square and aboveboard?"

Bletchley nodded agreement.

"You ought to have gone to the authorities," he said.

"Just what I did do, my dear fellow. Made a positive nuisance of myself pestering the police."

He poured himself out another drink.

"And what did I get for my pains? Polite inattention. Blind and deaf, that's what we were in this country. Another War with Germany was out of the question—there was peace in Europe—our relations with Germany were excellent. Natural sympathy between us nowadays. I was regarded as an old fossil, a War maniac, a diehard old sailor. What was the good of pointing out to people that the Germans were building the finest Air Force in Europe and not just to fly round and have picnics!"

Major Bletchley said explosively:

"Nobody believed it! Damned fools! Peace in our time. Appeasement. All a lot of blah!"

Haydock said, his face redder than usual with suppressed anger: "A War-monger, that's what they called me. The sort of chap, they said, who was an obstacle to peace. Peace! I knew what our Hun friends were at! And mind this, they prepare things a long time beforehand. I was convinced that Mr. Hahn was up to no good. I didn't like his foreign workmen. I didn't like the way he was spending money on this place. I kept on badgering away at people."

"Stout fellow," said Bletchley appreciatively.

"And finally," said the Commander, "I began to make an impression. We had a new Chief Constable down here—retired soldier. And he had the sense to listen to me. His fellows began to nose around. Sure enough, Hahn decamped. Just slipped out and disappeared one fine night. The police went over this place with a search warrant. In a safe which had been built-in in the dining room they found a wireless transmitter and some pretty damaging documents. Also a big store place under the garage for petrol—great tanks. I can tell you I was cock-a-hoop over that. Fellows at the club used to rag me about my German Spy complex. They dried up after that. Trouble with us in this country is that we're so absurdly unsuspicious."

"It's a crime. Fools—that's what we are—fools. Why don't we intern all these refugees?" Major Bletchley was well away.

"End of the story was I bought the place when it came into the market," continued the Commander, not to be sidetracked from his pet story. "Come in and have a look round, Meadowes?"

"Thanks. I'd like to."

Commander Haydock was as full of zest as a boy as he did the honours of the establishment. He threw open the big safe in the dining room to show where the secret wireless had been found. Tommy was taken out to the garage and was shown where the big petrol tanks had been concealed, and finally, after a superficial glance at the two excellent bathrooms, the special lighting, and the various kitchen "gadgets," he was taken down the steep concreted path to the little cove beneath, whilst Commander Haydock told him all over again how extremely useful the whole layout would be to an enemy in War time.

He was taken into the cave which gave the place its name and Haydock pointed out enthusiastically how it could have been used.

Major Bletchley did not accompany the two men on their tour, but remained peacefully sipping his drink on the terrace. Tommy gathered that the Commander's spy hunt with its successful issue was that good gentleman's principal topic of conversation and that his friends had heard it many times.

In fact, Major Bletchley said as much when they were walking
down to Sans Souci a little later.

"Good fellow, Haydock," he said. "But he's not content to let a good
thing alone. We've heard all about that business again and again
until we're sick of it. He's as proud of the whole bag of tricks up
there as a cat of its kittens."

The simile was not too far-fetched, and Tommy assented with a
smile.

The conversation then turning to Major Bletchley's own successful
unmasking of a dishonest bearer in 1923, Tommy's attention was free
to pursue its own inward line of thought punctuated by sympathetic
"Not reallys?"—"You don't say so?" and "What an extraordinary
business!" which was all Major Bletchley needed in the way of
encouragement.

More than ever now, Tommy felt that when the dying Farquhar
had mentioned Sans Souci he had been on the right track. Here, in
this out of the world spot, preparations had been made a long time
beforehand. The arrival of the German Hahn and his extensive in-
stallation showed clearly enough that this particular part of the coast
had been selected for a rallying point, a focus of enemy activity.

That particular game had been defeated by the unexpected activity
of the suspicious Commander Haydock. Round One had gone to Britain. But supposing that Smugglers' Rest had been only the first outpost
of a complicated scheme of attack? Smugglers' Rest, that is to say, had
represented sea communications. Its beach, inaccessible save for the
path down from above, would lend itself admirably to the plan. But it
was only a part of the whole.

Defeated on that part of the plan by Haydock, what had been the
enemy's response? Might not he have fallen back upon the next best
thing—that is to say, Sans Souci? The exposure of Hahn had come
about four years ago. Tommy had an idea, from what Sheila Perenna
had said, that it was very soon after that that Mrs. Perenna had returned to England and bought Sans Souci. The next move in the
game?

It would seem, therefore, that Leahampton was definitely an enemy
center—that there were already installations and affiliations in the
neighbourhood.

His spirits rose. The depression engendered by the harmless and
futile atmosphere of Sans Souci disappeared. Innocent as it seemed,

that innocence was no more than skin deep. Behind that innocuous mask things were going on.

And the focus of it all, so far as Tommy could judge, was Mrs. Perenna. The first thing to do was to know more about Mrs. Perenna, to penetrate behind her apparently simple routine of running her boarding establishment. Her correspondence, her acquaintances, her social or War working activities—somewhere in all these must lie the essence of her real activities. If Mrs. Perenna was the renowned woman agent, M, then it was she who controlled the whole of the Fifth Column activities in this country. Her identity would be known to few— only to those at the top. But communications she must have with her chiefs of staff and it was those communications that he and Tuppence had got to tap.

At the right moment, as Tommy saw well enough, Smugglers' Rest could be seized and held—by a few stalwarts operating from Sans Souci. That moment was not yet, but it might be very near.

Once the German Army was established in control of the channel ports in France and Belgium, they could concentrate on the invasion and subjugation of Britain, and things were certainly going very badly in France at the moment.

Britain's Navy was all-powerful on the sea, so the attack must come by air and by internal treachery—and if the threads of internal treachery were in Mrs. Perenna's keeping, there was no time to lose.

Major Bletchley's words chimed in with his thoughts:

"I saw, you know, that there was no time to lose. I got hold of Abdul, my sayce—good fellow, Abdul—"

The story droned on.

Tommy was thinking:

"Why Leahampton? Any reason? It's out of the main stream—bit of a backwater. Conservative, old-fashioned. All those points make it desirable. Is there anything else?"

There was a stretch of flat agricultural country behind it, running inland. A lot of pasture. Suitable, therefore, for the landing of troop-carrying airplanes or of parachute troops. But that was true of many other places. There was also a big chemical works where, it might be noted, Carl von Deinim was employed.

Carl von Deinim. How did he fit in? Only too well. He was not, as Grant had pointed out, the real head. A cog, only, in the machine. Liable to suspicion and internment at any moment. But in the meantime, he might have accomplished what had been his task. He had mentioned to Tuppence that he was working on decontamination problems and on the immunizing of certain gases. There were probabilities there —probabilities unpleasant to contemplate.

Carl, Tommy decided (a little reluctantly) was in it. A pity, because he rather liked the fellow. Well, he was working for his country— taking his life in his hands. Tommy had respect for such an adversary— down him by all means—a firing party was the end, but you knew that when you took on your job.

It was the people who betrayed their own land—from within—that really roused a slow vindictive passion in him. By God, he'd get them!

—"And that's how I got them!" The major wound up his story triumphantly. "Pretty smart bit of work, eh?"

Unblushingly Tommy said:

"Most ingenious thing I've heard in my life, Major."

II

Mrs. Blenkensop was reading a letter on thin foreign paper, stamped outside with the censor's mark.

"Dear Raymond," she murmured. "I was so happy about him out in Egypt, and now, it seems, there is a big change round. All *very* secret, of course, and he can't *say* anything—just that there really is a marvellous plan and that I'm to be ready for some *big surprises* soon. I'm glad to know where he's being sent, but I really don't see why—"

Bletchley grunted.

"Surely he's not allowed to tell you that?"

Tuppence gave a deprecating laugh and looked round the breakfast table as she folded up her precious letter.

"Oh! We have our methods," she said archly. "Dear Raymond knows that if only I know where he is or where he's going I don't worry quite so much. It's quite a simple way, too. Just a certain word, you know, and after it the initial letters of the next words spell out the place. Of course it makes rather a funny sentence sometimes—but Raymond is really most ingenious. I'm sure *nobody* would notice."

Little murmurs arose round the table. The moment was well chosen, everybody happened to be at the breakfast table together for once.

Bletchley, his face rather red, said:

"You'll excuse me, Mrs. Blenkensop, but that's a damned foolish thing to do. Movements of troops and air squadrons are just what the Germans want to know."

"Oh, but I never tell anyone," cried Tuppence. "I'm very, very careful."

"All the same it's an unwise thing to do—and your boy will get into trouble over it some day."

"Oh, I do hope not. I'm his *mother*, you see. A mother *ought* to know."

"Indeed and I think you're right," boomed out Mrs. O'Rourke. "Wild horses wouldn't drag the information from you—we know that."

"Letters can be read," said Bletchley.

"I'm very careful never to leave letters lying about," said Tuppence with an air of outraged dignity. "I always keep them locked up."

Bletchley shook his head doubtfully.

III

It was a grey morning with the wind blowing coldly from the sea. Tuppence was alone at the far end of the beach.

She took from her bag two letters that she had just called for at a small news agent's in the town.

She opened them.

DEAREST MOTHER,

Lots of funny things I could tell you only I mustn't. We're putting up a good show, I think. Five German planes before breakfast is to-day's market quotation. Bit of a mess at the moment and all that, but we'll get there all right in the end.

It's the way they machine gun the poor civilian devils on the roads that gets me. It makes us all see red. Gus and Trundles want to be remembered to you. They're still going strong.

Don't worry about me. I'm all right. Wouldn't have missed this show for the world. Love to old Carrot Top—have the W.C. given him a job yet?

Yours ever—

DEREK.

Tuppence's eyes were very bright and shining as she read and re-read this.

Then she opened the other letter.

Dearest Mum,

How's old Aunt Gracie? Going strong? I think you're wonderful to stick it. I couldn't.

No news. My job's very interesting, but so hush-hush I can't tell you about it. But I really do feel I'm doing something worth while. Don't fret about not getting any War work to do—it's so silly all these elderly women rushing about wanting to *do* things. They only really want people who are young and efficient. I wonder how Carrots is getting on at his job up in Scotland? Just filling up forms, I suppose. Still he'll be happy to feel he is doing something.

Lots of love.

Deborah.

Tuppence smiled.

She folded the letters, smoothed them lovingly and then under the shelter of a breakwater she struck a match and set them on fire. She waited until they were reduced to ashes.

Taking out her fountain pen and a small writing pad she wrote rapidly.

Langherne,
Cornwall.

Dearest Deb,

It seems so remote from the War here that I can hardly believe there is a War going on. Very glad to get your letter and know that your work is interesting.

Aunt Gracie has grown much more feeble and very hazy in her mind. I think she is glad to have me here. She talks a good deal about the old days and sometimes, I think, confuses me with my own mother. They are growing more vegetables than usual—have turned the rose garden into potatoes. I help old Sikes a bit. It makes me feel I am doing something in the War. Your father seems a bit disgruntled but I think, as you say, he too is glad to be doing something.

Love from your
Tuppenny Mother.

She took a fresh sheet.

Darling Derek,

A great comfort to get your letter. Send field postcards often if you haven't time to write.

I've come down to be with Aunt Gracie a bit. She is very feeble.

She will talk of you as though you were seven and gave me ten shillings yesterday to send you as a tip.

I'm still on the shelf and nobody wants my invaluable services! Extraordinary! Your father, as I told you, has got a job in the Ministry of Requirements. He is up North somewhere. Better than nothing, but not what he wanted, poor old Carrot Top. Still I suppose we've got to be humble and take a back seat and leave the War to you young idiots.

I won't say "Take care of yourself," because I gather that the whole point is that you should do just the opposite. But don't go and be stupid.

Lots of love.

TUPPENCE.

She put the letters into envelopes, addressed and stamped them and posted them on her way back to Sans Souci.

As she reached the bottom of the cliff her attention was caught by two figures standing talking a little way up.

Tuppence stopped dead. It was the same woman she had seen yesterday and talking to her was Carl von Deinim.

Regretfully Tuppence noted the fact that there was no cover. She could not get near them unseen and overhear what was being said.

Moreover, at that moment the young German turned his head and saw her. Rather abruptly, the two figures parted. The woman came rapidly down the hill, crossing the road and passing Tuppence on the other side.

Carl von Deinim waited until Tuppence came up to him.

Then, gravely and politely, he wished her good morning.

Tuppence said immediately:

"What a very odd looking woman that was to whom you were talking, Mr. von Deinim."

"Yes. It is a Central European type. She is a Czech."

"Really? A—a friend of yours?"

Tuppence's tone was a very good copy of the inquisitive voice of Aunt Gracie in her younger days.

"Not at all," said Carl stiffly. "I never saw the woman before."

"Oh, really. I thought—" Tuppence paused artistically.

"She asks me only for a direction. I speak German to her because she does not understand much English."

"I see. And she was asking the way somewhere?"

"She asked me if I knew a Mrs. Gottlieb near here. I do not, and she says she has, perhaps, got the name of the house wrong."

"I see," said Tuppence thoughtfully.

Mr. Rosenstein. Mrs. Gottlieb.

She stole a swift glance at Carl von Deinim. He was walking beside her with a set stiff face.

Tuppence felt a definite suspicion of this strange woman. And she felt almost convinced that when she had first caught sight of them, the woman and Carl had been already talking some time together.

Carl von Deinim?

Carl and Sheila that morning. *"You must be careful. . . ."*

Tuppence thought:

"I hope—I hope these young things *aren't* in it!"

Soft, she told herself, middle-aged and soft! That's what she was! The Nazi creed was a youth creed. Nazi agents would in all probability be young. Carl and Sheila. Tommy said Sheila wasn't in it. Yes, but Tommy was a man, and Sheila was beautiful with a queer breathtaking beauty.

Carl and Sheila, and behind them that enigmatic figure: Mrs. Perenna. Mrs. Perenna, sometimes the voluble, commonplace, guest house hostess, sometimes, for fleeting minutes, a tragic violent personality.

Tuppence went slowly upstairs to her bedroom.

That evening, when Tuppence went to bed, she pulled out the long drawer of her bureau. At one side of it was a small japanned box with a flimsy cheap lock. Tuppence slipped on gloves, unlocked the box, and opened it. A pile of letters lay inside. On the top was the one received that morning from "Raymond." Tuppence unfolded it with due precautions.

Then her lips set grimly. There had been an eyelash in the fold of the paper this morning. The eyelash was not there now.

She went to the washstand. There was a little bottle labelled innocently: "Grey powder" with a dose.

Adroitly Tuppence dusted a little of the powder onto the letter and onto the surface of the glossy japanned enamel of the box.

There were no fingerprints on either of them.

Again Tuppence nodded her head with a certain grim satisfaction. *For there should have been fingerprints—her own.*

A servant might have read letters out of curiosity, though it seemed unlikely—certainly unlikely that she should have gone to the trouble of finding a key to fit the box.

But a servant would not think of wiping off fingerprints.

Mrs. Perenna? Sheila? Somebody else? Somebody, at least, who was interested in the movements of British armed forces.

IV

Tuppence's plan of campaign had been simple in its outlines. First, a general sizing up of probabilities and possibilities. Second, an experiment to determine whether there was or was not an inmate of Sans Souci who was interested in troop movements and anxious to conceal the fact.

Third—who that person was?

It was concerning that third operation that Tuppence pondered as she lay in bed the following morning. Her train of thought was slightly hampered by Betty Sprot, who had pranced in at an early hour, preceding indeed the cup of somewhat tepid inky liquid known as Morning Tea.

Betty was both active and voluble. She had taken a great attachment to Tuppence. She climbed up on the bed and thrust an extremely tattered picture book under Tuppence's nose, commanding with brevity:

"Wead."

Tuppence read obediently:

"Goosey, goosey gander, whither will you wander?
Upstairs, downstairs, in my lady's chamber."

Betty rolled with mirth—repeating in an ecstasy:

"Uptares—uptares—uptares—" and then with a sudden climax: "Down—" and proceeded to roll off the bed with a thump.

This proceeding was repeated several times until it palled. Then Betty crawled about the floor, playing with Tuppence's shoes and muttering busily to herself in her own particular idiom:

"Ag da—bah pit—soo—soo dah—putch—"

Released to fly back to its own perplexities, Tuppence's mind forgot the child. The words of the nursery rhyme seemed to mock at her.

Goosey, goosey gander, whither shall ye wander?

Whither indeed? Goosey, that was her, Gander was Tommy. It was, at any rate, what they appeared to be! Tuppence had the heartiest contempt for Mrs. Blenkensop. Mr. Meadowes, she thought, was a little better—stolid, British, unimaginative—quite incredibly stupid. Both of them, she hoped, fitting nicely into the background of Sans Souci. Both such possible people to be there.

All the same, one must not relax—a slip was so easy. She had made one the other day—nothing that mattered, but just a sufficient indication to warn her to be careful. Such an easy approach to intimacy and good relations—an indifferent knitter asking for guidance. But she had forgotten that one evening, her fingers had slipped into their own practised efficiency, the needles clicking busily with the even note of the experienced knitter. And Mrs. O'Rourke had noticed it. Since then, she had carefully struck a medium course—not so clumsy as she had been at first—but not so rapid as she could be.

"Ag boo bate?" demanded Betty. She reiterated the question: "Ag boo bate?"

"Lovely, darling," said Tuppence absently. "Beautiful."

Satisfied, Betty relapsed into murmurs again.

Her next step, Tuppence thought, could be managed easily enough. That is to say with the connivance of Tommy. She saw exactly how to do it—

Lying there planning, time slipped by. Mrs. Sprot came in, breathless, to seek for Betty.

"Oh, here she is. I couldn't think where she had got to. Oh, Betty, you naughty girl—Oh, dear, Mrs. Blenkensop, I am so sorry."

Tuppence sat up in bed. Betty, with an angelic face, was contemplating her handiwork.

She had removed all the laces from Tuppence's shoes and had immersed them in a glass of water. She was prodding them now with a gleeful finger.

Tuppence laughed and cut short Mrs. Sprot's apologies.

"How frightfully funny. Don't worry, Mrs. Sprot, they'll recover all right. It's my fault. I should have noticed what she was doing. She was rather quiet."

"I know." Mrs. Sprot sighed. "Whenever they're quiet, it's a bad sign. I'll get you some more laces this morning, Mrs. Blenkensop."

"Don't bother," said Tuppence. "They'll dry none the worse."

Mrs. Sprot bore Betty away and Tuppence got up to put her plan into execution.

VI

TOMMY LOOKED RATHER gingerly at the packet that Tuppence thrust upon him.

"Is this it?"

"Yes. Be careful. Don't get it over you."

Tommy took a delicate sniff at the packet and replied with energy: "No, indeed. What is this frightful stuff?"

"Asafoetida," replied Tuppence. "A pinch of that and you will wonder why your boy friend is no longer attentive, as the advertisements say."

"Shades of B.O.," murmured Tommy.

Shortly after that, various incidents occurred.

The first was the Smell in Mr. Meadowes' room.

Mr. Meadowes, not a complaining man by nature, spoke about it mildly at first, then with increasing firmness.

Mrs. Perenna was summoned into conclave. With all the will in the world to resist, she had to admit that there was a smell. A pronounced, unpleasant smell. Perhaps, she suggested, the gas tap of the fire was leaking.

Bending down and sniffing dubiously, Tommy remarked that he did not think the smell came from there. Nor from under the floor. He himself thought, definitely—a dead rat.

Mrs. Perenna admitted that she had heard of such things—but she was sure there were no rats at Sans Souci. Perhaps a mouse—though she herself had never seen a mouse there.

Mr. Meadowes said with firmness that he thought the smell indicated at least a rat—and he added, still more firmly, that he was not going to sleep another night in the room until the matter had been seen to. He would ask Mrs. Perenna to change his room.

Mrs. Perenna said, Of course, she had just been about to suggest the same thing. She was afraid that the only room vacant was rather a small one and unfortunately it had no sea view, but if Mr. Meadowes did not mind that—

Mr. Meadowes did not. His only wish was to get away from the smell. Mrs. Perenna thereupon accompanied him to a small bedroom, the door of which happened to be just opposite the door of Mrs. Blenkensop's room, and summoned the adenoidal, semi-idiotic Beatrice to "move Mr. Meadowes' things." She would, she explained, send for "a man" to take up the floor and search for the origin of the smell.

Matters were settled satisfactorily on this basis.

II

The second incident was Mr. Meadowes' hay fever. That was what he called it at first. Later he admitted doubtfully that he might just possibly have caught cold. He sneezed a good deal, and his eyes ran. If there was a faint elusive suggestion of raw onion floating in the breeze in the vicinity of Mr. Meadowes' large silk handkerchief nobody noticed the fact and indeed a pungent amount of eau de cologne masked the more penetrating odour.

Finally, defeated by incessant sneezing and nose-blowing, Mr. Meadowes retired to bed for the day.

It was on the morning of that day that Mrs. Blenkensop received a letter from her son Douglas. So excited and thrilled was Mrs. Blenkensop that everybody at Sans Souci heard about it. The letter had not been censored at all, she explained, because fortunately one of Douglas's friends coming on leave had brought it, so for once Douglas had been able to write quite fully.

"And it just shows," declared Mrs. Blenkensop, wagging her head sagely, "how little we really know of what is going on."

After breakfast she went upstairs to her room, opened the japanned box and put the letter away. Between the folded pages were some unnoticeable grains of rice powder. She closed the box again, pressing her fingers firmly on its surface.

As she left her room she coughed, and from opposite came the sound of a highly histrionic sneeze.

Tuppence smiled and proceeded downstairs.

She had already made known her intention of going up to London for the day—to see her lawyer on some business and to do a little shopping.

Now she was given a good send-off by the assembled boarders and entrusted with various commissions—"only if you have time, of course."

Major Bletchley held himself aloof from this female chatter. He was reading his paper and uttering appropriate comments aloud. "Damned swines of Germans. Machine gunning civilian refugees on the roads. Damned brutes. If I were our people—"

Tuppence left him still outlining what he would do if he were in charge of operations.

She made a detour through the garden to ask Betty Sprot what she would like as a present from London.

Betty, ecstatically clasping a snail in two hot hands, gurgled appreciatively. In response to Tuppence's suggestions "A pussy? A picture book? Some coloured chalks to draw with?" Betty decided, "Betty dwar." So the coloured chalks were noted down on Tuppence's list.

As she passed on, meaning to rejoin the drive by the path at the end of the garden, she came unexpectedly upon Carl von Deinim. He was standing leaning on the wall. His hands were clenched, and as Tuppence approached he turned on her, his usually impassive face convulsed with emotion.

Tuppence paused involuntarily and asked:

"Is anything the matter?"

"Ach, yes, everything is the matter." His voice was hoarse and unnatural. "You have a saying here that a thing is neither fish, flesh, fowl nor good red herring, have you not?"

Tuppence nodded.

Carl went on bitterly:

"That is what I am. It cannot go on, that is what I say. It cannot go on. It would be best, I think, to end everything."

"What do you mean?"

The young man said:

"You have spoken kindly to me. You would, I think, understand. I fled from my own country because of injustice and cruelty. I came here to find freedom. I hated Nazi Germany. But alas, I am still a German. Nothing can alter that."

Tuppence murmured:

"You must have difficulties, I know—"

"It is not that. I am a German, I tell you. In my heart—in my feeling. Germany is still my country. When I read of German cities bombed, of German soldiers dying, of German aeroplanes brought down—they are my people who die. When that old fire-eating Major reads out from his paper, when he says 'those swine'—I am moved to fury—I cannot bear it."

He added quietly:

"And so I think it would be best, perhaps, to end it all. Yes, to end it."

Tuppence took hold of him firmly by the arm.

"Nonsense," she said robustly. "Of course you feel as you do. Anyone would. But you've got to stick it."

"I wish they would intern me. It would be easier so."

"Yes, probably it would. But in the meantime you're doing useful work—or so I've heard. Useful not only to England but to humanity. You're working on decontamination problems, aren't you?"

His face lit up slightly.

"Ah, yes, and I begin to have much success. A process very simple, easily made and not complicated to apply."

"Well," said Tuppence, "that's worth doing. Anything that mitigates suffering is worth while—and anything that's constructive and not destructive. Naturally we've got to call the other side names. They're doing just the same in Germany. Hundreds of Major Bletchleys—foaming at the mouth. I hate the Germans myself. 'The Germans,' I say, and feel waves of loathing. But when I think of individual Germans, mothers sitting anxiously waiting for news of their sons, and boys leaving home to fight, and peasants getting in the harvests, and little shopkeepers and some of the nice kindly German people I know, I feel quite different. I know then they are just human beings and that we're all feeling alike. That's the real thing. The other is just the War mask that you put on. It's a part of War—probably a necessary part—but it's ephemeral."

As she spoke she thought, as Tommy had done not long before, of Nurse Cavell's words: "Patriotism is not enough. I must have no hatred in my heart."

That saying of a most truly patriotic woman had always seemed to them both the high water mark of sacrifice.

Carl von Deinim took her hand and kissed it. He said:

"I thank you. What you say is good and true. I will have more fortitude."

"Oh, dear," thought Tuppence as she walked down the road into the town. "How very unfortunate that the person I like best in this place should be a German. It makes everything cock-eyed!"

III

Tuppence was nothing if not thorough. Although she had no wish to go to London, she judged it wise to do exactly as she had said she was going to do. If she merely made an excursion somewhere for the day, somebody might see her and the fact would get round to Sans Souci.

No, Mrs. Blenkensop had said she was going to London and to London she must go.

She purchased a third return and was just leaving the booking office window when she ran into Sheila Perenna.

"Hullo," said Sheila. "Where are you off to? I just came to see about a parcel which seems to have gone astray."

Tuppence explained her plans.

"Oh, yes, of course," said Sheila carelessly. "I do remember you saying something about it, but I hadn't realized it was today you were going. I'll come and see you into the train."

Sheila was more animated than usual. She looked neither bad tempered nor sulky. She chatted quite amiably about small details of daily life at Sans Souci. She remained talking to Tuppence until the train left the station.

After waving from the window and watching the girl's figure recede, Tuppence sat down in her corner seat again and gave herself up to serious meditation.

Was it, she wondered, an accident that Sheila had happened to be at the station just at that time? Or was it a proof of enemy thoroughness? Did Mrs. Perenna want to make quite sure that the garrulous Mrs. Blenkensop really *had* gone to London?

It looked very much like it.

IV

It was not until the next day that Tuppence was able to have a conference with Tommy. They had agreed never to attempt to communicate with each other under the roof of Sans Souci.

Mrs. Blenkensop met Mr. Meadowes as the latter, his hay fever somewhat abated, was taking a gentle stroll on the front. They sat down on one of the promenade seats.

"Well?" said Tuppence.

Slowly, Tommy nodded his head. He looked rather unhappy.

"Yes," he said. "I got something. But, Lord, what a day. Perpetually with an eye to the crack of the door. I've got quite a stiff neck."

"Never mind your neck," said Tuppence unfeelingly. "Tell me."

"Well, the maids went in to do the bed and the room, of course. And Mrs. Perenna went in—but that was when the maids were there and she was just blowing them up about something. And the kid ran in once and came out with a woolly dog."

"Yes, yes. Anyone else?"

"One person," said Tommy slowly.

"Who?"

"Carl von Deinim."

"Oh." Tuppence felt a swift pang. So, after all—

"When?" she asked.

"Lunch time. He came out from the dining room early, came up to his room, then sneaked across the passage and into yours. He was there about a quarter of an hour."

He paused.

"That settles it, I think?"

Tuppence nodded.

Yes, it settled it all right. Carl von Deinim could have no reason for going into Mrs. Blenkensop's bedroom and remaining there for a quarter of an hour save one. His complicity was proved. He must be, Tuppence thought, a marvellous actor . . .

His words to her that morning had rung so very true. Well, perhaps they had been true in a way. To know when to use the truth was the essence of successful deception. Carl von Deinim was a patriot all right, he was an enemy agent working for his country. One could respect him for that. Yes—but destroy him too.

"I'm sorry," she said slowly.

"So am I," said Tommy. "He's a good chap."

Tuppence said:

"You and I might be doing the same thing in Germany."

Tommy nodded. Tuppence went on.

"Well, we know more or less where we are. Carl von Deinim working in with Sheila and her mother. Probably Mrs. Perenna is the big noise. Then there is that foreign woman who was talking to Carl yesterday. She's in it somehow."

"What do we do now?"

"We must go through Mrs. Perenna's room some time. There might be something there that would give us a hint. And we must tail her—see where she goes and whom she meets. Tommy, let's get Albert down here."

Tommy considered the point.

Some years ago, Albert, a page boy in a hotel, had joined forces with the young Beresfords and shared their adventures. Afterwards he had entered their service and been the sole domestic prop of the establishment. Some six years ago he had married and was now the proud proprietor of The Duck and Dog pub in South London.

Tuppence continued rapidly:

"Albert will be thrilled. We'll get him down here. He can stay at that pub near the station and he can shadow the Perennas for us—or anyone else."

"What about Mrs. Albert?"

"She was going to her mother in Wales with the children last Monday. Because of Air Raids. It all fits in perfectly."

"Yes, that's a good idea, Tuppence. Either of us following the woman about would be rather conspicuous. Albert will be perfect. Now another thing—I think we ought to watch out for that so-called Czech woman who was talking to Carl and hanging about here. It seems to me that she probably represents the other end of the business—and that's what we're anxious to find."

"Oh, yes, I do agree. She comes here for orders, or to take messages. Next time we see her, one of us must follow her and find out more about her."

"What about looking through Mrs. Perenna's room—and Carl's, too, I suppose?"

"I don't suppose you'll find anything in his. After all, as a German, the police are liable to search it and so he'd be careful not to have anything suspicious. The Perenna is going to be difficult. When she's out of the house, Sheila is often here, and there's Betty and Mrs. Sprot running about all over the landings, and Mrs. O'Rourke spends a lot of time in her bedroom."

She paused.

"Lunch time is the best."

"Master Carl's time?"

"Exactly. I could have a headache and go to my room— No, some-one might come up and want to minister to me. I know, I'll just come in quietly before lunch and go up to my room without telling anyone. Then, after lunch, I can say I had a headache."

"Hadn't I better do it? My hay fever could recrudesce tomorrow."

"I think it had better be me. If I'm caught I could always say I was looking for aspirin or something. One of the gentlemen boarders in Mrs. Perenna's room would cause far more speculation."

Tommy grinned.

"Of a scandalous character."

Then the smile died. He looked grave and anxious.

"As soon as we can, old thing. The news is bad today. We must get on to something soon."

v

Tommy continued his walk and presently entered the post office, where he put through a call to Mr. Grant, and reported "the recent operation was successful and our friend C is definitely involved."

Then he wrote a letter and posted it. It was addressed to Mr. Albert Batt, The Duck and Dog, Glamorgan St., Kensington.

Then he bought himself a weekly paper which professed to inform the English world of what was really going to happen and strolled innocently back in the direction of Sans Souci.

Presently he was hailed by the hearty voice of Commander Haydock leaning from his two seater car and shouting, "Hullo, Meadowes, want a lift?"

Tommy accepted the lift gratefully and got in.

"So you read that rag, do you?" demanded Haydock, glancing at the scarlet cover of the *Inside Weekly News*.

Mr. Meadowes displayed the slight confusion of all readers of the periodical in question when challenged.

"Awful rag," he agreed. "But sometimes, you know, they really do seem to know what's going on behind the scenes."

"And sometimes they're wrong."

"Oh, quite so."

"Truth of it is," said Commander Haydock, steering rather erratically round a one-way island and narrowly missing collision with a large van, "when the beggars are right, you remember it, and when they're wrong you forget it."

"Do you think there's any truth in this rumour about Stalin having approached us?"

"Wishful thinking, my boy, wishful thinking," said Commander Haydock. "The Russkys are as crooked as Hell and always have been. Don't trust 'em, that's what I say. Hear you've been under the weather?"

"Just a touch of hay fever. I get it about this time of year."

"Yes, of course. Never suffered from it myself, but I had a pal who did. Used to lay him out regularly every June. Feeling fit enough for a game of golf?"

Tommy said he'd like it very much.

"Right. What about tomorrow? Tell you what, I've got to go to a meeting about this Parashot business, raising a corps of local volunteers—jolly good idea, if you ask me. Time we were all made to pull our weight. So shall we have a round about six?"

"Thanks very much. I'd like to."

"Good. Then that's settled."

The Commander drew up abruptly at the gate of Sans Souci.

"How's the fair Sheila?" he asked.

"Quite well, I think. I haven't seen much of her."

Haydock gave his loud barking laugh.

"Not as much as you'd like to, I bet! Good looking girl, that, but damned rude. She sees too much of that German fellow. Damned unpatriotic, I call it. Daresay she's got no use for old fogies like you or me, but there are plenty of nice lads going about in our own services. Why take up with a bloody German? That sort of thing riles me."

Mr. Meadowes said:

"Be careful, he's just coming up the hill behind us."

"Don't care if he does hear! Rather hope he does. I'd like to kick Master Carl's behind for him. Any decent German's fighting for his country—not slinking over here to get out of it!"

"Well," said Tommy. "It's one less German to invade England at all events."

"You mean he's here already? Ha, ha! rather good, Meadowes! Not that I believe this tommyrot about invasion. We never have been invaded and never will be. We've got a Navy, thank God!"

With which patriotic announcement the Commander let in his clutch with a jerk and the car leaped forward up the hill to Smugglers' Rest.

VI

Tuppence arrived at the gate of Sans Souci at twenty minutes to two. She turned off from the drive and went through the garden and into the house through the open drawing room window. A smell of Irish stew and the clatter of plates and murmur of voices came from afar. Sans Souci was hard at work on its midday meal.

Tuppence waited by the drawing room door until Martha, the maid, had passed across the hall and into the dining room, then she ran quickly up the stairs, shoeless.

She went into the room, put on her soft felt bedroom slippers, and then went along the landing and into Mrs. Perenna's room.

Once inside she looked round her and felt a certain distaste sweep over her. Not a nice job, this. Quite unpardonable if Mrs. Perenna was simply Mrs. Perenna. Prying into people's private affairs—

Tuppence shook herself, an impatient terrier shake that was a reminiscence of her girlhood. *There was a War on!*

She went over to the dressing table.

Quick and deft in her movements, she had soon gone through the contents of the drawers there. In the tall bureau, one of the drawers was locked. That seemed more promising.

Tommy had been entrusted with certain tools and had received some brief instruction on the manipulation of them. These indications he had passed on to Tuppence.

A deft twist or two of the wrist and the drawer yielded.

There was a cash box containing twenty pounds in notes and some piles of silver—also a jewel case. And there was a heap of papers. These last were what interested Tuppence most. Rapidly she went through them; necessarily it was a cursory glance. She could not afford time for more.

Papers relating to a mortgage on Sans Souci, a bank account, letters. Time flew past, Tuppence skimmed through the documents, concentrating furiously on anything that might bear a double meaning. Two letters from a friend in Italy, rambling discursive letters, seemingly quite harmless. But possibly not so harmless as they sounded. A letter from one Simon Mortimer, of London—a dry business-like letter containing so little of moment that Tuppence wondered why it had been kept. Was Mr. Mortimer not so harmless as he seemed? At the bottom of the pile a letter in faded ink signed Pat and beginning *"This will be the last letter I'll be writing you, Eileen my darling—"*

No, not that! Tuppence could not bring herself to read that! She refolded it, tidied the letters on top of it and then, suddenly alert, pushed the drawer to—no time to re-lock it—and when the door opened and Mrs. Perenna came in, she was searching vaguely amongst the bottles on the washstand.

Mrs. Blenkensop turned a flustered, but foolish face towards her hostess.

"Oh, Mrs. Perenna, do forgive me. I came in with such a blinding headache, and I thought I would lie down on my bed with a little aspirin, and I couldn't find mine, so I thought you wouldn't mind—I know you must have some because you offered it to Miss Minton the other day."

Mrs. Perenna swept into the room. There was a sharpness in her voice as she said:

"Why, of course, Mrs. Blenkensop, why ever didn't you come and ask me?"

"Well, of course, yes, I should have done really. But I knew you were all at lunch, and I do so hate, you know, making a *fuss—*"

Passing Tuppence, Mrs. Perenna caught up the bottle of aspirin from the washstand.

"How many would you like?" she demanded crisply.

Mrs. Blenkensop accepted three. Escorted by Mrs. Perenna she crossed to her own room and hastily demurred to the suggestion of a hot water bottle.

Mrs. Perenna used her parting shot as she left the room.

"But you have some aspirin of your own, Mrs. Blenkensop. I've seen it."

Tuppence cried quickly:

"Oh, I know. I know I've got some somewhere, but, so stupid of me, I simply couldn't lay my hands on it."

Mrs. Perenna said, with a flash of her big white teeth:

"Well, have a good rest until tea time."

She went out, closing the door behind her. Tuppence drew a deep breath, lying on her bed rigidly lest Mrs. Perenna should return.

Had the other suspected anything? Those teeth, so big and so white —the better to eat you with, my dear. Tuppence always thought of that when she noticed those teeth. Mrs. Perenna's hands, too, big, cruel-looking hands.

She had appeared to accept Tuppence's presence in her bedroom quite naturally. But later she would find the bureau drawer unlocked. Would she suspect then? Or would she think she had left it unlocked herself by accident? One did do such things. Had Tuppence been able to replace the papers in such a way that they looked much the same as before?

Surely, even if Mrs. Perenna did notice anything amiss she would be more likely to suspect one of the servants than she would "Mrs. Blenkensop." And if she did suspect the latter, wouldn't it be a mere case of suspecting her of undue curiosity? There were people, Tuppence knew, who did poke and pry.

But then, if Mrs. Perenna were the renowned German agent, M, she would be suspicious of counterespionage.

Had anything in her bearing revealed undue alertness?

She had seemed natural enough—only that one sharply pointed remark about the aspirin.

Suddenly, Tuppence sat up on her bed. She remembered that her aspirin, together with some iodine and a bottle of soda mints were all together at the back of the writing table drawer where she had shoved them when unpacking.

It would seem, therefore, that she was not the only person to snoop in other people's rooms. Mrs. Perenna had got there first.

VII

On the following day Mrs. Sprot went up to London.

A few tentative remarks on her part had led immediately to various offers on the part of the inhabitants of Sans Souci to look after Betty.

When Mrs. Sprot, with many final adjurations to Betty to be a very good girl, had departed, Betty attached herself to Tuppence, who had elected to take morning duty.

"Play," said Betty. "Play hide seek."

She was talking more easily every day and had adopted a most fetching habit of laying her head on one side, fixing her interlocutor with a bewitching smile and murmuring:

"*Peese.*"

Tuppence had intended taking her for a walk, but it was raining hard, so the two of them adjourned to the bedroom where Betty led the way to the bottom drawer of the bureau where her playthings were kept.

"Hide Bonzo, shall we?" asked Tuppence.

But Betty had changed her mind and demanded instead:

"Wead me story."

Tuppence pulled out a rather tattered book from one end of the cupboard—to be interrupted by a squeal from Betty.

"No, no. Narsty . . . Bad . . ."

Tuppence stared at her in surprise and then down at the book, which was a coloured version of *Little Jack Horner*.

"Was Jack a bad boy?" she asked. "Because he pulled out a plum?"

Betty reiterated with emphasis:

"Ba-a-ad!" and with a terrific effort, "Dirrty!"

She seized the book from Tuppence and replaced it in the line, then tugged out an identical book from the other end of the shelf, announcing with a beaming face:

"K-k-klean ni-i-ice Jackorner!"

Tuppence realized that the dirty and worn books had been replaced by new and cleaner editions and was rather amused. Mrs. Sprot was very much what Tuppence thought of as "the hygienic mother." Always terrified of germs, of impure food, or of the child suckling a soiled toy.

Tuppence, brought up in a free and easy Rectory life, was always rather contemptuous of exaggerated hygiene and had brought up her own two children to absorb what she called a "reasonable amount" of dirt. However, she obediently took out the clean copy of Jack Horner and read it to the child with the comments proper to the occasion. Betty murmuring, "*That's* Jack!— Plum!— In a *Pie*," pointing out these interesting objects with a sticky finger that bade fair to soon consign this second copy to the scrap heap. They proceeded to *Goosey Goosey Gander* and the *Old Woman Who Lived in a Shoe*, and then Betty hid the books and Tuppence took an amazingly long time to find each of them, to Betty's great glee, and so the morning passed rapidly away.

After lunch Betty had her rest and it was then that Mrs. O'Rourke invited Tuppence into her room.

Mrs. O'Rourke's room was very untidy and smelled strongly of peppermint and stale cake, with a faint odour of moth balls added. There were photographs on every table of Mrs. O'Rourke's children and grandchildren and nieces and nephews and great nieces and great nephews. There were so many of them that Tuppence felt as though she were looking at a realistically produced play of the late Victorian period.

" 'Tis a grand way you have with children, Mrs. Blenkensop," observed Mrs. O'Rourke genially.

"Oh, well," said Tuppence, "with my own two—"

Mrs. O'Rourke cut in quickly:

"Two? It was three boys I understood you had?"

"Oh, yes, three. But two of them are very near in age and I was thinking of the days spent with them."

"Ah! I see. Sit down now, Mrs. Blenkensop. Make yourself at home."

Tuppence sat down obediently and wished that Mrs. O'Rourke did not always make her feel so uncomfortable. She felt now exactly like Hansel or Gretel accepting the witch's invitation.

"Tell me now," said Mrs. O'Rourke. "What do you think of Sans Souci?"

Tuppence began a somewhat gushing speech of eulogy, but Mrs. O'Rourke cut her short without ceremony.

"What I'd be asking you is if you don't feel there's something odd about the place?"

"Odd? No, I don't think so."

"Not about Mrs. Perenna? You're interested in her, you must allow. I've seen you watching her and watching her."

Tuppence flushed.

"She—she's an interesting woman."

"She is not then," said Mrs. O'Rourke. "She's a commonplace woman enough—that is if she's what she seems. But perhaps she isn't. Is that your idea?"

"Really, Mrs. O'Rourke, I don't know *what* you mean."

"Have you ever stopped to think that many of us are that way—different to what we seem on the surface. Mr. Meadowes, now. He's a puzzling kind of man. Sometimes I'd say he was a typical Englishman, stupid to the core, and there's other times I'll catch a look or a word that's not stupid at all. It's odd that, don't you think so?"

Tuppence said firmly:

"Oh, I really think Mr. Meadowes is *very* typical."

"There are others. Perhaps you'll know who I'll be meaning?"

Tuppence shook her head.

"The name," said Mrs. O'Rourke encouragingly, "begins with an S."
She nodded her head several times.

With a sudden spark of anger and an obscure impulse to spring to
the defense of something young and vulnerable, Tuppence said
sharply:

"Sheila's just a rebel. One usually is, at that age."

Mrs. O'Rourke nodded her head several times, looking just like an
obese china mandarin that Tuppence remembered on her Aunt
Gracie's mantelpiece. A vast smile tilted up the corners of her mouth.
She said softly:

"You mayn't know it, but Miss Minton's Christian name is Sophia."

"Oh!" Tuppence was taken aback. "Was it Miss Minton you meant?"

"It was not," said Mrs. O'Rourke.

Tuppence turned away to the window. Queer how this old woman
could affect her, spreading about her an atmosphere of unrest and
fear. "Like a mouse between a cat's paws," thought Tuppence. "That's
what I feel like . . ."

This vast smiling monumental old woman, sitting there, almost purring—and yet there was the pat-pat of paws playing with something
that wasn't, in spite of the purring, to be allowed to get away . . .

Nonsense—all nonsense! I imagine these things, thought Tuppence,
staring out of the window into the garden. The rain had stopped.
There was a gentle patter of raindrops off the trees.

Tuppence thought: "It isn't all my fancy. I'm not a fanciful person.
There is something, some focus of evil here. If I could see—"

Her thoughts broke off abruptly.

At the bottom of the garden the bushes parted slightly. In the gap
a face appeared, staring stealthily up at the house. It was the face of
the foreign woman who had stood talking to Carl von Deinim in the
road.

It was so still, so unblinking in its regard, that it seemed to Tuppence as though it was not human. Staring, staring up at the windows of Sans Souci. It was devoid of expression, and yet there was—
yes, undoubtedly there was, menace about it. Immobile, implacable. It
represented some spirit, some force, alien to Sans Souci and the
commonplace banality of English guest house life. So, Tuppence
thought, might Jael have looked, waiting to drive the nail through the
forehead of sleeping Sisera.

These thoughts took only a second or two to flash through Tuppence's mind. Turning abruptly from the window, she murmured

something to Mrs. O'Rourke, hurried out of the room and ran down stairs and out of the front door.

Turning to the right, she ran down the side garden path to where she had seen the face. There was no one there now. Tuppence went through the shrubbery and out on to the road and looked up and down the hill. She could see no one. Where had the woman gone?

Vexed, she turned and went back into the grounds of Sans Souci. Could she have imagined the whole thing? No, the woman had been there.

Obstinately she wandered round the garden, peering behind bushes. She got very wet and found no trace of the strange woman. She retraced her steps to the house with a vague feeling of foreboding—a queer formless dread of something about to happen.

She did not guess, would never have guessed, what that something was going to be.

II

Now that the weather had cleared, Miss Minton was dressing Betty preparatory to taking her out for a walk. They were going down to the town to buy a celluloid duck to sail in Betty's bath.

Betty was very excited and capered so violently that it was extremely difficult to insert her arms into the woolly pullover. The two set off together, Betty chattering violently: "Byaduck. Byaduck. For Bettibarf. For Bettibarf," and deriving great pleasure from a ceaseless reiteration of these important facts.

Two matches, left carelessly crossed on the marble table in the hall, informed Tuppence that Mr. Meadowes was spending the afternoon on the trail of Mrs. Perenna. Tuppence betook herself to the drawing room and the company of Mr. and Mrs. Cayley.

Mr. Cayley was in a fretful mood. He had come to Leahampton, he explained, for absolute rest and quiet, and what quiet could there be with a child in the house? All day long it went on, screaming and running about, jumping up and down on the floors—

His wife murmured pacifically that Betty was really a dear little mite, but the remark met with no favour.

"No doubt, no doubt," said Mr. Cayley, wriggling his long neck. "But her mother should keep her quiet. There are other people to consider. Invalids, people whose nerves need repose."

Tuppence said: "It's not easy to keep a child of that age quiet. It's not natural—there would be something wrong with the child if she was quiet."

Mr. Cayley gobbled angrily:

"Nonsense—nonsense—this foolish modern spirit. Letting children do exactly as they please. A child should be made to sit down quietly and—and nurse a doll—or read, or something."

"She's not three yet," said Tuppence, smiling. "You can hardly expect her to be able to read."

"Well, something must be done about it. I shall speak to Mrs. Perenna. The child was singing, singing in her bed before seven o'clock this morning. I had had a bad night and just dropped off towards morning—and it woke me right up."

"It's very important that Mr. Cayley should get as much sleep as possible," said Mrs. Cayley anxiously. "The doctor said so."

"You should go to a nursing home," said Tuppence.

"My dear lady, such places are ruinously expensive and besides it's not the right atmosphere. There is a suggestion of illness that reacts unfavourably on my sub-conscious."

"Bright society, the doctor said," Mrs. Cayley explained helpfully. "A normal life. He thought a guest house would be better than just taking a furnished house. Mr. Cayley would not be so likely to brood, and would be stimulated by exchanging ideas with other people."

Mr. Cayley's method of exchanging ideas was, so far as Tuppence could judge, a mere recital of his own ailments and symptoms and the exchange consisted in the sympathetic or unsympathetic reception of them.

Adroitly, Tuppence changed the subject.

"I wish you would tell me," she said, "of your own views on life in Germany. You told me you had travelled there a good deal in recent years. It would be interesting to have the point of view of an experienced man of the world like yourself. I can see you are the kind of man, quite unswayed by prejudice, who could really give a clear account of conditions there."

Flattery, in Tuppence's opinion, should always be laid on with a trowel where a man was concerned. Mr. Cayley rose at once to the bait.

"As you say, dear lady, I am capable of taking a clear unprejudiced view. Now, in my opinion—"

What followed constituted a monologue. Tuppence, throwing in an occasional "Now that's very interesting," or "What a shrewd observer you are," listened with an attention that was not assumed for the occasion. For Mr. Cayley, carried away by the sympathy of his listener, was displaying himself as a decided admirer of the Nazi system. How much better it would have been, he hinted, if he did not say, for England and Germany to have allied themselves against the rest of Europe.

The return of Miss Minton and Betty, the celluloid duck duly obtained, broke in upon the monologue, which had extended unbroken for nearly two hours. Looking up, Tuppence caught rather a curious expression on Mrs. Cayley's face. She found it hard to define. It might be merely pardonable wifely jealousy at the monopoly of her husband's attention by another woman. It might be alarm at the fact that Mr. Cayley was being too outspoken in his political views. It certainly expressed dissatisfaction.

Tea was the next move and hard on that came the return of Mrs. Sprot from London, exclaiming:

"I do hope Betty's been good and not troublesome? Have you been a good girl, Betty?" To which Betty replied laconically by the single word:

"Dam!"

This, however, was not to be regarded as an expression of disapproval at her mother's return, but merely as a request for blackberry preserve.

It elicited a deep chuckle from Mrs. O'Rourke and a reproachful: "Please, Betty, dear," from the young lady's parent.

Mrs. Sprot then sat down, drank several cups of tea, and plunged into a spirited narrative of her purchases in London, the crowd on the train, what a soldier recently returned from France had told the occupants of her carriage, and what a girl behind the stocking counter had told her of a recent air raid in one of the suburbs.

The conversation was, in fact, completely normal. It was prolonged afterwards on the terrace outside, for the sun was now shining and the wet day a thing of the past.

Betty rushed happily about, making mysterious expeditions into the bushes and returning with a laurel leaf, or a heap of pebbles which she placed in the lap of one of the grown-ups with a confused and unintelligible explanation of what it represented. Fortunately she required little co-operation in her game, being satisfied with an occasional "How nice, darling. Is it really?"

Never had there been an evening more typical of Sans Souci at its most harmless. Chatter, gossip, speculations as to the course of the war—can France rally? Will Weygand pull things together? What is Russia likely to do? Could Hitler invade England if he tried? Will Paris fall if the "bulge" is not straightened out? Was it true that . . . ? It had been said that . . . And it was rumoured that . . .

Political and military scandal was happily bandied about.

Tuppence thought to herself: "Chatterbugs a danger? Nonsense, they're a safety valve. People *enjoy* these rumours. It gives them the stimulation to carry on with their own private worries and anxieties." She contributed a nice tidbit prefixed by, "My son told me—of course this is *quite* private, you understand—"

Suddenly, with a start, Mrs. Sprot glanced at her watch.

"Goodness, it's nearly seven. I ought to have put that child to bed hours ago. Betty—Betty!"

It was some time since Betty had returned to the terrace, though no one had noticed her defection.

Mrs. Sprot called her with rising impatience.

"Bett-eeee! Where can the child be?"

Mrs. O'Rourke said, with her deep laugh:

"Up to mischief, I've no doubt of it. 'Tis always the way when there's peace."

"Betty! I want you."

There was no answer and Mrs. Sprot rose impatiently.

"I suppose I must go and look for her. I wonder where she can be?"

Miss Minton suggested that she was hiding somewhere and Tuppence, with memories of her own childhood, suggested the kitchen. But Betty could not be found, either inside or outside the house. They went round the garden calling, looking all over the bedrooms. There was no Betty anywhere.

Mrs. Sprot began to get annoyed.

"It's very naughty of her—very naughty indeed! Do you think she can have gone out on the road?"

Together she and Tuppence went out to the gate and looked up and down the hill. There was no one in sight except a tradesman's boy with a bicycle standing talking to a maid at the door of St. Lucian's opposite.

On Tuppence's suggestion, she and Mrs. Sprot crossed the road and the latter asked if either of them had noticed a little girl. They both shook their heads and then the servant asked, with sudden recollection:

"A little girl in a green checked gingham dress?"

Mrs. Sprot said eagerly:

"That's right."

"I saw her about half an hour ago—going down the road with a woman."

Mrs. Sprot said, with astonishment:

"With a woman? What sort of a woman?"

The girl seemed slightly embarrassed.

"Well, what I'd call an odd looking kind of woman. A foreigner she was. Queer clothes. A kind of shawl thing and no hat, and a strange sort of face—queer like, if you know what I mean. I've seen her about once or twice lately, and to tell the truth I thought she was a bit wanting— If you know what I mean," she added helpfully.

In a flash Tuppence remembered the face she had seen that afternoon peering through the bushes and the foreboding that had swept over her.

But she had never thought of the woman in connection with the child, could not understand it now.

She had little time for meditation, however. Mrs. Sprot almost collapsed against her.

"Oh, Betty, my little girl. She's been kidnapped. She—what did the woman look like—a gypsy?"

Tuppence shook her head energetically.

"No, she was fair, very fair, a broad face with high cheek bones and blue eyes set very far apart."

She saw Mrs. Sprot staring at her and hastened to explain.

"I saw the woman this afternoon—peering through the bushes at the bottom of the garden. And I've noticed her hanging about. Carl von Deinim was speaking to her one day. It must be the same woman."

The servant girl chimed in to say:

"That's right. Fair-haired, she was. And wanting, if you ask me. Didn't understand nothing that was said to her."

"Oh, God," moaned Mrs. Sprot. "What shall I do?"

Tuppence passed an arm round her.

"Come back to the house, have a little brandy and then we'll ring up the police. It's all right. We'll get her back."

Mrs. Sprot went with her meekly, murmuring in a dazed fashion:

"I can't imagine how Betty would go like that with a stranger."

"She's very young," said Tuppence. "Not old enough to be shy."

Mrs. Sprot cried out weakly:

"Some dreadful German woman, I expect. She'll kill my Betty."

"Nonsense," said Tuppence robustly. "It will be all right. I expect she's just some woman who's not quite right in her head." But she did not believe her own words—did not believe for one moment that that calm blond woman was an irresponsible lunatic.

Carl! Would Carl know? Had Carl something to do with this?

A few minutes later she was inclined to doubt this. Carl von Deinim, like the rest, seemed amazed, unbelieving, completely surprised.

As soon as the facts were made plain, Major Bletchley assumed control.

"Now then, dear lady," he said to Mrs. Sprot, "sit down here—just drink a little drop of this—brandy—it won't hurt you—and I'll get straight on to the police station."

Mrs. Sprot murmured:

"Wait a minute—there might be something—"

She hurried up the stairs and along the passage to hers and Betty's room.

A minute or two later they heard her footsteps running wildly along the landing. She rushed down the stairs like a demented woman and clutched Major Bletchley's hand from the telephone receiver, which he was just about to lift.

"No, no," she panted. "You mustn't—you mustn't . . ."

And sobbing wildly, she collapsed into a chair.

They crowded around her. In a minute or two, she recovered her composure. Sitting up, with Mrs. Cayley's arm round her, she held something out for them to see.

"I found this—on the floor of my room. It had been wrapped round a stone and thrown through the window. Look—look what it says."

Tommy took it from her and unfolded it.

It was a note, written in a queer stiff foreign handwriting, big and bold.

WE HAVE GOT YOUR CHILD IN SAFE KEEPING. YOU WILL BE TOLD WHAT TO DO IN DUE COURSE. IF YOU GO TO THE POLICE YOUR CHILD WILL BE KILLED. SAY NOTHING. WAIT FOR INSTRUCTIONS. IF NOT— X.

Mrs. Sprot was moaning faintly:

"Betty—Betty—"

Everyone was talking at once. "The dirty murdering scoundrels!" from Mrs. O'Rourke. "Brutes!" from Sheila Perenna. "Fantastic, fantastic—I don't believe a word of it. Silly practical joke," from Mr. Cayley. "Oh, the dear, wee mite," from Miss Minton. "I do not understand. It is incredible," from Carl von Deinim. And above everyone else the strenuous voice of Major Bletchley:

"Damned nonsense. Intimidation. We must inform the police at once. They'll soon get to the bottom of it."

Once more he moved towards the telephone. This time a scream of outraged motherhood from Mrs. Sprot stopped him.

He shouted:

"But, my dear Madam, it's *got* to be done. This is only a crude device to prevent you getting on the track of these scoundrels."

"They'll kill her."

"Nonsense. They wouldn't dare."

"I won't have it, I tell you. I'm her mother. It's for me to say."

"I know. I know. That's what they're counting on—your feeling like that. Very natural. But you must take it from me, a soldier and an experienced man of the world, the police are what we need."

"*No!*"

Bletchley's eyes went round seeking allies.

"Meadowes, you agree with me?"

Slowly, Tommy nodded.

"Cayley? Look, Mrs. Sprot, both Meadowes and Cayley agree."

Mrs. Sprot said, with sudden energy:

"Men! All of you! Ask the women!"

Tommy's eyes sought Tuppence. Tuppence said, her voice low and shaken:

"I—I agree with Mrs. Sprot."

She was thinking, "Deborah! Derek! If it were them. I'd feel like her. Tommy and the others are right, I've no doubt, but all the same I couldn't do it. I couldn't risk it."

Mrs. O'Rourke was saying:

"No mother alive could risk it and that's a fact."

Mrs. Cayley murmured:

"I do think, you know, that—well—" and tailed off into incoherence.

Miss Minton said tremulously:

"Such awful things happen. We'd never forgive ourselves if anything happened to dear little Betty."

Tuppence said sharply:

"You haven't said anything, Mr. von Deinim?"

Carl's blue eyes were very bright. His face was a mask. He said slowly and stiffly:

"I am a foreigner. I do not know your English police. How competent they are—how quick."

Someone had come into the hall. It was Mrs. Perenna; her cheeks were flushed. Evidently she had been hurrying up the hill. She said:

"What's all this?" And her voice was commanding, imperious, not the complaisant guest house hostess, but a woman of force.

They told her—a confused tale told by too many people, but she grasped it quickly.

And with her grasping of it, the whole thing seemed, in a way, to be passed up to her for judgment. She was the supreme court.

She held the hastily scrawled note a minute, then she handed it back. Her words came sharp and authoritative.

"The police? They'll be no good. You can't risk their blundering. Take the law into your own hands. Go after the child yourself."

Bletchley said, shrugging his shoulders:

"Very well. If you won't call in the police, it's the best thing to be done."

Tommy said:

"They can't have got much of a start."

"Half an hour, the maid said," Tuppence put in.

"Haydock," said Bletchley. "Haydock's the man to help us. He's got a car. The woman's unusual looking, you say? And a foreigner? Ought to leave a trail that we can follow. Come on, there's no time to be lost. You'll come along, Meadowes?"

Mrs. Sprot got up.

"I'm coming, too."

"Now, my dear lady, leave it to us—"

"I'm coming, too."

"Oh, well—"

He gave in—murmuring something about the female of the species being deadlier than the male.

III

In the end Commander Haydock, taking in the situation with commendable Naval rapidity, drove the car. Tommy sat beside him, and behind were Bletchley, Mrs. Sprot and Tuppence. Not only did Mrs. Sprot cling to her, but Tuppence was the only one (with the exception of Carl von Deinim) who knew the mysterious kidnapper by sight.

The Commander was a good organizer and a quick worker. In next to no time, he had filled up the car with petrol, tossed a map of the district and a larger scale map of Leahampton itself to Bletchley and was ready to start off.

Mrs. Sprot had run upstairs again, presumably to her room to get a coat. But when she got into the car and they had started down the hill she disclosed to Tuppence something in her handbag. It was a small pistol.

She said quietly:

"I got it from Major Bletchley's room. I remember his mentioning one day that he had one."

Tuppence looked a little dubious.

"You don't think that—"

Mrs. Sprot said, her mouth a thin line:

"It may come in useful."

Tuppence sat marvelling at the strange forces maternity will set loose in an ordinary, commonplace young woman. She could visualize Mrs. Sprot, the kind of woman who would normally declare herself frightened to death of firearms, coolly shooting down any person who had harmed her child.

They drove first, on the Commander's suggestion, to the railway station. A train had left Leahampton about twenty minutes earlier and it was possible that the fugitives had gone by it.

At the station they separated, the Commander taking the ticket collector, Tommy the booking office, and Bletchley the porters outside. Tuppence and Mrs. Sprot went into the Ladies' Room on the chance that the woman had gone in there to change her appearance before taking the train.

One and all drew blank. It was now more difficult to shape a course. In all probability, as Haydock pointed out, the kidnappers had had a car waiting, and once Betty had been persuaded to come away with the woman, they had made their getaway in that. It was here, as Bletchley pointed out once more, that the co-operation of the police was so vital. It needed an organization of that kind who could send out messages all over the country, covering the different roads.

Mrs. Sprot merely shook her head, her lips pressed tightly together.

Tuppence said:

"We must put ourselves in their places. Where would they have waited in the car? Somewhere as near Sans Souci as possible, but where a car wouldn't be noticed. Now let's *think*. The woman and Betty walk down the hill together. At the bottom is the esplanade. The car might have been drawn up there. So long as you don't leave it un-attended you can stop there for quite a while. The only other places are the Car Park in James Square, also quite near, or else one of the small streets that lead off from the esplanade."

It was at that moment that a small man, with a diffident manner and pince-nez, stepped up to them and said, stammering a little:

"Excuse me. . . . No offense, I hope . . . but I c-c-couldn't help overhearing what you were asking the porter just now." (He now di-rected his remarks to Major Bletchley.) "I was not listening, of course; just came down to see about a parcel—extraordinary how long things are delayed just now—movements of troops, they say—but really most difficult when it's perishable—the parcel, I mean—and so, you see, I hap-pened to overhear—and really it did seem the most wonderful coincidence . . ."

Mrs. Sprot sprang forward. She seized him by the arm.

"You've seen her? You've seen my little girl?"

"Oh, really, your little girl, you say? Now fancy that—"

Mrs. Sprot cried: "Tell me." And her fingers bit into the little man's arm so that he winced.

Tuppence said quickly:

"Please tell us anything you have seen as quickly as you can. We shall be most grateful if you will."

"Oh, well, really, of course, it may be nothing at all. But the descrip-tion fitted so well—"

Tuppence felt the woman beside her trembling, but she herself strove to keep her manner calm and unhurried. She knew the type with which they were dealing—fussy, muddle-headed, diffident, inca-pable of going straight to the point and worse if hurried. She said:

"Please tell us."

"It was only—my name is Robbins, by the way, Edward Robbins—"

"Yes, Mr. Robbins."

"I live at Whiteways, in Ernes Cliff Road, one of those new houses on the new road—most labour saving, and really *every* convenience, and a beautiful view and the downs only a stone's throw away."

With a glance Tuppence quelled Major Bletchley, who she saw was about to break out, and she said:

"And you saw the little girl we are looking for?"

"Yes, I really think it *must* be. A little girl with a foreign looking woman, you said? It was really the woman I noticed. Because, of course, we are all on the lookout nowadays for Fifth Columnists, aren't we? A sharp lookout, that is what they say, and I always try to do so, and so, as I say, I noticed the woman. A nurse, I thought, or a maid—a lot of spies came over here in that capacity, and this woman was most unusual looking and walking up the road and on to the downs—with a little girl—and the little girl seemed tired and rather lagging, and half past seven, well, most children go to bed then, so I looked at the woman pretty sharply. I think it flustered her. She hurried to the road, pulling the child after her, and finally picked her up and went on up the path out on to the cliff, which I thought *strange*, you know, because there are no houses there at all—nothing—not until you get to White-haven—about five miles over the downs—a favourite walk for hikers. But in this case I thought it odd. I wondered if the woman was going to signal, perhaps. One hears of so much enemy activity and she certainly looked uneasy when she saw me staring at her."

Commander Haydock was back in the car and had started the engine. He said:

"Ernes Cliff Road, you say? That's right the other side of the town, isn't it?"

"Yes, you go along the esplanade and past the old town and then up—"

The others had jumped in, not listening further to Mr. Robbins. Tuppence called out:

"Thank you, Mr. Robbins," and they drove off leaving him staring after them with his mouth open.

They drove rapidly through the town, avoiding accidents more by good luck than by skill. But the luck held. They came out at last at a mass of straggling building development, somewhat marred by proximity to the gas works. A series of little roads led up towards the downs, stopping abruptly a short way up the hill. Ernes Cliff Road was the third of these.

Commander Haydock turned smartly into it and drove up. At the end the road petered out on to bare hillside up which a footpath meandered.

"Better get out and walk here," said Bletchley.

Haydock said dubiously:

"Could almost take the car up. Ground's firm enough. Bit bumpy but I think she could do it."

Mrs. Sprot cried:

"Oh, yes, please, please. . . . We must be quick."

The Commander murmured to himself.

"Hope to goodness we're after the right lot. That little pip-squeak may have seen any woman with a kid."

The car groaned uneasily as she ploughed her way up over the rough ground. The gradient was severe, but the turf was short and springy. They came out without mishap on the top of the rise. Here the view was less interrupted till it rested in the distance on the curve of Whitehaven Bay.

Bletchley said:

"Not a bad idea. The woman could spend the night up here if need be, drop down into Whitehaven tomorrow morning and take a train there."

Haydock said:

"No signs of them as far as I can see."

He was standing up holding to his eyes some field glasses that he had thoughtfully brought with him. Suddenly his figure became tense as he focussed the glasses on two small moving dots.

"Got 'em, by Jove. . . ."

He dropped into the driver's seat again and the car bucketed forward. The chase was a short one now. Shot up in the air, tossed from side to side, the occupants of the car gained rapidly on those two small dots. They could be distinguished now—a tall figure and a short one—nearer still, a woman holding a child by the hand—still nearer, yes, a child in a green gingham frock. Betty.

Mrs. Sprot gave a strangled cry.

"All right now, my dear," said Major Bletchley, patting her kindly. "We've got 'em."

They went on. Suddenly the woman turned and saw the car advancing towards her.

With a cry she caught up the child in her arms and began running. She ran, not forward, but sideways towards the edge of the cliff.

The car, after a few yards, could not follow, the ground was too uneven and blocked with big boulders. It stopped and the occupants tumbled out.

Mrs. Sprot was out first and running wildly after the two fugitives. The others followed her.

When they were within twenty yards, the other woman turned at bay. She was standing now at the very edge of the cliff. With a hoarse cry she clutched the child closer.

Haydock cried out:

"My God, she's going to throw the kid over the cliff. . . ."

The woman stood there, clutching Betty tightly. Her face was disfigured with a frenzy of hate. She uttered a long hoarse sentence that none of them understood. And still she held the child and looked from time to time at the drop below—not a yard from where she stood.

It seemed clear that she was threatening to throw the child over the cliff.

All of them stood there, dazed, terrified, unable to move for fear of precipitating a catastrophe.

Haydock was tugging at his pocket. He pulled out a service revolver. He shouted:

"Put that child down—or I fire."

The foreign woman laughed. She held the child closer to her breast. The two figures were moulded into one.

Haydock muttered:

"I daren't shoot. I'd hit the child."

Tommy said:

"The woman's crazy. She'll jump over with the child in another moment."

Haydock said again, helplessly:

"I daren't shoot—"

But at that moment a shot rang out. The woman swayed and fell, the child still clasped in her arms.

The men ran forward. Mrs. Sprot stood swaying, the smoking pistol in her hand, her eyes dilated.

She took a few stiff steps forward.

Tommy was kneeling by the bodies. He turned them gently. He saw the woman's face—noted appreciatively its strange wild beauty. The eyes opened, looked at him, then went blank. With a little sigh, the woman died, shot through the head.

Unhurt, little Betty Sprot wriggled out and ran towards her mother who was standing like a statue.

Then, at last, Mrs. Sprot crumpled. She flung away the pistol and dropped down, clutching the child to her.

She cried:

"She's safe—she's safe— Oh, Betty—*Betty*." And then, in a low, awed whisper:

"Did I—did I—kill her?"

Tuppence said firmly:

"Don't think about it—don't think about it. Think about Betty. Just think about Betty."

Mrs. Sprot held the child close against her, sobbing.

Tuppence went forward to join the men.

Haydock murmured:

"Bloody miracle. I couldn't have brought off a shot like that. Don't believe the woman's ever handled a pistol before either—sheer instinct. A miracle, that's what it is."

Tuppence said:

"Thank God! It was a near thing!" And she looked down at the sheer drop to the sea below and shuddered.

VIII

IT WAS NOT until some days later that Mrs. Blenkensop and Mr. Meadowes were able to meet and compare notes.

The intervening days had been busy. The dead woman had been identified as Vanda Polonska, a Polish refugee who had entered the country soon after the outbreak of war. Very little was known about her, but she appeared to have received certain sums of money from an unknown source which pointed to the probability of her being an enemy agent of some kind.

"And so it's a blank wall as usual," said Tommy gloomily.

Tuppence nodded.

"Yes, they seal up both ends, don't they? No papers, no hints of any kind as to who she had dealings with."

"Too damned efficient," said Tommy.

He added:

"You know, Tuppence, I don't like the look of things."

Tuppence assented. The news was indeed far from reassuring.

The French Army was in retreat and it seemed doubtful if the tide could be turned. Evacuation from Dunkerque was in progress. It was clearly a matter of a few days only before Paris fell. There was a general dismay at the revelation of lack of equipment and of material for resisting the Germans' great mechanized units.

Tommy said:

"Is it only our usual muddling and slowness? Or has there been deliberate engineering behind this?"

"The latter, I think, but they'll never be able to prove it."

"No. Our adversaries are too darned clever for that."

"We are combing out a lot of the rot now."

"Oh, yes, we're rounding up the obvious people, but I don't believe we've got at the brains that are behind it all. Brains, organization, a whole carefully thought-out plan—a plan which uses our habits of dilatoriness, and our petty feuds, and our slowness for its own ends."

Tuppence said:

"That's what we're here for—and we haven't got results."

"We've done something," Tommy reminded her.

"Carl von Deinim and Vanda Polonska, yes. The small fry."

"You think they were working together?"

"I think they must have been," said Tuppence thoughtfully. "Remember, I saw them talking."

"Then Carl von Deinim must have engineered the kidnapping."

"I suppose so."

"But why?"

"I don't know," said Tuppence. "That's what I keep thinking and thinking about. It doesn't make sense."

"Why kidnap that particular child? Who are the Sprots? They've no money—so it isn't ransom. They're neither of them employed by the Government in any capacity."

"I know, Tommy. It just doesn't make any sense at all."

"Hasn't Mrs. Sprot any idea herself?"

"That woman," said Tuppence scornfully, "hasn't got the brains of a hen. She doesn't think at all. Just says it's the sort of thing the wicked Germans would do."

"Silly ass," said Tommy. "The Germans are efficient. If they send one of their agents to kidnap a brat, it's for some reason."

"I've a feeling, you know," said Tuppence, "that Mrs. Sprot could get at the reason if only she'd think about it. There must be something

—some piece of information that she herself has inadvertently got hold of, perhaps without knowing what it is exactly."

"*Say nothing. Wait for instructions.*" Tommy quoted from the note found on Mrs. Sprot's bedroom floor. "Damn it all, that means something."

"Of course it does—it must. The only thing I can think of is that Mrs. Sprot, or her husband, has been given something to keep by someone else—given it, perhaps, just because they are such humdrum ordinary people that no one would ever suspect they had it—whatever 'it' may be."

"It's an idea, that."

"I know—but it's awfully like a spy story. It doesn't seem real somehow."

"Have you asked Mrs. Sprot to rack her brains a bit?"

"Yes, the trouble is that she isn't really interested. All she cares about is getting Betty back—that, and having hysterics because she's shot someone."

"Funny creatures, women," mused Tommy. "There was that woman, went out that day like an avenging fury, she'd have shot down a regiment in cold blood without turning a hair just to get her child back, and then, having shot the kidnapper by a perfectly incredible fluke, she breaks down and comes all over squeamish about it."

"The coroner exonerated her all right," said Tuppence.

"Naturally. By Jove, I wouldn't have risked firing when she did." Tuppence said:

"No more would she, probably, if she'd known more about it. It was sheer ignorance of the difficulty of the shot that made her bring it off." Tommy nodded.

"Quite Biblical," he said. "David and Goliath."

"Oh!" said Tuppence.

"What is it, old thing?"

"I don't quite know. When you said that something twanged somewhere in my brain, and now it's gone again!"

"Very useful," said Tommy.

"Don't be scathing. That sort of thing does happen sometimes."

"Gentleman who drew a bow at a venture, was that it?"

"No, it was—wait a minute—I think it was something to do with Solomon."

"Cedars, temples, a lot of wives and concubines?"

"Stop," said Tuppence, putting her hands to her ears. "You're making it worse."

"Jews?" said Tommy hopefully. "Tribes of Israel?"

But Tuppence shook her head. After a minute or two she said: "I wish I could remember who it was that woman reminded me of."

"The late Vanda Polonska?"

"Yes. The first time I saw her her face seemed vaguely familiar."

"Do you think you had come across her somewhere else?"

"No, I'm sure I hadn't."

"Mrs. Perenna and Sheila are a totally different type."

"Oh, yes, it wasn't them. You know, Tommy, about those two. I've been thinking."

"To any good purpose?"

"I'm not sure. It's about that note—the one Mrs. Sprot found on the floor in her room when Betty was kidnapped."

"Well?"

"All that about its being wrapped round a stone and thrown through the window is rubbish. It was put there by someone—ready for Mrs. Sprot to find—and I think it was Mrs. Perenna who put it there."

"Mrs. Perenna, Carl, Vanda Polonska—all working together."

"Yes. Did you notice how Mrs. Perenna came in just at the critical moment and clinched things—not to ring up the police? She took command of the whole situation."

"So she's still your selection for M?"

"Yes, isn't she yours?"

"I suppose so," said Tommy slowly.

"Why, Tommy, have you got another idea?"

"It's probably an awfully dud one."

"Tell me."

"No, I'd rather not. I've nothing to go on. Nothing whatever. But if I'm right, it's not M we're up against, but N."

He thought to himself:

"Bletchley. I suppose he's all right. Why shouldn't he be? He's a true enough type—almost too true, and after all, it was he who wanted to ring up the police. Yes, but he could have been pretty sure that the child's mother wouldn't stand for the idea. The threatening note made sure of that. He could afford to urge the opposite point of view—"

And that brought him back again to the vexing, teasing problem to which as yet he could find no answer.

Why kidnap Betty Sprot?

II

There was a car standing outside Sans Souci bearing the word PO-LICE on it.

Absorbed in her own thoughts Tuppence took little notice of that. She turned in at the drive and entering the front door went straight upstairs to her own room.

She stopped, taken aback, on the threshold, as a tall figure turned away from the window.

"Dear me," said Tuppence. "Sheila?"

The girl came straight towards her. Now Tuppence saw her more clearly, saw the blazing eyes deep set in the white tragic face.

Sheila said:

"I'm glad you've come. I've been waiting for you."

"What's the matter?"

The girl's voice was quiet and devoid of emotion. She said:

"They have arrested Carl!"

"The police?"

"Yes."

"Oh, dear," said Tuppence. She felt inadequate to the situation.

Quiet as Sheila's voice had been, Tuppence was under no misapprehension as to what lay behind it.

Whether they were fellow conspirators or not, this girl loved Carl von Deinim, and Tuppence felt her heart aching in sympathy with this tragic young creature.

Sheila said:

"What shall I do?"

The simple forlorn question made Tuppence wince. She said helplessly:

"Oh, my dear."

Sheila said, and her voice was like a mourning harp:

"They've taken him away. I shall never see him again."

She cried out:

"What shall I do? What shall I do?" And flinging herself down on her knees by the bed, she wept her heart out.

Tuppence stroked the dark head. She said presently, in a weak voice:

"It—it may not be true. Perhaps they are only going to intern him. After all, he is an enemy alien, you know."

"That's not what they said. They're searching his room now."

Tuppence said slowly, "Well, if they find nothing—"

"They will find nothing, of course! What should they find?"

"I don't know. I thought perhaps you might?"

"I?"

Her scorn, her amazement were too real to be feigned. Any suspicions Tuppence had had that Sheila Perenna was involved died at this moment. The girl knew nothing, had never known anything.

Tuppence said:

"If he is innocent—"

Sheila interrupted her.

"What does that matter? The police will make a case against him."

Tuppence said sharply:

"Nonsense, my dear child, that really isn't true."

"The English police will do anything. My Mother says so."

"Your Mother may say so, but she's wrong. I assure you that it isn't so."

Sheila looked at her doubtfully for a minute or two. Then she said:

"Very well. If you say so. I trust you."

Tuppence felt very uncomfortable. She said sharply:

"You trust too much, Sheila. You may have been unwise to trust Carl."

"Are you against him, too? I thought you liked him. He thinks so, too."

Touching young things—with their faith in one's liking for them. And it was true—she had liked Carl—she did like him.

Rather wearily she said:

"Listen, Sheila, liking or not liking has nothing to do with facts. This country and Germany are at war. There are many ways of serving one's country. One of them is to get information—and to work behind the lines. It is a brave thing to do, for when you are caught, it is"—her voice broke a little—"the end."

Sheila said:

"You think Carl—"

"Might be working for his country that way? It is a possibility, isn't it?"

"No," said Sheila.

"It would be his job, you see, to come over here as a refugee, to appear to be violently anti-Nazi and then to gather information."

Sheila said quietly:

"It's not true. I know Carl. I know his heart and his mind. He cares most for science—for his work—for the truth and the knowledge in it. He is grateful to England for letting him work here. Sometimes, when people say cruel things, he feels German and bitter. But he hates the Nazis always and what they stand for—their denial of freedom."

Tuppence said:

"He would say so, of course."

Sheila turned reproachful eyes upon her.

"So you believe he is a spy?"

"I think it is"—Tuppence hesitated—"a possibility."

Sheila walked to the door.

"I see. I'm sorry I came to ask you to help us."

"But what did you think I could do, dear child?"

"You know people. Your sons are in the Army and Navy and I've heard you say more than once that they knew influential people. I thought perhaps you could get them to—to do—something?"

Tuppence thought of those mythical creatures, Douglas and Raymond and Cyril.

"I'm afraid," she said, "that they couldn't do anything."

Sheila flung her head up. She said passionately:

"Then there's no hope for us. They'll take him away and shut him up, and one day, early in the morning, they'll stand him against a wall and shoot him—and that will be the end."

She went out, shutting the door behind her.

"Oh, damn, damn, damn the Irish!" thought Tuppence in a fury of mixed feelings. "Why have they got that terrible power of twisting things until you don't know where you are? If Carl von Deinim's a spy, he deserves to be shot. I must hang on to that, not let that girl with her Irish voice bewitch me into thinking it's the tragedy of a hero and a martyr!"

She recalled the voice of a famous actress speaking a line from *Riders to the Sea.*

"It's the fine quiet time they'll be having. . . ."

Poignant . . . carrying you away on a tide of feeling . . .

She thought, "If it weren't true. Oh, if only it weren't true. . . ."

Yet, knowing what she did, how could she doubt?

III

The fisherman on the end of the Old Pier cast in his line and then reeled it cautiously in.

"No doubt whatever, I'm afraid," he said.

"You know," said Tommy, "I'm sorry about it. He's—well, he's a nice chap."

"They are, my dear fellow, they usually are. It isn't the skunks and the rats of a land who volunteer to go to the enemy's country. It's the brave men. We know that well enough. But there it is, the case is proved."

"No doubt whatever, you say?"

"No doubt at all. Among his chemical formulae was a list of people in the factory to be approached, as possible Fascist sympathizers. There was also a very clever scheme of sabotage and a chemical process that, applied to fertilizers, would have devastated large areas of food stocks. All well up Master Carl's street."

Rather unwillingly, Tommy said, secretly anathematizing Tuppence who had made him promise to say it:

"I suppose it's not possible that these things could have been planted on him?"

Mr. Grant smiled, rather a diabolical smile.

"Oh," he said. "Your wife's idea, no doubt."

"Well—er—yes, as a matter of fact it is."

"He's an attractive lad," said Mr. Grant tolerantly.

Then he went on:

"No, seriously, I don't think we can take that suggestion into account. He'd got a supply of secret ink, you know. That's a pretty good clinching test. And it wasn't obvious as it would have been if planted. It wasn't 'the mixture to be taken when required' on the washstand or anything like that. In fact, it was damned ingenious. Only come across the method once before and then it was waistcoat buttons. Steeped in the stuff, you know. When the fellow wants to use it, he soaks a button in water. Carl von Deinim's wasn't buttons. It was a shoe-lace. Pretty neat."

"Oh!" Something stirred in Tommy's mind—vague—wholly nebulous. . . .

Tuppence was quicker. As soon as he retailed the conversation to her, she seized on the salient point.

"A shoe-lace? Tommy, that explains it!"

"What?"

"Betty, you idiot! Don't you remember that funny thing she did in my room, taking out my laces and soaking them in water. I thought at the time it was a funny thing to think of doing. But, of course, she'd seen Carl do it and was imitating him. He couldn't risk her talking about it and so he arranged with that woman for her to be kidnapped."

Tommy said, "Then that's cleared up."

"Yes. It's nice when things begin to fall into shape. You can put them behind you and get on a bit."

"We need to get on."

Tuppence nodded.

The times were gloomy indeed. France had astonishingly and suddenly capitulated—to the bewilderment and dismay of her own people.

The destination of the French Navy was in doubt.

Now the coasts of France were entirely in the hands of Germany and the talk of invasion was no longer a remote contingency.

Tommy said:

"Carl von Deinim was only a link in the chain. Mrs. Perenna's the fountain head."

"Yes, we've got to get the goods on her. But it won't be easy."

"No. After all, if she's the brains of the whole thing, one can't expect it to be."

"Was M Mrs. Perenna?"

Tommy supposed she must be. He said slowly:

"You really think the girl isn't in this at all?"

"I'm quite sure of it."

Tommy sighed.

"Well, you should know. But if so, it's tough luck on her. First the man she loves—and then her mother. She's not going to have much left, is she?"

"We can't help that."

"Yes, but supposing we're wrong—that M or N is someone else?"

Tuppence said rather coldly:

"So you're still harping on that? Are you sure it isn't a case of wishful thinking?"

"What do you mean?"

"Sheila Perenna—that's what I mean."

"Aren't you being rather absurd, Tuppence?"

"No, I'm not. She's got round you, Tommy, just like any other man—"

Tommy replied angrily:

"Not at all. It's simply that I've got my own ideas."

"Which are?"

"I think I'll keep them to myself for a bit. We'll see which of us is right."

"Well, I think we've got to go all out after Mrs. Perenna. Find out where she goes, whom she meets—everything. There must be a link somewhere. You'd better put Albert on to her this afternoon."

"You can do that. I'm busy."

"Why, what are you doing?"

Tommy said:

"I'm playing golf."

IX

"SEEMS QUITE LIKE old times, doesn't it, Madam?" said Albert. He beamed happily. Though now, in his middle years, running somewhat to fat, Albert had still the romantic boy's heart which had first led him into associations with Tommy and Tuppence in their young and adventurous days.

"Remember how you first came across me?" demanded Albert. "Cleanin' of the brasses, I was, in those top notch flats. Coo, wasn't that hall porter a nasty bit of goods? Always on to me, he was. And the day you come along and strung me a tale! Pack of lies it was, too, all about a crook called Ready Rita. Not but what some of it didn't turn out to be true. And since then, as you might say, I've never looked back. Many's the adventure we had afore we all settled down, so to speak."

Albert sighed, and by a natural association of ideas Tuppence inquired after the health of Mrs. Albert.

"Oh, the Missus is all right—but she doesn't take to the Welsh much, she says. Thinks they ought to learn proper English, and as for raids—why, they've had two there already, and holes in the field what you could put a motor car in, so she says. So—how's that for safety? Might as well be in Kensington, she says, where she wouldn't have to see all them melancholy trees and could get good clean milk in a bottle."

"I don't know," said Tuppence, suddenly stricken, "that we ought to get you into this, Albert."

"Nonsense, Madam," said Albert. "Didn't I try and join up and they was so haughty they wouldn't look at me. Wait for my age group to be called up, they said. And me in the pink of health and only too eager to get at them perishing Germans—if you'll excuse the language. You just tell me how I can put a spoke in their wheel and spoil their goings on—and I'm there. Fifth Column, that's what we're up against, so the papers say—though what's happened to the other four they don't mention. But the long and short of it is, I'm ready to assist you and Captain Beresford in any way you like to indicate."

"Good. Now I'll tell you what we want you to do."

II

"How well do you know Bletchley?" asked Tommy, as he stepped off the tee and watched with approval his ball leaping down the centre of the fairway.

Commander Haydock who had also done a good drive had a pleased expression on his face as he shouldered his clubs and replied:

"Bletchley? Let me see. Oh! About nine months or so. He came here last Autumn."

"Friend of friends of yours, I think you said?" Tommy suggested mendaciously.

"Did I?" The Commander looked a little surprised. "No, I don't think so. Rather fancy I met him here at the Club."

"Bit of a mystery man, I gather?"

The Commander was clearly surprised this time.

"Mystery man? Old Bletchley?" He sounded frankly incredulous. Tommy sighed inwardly. He supposed he was imagining things.

He played his next shot—and topped it. Haydock had a good iron shot that stopped just short of the green. As he rejoined the other, he said:

"What on earth makes you call Bletchley a mystery man? I should have said he was a painfully prosaic chap—typical Army. Bit set in his ideas and all that—narrow life, an Army life—but mystery!"

Tommy said vaguely:

"Oh, well, I just got the idea from something somebody said—"

They got down to the business of putting. The Commander won the hole.

"Three up and two to play," he remarked with satisfaction.

Then, as Tommy had hoped, his mind, free of the preoccupation of the match, harked back to what Tommy had said.

"What sort of mystery do you mean?" he asked.

Tommy shrugged his shoulders.

"Oh, it was just that nobody seemed to know much about him."

"He was in the Rugbyshires."

"Oh, you know that definitely?"

"Well, I—well, no, I don't know myself. I say, Meadowes, what's the idea? Nothing wrong about Bletchley, is there?"

"No, no, of course not." Tommy's disclaimer came hastily. He had started his hare. He could now sit back and watch the Commander's mind dodging after it.

"Always struck me as an almost absurdly typical sort of chap," said Haydock.

"Just so, just so."

"Ah, yes—see what you mean. Bit too much of a type, perhaps?"

"I'm leading the witness," thought Tommy. "Still perhaps something may crop up out of the old boy's mind."

"Yes, I do see what you mean," the Commander went on thoughtfully. "And now I come to think of it I've never actually come across anyone who knew Bletchley before he came down here. He doesn't have any old pals to stay—nothing of that kind."

"Ah!" said Tommy—and added, "Shall we play the bye? Might as well get a bit more exercise. It's a lovely evening."

They drove off, then separated to play their next shots. When they met again on the green, Haydock said abruptly:

"Tell me what you heard about him?"

"Nothing—nothing at all."

"No need to be so cautious with me, Meadowes. I hear all sorts of rumours. You understand? Everyone comes to me. I'm known to be pretty keen on the subject. What's the idea—that Bletchley isn't what he seems to be?"

"It was only the merest suggestion."

"What do they think he is? A Hun? Nonsense, the man's as English as you and I."

"Oh, yes, I'm sure he's quite all right."

"Why, he's always yelling for more foreigners to be interned. Look how violent he was against that young German chap—and quite right, too, it seems. I heard unofficially from the Chief Constable that they found enough to hang von Deinim a dozen times over. He'd got a scheme to poison the water supply of the whole country and he was actually working out a new gas—working on it in one of our factories. My God, the shortsightedness of our people! Fancy letting the fellow inside the place to begin with. Believe anything, our Government would! A young fellow has only to come to this country just before war starts and whine a bit about persecution and they shut both eyes and let him into all our secrets. They were just as dense about that fellow Hahn—"

Tommy had no intention of letting the Commander run ahead on the well-grooved track. He deliberately missed a putt.

"Hard lines," cried Haydock. He played a careful shot. The ball rolled into the hole.

"My hole. A bit off your game today. What were we talking about?"

Tommy said firmly:

"About Bletchley being perfectly all right."

"Of course. Of course. I wonder now—I did hear a rather funny story about him—didn't think anything of it at the time—"

Here, to Tommy's annoyance, they were hailed by two other men. The four returned to the clubhouse together and had drinks. After that, the Commander looked at his watch and remarked that he and Meadowes must be getting along. Tommy had accepted an invitation to supper with the Commander.

Smugglers' Rest was in its usual condition of apple pie order. A tall middle-aged manservant waited on them with the professional deftness of a waiter. Such perfect service was somewhat unusual to find outside of a London restaurant.

When the man had left the room, Tommy commented on the fact.

"Yes, I was lucky to get Appledore."

"How did you get hold of him?"

"He answered an advertisement as a matter of fact. He had excellent references, was clearly far superior to any of the others who applied and asked remarkably low wages. I engaged him on the spot."

Tommy said with a laugh:

"The war has certainly robbed us of most of our good restaurant service. Practically all good waiters were foreigners. It doesn't seem to come naturally to the Englishman."

"Bit too servile, that's why. Bowing and scraping doesn't come kindly to the English bulldog."

Sitting outside, sipping coffee, Tommy gently asked:

"What was it you were going to say on the links? Something about a funny story—apropos to Bletchley."

"What was it now? Hullo, did you see that? Light being shown out at sea. Where's my telescope!"

Tommy sighed. The stars in their courses seemed to be fighting against him. The Commander fussed into the house and out again, swept the horizon with his glass, outlined a whole system of signalling by the enemy to likely spots on shore, most of the evidence for which seemed to be non-existent, and proceeded to give a gloomy picture of a successful invasion in the near future.

"No organization, no proper co-ordination. You're a L.D.V. yourself, Meadowes—you know what it's like. With a man like old Andrews in charge—"

This was well-worn ground. It was Commander Haydock's pet grievance. He ought to be the man in command and he was quite determined to oust Col. Andrews if it could possibly be done.

The manservant brought out whisky and liqueurs while the Commander was still holding forth.

"—and we're still honeycombed with spies—riddled with 'em. It was the same in the last war—hairdressers, waiters—"

Tommy, leaning back, catching the profile of Appledore as the latter hovered deft-footed, thought—"Waiters? You could call that fellow Fritz easier than Appledore. . . ."

Well, why not? The fellow spoke perfect English, true, but then many Germans did. They had perfected their English by years in English restaurants. And the racial type was not unlike. Fair-haired, blue-eyed—often betrayed by the shape of the head—yes, the head—where had he seen a head lately?

He spoke on an impulse. The words fitted in appropriately enough with what the Commander was just saying.

"All these damned forms to fill in. No good at all, Meadowes. Series of idiotic questions—"

Tommy said:

"I know. Such as—'What is your name? Answer N or M.'"

There was a swerve—a crash. Appledore, the perfect servant, had blundered. A stream of crème de menthe soaked over Tommy's cuff and hand.

The man stammered, "Sorry, sir."

Haydock blazed out in fury.

"You damned clumsy fool! What the Hell do you think you're doing?"

His usually red face was quite purple with anger. Tommy thought: "Talk of an Army temper—Navy beats it hollow!" Haydock continued with a stream of abuse. Appledore was abject in apologies.

Tommy felt uncomfortable for the man, but suddenly, as though by magic, the Commander's wrath passed and he was his hearty self again.

"Come along and have a wash. Beastly stuff. It would be the crème de menthe."

Tommy followed him **indoors** and was soon in the sumptuous bathroom with the innumerable **gadgets**. He carefully washed off the sticky sweet stuff. The Commander talked from the bedroom next door. He sounded a little shamefaced.

"Afraid I let myself go a bit. Poor old Appledore—he knows I let go a bit more than I mean always."

Tommy turned from the washbasin drying his hands. He did not notice that a cake of soap had slipped onto the floor. His foot stepped on it. The linoleum was highly polished.

A moment later Tommy was doing a wild ballet dancer step. He shot across the bathroom, arms outstretched. One came up heavily against the right hand tap of the bath, the other pushed heavily against the side of a small bathroom cabinet. It was an extravagant gesture never likely to be achieved except by some catastrophe such as had just occurred.

His foot skidded heavily against the end panel of the bath.

The thing happened like a conjuring trick. The bath slid out from the ball, turning on a concealed pivot. Tommy found himself looking into a dim recess. He had no doubt whatever as to what occupied that recess. It contained a transmitting wireless apparatus.

The Commander's voice had ceased. He appeared suddenly in the doorway. And with a click, several things fell into place in Tommy's brain.

Had he been blind up to now? That jovial florid face—the face of a "hearty Englishman"—was only a mask. Why had he not seen it all along for what it was—the face of a bad-tempered, overbearing Prussian officer. Tommy was helped, no doubt, by the incident that had just happened. For it recalled to him another incident, a Prussian bully turning on a subordinate and rating him with the Junker's true insolence. So had Commander Haydock turned on his subordinate that evening when the latter had been taken unawares.

And it all fitted in—it fitted in like magic. The double bluff. The enemy agent Hahn, sent first, preparing the place, employing foreign workmen, drawing attention to himself and proceeding finally to the next stage in the plan, his own unmasking by the gallant British sailor Commander Haydock. And then how natural that the Englishman should buy the place and tell the story to everyone, boring them by constant repetition. And so M, securely settled in his appointed place with sea communications and his secret wireless and his staff officers at Sans Souci close at hand, N is ready to carry out Germany's plan.

Tommy was unable to resist a flash of genuine admiration. The whole thing had been so perfectly planned. He himself had never suspected Haydock—he had accepted Haydock as the genuine article—only a completely unforeseen accident had given the show away.

All this passed through Tommy's mind in a few seconds. He knew, only too well, that he was, that he must necessarily be in deadly peril. If only he could act the part of the credulous thick-headed Englishman well enough.

He turned to Haydock with what he hoped was a natural sounding laugh.

"By Jove, one never stops getting surprises at your place. Was this another of Hahn's little gadgets? You didn't show me this the other day."

Haydock was standing very still. There was a tensity about his big body as it stood there blocking the door.

"More than a match for me," Tommy thought. "And there's that confounded servant, too."

For an instant Haydock stood as though moulded in stone, then he relaxed. He said with a laugh:

"Damned funny, Meadowes. You went skating over the floor like a ballet dancer! Don't suppose a thing like that would happen once in a thousand times. Dry your hands and come along into the other room."

Tommy followed him out of the bathroom. He was alert and tense in every muscle. Somehow or other he must get safely away from this house with his knowledge. Could he succeed in fooling Haydock? The latter's tone sounded natural enough.

With an arm round Tommy's shoulders, a casual arm, perhaps (or perhaps not), Haydock shepherded him into the sitting room. Turning, he shut the door behind them.

"Look here, old boy, I've got something to say to you."

His voice was friendly, natural—just a shade embarrassed. He motioned to Tommy to sit down.

"It's a bit awkward," he said. "Upon my word, it's a bit awkward! Nothing for it, though, but to take you into my confidence. Only you'll have to keep dark about it, Meadowes. You understand that?"

Tommy endeavoured to throw an expression of eager interest upon his face.

Haydock sat down and drew his chair confidentially close.

"You see, Meadowes, it's like this. Nobody's supposed to know it but I'm working on Intelligence. M.I.42 B.X.—that's my department. Ever heard of it?"

Tommy shook his head and intensified the eager expression.

"Well, it's pretty secret. Kind of inner ring, if you know what I mean. We transmit certain information from here—but it would be absolutely fatal if that fact got out, you understand?"

"Of course, of course," said Mr. Meadowes. "Most interesting! Naturally you can count on me not to say a word."

"Yes, that's absolutely vital. The whole thing is extremely confidential."

"I quite understand. Your work must be most thrilling. Really most thrilling. I should like so much to know more about it—but I suppose I mustn't ask that?"

"No, I'm afraid not. It's very secret, you see."

"Oh, yes, I see. I really do apologize—a most extraordinary accident—"

He thought to himself:

"Surely he can't be taken in? He can't imagine I'd fall for this stuff?"

It seemed incredible to him. Then he reflected that vanity had been the undoing of many men. Commander Haydock was a clever man, a big fellow—this miserable chap Meadowes was a stupid Britisher— the sort of man who would believe anything! If only Haydock continued to think that.

Tommy went on talking. He displayed keen interest and curiosity. He knew he mustn't ask questions but—he supposed Commander Haydock's work must be very dangerous? Had he ever been in Germany, working there?

Haydock replied genially enough. He was intensely the British sailor now—the Prussian officer had disappeared. But Tommy, watching him with a new vision, wondered how he could ever have been deceived. The shape of the head—the line of the jaw—nothing British about them.

Presently Mr. Meadowes rose. It was the supreme test. Would it go off all right?

"I really must be going now—getting quite late—feel terribly apologetic, but can assure you will not say a word to anybody."

("It's now or never. Will he let me go or not? I must be ready—a straight to his jaw would be best—")

Talking amiably and with pleasurable excitement, Mr. Meadowes edged towards the door.

He was in the hall . . . he had opened the front door . . .

Through a door on the right he caught a glimpse of Appledore setting the breakfast things ready on a tray for the morning. ("The damned fool was going to let him get away with it!")

The two men stood in the porch, chatting—fixing up another match for next Saturday.

Tommy thought grimly: "There'll be no next Saturday for you, my boy."

Voices came from the road outside. Two men returning from a tramp on the headland. They were men that both Tommy and the Commander knew slightly. Tommy hailed them. They stopped. Haydock and he exchanged a few words with them, all standing at the gate, then Tommy waved a genial farewell to his host and stepped off with the two men.

He had got away with it.

Haydock, damned fool, had been taken in!

He heard Haydock go back to his house, go in and shut the door. Tommy tramped cheerfully down the hill with his two new-found friends.

Weather looked likely to change.

Old Monroe was off his game again.

That fellow Ashby refused to join the L.D.V. Said it was no damned good. Pretty thick, that. Young Marsh, the assistant caddy master, was a conscientious objector. Didn't Meadowes think that matter ought to be put up to the committee? There had been a pretty bad raid on Southampton, the night before last—quite a lot of damage done. What did Meadowes think about Spain? Were they turning nasty? Of course, ever since the French collapse—

Tommy could have shouted aloud. Such good casual normal talk. A stroke of providence that these two men had turned up just at that moment.

He said goodbye to them at the gate of Sans Souci and turned in.

He walked the drive whistling softly to himself.

He had just turned the dark corner by the rhododendrons when something heavy descended on his head. He crashed forward, pitching into blackness and oblivion.

X

"Did you say three spades, Mrs. Blenkensop?"

Yes, Mrs. Blenkensop had said three spades. Mrs. Sprot, returning breathless from the telephone, saying: "And they've changed the time of the A.R.P. exam. again, it's *too* bad," demanded to have the bidding again.

Miss Minton, as usual, delayed things by ceaseless reiterations.

"Was it two clubs I said? Are you sure? I rather thought, you know, that it might have been on no trump— Oh, yes, of course, I remember now. Mrs. Cayley said one heart, didn't she? I was going to say one no trump, although I hadn't quite got the count, but I do think one should play a plucky game—and then Mrs. Cayley said one heart and so I had to go two clubs. I always think it's so difficult when one has two short suits—"

Sometimes, Tuppence thought to herself, it would save time if Miss Minton just put her hand down on the table to show them all. She was quite incapable of not telling exactly what was in it.

"So now we've got it right," said Miss Minton triumphantly. "One heart, two clubs."

"Two spades," said Tuppence.

"I passed, didn't I?" said Mrs. Sprot.

They looked at Mrs. Cayley, who was leaning forward listening. Miss Minton took up the tale.

"Then Mrs. Cayley said two hearts and I said three diamonds."

"And I said three spades," said Tuppence.

"Pass," said Mrs. Sprot.

Mrs. Cayley sat in silence. At last she seemed to become aware that everyone was looking at her.

"Oh, dear." She flushed. "I'm so sorry. I thought perhaps Mr. Cayley needed me. I hope he's all right out there on the terrace."

She looked from one to the other of them.

"Perhaps, if you don't mind, I'd better just go and *see*. I heard rather an odd noise. Perhaps he's dropped his book."

She fluttered out of the window. Tuppence gave an exasperated sigh.

"She ought to have a string tied to her wrist," she said. "Then he could pull it when he wanted her."

"Such a devoted wife," said Miss Minton. "It's very nice to see it, isn't it?"

"Is it?" said Tuppence, who was feeling far from good-tempered.

The three women sat in silence for a minute or two.

"Where's Sheila tonight?" asked Miss Minton.

"She went to the pictures," said Mrs. Sprot.

"Where's Mrs. Perenna?" asked Tuppence.

"She said she was going to do accounts in her room," said Miss Minton. "Poor dear. So tiring, doing accounts."

"She's not been doing accounts all the evening," said Mrs. Sprot, "because she came in just now when I was telephoning in the hall."

"I wonder where she'd been," said Miss Minton, whose life was taken up with such small wonderments. "Not to the pictures, they wouldn't be out yet."

"She hadn't got a hat on," said Mrs. Sprot. "Nor a coat. Her hair was all anyhow and I think she'd been running or something. Quite out of breath. She ran upstairs without a word and she glared—positively glared at me—and I'm sure *I* hadn't done anything."

Mrs. Cayley reappeared at the window.

"Fancy," she said. "Mr. Cayley has walked all round the garden by himself. He quite enjoyed it, he said. Such a mild night."

She sat down again.

"Let me see— Oh, do you think we could have the bidding over again?"

Tuppence suppressed a rebellious sigh. They had the bidding all over again and she was left to play three spades.

Mrs. Perenna came in just as they were cutting for the next deal.

"Did you enjoy your walk?" asked Miss Minton.

Mrs. Perenna stared at her. It was a fierce and unpleasant stare. She said:

"I've not been out."

"Oh—oh—I thought Mrs. Sprot said you'd come in just now."

Mrs. Perenna said:

"I just went outside to look at the weather."

Her tone was disagreeable. She threw a hostile glance at the meek Mrs. Sprot, who flushed and looked frightened.

"Just fancy," said Mrs. Cayley, contributing her item of news, "Mr. Cayley walked all round the garden."

Mrs. Perenna said sharply:

"Why did he do that?"

Mrs. Cayley said:

"It is such a mild night. He hasn't even put on his second muffler and he *still* doesn't want to come in. I do *hope* he won't get a chill."

Mrs. Perenna said:

"There are worse things than chills. A bomb might come any minute and blow us all to bits!"

"Oh, dear, I hope it won't."

"Do you? *I* rather wish it would."

Mrs. Perenna went out of the window. The four bridge players stared after her.

"She seems very *odd* tonight," said Mrs. Sprot.

Miss Minton leaned forward.

"You don't think, do you—" She looked from side to side. They all leaned nearer together. Miss Minton said in a sibilant whisper:

"You don't suspect, do you, that she *drinks?*"

"Oh, dear," said Mrs. Cayley, "I wonder now. That would explain it. She really is so—so unaccountable sometimes. What do you think, Mrs. Blenkensop?"

"Oh, I don't *really* think so. I think she's worried about something. Er—it's your call, Mrs. Sprot."

"Dear me, what shall I say?" asked Mrs. Sprot, surveying her hand.

Nobody volunteered to tell her, though Miss Minton, who had been gazing with unabashed interest into her hand might have been in a position to advise.

"That isn't Betty, is it?" demanded Mrs. Sprot, her head upraised.

"No, it isn't," said Tuppence firmly.

She felt that she might scream unless they could get on with the game.

Mrs. Sprot looked at her hand vaguely, her mind still apparently maternal. Then she said:

"Oh, one diamond, I *think*."

The call went round. Mrs. Cayley led.

"When in doubt lead a trump, they say," she twittered, and laid down the nine of diamonds.

A deep genial voice said:

"'Tis the curse of Scotland that you've played there!"

Mrs. O'Rourke stood in the window. She was breathing deeply— her eyes were sparkling. She looked sly and malicious. She advanced into the room.

"Just a nice quiet game of bridge, is it?"

"What's that in your hand?" asked Mrs. Sprot, with interest.

"'Tis a hammer," said Mrs. O'Rourke amiably. "I found it lying in the drive. No doubt someone left it there."

"It's a funny place to leave a hammer," said Mrs. Sprot doubtfully.

"It is that," agreed Mrs. O'Rourke.

She seemed in a particularly good humour. Swinging the hammer by its handle she went out into the hall.

"Let me see," said Miss Minton. "What's trumps?"

The game proceeded for five minutes without further interruption, and then Major Bletchley came in. He had been to the pictures and proceeded to tell them in detail the plot of *Wandering Minstrel*, laid in the reign of Richard the First. The Major, as a military man, criticized at some length the Crusading battle scenes.

The rubber was not finished, for Mrs. Cayley, looking at her watch, discovered the lateness of the.hour with shrill little cries of horror and rushed out to Mr. Cayley. The latter, as a neglected invalid, enjoying himself a great deal, coughing in a sepulchral manner shivering dramatically and saying several times:

"*Quite* all right, my dear. I hope you enjoyed your game. It doesn't matter about *me* at all. Even if I *have* caught a severe chill, what does it really matter? There's a war on!"

II

At breakfast the next morning, Tuppence was aware at once of a certain tension in the atmosphere.

Mrs. Perenna, her lips pursed very tightly together, was distinctly acrid in the few remarks she made. She left the room with what could only be described as a flounce.

Major Bletchley, spreading marmalade thickly on his toast, gave vent to a deep chuckle.

"Touch of frost in the air," he remarked. "Well, well! Only to be expected, I suppose."

"Why, what has happened?" demanded Miss Minton, leaning forward eagerly, her thin neck twitching with pleasurable anticipation.

"Don't know that I ought to tell tales out of school," replied the Major irritatingly.

"Oh! Major Bletchley!"

"Do tell us," said Tuppence.

Major Bletchley looked thoughtfully at his audience: Miss Minton, Mrs. Blenkensop, Mrs. Cayley and Mrs. O'Rourke. Mrs. Sprot and Betty had just left. He decided to talk.

"It's Meadowes," he said. "Been out on the tiles all night. Hasn't come home yet."

"What?" exclaimed Tuppence.

Major Bletchley threw her a pleased and malicious glance. He enjoyed the discomfiture of the designing widow.

"Bit of a gay dog, Meadowes," he chortled. "The Perenna's annoyed. Naturally."

"Oh, dear," said Miss Minton, flushing painfully. Mrs. Cayley looked shocked. Mrs. O'Rourke merely chuckled.

"Mrs. Perenna told me already," she said. "Ah, well, the boys will be boys."

Miss Minton said eagerly:

"Oh, but surely—perhaps Mr. Meadowes has met with an accident. In the blackout, you know."

"Good old blackout," said Major Bletchley. "Responsible for a lot. I can tell you, it's been an eye-opener being on patrol in the L.D.V. Stopping cars and all that. The amount of wives just 'seeing their husbands home.' And different names on their identity cards! And the wife or the husband coming back the other way alone a few hours later. Ha Ha!" He chuckled, then quickly composed his face as he received the full blast of Mrs. Blenkensop's disapproving stare.

"Human nature—a bit humorous, eh?" he said appeasingly.

"Oh, but Mr. Meadowes," bleated Miss Minton. "He may really have met with an accident. Been knocked down by a car."

"That'll be his story, I expect," said the Major. "Car hit him and knocked him out and he came to in the morning."

"He may have been taken to hospital."

"They'd have let us know. After all, he's carrying his identity card, isn't he?"

"Oh, dear," said Mrs. Cayley. "I wonder what Mr. Cayley will say?"

This rhetorical question remained unanswered. Tuppence, rising with an assumption of affronted dignity, got up and left the room.

Major Bletchley chuckled when the door closed behind her.

"Poor old Meadowes," he said. "The fair widow's annoyed about it. Thought she'd got her hooks into him."

"Oh, Major *Bletchley*," bleated Miss Minton.

Major Bletchley winked.

"Remember Sam in Dickens. *Beware of widders, Sammy.*"

III

Tuppence was a little upset by Tommy's unannounced absence, but she tried to reassure herself. He might possibly have struck some hot trail and gone off upon it. The difficulties of communication with each other under such circumstances had been foreseen by them both, and they had agreed that the other one was not to be unduly perturbed by unexplained absences. They had arranged certain contrivances between them for such emergencies.

Mrs. Perenna had, according to Mrs. Sprot, been out last night. The vehemence of her own denial of the fact only made that absence of hers more interesting to speculate upon.

It was possible that Tommy had trailed her on her secret errand and had found something worth following up.

Doubtless he would communicate with Tuppence in his special way, or else turn up, very shortly.

Nevertheless, Tuppence was unable to avoid a certain feeling of uneasiness. She decided that in her rôle of Mrs. Blenkensop it would be perfectly natural to display some curiosity and even anxiety. She went without more ado in search of Mrs. Perenna.

Mrs. Perenna was inclined to be short with her upon the subject. She made it clear that such conduct on the part of one of her lodgers was not to be condoned or glossed over.

Tuppence exclaimed breathlessly:

"Oh, but he may have met with an *accident*. I'm sure he *must* have done. He's not at all that sort of man—not at all loose in his ideas, or *anything* of that kind. He must have been run down by a car or something."

"We shall probably soon hear one way or another," said Mrs. Perenna.

But the day wore on and there was no sign of Mr. Meadowes.

In the evening, Mrs. Perenna, urged on by the pleas of her boarders, agreed extremely reluctantly to ring up the police.

A sergeant called at the house with a notebook and took particulars. Certain facts were then elicited. Mr. Meadowes had left Commander Haydock's house at half past ten. From there he had walked with a Mr. Walters and a Dr. Curtis as far as the gate of Sans Souci, where he had said goodbye to them and turned into the drive.

From that moment, Mr. Meadowes seemed to have disappeared into space.

In Tuppence's mind, two possibilities emerged from this.

When walking up the drive, Tommy may have seen Mrs. Perenna coming towards him, have slipped into the bushes and then have followed her. Having observed her rendezvous with some unknown person, he might then have followed the latter, whilst Mrs. Perenna returned to Sans Souci. In that case, he was probably very much alive, and busy on a trail. In which case the well-meant endeavours of the police to find him might prove most embarrassing.

The other possibility was not so pleasant. It resolved itself into two pictures—one that of Mrs. Perenna returning "out of breath and dishevelled"—the other, one that would not be laid aside, a picture of Mrs. O'Rourke standing smiling in the window, holding a heavy hammer.

That hammer had horrible possibilities.

For what should a hammer be doing lying outside?

As to who had wielded it, that was most difficult. A good deal depended on the exact time Mrs. Perenna had re-entered the house. It was certainly somewhere in the neighbourhood of half past ten, but none of the bridge party happened to have noted the time exactly. Mrs. Perenna had declared vehemently that she had not been out except just to look at the weather. But one does not get out of breath just looking at the weather. It was clearly extremely vexing to her to have been seen by Mrs. Sprot. With ordinary luck the four ladies might have been safely accounted for as busy playing bridge.

What had the time been exactly?

Tuppence found everybody extremely vague on the subject.

If the time agreed, Mrs. Perenna was clearly the most likely suspect. But there were other possibilities. Of the inhabitants of Sans Souci, three had been out at the time of Tommy's return. Major Bletchley had been out at the cinema—but he had been to it alone, and the way that he had insisted on retailing the whole picture so meticulously might suggest to a suspicious mind that he was deliberately establishing an *alibi*.

Then there was the valetudinarian Mr. Cayley who had gone for a walk all round the garden. But for the accident of Mrs. Cayley's anxiety over her spouse, no one might have ever heard of that walk and might have imagined Mr. Cayley to have remained securely encased in rugs like a mummy in his chair on the terrace. (Rather unlike him, really, to risk the contamination of the night air so long.)

And there was Mrs. O'Rourke herself, swinging the hammer, and smiling . . .

IV

"What's the matter, Deb? You're looking worried, my sweet."

Deborah Beresford started and then laughed, looking frankly into Tony Marsdon's sympathetic brown eyes. She liked Tony. He had brains—was one of the most brilliant beginners in the coding department—and was thought likely to go far.

Deborah enjoyed her job, though she found it made somewhat strenuous demands on her powers of concentration. It was tiring, but it was worth while and it gave her a pleasant feeling of importance. This was real work—not just hanging about a hospital waiting for a chance to nurse.

She said:

"Oh, nothing. Just *family! You* know."

"Families *are* a bit trying. What's yours been up to?"

"It's my mother. To tell the truth I'm just a bit worried about her."

"Why? What's happened?"

"Well, you see, she went down to Cornwall to a frightfully trying old aunt of mine. Seventy-eight and completely ga ga."

"Sounds grim," commented the young man sympathetically.

"Yes, it was really very noble of mother. But she was rather hipped anyway because nobody seemed to want her in this war. Of course, she nursed and did things in the last one—but it's all quite different now, and they don't want these middle-aged people. They want people who are young and on the spot. Well, as I say, mother got a bit hipped over it all, and so she went off down to Cornwall to stay with Aunt Gracie, and she's been doing a bit in the garden, extra vegetable growing and all that."

"Quite sound," commented Tony.

"Yes, much the best thing she could do. She's quite active still, you know," said Deborah kindly.

"Well, that sounds all right."

"Oh, yes, it isn't *that*. I was quite happy about her—had a letter only two days ago sounding quite cheerful."

"What's the trouble, then?"

"The trouble is that I told Charles, who was going down to see his people in that part of the world, to go and look her up. And he did. And she wasn't there."

"Wasn't *there*?"

"No. And she hadn't been there! Not at all apparently!"

Tony looked a little embarrassed.

"Rather odd," he murmured. "Where's—I mean—your father?"

"Carrot Top? Oh, he's in Scotland somewhere. In one of those dreadful Ministries where they file papers in triplicate all day long."

"Your mother hasn't gone to join him perhaps?"

"She can't. He's in one of those area things where wives can't go."

"Oh—er—well, I suppose she's just sloped off somewhere."

Tony was decidedly embarrassed now—especially with Deborah's large worried eyes fixed plaintively upon him.

"Yes, but why? It's so *queer*. All her letters—talking about Aunt Gracie and the garden and everything."

"I know, I know," said Tony hastily. "Of course, she'd want you to think—I mean—nowadays—well, people *do* slope off now and again, if you know what I mean—"

Deborah's gaze, from being plaintive, became suddenly wrathful.

"If you think mother's just gone off week-ending with someone you're absolutely wrong. Absolutely. Mother and father are devoted to each other—really devoted. It's quite a joke in the family. She'd never—"

Tony said hastily:

"Of course not. Sorry. I really didn't mean—"

Deborah, her wrath appeased, creased her forehead.

"The odd thing is that someone the other day said they'd seen mother in Leahampton, of all places, and of course I said it couldn't be her because she was in Cornwall, but now I wonder—"

Tony, his match held to a cigarette, paused suddenly and the match went out.

"Leahampton?" he said sharply.

"Yes. Just the last place you could imagine mother going off to. Nothing to do and all old Colonels and maiden ladies."

"Doesn't sound a likely spot, certainly," said Tony.

He lit his cigarette and asked casually:

"What did your mother do in the last war?"

Deborah answered mechanically:

"Oh, nursed a bit and drove a General—army, I mean, not a bus. All the usual sort of things."

"Oh, I thought perhaps she'd been like you—in the Intelligence."

"Oh, mother would never have had the head for this sort of work. I believe, though, that after the war she and father did do something in the sleuthing line. Secret papers and master spies—that sort of thing. Of course, the darlings exaggerate it all a good deal and make it all sound as though it had been frightfully important. We don't really encourage them to talk about it much because you know what one's family is—the same old story over and over again."

"Oh, rather," said Tony Marsdon heartily. "I quite agree."

It was on the following day that Deborah, returning to her lodging house, was puzzled by something unfamiliar in the appearance of her room.

It took her a few minutes to fathom what it was. Then she rang the bell and demanded angrily of her landlady what had happened to the big photograph that always stood on the top of the chest of drawers.

Mrs. Rowley was aggrieved and resentful.

She couldn't say, she was sure. She hadn't touched it herself. Maybe Gladys—

But Gladys also denied having removed it. The man had been there about the gas, she said hopefully.

But Deborah declined to believe that an employé of the Gas Company would have taken a fancy to and removed the portrait of a middle-aged lady.

Far more likely, in Deborah's opinion, that Gladys had smashed the photograph frame and had hastily removed all traces of the crime to the dustbin.

Deborah didn't make a fuss about it. Sometime or other she'd get her mother to send her another photo.

She thought to herself with rising vexation:

"What's the old darling up to? She might tell me. Of course, it's absolute nonsense to suggest, as Tony did, that she's gone off with someone, but all the same it's very queer . . ."

XI

IT WAS TUPPENCE'S turn to talk to the fisherman on the end of the pier.

She had hoped against hope that Mr. Grant might have some comfort for her. But her hopes were soon dashed.

He stated definitely that no news of any kind had come from Tommy.

Tuppence said, trying her best to make her voice assured and business-like:

"There's no reason to suppose that anything has—happened to him?"

"None whatever. But let's suppose it has."

"What?"

"I'm saying—supposing it has. What about you?"

"Oh, I see—I—carry on, of course."

"That's the stuff. *There is time to weep after the battle.* We're in the thick of the battle now. And time is short. One piece of information you brought us has been proved correct. You overheard a reference to the *fourth.* The fourth referred to is the fourth of next month. It's the date fixed for the big attack on this country."

"You're sure?"

"Fairly sure. They're methodical people, our enemies. All their plans neatly made and worked out. Wish we could say the same of ourselves. Planning isn't our strong point. Yes, the Fourth is The Day. All these raids aren't the real thing—they're mostly reconnaissance—testing our defences and our reflexes to air attack. On the fourth comes the real thing."

"But if you know that—"

"We know The Day is fixed. We know, or think we know, roughly, *where* . . . (But we may be wrong there.) We're as ready as we can be. But it's the old story of the siege of Troy. They knew, as we know, all about the forces without. It's the forces within we want to know about. The men in the Wooden Horse! For they are the men who can deliver up the keys of the fortress. A dozen men in high places, in command in vital spots, by issuing conflicting orders, can throw the country into just that state of confusion necessary for the German plan to succeed. We've *got* to have inside information in time."

Tuppence said despairingly:

"I feel so futile—so inexperienced."

"Oh, you needn't worry about that. We've got experienced people working, all the experience and talent we've got—but when there's treachery within we can't tell who to trust. You and Beresford are the irregular forces. Nobody knows about you. That's why you've got a chance to succeed—that's why you *have* succeeded up to a certain point."

"Can't you put some of your people on to Mrs. Perenna? There *must* be some of them you can trust absolutely?"

"Oh, we've done that. Working from 'information received that Mrs. Perenna is a member of the I.R.A. with anti-British sympathies.' That's true enough, by the way—but we can't get proof of anything further. Not of the vital facts we want. So stick to it, Mrs. Beresford. Go on, and do your darnedest."

"The fourth," said Tuppence. "That's barely a week ahead?"

"It's a week exactly."

Tuppence clenched her hands.

"We *must* get *something!* I say *we* because I believe Tommy is on to something, and that that's why he hasn't come back. He's following up a lead. If I could only get something, too. I wonder now. If I—"

She frowned, planning a new form of attack.

II

"You see, Albert, it's a possibility."

"I see what you mean, Madam, of course. But I don't like the idea very much, I must say."

"I think it might work."

"Yes, Madam, but it's exposing yourself to attack—that's what I don't like—and I'm sure the master wouldn't like it."

"We've tried all the usual ways. That is to say, we've done what we could keeping under cover. It seems to me that now the only chance is to come out into the open."

"You are aware, Madam, that thereby you may be sacrificing an advantage?"

"You're frightfully B.B.C. in your language this afternoon, Albert," said Tuppence, with some exasperation.

Albert looked slightly taken aback and reverted to a more natural form of speech.

"I was listening to a very interesting talk on pond life last night," he explained.

"We've no time to think about pond life now," said Tuppence.

"Where's Captain Beresford, that's what I'd like to know?"

"So should I," said Tuppence, with a pang.

"Don't seem natural, his disappearing without a word. He ought to have tipped you the wink by now. That's why—"

"Yes, Albert?"

"What I mean is, if *he's* come out in the open, perhaps *you'd* better not."

He paused to arrange his ideas and then went on.

"I mean, they've blown the gaff on *him,* but *they mayn't know about you*—and so it's up to you to keep under cover still."

"I wish I could make up my mind," sighed Tuppence.

"Which way were you thinking of managing it, Madam?"

Tuppence murmured thoughtfully:

"I thought I might lose a letter I'd written—make a lot of fuss about it, seem very upset. Then it would be found in the hall and Beatrice would probably put it on the hall table. Then the right person would get a look at it."

"What would be in the letter?"

"Oh, roughly—that I'd been successful in discovering the identity of the person in question and that I was to make a full report personally tomorrow. Then, you see, Albert, N or M would have to come out in the open and have a shot at eliminating me."

"Yes, and maybe they'd manage it, too."

"Not if I was on my guard. They'd have, I think, to decoy me away somewhere—some lonely spot. That's where you'd come in—because they don't know about you."

"I'd follow them up and catch them red-handed, so to speak?"

Tuppence nodded.

"That's the idea. I must think it out carefully—I'll meet you tomorrow."

III

Tuppence was just emerging from the local lending library with what had been recommended to her as a "nice book" clasped under her arm when she was startled by a voice saying:

"Mrs. Beresford."

She turned abruptly to see a tall, dark young man with an agreeable but slightly embarrassed smile.

He said:

"Er—I'm afraid you don't remember me?"

Tuppence was thoroughly used to the formula. She could have predicted with accuracy the words that were coming next.

"I—er—came to the flat with Deborah one day."

Deborah's friends! So many of them, and all, to Tuppence, looking singularly alike! Some dark like this young man, some fair, an occasional red-haired one—but all cast in the same mould—pleasant, well-mannered, their hair, in Tuppence's view, just slightly too long. (But when this was hinted, Deborah would say, "Oh, *mother*, don't be so terribly 1916. I can't *stand* short hair.")

Annoying to have run across and been recognized by one of Deborah's young men just now. However, she could probably soon shake him off.

"I'm Antony Marsdon," explained the young man.

Tuppence murmured mendaciously, "Oh, of course," and shook hands.

Tony Marsdon went on:

"I'm awfully glad to have found you, Mrs. Beresford. You see, I'm working at the same job as Deborah, and as a matter of fact something rather awkward has happened."

"Yes?" said Tuppence. "What is it?"

"Well, you see, Deborah's found out that you're not down in Cornwall as she thought, and that makes it a bit awkward, doesn't it, for you?"

"Oh, bother," said Tuppence, concerned. "How did she find out?"

Tony Marsdon explained. He went on rather diffidently:

"Deborah, of course, has no idea of what you're really doing."

He paused discreetly, and then went on:

"It's important, I imagine, that she shouldn't know. My job, actually, is rather the same line. I'm supposed to be just a beginner in the Coding Department. Really my instructions are to express views that are mildly Fascist—admiration of the German system, insinuations that a working alliance with Hitler wouldn't be a bad thing—all that sort of thing—just to see what response I get. There's a good deal of rot going on, you see, and we want to find out who's at the bottom of it."

"Not everywhere," thought Tuppence.

"But as soon as Deb told me about you," continued the young man, "I thought I'd better come straight down and warn you so that you could cook up a likely story. You see, I happen to know what you are doing and that it's of vital importance. It would be fatal if any hint of who you are got about. I thought perhaps you could make it seem as though you'd joined Captain Beresford in Scotland or wherever he is. You might say that you'd been allowed to work with him there."

"I might do that, certainly," said Tuppence thoughtfully.

Tony Marsdon said anxiously:

"You don't think I'm butting in?"

"No, no, I'm very grateful to you."

Tony said rather inconsequentially:

"I'm—well—you see—I'm rather fond of Deborah."

Tuppence flashed him an amused quick glance.

How far away it seemed, that world of attentive young men and Deb with her rudeness to them that never seemed to put them off. This young man was, she thought, quite an attractive specimen.

She put aside what she called to herself "peace time thoughts" and concentrated on the present situation.

After a moment or two she said slowly:

"My husband isn't in Scotland."

"Isn't he?"

"No, he's down here with me. At least he was! Now—he's disappeared."

"I say, that's bad—or isn't it? Was he on to something?"

Tuppence nodded.

"I think so. That's why I don't think that his disappearing like this is really a bad sign. I think, sooner or later, he'll communicate with me—in his own way." She smiled a little.

Tony said, with some slight embarrassment:

"Of course, you know the game well, I expect. But you ought to be careful."

Tuppence nodded.

"I know what you mean. Beautiful heroines in books are always easily decoyed away. But Tommy and I have our methods. We've got a slogan." She smiled. *"Penny plain and tuppence coloured."*

"What?" The young man stared at her as though she had gone mad.

"I ought to explain that my family nickname is Tuppence."

"Oh, I see." The young man's brow cleared. "Ingenious—what?"

"I hope so."

"I don't want to butt in—but couldn't I help in any way?"

"Yes," said Tuppence thoughtfully, "I think perhaps you might."

XII

AFTER LONG AEONS of unconsciousness, Tommy began to be aware of a fiery ball swimming in space. In the centre of the fiery ball was a core of pain, the universe shrank, the fiery ball swung more slowly—he discovered suddenly that the nucleus of it was his own aching head.

Slowly he became aware of other things—of cold cramped limbs, of hunger, of an inability to move his lips.

Slower and slower swung the fiery ball . . . It was now Thomas Beresford's head and it was resting on solid ground. Very solid ground. In fact on something suspiciously like stone.

Yes, he was lying on hard stones, and he was in pain, unable to move, extremely hungry, cold and uncomfortable.

Surely, although Mrs. Perenna's beds had never been unduly soft, this could not be—

Of course—Haydock! The wireless! The German waiter! Turning in at the gates of Sans Souci . . .

Someone, creeping up behind him, had struck him down. That was the reason of his aching head.

And he'd thought he'd got away with it all right! So Haydock, after all, hadn't been quite such a fool?

Haydock? Haydock had gone back into Smugglers' Rest and closed the door. How had he managed to get down the hill and be waiting for Tommy in the grounds of Sans Souci?

It couldn't be done. Not without Tommy seeing him.

The manservant, then? Had he been sent ahead to lie in wait? But surely, as Tommy had crossed the hall, he had seen Appledore in the kitchen of which the door was slightly ajar. Or did he only fancy he had seen him? Perhaps that was the explanation.

Anyway it didn't matter. The thing to do was to find out where he was now.

His eyes, becoming accustomed to the darkness, picked out a small rectangle of dim light. A window or small grating. The air smelled chill and musty. He was, he fancied, lying in a cellar. His hands and feet were tied and a gag in his mouth was secured by a bandage.

"Seems rather as though I'm for it," thought Tommy.

He tried gingerly to move his limbs or body, but he could not succeed.

At that moment, there was a faint creaking sound and a door somewhere behind him was pushed open. A man with a candle came in. He set down the candle on the floor. Tommy recognized Appledore. The latter disappeared again and then returned carrying a tray on which were a jug of water, a glass and some bread and cheese.

Stooping down he first tested the cords binding the other's limbs. He then touched the gag.

He said in a quiet level voice:

"I am about to take this off. You will then be able to eat and drink. If, however, you make the slightest sound, I shall replace it immediately."

Tommy tried to nod his head, which proved impossible, so he opened and shut his eyes several times instead.

Appledore, taking this for consent, carefully unknotted the bandage.

His mouth freed, Tommy spent some few minutes easing his jaw. Appledore held the glass of water to his lips. He swallowed at first with difficulty, then more easily. The water did him a world of good.

He murmured stiffly:

"That's better. I'm not quite so young as I was. Now for the eats, Fritz—or is it Franz?

The man said quietly:

"My name here is Appledore."

He held the slice of bread and cheese up and Tommy bit at it hungrily.

The meal washed down with some more water, he then asked:

"And what's the next part of the programme?"

For answer, Appledore picked up the gag again.

Tommy said quickly:

"I want to see Commander Haydock."

Appledore shook his head. Deftly he replaced the gag and went out.

Tommy was left to meditate in darkness. He was awakened from a confused sleep by the sound of the door reopening. This time Haydock and Appledore came in together. The gag was removed and the cords that held his arms were loosened so that he could sit up and stretch his arms.

Haydock had an automatic pistol with him.

Tommy, without much inward confidence, began to play his part.

He said indignantly:

"Look here, Haydock, what's the meaning of all this? I've been set upon—kidnapped—"

The Commander was gently shaking his head.

He said:

"Don't waste your breath. It's not worth it."

"Just because you're a member of our Secret Service, you think you can—"

Again the other shook his head.

"No, no, Meadowes. You weren't taken in by that story. No need to keep up the pretense."

But Tommy showed no signs of discomfiture. He argued to himself that the other could not really be sure. If he continued to play his part—

"Who the devil do you think you are?" he demanded. "However great your powers you've no right to behave like this. I'm perfectly capable of holding my tongue about any of our vital secrets!"

The other said coldly:

"You do your stuff very well, but I may tell you that it's immaterial to me whether you're a member of the British Intelligence, or merely a muddling amateur—"

"Of all the damned cheek—"

"Cut it out, Meadowes."

"I tell you—"

Haydock thrust a ferocious face forwards.

"Be quiet, damn you. Earlier on it would have mattered to find out who you were and who sent you. Now it doesn't matter. The time's short, you see. And you didn't have the chance to report to anyone what you'd found out."

"The police will be looking for me as soon as I'm reported missing."

Haydock showed his teeth in a sudden gleam.

"I've had the police here this evening. Good fellows—both friends of mine. They asked me all about Mr. Meadowes. Very concerned about his disappearance. How he seemed that evening—what he said. They never dreamed, how should they, that the man they were talking about was practically underneath their feet where they were sitting. It's quite clear, you see, that you left this house well and alive. They'd never dream of looking for you here."

"You can't keep me here forever," Tommy said vehemently.

Haydock said with a resumption of his most British manner:

"It won't be necessary, my dear fellow. Only until tomorrow night. There's a boat due in at my little cove—and we're thinking of sending you on a voyage for your health—though actually I don't think you'll be alive, or even on board, when they arrive at their destination."

"I wonder you didn't knock me on the head straight away."

"It's such hot weather, my dear fellow. Just occasionally our sea communications are interrupted, and if that were to be so—well, a dead body on the premises has a way of announcing its presence."

"I see," said Tommy.

He did see. The issue was perfectly clear. He was to be kept alive until the boat arrived. Then he would be killed—or drugged—and taken out to sea. Nothing would ever connect his body, when found, with Smugglers' Rest.

"I just came along," continued Haydock, speaking in the most natural manner, "to ask whether there is anything we could—er—do for you—afterwards?"

Tommy reflected. Then he said:

"Thanks—but I won't ask you to take a lock of my hair to the little woman in St. John's Wood, or anything of that kind. She'll miss me when pay day comes along—but I daresay she'll soon find a friend elsewhere."

At all costs, he felt, he must create the impression that he was playing a lone hand. So long as no suspicion attached itself to Tuppence then the game might still be won through, though he was not there to play it.

"As you please," said Haydock. "If you did care to send a message to—your friend—we would see that it was delivered."

So he was, after all, anxious to get a little information about this unknown Mr. Meadowes? Very well, then, Tommy would keep him guessing.

He shook his head.

"Nothing doing," he said.

"Very well." With an appearance of the utmost indifference Haydock nodded to Appledore. The latter replaced the bonds and the gag. The two men went out, locking the door behind them.

Left to his reflections, Tommy felt anything but cheerful. Not only was he faced with the prospect of rapidly approaching death but he had no means of leaving any clue behind him as to the information he had discovered.

His body was completely helpless. His brain felt singularly inactive. Could he, he wondered, have utilized Haydock's suggestion of a message? Perhaps if his brain had been working better . . . But he could think of nothing helpful.

There was, of course, still Tuppence. But what could Tuppence do? As Haydock had just pointed out, Tommy's disappearance would not be connected with him. Tommy had left Smugglers' Rest alive and well. The evidence of two independent witnesses would confirm that. Whoever Tuppence might suspect, it would not be Haydock. And she might not suspect at all. She might think that he was merely following up a trail.

Damn it all, if only he had been more on his guard—

There was a little light in the cellar. It came through the grating which was high up in one corner. If only he could get his mouth free, could shout for help. Somebody might hear, though it was very unlikely.

For the next half hour he busied himself straining at the cords that bound him and trying to bite through the gag. It was all in vain, however. The people who had adjusted those things knew their business.

It was, he judged, late afternoon. Haydock, he fancied, had gone out; he had heard no sounds from overhead.

Confound it all, he was probably playing golf, speculating at the clubhouse over what could have happened to Meadowes!

"Dined with me night before last—seemed quite normal then. Just vanished into the blue."

Tommy writhed with fury. That hearty English manner! Was everyone blind not to see that bullet-headed Prussian skull? He himself hadn't seen it. Wonderful what a first class actor could get away with.

So here he was—a failure—an ignominious failure—trussed up like a chicken, with no one to guess where he was.

If only Tuppence could have second sight! She might suspect. She had, sometimes, an uncanny insight . . .

What was that?

He strained his ears listening to a far-off sound.

Only some man humming a tune.

And here he was, unable to make a sound to attract anyone's attention.

The humming came nearer. A most untuneful noise.

But the tune, though mangled, was recognizable. It dated from the last war—had been revived for this one.

"If you were the only girl in the world and I was the only boy."

How often he had hummed that in 1917.

Dash this fellow. Why couldn't he sing in tune?

Suddenly Tommy's body grew taut and rigid. Those particular lapses were strangely familiar. Surely there was only one person who always went wrong in that one particular place and in that one particular way!

"Albert, by Gosh!" thought Tommy.

Albert prowling round Smugglers' Rest. Albert quite close at hand, and here was he, trussed up, unable to move hand or foot, unable to make a sound . . .

Wait a minute. Was he?

There was just one sound—not so easy with the mouth shut as with the mouth open, but it could be done.

Desperately Tommy began to snore. He kept his eyes closed, ready to feign a deep sleep if Appledore should come down, and he snored, he snored . . .

Short snore, short snore, short snore—pause—long snore, long snore, long snore—pause—short snore, short snore, short snore . . .

II

Albert, when Tuppence had left him, was deeply perturbed.

With the advance of years he had become a person of slow mental processes, but those processes were tenacious.

The state of affairs in general seemed to him quite wrong.

The War was all wrong to begin with.

"Those Germans," thought Albert gloomily and almost without rancour. Heiling Hitler and goose-stepping and over-running the world and bombing and machine-gunning and generally making pestilential nuisances of themselves. They'd got to be stopped, no two ways about it—and so far it seemed as though nobody had been able to stop them.

And now here was Mrs. Beresford, a nice lady if there ever was one, getting herself mixed up in trouble and looking out for more trouble, and how was he going to stop her? Didn't look as though he could. Up against this Fifth Column and a nasty lot they must be. Some of 'em English born, too! A disgrace, that was!

And the master who was always the one to hold the missus back from her impetuous ways—the master was missing.

Albert didn't like that at all. It looked to him as though "those Germans" might be at the bottom of that.

Yes, it looked bad, it did. Looked as though he might have copped one.

Albert was not given to the exercise of deep reasoning. Like most Englishmen, he felt something strongly and proceeded to muddle around until he had, somehow or other, cleared up the mess. Deciding that the master had got to be found, Albert, rather after the manner of a faithful dog, set out to find him.

He acted upon no settled plan, but proceeded in exactly the same way as he was wont to embark upon the search for his wife's handbag or his own spectacles when either of those essential articles was mislaid. That is to say, he went to the place where he had last seen the missing objects and started from there.

In this case, the last thing known about Tommy was that he had dined with Commander Haydock at Smugglers' Rest and had then returned to Sans Souci and had been last seen turning in at the gate.

Albert, accordingly, climbed the hill as far as the gate of Sans Souci and spent some five minutes staring hopefully at the gate. Nothing of a scintillating character having occurred to him, he sighed and wandered slowly up the hill to Smugglers' Rest.

Albert, too, had visited the Ornate Cinema that week, and had been powerfully impressed by the theme of *Wandering Minstrel*. Romantic, it was! He could not but be struck by the similarity of his own predicament. He, like that hero of the screen, Gary Cooper, was a faithful Blondel seeking his imprisoned master. Like Blondel, he had fought at that master's side in bygone days. Now his master was betrayed by treachery, and there was none but his faithful Blondel to seek for him and restore him to the loving arms of Queen Berengaria.

Albert heaved a sigh as he remembered the melting strains of *Richard, O mon roi* which the faithful troubadour had crooned so feelingly beneath tower after tower.

Pity he himself wasn't better at picking up a tune. Took him a long time to get hold of a tune, it did. His lips shaped themselves into a tentative whistle. Begun playing the old tunes again lately, they had.

"If you were the only girl in the world and I was the only boy—"

Albert paused to survey the neat white painted gate of Smugglers' Rest. That was it, that was where the master had gone to dinner.

He went up the hill a little further and came out on the downs. Nothing here. Nothing but grass and a few sheep.

The gate of Smugglers' Rest swung open and a car passed out. A big man in plus fours with golf clubs drove out and down the hill.

"That would be Commander Haydock, that would," Albert deduced.

He wandered down again and stared at Smugglers' Rest. A tidy little place. Nice bit of garden. Nice view.

He eyed it benignly.

"I would say such wonderful things to you," he hummed.

Through a side door of the house a man came out with a hoe and passed out of sight through a little gate.

Albert, who grew nasturtiums and a bit of lettuce in his back garden, was instantly interested.

He edged nearer to Smugglers' Rest and passed through the open gate. Yes, tidy little place.

He circled slowly round it. Some way below him, reached by steps, was a flat plateau planted as a vegetable garden. The man who had come out of the house was busy down there.

Albert watched him with interest for some minutes. Then he turned to contemplate the house.

Tidy little place, he thought for the third time. Just the sort of place a retired Naval gentleman would like to have. This was where the master had dined that night.

Slowly Albert circled round and round the house. He looked at it much as he had looked at the gate of Sans Souci—hopefully, as though asking it to tell him something.

And as he went he hummed softly to himself, a twentieth century Blondel in search of his master.

"There would be such wonderful things to do," hummed Albert. "I would say such wonderful things to you. There would be such wonderful things to do—" Gone wrong somewhere, hadn't he? He'd hummed that bit before.

Hullo! Funny. So the Commander kept pigs, did he? A long drawn grunt came to him. Funny—seemed almost as though it were underground. Funny place to keep pigs.

Couldn't be pigs. No, it was someone having a bit of shut-eye. Bit of shut-eye in the cellar, so it seemed . . .

Right kind of day for a snooze, but funny place to go for it. Humming like a bumble bee, Albert approached nearer.

That's where it was coming from—through that little grating. Grunt, grunt, grunt. Snoooooore. Snoooooore. Snoooooore—grunt, grunt, grunt. Funny sort of snore—reminded him of something . . .

"Coo!" said Albert. "That's what it is—S.O.S.—Dot, dot, dot, dash, dash, dash, dot, dot, dot."

He looked round him with a quick glance.

Then, kneeling down, he tapped a soft message on the iron grille of the little window of the cellar.

XIII

Although Tuppence went to bed in an optimistic frame of mind, she suffered a severe reaction in those waking hours of early dawn when human morale sinks to its lowest.

On descending to breakfast, however, her spirits were raised by the sight of a letter on her plate addressed in a painfully backhanded script.

This was no communication from Douglas, Raymond or Cyril, or any other of the camouflaged correspondence that arrived punctually for her, and which included this morning a brightly coloured Bonzo postcard with a scrawled "Sorry I haven't written before. All well, Maudie" on it.

Tuppence thrust this aside and opened the letter.

DEAR PATRICIA [it ran],
Auntie Grace is, I am afraid, much worse today. The doctors do not actually say she is sinking, but I am afraid that there cannot be much hope. If you want to see her before the end I think it would be well to come today. If you will take the 10:20 train to Yarrow, a friend will meet you with his car.

Shall look forward to seeing you again, dear, in spite of the melancholy reason.

Yours ever,
PENELOPE PLAYNE.

It was all Tuppence could do to restrain her jubilation.

Good old Penny Playne.

With some difficulty she assumed a mourning expression—and sighed heavily as she laid the letter down.

To the two sympathetic listeners present, Mrs. O'Rourke and Miss Minton, she imparted the contents of the letter, and enlarged freely on the personality of Aunt Gracie, her indomitable spirit, her indifference to air raids and danger, and her vanquishment by illness. Miss Minton tended to be curious as to the exact nature of Aunt Gracie's sufferings and compared them interestedly with the diseases of her own cousin Selina. Tuppence, hovering slightly between dropsy and diabetes, found herself slightly confused, but compromised on complications with the kidneys. Mrs. O'Rourke displayed an avid interest as to whether Tuppence would benefit pecuniarily by the old lady's death and learned that dear Cyril had always been Aunt Gracie's favourite grand-nephew as well as being her god-son.

After breakfast Tuppence rang up the tailor's and cancelled a fitting of a coat and skirt for that afternoon, and then sought out Mrs. Perenna and explained that she might be away from home for a night or two.

Mrs. Perenna expressed the usual conventional sentiments. She looked tired this morning, and had an anxious harassed expression.

"Still no news of Mr. Meadowes," she said. "It really is *most* odd, is it not?"

"I'm sure he must have met with an accident," sighed Mrs. Blenkensop. "I always said so."

"Oh, but surely, Mrs. Blenkensop, the accident would have been reported by this time."

"Well, what do you think?" asked Tuppence.

Mrs. Perenna shook her head.

"I really don't know *what* to say. I quite agree that he can't have gone away of his own free will. He would have sent word by now."

"It was always a most unjustified suggestion," said Mrs. Blenkensop warmly. "That horrid Major Bletchley started it. No, if it isn't an accident, it must be loss of memory. I believe that is far more common than is generally known, especially at times of stress like those we are living through now."

Mrs. Perenna nodded her head. She pursed up her lips with rather a doubtful expression. She shot a quick look at Tuppence.

"You know, Mrs. Blenkensop," she said, "we don't know very much *about* Mr. Meadowes, do we?"

Tuppence said sharply: "What do you mean?"

"Oh, please don't take me up so sharply. *I* don't believe it—not for a minute."

"Don't believe what?"

"This story that's going around."

"What story? I haven't heard anything."

"No—well—perhaps people wouldn't tell you. I don't really know how it started. I've an idea that Mr. Cayley mentioned it first. Of course he's rather a suspicious man, if you know what I mean?"

Tuppence contained herself with as much patience as possible.

"Please tell me," she said.

"Well, it was just a suggestion, you know, that Mr. Meadowes might be an enemy agent—one of these dreadful Fifth Column people."

Tuppence put all she could of an outraged Mrs. Blenkensop into her indignant:

"I never *heard* of such an absurd idea!"

"No. I don't think there's anything in it. But, of course, Mr. Meadowes *was* seen about a good deal with that German boy—and I believe he asked a lot of questions about the chemical processes at the factory—and so people think that perhaps the two of them might have been working together."

Tuppence said:

"*You* don't think there's any doubt about Carl, do you, Mrs. Perenna?"

She saw a quick spasm distort the other woman's face.

"I wish I *could* think it was not true."

Tuppence said gently:

"Poor Sheila . . ."

Mrs. Perenna's eyes flashed.

"Her heart's broken, the poor child. Why should it be that way? Why couldn't it be someone else she set her heart upon?"

Tuppence shook her head.

"Things don't happen that way."

"You're right." The other spoke in a deep, bitter voice. "It's got to be the way things tear you to pieces . . . It's got to be sorrow and bitterness and dust and ashes. I'm sick of the cruelty—the unfairness of this world. I'd like to smash it and break it—and let us all start again near to the earth and without these rules and laws and the tyranny of nation over nation. I'd like—"

A cough interrupted her. A deep, throaty cough. Mrs. O'Rourke was standing in the doorway, her vast bulk filling the aperture completely.

"Am I interrupting now?" she demanded.

Like a sponge across a slate, all evidence of Mrs. Perenna's outburst vanished from her face—leaving in its wake only the mild worried face of the proprietress of a guest house whose guests were causing trouble.

"No, indeed, Mrs. O'Rourke," she said. "We were just talking about what had become of Mr. Meadowes. It's amazing the police can find no trace of him."

"Ah, the police!" said Mrs. O'Rourke in tones of easy contempt. "What good would they be? No good at all, at all! Only fit for finding motor cars, and dropping on poor wretches who haven't taken out their dog licenses."

"What's your theory, Mrs. O'Rourke?" asked Tuppence.

"You'll have been hearing the story that's going about?"

"About his being a Fascist, and an enemy agent—yes," said Tuppence coldly.

"It might be true now," said Mrs. O'Rourke thoughtfully, "for there's been something about the man that's intrigued me from the beginning. I've watched him, you know." She smiled directly at Tuppence—and like all Mrs. O'Rourke's smiles it had a vaguely terrifying quality—

the smile of an ogress. "He'd not the look of a man who'd retired from business and had nothing to do with himself. If I was backing my judgment, I'd say he came here with a purpose."

"And when the police got on his track he disappeared, is that it?" demanded Tuppence.

"It might be so," said Mrs. O'Rourke. "What's your opinion, Mrs. Perenna?"

"I don't know," sighed Mrs. Perenna. "It's a most vexing thing to happen. It makes so much *talk*."

"Ah! talk won't hurt you. They're happy now out there on the terrace wondering and surmising. They'll have it in the end that the quiet inoffensive man was going to blow us all up in our beds with bombs."

"You haven't told us what you think," said Tuppence.

Mrs. O'Rourke smiled, that same slow ferocious smile.

"I'm thinking that the man is safe somewhere—quite safe . . ."

Tuppence thought:

"She might say that if she knew . . . But he isn't where she thinks he is!"

She went up to her room to get ready. Betty Sprot came running out of the Cayleys' bedroom with a smile of mischievous and impish glee on her face.

"What have you been up to, minx?" demanded Tuppence.

Betty gurgled.

"Goosey, goosey gander . . ."

Tuppence chanted:

"Whither will you wander? *Up*stairs!" She snatched up Betty high over her head. "*Downstairs!*" She rolled her on the floor—

At this minute Mrs. Sprot appeared and Betty was led off to be attired for her walk.

"Hide?" said Betty hopefully. "Hide?"

"You can't play hide and seek now," said Mrs. Sprot.

Tuppence went into her room and donned her hat. (A nuisance having to wear a hat—Tuppence Beresford never did—but Patricia Blenkensop would certainly wear one, Tuppence felt.)

Somebody, she noted, had altered the position of the hats in her hat cupboard. Had someone been searching her room? Well, let them. They wouldn't find anything to cast doubt on blameless Mrs. Blenkensop.

She left Penelope Playne's letter artistically on the dressing table and went downstairs and out of the house.

It was ten o'clock as she turned out of the gate. Plenty of time. She looked up at the sky and in doing so stepped into a dark puddle by the gatepost, but without apparently noticing it she went on.

Her heart was dancing wildly. Success—success—they were going to succeed.

II

Yarrow was a small country station where the village was some distance from the railway.

Outside the station a car was waiting. A good looking young man was driving it. He touched his peaked cap to Tuppence, but the gesture seemed hardly natural.

Tuppence kicked the off side tire dubiously.

"Isn't this rather flat?"

"We haven't far to go, Madam."

She nodded and got in.

They drove, not towards the village, but towards the downs. After winding up over a hill, they took a side track that dropped sharply into a deep cleft. From the shadow of a small copse of trees a figure stepped out to meet them.

The car stopped and Tuppence, getting out, went to meet Antony Marsdon.

"Beresford's all right," he said quickly. "We located him yesterday. He's a prisoner—the other side got him—and for good reasons he's remaining put for another twelve hours. You see, there's a small boat due in at a certain spot—and we want to catch her badly. That's why Beresford's lying low—we don't want to give the show away until the last minute."

He looked at her anxiously.

"You do understand, don't you?"

"Oh, yes!" Tuppence was staring at a curious tangled mass of canvas material half hidden by the trees.

"He'll be absolutely all right," continued the young man earnestly.

"Of course Tommy will be all right," said Tuppence impatiently. "You needn't talk to me as though I were a child of two. We're both ready to run a few risks. What's that thing over there?"

"Well—" the young man hesitated. "That's just it. I've been ordered to put a certain proposition before you. But—but, well, frankly, I don't like doing it. You see—"

Tuppence treated him to a cold stare.

"Why don't you like doing it?"

"Well—dash it—you're Deborah's mother. And I mean—what would Deb say to me if—if—"

"If I got it in the neck?" inquired Tuppence. "Personally, if I were you, I shouldn't mention it to her. The man who said explanations were a mistake was quite right."

Then she smiled kindly at him.

"My dear boy, I know exactly how you feel. That it's all very well for you and Deborah and the young generally to run risks, but that the mere middle-aged must be shielded. All complete nonsense, because if anyone is going to be liquidated it is much better it should be the middle-aged who have had the best part of their lives. Anyway, stop looking upon me as that sacred object, Deborah's mother, and just tell me what dangerous and unpleasant job there is for me to do."

"You know," said the young man with enthusiasm, "I think you're splendid, simply splendid."

"Cut out the compliments," said Tuppence. "I'm admiring myself a good deal, so there's no need for you to chime in. What exactly is the big idea?"

Tony indicated the mass of crumpled material with a gesture.

"That," he said, "is the remains of a parachute."

"Aha," said Tuppence. Her eyes sparkled.

"There was just an isolated parachutist," went on Marsdon. "Fortunately the L.D.V.'s around here are quite a bright lot. The descent was spotted, and they got her."

"Her?"

"Yes, her! Woman dressed as a hospital nurse."

"I'm sorry she wasn't a nun," said Tuppence. "There have been so many good stories going around about nuns paying their fares in buses with hairy muscular arms."

"Well, she wasn't a nun and she wasn't a man in disguise. She was a woman of medium height, middle-aged, with dark hair and of slight build."

"In fact," said Tuppence, "a woman not unlike me?"

"You've hit it exactly," said Tony.

"Well?" said Tuppence.

Marsdon said slowly:

"The next part of it is up to you."

Tuppence smiled. She said:

"I'm on all right. Where do I go and what do I do?"

"I say, Mrs. Beresford, you really *are* a sport. Magnificent nerve you've got."

"Where do I go and what do I do?" repeated Tuppence impatiently.

"The instructions are very meagre, unfortunately. In the woman's pocket there was a piece of paper with these words on it in German: 'Walk to Leatherbarrow—due east from the stone cross. 14 St. Asalph's Road. Dr. Binion.'"

Tuppence looked up. On the hill top near by was a stone cross.

"That's it," said Tony. "Signposts have been removed, of course. But Leatherbarrow's a biggish place and walking due east from the cross you're bound to strike it."

"How far?"

"Five miles at least."

Tuppence made a slight grimace.

"Healthy walking exercise before lunch," she commented. "I hope Dr. Binion offers me lunch when I get there."

"Do you know German, Mrs. Beresford?"

"Hotel variety only. I shall have to be firm about speaking English— say my instructions were to do so."

"It's an awful risk," said Marsdon.

"Nonsense. Who's to imagine there's been a substitution? Or does everyone know for miles round that there's been a parachutist brought down?"

"The two L.D.V. men who reported it are being kept by the Chief Constable. Don't want to risk their telling their friends how clever they have been!"

"Somebody else may have seen it—or heard about it?"

Tony smiled.

"My dear Mrs. Beresford, every single day, word goes round that one, two, three, four, up to a hundred parachutists have been seen!"

"That's probably quite true," agreed Tuppence. "Well, lead me to it."

Tony said:

"We've got the kit here—and a policewoman who's an expert in the art of makeup. Come with me."

Just inside the copse there was a tumble-down shed. At the door of it was a competent looking middle-aged woman.

She looked at Tuppence and nodded approvingly.

Inside the shed, seated on an upturned packing case, Tuppence submitted herself to expert ministrations. Finally the operator stood back, nodded approvingly and remarked:

"There now, I think we've made a very nice job of it. What do you think, sir?"

"Very good indeed," said Tony.

Tuppence stretched out her hand and took the mirror the other woman held. She surveyed her own face earnestly and could hardly repress a cry of surprise.

The eyebrows had been trimmed to an entirely different shape, altering the whole expression. Small pieces of adhesive plaster hidden by curls pulled forward over the ears had tightened the skin of the face and altered its contours. A small amount of nose putty had altered the shape of the nose, giving Tuppence an unexpectedly beak-like profile. Skilful makeup had added several years to her age, with heavy lines running down each side of the mouth. The whole face had a complacent, rather foolish look.

"It's frightfully clever," said Tuppence admiringly. She touched her nose gingerly.

"You must be careful," the other woman warned her. She produced two slices of thin india-rubber. "Do you think you could bear to wear these in your cheeks?"

"I suppose I shall have to," said Tuppence gloomily.

She slipped them in and worked her jaws carefully.

"It's not really too uncomfortable," she had to admit.

Tony then discreetly left the shed and Tuppence shed her own clothing and got into the nurse's kit. It was not too bad a fit, though inclined to strain a little over the shoulders. The dark blue bonnet put the final touch to her new personality. She rejected, however, the stout square-toed shoes.

"If I've got to walk five miles," she said decidedly, "I'll do it in my own shoes."

They both agreed that this was reasonable—particularly as Tuppence's own shoes were dark blue brogues that went well with the uniform.

She looked with interest into the dark blue handbag—powder—no lipstick—two pounds fourteen and sixpence in English money, a handkerchief and an identity card in the name of Freda Elton, 4 Manchester Road, Sheffield.

Tuppence transferred her own powder and lipstick and stood up, prepared to set out.

Tony Marsdon turned his head away. He said gruffly:

"I feel a swine letting you do this."

"I know just how you feel."

"But, you see, it's absolutely vital—that we should get some idea of just where and how the attack will come."

Tuppence patted him on the arm.

"Don't worry, my child. Believe it or not, I'm enjoying myself."

Tony Marsdon said again:

"I think you're simply wonderful!"

III

Somewhat weary, Tuppence stood outside 14 St. Asalph's Road and noted that Dr. Binion was a dental surgeon and not a doctor.

From the corner of her eye she noted Tony Marsdon. He was sitting in a racy looking car outside a house further down the street.

It had been judged necessary for Tuppence to walk to Leatherbarrow exactly as instructed, since if she had been driven there in a car the fact might have been noted.

It was certainly true that two enemy aircraft had passed over the downs, circling low before making off, and they could have noted the nurse's lonely figure walking across country.

Tony, with the expert policewoman, had driven off in the opposite direction and had made a big detour before approaching Leatherbarrow and taking up his position in St. Asalph's Road.

Everything was now set.

"The arena doors open," murmured Tuppence. "Enter one Christian en route for the lions. Oh, well, nobody can say I'm not seeing life."

She crossed the road and rang the bell, wondering as she did so, exactly how much Deborah liked that young man.

The door was opened by an elderly woman with a stolid peasant face—not an English face.

"Dr. Binion?" said Tuppence.

The woman looked her slowly up and down.

"You will be Nurse Elton, I suppose."

"Yes."

"Then you will come up to the doctor's surgery."

She stood back, the door closed behind Tuppence, who found herself standing in a narrow linoleum lined hall.

The maid preceded her upstairs and opened a door on the next floor.

"Please to wait. The doctor will come to you."

She went out, shutting the door behind her.

A very ordinary dentist's surgery—the appointments somewhat old and shabby.

Tuppence looked at the dentist's chair and smiled to think that for once it held none of the usual terrors. She had the "dentist feeling" all right—but from quite different causes.

Presently the door would open and "Dr. Binion" would come in. Who would Dr. Binion be? A stranger? Or someone she had seen before? If it was the person she was half expecting to see—

The door opened.

The man who entered was not at all the person Tuppence had half fancied she might see! It was someone she had never considered as a likely starter.

It was Commander Haydock.

XIV

A FLOOD OF wild surmises as to the part Commander Haydock had played in Tommy's disappearance surged through Tuppence's brain, but she thrust them resolutely aside. This was a moment for keeping all her wits about her.

Would or would not the Commander recognize her? It was an interesting question.

She had so steeled herself beforehand to display no recognition or surprise herself, no matter whom she might see, that she felt reasonably sure that she herself had displayed no signs untoward to the situation.

She rose now to her feet and stood there, standing in a respectful attitude, as befitted a mere German woman in the presence of a Lord of creation.

"So you have arrived," said the Commander.

He spoke in English and his manner was precisely the same as usual.

"Yes," said Tuppence, and added, as though presenting her credentials: "Nurse Elton."

Haydock smiled as though at a joke.

"Nurse Elton! Excellent."

He looked at her approvingly.

"You look absolutely right," he said kindly.

Tuppence inclined her head, but said nothing. She was leaving the initiative to him.

"You know, I suppose, what you have to do?" went on Haydock. "Sit down, please."

Tuppence sat down obediently. She replied:

"I was to take detailed instructions from you."

"Very proper," said Haydock. There was a faint suggestion of mockery in his voice.

He said:

"You know the day?"

Tuppence made a rapid decision.

"The fourth!"

Haydock looked startled. A heavy frown creased his forehead.

"So you know that, do you?" he muttered.

There was a pause, then Tuppence said:

"You will tell me, please, what I have to do?"

Haydock said:

"All in good time, my dear."

He paused a minute and then asked:

"You have heard, no doubt, of Sans Souci?"

"No," said Tuppence.

"You haven't?"

"No," said Tuppence firmly.

"Let's see how you deal with that one!" she thought.

There was a queer smile on the Commander's face. He said:

"So you haven't heard of Sans Souci? That surprises me very much—since I was under the impression, you know, *that you'd been living there for the last month . . .*"

There was a dead silence. The Commander said:

"What about that, Mrs. Blenkensop?"

"I don't know what you mean, Dr. Binion. I landed by parachute this morning."

Again Haydock smiled—definitely an unpleasant smile.

He said:

"A few yards of canvas thrust into a bush create a wonderful illusion. And I am not Dr. Binion, dear lady. Dr. Binion is, officially, my dentist—he is good enough to lend me his surgery now and again."

"Indeed?" said Tuppence.

"Indeed, Mrs. Blenkensop! Or perhaps you would prefer me to address you by your real name of Beresford?"

Again there was a poignant silence. Tuppence drew a deep breath. Haydock nodded.

"The game's up, you see. 'You've walked into my parlour,' said the spider to the fly."

There was a faint click and a gleam of blue steel showed in his hand. His voice took on a grim note as he said:

"And I shouldn't advise you to make any noise or try to arouse the neighbourhood! You'd be dead before you got so much as a yelp out, and even if you did manage to scream it wouldn't arouse attention. Patients under gas, you know, often cry out."

Tuppence said composedly:

"You seem to have thought of everything. Has it occurred to you that I have friends who know where I am?"

"Ah! Still harping on the blue-eyed boy—actually brown eyed! Young Antony Marsdon. I'm sorry, Mrs. Beresford, but young Antony happens to be one of our most stalwart supporters in this country. As I said just now, a few yards of canvas creates a wonderful effect. You swallowed the parachute idea quite easily."

"I don't see the point of all this rigmarole!"

"Don't you? We don't want your friends to trace you too easily, you see. If they pick up your trail it will lead to Yarrow and to a man in a car. The fact that a hospital nurse, of quite different facial appearance, walked into Leatherbarrow between one and two will hardly be connected with your disappearance."

"Very elaborate," said Tuppence.

Haydock said:

"I admire your nerve, you know. I admire it very much. I'm sorry to have to coerce you—but it's vital that we should know just exactly how much you did discover at Sans Souci."

Tuppence did not answer.

Haydock said quietly:

"I'd advise you, you know, to come clean. There are certain—possibilities—in a dentist's chair and instruments."

Tuppence merely threw him a scornful look.

Haydock leaned back in his chair. He said slowly:

"Yes—I daresay you've got a lot of fortitude—your type often has. But what about the other half of the picture?"

"What do you mean?"

"I'm talking about Thomas Beresford, your husband, who has lately been living at Sans Souci under the name of Mr. Meadowes, and who is now very conveniently trussed up in the cellar of my house."

Tuppence said sharply:

"I don't believe it."

"Because of the Penny Playne letter? Don't you realize that that was just a smart bit of work on the part of young Antony. You played into his hands nicely when you gave him the code."

Tuppence's voice trembled.

"Then Tommy—then Tommy—"

"Tommy," said Commander Haydock, "is where he has been all along—completely in my power! It's up to you now. If you answer my questions satisfactorily, there's a chance for him. If you don't—well, the original plan holds. He'll be knocked on the head, taken out to sea and put overboard."

Tuppence was silent for a minute or two—then she said:

"What do you want to know?"

"I want to know who employed you, what your means of communication with that person or persons are, what you have reported so far, and exactly what you know?"

Tuppence shrugged her shoulders.

"I could tell you what lies I chose," she pointed out.

"No, because I shall proceed to test what you say." He drew his chair a little nearer. His manner was now definitely appealing—"My dear woman—I know just what you feel about it all, but do believe me when I say I really do admire both you and your husband immensely. You've got grit and pluck. It's people like you who will be needed in the new State—the State that will arise in this country when your present imbecile Government is vanquished. We want to turn some of our enemies into friends—those that are worth while. If I have to give the order that ends your husband's life, I shall do it—it's my duty—but I shall feel really badly about having to do it! He's a fine fellow— quiet, unassuming and clever. Let me impress upon you what so few people in this country seem to understand. Our Leader does not intend to conquer this country in the sense that you all think. He aims at creating a new Britain—a Britain strong in its own power—ruled over, *not* by Germans, but by *Englishmen*. And the best *type* of Englishmen—Englishmen with brains and breeding and courage. *A brave new world*, as Shakespeare puts it."

He leaned forward.

"We want to do away with muddle and inefficiency. With bribery and corruption. With self-seeking and money-grubbing—*and in this new state we want people like you and your husband*—brave and resourceful—enemies that have been, friends to be. You would be surprised if you knew how many there are in this country, as in others, who have sympathy with and belief in our aims. Among us all we will create a new Europe—a Europe of peace and progress. Try and see it that way—because, I assure you—it *is* that way . . ."

His voice was compelling, magnetic. Leaning forward, he looked the embodiment of a straightforward British sailor.

Tuppence looked at him and searched her mind for a telling phrase. She was only able to find one that was both childish and rude.

"Goosey, goosey gander!" said Tuppence. . . .

II

The effect was so magical that she was quite taken aback.

Haydock jumped to his feet, his face went dark purple with rage, and in a second all likeness to a hearty British sailor had vanished. She saw what Tommy had once seen—an infuriated Prussian.

He swore at her fluently in German. Then, changing to English, he shouted:

"You infernal little fool! Don't you realize you give yourself away completely answering like that? You've done for yourself now—you and your precious husband."

Raising his voice he called:

"Anna!"

The woman who had admitted Tuppence came into the room. Haydock thrust the pistol into her hand.

"Watch her. Shoot if necessary."

He stormed out of the room.

Tuppence looked appealingly at Anna, who stood in front of her with an impressive face.

"Would you really shoot me?" said Tuppence.

Anna answered quietly:

"You need not try to get round me. In the last war my son was killed, my Otto. I was thirty-eight, then—I am sixty-two now—but I have not forgotten."

Tuppence looked at the broad, impassive face. It reminded her of the Polish woman, Vanda Polonska. That same frightening ferocity and singleness of purpose. Motherhood—unrelenting! So, no doubt, felt many a quiet Mrs. Jones and Mrs. Smith all over England. There was no arguing with the female of the species—the mother deprived of her young.

Something stirred in the recesses of Tuppence's brain—some nagging recollection—something that she had always known but had never succeeded in getting into the forefront of her mind. Solomon—Solomon came into it somewhere . . .

The door opened. Commander Haydock came back into the room.

He howled out, beside himself with rage:

"Where is it? Where have you hidden it?"

Tuppence stared at him. She was completely taken aback. What he was saying did not make sense to her.

She had taken nothing and hidden nothing.

Haydock said to Anna:

"Get out."

The woman handed the pistol to him and left the room promptly.

Haydock dropped into a chair and seemed to be striving to pull himself together. He said:

"You can't get away with it, you know. I've got you—and I've got ways of making people speak—not pretty ways. You'll have to tell the truth in the end. Now then, *what have you done with it?*"

Tuppence was quick to see that here, at least, was something that gave her the possibility of bargaining. If only she could find out what it was she was supposed to have in her possession.

She said cautiously:

"How do you know I've got it?"

"From what you said, you damned little fool. You haven't got it on you—that we know, since you changed completely into this kit."

"Suppose I posted it to someone?" said Tuppence.

"Don't be a fool. Everything you posted since yesterday has been examined. You didn't post it. No, there's only one thing you *could* have done. Hidden it in Sans Souci before you left this morning. I give you just three minutes to tell me where that hiding place is."

He put his watch down on the table.

"*Three minutes, Mrs. Thomas Beresford.*"

The clock on the mantelpiece ticked.

Tuppence sat quite still with a blank impassive face.

It revealed nothing of the racing thoughts behind it.

In a flash of bewildering light she saw everything—saw the whole business revealed in terms of blinding clarity and realized at last who was the centre and pivot of the whole organization.

It came quite as a shock to her when Haydock said:

"Ten seconds more . . ."

Like one in a dream she watched him, saw the pistol arm rise, heard him count:

"One, two, three, four, five—"

He had reached *eight* when the shot rang out and he collapsed forward on his chair, an expression of bewilderment on his broad red face. So intent had he been on watching his victim that he had been unaware of the door behind him slowly opening.

In a flash Tuppence was on her feet. She pushed her way past the uniformed men in the doorway, and seized on a tweed clad arm.

"*Mr. Grant.*"

"Yes, yes, my dear, it's all right now—you've been wonderful—"

Tuppence brushed aside these reassurances.

"*Quick!* There's no time to lose. You've got a car here?"

"Yes." He stared.

"A fast one? We must get to Sans Souci *at once*. If only we're in time. Before they telephone here, and get no answer."

Two minutes later they were in the car, and it was threading its way through the streets of Leatherbarrow. Then they were out in the open country and the needle of the speedometer was rising.

Mr. Grant asked no questions. He was content to sit quietly whilst Tuppence watched the speedometer in an agony of apprehension. The chauffeur had been given his orders and he drove with all the speed of which the car was capable.

Tuppence spoke only once.

"Tommy?"

"Quite all right. Released half an hour ago."

She nodded.

Now, at last, they were nearing Leahampton. They darted and twisted through the town, up the hill.

Tuppence jumped out and she and Mr. Grant ran up the drive. The hall door, as usual, was open. There was no one in sight. Tuppence ran lightly up the stairs.

She just glanced inside her own room in passing, and noted the confusion of open drawers and disordered bed. She nodded and passed on, along the corridor and into the room occupied by Mr. and Mrs. Cayley.

The room was empty. It looked peaceful and smelled slightly of medicines.

Tuppence ran across to the bed and pulled at the coverings.

They fell to the ground and Tuppence ran her hand under the

mattress. She turned triumphantly to Mr. Grant with a tattered child's picture book in her hand.

"Here you are. It's all in here—"

"What on—"

They turned. Mrs. Sprot was standing in the doorway staring.

"And now," said Tuppence, *"let me introduce you to M!* Yes. Mrs. Sprot! I ought to have known it all along."

It was left to Mrs. Cayley, arriving in the doorway a moment later, to introduce the appropriate anti-climax.

"Oh, *dear,*" said Mrs. Cayley, looking with dismay at her spouse's dismantled bed. "Whatever *will* Mr. Cayley say?"

XV

"I ought to have known it all along," said Tuppence.

She was reviving her shattered nerves by a generous tot of old brandy, and was beaming alternately at Tommy and at Mr. Grant—and at Albert, who was sitting in front of a pint of beer and grinning from ear to ear.

"Tell us all about it, Tuppence," urged Tommy.

"You first," said Tuppence.

"There's not much for me to tell," said Tommy. "Sheer accident let me into the secret of the wireless transmitter. I thought I'd got away with it, but Haydock was too smart for me."

Tuppence nodded and said:

"He telephoned to Mrs. Sprot at once. And she ran out into the drive and lay in wait for you with the hammer. She was only away from the bridge table for about three minutes. I *did* notice she was a little out of breath—but I never suspected her."

"After that," said Tommy, "the credit belongs entirely to Albert. He came sniffing round like a faithful dog. I did some impassioned Morse snoring and he cottoned on to it. He went off to Mr. Grant with the news and the two of them came back late that night. More snoring! Result was, I agreed to remain put so as to catch the sea forces when they arrived."

Mr. Grant added his quota.

"When Haydock went off this morning, our people took charge at Smugglers' Rest. We nabbed the boat this evening."

"And now, Tuppence," said Tommy. "Your story."

"Well, to begin with, I've been the most frightful fool all along! I suspected everybody here except Mrs. Sprot! I *did* once have a terrible feeling of menace, as though I was in danger—that was after I overheard that telephone message about the 4th of the month. There were three people there at the time—I put down my feeling of apprehension to either Mrs. Perenna or Mrs. O'Rourke. Quite wrong—it was the colourless Mrs. Sprot who was the really dangerous personality.

"I went muddling on, as Tommy knows, until after he disappeared. Then I was just cooking up a plan with Albert when suddenly, out of the blue, Antony Marsdon turned up. It seemed all right to begin with—the usual sort of young man that Deb often has in tow. But two things made me think a bit. First, I became more and more sure as I talked to him that I *hadn't* seen him before and that he never *had* been to the flat. The second was that, though he seemed to know all about *my* working at Leahampton, he assumed that *Tommy* was in Scotland. Now that seemed all wrong. If he knew about anyone, it would be *Tommy* he knew about, since I was more or less unofficial. That struck me as very odd.

"Mr. Grant had told me that Fifth Columnists were everywhere—in the most unlikely places. So why shouldn't one of them be working in Deborah's show? I wasn't convinced, but I *was* suspicious enough to lay a trap for him. I told him that Tommy and I had fixed up a code for communicating with each other. Our real one, of course, was a Bonzo postcard, but I told Antony a fairy tale about the *Penny Plain, Twopence Coloured* saying.

"As I hoped, he rose to it beautifully! I got a letter this morning which gave him away completely.

"The arrangements had been all worked out beforehand. All I had to do was to ring up a tailor and cancel a fitting. That was an intimation that the fish had risen."

"Coo-er!" said Albert. "It didn't half give me a turn. I drove up with a baker's van and we dumped a pool of stuff just outside the gate. Aniseed, it was—or smelled like it."

"And then"—Tuppence took up the tale—"I came out and walked in it. Of course it was easy for the baker's van to follow me to the station and someone came up behind me and heard me book to Yarrow. It was after that that it might have been difficult."

"The dogs followed the scent well," said Mr. Grant. "They picked it up at Yarrow station and again on the track the tire had made after you rubbed your shoe on it. It led us down to the copse and up again to the stone cross and after you where you had walked over the downs. The enemy had no idea we could follow you easily after they themselves had seen you start and driven off themselves."

"All the same," said Albert, "it gives me a turn. Knowing you were in that house and not knowing what might come to you. Got in a back window, we did, and nabbed the foreign woman as she came down the stairs. Come in just in the nick of time, we did."

"I knew you'd come," said Tuppence. "The thing was for me to spin things out as long as I could. I'd have pretended to tell if I hadn't seen the door opening. What was really exciting was the way I suddenly saw the whole thing and what a fool I'd been."

"How did you see it?" asked Tommy.

"*Goosey, goosey gander*," said Tuppence promptly. "When I said that to Commander Haydock he went absolutely livid. And not just because it was silly and crude. No, I saw at once that it *meant* something to him. And then there was the expression on that woman's face —Anna—it was like the Polish woman's, and then, of course, I thought of Solomon and I saw the whole thing."

Tommy gave a sigh of exasperation.

"Tuppence, if you say that once again, I'll shoot you myself. Saw all *what*? And what on earth has Solomon got to do with it?"

"Do you remember that two women came to Solomon with a baby and both said it was hers, but Solomon said, 'Very well, cut it in two.' And the false mother said, 'All right.' But the real mother said, 'No, let the other woman have it.' You see, she couldn't face her child being killed. Well, that night that Mrs. Sprot shot the other woman, you all said what a miracle it was and how easily she might have shot the child. Of course, it ought to have been quite plain then! If it *had* been her child, she *couldn't* have risked that shot for a minute. It meant that Betty *wasn't* her child. And that's why she absolutely *had* to shoot the other woman."

"Why?"

"Because, of course, the other woman was *the child's real mother*." Tuppence's voice shook a little.

"Poor thing—poor hunted thing. She came over a penniless refugee and gratefully agreed to let Mrs. Sprot adopt her baby."

"Why did Mrs. Sprot want to adopt the child?"

"*Camouflage!* Supreme psychological camouflage. You just can't conceive of a master spy dragging her kid into the business. That's the main reason why I never considered Mrs. Sprot seriously. Simply because of the child. But Betty's real mother had a terrible hankering for her baby and she found out Mrs. Sprot's address and came down here. She hung about waiting for her chance, and at last she got it and went off with the child.

"Mrs. Sprot, of course, was frantic. At all costs she didn't want the police. So she wrote that message and pretended she found it in her bedroom, and roped in Commander Haydock to help. Then, when we'd tracked down the wretched woman, she was taking no chances and shot her. . . . Far from not knowing anything about firearms, she was a very fine shot! Yes, she killed that wretched woman—and because of that I've no pity for her. She was bad through and through."

Tuppence paused, then she went on:

"Another thing that ought to have given me a hint was the likeness between Vanda Polonska and Betty. It was *Betty* the woman reminded me of all along. And then the child's absurd play with my shoe-laces. How much more likely that she'd seen her so-called mother do that— not Carl von Deinim! But as soon as Mrs. Sprot saw what the child was doing, she planted a lot of evidence in Carl's room for us to find and added the master touch of a shoe-lace dipped in secret ink."

"I'm glad that Carl wasn't in it," said Tommy. "I liked him."

"He's not been shot, has he?" asked Tuppence anxiously, noting the past tense.

Mr. Grant shook his head.

"He's all right," he said. "As a matter of fact I've got a little surprise for you there."

Tuppence's face lit up as she said:

"I'm terribly glad—for Sheila's sake! Of course we were idiots to go on barking up the wrong tree after Mrs. Perenna."

"She was mixed up in some I.R.A. activities, nothing more," said Mr. Grant.

"I suspected Mrs. O'Rourke a little—and sometimes the Cayleys—"

"And I suspected Bletchley," put in Tommy.

"And all the time," said Tuppence, "it was that milk and water creature we just thought of as—Betty's mother."

"Hardly milk and water," said Mr. Grant. "A very dangerous woman and a very clever actress. And, I'm sorry to say, English by birth."

Tuppence said:

"Then I've no pity or admiration for her—it wasn't even her country she was working for." She looked with fresh curiosity at Mr. Grant. "You found what you wanted?"

Mr. Grant nodded.

"It was all in that battered set of duplicate children's books."

"The ones that Betty said were *nasty*," Tuppence exclaimed.

"They *were* nasty," said Mr. Grant drily. "*Little Jack Horner* contained very full details of our naval dispositions. *Johnny Head in Air* did the same for the Air Force. Military matters were appropriately embodied in *There Was a Little Man and He Had a Little Gun*."

"And *Goosey, Goosey Gander?*" asked Tuppence.

Mr. Grant said:

"Treated with the appropriate reagent, that book contains, written in invisible ink, a full list of all prominent personages who are pledged to assist an invasion of this country. Amongst them were two Chief Constables, an Air Vice-Marshal, two Generals, the Head of an Armaments Works, a Cabinet Minister, many Police Superintendents, Commanders of Local Volunteer Defense Organizations, and various military and naval lesser fry, as well as members of our own Intelligence Force."

Tommy and Tuppence stared.

"Incredible!" said the former.

Grant shook his head.

"You do not know the force of the German propaganda. It appeals to something in man, some desire or lust for power. These people were ready to betray their country not for money, but in a kind of megalomaniacal pride in what they, *they themselves*, were going to achieve for that country. In every land it has been the same. It is the Cult of Lucifer—Lucifer, Son of the Morning. Pride and a desire for *personal glory!*"

He added:

"You can realize that, with such persons to issue contradictory orders and confuse operations, the threatened invasion would have had every chance to succeed."

"And now?" said Tuppence.

Mr. Grant smiled.

"And now," he said, *"let them come! We'll be ready for them!"*

XVI

"DARLING," SAID DEBORAH. "Do you know I almost thought the most terrible things about you?"

"Did you?" said Tuppence. "When?"

Her eyes rested affectionately on her daughter's dark head.

"That time when you sloped off to Scotland to join father and I thought you were with Aunt Gracie. I almost thought you were having an affair with someone."

"Oh, Deb, did you?"

"Not really, of course. Not at your age. And, of course, I know you and Carrot Top are devoted to each other. It was really an idiot called Tony Marsdon who put it into my head. Do you know, mother —I think I might tell you—he was found afterwards to be a Fifth Columnist. He always did talk rather oddly—how things would be just the same, perhaps better, if Hitler did win."

"Did you—er—like him at all?"

"Tony? Oh, no—he was always rather a bore. I must dance this."

She floated away in the arms of a fair-haired young man, smiling up at him sweetly. Tuppence followed their revolutions for a few minutes, then her eyes shifted to where a tall young man in Air Force uniform was dancing with a fair-haired slender girl.

"I do think, Tommy," said Tuppence, "that our children are rather nice."

"Here's Sheila," said Tommy.

He got up as Sheila Perenna came towards their table.

She was dressed in an emerald evening dress which showed up her dark beauty. It was a sullen beauty tonight and she greeted her host and hostess somewhat ungraciously.

"I've come, you see," she said, "as I promised. But I can't think why you wanted to ask me."

"Because we like you," said Tommy, smiling.

"Do you really?" said Sheila. "I can't think why. I've been perfectly foul to you both."

She paused and murmured:

"But I am grateful."

Tuppence said:

"We must find a nice partner to dance with you."

"I don't want to dance. I loathe dancing. I came just to see you two."

"You will like the partner we've asked to meet you," said Tuppence, smiling.

"I—" Sheila began. Then stopped—for Carl von Deinim was walking across the floor.

Sheila looked at him like one dazed. She muttered:

"You—"

"I, myself," said Carl.

There was something a little different about Carl von Deinim this evening. Sheila stared at him, a trifle perplexed. The colour had come up in her cheeks, turning them a deep glowing red.

She said a little breathlessly:

"I knew that you would be all right now—but I thought they would still keep you interned?"

Carl shook his head.

"There is no reason to intern me."

He went on.

"You have got to forgive me, Sheila, for deceiving you. I am not, you see, Carl von Deinim at all. I took his name for reasons of my own."

He looked questioningly at Tuppence, who said:

"Go ahead. Tell her."

"Carl von Deinim was my friend. I knew him in England some years ago. I renewed acquaintanceship with him in Germany just before the war. I was there then on special business for this country."

"You were in the Intelligence?" asked Sheila.

"Yes. When I was there, queer things began to happen. Once or twice I had some very near escapes. My plans were known when they should not have been known. I realized that there was something very wrong and that 'the rot,' to express it in their terms, had penetrated actually into the service in which I was. I had been let down by my own people. Carl and I had a certain superficial likeness (my grandmother was a German), hence my suitability for work in Germany. Carl was not a Nazi. He was interested solely in his job—a job I myself had also practised—research chemistry. He decided, shortly before war broke out, to escape to England. His brothers had been sent to concentration camps. There would, he thought, be great difficulties in the way of his own escape, but in an almost miraculous fashion all these difficulties smoothed themselves out. The fact, when he mentioned it to me, made me somewhat suspicious. Why were the authorities making it so easy for von Deinim to leave Germany when his brothers and other relations were in concentration camps and he himself was suspected because of his anti-Nazi sympathies? It seemed as though they wanted him in England for some reason. My own position was becoming increasingly precarious. Carl's lodgings were in the same house as mine and one day I found him, to my sorrow, lying dead on his bed. He had succumbed to depression and taken his own life, leaving a letter behind which I read and pocketed.

"I decided then to effect a substitution. I wanted to get out of Germany—and I wanted to know why Carl was being encouraged to do so. I dressed his body in my clothes and laid it on my bed. It was disfigured by the shot he had fired into his head. My landlady, I knew, was semi-blind.

"With Carl von Deinim's papers I travelled to England and went to the address to which he had been recommended to go. That address was Sans Souci.

"Whilst I was there I played the part of Carl von Deinim and never relaxed. I found arrangements had been made for me to work in the chemical factory there. At first I thought that the idea was I should be compelled to do work for the Nazis. I realized later that the part for which my poor friend had been cast was that of scapegoat.

"When I was arrested on faked evidence, I said nothing. I wanted to leave the revelation of my own identity as late as possible. I wanted to see what would happen.

"It was only a few days ago that I was recognized by one of our people and the truth came out."

Sheila said reproachfully:

"You should have told me."

He said gently:

"If you feel like that—I am sorry."

His eyes looked into hers. She looked at him angrily and proudly—then the anger melted. She said:

"I suppose you had to do what you did. . . . "

"Darling—"

He caught himself up.

"Come and dance. . . ."

They moved off together.

Tuppence sighed.

"What's the matter?" said Tommy.

"I do hope Sheila will go on caring for him now that he isn't a German outcast with everyone against him."

"She looks as though she cared all right."

"Yes, but the Irish are terribly perverse. And Sheila is a born rebel."

"Why did he search your room that day? That's what led us up the garden path so terribly."

Tommy gave a laugh.

"I gather he thought Mrs. Blenkensop wasn't a very convincing person. In fact—while we were suspecting him he was suspecting us."

"Hullo, you two," said Derek Beresford as he and his partner danced past his parents' table. "Why don't you come and dance?"

He smiled encouragingly at them.

"They are so kind to us, bless 'em," said Tuppence.

Presently the twins and their partners returned and sat down.

Derek said to his father:

"Glad you got a job all right. Not very interesting I suppose?"

"Mainly routine," said Tommy.

"Never mind, you're doing something. That's the great thing."

"And I'm glad mother was allowed to go and work, too," said Deborah. "She looks ever so much happier. It wasn't too dull, was it, mother?"

"I didn't find it at all dull," said Tuppence.

"Good," said Deborah. She added, "When the war's over, I'll be able to tell you something about my job. It's really frightfully interesting, but very confidential."

"How thrilling," said Tuppence.

"Oh, it is! Of course, it's not so thrilling as flying—"

She looked enviously at Derek.

She said, "He's going to be recommended for—"

Derek said quickly:

"Shut up, Deb."

Tommy said:

"Hullo, Derek, what have you been up to?"

"Oh, nothing much—sort of show all of us are doing. Don't know why they pitched on me," murmured the young airman, his face scarlet. He looked as embarrassed as though he had been accused of the most deadly of sins.

He got up and the fair-haired girl got up, too.

Derek said:

"Mustn't miss any of this—last night of my leave."

"Come on, Charley," said Deborah.

The two of them floated away with their partners.

Tuppence prayed inwardly:

"Oh, let them be safe—don't let anything happen to them. . . ."

She looked up to meet Tommy's eyes. He said, "About that child—shall we?"

"Betty? Oh, Tommy, I'm so glad you've thought of it, too! I thought it was just me being maternal. You really mean it?"

"That we should adopt her? Why not? She's had a raw deal, and it will be fun for us to have something young growing up."

"Oh, Tommy!"

She stretched out her hand and squeezed his. They looked at each other.

"We always do want the same things," said Tuppence happily.

Deborah, passing Derek on the floor, murmured to him:

"Just look at those two—actually holding hands! They're rather sweet, aren't they. We must do all we can to make up to them for having such a dull time in this war. . . ."

Murder in Mesopotamia

FOREWORD

GILES REILLY, M.D.

THE EVENTS CHRONICLED in this narrative took place some four years ago. Circumstances have rendered it necessary, in my opinion, that a straightforward account of them should be given to the public. There have been the wildest and most ridiculous rumours suggesting that important evidence was suppressed and other nonsense of that kind. Those misconstructions have appeared more especially in the American press.

For obvious reasons it was desirable that the account should not come from the pen of one of the expedition staff, who might reasonably be supposed to be prejudiced.

I therefore suggested to Miss Amy Leatheran that she should undertake the task. She is obviously the person to do it. She has a professional character of the highest, she is not biased by having any previous connection with the University of Pittstown Expedition to Iraq and she was an observant and intelligent eye-witness.

It was not very easy to persuade Miss Leatheran to undertake this task—in fact, persuading her was one of the hardest jobs of my professional career—and even after it was completed she displayed a curious reluctance to let me see the manuscript. I discovered that this was partly due to some critical remarks she had made concerning my daughter Sheila. I soon disposed of that, assuring her that as children criticize their parents freely in print nowadays, parents are only too delighted when their offspring come in for their share of abuse! Her other objection was extreme modesty about her literary style. She hoped I would "put the grammar right and all that." I have, on the contrary, refused to alter so much as a single word. Miss Leatheran's style in my opinion is vigorous, individual and entirely apposite. If she calls Hercule Poirot "Poirot" in one paragraph and "Mr. Poirot" in the next, such a variation is both interesting and suggestive. At one moment she is, so to speak, "remembering her manners" (and hospital nurses are great sticklers for etiquette) and at the next her interest in what she is telling is that of a pure human being—cap and cuffs forgotten!

The only thing I have done is to take the liberty of writing a first chapter—aided by a letter kindly supplied by one of Miss Leatheran's friends. It is intended to be in the nature of a frontispiece—that is, it gives a rough sketch of the narrator.

I
FOREWORD

In the hall of the Tigris Palace Hotel in Baghdad a hospital nurse was finishing a letter. Her fountain-pen drove briskly over the paper.

". . . Well, dear, I think that's really all my news. I must say it's been nice to see a bit of the world—though England for me every time, thank you! The *dirt* and the *mess* in Baghdad you wouldn't believe—and not romantic at all like you'd think from the Arabian Nights! Of course, it's pretty just on the river, but the town itself is just awful—and no proper shops at all. Major Kelsey took me through the bazaars, and of course there's no denying they're *quaint*—but just a lot of rubbish and hammering away at copper pans till they make your head ache—and not what I'd like to use myself unless I was sure about the cleaning. You've got to be so careful of verdigris with copper pans.

"I'll write and let you know if anything comes of the job that Dr. Reilly spoke about. He said this American gentleman was in Baghdad now and might come and see me this afternoon. It's for his wife—she has 'fancies,' so Dr. Reilly said. He didn't say any more than that, and of course, dear, one knows what that *usually means* (but I hope not actually D.T.'s!). Of course, Dr. Reilly didn't say anything—but he had a look—if you know what I mean. This Dr. Leidner is an archæologist and is digging up a mound out in the desert somewhere for some American museum.

"Well, dear, I will close now. I thought what you told me about little Stubbins was simply *killing!* Whatever did Matron say?

"No more now.

"Yours ever,

"Amy Leatheran."

Enclosing the letter in an envelope, she addressed it to Sister Curshaw, St. Christopher's Hospital, London.

As she put the cap on her fountain-pen, one of the native boys approached her.

"A gentleman come see you. Dr. Leidner."

Nurse Leatheran turned. She saw a man of middle height with slightly stooping shoulders, a brown beard and gentle tired eyes.

Dr. Leidner saw a woman of thirty-five of erect, confident bearing. He saw a good-humoured face with slightly prominent blue eyes and glossy brown hair. She looked, he thought, just what a hospital nurse for a nervous case ought to look. Cheerful, robust, shrewd and matter of fact.

Nurse Leatheran, he thought, would do.

II

INTRODUCING AMY LEATHERAN

I DON'T PRETEND to be an author or to know anything about writing. I'm doing this simply because Dr. Reilly asked me to, and somehow when Dr. Reilly asks you to do a thing you don't like to refuse.

"Oh, but, doctor," I said, "I'm not literary—not literary at all."

"Nonsense!" he said. "Treat it as case notes, if you like."

Well, of course, you *can* look at it that way.

Dr. Reilly went on. He said that an unvarnished plain account of the Tell Yarimjah business was badly needed.

"If one of the interested parties writes it, it won't carry conviction. They'll say it's biased one way or another."

And of course that was true, too. I was in it all and yet an outsider, so to speak.

"Why don't you write it yourself, doctor?" I asked.

"I wasn't on the spot—you were. Besides," he added with a sigh, "my daughter won't let me."

The way he knuckles under to that chit of a girl of his is downright disgraceful. I had half a mind to say so, when I saw that his eyes were twinkling. That was the worst of Dr. Reilly. You never knew whether he was joking or not. He always said things in the same slow melancholy way—but half the time there was a twinkle underneath it.

"Well," I said doubtfully. "I suppose I *could*."

"Of course you could."

"Only I don't quite know how to set about it."

"There's a good precedent for that. Begin at the beginning, go on to the end and then leave off."

"I don't even know quite where and what the beginning was," I said doubtfully.

"Believe me, nurse, the difficulty of beginning will be nothing to the difficulty of knowing how to stop. At least that's the way it is with me when I have to make a speech. Some one's got to catch hold of my coat-tails and pull me down by main force."

"Oh, you're joking, doctor."

"It's profoundly serious I am. Now what about it?"

Another thing was worrying me. After hesitating a moment or two I said:

"You know, doctor, I'm afraid I might tend to be—well, a little *personal* sometimes."

"God bless my soul, woman, the more personal you are the better! This is a story of human beings—not dummies! Be personal—be prejudiced—be catty—be anything you please! Write the thing your own way. We can always prune out the bits that are libellous afterwards! You go ahead. You're a sensible woman, and you'll give a sensible common-sense account of the business."

So that was that, and I promised to do my best.

And here I am beginning, but as I said to the doctor, it's difficult to know just where to start.

I suppose I ought to say a word or two about myself. I'm thirty-two and my name is Amy Leatheran. I took my training at St. Christopher's and after that did two years' maternity. I did a certain amount of private work and I was for four years at Miss Bendix's Nursing Home in Devonshire Place. I came out to Iraq with a Mrs. Kelsey. I'd attended her when her baby was born. She was coming out to Baghdad with her husband and had already got a children's nurse booked who had been for some years with friends of hers out there. Their children were coming home and going to school, and the nurse had agreed to go to Mrs. Kelsey when they left. Mrs. Kelsey was delicate and nervous about the journey out with so young a child, so Major Kelsey arranged that I should come out with her and look after her and the baby. They would pay my passage home unless we found some one needing a nurse for the return journey.

Well, there is no need to describe the Kelseys—the baby was a little love and Mrs. Kelsey quite nice, though rather the fretting kind. I enjoyed the voyage very much. I'd never been a long trip on the sea before.

Dr. Reilly was on board the boat. He was a black-haired, long-faced man who said all sorts of funny things in a low, sad voice. I think he enjoyed pulling my leg and used to make the most extraordinary statements to see if I would swallow them. He was the civil surgeon at a place called Hassanieh—a day and a half's journey from Baghdad.

I had been about a week in Baghdad when I ran across him and he asked when I was leaving the Kelseys. I said that it was funny his asking that because as a matter of fact the Wrights (the other people I mentioned) were going home earlier than they had meant to and their nurse was free to come straightaway.

He said that he had heard about the Wrights and that that was why he had asked me.

"As a matter of fact, nurse, I've got a possible job for you."

"A case?"

He screwed his face up as though considering.

"You could hardly call it a case. It's just a lady who has—shall we say—fancies?"

"Oh!" I said.

(One usually knows what *that* means—drink or drugs!)

Dr. Reilly didn't explain further. He was very discreet.

"Yes," he said. "A Mrs. Leidner. Husband's an American—an American Swede to be exact. He's the head of a large American dig."

And he explained how this expedition was excavating the site of a big Assyrian city something like Nineveh. The expedition house was not actually very far from Hassanieh, but it was a lonely spot and Dr. Leidner had been worried for some time about his wife's health.

"He's not been very explicit about it, but it seems she has these fits of recurring nervous terrors."

"Is she left alone all day amongst natives?" I asked.

"Oh, no, there's quite a crowd—seven or eight. I don't fancy she's ever alone in the house. But there seems to be no doubt that she's worked herself up into a queer state. Leidner has any amount of work on his shoulders, but he's crazy about his wife and it worries him to know she's in this state. He felt he'd be happier if he knew that some responsible person with expert knowledge was keeping an eye on her."

"And what does Mrs. Leidner herself think about it?"

Dr. Reilly answered gravely.

"Mrs. Leidner is a very lovely lady. She's seldom of the same mind about anything two days on end. But on the whole she favours the idea." He added, "She's an odd woman. A mass of affectation and, I should fancy, a champion liar—but Leidner seems honestly to believe that she is scared out of her life by something or other."

"What did she herself say to you, doctor?"

"Oh, she hasn't consulted me! She doesn't like me anyway—for several reasons. It was Leidner who came to me and propounded this plan. Well, nurse, what do you think of the idea? You'd see something of the country before you go home—they'll be digging for another two months. And excavation is quite interesting work."

After a moment's hesitation while I turned the matter over in my mind:

"Well," I said. "I really think I might try it."

"Splendid," said Dr. Reilly, rising. "Leidner's in Baghdad now. I'll tell him to come round and see if he can fix things up with you."

Dr. Leidner came to the hotel that afternoon. He was a middle-aged man with a rather nervous, hesitating manner. There was something gentle and kindly and rather helpless about him.

He sounded very devoted to his wife, but he was very vague about what was the matter with her.

"You see," he said, tugging at his beard in a rather perplexed manner that I later came to know to be characteristic of him, "my wife is really in a very nervous state. I—I'm quite worried about her."

"She is in good physical health?" I asked.

"Yes—oh, yes, I think so. No, I should not think there was anything the matter with her physically. But she—well—imagines things, you know."

"What kind of things?" I asked.

But he shied off from the point, merely murmuring perplexedly:

"She works herself up over nothing at all. . . . I really can see no foundations for these fears."

"Fears of what, Dr. Leidner?"

He said vaguely, "Oh, just—nervous terrors, you know."

Ten to one, I thought to myself, it's drugs. And he doesn't realize it! Lots of men don't. Just wonder why their wives are so jumpy and have such extraordinary changes of mood.

I asked whether Mrs. Leidner herself approved of the idea of my coming.

His face lighted up.

"Yes. I was surprised. Most pleasurably surprised. She said it was a very good idea. She said she would feel very much safer."

The word struck me oddly. *Safer.* A very queer word to use. I began to surmise that Mrs. Leidner might be a mental case.

He went on with a kind of boyish eagerness.

"I'm sure you'll get on very well with her. She's really a very charming woman." He smiled disarmingly. "She feels you'll be the greatest comfort to her. I felt the same as soon as I saw you. You look, if you will allow me to say so, so splendidly healthy and full of common sense. I'm sure you're just the person for Louise."

"Well, we can but try, Dr. Leidner," I said cheerfully. "I'm sure I hope I can be of use to your wife. Perhaps she's nervous of natives and coloured people?"

"Oh, dear me, no." He shook his head, amused at the idea. "My wife likes Arabs very much—she appreciates their simplicity and their sense of humour. This is only her second season—we have been married less than two years—but she already speaks quite a fair amount of Arabic."

I was silent for a moment or two, then I had one more try.

"Can't you tell me at all what it is your wife is afraid of, Dr. Leidner?" I asked.

He hesitated. Then he said slowly, "I hope—I believe—that she will tell you that herself."

And that's all I could get out of him.

III

GOSSIP

It was arranged that I should go to Tell Yarimjah the following week.
Mrs. Kelsey was settling into her house at Alwiyah, and I was glad
to be able to take a few things off her shoulders.

During that time I heard one or two allusions to the Leidner expedition. A friend of Mrs. Kelsey's, a young squadron-leader, pursed
his lips in surprise as he exclaimed:

"Lovely Louise. So that's her latest!" He turned to me. "That's our
nickname for her, nurse. She's always known as Lovely Louise."

"Is she so very handsome then?" I asked.

"It's taking her at her own valuation. *She* thinks she is!"

"Now don't be spiteful, John," said Mrs. Kelsey. "You know it's not
only she who thinks so! Lots of people have been very smitten by her."

"Perhaps you're right. She's a bit long in the tooth, but she has a
certain attraction."

"You were completely bowled over yourself," said Mrs. Kelsey,
laughing.

The squadron-leader blushed and admitted rather shamefacedly:

"Well, she has a way with her. As for Leidner himself, he worships
the ground she walks on—and all the rest of the expedition has to worship too! It's expected of them!"

"How many are there altogether?" I asked.

"All sorts and nationalities, nurse," said the squadron-leader cheerfully. "An English architect, a French Father from Carthage—he does
the inscriptions—tablets and things, you know. And then there's Miss
Johnson. She's English too—sort of general bottle-washer. And a little
plump man who does the photography—he's an American. And the
Mercados. Heaven knows what nationality they are—Dagos of some
kind! She's quite young—a snaky-looking creature—and oh! doesn't she
hate Lovely Louise! And there are a couple of youngsters, and that's
the lot. A few odd fish, but nice on the whole—don't you agree,
Pennyman?"

He was appealing to an elderly man who was sitting thoughtfully twirling a pair of pince-nez.

The latter started and looked up.

"Yes—yes—very nice indeed. Taken individually, that is. Of course, Mercado is rather a queer fish—"

"He has such a very *odd* beard," put in Mrs. Kelsey. "A queer limp kind."

Major Pennyman went on without noticing her interruption.

"The young 'uns are both nice. The American's rather silent, and the English boy talks a bit too much. Funny, it's usually the other way round. Leidner himself is a delightful fellow—so modest and unassuming. Yes, individually they are all pleasant people. But somehow or other, I may have been fanciful, but the last time I went to see them I got a queer impression of something being wrong. I don't know what it was exactly. . . . Nobody seemed quite natural. There was a queer atmosphere of tension. I can explain best what I mean by saying that they all passed the butter to each other too politely."

Blushing a little, because I don't like airing my own opinions too much, I said:

"If people are too much cooped up together it's got a way of getting on their nerves. I know that myself from experience in hospital."

"That's true," said Major Kelsey, "but it's early in the season, hardly time for that particular irritaton to have set in."

"An expedition is probably like our life here in miniature," said Major Pennyman. "It has its cliques and rivalries and jealousies."

"It sounds as though they'd got a good many new-comers this year," said Major Kelsey.

"Let me see." The squadron-leader counted them off on his fingers. "Young Coleman is new, so is Reiter. Emmott was out last year and so were the Mercados. Father Lavigny is a new-comer. He's come in place of Dr. Byrd, who was ill this year and couldn't come out. Carey, of course, is an old hand. He's been out ever since the beginning, five years ago. Miss Johnson's been out nearly as many years as Carey."

"I always thought they got on so well together at Tell Yarimjah," remarked Major Kelsey. "They seemed like a happy family—which is really surprising when one considers what human nature is! I'm sure Nurse Leatheran agrees with me."

"Well," I said. "I don't know that you're not right! The rows I've known in hospital and starting often from nothing more than a dispute about a pot of tea."

"Yes, one tends to get petty in close communities," said Major Pennyman. "All the same I feel there must be something more to it in this case. Leidner is such a gentle, unassuming man, with really a remarkable amount of tact. He's always managed to keep his expedition happy and on good terms with each other. And yet I *did* notice that feeling of tension the other day."

Mrs. Kelsey laughed.

"And you don't see the explanation? Why, it leaps to the eye!"

"What do you mean?"

"*Mrs.* Leidner, of course."

"Oh, come, Mary," said her husband, "she's a charming woman—not at all the quarrelsome kind."

"I didn't say she was quarrelsome. She *causes* quarrels!"

"In what way? And why should she?"

"Why? Why? Because she's bored. She's not an archæologist, only the wife of one. She's bored shut away from any excitements and so she provides her own drama. She amuses herself by setting other people by the ears."

"Mary, you don't know in the least. You're merely imagining."

"Of course I'm imagining! But you'll find I'm right. Lovely Louise doesn't look like the Mona Lisa for nothing! She mayn't mean any harm, but she likes to see what will happen."

"She's devoted to Leidner."

"Oh! I dare say. I'm not suggesting vulgar intrigues. But she's an *allumeuse*, that woman."

"Women are so sweet to each other," said Major Kelsey.

"I know. Cat, cat, cat, that's what you men say. But we're usually right about our own sex."

"All the same," said Major Pennyman thoughtfully, "assuming all Mrs. Kelsey's uncharitable surmises to be true, I don't think it would quite account for that curious sense of tension—rather like the feeling there is before a thunderstorm. I had the impression very strongly that the storm might break any minute."

"Now don't frighten nurse," said Mrs. Kelsey. "She's going there in three days' time and you'll put her right off."

"Oh, you won't frighten me," I said, laughing.

All the same I thought a good deal about what had been said. Dr. Leidner's curious use of the word "safer" recurred to me. Was it his wife's secret fear, unacknowledged or expressed perhaps, that was reacting on the rest of the party? Or was it the actual tension (or perhaps the unknown cause of it) that was reacting on *her* nerves?

I looked up the word "allumeuse" that Mrs. Kelsey had used in a dictionary, but couldn't get any sense out of it.

"Well," I thought to myself, "I must wait and see."

IV

I ARRIVE IN HASSANIEH

THREE DAYS LATER I left Baghdad.

I was sorry to leave Mrs. Kelsey and the baby, who was a little love and was thriving splendidly, gaining her proper number of ounces every week. Major Kelsey took me to the station and saw me off. I should arrive at Kirkuk the following morning, and there some one was to meet me.

I slept badly. I never sleep very well in a train and I was troubled by dreams.

The next morning, however, when I looked out of the window it was a lovely day and I felt interested and curious about the people I was going to see.

As I stood on the platform hesitating and looking about me I saw a young man coming towards me. He had a round pink face, and really, in all my life, I have never seen any one who seemed so exactly like a young man out of one of Mr. P. G. Wodehouse's books.

"Hallo, 'allo, 'allo," he said. "Are you Nurse Leatheran? Well, I mean you must be—I can see that. Ha ha! My name's Coleman. Dr. Leidner sent me along. How are you feeling? Beastly journey and all that? Don't I know these trains! Well, here we are—had any breakfast? This your kit? I say, awfully modest, aren't you? Mrs. Leidner has four suitcases and a trunk—to say nothing of a hat-box and a patent pillow, and this, that and the other. Am I talking too much? Come along to the old bus."

There was what I heard called later a station wagon waiting outside. It was a little like a wagonette, a little like a lorry and a little like a car. Mr. Coleman helped me in, explaining that I had better sit next to the driver so as to get less jolting.

Jolting! I wonder the whole contraption didn't fall to pieces! And nothing like a road—just a sort of track all ruts and holes. Glorious East indeed! When I thought of our splendid arterial roads in England it made me quite homesick.

Mr. Coleman leaned forward from his seat behind me and yelled in my ear a good deal.

"Track's in pretty good condition," he shouted just after we had all been thrown up in our seats till we nearly touched the roof.

And apparently he was speaking quite seriously.

"Very good for you—jogs the liver," he said. "You ought to know that, nurse."

"A stimulated liver won't be much good to me if my head's split open," I observed tartly.

"You should come along here after it's rained! The skids are glorious. Most of the time one's going sideways."

To this I did not respond.

Presently we had to cross the river, which we did on the craziest ferry-boat you can imagine. To my mind it was a mercy we ever got across, but every one seemed to think it was quite usual.

It took us about four hours to get to Hassanieh, which, to my surprise, was quite a big place. Very pretty it looked, too, before we got there from the other side of the river—standing up quite white and fairy-like with minarets. It was a bit different, though, when one had crossed the bridge and come right into it. Such a smell, and everything ramshackle and tumble-down, and mud and mess everywhere.

Mr. Coleman took me to Dr. Reilly's house, where, he said, the doctor was expecting me to lunch.

Dr. Reilly was just as nice as ever, and his house was nice too, with a bathroom and everything spick and span. I had a nice bath, and by the time I got back into my uniform and came down I was feeling fine.

Lunch was just ready and we went in, the doctor apologizing for his daughter, whom he said was always late.

We'd just had a very good dish of eggs in sauce when she came in and Dr. Reilly said, "Nurse, this is my daughter Sheila."

She shook hands, hoped I'd had a good journey, tossed off her hat, gave a cool nod to Mr. Coleman and sat down.

"Well, Bill," she said. "How's everything?"

He began to talk to her about some party or other that was to come off at the club, and I took stock of her.

I can't say I took to her much. A thought too cool for my liking. An off-hand sort of girl, though good-looking. Black hair and blue eyes— a pale sort of face and the usual lip-sticked mouth. She'd a cool, sarcastic way of talking that rather annoyed me. I had a probationer like her under me once—a girl who worked well, I'll admit, but whose manner always riled me.

It looked to me rather as though Mr. Coleman was gone on her. He stammered a bit, and his conversation became slightly more idiotic than it was before, if that was possible! He reminded me of a large stupid dog wagging its tail and trying to please.

After lunch Dr. Reilly went off to the hospital, and Mr. Coleman had some things to get in the town, and Miss Reilly asked me whether I'd like to see round the town a bit or whether I'd rather stop in the house. Mr. Coleman, she said, would be back to fetch me in about an hour.

"Is there anything to see?" I asked.

"There are some picturesque corners," said Miss Reilly. "But I don't know that you'd care for them. They're extremely dirty."

The way she said it rather nettled me. I've never been able to see that picturesqueness excuses dirt.

In the end she took me to the club, which was pleasant enough, over-looking the river, and there were English papers and magazines there.

When we got back to the house Mr. Coleman wasn't there yet, so we sat down and talked a bit. It wasn't easy somehow.

She asked me if I'd met Mrs. Leidner yet.

"No," I said. "Only her husband."

"Oh," she said. "I wonder what you'll think of her?"

I didn't say anything to that. And she went on:

"I like Dr. Leidner very much. Everybody likes him."

That's as good as saying, I thought, that you don't like his wife.

I still didn't say anything and presently she asked abruptly:

"What's the matter with her? Did Dr. Leidner tell you?"

I wasn't going to start gossiping about a patient before I got there even, so I said evasively:

"I understand she's a bit run down and wants looking after."

She laughed—a nasty sort of laugh—hard and abrupt.

"Good God," she said. "Aren't nine people looking after her already enough?"

"I suppose they've all got their work to do," I said.

"Work to do? Of course they've got work to do. But Louise comes first—she sees to that all right."

"No," I said to myself. "You *don't* like her."

"All the same," went on Miss Reilly, "I don't see what she wants with a professional hospital nurse. I should have thought amateur assistance was more in her line; not some one who'll jam a thermometer in her mouth, and count her pulse and bring everything down to hard facts."

Well, I must admit it, I was curious.

"You think there's nothing the matter with her?" I asked.

"Of course there's nothing the matter with her! The woman's as strong as an ox. 'Dear Louise hasn't slept.' 'She's got black circles under her eyes.' Yes—put there with a blue pencil! Anything to get attention, to have everybody hovering round her, making a fuss of her!"

There was something in that, of course. I had (what nurse hasn't?) come across many cases of hypochondriacs whose delight it is to keep a whole household dancing attendance. And if a doctor or a nurse were to say to them, "There's nothing on earth the matter with you!" well, to begin with they wouldn't believe it, and their indignation would be as genuine as indignation can be.

Of course it was quite possible that Mrs. Leidner might be a case of this kind. The husband, naturally, would be the first to be deceived. Husbands, I've found, are a credulous lot where illness is concerned. But all the same, it didn't quite square with what I'd heard. It didn't, for instance, fit in with that word "safer."

Funny how that word had got kind of stuck in my mind.

Reflecting on it, I asked:

"Is Mrs. Leidner a nervous woman? Is she nervous, for instance, of living out far from anywhere?"

"What is there to be nervous of? Good heavens, there are ten of them! And they've got guards too—because of the antiquities. Oh, no, she's not nervous—at least—"

She seemed struck by some thought and stopped—going on slowly after a minute or two.

"It's odd your saying that."

"Why?"

"Flight-Lieutenant Jervis and I rode over the other day. It was in the morning. Most of them were up on the dig. She was sitting writing a letter and I suppose she didn't hear us coming. The boy who brings you in wasn't about for once, and we came straight up on to the veranda. Apparently she saw Flight-Lieutenant Jervis's shadow thrown on the wall—and she fairly screamed! Apologized, of course. Said she thought it was a strange man. A bit odd, that. I mean, even if it was a strange man, why get the wind up?"

I nodded thoughtfully.

Miss Reilly was silent, then burst out suddenly.

"I don't know what's the matter with them there this year. They've all got the jumps. Johnson goes about so glum she can't open her mouth. David never speaks if he can help it. Bill, of course, never stops, and somehow his chatter seems to make the others worse. Carey goes about looking as though something would snap any minute. And they all watch each other as though—as though— Oh, I don't know, but it's *queer*."

It was odd, I thought, that two such dissimilar people as Miss Reilly and Major Pennyman should have been struck in the same manner.

Just then Mr. Coleman came bustling in. Bustling was just the word for it. If his tongue had hung out and he had suddenly produced a tail to wag you wouldn't have been surprised.

"Hallo-allo," he said. "Absolutely the world's best shopper—that's me. Have you shown nurse all the beauties of the town?"

"She wasn't impressed," said Miss Reilly dryly.

"I don't blame her," said Mr. Coleman heartily. "Of all the one-horse tumble-down places!"

"Not a lover of the picturesque or the antique, are you, Bill? I can't think why you are an archæologist."

"Don't blame me for that. Blame my guardian. He's a learned bird —fellow of his college—browses among books in bedroom slippers— that kind of man. Bit of a shock for him to have a ward like me."

"I think it's frightfully stupid of you to be forced into a profession you don't care for," said the girl sharply.

"Not forced, Sheila, old girl, not forced. The old man asked if I had any special profession in mind, and I said I hadn't, and so he wangled a season out here for me."

"But haven't you any idea really what you'd *like* to do? You *must* have!"

"Of course I have. My idea would be to give work a miss altogether. What I'd like to do is to have plenty of money and go in for motor-racing."

"You're absurd!" said Miss Reilly.

She sounded quite angry.

"Oh, I realize that it's quite out of the question," said Mr. Coleman cheerfully. "So, if I've got to do something, I don't much care what it is so long as it isn't mugging in an office all day long. I was quite agreeable to seeing a bit of the world. Here goes, I said, and along I came."

"And a fat lot of use you must be, I expect!"

"There you're wrong. I can stand up on the dig and shout 'Y'Allah' with anybody! And as a matter of fact I'm not so dusty at drawing. Imitating handwriting used to be my specialty at school. I'd have made a first-class forger. Oh, well, I may come to that yet. If my Rolls-Royce splashes you with mud as you're waiting for a bus, you'll know that I've taken to crime."

Miss Reilly said coldly:

"Don't you think it's about time you started instead of talking so much?"

"Hospitable, aren't we, nurse?"

"I'm sure Nurse Leatheran is anxious to get settled in."

"You're always sure of everything," retorted Mr. Coleman with a grin.

That was true enough, I thought. Cock-sure little minx.

I said dryly:

"Perhaps we'd better start, Mr. Coleman."

"Right you are, nurse."

I shook hands with Miss Reilly and thanked her, and we set off.

"Damned attractive girl, Sheila," said Mr. Coleman. "But always ticking a fellow off."

We drove out of the town and presently took a kind of track between green crops. It was very bumpy and full of ruts.

After about half an hour Mr. Coleman pointed to a big mound by the river bank ahead of us and said:

"Tell Yarimjah."

I could see little black figures moving about it like ants.

As I was looking they suddenly began to run all together down the side of the mound.

"Fidos," said Mr. Coleman. "Knocking off time. We knock off an hour before sunset."

The expedition house lay a little way back from the river.

The driver rounded a corner, bumped through an extremely narrow arch and there we were.

The house was built round a courtyard. Originally it had occupied only the south side of the courtyard with a few unimportant out-buildings on the east. The expedition had continued the building on

the other two sides. As the plan of the house was to prove of special
interest later, I append a rough sketch of it below.

All the rooms opened on to the courtyard, and most of the windows—
the exception being in the original south building where there were

windows giving on the outside country as well. These windows,
however, were barred on the outside. In the south-west corner a staircase ran up to a long flat roof with a parapet running the length of
the south side of the building which was higher than the other three
sides.

Mr. Coleman led me along the east side of the courtyard and round
to where a big open verandah occupied the centre of the south side.
He pushed open a door at one side of it and we entered a room where
several people were sitting round a tea table.

"Toodle-oodle-oo!" said Mr. Coleman. "Here's Sairey Gamp."

The lady who was sitting at the head of the table rose and came to
greet me.

I had my first glimpse of Louise Leidner.

V

TELL YARIMJAH

I DON'T MIND admitting that my first impression on seeing Mrs. Leidner was one of downright surprise. One gets into the way of imagining a person when one hears them talked about. I'd got it firmly into my head that Mrs. Leidner was a dark, discontented kind of woman. The nervy kind, all on edge. And then, too, I'd expected her to be—well, to put it frankly—a bit vulgar.

She wasn't a bit like what I'd imagined her! To begin with, she was very fair. She wasn't a Swede, like her husband, but she might have been as far as looks went. She had that blonde Scandinavian fairness that you don't very often see. She wasn't a young woman. Midway between thirty and forty, I should say. Her face was rather haggard, and there was some grey hair mingled with the fairness. Her eyes, though, were lovely. They were the only eyes I've ever come across that you might truly describe as violet. They were very large, and there were faint shadows underneath them. She was very thin and fragile-looking, and if I say that she had an air of intense weariness and was at the same time very much alive, it sounds like nonsense— but that's the feeling I got. I felt, too, that she was a lady through and through. And that means something—even nowadays.

She put out her hand and smiled. Her voice was low and soft with an American drawl in it.

"I'm so glad you've come, nurse. Will you have some tea? Or would you like to go to your room first?"

I said I'd have tea, and she introduced me to the people sitting round the table.

"This is Miss Johnson—and Mr. Reiter. Mrs. Mercado. Mr. Emmott. Father Lavigny. My husband will be in presently. Sit down here between Father Lavigny and Miss Johnson."

I did as I was bid and Miss Johnson began talking to me, asking about my journey and so on.

I liked her. She reminded me of a matron I'd had in my probationer days whom we had all admired and worked hard for.

She was getting on for fifty, I should judge, and rather mannish in appearance, with iron-grey hair cropped short. She had an abrupt, pleasant voice, rather deep in tone. She had an ugly rugged face with an almost laughably turned-up nose which she was in the habit of rubbing irritably when anything troubled or perplexed her. She wore a tweed coat and skirt made rather like a man's. She told me presently that she was a native of Yorkshire.

Father Lavigny I found just a bit alarming. He was a tall man with a great black beard and pince-nez. I had heard Mrs. Kelsey say that there was a French monk there, and I now saw that Father Lavigny was wearing a monk's robe of some white woollen material. It surprised me rather, because I always understood that monks went into monasteries and didn't come out again.

Mrs. Leidner talked to him mostly in French, but he spoke to me in quite fair English. I noticed that he had shrewd, observant eyes which darted about from face to face.

Opposite me were the other three. Mr. Reiter was a stout, fair young man with glasses. His hair was rather long and curly, and he had very round blue eyes. I should think he must have been a lovely baby, but he wasn't much to look at now! In fact he was just a little like a pig. The other young man had very short hair cropped close to his head. He had a long, rather humorous face and very good teeth, and he looked very attractive when he smiled. He said very little, though, just nodded if spoken to or answered in monosyllables. He, like Mr. Reiter, was an American. The last person was Mrs. Mercado, and I couldn't have a good look at her because whenever I glanced in her direction I always found her staring at me with a kind of hungry stare that was a bit disconcerting to say the least of it. You might have thought a hospital nurse was a strange animal the way she was looking at me. No manners at all!

She was quite young—not more than about twenty-five—and sort of dark and slinky-looking, if you know what I mean. Quite nice-looking in a kind of way, but rather as though she might have what my mother used to call "a touch of the tar-brush." She had on a very vivid pullover and her nails matched it in colour. She had a thin bird-like eager face with big eyes and rather a tight, suspicious mouth.

The tea was very good—a nice strong blend—not like the weak China stuff that Mrs. Kelsey always had and that had been a sore trial to me.

There was toast and jam and a plate of rock buns and a cutting cake. Mr. Emmott was very polite passing me things. Quiet as he was he always seemed to notice when my plate was empty.

Presently Mr. Coleman bustled in and took the place beyond Miss Johnson. There didn't seem to be anything the matter with *his* nerves. He talked away nineteen to the dozen.

Mrs. Leidner sighed once and cast a wearied look in his direction but it didn't have any effect. Nor did the fact that Mrs. Mercado, to whom he was addressing most of his conversation, was far too busy watching me to do more than make perfunctory replies.

Just as we were finishing, Dr. Leidner and Mr. Mercado came in from the dig.

Dr. Leidner greeted me in his nice kind manner. I saw his eyes go quickly and anxiously to his wife's face and he seemed to be relieved by what he saw there. Then he sat down at the other end of the table and Mr. Mercado sat down in the vacant place by Mrs. Leidner. He was a tall, thin, melancholy man, a good deal older than his wife, with a sallow complexion and a queer, soft, shapeless-looking beard. I was glad when he came in, for his wife stopped staring at me and transferred her attention to him, watching him with a kind of anxious impatience that I found rather odd. He himself stirred his tea dreamily and said nothing at all. A piece of cake lay untasted on his plate.

There was still one vacant place, and presently the door opened and a man came in.

The moment I saw Richard Carey I felt he was one of the handsomest men I'd seen for a long time—and yet I doubt if that were really so. To say a man is handsome and at the same time to say he looks like a death's head sounds a rank contradiction, and yet it was true. His head gave the effect of having the skin stretched unusually tightly over the bones—but they were beautiful bones. The lean line of jaw and temple and forehead was so sharply outlined that he reminded me of a bronze statue. Out of this lean brown face looked two of the brightest and most intensely blue eyes I have ever seen. He stood about six foot and was, I should imagine, a little under forty years of age.

Dr. Leidner said:

"This is Mr. Carey, our architect, nurse."

He murmured something in a pleasant, inaudible English voice and sat down by Mrs. Mercado.

Mrs. Leidner said:

"I'm afraid the tea is a little cold, Mr. Carey." He said:

"Oh, that's quite all right, Mrs. Leidner. My fault for being late. I wanted to finish plotting those walls."

Mrs. Mercado said, "Jam, Mr. Carey?"

Mr. Reiter pushed forward the toast.

And I remember Major Pennyman saying:

"I can explain best what I mean by saying that they all passed the butter to each other a shade too politely."

Yes, there was something a little odd about it. . . .

A shade formal. . . .

You'd have said it was a party of strangers—not people who had known each other—some of them—for quite a number of years.

VI

FIRST EVENING

AFTER TEA MRS. LEIDNER took me to show me my room.

Perhaps here I had better give a short description of the arrangement of the rooms. This was very simple and can easily be understood by a reference to the plan.

On either side of the big open porch were doors leading into the two principal rooms. That on the right led into the dining-room, where we had had tea. The one on the other side led into an exactly similar room (I have called it the living-room) which was used as a sitting-room and kind of informal workroom—that is, a certain amount of drawing (other than the strictly architectural) was done there, and the more delicate pieces of pottery were brought there to be pieced together. Through the living-room one passed into the antiquities-room where all the finds from the dig were brought in and stored on shelves and in pigeon-holes, and also laid out on big benches and tables. From the antika-room there was no exit save through the living-room.

Beyond the antika-room, but reached through a door which gave on the courtyard, was Mrs. Leidner's bedroom. This, like the other rooms on that side of the house, had a couple of barred windows looking out over the ploughed countryside. Round the corner next to Mrs. Leidner's room, but with no actual communicating door, was Dr. Leidner's room. This was the first of the rooms on the east side of the building. Next to it was the room that was to be mine. Next to me was Miss Johnson's, with Mr. and Mrs. Mercado's beyond. After that came two so-called bathrooms.

(When I once used that last term in the hearing of Dr. Reilly he laughed at me and said a bathroom was either a bathroom or not a bathroom! All the same, when you've got used to taps and proper plumbing, it seems strange to call a couple of mud-rooms with a tin hip-bath in each of them, and muddy water brought in kerosene tins, *bathrooms!*)

All this side of the building had been added by Dr. Leidner to the original Arab house. The bedrooms were all the same, each with a window and a door giving on to the courtyard.

Along the north side were the drawing-office, the laboratory and the photographic rooms.

To return to the verandah, the arrangement of rooms was much the same on the other side. There was the dining-room leading into the office where the files were kept and the cataloguing and typing were done. Corresponding to Mrs. Leidner's room was that of Father Lavigny, who was given the largest bedroom; he used it also for the decoding—or whatever you call it—of tablets.

In the south-west corner was the staircase running up to the roof. On the west side were first the kitchen quarters and then four small bedrooms used by the young men—Carey, Emmott, Reiter and Coleman.

At the north-west corner was the photographic-room with the dark-room leading out of it. Next to that the laboratory. Then came the only entrance—the big arched doorway through which we had entered. Outside were sleeping quarters for the native servants, the guard-house for the soldiers, and stables, etc., for the water horses. The drawing-office was to the right of the archway occupying the rest of the north side.

I have gone into the arrangements of the house rather fully here because I don't want to have to go over them again later.

As I say, Mrs. Leidner herself took me round the building and finally established me in my bedroom, hoping that I should be comfortable and have everything I wanted.

The room was nicely though plainly furnished—a bed, a chest of drawers, a wash-stand and a chair.

"The boys will bring you hot water before lunch and dinner—and in the morning, of course. If you want it any other time, go outside and clap your hands, and when the boy comes say, *jib mai' har.* Do you think you can remember that?"

I said I thought so and repeated it a little haltingly.

"That's right. And be sure and shout it. Arabs don't understand anything said in an ordinary 'English' voice."

"Languages are funny things," I said. "It seems odd there should be such a lot of different ones."

Mrs. Leidner smiled.

"There is a church in Palestine in which the Lord's Prayer is written up in—ninety, I think it is—different languages."

"Well!" I said, "I must write and tell my old aunt that. She *will* be interested."

Mrs. Leidner fingered the jug and basin absently and shifted the soap-dish an inch or two.

"I do hope you'll be happy here," she said. "And not get too bored."

"I'm not often bored," I assured her. "Life's not long enough for that."

She did not answer. She continued to toy with the wash-stand as though abstracted.

Suddenly she fixed her dark violet eyes on my face.

"What exactly did my husband tell you, nurse?"

Well, one usually says the same thing to a question of that kind.

"I gathered you were a bit run-down and all that, Mrs. Leidner," I said glibly. "And that you just wanted some one to look after you and take any worries off your hands."

She bent her head slowly and thoughtfully.

"Yes," she said. "Yes—that will do very well."

That was just a little bit enigmatic, but I wasn't going to question it. Instead I said:

"I hope you'll let me help you with anything there is to do in the house. You mustn't let me be idle."

She smiled a little.

"Thank you, nurse."

Then she sat down on the bed and, rather to my surprise, began to cross-question me rather closely. I say rather to my surprise because, from the moment I set eyes on her, I felt sure that Mrs. Leidner was a lady. And a lady, in my experience, very seldom displays curiosity about one's private affairs.

But Mrs. Leidner seemed anxious to know everything there was to know about me. Where I'd trained and how long ago. What had brought me out to the East. How it had come about that Dr. Reilly had recommended me. She even asked me if I had ever been in America or had any relations in America. One or two other questions she asked me that seemed quite purposeless at the time, but of which I saw the significance later.

Then, suddenly, her manner changed. She smiled—a warm sunny smile—and she said, very sweetly, that she was very glad I had come and that she was sure I was going to be a comfort to her.

She got up from the bed and said:

"Would you like to come up to the roof and see the sunset? It's usually very lovely about this time."

I agreed willingly.

As we went out of the room she asked:

"Were there many other people on the train from Baghdad? Any men?"

I said that I hadn't noticed anybody in particular. There had been two Frenchmen in the restaurant-car the night before. And a party of three men who I gathered from their conversation had to do with the Pipe line.

She nodded and a faint sound escaped her. It sounded like a small sigh of relief.

We went up to the roof together.

Mrs. Mercado was there, sitting on the parapet, and Dr. Leidner was bending over looking at a lot of stones and broken pottery that were laid out in rows. There were big things he called querns, and pestles and celts and stone axes, and more broken bits of pottery with queer patterns on them than I've ever seen all at once.

"Come over here," called out Mrs. Mercado. "Isn't it *too,* too beautiful?"

It certainly was a beautiful sunset. Hassanieh in the distance looked quite fairy-like with the setting sun behind it, and the River Tigris flowing between its wide banks looked like a dream river rather than a real one.

"Isn't it lovely, Eric?" said Mrs. Leidner.

The doctor looked up with abstracted eyes, murmured, "Lovely, lovely," perfunctorily and went on sorting potsherds.

Mrs. Leidner smiled and said:

"Archæologists only look at what lies beneath their feet. The sky and the heavens don't exist for them."

Mrs. Mercado giggled.

"Oh, they're very queer people—you'll soon find *that* out, nurse," she said.

She paused and then added:

"We are all *so* glad you've come. We've been so very worried about our dear Mrs. Leidner, haven't we, Louise?"

"Have you?"

Her voice was not encouraging.

"Oh, yes. She really has been *very* bad, nurse. All sorts of alarms and excursions. You know when anybody says to me of some one, 'It's just nerves,' I always say: But what could be *worse?* Nerves are the core and centre of one's being, aren't they?"

"Puss, puss," I thought to myself.

Mrs. Leidner said dryly:

"Well, you needn't be worried about me any more, Marie. Nurse is going to look after me."

"Certainly I am," I said cheerfully.

"I'm sure that will make all the difference," said Mrs. Mercado. "We've all felt that she ought to see a doctor or do *something.* Her nerves have really been all to pieces, haven't they, Louise dear?"

"So much so that I seem to have got on *your* nerves with them," said Mrs. Leidner. "Shall we talk about something more interesting than my wretched ailments?"

I understood then that Mrs. Leidner was the sort of woman who could easily make enemies. There was a cool rudeness in her tone (not that I blamed her for it) which brought a flush to Mrs. Mercado's rather sallow cheeks. She stammered out something, but Mrs. Leidner had risen and had joined her husband at the other end of the roof. I doubt if he heard her coming till she laid her hand on his shoulder, then he looked up quickly. There was affection and a kind of eager questioning in his face.

Mrs. Leidner nodded her head gently. Presently, her arm through his, they wandered to the far parapet and finally down the steps together.

"He's devoted to her, isn't he?" said Mrs. Mercado.

"Yes," I said. "It's very nice to see."

She was looking at me with a queer, rather eager sidelong glance.

"What do you think is really the matter with her, nurse?" she asked, lowering her voice a little.

"Oh, I don't suppose it's much," I said cheerfully. "Just a bit run-down, I expect."

Her eyes still bored into me as they had done at tea. She said abruptly:

"Are you a mental nurse?"

"Oh, dear no!" I said. "What made you think that?"

She was silent for a moment, then she said:

"Do you know how queer she's been? Did Dr. Leidner tell you?"

I don't hold with gossiping about my cases. On the other hand, it's my experience that it's often very hard to get the truth out of the relatives, and until you know the truth you're often working in the dark and doing no good. Of course, when there's a doctor in charge, it's different. He tells you what it's necessary for you to know. But in this case there wasn't a doctor in charge. Dr. Reilly had never been called in professionally. And in my own mind I wasn't at all sure that Dr. Leidner had told me all he could have done. It's often the husband's instinct to be reticent—and more honour to him, I say. But all the same, the more I knew the better I could tell which line to take. Mrs. Mercado (whom I put down in my own mind as a thoroughly spiteful little cat) was clearly dying to talk. And frankly, on the human side as well as the professional, I wanted to hear what she had to say. You can put it that I was just every-day curious if you like.

I said, "I gather Mrs. Leidner's not been quite her normal self lately?"

Mrs. Mercado laughed disagreeably.

"Normal? I should say not. Frightening us to death. One night it was fingers tapping on her window. And then it was a hand without an arm attached. But when it came to a yellow face pressed against the window—and when she rushed to the window there was nothing there—well, I ask you, it *is* a bit creepy for all of us."

"Perhaps somebody was playing a trick on her," I suggested.

"Oh, no, she fancied it all. And only three days ago at dinner they were firing off shots in the village—nearly a mile away—and she jumped up and screamed out—it scared us all to death. As for Dr. Leidner, he rushed to her and behaved in the most ridiculous way. 'It's nothing, darling, it's nothing at all,' he kept saying. I think, you know, nurse, men sometimes *encourage* women in these hysterical fancies. It's a pity because it's a bad thing. Delusions shouldn't be encouraged."

"Not if they *are* delusions," I said dryly.

"What else could they be?"

I didn't answer because I didn't know what to say. It was a funny business. The shots and the screaming were natural enough—for any one in a nervous condition, that is. But this queer story of a spectral face and hand was different. It looked to me like one of two things —either Mrs. Leidner had made the story up (exactly as a child shows off by telling lies about something that never happened in order to make herself the centre of attraction) or else it was, as I had suggested, a deliberate practical joke. It was the sort of thing, I reflected, that an unimaginative hearty sort of young fellow like Mr. Coleman might think very funny. I decided to keep a close watch on him. Nervous patients can be scared nearly out of their minds by a silly joke.

Mrs. Mercado said with a sideways glance at me.

"She's very romantic-looking, nurse, don't you think so? The sort of woman things *happen* to."

"Have many things happened to her?" I asked.

"Well, her first husband was killed in the war when she was only twenty. I think that's very pathetic and romantic, don't you?"

"It's one way of calling a goose a swan," I said dryly.

"Oh! nurse. What an extraordinary remark!"

It was really a very true one. The amount of women you hear say, "If Donald—or Arthur—or whatever his name was—had *only* lived." And I sometimes think but if he had, he'd have been a stout, unromantic, short-tempered, middle-aged husband as likely as not.

It was getting dark and I suggested that we should go down. Mrs. Mercado agreed and asked if I would like to see the laboratory. "My husband will be there—working."

I said I would like to very much and we made our way there. The place was lighted by a lamp but it was empty. Mrs. Mercado showed me some of the apparatus and some copper ornaments that were being treated, and also some bones coated with wax.

"Where can Joseph be?" said Mrs. Mercado.

She looked into the drawing-office, where Carey was at work. He hardly looked up as we entered, and I was struck by the extraordinary look of strain on his face. It came to me suddenly: "This man is at the end of his tether. Very soon, something will snap." And I remembered somebody else had noticed that same tenseness about him.

As we went out again I turned my head for one last look at him. He was bent over his paper, his lips pressed very closely together, and that "death's head" suggestion of his bones very strongly marked. Perhaps it was fanciful, but I thought that he looked like a knight of old who was going into battle and knew he was going to be killed.

And again I felt what an extraordinary and quite unconscious power of attraction he had.

We found Mr. Mercado in the living-room. He was explaining the idea of some new process to Mrs. Leidner. She was sitting on a straight wooden chair, embroidering flowers in fine silks, and I was struck anew by her strange, fragile, unearthly appearance. She looked a fairy creature more than flesh and blood.

Mrs. Mercado said, her voice high and shrill:

"Oh, *there* you are, Joseph. We thought we'd find you in the lab."

He jumped up looking startled and confused, as though her entrance had broken a spell. He said stammeringly:

"I—I must go now. I'm in the middle of—the middle of—"

He didn't complete the sentence but turned towards the door.

Mrs. Leidner said in her soft, drawling voice:

"You must finish telling me some other time. It was very interesting."

She looked up at us, smiled rather sweetly but in a far-away manner, and bent over her embroidery again.

In a minute or two she said:

"There are some books over there, nurse. We've got quite a good selection. Choose one and sit down."

I went over to the bookshelf. Mrs. Mercado stayed for a minute or two, then, turning abruptly, she went out. As she passed me I saw her face and I didn't like the look of it. She looked wild with fury.

In spite of myself I remembered some of the things Mrs. Kelsey had said and hinted about Mrs. Leidner. I didn't like to think they were true because I liked Mrs. Leidner, but I wondered, nevertheless, if there mightn't perhaps be a grain of truth behind them.

I didn't think it was all her fault, but the fact remained that dear ugly Miss Johnson, and that common little spitfire Mrs. Mercado, couldn't hold a candle to her in looks or in attraction. And after all, men are men all over the world. You soon see a lot of that in my profession.

Mercado was a poor fish, and I don't suppose Mrs. Leidner really cared two hoots for his admiration—but his wife cared. If I wasn't mistaken, she minded badly and would be quite willing to do Mrs. Leidner a bad turn if she could.

I looked at Mrs. Leidner sitting there and sewing at her pretty flowers, so remote and far away and aloof. I felt somehow I ought to warn her. I felt that perhaps she didn't know how stupid and unreasoning and violent jealousy and hate can be—and how little it takes to set them smouldering.

And then I said to myself, "Amy Leatheran, you're a fool. Mrs. Leidner's no chicken. She's close on forty if she's a day, and she must know all about life there is to know."

But I felt that all the same perhaps she didn't.

She had such a queer untouched look.

I began to wonder what her life had been. I knew she'd only married Dr. Leidner two years ago. And according to Mrs. Mercado her first husband had died nearly twenty years ago.

I came and sat down near her with a book, and presently I went and washed my hands for supper. It was a good meal—some really excellent curry. They all went to bed early and I was glad for I was tired.

Dr. Leidner came with me to my room to see I had all I wanted.

He gave me a warm handclasp and said eagerly:

"She likes you, nurse. She's taken to you at once. I'm so glad. I feel everything's going to be all right now."

His eagerness was almost boyish.

I felt, too, that Mrs. Leidner had taken a liking to me, and I was pleased it should be so.

But I didn't quite share his confidence. I felt, somehow, that there was more to it all than he himself might know.

There was *something*—something I couldn't get at. But I felt it in the air.

My bed was comfortable, but I didn't sleep well for all that. I dreamt too much.

The words of a poem by Keats, that I'd had to learn as a child, kept running through my head. I kept getting them wrong and it worried me. It was a poem I'd always hated—I suppose because I'd had to learn it whether I wanted to or not. But somehow when I woke up in the dark I saw a sort of beauty in it for the first time.

"*Oh, say what ails thee, knight at arms, alone—and* (what was it?)— *palely loitering . . . ?*" I saw the knight's face in my mind for the first time—and it was Mr. Carey's face—a grim, tense, bronzed face like some of those poor young men I remembered as a girl during the war . . . and I felt sorry for him—and then I fell off to sleep again and I saw that the Belle Dame sans Merci was Mrs. Leidner and she was leaning sideways on a horse with an embroidery of flowers in her hands—and then the horse stumbled and everywhere there were bones coated in wax, and I woke up all goose-flesh and shivering, and told myself that curry never *had* agreed with me at night.

VII

THE MAN AT THE WINDOW

I THINK I'D better make it clear right away that there isn't going to be any local colour in this story. I don't know anything about archæology and I don't know that I very much want to. Messing about with people and places that are buried and done with doesn't make sense to me. Mr. Carey used to tell me that I hadn't got the archæological temperament and I've no doubt he was quite right.

The very first morning after my arrival Mr. Carey asked if I'd like to come and see the palace he was—*planning* I think he called it. Though how you can plan for a thing that's happened long ago I'm sure I don't know! Well, I said I'd like to, and to tell the truth, I was a bit excited about it. Nearly three thousand years old that palace was, it appeared. I wondered what sort of palaces they had in those days, and if it would be like the pictures I'd seen of Tutankhamen's tomb furniture. But would you believe it, there was nothing to see but *mud!* Dirty mud walls about two feet high—and that's all there was to it. Mr. Carey took me here and there telling me things—how this was the great court, and there were some chambers here and an upper storey and various other rooms that opened off the central court. And all I thought was, "But how does he *know?*" though, of course, I was too polite to say so. I can tell you it *was* a disappointment! The whole excavation looked like nothing but mud to me—no marble or gold or anything handsome—my aunt's house in Cricklewood would have made a much more imposing ruin! And those old Assyrians or whatever they were called themselves *kings*. When Mr. Carey had shown me his old "palace," he handed me over to Father Lavigny, who showed me the rest of the mound. I was a little afraid of Father Lavigny, being a monk and a foreigner and having such a deep voice and all, but he was very kind—though rather vague. Sometimes I felt it wasn't much more real to him than it was to me.

Mrs. Leidner explained that later. She said that Father Lavigny was only interested in "written documents"—as she called them. They wrote everything on clay, these people, queer heathenish-looking marks too, but quite sensible. There were even school tablets—the teacher's lesson on one side and the pupil's effort on the back of it. I confess that that did interest me rather—it seemed so human, if you know what I mean.

Father Lavigny walked round the work with me and showed me what were temples or palaces and what were private houses, and also a place which he said was an early Akkadian cemetery. He spoke in a funny jerky way, just throwing in a scrap of information and then reverting to other subjects.

He said:

"It is strange that you have come here. Is Mrs. Leidner really ill, then?"

"Not exactly ill," I said cautiously.

He said:

"She is an odd woman. A dangerous woman, I think."

"Now what do you mean by that?" I said. "Dangerous? How dangerous?"

He shook his head thoughtfully.

"I think she is ruthless," he said. "Yes, I think she could be absolutely ruthless."

"If you'll excuse me," I said, "I think you're talking nonsense."

He shook his head.

"You do not know women as I do," he said.

And that was a funny thing, I thought, for a monk to say. But of course I suppose he might have heard a lot of things in confession. But that rather puzzled me, because I wasn't sure if monks heard confessions or if it was only priests. I supposed he *was* a monk with that long woollen robe—all sweeping up the dirt—and the rosary and all!

"Yes, she could be ruthless," he said musingly. "I am quite sure of that. And yet—though she is so hard—like stone, like marble—yet she is afraid. What is she afraid of?"

That, I thought, is what we should all like to know!

At least it was possible that her husband did know, but I didn't think any one else did.

He fixed me with a sudden bright, dark eye.

"It is odd here? You find it odd? Or quite natural?"

"Not quite natural," I said, considering. "It's comfortable enough as far as the arrangements go—but there isn't quite a comfortable feeling."

"It makes *me* uncomfortable. I have the idea"—he became suddenly a little more foreign—"that something prepares itself. Dr. Leidner, too, he is not quite himself. Something is worrying him also."

"His wife's health?"

"That perhaps. But there is more. There is—how shall I say it—an uneasiness."

And that was just it, there was an uneasiness.

We didn't say any more just then, for Dr. Leidner came towards us. He showed me a child's grave that had just been uncovered. Rather pathetic it was—the little bones—and a pot or two and some little specks that Dr. Leidner told me were a bead necklace.

It was the workmen that made me laugh. You never saw such a lot of scarecrows—all in long petticoats and rags, and their heads tied up as though they had toothache. And every now and then, as they went to and fro carrying away baskets of earth, they began to sing —at least I suppose it was meant to be singing—a queer sort of monotonous chant that went on and on over and over again. I noticed that most of their eyes were terrible—all covered with discharge, and one or two looked half blind. I was just thinking what a miserable lot they were when Dr. Leidner said, "Rather a fine-looking lot of men, aren't they?" and I thought what a queer world it was and how two different people could see the same thing each of them the other way round. I haven't put that very well, but you can guess what I mean.

After a bit Dr. Leidner said he was going back to the house for a mid-morning cup of tea. So he and I walked back together and he told me things. When *he* explained, it was all quite different. I sort of *saw* it all—how it used to be—the streets and the houses, and he showed me ovens where they baked bread and said the Arabs used much the same kind of ovens nowadays.

We got back to the house and found Mrs. Leidner had got up. She was looking better to-day, not so thin and worn. Tea came in almost at once and Dr. Leidner told her what had turned up during the morning on the dig. Then he went back to work and Mrs. Leidner asked me if I would like to see some of the finds they had made up to date. Of course I said "Yes," so she took me through into the antika-room. There was a lot of stuff lying about—mostly broken pots it seemed to me—or else ones that were all mended and stuck together. The whole lot might have been thrown away, I thought.

"Dear, dear," I said, "it's a pity they're all so broken, isn't it? Are they really worth keeping?"

Mrs. Leidner smiled a little and she said:

"You mustn't let Eric hear you. Pots interest him more than any-thing else, and some of these are the oldest things we have—perhaps as much as seven thousand years old." And she explained how some of them came from a very deep cut on the mound down towards the bottom, and how, thousands of years ago, they had been broken and mended with bitumen, showing people prized their things just as much then as they do nowadays.

"And now," she said, "we'll show you something more exciting." And she took down a box from the shelf and showed me a beauti-ful gold dagger with dark-blue stones in the handle.

I exclaimed with pleasure.

Mrs. Leidner laughed.

"Yes, everybody likes gold! Except my husband."

"Why doesn't Dr. Leidner like it?"

"Well, for one thing it comes expensive. You have to pay the work-men who find it the weight of the object in gold."

"Good gracious!" I exclaimed. "But why?"

"Oh, it's a custom. For one thing it prevents them from stealing. You see, if they *did* steal it wouldn't be for the archæological value but for the intrinsic value. They could melt it down. So we make it easy for them to be honest."

She took down another tray and showed me a really beautiful gold drinking-cup with a design of rams' heads on it.

Again I exclaimed.

"Yes, it is beautiful, isn't it? These came from a prince's grave. We found other royal graves but most of them had been plundered. This cup is our best find. It is one of the most lovely ever found anywhere. Early Akkadian. Unique."

Suddenly, with a frown, Mrs. Leidner brought the cup up close to her eyes and scratched at it delicately with her nail.

"How extraordinary! There's actually wax on it. Some one must have been in here with a candle."

She detached the little flake and replaced the cup in its place.

After that she showed me some queer little terra-cotta figurines —but most of them were just rude. Nasty minds those old people had, I say.

When we went back to the porch Mrs. Mercado was sitting polish-ing her nails. She was holding them out in front of her admiring the effect. I thought myself that anything more hideous than that orange red could hardly have been imagined.

Mrs. Leidner had brought with her from the antika-room a very delicate little saucer broken in several pieces, and this she now proceeded to join together. I watched her for a minute or two and then asked if I could help.

"Oh, yes, there are plenty more." She fetched quite a supply of broken pottery and we set to work. I soon got into the hang of it and she praised my ability. I suppose most nurses are handy with their fingers.

"How busy everybody is," said Mrs. Mercado. "It makes me feel dreadfully idle. Of course I *am* idle."

"Why shouldn't you be if you like?" said Mrs. Leidner.

Her voice was quite uninterested.

At twelve we had lunch. Afterwards Dr. Leidner and Mr. Mercado cleaned some pottery, pouring a solution of hydrochloric acid over it. One pot went a lovely plum colour and a pattern of bulls' horns came out on another one. It was really quite magical. All the dried mud that no washing would remove sort of foamed and boiled away.

Mr. Carey and Mr. Coleman went out on the dig and Mr. Reiter went off to the photographic room.

"What will you do, Louise?" Dr. Leidner asked his wife. "I suppose you'll rest for a bit?"

I gathered that Mrs. Leidner usually lay down every afternoon.

"I'll rest for about an hour. Then perhaps I'll go out for a short stroll."

"Good. Nurse will go with you, won't you?"

"Of course," I said.

"No, no," said Mrs. Leidner. "I like going alone. Nurse isn't to feel so much on duty that I'm not allowed out of her sight."

"Oh, but I'd like to come," I said.

"No, really, I'd rather you didn't." She was quite firm—almost peremptory. "I must be by myself every now and then. It's necessary to me."

I didn't insist, of course. But as I went off for a short sleep myself it struck me as odd that Mrs. Leidner, with her nervous terrors, should be quite content to walk by herself without any kind of protection.

When I came out of my room at half-past three the courtyard was deserted save for a little boy with a large copper bath who was washing pottery, and Mr. Emmott, who was sorting and arranging it. As I went towards them Mrs. Leidner came in through the archway. She looked more alive than I had seen her yet. Her eyes shone and she looked uplifted and almost gay.

Dr. Leidner came out from the laboratory and joined her. He was showing her a big dish with bulls' horns on it.

"The prehistoric levels are being extraordinarily productive," he said. "It's been a good season so far. Finding that tomb right at the beginning was a real piece of luck. The only person who might complain is Father Lavigny. We've had hardly any tablets so far."

"He doesn't seem to have done very much with the few we have had," said Mrs. Leidner dryly. "He may be a very fine epigraphist but he's a remarkably lazy one. He spends all his afternoons sleeping."

"We miss Byrd," said Dr. Leidner. "This man strikes me as slightly unorthodox—though, of course, I'm not competent to judge. But one or two of his translations have been surprising to say the least of it. I can hardly believe, for instance, that he's right about that inscribed brick, and yet he must know."

After tea Mrs. Leidner asked me if I would like to stroll down to the river. I thought that perhaps she feared that her refusal to let me accompany her earlier in the afternoon might have hurt my feelings.

I wanted her to know that I wasn't the touchy kind, so I accepted at once.

It was a lovely evening. A path led between barley fields and then through some flowering fruit trees. Finally we came to the edge of the Tigris. Immediately on our left was the Tell with the workmen singing in their queer monotonous chant. A little to our right was a big water-wheel which made a queer groaning noise. It used to set my teeth on edge at first. But in the end I got fond of it and it had a queer soothing effect on me. Beyond the water-wheel was the village from which most of the workmen came.

"It's rather beautiful, isn't it?" said Mrs. Leidner.

"It's very peaceful," I said. "It seems funny to me to be so far away from everywhere."

"Far from everywhere," repeated Mrs. Leidner. "Yes. Here at least one might expect to be safe."

I glanced at her sharply, but I think she was speaking more to herself than to me, and I don't think she realized that her words had been revealing.

We began to walk back to the house.

Suddenly Mrs. Leidner clutched my arm so violently that I nearly cried out.

"Who's that, nurse? What's he doing?"

Some little distance ahead of us, just where the path ran near the expedition house, a man was standing. He wore European clothes and he seemed to be standing on tiptoe and trying to look in at one of the windows.

As we watched he glanced round, caught sight of us, and immediately continued on the path towards us. I felt Mrs. Leidner's clutch tighten.

"Nurse," she whispered. "Nurse . . ."

"It's all right, my dear, it's all right," I said reassuringly.

The man came along and passed us. He was an Iraqi, and as soon as she saw him near to, Mrs. Leidner relaxed with a sigh.

"He's only an Iraqi after all," she said.

We went on our way. I glanced up at the windows as I passed. Not only were they barred, but they were too high from the ground to permit of any one seeing in, for the level of the ground was lower here than on the inside of the courtyard.

"It must have been just curiosity," I said.

Mrs. Leidner nodded.

"That's all. But just for a minute I thought—"

She broke off.

I thought to myself, "You thought *what?* That's what I'd like to know? *What* did you think?"

But I knew one thing now—that Mrs. Leidner was afraid of a definite flesh and blood person.

VIII

NIGHT ALARM

IT'S A LITTLE difficult to know exactly what to note in the week that followed my arrival at Tell Yarimjah.

Looking back as I do from my present standpoint of knowledge I can see a good many little signs and indications that I was quite blind to at the time.

To tell the story properly, however, I think I ought to try and re-capture the point of view that I actually held—puzzled, uneasy, and increasingly conscious of something wrong.

For one thing *was* certain, that curious sense of strain and constraint was *not* imagined. It was genuine. Even Bill Coleman the insensitive commented upon it.

"This place gets under my skin," I heard him say. "Are they always such a glum lot?"

It was David Emmott to whom he spoke, the other assistant. I had taken rather a fancy to Mr. Emmott; his taciturnity was not, I felt sure, unfriendly. There was something about him that seemed very steadfast and reassuring in an atmosphere where one was uncertain what any one was feeling or thinking.

"No," he said in answer to Mr. Coleman. "It wasn't like this last year."

But he didn't enlarge on the theme, or say any more.

"What I can't make out is what it's all about," said Mr. Coleman in an aggrieved voice.

Emmott shrugged his shoulders but didn't answer.

I had a rather enlightening conversation with Miss Johnson. I liked her very much. She was capable, practical and intelligent. She had, it was quite obvious, a distinct hero worship for Dr. Leidner.

On this occasion she told me the story of his life since his young days. She knew every site he had dug, and the results of the dig. I would almost dare swear she could quote from every lecture he had ever delivered. She considered him, she told me, quite the finest field archæologist living.

"And he's so simple. So completely unworldly. He doesn't know the meaning of the word conceit. Only a really great man could be so simple."

"That's true enough," I said. "Big people don't need to throw their weight about."

"And he's so light-hearted too. I can't tell you what fun we used to have—he and Richard Carey and I—the first years we were out here. We were such a happy party. Richard Carey worked with him in Palestine, of course. Theirs is a friendship of ten years or so. Oh, well, I've known him for seven."

"What a handsome man Mr. Carey is," I said.

"Yes—I suppose he is."

She said it rather curtly.

"But he's just a little bit quiet, don't you think?"

"He usedn't to be like that," said Miss Johnson quickly. "It's only since—"

She stopped abruptly.

"Only since—?" I prompted.

"Oh, well." Miss Johnson gave a characteristic motion of her shoulders. "A good many things are changed nowadays."

I didn't answer. I hoped she would go on—and she did—prefacing her remarks with a little laugh as though to detract from their importance.

"I'm afraid I'm rather a conservative old fogy. I sometimes think that if an archæologist's wife isn't really interested, it would be wiser for her not to accompany the expedition. It often leads to friction."

"Mrs. Mercado—" I suggested.

"Oh, her!" Miss Johnson brushed the suggestion aside. "I was really thinking of Mrs. Leidner. She's a very charming woman—and one can quite understand why Dr. Leidner 'fell for her'—to use a slang term. But I can't help feeling she's out of place here. She—it unsettles things."

So Miss Johnson agreed with Mrs. Kelsey that it was Mrs. Leidner who was responsible for the strained atmosphere. But then where did Mrs. Leidner's own nervous fears come in?

"It unsettles *him*," said Miss Johnson earnestly. "Of course, I'm— well, I'm like a faithful but jealous old dog. I don't like to see him so worn out and worried. His whole mind ought to be on the work —not taken up with his wife and her silly fears! If she's nervous of coming to out-of-the-way places, she ought to have stayed in America.

I've no patience with people who come to a place and then do nothing but grouse about it!"

And then, a little fearful of having said more than she meant to say, she went on:

"Of course I admire her very much. She's a lovely woman and she's got great charm of manner when she chooses."

And there the subject dropped.

I thought to myself that it was always the same way—wherever women are cooped up together, there's bound to be jealousy. Miss Johnson clearly didn't like her chief's wife (that was perhaps natural) and unless I was much mistaken Mrs. Mercado fairly hated her.

Another person who didn't like Mrs. Leidner was Sheila Reilly. She came out once or twice to the dig, once in a car and twice with some young man on a horse—on two horses I mean, of course. It was at the back of my mind that she had a weakness for the silent young American, Emmott. When he was on duty at the dig she used to stay talking to him, and I thought, too, that *he* admired *her*.

One day, rather injudiciously, I thought, Mrs. Leidner commented upon it at lunch.

"The Reilly girl is still hunting David down," she said with a little laugh. "Poor David, she chases you up on the dig even! How foolish girls are!"

Mr. Emmott didn't answer, but under his tan his face got rather red. He raised his eyes and looked right into hers with a very curious expression—a straight, steady glance with something of a challenge in it.

She smiled very faintly and looked away.

I heard Father Lavigny murmur something, but when I said "Pardon?" he merely shook his head and did not repeat his remark.

That afternoon Mr. Coleman said to me:

"Matter of fact I didn't like Mrs. L any too much at first. She used to jump down my throat every time I opened my mouth. But I've begun to understand her better now. She's one of the kindest women I've ever met. You find yourself telling her all the foolish scrapes you ever got into before you know where you are. She's got her knife into Sheila Reilly, I know, but then Sheila's been damned rude to her once or twice. That's the worst of Sheila—she's got no manners. And a temper like the devil!"

That I could well believe. Dr. Reilly spoilt her.

"Of course she's bound to get a bit full of herself, being the only young woman in the place. But that doesn't excuse her talking to Mrs. Leidner as though Mrs. Leidner were her great-aunt. Mrs. L's not exactly a chicken, but she's a damned good-looking woman. Rather like those fairy women who come out of marshes with lights and lure you away." He added bitterly, "You wouldn't find Sheila luring any one. All she does is to tick a fellow off."

I only remember two other incidents of any kind of significance.

One was when I went to the laboratory to fetch some acetone to get the stickiness off my fingers from mending the pottery. Mr. Mercado was sitting in a corner, his head was laid down on his arms and I fancied he was asleep. I took the bottle I wanted and went off with it.

That evening, to my great surprise, Mrs. Mercado tackled me.

"Did you take a bottle of acetone from the lab?"

"Yes," I said. "I did."

"You know perfectly well that there's a small bottle always kept in the antika-room."

She spoke quite angrily.

"Is there? I didn't know."

"I think you did! You just wanted to come spying round. I know what hospital nurses are."

I stared at her.

"I don't know what you're talking about, Mrs. Mercado," I said with dignity. "I'm sure I don't want to spy on any one."

"Oh, no! Of course not. Do you think I don't know what you're here for?"

Really, for a minute or two I thought she must have been drinking. I went away without saying any more. But I thought it was very odd.

The other thing was nothing very much. I was trying to entice a pi dog pup with a piece of bread. It was very timid, however, like all Arab dogs—and was convinced I meant no good. It slunk away and I followed it—out through the archway and round the corner of the house. I came round so sharply that before I knew I had cannoned into Father Lavigny and another man who were standing together— and in a minute I realized that the second man was the same one Mrs. Leidner and I had noticed that day trying to peer through the window.

I apologized and Father Lavigny smiled, and with a word of farewell greeting to the other man he returned to the house with me.

"You know," he said, "I am very ashamed. I am a student of Oriental languages and none of the men on the work can understand me! It is humiliating, do you not think? I was trying my Arabic on that man, who is a townsman, to see if I got on better—but it still wasn't very successful. Leidner says my Arabic is too pure."

That was all. But it just passed through my head that it was odd the same man should still be hanging round the house.

That night we had a scare.

It must have been about two in the morning. I'm a light sleeper, as most nurses have to be. I was awake and sitting up in bed by the time that my door opened.

"Nurse, nurse!"

It was Mrs. Leidner's voice, low and urgent.

I struck a match and lighted the candle.

She was standing by the door in a long blue dressing-gown. She was looking petrified with terror.

"There's some one—some one—in the room next to mine. . . . I heard him—scratching on the wall."

I jumped out of bed and came to her.

"It's all right," I said. "I'm here. Don't be afraid, my dear."

She whispered:

"Get Eric."

I nodded and ran out and knocked on his door. In a minute he was with us. Mrs. Leidner was sitting on my bed, her breath coming in great gasps.

"I heard him," she said. "I hear him—scratching on the wall."

"Some one in the antika-room?" cried Dr. Leidner.

He ran out quickly—and it just flashed across my mind how differently these two had reacted. Mrs. Leidner's fear was entirely personal, but Dr. Leidner's mind leaped at once to his precious treasures.

"The antika-room!" breathed Mrs. Leidner. "Of course! How stupid of me."

And rising and pulling her gown round her, she bade me come with her. All traces of her panic-stricken fear had vanished.

We arrived in the antika-room to find Dr. Leidner and Father Lavigny. The latter had also heard a noise, had risen to investigate, and had fancied he saw a light in the antika-room. He had delayed to put on slippers and snatch up a torch and had found no one by the time he got there. The door, moreover, was duly locked, as it was supposed to be at night.

Whilst he was assuring himself that nothing had been taken, Dr. Leidner had joined him.

Nothing more was to be learned. The outside archway door was locked. The guard swore nobody could have got in from outside, but as they had probably been fast asleep this was not conclusive. There were no marks or traces of an intruder and nothing had been taken.

It was possible that what had alarmed Mrs. Leidner was the noise made by Father Lavigny taking down boxes from the shelves to assure himself that all was in order.

On the other hand, Father Lavigny himself was positive that he had (a) heard footsteps passing his window and (b) seen the flicker of a light, possibly a torch, in the antika-room.

Nobody else had heard or seen anything.

The incident is of value in my narrative because it led to Mrs. Leidner's unburdening herself to me on the following day.

IX

MRS. LEIDNER'S STORY

WE HAD JUST finished lunch. Mrs. Leidner went to her room to rest as usual. I settled her on her bed with plenty of pillows and her book, and was leaving the room when she called me back.

"Don't go, nurse, there's something I want to say to you."

I came back into the room.

"Shut the door."

I obeyed.

She got up from the bed and began to walk up and down the room. I could see that she was making up her mind to something and I didn't like to interrupt her. She was clearly in great indecision of mind.

At last she seemed to have nerved herself to the required point. She turned to me and said abruptly:

"Sit down."

I sat down by the table very quietly. She began nervously:

"You must have wondered what all this is about?"

I just nodded without saying anything.

"I've made up my mind to tell you—everything! I must tell some one or I shall go mad."

"Well," I said. "I think really it would be just as well. It's not easy to know the best thing to do when one's kept in the dark."

She stopped in her uneasy walk and faced me.

"Do you know what I'm frightened of?"

"Some man," I said.

"Yes—but I didn't say whom—I said what."

I waited.

She said:

"*I'm afraid of being killed!*"

Well, it was out now. I wasn't going to show any particular concern. She was near enough hysterics as it was.

"Dear me," I said. "So that's it, is it?"

Then she began to laugh. She laughed and she laughed—and the tears ran down her face.

"The way you said that!" she gasped. "The way you said it . . ."

"Now, now," I said. "This won't do." I spoke sharply. I pushed her into a chair, went over to the wash-stand and got a cold sponge and bathed her forehead and wrists.

"No more nonsense," I said. "Tell me calmly and sensibly all about it."

That stopped her. She sat up and spoke in her natural voice.

"You're a treasure, nurse," she said. "You make me feel as though I'm six. I'm going to tell you."

"That's right," I said. "Take your time and don't hurry."

She began to speak, slowly and deliberately.

"When I was a girl of twenty I married. A young man in one of our state departments. It was in 1918."

"I know," I said. "Mrs. Mercado told me. He was killed in the war." But Mrs. Leidner shook her head.

"That's what she thinks. That's what everybody thinks. The truth is something quite different. I was a queer patriotic, enthusiastic girl, nurse, full of idealism. When I'd been married a few months I discovered—by a quite unforseeable accident—that my husband was a spy in German pay. I learned that the information supplied by him had led directly to the sinking of an American transport and the loss of hundreds of lives. I don't know what most people would have done. . . . But I'll tell you what I did. I went straight to my father, who was in the War Department, and told him the truth. Frederick *was* killed in the war—but he was killed in America—shot as a spy."

"Oh, dear, dear!" I ejaculated. "How terrible!"

"Yes," she said. "It was terrible. He was so kind, too—so gentle. . . . And all the time . . . But I never hesitated. Perhaps I was wrong."

"It's difficult to say," I said. "I'm sure I don't know what one would do."

"What I'm telling you was never generally known outside the state departments. Ostensibly my husband had gone to the front and had been killed. I had a lot of sympathy and kindness shown me as a war widow."

Her voice was bitter and I nodded comprehendingly.

"Lots of people wanted to marry me, but I always refused. I'd had too bad a shock. I didn't feel I could ever *trust* any one again."

"Yes, I can imagine feeling like that."

"And then I became very fond of a certain young man. I wavered. An amazing thing happened! I got an anonymous letter—from Frederick—saying that if I ever married another man, he'd kill me!"

"From Frederick? From your dead husband?"

"Yes. Of course, I thought at first I was mad or dreaming. . . . At last I went to my father. He told me the truth. My husband hadn't been shot after all. He'd escaped—but his escape did him no good. He was involved in a train wreck a few weeks later and his dead body was found amongst others. My father had kept the fact of his escape from me, and since the man had died anyway he had seen no reason to tell me anything until now.

"But the letter I received opened up entirely new possibilities. Was it perhaps a fact that my husband was still alive?

"My father went into the matter as carefully as possible. And he declared that as far as one could humanly be sure the body that was buried as Frederick's *was* Frederick's. There had been a certain amount of disfiguration, so that he could not speak with absolute cast-iron certainty, but he reiterated his solemn belief that Frederick was dead and that this letter was a cruel and malicious hoax.

"The same thing happened more than once. If I seemed to be on intimate terms with any man, I would receive a threatening letter."

"In your husband's handwriting?"

She said slowly:

"That is difficult to say. I had no letters of his. I had only my memory to go by."

"There was no allusion or special form of words used that could make you sure?"

"No. There *were* certain terms—nicknames, for instance—private between us—if one of those had been used or quoted, then I should have been quite sure."

"Yes," I said thoughtfully. "That is odd. It looks as though it *wasn't* your husband. But is there any one else it could be?"

"There is a possibility. Frederick had a younger brother—a boy of ten or twelve at the time of our marriage. He worshipped Frederick and Frederick was devoted to him. What happened to this boy, William his name was, I don't know. It seems to me possible that, adoring his brother as fanatically as he did, he may have grown up regarding me as directly responsible for his death. He had always been jealous of me and may have invented this scheme by way of punishment."

"It's possible," I said. "It's amazing the way children do remember if they've had a shock."

"I know. This boy may have dedicated his life to revenge."

"Please go on."

"There isn't very much more to tell. I met Eric three years ago. I meant never to marry. Eric made me change my mind. Right up to our wedding day I waited for another threatening letter. None came. I decided that whoever the writer might be, he was either dead, or tired of his cruel sport. *Two days after our marriage I got this.*"

Drawing a small attaché-case which was on the table towards her, she unlocked it, took out a letter and handed it to me.

The ink was slightly faded. It was written in a rather womanish hand with a forward slant.

You have disobeyed. Now you cannot escape. You must be Frederick Bosner's wife only! You have got to die.

"I was frightened—but not so much as I might have been to begin with. Being with Eric made me feel safe. Then, a month later, I got a second letter."

I have not forgotten. I am making my plans. You have got to die. Why did you disobey?

"Does your husband know about this?"

Mrs. Leidner answered slowly.

"He knows that I am threatened. I showed him both letters when the second one came. He was inclined to think the whole thing a hoax. He thought also that it might be some one who wanted to blackmail me by pretending my first husband was alive."

She paused and then went on.

"A few days after I received the second letter we had a narrow escape from death by gas poisoning. Somebody entered our apartment after we were asleep and turned on the gas. Luckily I woke and smelled the gas in time. Then I lost my nerve. I told Eric how I had been persecuted for years, and I told him that I was sure this madman, whoever he might be, did really mean to kill me. I think that for the first time I really did think it *was* Frederick. There was always something a little ruthless behind his gentleness.

"Eric was still, I think, less alarmed than I was. He wanted to go to the police. Naturally I wouldn't hear of that. In the end we agreed that I should accompany him here, and that it might be wise if I didn't return to America in the summer but stayed in London and Paris.

"We carried out our plan and all went well. I felt sure that now eve-

rything would be all right. After all, we had put half the globe between ourselves and my enemy.

"And then—a little over three weeks ago—I received a letter—with
an Iraq stamp on it."

She handed me a third letter.

*You thought you could escape. You were wrong. You shall not be
false to me and live. I have always told you so. Death is coming very
soon.*

"And a week ago—*this!* Just lying on the table here. It had not even
gone through the post."

I took the sheet of paper from her. There was just one phrase
scrawled across it.

I have arrived.

She stared at me.

"You see? You understand? He's going to kill me. It may be Frederick—it may be little William—*but he's going to kill me.*"

Her voice rose shudderingly. I caught her wrist.

"Now—now," I said warningly. "Don't give way. We'll look after
you. Have you got any sal volatile?"

She nodded towards the wash-stand and I gave her a good dose.

"That's better," I said, as the colour returned to her cheeks.

"Yes, I'm better now. But oh, nurse, do you see why I'm in this
state. When I saw that man looking in through my window, I
thought: *He's come.* . . . Even when *you* arrived I was suspicious. I thought you might be a man in disguise—"

"The idea!"

"Oh, I know it sounds absurd. But you might have been in league
with him perhaps—not a hospital nurse at all."

"But that's nonsense!"

"Yes, perhaps. But I've got beyond sense."

Struck by a sudden idea, I said:

"You'd *recognize* your husband, I suppose?"

She answered slowly.

"I don't even know that. It's over fifteen years ago. I mightn't recognize his face."

Then she shivered.

"I saw it one night—but it was a *dead* face. There was a tap, tap, tap
on the window. And then I saw a face, a dead face, ghastly and grinning against the pane. I screamed and screamed. . . . And they said
there wasn't anything there!"

I remembered Mrs. Mercado's story.

"You don't think," I said hesitatingly, "that you *dreamt* that?"

"I'm sure I didn't!"

I wasn't so sure. It was the kind of nightmare that was quite likely under the circumstances and that easily might be taken for a waking occurrence. However, I never contradict a patient. I soothed Mrs. Leidner as best I could and pointed out that if any stranger arrived in the neighbourhood it was pretty sure to be known.

I left her, I think, a little comforted, and I went in search of Dr. Leidner and told him of our conversation.

"I'm glad she's told you," he said simply. "It has worried me dreadfully. I feel sure that all those faces and tappings on the window-pane have been sheer imagination on her part. I haven't known what to do for the best. What do you think of the whole thing?"

I didn't quite understand the tone in his voice, but I answered promptly enough.

"It's possible," I said, "that these letters may be just a cruel and malicious hoax."

"Yes, that is quite likely. But what are we to *do?* They are driving her mad. I don't know what to think."

I didn't either. It had occurred to me that possibly a woman might be concerned. Those letters had a feminine note about them. Mrs. Mercado was at the back of my mind.

Supposing that by some chance she had learnt the facts of Mrs. Leidner's first marriage. She might be indulging her spite by terrorizing the other woman.

I didn't quite like to suggest such a thing to Dr. Leidner. It's so difficult to know how people are going to take things.

"Oh, well," I said cheerfully, "we must hope for the best. I think Mrs. Leidner seems happier already from just talking about it. That's always a help, you know. It's bottling things up that makes them get on your nerves."

"I'm very glad she has told you," he repeated. "It's a good sign. It shows she likes and trusts you. I've been at my wit's end to know what to do for the best."

It was on the tip of my tongue to ask him whether he'd thought of giving a discreet hint to the local police, but afterwards I was glad I hadn't done so.

What happened was this. On the following day Mr. Coleman was going in to Hassanieh to get the workmen's pay. He was also taking in all our letters to catch the air mail.

The letters, as written, were dropped into a wooden box on the dining-room window-sill. Last thing that night Mr. Coleman took them out and was sorting them out into bundles and putting rubber-bands round them.

Suddenly he gave a shout.

"What is it?" I asked.

He held out a letter with a grin.

"It's our Lovely Louise—she really *is* going balmy. She's addressed a letter to some one at 42nd Street, Paris, France. I don't think that can be right, do you? Do you mind taking it to her and asking what she *does* mean? She's just gone off to bed."

I took it from him and ran off to Mrs. Leidner with it and she amended the address.

It was the first time I had seen Mrs. Leidner's handwriting, and I wondered idly where I had seen it before, for it was certainly quite familiar to me.

It wasn't until the middle of the night that it suddenly came to me.

Except that it was bigger and rather more straggling, *it was extraordinarily like the writing on the anonymous letters.*

New ideas flashed through my head.

Had Mrs. Leidner conceivably written those letters *herself?*

And did Dr. Leidner half suspect the fact?

X

SATURDAY AFTERNOON

Mrs. Leidner told me her story on a Friday.

On Saturday morning there was a feeling of slight anticlimax in the air.

Mrs. Leidner, in particular, was inclined to be very off-hand with me and rather pointedly avoided any possibility of a *tête-à-tête*. Well, *that* didn't surprise me! I've had the same thing happen to me again and again. Ladies tell their nurses things in a sudden burst of confidence, and then, afterwards, they feel uncomfortable about it and wish they hadn't! It's only human nature.

I was very careful not to hint or remind her in any way of what she had told me. I purposely kept my conversation as matter-of-fact as possible.

Mr. Coleman had started in to Hassanieh in the morning, driving himself in the lorry with the letters in a knapsack. He also had one or two commissions to do for the members of the expedition. It was pay-day for the men, and he would have to go to the bank and bring out the money in coins of small denominations. All this was a long business and he did not expect to be back until the afternoon. I rather suspected he might be lunching with Sheila Reilly.

Work on the dig was usually not very busy on the afternoon of pay-day as at three-thirty the paying-out began.

The little boy, Abdullah, whose business it was to wash pots, was established as usual in the centre of the courtyard, and again as usual, kept up his queer nasal chant. Dr. Leidner and Mr. Emmott were going to put in some work on the pottery until Mr. Coleman returned, and Mr. Carey went up to the dig.

Mrs. Leidner went to her room to rest. I settled her as usual and then went to my own room, taking a book with me as I did not feel sleepy. It was then about a quarter to one, and a couple of hours passed quite pleasantly. I was reading *Death in a Nursing Home*— really a most exciting story—though I don't think the author knew much about the way nursing homes are run! At any rate I've never known a nursing home like that! I really felt inclined to write to the author and put him right about a few points.

When I put the book down at last (it was the red-haired parlour-maid and I'd never suspected her once!) and looked at my watch I was quite surprised to find it was twenty minutes to three!

I got up, straightened my uniform, and came out into the courtyard.

Abdullah was still scrubbing and still singing his depressing chant, and David Emmott was standing by him sorting the scrubbed pots, and putting the ones that were broken into boxes to await mending. I strolled over towards them just as Dr. Leidner came down the staircase from the roof.

"Not a bad afternoon," he said cheerfully. "I've made a bit of a clearance up there. Louise will be pleased. She's complained lately that there's not room to walk about. I'll go and tell her the good news."

He went over to his wife's door, tapped on it and went in.

It must, I suppose, have been about a minute and a half later that he came out again. I happened to be looking at the door when he did so. It was like a nightmare. He had gone in a brisk, cheerful man. He came out like a drunken one—reeling a little on his feet, and with a queer dazed expression on his face.

"Nurse—" he called in a queer, hoarse voice. "Nurse—"

I saw at once something was wrong, and I ran across to him. He looked awful—his face was all grey and twitching, and I saw he might collapse any minute.

"My wife . . ." he said. "My wife . . . Oh, my God . . ."

I pushed past him into the room. Then I caught my breath.

Mrs. Leidner was lying in a dreadful huddled heap by the bed.

I bent over her. She was quite dead—must have been dead an hour at least. The cause of death was perfectly plain—a terrific blow on the front of the head just over the right temple. She must have got up from the bed and been struck down where she stood.

I didn't handle her more than I could help.

I glanced round the room to see if there was anything that might give a clue, but nothing seemed out of place or disturbed. The windows were closed and fastened, and there was no place where the murderer could have hidden. Obviously he had been and gone long ago.

I went out, closing the door behind me.

Dr. Leidner had collapsed completely now. David Emmott was with him and turned a white, inquiring face to me.

In a few low words I told him what had happened.

As I had always suspected, he was a first-class person to rely on in trouble. He was perfectly calm and self-possessed. Those blue eyes of his opened very wide, but otherwise he gave no sign at all.

He considered for a moment and then said:

"I suppose we must notify the police as soon as possible. Bill ought to be back any minute. What shall we do with Leidner?"

"Help me to get him into his room."

He nodded.

"Better lock this door first, I suppose," he said.

He turned the key in the lock of Mrs. Leidner's door, then drew it out and handed it to me.

"I guess you'd better keep this, nurse. Now then."

Together we lifted Dr. Leidner and carried him into his own room and laid him on his bed. Mr. Emmott went off in search of brandy. He returned, accompanied by Miss Johnson.

Her face was drawn and anxious, but she was calm and capable, and I felt satisfied to leave Dr. Leidner in her charge.

I hurried out into the courtyard. The station wagon was just coming in through the archway. I think it gave us all a shock to see Bill's pink, cheerful face as he jumped out with his familiar "Hallo, 'allo, 'allo! Here's the oof!" He went on gaily, "No highway robberies—"

He came to a halt suddenly. "I say, is anything up? What's the matter with you all? You look as though the cat had killed your canary."

Mr. Emmott said shortly:

"Mrs. Leidner's dead—killed."

"*What?*" Bill's jolly face changed ludicrously. He stared, his eyes goggling. "Mother Leidner dead! You're pulling my leg."

"Dead?" It was a sharp cry. I turned to see Mrs. Mercado behind me. "Did you say Mrs. Leidner had been *killed?*"

"Yes," I said. "Murdered."

"No!" she gasped. "Oh, no! I won't believe it. Perhaps she's committed suicide."

"Suicides don't hit themselves on the head," I said dryly. "It's murder all right, Mrs. Mercado."

She sat down suddenly on an upturned packing-case.

She said, "Oh, but this is horrible—*horrible* . . ."

Naturally it was horrible. We didn't need *her* to tell us so! I wondered if perhaps she was feeling a bit remorseful for the harsh feelings she had harboured against the dead woman, and all the spiteful things she had said.

After a minute or two she asked rather breathlessly:
"What are you going to do?"

Mr. Emmott took charge in his quiet way.

"Bill, you'd better get in again to Hassanieh as quick as you can. I don't know much about the proper procedure. Better get hold of Captain Maitland, he's in charge of the police here, I think. Get Dr. Reilly first. He'll know what to do."

Mr. Coleman nodded. All the facetiousness was knocked out of him. He just looked young and frightened. Without a word he jumped into the station wagon and drove off.

Mr. Emmott said rather uncertainly, "I suppose we ought to have a hunt round." He raised his voice and called:

"Ibrahim!"

"Na'am."

The house-boy came running. Mr. Emmott spoke to him in Arabic. A vigorous colloquy passed between them. The boy seemed to be emphatically denying something.

At last Mr. Emmott said in a perplexed voice:

"He says there's not been a soul here this afternoon. No stranger of any kind. I suppose the fellow must have slipped in without their seeing him."

"Of course he did," said Mrs. Mercado. "He slunk in when the boys weren't looking."

"Yes," said Mr. Emmott.

The slight uncertainty in his voice made me look at him inquiringly.

He turned and spoke to the little pot-boy, Abdullah, asking him a question.

The boy replied vehemently at length.

The puzzled frown on Mr. Emmott's brow increased.

"I don't understand it," he murmured under his breath. "I don't understand it at all."

But he didn't tell me what he didn't understand.

XI

AN ODD BUSINESS

I'M ADHERING AS far as possible to telling only my personal part in the business. I pass over the events of the next two hours, the arrival of Captain Maitland and the police and Dr. Reilly. There was a good deal of general confusion, questioning, all the routine business, I suppose.

In my opinion we began to get down to brass tacks about five o'clock when Dr. Reilly asked me to come with him into the office.

He shut the door, sat down in Dr. Leidner's chair, motioned me to sit down opposite him, and said briskly:

"Now, then, nurse, let's get down to it. There's something damned odd here."

I settled my cuffs and looked at him inquiringly.

He drew out a notebook.

"This is for my own satisfaction. Now, what time was it exactly when Dr. Leidner found his wife's body?"

"I should say it was almost exactly a quarter to three," I said.

"And how do you know that?"

"Well, I looked at my watch when I got up. It was twenty to three then."

"Let's have a look at this watch of yours."

I slipped it off my wrist and held it out to him.

"Right to the minute. Excellent woman. Good, that's *that* fixed. Now did you form any opinion as to how long she'd been dead?"

"Oh, really, doctor," I said, "I shouldn't like to say."

"Don't be so professional. I want to see if your estimate agrees with mine."

"Well, I should say she'd been dead at least an hour."

"Quite so. I examined the body at half-past four and I'm inclined to put the time of death between 1.15 and 1.45. We'll say half-past one at a guess. That's near enough."

He stopped and drummed thoughtfully with his fingers on the table.

"Damned odd, this business," he said. "Can you tell me about it—you were resting, you say? Did you hear anything?"

"At half-past one? No, doctor. I didn't hear anything at half-past one or at any other time. I lay on my bed from a quarter to one until twenty to three and I didn't hear anything except that droning noise the Arab boy makes, and occasionally Mr. Emmott shouting up to Dr. Leidner on the roof."

"The Arab boy—yes."

He frowned.

At that moment the door opened and Dr. Leidner and Captain Maitland came in. Captain Maitland was a fussy little man with a pair of shrewd grey eyes.

Dr. Reilly rose and pushed Dr. Leidner into his chair.

"Sit down, man. I'm glad you've come. We shall want you. There's something very queer about this business."

Dr. Leidner bowed his head.

"I know." He looked at me. "My wife confided the truth to Nurse Leatheran. We mustn't keep anything back at this juncture, nurse, so please tell Captain Maitland and Dr. Reilly just what passed between you and my wife yesterday."

As nearly as possible I gave our conversation verbatim.

Captain Maitland uttered an occasional ejaculation. When I had finished he turned to Dr. Leidner.

"And this is all true, Leidner—eh?"

"Every word Nurse Leatheran has told you is correct."

"What an extraordinary story," said Dr. Reilly. "You can produce these letters?"

"I have no doubt they will be found amongst my wife's belongings."

"She took them out of the attaché-case on her table," I said.

"Then they are probably still there."

He turned to Captain Maitland and his usually gentle face grew hard and stern.

"There must be no question of hushing this story up, Captain Maitland. The one thing necessary is for this man to be caught and punished."

"You believe it actually is Mrs. Leidner's former husband?" I asked.

"Don't you think so, nurse?" asked Captain Maitland.

"Well, I think it is open to doubt," I said hesitatingly.

"In any case," said Dr. Leidner, "the man is a murderer—and I

should say a dangerous lunatic also. He *must* be found, Captain Maitland. He must. It should not be difficult."

Dr. Reilly said slowly:

"It may be more difficult than you think . . . eh, Maitland?"

Captain Maitland tugged at his moustache without replying.

Suddenly I gave a start.

"Excuse me," I said, "but there's something perhaps I ought to
mention."

I told my story of the Iraqi we had seen trying to peer through the
window, and of how I had seen him hanging about the place two
days ago trying to pump Father Lavigny.

"Good," said Captain Maitland, "we'll make a note of that. It will
be something for the police to go on. The man may have some connection with the case."

"Probably paid to act as a spy," I suggested. "To find out when the
coast was clear."

Dr. Reilly rubbed his nose with a harassed gesture.

"That's the devil of it," he said. "Supposing the coast wasn't clear—
eh?"

I stared at him in a puzzled fashion.

Captain Maitland turned to Dr. Leidner.

"I want you to listen to me very carefully, Leidner. This is a re-
view of the evidence we've got up to date. After lunch, which was
served at twelve o'clock and was over by five and twenty to one, your
wife went to her room accompanied by Nurse Leatheran, who settled
her comfortably. You yourself went up to the roof, where you spent
the next two hours, is that right?"

"Yes."

"Did you come down from the roof at all during that time?"

"No."

"Did any one come up to you?"

"Yes, Emmott did pretty frequently. He went to and fro between
me and the boy, who was washing pottery down below."

"Did you yourself look over into the courtyard at all?"

"Once or twice—usually to call to Emmott about something."

"On each occasion the boy was sitting in the middle of the courtyard
washing pots?"

"Yes."

"What was the longest period of time when Emmott was with you
and absent from the courtyard?"

Dr. Leidner considered.

"It's difficult to say—perhaps ten minutes. Personally I should say two or three minutes, but I know by experience that my sense of time is not very good when I am absorbed and interested in what I am doing."

Captain Maitland looked at Dr. Reilly. The latter nodded. "We'd better get down to it," he said.

Captain Maitland took out a small notebook and opened it.

"Look here, Leidner, I'm going to read to you exactly what every member of your expedition was doing between one and two this afternoon."

"But surely—"

"Wait. You'll see what I'm driving at in a minute. First Mr. and Mrs. Mercado. Mr. Mercado says he was working in his laboratory. Mrs. Mercado says she was in her bedroom shampooing her hair. Miss Johnson says she was in the living-room taking impressions of cylinder seals. Mr. Reiter says he was in the dark-room developing plates. Father Lavigny says he was working in his bedroom. As to the two remaining members of the expedition, Carey and Coleman, the former was up on the dig and Coleman was in Hassanieh. So much for the members of the expedition. Now for the servants. The cook—your Indian chap—was sitting immediately outside the archway chatting to the guard and plucking a couple of fowls. Ibrahim and Mansur, the house-boys, joined him there at about 1.15. They both remained there laughing and talking until 2.30—*by which time your wife was already dead.*"

Dr. Leidner leaned forward.

"I don't understand—you puzzle me. What are you hinting at?"

"Is there any means of access to your wife's room except by the door into the courtyard?"

"No. There are two windows, but they are heavily barred—and besides, I think they were shut."

He looked at me questioningly.

"They were closed and latched on the inside," I said promptly.

"In any case," said Captain Maitland, "even if they had been open, no one could have entered or left the room that way. My fellows and I have assured ourselves of that. It is the same with all the other windows giving on the open country. They all have iron bars and all the bars are in good condition. To have got into your wife's room, a stranger *must* have come through the arched doorway into the courtyard. But we have the united assurances of the guard, the cook and the house-boy that *nobody did so.*"

Dr. Leidner sprang up.

"What do you mean? What do you mean?"

"Pull yourself together, man," said Dr. Reilly quietly. "I know it's a shock, but it's got to be faced. *The murderer didn't come from outside*—so he must have come from *inside*. It looks as though Mrs. Leidner must have been murdered *by a member of your own expedition.*"

XII
"I DIDN'T BELIEVE . . ."

"No. No!"

Dr. Leidner sprang up and walked up and down in an agitated manner.

"It's impossible what you say, Reilly. Absolutely impossible. One of us? Why, every single member of the expedition was devoted to Louise!"

A queer little expression pulled down the corners of Dr. Reilly's mouth. Under the circumstances it was difficult for him to say anything, but if ever a man's silence was eloquent his was at that minute.

"Quite impossible," reiterated Dr. Leidner. "They were all devoted to her. Louise had such wonderful charm. Every one felt it."

Dr. Reilly coughed.

"Excuse me, Leidner, but after all that's only your opinion. If any member of the expedition had disliked your wife they would naturally not advertise the fact to you."

Dr. Leidner looked distressed.

"True—quite true. But all the same, Reilly, I think you are wrong. I'm sure every one was fond of Louise."

He was silent for a moment or two and then burst out.

"This idea of yours is infamous. It's—it's frankly incredible."

"You can't get away from—er—the facts," said Captain Maitland.

"Facts? Facts? Lies told by an Indian cook and a couple of Arab house-boys. You know these fellows as well as I do, Reilly; so do you, Maitland. Truth as truth means nothing to them. They say what you want them to say as a mere matter of politeness."

"In this case," said Dr. Reilly dryly, "they are saying what we *don't* want them to say. Besides, I know the habits of your household fairly well. Just outside the gate is a kind of social club. Whenever I've been over here in the afternoon I've always found most of your staff there. It's the natural place for them to be."

"All the same I think you are assuming too much. Why shouldn't this man—this devil—have got in earlier and concealed himself some-where?"

"I agree that that is not actually impossible," said Dr. Reilly coolly. "Let us assume that a stranger *did* somehow gain admission unseen. He would have to remain concealed until the right moment (and he certainly couldn't have done so in Mrs. Leidner's room, there is no cover there) and take the risk of being seen entering the room and leaving it—with Emmott and the boy in the courtyard most of the time."

"The boy. I'd forgotten the boy," said Dr. Leidner. "A sharp little chap. But surely, Maitland, the boy *must* have seen the murderer go into my wife's room?"

"We've elucidated that. The boy was washing pots the whole after-noon with one exception. Somewhere around half-past one—Emmott can't put it closer than that—he went up to the roof and was with you for ten minutes—that's right, isn't it?"

"Yes. I couldn't have told you the exact time but it must have been about that."

"Very good. Well, during that ten minutes, the boy, seizing his chance to be idle, strolled out and joined the others outside the gate for a chat. When Emmott came down he found the boy absent and called him angrily, asking him what he meant by leaving his work. As far as I can see, *your wife must have been murdered during that ten minutes.*"

With a groan, Dr. Leidner sat down and hid his face in his hands.

Dr. Reilly took up the tale, his voice quiet and matter-of-fact.

"The time fits in with my evidence," he said. "She'd been dead about three hours when I examined her. The only question is—who did it?"

There was a silence. Dr. Leidner sat up in his chair and passed a hand over his forehead.

"I admit the force of your reasoning, Reilly," he said quietly. "It certainly *seems* as though it were what people call 'an inside job.' But I feel convinced that somewhere or other there is a mistake. It's plau-sible but there must be a flaw in it. To begin with, you are assuming that an amazing coincidence has occurred."

"Odd that you should use that word," said Dr. Reilly.

Without paying any attention Dr. Leidner went on:

"My wife receives threatening letters. She has reason to fear a cer-tain person. Then she is—killed. And you ask me to believe that she is killed—not by that person—but by some one entirely different! I say that that is ridiculous."

"It seems so—yes," said Dr. Reilly meditatively.

He looked at Captain Maitland. "Coincidence—eh? What do you say, Maitland? Are you in favour of the idea? Shall we put it up to Leidner?"

Captain Maitland gave a nod.

"Go ahead," he said shortly.

"Have you ever heard of a man called Hercule Poirot, Leidner?"

Dr. Leidner stared at him, puzzled.

"I think I have heard the name, yes," he said vaguely. "I once heard a Mr. Van Aldin speak of him in very high terms. He is a private detective, is he not?"

"That's the man."

"But surely he lives in London, so how will that help us?"

"He lives in London, true," said Dr. Reilly, "but this is where the coincidence comes in. He is now, not in London, but in Syria, and *he will actually pass through Hassanieh on his way to Baghdad tomorrow!*"

"Who told you this?"

"Jean Berat, the French consul. He dined with us last night and was talking about him. It seems he has been disentangling some military scandal in Syria. He's coming through here to visit Baghdad, and afterwards returning through Syria to London. How's that for a coincidence?"

Dr. Leidner hesitated a moment and looked apologetically at Captain Maitland.

"What do you think, Captain Maitland?"

"Should welcome co-operation," said Captain Maitland promptly. "My fellows are good scouts at scouring the countryside and investigating Arab blood feuds, but frankly, Leidner, this business of your wife's seems to me rather out of my class. The whole thing looks confoundedly fishy. I'm more than willing to have the fellow take a look at the case."

"You suggest that I should appeal to this man Poirot to help us?" said Dr. Leidner. "And suppose he refuses?"

"He won't refuse," said Dr. Reilly.

"How do you know?"

"Because I'm a professional man myself. If a really intricate case of say—cerebrospinal meningitis comes my way and I'm invited to take a hand, I shouldn't be able to refuse. This isn't an ordinary crime, Leidner."

"No," said Dr. Leidner. His lips twitched with sudden pain.

"Will you then, Reilly, approach this Hercule Poirot on my behalf?"

"I will."

Dr. Leidner made a gesture of thanks.

"Even now," he said slowly, "I can't realize it—that Louise is really dead."

I could bear it no longer.

"Oh! Dr. Leidner," I burst out. "I—I can't tell you how badly I feel about this. I've failed so badly in my duty. It was my job to watch over Mrs. Leidner—to keep her from harm."

Dr. Leidner shook his head gravely.

"No, no, nurse, you've nothing to reproach yourself with," he said slowly. "It's I, God forgive me, who am to blame. . . . I *didn't believe—* all along I didn't believe . . . I didn't dream for one moment that there was any *real* danger. . . ."

He got up. His face twitched.

"*I let her go to her death.* . . . Yes, I let her go to her death—*not believing—*"

He staggered out of the room.

Dr. Reilly looked at me.

"I feel pretty culpable too," he said. "I thought the good lady was playing on his nerves."

"I didn't take it really seriously either," I confessed.

"We were all three wrong," said Dr. Reilly gravely.

"So it seems," said Captain Maitland.

XIII
HERCULE POIROT ARRIVES

I DON'T THINK I shall ever forget my first sight of Hercule Poirot. Of course, I got used to him later on, but to begin with it was a shock, and I think every one else must have felt the same!

I don't know what I'd imagined—something rather like Sherlock Holmes—long and lean with a keen, clever face. Of course, I knew he was a foreigner, but I hadn't expected him to be *quite* as foreign as he was, if you know what I mean.

When you saw him you just wanted to laugh! He was like something on the stage or at the pictures. To begin with, he wasn't above five foot five, I should think—an odd plump little man, quite old, with an enormous moustache, and a head like an egg. He looked like a hairdresser in a comic play!

And this was the man who was going to find out who killed Mrs. Leidner!

I suppose something of my disgust must have shown in my face, for almost straightaway he said to me with a queer kind of twinkle:

"You disapprove of me, *ma sœur?* Remember, the pudding proves itself only when you eat it."

The proof of the pudding's in the eating, I *suppose* he meant.

Well, that's a true enough saying, but I couldn't say I felt much confidence myself!

Dr. Reilly brought him out in his car soon after lunch on Sunday, and his first procedure was to ask us all to assemble together.

We did so in the dining-room, all sitting round the table. Mr. Poirot sat at the head of it with Dr. Leidner one side and Dr. Reilly the other.

When we were all assembled, Dr. Leidner cleared his throat and spoke in his gentle, hesitating voice.

"I dare say you have all heard of M. Hercule Poirot. He was passing through Hassanieh to-day, and has very kindly agreed to break his journey to help us. The Iraq police and Captain Maitland are, I am sure, doing their very best, but—but there are circumstances in the case"—he floundered and shot an appealing glance at Dr. Reilly— "there may, it seems, be difficulties. . . ."

"It is not all the square and overboard—no?" said the little man at the top of the table. Why, he couldn't even speak English properly!

"Oh, he *must* be caught!" cried Mrs. Mercado. "It would be unbearable if he got away!"

I noticed the little foreigner's eyes rest on her appraisingly.

"He? Who is *he*, madame?" he asked.

"Why, the murderer, of course."

"Ah! the murderer," said Hercule Poirot.

He spoke as though the murderer was of no consequence at all! We all stared at him. He looked from one face to another.

"It is likely, I think," he said, "that you have none of you been brought in contact with a case of murder before?"

There was a general murmur of assent.

Hercule Poirot smiled.

"It is clear, therefore, that you do not understand the A.B.C. of the position. There are unpleasantnesses! Yes, there are a lot of unpleasantnesses. To begin with, there is *suspicion*."

"Suspicion?"

It was Miss Johnson who spoke. Mr. Poirot looked at her thoughtfully. I had an idea that he regarded her with approval. He looked as though he were thinking, "Here is a sensible, intelligent person!"

"Yes, mademoiselle," he said. "Suspicion! Let us not make the bones about it. *You are all under suspicion here in this house.* The cook, the house-boy, the scullion, the pot-boy—yes, and all the members of the expedition too."

Mrs. Mercado started up, her face working.

"How *dare* you? How dare you say such a thing! This is odious— unbearable! Dr. Leidner—you can't sit here and let this man—and let this man—"

Dr. Leidner said wearily:

"Please try and be calm, Marie."

Mr. Mercado stood up too. His hands were shaking and his eyes were bloodshot.

"I agree. It is an outrage—an insult—"

"No, no," said Mr. Poirot. "I do not insult you. I merely ask you all to face facts. *In a house where murder has been committed, every inmate comes in for a certain share of suspicion.* I ask you what evidence is there that the murderer came from outside at all?"

Mrs. Mercado cried:

"But of course he did! It stands to reason! Why—" She stopped and said more slowly, "anything else would be incredible!"

"You are doubtless correct, madame," said Poirot with a bow. "I explain to you only how the matter must be approached. First I assure myself of the fact that every one in this room is innocent. After that I seek the murderer elsewhere."

"Is it not possible that that may be a little late in the day?" asked Father Lavigny suavely.

"The tortoise, *mon père*, overtook the hare."

Father Lavigny shrugged his shoulders.

"We are in your hands," he said resignedly. "Convince yourself as soon as may be of our innocence in this terrible business."

"As rapidly as possible. It was my duty to make the position clear to you, so that you may not resent the impertinence of any questions I may have to ask. Perhaps, *mon père*, the Church will set an example?"

"Ask any questions you please of me," said Father Lavigny gravely.

"This is your first season out here?"

"Yes."

"And you arrived—when?"

"Three weeks ago almost to a day. That is, on the 27th of February."

"Coming from?"

"The Order of the *Pères Blancs* at Carthage."

"Thank you, *mon père*. Were you at any time acquainted with Mrs. Leidner before coming here?"

"No, I had never seen the lady until I met her here."

"Will you tell me what you were doing at the time of the tragedy?"

"I was working on some cuneiform tablets in my own room."

I noticed that Poirot had at his elbow a rough plan of the building.

"That is the room at the south-west corner corresponding to that of Mrs. Leidner on the opposite side?"

"Yes."

"At what time did you go to your room?"

"Immediately after lunch. I should say at about twenty minutes to one."

"And you remained there until—when?"

"Just before three o'clock. I had heard the station wagon come back —and then I heard it drive off again. I wondered why, and came out to see."

"During the time that you were there did you leave the room at all?"

"No, not once."

"And you heard or saw nothing that might have any bearing on the tragedy?"

"No."

"You have no window giving on the courtyard in your room?"

"No, both the windows give on the countryside."

"Could you hear at all what was happening in the courtyard?"

"Not very much. I heard Mr. Emmott passing my room and going up to the roof. He did so once or twice."

"Can you remember at what time?"

"No, I'm afraid I can't. I was engrossed in my work, you see."

There was a pause and then Poirot said:

"Can you say or suggest anything at all that might throw light on this business. Did you, for instance, notice anything in the days preceding the murder?"

Father Lavigny looked slightly uncomfortable.

He shot a half-questioning look at Dr. Leidner.

"That is rather a difficult question, monsieur," he said gravely. "If you ask me, I must reply frankly that in my opinion Mrs. Leidner was clearly in dread of some one or something. She was definitely nervous about strangers. I imagine she had a reason for this nervousness of hers—but I *know* nothing. She did not confide in me."

Poirot cleared his throat and consulted some notes that he held in his hand.

"Two nights ago I understand there was a scare of burglary."

Father Lavigny replied in the affirmative and retailed his story of the light seen in the antika-room and the subsequent futile search.

"You believe, do you not, that some unauthorized person was on the premises at that time?"

"I don't know what to think," said Father Lavigny frankly. "Nothing was taken or disturbed in any way. It might have been one of the house-boys—"

"Or a member of the expedition?"

"Or a member of the expedition. But in that case there would be no reason for the person not admitting the fact."

"But it *might* equally have been a stranger from outside?"

"I suppose so."

"Supposing a stranger *had* been on the premises, could he have concealed himself successfully during the following day and until the afternoon of the day following that?"

He asked the question half of Father Lavigny and half of Dr. Leidner. Both men considered the question carefully.

"I hardly think it would be possible," said Dr. Leidner at last with some reluctance. "I don't see where he could possibly conceal himself, do you, Father Lavigny?"

"No—no—I don't."

Both men seemed reluctant to put the suggestion aside.

Poirot turned to Miss Johnson.

"And you, mademoiselle? Do you consider such a hypothesis feasible?"

After a moment's thought Miss Johnson shook her head.

"No," she said. "I don't. Where could any one hide? The bedrooms are all in use and, in any case, are sparsely furnished. The dark-room, the drawing-office and the laboratory were all in use the next day—so were all these rooms. There are no cupboards or corners. Perhaps, if the servants were in collusion—"

"That is possible, but unlikely," said Poirot.

He turned once more to Father Lavigny.

"There is another point. The other day Nurse Leatheran here noticed you talking to a man outside. She had previously noticed that same man trying to peer in at one of the windows on the outside. It rather looks as though the man were hanging round the place deliberately."

"That is possible, of course," said Father Lavigny thoughtfully.

"Did you speak to this man first, or did he speak to you?"

Father Lavigny considered for a moment or two.

"I believe—yes, I am sure, that he spoke to me."

"What did he say?"

Father Lavigny made an effort of memory.

"He said, I think, something to the effect was this the American expedition house? And then something else about the Americans employing a lot of men on the work. I did not really understand him very well, but I endeavoured to keep up a conversation so as to improve my Arabic. I thought, perhaps, that being a townee he would understand me better than the men on the dig do."

"Did you converse about anything else?"

"As far as I remember, I said Hassanieh was a big town—and we then agreed that Baghdad was bigger—and I think he asked whether I was an Armenian or a Syrian Catholic—something of that kind."

Poirot nodded.

"Can you describe him?"

Again Father Lavigny frowned in thought.

"He was rather a short man," he said at last, "and squarely built. He had a very noticeable squint and was of fair complexion."

Mr. Poirot turned to me.

"Does that agree with the way you would describe him?" he asked.

"Not exactly," I said hesitatingly. "I should have said he was tall rather than short, and very dark complexioned. He seemed to me of a rather slender build. I didn't notice any squint."

Mr. Poirot gave a despairing shrug of the shoulders.

"It is always so! If you were of the police how well you would know it! The description of the same man by two different people—never does it agree. Every detail is contradicted."

"I'm fairly sure about the squint," said Father Lavigny. "Nurse Leatheran may be right about the other points. By the way, when I said *fair,* I only meant fair for an *Iraqi.* I expect nurse would call that dark."

"Very dark," I said obstinately. "A dirty dark-yellow colour."

I saw Dr. Reilly bite his lip and smile.

Poirot threw up his hands.

"*Passons!*" he said. "This stranger hanging about, he may be important—he may not. At any rate he must be found. Let us continue our inquiry."

He hesitated for a minute, studying the faces turned towards him round the table, then, with a quick nod, he singled out Mr. Reiter.

"Come, my friend," he said. "Let us have your account of yesterday afternoon."

Mr. Reiter's pink, plump face flushed scarlet.

"Me?" he said.

"Yes, you. To begin with, your name and your age?"

"Carl Reiter, twenty-eight."

"American—yes?"

"Yes, I come from Chicago."

"This is your first season?"

"Yes. I'm in charge of the photography."

"Ah, yes. And yesterday afternoon, how did you employ yourself?"

"Well—I was in the dark-room most of the time."

"*Most* of the time—eh?"

"Yes. I developed some plates first. Afterwards I was fixing up some objects to photograph."

"Outside?"

"Oh, no, in the photographic room."

"The dark-room opens out of the photographic room?"

"Yes."

"And so you never came outside the photographic room?"

"No."

"Did you notice anything that went on in the courtyard?"

The young man shook his head.

"I wasn't noticing anything," he explained. "I was busy. I heard the car come back, and as soon as I could leave what I was doing I came out to see if there was any mail. It was then that I—heard."

"And you began your work in the photographic room—when?"

"At ten minutes to one."

"Were you acquainted with Mrs. Leidner before you joined this expedition?"

The young man shook his head.

"No, sir. I never saw her till I actually got here."

"Can you think of *anything*—any incident—however small—that might help us?"

Carl Reiter shook his head.

He said helplessly:

"I guess I don't know anything at all, sir."

"Mr. Emmott?"

David Emmott spoke clearly and concisely in his pleasant soft American voice.

"I was working with the pottery from a quarter to one till a quarter to three—overseeing the boy Abdullah, sorting it, and occasionally going up to the roof to help Dr. Leidner."

"How often did you go up to the roof?"

"Four times, I think."

"For how long?"

"Usually a couple of minutes—not more. But on one occasion after I'd been working a little over half an hour I stayed as long as ten minutes—discussing what to keep and what to fling away."

"And I understand that when you came down you found the boy had left his place?"

"Yes. I called him angrily and he reappeared from outside the archway. He had gone out to gossip with the others."

"That was the only time he left his work?"

"Well, I sent him up once or twice to the roof with pottery."

Poirot said gravely:

"It is hardly necessary to ask you, Mr. Emmott, whether you saw any one enter or leave Mrs. Leidner's room during that time?"

Mr. Emmott replied promptly.

"I saw no one at all. Nobody even came out into the courtyard during the two hours I was working."

"And to the best of your belief it was half-past one when both you and the boy were absent and the courtyard was empty?"

"It couldn't have been far off that time. Of course, I can't say *exactly*."

Poirot turned to Dr. Reilly.

"That agrees with your estimate of the time of death, doctor?"

"It does," said Dr. Reilly.

Mr. Poirot stroke his great curled moustaches.

"I think we can take it," he said gravely, "that Mrs. Leidner met her death during that ten minutes."

XIV
ONE OF US?

THERE WAS A little pause—and in it a wave of horror seemed to float round the room.

I think it was at that moment that I first believed Dr. Reilly's theory to be right.

I *felt* that the murderer was in the room. Sitting with us—listening. *One of us . . .*

Perhaps Mrs. Mercado felt it too. For she suddenly gave a short sharp cry.

"I can't help it," she sobbed. "I—it's so *terrible!*"

"Courage, Marie," said her husband.

He looked at us apologetically.

"She is so sensitive. She feels things so much."

"I—I was so fond of Louise," sobbed Mrs. Mercado.

I don't know whether something of what I felt showed in my face, but I suddenly found that Mr. Poirot was looking at me, and that a slight smile hovered on his lips.

I gave him a cold glance, and at once he resumed his inquiry.

"Tell me, madame," he said, "of the way you spent yesterday afternoon?"

"I was washing my hair," sobbed Mrs. Mercado. "It seems awful not to have known anything about it. I was quite happy and busy."

"You were in your room?"

"Yes."

"And you did not leave it?"

"No. Not till I heard the car. Then I came out and I heard what had happened. Oh, it was *awful!*"

"Did it surprise you?"

Mrs. Mercado stopped crying. Her eyes opened resentfully.

"What do you mean, M. Poirot? Are you suggesting—"

"What should I mean, madame? You have just told us how fond you were of Mrs. Leidner. She might, perhaps, have confided in you."

"Oh, I see. . . . No—no, dear Louise never told me anything—anything *definite*, that is. Of course, I could see she was terribly worried and nervous. And there were those strange occurrences—hands tapping on the window and all that."

"Fancies, I remember you said," I put in, unable to keep silent.

I was glad to see that she looked momentarily disconcerted.

Once again I was conscious of Mr. Poirot's amused eye glancing in my direction.

He summed up in a business-like way.

"It comes to this, madame, you were washing your hair—you heard nothing and you saw nothing. Is there anything at all you can think of that would be a help to us in any way?"

Mrs. Mercado took no time to think.

"No, indeed there isn't. It's the deepest mystery! But I should say there is no doubt—no doubt *at all* that the murderer came from outside. Why, it stands to reason."

Poirot turned to her husband.

"And you, monsieur, what have you to say?"

Mr. Mercado started nervously. He pulled at his beard in an aimless fashion.

"Must have been. Must have been," he said. "Yet how could any one wish to harm her? She was so gentle—so kind—" He shook his head. "Whoever killed her must have been a fiend—yes, a fiend!"

"And you yourself, monsieur, how did you pass yesterday afternoon?"

"I?" he stared vaguely.

"You were in the laboratory, Joseph," his wife prompted him.

"Ah, yes, so I was—so I was. My usual tasks."

"At what time did you go there?"

Again he looked helplessly and inquiringly at Mrs. Mercado.

"At ten minutes to one, Joseph."

"Ah, yes, at ten minutes to one."

"Did you come out in the courtyard at all?"

"No—I don't think so." He considered. "No, I am sure I didn't."

"When did you hear of the tragedy?"

"My wife came and told me. It was terrible—shocking. I could hardly believe it. Even now, I can hardly believe it is true."

Suddenly he began to tremble.

"It is horrible—horrible . . ."

Mrs. Mercado came quickly to his side.

"Yes, yes, Joseph, we all feel that. But we mustn't give way. It makes it so much more difficult for poor Dr. Leidner."

I saw a spasm of pain pass across Dr. Leidner's face, and I guessed that this emotional atmosphere was not easy for him. He gave a half glance at Poirot as though in appeal. Poirot responded quickly.

"Miss Johnson?" he said.

"I'm afraid I can tell you very little," said Miss Johnson. Her cultured well-bred voice was soothing after Mrs. Mercado's shrill treble. She went on:

"I was working in the living-room—taking impressions of some cylinder seals on plasticine."

"And you saw or noticed nothing?"

"No."

Poirot gave her a quick glance. His ear had caught what mine had —a faint note of indecision.

"Are you quite sure, mademoiselle? Is there something that comes back to you vaguely?"

"No—not really—"

"Something you saw, shall we say, out of the corner of your eye hardly knowing you saw it."

"No, certainly not," she replied positively.

"Something you *heard* then. Ah, yes, something you are not quite sure whether you heard or not?"

Miss Johnson gave a short vexed laugh.

"You press me very closely, M. Poirot. I'm afraid you are encouraging me to tell you what I am, perhaps, only imagining."

"Then there *was* something you—shall we say—imagined?"

Miss Johnson said slowly, weighing her words in a detached way:

"I have imagined—since—that at some time during the afternoon I heard a very faint cry. . . . What I mean is that I dare say I *did* hear a cry. All the windows in the living-room were open and one hears all sorts of sounds from people working in the barley fields. But you see—since—I've got the idea into my head that it was—that it was Mrs. Leidner I heard. And that's made me rather unhappy. Because if I'd jumped up and run along to her room—well, who knows? I might have been in time . . ."

Dr. Reilly interposed authoritatively.

"Now, don't start getting that into your head," he said. "I've no doubt but that Mrs. Leidner (forgive me, Leidner) was struck down almost as soon as the man entered the room, and it was that blow that killed her. No second blow was struck. Otherwise she would have had time to call for help and make a real outcry."

"Still, I might have caught the murderer," said Miss Johnson.

"What time was this, mademoiselle?" asked Poirot. "In the neighbourhood of half-past one?"

"It must have been about that time—yes." She reflected a minute.

"That would fit in," said Poirot thoughtfully. "You heard nothing else—the opening or shutting of a door, for instance?"

Miss Johnson shook her head.

"No, I do not remember anything of that kind."

"You were sitting at a table, I presume. Which way were you facing? The courtyard? The antika-room? The verandah? Or the open countryside?"

"I was facing the courtyard."

"Could you see the boy Abdullah washing pots from where you were?"

"Oh, yes, if I looked up, but of course, I was very intent on what I was doing. All my attention was on that."

"If any one had passed the courtyard window, though, you would have noticed it?"

"Oh, yes, I am almost sure of that."

"And nobody did so?"

"No."

"But if any one had walked, say, across the middle of the courtyard, would you have noticed that?"

"I think—probably not—unless, as I said before, I had happened to look up and out of the window."

"You did not notice the boy Abdullah leave his work and go out to join the other servants?"

"No."

"Ten minutes," mused Poirot. "That fatal ten minutes."

There was a momentary silence.

Miss Johnson lifted her head suddenly and said:

"You know, M. Poirot, I think I have unintentionally misled you. On thinking it over, I do not believe that I could possibly have heard any cry uttered in Mrs. Leidner's room from where I was. The antika-room lay between me and her—and I understand her windows were found closed."

"In any case, do not distress yourself, mademoiselle," said Poirot kindly. "It is not really of much importance."

"No, of course not. I understand that. But you see, it *is* of importance to me, because I feel I might have done something."

"Don't distress yourself, dear Anne," said Dr. Leidner with affection. "You must be sensible. What you heard was probably one Arab bawling to another some distance away in the fields."

Miss Johnson flushed a little at the kindliness of his tone. I even saw tears spring to her eyes. She turned her head away and spoke even more gruffly than usual.

"Probably was. Usual thing after a tragedy—start imagining things that aren't so at all."

Poirot was once more consulting his notebook.

"I do not suppose there is much more to be said. Mr. Carey?"

Richard Carey spoke slowly—in a wooden, mechanical manner.

"I'm afraid I can add nothing helpful. I was on duty at the dig. The news was brought to me there."

"And you know or can think of nothing helpful that occurred in the days immediately preceding the murder?"

"Nothing at all."

"Mr. Coleman?"

"I was right out of the whole thing," said Mr. Coleman with—was it just a shade of regret—in his tone. "I went into Hassanieh yesterday morning to get the money for the men's wages. When I came back Emmott told me what had happened and I went back in the bus to get the police and Dr. Reilly."

"And beforehand?"

"Well, sir, things were a bit jumpy—but you know that already. There was the antika-room scare and one or two before that—hands and faces at the window—you remember, sir," he appealed to Dr. Leidner, who bent his head in assent. "I think, you know, that you'll find some Johnny *did* get in from outside. Must have been an artful sort of beggar."

Poirot considered him for a minute or two in silence.

"You are an Englishman, Mr. Coleman?" he asked at last.

"That's right, sir. All British. See the trademark. Guaranteed genuine."

"This is your first season?"

"Quite right."

"And you are passionately keen on archæology?"

This description of himself seemed to cause Mr. Coleman some embarrassment. He got rather pink and shot the side look of a guilty schoolboy at Dr. Leidner.

"Of course—it's all very interesting," he stammered. "I mean—I'm not exactly a brainy chap . . ."

He broke off rather lamely. Poirot did not insist.

He tapped thoughtfully on the table with the end of his pencil and carefully straightened an inkpot that stood in front of him.

"It seems then," he said, "that that is as near as we can get for the moment. If any one of you thinks of something that has for the time being slipped his or her memory do not hesitate to come to me with it. It will be well now, I think, for me to have a few words alone with Dr. Leidner and Dr. Reilly."

It was the signal for a breaking up of the party. We all rose and filed out of the door. When I was half-way out, however, a voice recalled me.

"Perhaps," said Mr. Poirot, "Nurse Leatheran will be so kind as to remain. I think her assistance will be valuable to us."

I came back and resumed my seat at the table.

XV

POIROT MAKES A SUGGESTION

Dr. Reilly had risen from his seat. When every one had gone out he carefully closed the door. Then, with an inquiring glance at Poirot, he proceeded to shut the window giving on the courtyard. The others were already shut. Then he, too, resumed his seat at the table.

"*Bien!*" said Poirot. "We are now private and undisturbed. We can speak freely. We have heard what the members of the expedition have to tell us and— But yes, *ma sœur*, what is it that you think?"

I got rather red. There was no denying that the queer little man had sharp eyes. He'd seen the thought passing through my mind—I suppose my face *had* shown a bit too clearly what I was thinking!

"Oh, it's nothing—" I said, hesitating.

"Come on, nurse," said Dr. Reilly. "Don't keep the specialist waiting."

"It's nothing really," I said hurriedly. "It only just passed through my mind, so to speak, that perhaps even if any one did know or suspect something it wouldn't be easy to bring it out in front of everybody else—or even, perhaps, in front of Dr. Leidner."

Rather to my astonishment, M. Poirot nodded his head in vigorous agreement.

"Precisely. Precisely. It is very just what you say there. But I will explain. That little reunion we have just had—it served a purpose. In England before the races you have a parade of the horses, do you not? They go in front of the grandstand so that every one may have an opportunity of seeing and judging them. That is the purpose of my little assembly. In the sporting phrase, I run my eye over the possible starters."

Dr. Leidner cried out violently, "I do not believe for one minute that *any* member of my expedition is implicated in this crime!"

Then, turning to me, he said authoritatively:

"Nurse, I should be much obliged if you would tell M. Poirot here and now exactly what passed between my wife and you two days ago."

Thus urged, I plunged straightaway into my story, trying as far as possible to recall the exact words and phrases Mrs. Leidner had used.

When I had finished, M. Poirot said:

"Very good. Very good. You have the mind neat and orderly. You will be of great service to me here."

He turned to Dr. Leidner.

"You have these letters?"

"I have them here. I thought that you would want to see them first thing."

Poirot took them from him, read them, and scrutinized them carefully as he did so. I was rather disappointed that he didn't dust powder over them or examine them with a microscope or anything like that—but I realized that he wasn't a very young man and that his methods were probably not very up to date. He just read them in the way that any one might read a letter.

Having read them he put them down and cleared his throat.

"Now," he said, "let us proceed to get our facts clear and in order. The first of these letters was received by your wife shortly after her marriage to you in America. There had been others but these she destroyed. The first letter was followed by a second. A very short time after the second arrived you both had a near escape from coal gas poisoning. You then came abroad and for nearly two years no further letters were received. They started again at the beginning of your season this year—that is to say, within the last three weeks. That is correct?"

"Absolutely."

"Your wife displayed every sign of panic and, after consulting Dr. Reilly, you engaged Nurse Leatheran here to keep your wife company and allay her fears?"

"Yes."

"Certain incidents occurred—hands tapping at the window—a spectral face—noises in the antika-room. You did not witness any of these phenomena yourself?"

"No."

"In fact nobody did except Mrs. Leidner?"

"Father Lavigny saw a light in the antika-room."

"Yes, I have not forgotten that."

He was silent for a minute or two, then he said:

"Had your wife made a will?"

"I do not think so."

"Why was that?"

"It did not seem worth it from her point of view."

"Is she not a wealthy woman?"

"Yes, during her lifetime. Her father left her a considerable sum of money in trust. She could not touch the principal. At her death it was to pass to any children she might have—and failing children to the Pittstown Museum."

Poirot drummed thoughtfully on the table.

"Then we can, I think," he said, "eliminate one motive from the case. It is, you comprehend, what I look for first. *Who benefits by the deceased's death?* In this case it is a museum. Had it been otherwise, had Mrs. Leidner died intestate but possessed of a considerable fortune, I should imagine that it would prove an interesting question as to who inherited the money—you—or a former husband. But there would have been this difficulty, the former husband would have had to resurrect himself in order to claim it, and I should imagine that he would then be in danger of arrest, though I hardly fancy that the death penalty would be exacted so long after the war. However, these speculations need not arise. As I say, I settle first the question of money. For the next step I proceed always to suspect the husband or wife of the deceased! In this case, in the first place, you are proved never to have gone near your wife's room yesterday afternoon, in the second place, you lose instead of gain by your wife's death, and in the third place—"

He paused.

"Yes?" said Dr. Leidner.

"In the third place," said Poirot slowly. "I can, I think, appreciate devotion when I see it. I believe, Dr. Leidner, that your love for your wife was the ruling passion of your life. It is so, is it not?"

Dr. Leidner answered quite simply:

"Yes."

Poirot nodded.

"Therefore," he said, "we can proceed."

"Here, here, let's get down to it," said Dr. Reilly with some impatience.

Poirot gave him a reproving glance.

"My friend, do not be impatient. In a case like this everything must be approached with order and method. In fact, that is my rule in every case. Having disposed of certain possibilities, we now approach a very important point. It is vital that, as you say—all the cards should be on the table—there must be nothing kept back."

"Quite so," said Dr. Reilly.

"That is why I demand the whole truth," went on Poirot.

Dr. Leidner looked at him in surprise.

"I assure you, M. Poirot, that I have kept nothing back. I have told you everything that I know. There have been no reserves."

"*Tout de même,* you have not told me *everything.*"

"Yes, indeed. I cannot think of any detail that has escaped me."

He looked quite distressed.

Poirot shook his head gently.

"No," he said. "*You have not told me, for instance, why you installed Nurse Leatheran in the house.*"

Dr. Leidner looked completely bewildered.

"But I have explained that. It is obvious. My wife's nervousness— her fears . . ."

Poirot leaned forward. Slowly and emphatically he wagged a finger up and down.

"No, no, no. There is something there that is not clear. Your wife is in danger, yes—she is threatened with death, yes. You send—*not for the police*—not for a private detective even—but for a *nurse!* It does not make the sense, that!"

"I—I—" Dr. Leidner stopped. The colour rose in his cheeks. "I thought—" He came to a dead stop.

"Now we are coming to it," Poirot encouraged him. "You thought —what?"

Dr. Leidner remained silent. He looked harassed and unwilling.

"See you," Poirot's tone became winning and appealing, "it all rings true what you have told me, except for that. Why a *nurse?* There is an answer—yes. In fact, there can be only one answer. *You did not believe yourself in your wife's danger.*"

And then with a cry Dr. Leidner broke down.

"God help me," he groaned. "I didn't. I didn't."

Poirot watched him with the kind of attention a cat gives a mouse-hole—ready to pounce when the mouse shows itself.

"What *did* you think then?" he asked.

"I don't know. I don't know . . ."

"But you do know. You know perfectly. Perhaps I can help you— with a guess. *Did you, Dr. Leidner, suspect that these letters were all written by your wife herself?*"

There wasn't any need for him to answer. The truth of Poirot's guess was only too apparent. The horrified hand he held up, as though begging for mercy, told its own tale.

I drew a deep breath. So I *had* been right in my half-formed guess! I recalled the curious tone in which Dr. Leidner had asked me what I thought of it all. I nodded my head slowly and thoughtfully, and suddenly awoke to the fact that M. Poirot's eyes were on me.

"Did you think the same, nurse?"

"The idea did cross my mind," I said truthfully.

"For what reason?"

I explained the similarity of the handwriting on the letter that Mr. Coleman had shown me.

Poirot turned to Dr. Leidner.

"Had you, too, noticed that similarity?"

Dr. Leidner bowed his head.

"Yes, I did. The writing was small and cramped—not big and generous like Louise's, but several of the letters were formed the same way. I will show you."

From an inner breast pocket he took out some letters and finally selected a sheet from one which he handed to Poirot. It was part of a letter written to him by his wife. Poirot compared it carefully with the anonymous letters.

"Yes," he murmured. "Yes. There are several similarities—a curious way of forming the letter *s*, a distinctive *e*. I am not a handwriting expert—I cannot pronounce definitely (and for that matter, I have never found two handwriting experts who agree on any point whatsoever)—but one can at least say this—the similarity between the two handwritings is very marked. It seems highly probable that they were all written by the same person. But it is not *certain*. We must take all contingencies into mind."

He leaned back in his chair and said thoughtfully:

"There are three possibilities. First, the similarity of the handwriting is pure coincidence. Second, that these threatening letters were written by Mrs. Leidner herself for some obscure reason. Third, that they were written by some one *who deliberately copied her handwriting*. Why? There seems no sense in it. One of these three possibilities must be the correct one."

He reflected for a minute or two and then, turning to Dr. Leidner, he asked, with a resumal of his brisk manner.

"When the possibility that Mrs. Leidner herself was the author of these letters first struck you, what theory did you form?"

Dr. Leidner shook his head.

"I put the idea out of my head as quickly as possible. I felt it was monstrous."

"Did you search for no explanation?"

"Well," he hesitated, "I wondered if worrying and brooding over the past had perhaps affected my wife's brain slightly. I thought she might possibly have written those letters to herself without being conscious of having done so. That is possible, isn't it?" he added, turning to Dr. Reilly.

Dr. Reilly pursed up his lips.

"The human brain is capable of almost anything," he replied vaguely.

But he shot a lightning glance at Poirot, and as if in obedience to it, the latter abandoned the subject.

"The letters are an interesting point," he said. "But we must concentrate on the case as a whole. There are, as I see it, three possible solutions."

"Three?"

"Yes. Solution one: the simplest. You wife's first husband is still alive. He first threatens her and then proceeds to carry out his threats. If we accept this solution, our problem is to discover how he got in or out without being seen.

"Solution two: Mrs. Leidner, for reasons of her own (reasons probably more easily understood by a medical man than a layman), writes herself threatening letters. The gas business is staged by her (remember, it was she who roused you by telling you she smelt gas). But, *if Mrs. Leidner wrote herself the letters, she cannot be in danger from the supposed writer*. We must, therefore, look elsewhere for the murderer. We must look, in fact, amongst the members of your staff. Yes," in answer to a murmur of protest from Dr. Leidner, "that is the only logical conclusion. To satisfy a private grudge one of them killed her. That person, I may say, was probably aware of the letters—or was at any rate aware that Mrs. Leidner feared or was pretending to fear some one. That fact, in the murderer's opinion, rendered the murder quite safe for him. He felt sure it would be put down to a mysterious outsider—the writer of the threatening letters.

"A variant of this solution is that the murderer actually wrote the letters himself, being aware of Mrs. Leidner's past history. But in that case it is not quite clear *why* the criminal should have copied Mrs. Leidner's own handwriting since, as far as we can see, it would be more to his or her advantage that they should appear to be written by an outsider.

"The third solution is the most interesting to my mind. I suggest that the letters are genuine. They are written by Mrs. Leidner's first husband (or his younger brother), *who is actually one of the expedition staff.*"

XVI
THE SUSPECTS

Dr. Leidner sprang to his feet.

"Impossible! Absolutely impossible! The idea is absurd!"

Mr. Poirot looked at him quite calmly but said nothing.

"You mean to suggest that my wife's former husband is one of the expedition *and that she didn't recognize him?*"

"Exactly. Reflect a little on the facts. Nearly twenty years ago your wife lived with this man for a few months. Would she know him if she came across him after that lapse of time? I think not. His face will have changed, his build will have changed—his voice may not have changed so much, but that is a detail he can attend to himself. And remember, *she is not looking for him amongst her own household.* She visualizes him as somewhere *outside*—a stranger. No, I do not think she would recognize him. And there is a second possibility. The young brother—the child of those days who was so passionately devoted to his elder brother. He is now a man. Will she recognize a child of ten or twelve years old in a man nearing thirty? Yes, there is young William Bosner to be reckoned with. Remember, his brother in his eyes may not loom as a traitor but as a patriot, a martyr for his own country—Germany. In his eyes *Mrs. Leidner* is the traitor—the monster who sent his beloved brother to death! A susceptible child is capable of great hero worship, and a young mind can easily be obsessed by an idea which persists into adult life."

"Quite true," said Dr. Reilly. "The popular view that a child forgets easily is not an accurate one. Many people go right through life in the grip of an idea which has been impressed on them in very tender years."

"*Bien.* You have these two possibilities. Frederick Bosner, a man by now of fifty odd, and William Bosner, whose age would be something short of thirty. Let us examine the members of your staff from these two points of view."

"This is fantastic," murmured Dr. Leidner. "*My* staff! The members of my own expedition."

"And consequently considered above suspicion," said Poirot dryly. "A very useful point of view. *Commençons!* Who could emphatically *not* be Frederick or William?"

"The women."

"Naturally. Miss Johnson and Mrs. Mercado are crossed off. Who else?"

"Carey. He and I have worked together for years before I even met Louise—"

"And also he is the wrong age. He is, I should judge, thirty-eight or nine, too young for Frederick, too old for William. Now for the rest. There is Father Lavigny and Mr. Mercado. Either of them might be Frederick Bosner."

"But, my dear sir," cried Dr. Leidner in a voice of mingled irritation and amusement, "Father Lavigny is known all over the world as an epigraphist and Mercado has worked for years in a well-known museum in New York. It is *impossible* that either of them should be the man you think!"

Poirot waved an airy hand.

"Impossible—impossible—I take no account of the word! The impossible, always I examine it very closely! But we will pass on for the moment. Who else have you? Carl Reiter, a young man with a German name, David Emmott—"

"He has been with me two seasons, remember."

"He is a young man with the gift of patience. *If* he committed a crime, it would not be in a hurry. All would be very well prepared."

Dr. Leidner made a gesture of despair.

"And lastly, William Coleman," continued Poirot.

"He is an Englishman."

"*Pourquoi pas?* Did not Mrs. Leidner say that the boy left America and could not be traced? He might easily have been brought up in England."

"You have an answer to everything," said Dr. Leidner.

I was thinking hard. Right from the beginning I had thought Mr. Coleman's manner rather more like a P. G. Wodehouse book than like a real live young man. Had he really been playing a part all the time?

Poirot was writing in a little book.

"Let us proceed with order and method," he said. "On the first count we have two names. Father Lavigny and Mr. Mercado. On the second we have Coleman, Emmott and Reiter.

"Now let us pass to the opposite aspect of the matter—means and opportunity. *Who amongst the expedition had the means and the opportunity of committing the crime?* Carey was on the dig, Coleman was in Hassanieh, you yourself were on the roof. That leaves us Father Lavigny, Mr. Mercado, Mrs. Mercado, David Emmott, Carl Reiter, Miss Johnson and Nurse Leatheran."

"Oh!" I exclaimed, and I bounded in my chair.

Mr. Poirot looked at me with twinkling eyes.

"Yes, I'm afraid, *ma sœur*, that you have got to be included. It would have been quite easy for you to have gone along and killed Mrs. Leidner while the courtyard was empty. You have plenty of muscle and strength, and she would have been quite unsuspicious until the moment the blow was struck."

I was so upset that I couldn't get a word out. Dr. Reilly, I noticed, was looking highly amused.

"Interesting case of a nurse who murdered her patients one by one," he murmured.

Such a look as I gave him!

Dr. Leidner's mind had been running on a different tack.

"Not Emmott, M. Poirot," he objected. "You can't include him. He was on the roof with me, remember, during that ten minutes."

"Nevertheless we cannot exclude him. He could have come down, gone straight to Mrs. Leidner's room, killed her, and *then* called the boy back. Or he might have killed her on one of the occasions when he had *sent the boy up to you.*"

Dr. Leidner shook his head, murmuring:

"What a nightmare! It's all so—fantastic."

To my surprise Poirot agreed.

"Yes, that is true. *This is a fantastic crime.* One does not often come across them. Usually murder is very sordid—very simple. But this is unusual murder . . . I suspect, Dr. Leidner, that your wife was an unusual woman."

He had hit the nail on the head with such accuracy that I jumped.

"Is that true, nurse?" he asked.

Dr. Leidner said quietly:

"Tell him what Louise was like, nurse. You are unprejudiced."

I spoke quite frankly.

"She was very lovely," I said. "You couldn't help admiring her and wanting to do things for her. I've never met any one like her before."

"Thank you," said Dr. Leidner and smiled at me.

"That is valuable testimony coming from an outsider," said Poirot politely. "Well, let us proceed. Under the heading of *means and opportunity* we have seven names. Nurse Leatheran, Miss Johnson, Mrs. Mercado, Mr. Mercado, Mr. Reiter, Mr. Emmott and Father Lavigny."

Once more he cleared his throat. I've always noticed that foreigners can make the oddest noises.

"Let us for the moment assume that our third theory is correct. That is, that the murderer is Frederick or William Bosner, and that Frederick or William Bosner is a member of the expedition staff. By comparing both lists we can narrow down our suspects on this count to four. Father Lavigny, Mr. Mercado, Carl Reiter and David Emmott."

"Father Lavigny is out of the question," said Dr. Leidner with decision. "He is one of the *Pères Blancs* in Carthage."

"And his beard's quite real," I put in.

"*Ma sœur*," said Poirot, "a murderer of the first class *never* wears a false beard!"

"How do you know the murderer is of the first class?" I asked rebelliously.

"Because if he were not, the whole truth would be plain to me at this instant—and it is not."

That's pure conceit, I thought to myself.

"Anyway," I said, reverting to the beard, "it must have taken quite a time to grow."

"That is a practical observation," said Poirot. Dr. Leidner said irritably:

"But it's ridiculous—quite ridiculous. Both he and Mercado are well-known men. They've been known for years."

Poirot turned to him.

"You have not the true vision. You do not appreciate an important point. *If Frederick Bosner is not dead—what has he been doing all these years?* He must have taken a different name. He must have built himself up a career."

"As a *Père Blanc?*" asked Dr. Reilly sceptically.

"It is a little fantastic that, yes," confessed Poirot. "But we cannot put it right out of court. Besides, there are other possibilities."

"The young 'uns?" said Reilly. "If you want my opinion, on the face of it there's only one of your suspects that's even plausible."

"And that is?"

"Young Carl Reiter. There's nothing actually against him, but come down to it and you've got to admit a few things—he's the right age, he's got a German name, he's new this year and he had the opportunity all right. He'd only got to pop out of his photographic place, cross the courtyard to do his dirty work and hare back again while the coast was clear. If any one were to have dropped into the photographic room while he was out of it, he can always say later that he was in the dark-room. I don't say he's your man but if you are going to suspect some one I say he's by far and away the most likely."

M. Poirot didn't seem very receptive. He nodded gravely but doubtfully.

"Yes," he said. "He is the most plausible, but it may not be so simple as all that."

Then he said:

"Let us say no more at present. I would like now if I may to examine the room where the crime took place."

"Certainly." Dr. Leidner fumbled in his pockets then looked at Dr. Reilly.

"Captain Maitland took it," he said.

"Maitland gave it to me," said Reilly. "He had to go off on that Kurdish business."

He produced the key.

Dr. Leidner said hesitatingly:

"Do you mind—if I don't— Perhaps, nurse—"

"Of course. Of course," said Poirot. "I quite understand. Never do I wish to cause you unnecessary pain. If you will be good enough to accompany me, *ma sœur.*"

"Certainly," I said.

XVII

THE STAIN BY THE WASH-STAND

MRS. LEIDNER'S BODY had been taken to Hassanieh for the post-mortem, but otherwise her room had been left exactly as it was. There was so little in it that it had not taken the police long to go over it.

To the right of the door as you entered was the bed. Opposite the door were the two barred windows giving on the countryside. Between them was a plain oak table with two drawers that served Mrs. Leidner as a dressing-table. On the east wall there was a line of hooks with dresses hung up protected by cotton bags and a deal chest of drawers. Immediately to the left of the door was the wash-stand. In the middle of the room was a good-sized plain oak table with a blotter and inkstand and a small attaché-case. It was in the latter that Mrs. Leidner had kept the anonymous letters. The curtains were short strips of native material—white striped with orange. The floor was of stone with some goatskin rugs on it, three narrow ones of brown striped with white in front of the two windows and the wash-stand, and a larger better quality one of white with brown stripes lying between the bed and the writing-table.

There were no cupboards or alcoves or long curtains—nowhere, in fact, where any one could have hidden. The bed was a plain iron one with a printed cotton quilt. The only trace of luxury in the room were three pillows all made of the best soft and billowy down. Nobody but Mrs. Leidner had pillows like these.

In a few brief dry words Dr. Reilly explained where Mrs. Leidner's body had been found—in a heap on the rug beside the bed.

To illustrate his account, he beckoned me to come forward.

"If you don't mind, nurse?" he said.

I'm not squeamish. I got down on the floor and arranged myself as far as possible in the attitude in which Mrs. Leidner's body had been found.

"Leidner lifted her head when he found her," said the doctor. "But

I questioned him closely and it's obvious that he didn't actually change her position."

"It seems quite straightforward," said Poirot. "She was lying on the bed, asleep or resting—some one opens the door, she looks up, rises to her feet—"

"And he struck her down," finished the doctor. "The blow would produce unconsciousness and death would follow very shortly. You see—"

He explained the injury in technical language.

"Not much blood, then?" said Poirot.

"No, the blood escaped internally into the brain."

"*Eh bien,*" said Poirot, "that seems straightforward enough—except for one thing. If the man who entered was a stranger, why did not Mrs. Leidner cry out at once for help? If she had screamed she would have been heard. Nurse Leatheran here would have heard her, and Emmott and the boy."

"That's easily answered," said Dr. Reilly dryly. "*Because it wasn't a stranger.*"

Poirot nodded.

"Yes," he said meditatively. "She may have been *surprised* to see the person—but she was not *afraid.* Then, as he struck, she *may* have uttered a half cry—too late."

"The cry Miss Johnson heard?"

"Yes, if she *did* hear it. But on the whole I doubt it. These mud walls are thick and the windows were closed."

He stepped up to the bed.

"You left her actually lying down?" he asked me. I explained exactly what I had done.

"Did she mean to sleep or was she going to read?"

"I gave her two books—a light one and a volume of memoirs. She usually read for a while and then sometimes dropped off for a short sleep."

"And she was—what shall I say—quite as usual?"

I considered.

"Yes. She seemed quite normal and in good spirits," I said. "Just a shade off-hand, perhaps, but I put that down to her having confided in me the day before. It makes people a little uncomfortable sometimes."

Poirot's eyes twinkled.

"Ah, yes, indeed, me, I know that well."

He looked round the room.

"And when you came in here after the murder, was everything as you had seen it before?"

I looked round also.

"Yes, I think so. I don't remember anything being different."

"There was no sign of the weapon with which she was struck?"

"No."

Poirot looked at Dr. Reilly.

"What was it in your opinion?"

The doctor replied promptly.

"Something pretty powerful of a fair size and without any sharp corners or edges. The rounded base of a statue, say—something like that. Mind you, I'm not suggesting that that *was* it. But that type of thing. The blow was delivered with great force."

"Struck by a strong arm? A man's arm?"

"Yes—unless—"

"Unless—what?"

Dr. Reilly said slowly:

"It is just possible that Mrs. Leidner might have been on her knees —in which case, the blow being delivered from above with a heavy implement, the force needed would not have been so great."

"*On her knees,*" mused Poirot. "It is an idea—that."

"It's only an idea, mind," the doctor hastened to point out. "There's absolutely nothing to indicate it."

"But it's possible."

"Yes. And after all, in view of the circumstances, it's not fantastic. Her fear might have led her to kneel in supplication rather than to scream when her instinct would tell her it was too late—that nobody could get there in time."

"Yes," said Poirot thoughtfully. "It is an idea. . . ."

It was a very poor one, I thought. I couldn't for one moment imagine Mrs. Leidner on her knees to any one.

Poirot made his way slowly round the room. He opened the windows, tested the bars, passed his head through and satisfied himself that by no means could his shoulders be made to follow his head.

"The windows were shut when you found her," he said. "Were they also shut when you left her at a quarter to one?"

"Yes, they were always shut in the afternoon. There is no gauze over these windows as there is in the living-room and dining-room. They are kept shut to keep out the flies."

"And in any case no one could get in that way," mused Poirot. "And the walls are of the most solid—mud-brick—and there are no trap-doors and no sky-lights. No, there is only one way into this room —*through the door*. And there is only one way to the door—through the courtyard. And there is only one entrance to the courtyard—*through the archway*. And outside the archway there were five people and they all tell the same story, and I do not think, me, that they are lying. . . . No, they are not lying. They are not bribed to silence. The murderer was *here*. . . ."

I didn't say anything. Hadn't I felt the same thing just now when we were all cooped up round that table?

Slowly Poirot prowled round the room. He took up a photograph from the chest of drawers. It was of an elderly man with a white goatee beard. He looked inquiringly at me.

"Mrs. Leidner's father," I said. "She told me so."

He put it down again and glanced over the articles on the dressing-table—all of plain tortoiseshell—simple but good. He looked up at a row of books on a shelf, repeating the titles aloud.

"*Who Were the Greeks? Introduction to Relativity. Life of Lady Hester Stanhope. Crewe Train. Back to Methuselah. Linda Condon.* Yes, they tell us something, perhaps.

"She was not a fool, your Mrs. Leidner. She had a mind."

"Oh! she was a *very* clever woman," I said eagerly. "Very well read and up in everything. She wasn't a bit ordinary."

He smiled as he looked over at me.

"No," he said. "I've already realized that."

He passed on. He stood for some moments at the wash-stand where there was a big array of bottles and toilet creams.

Then, suddenly, he dropped on his knees and examined the rug.

Dr. Reilly and I came quickly to join him. He was examining a small dark brown stain, almost invisible on the brown of the rug. In fact it was only just noticeable where it impinged on one of the white stripes.

"What do you say, doctor?" he said. "Is that blood?"

Dr. Reilly knelt down.

"Might be," he said. "I'll make sure if you like?"

"If you would be so amiable."

Mr. Poirot examined the jug and basin. The jug was standing on the side of the wash-stand. The basin was empty, but beside the wash-stand there was an old kerosene tin containing slop water.

He turned to me.

"Do you remember, nurse? Was this jug *out* of the basin or *in* it when you left Mrs. Leidner at a quarter to one?"

"I can't be sure," I said after a minute or two. "I rather think it was standing in the basin."

"Ah?"

"But you see," I said hastily, "I only think so because it usually was. The boys leave it like that after lunch. I just feel that if it hadn't been in I should have noticed it."

He nodded quite appreciatively.

"Yes, I understand that. It is your hospital training. If everything had not been just so in the room, you would quite unconsciously have set it to rights hardly noticing what you were doing. And after the murder? Was it like it is now?"

I shook my head.

"I didn't notice then," I said. "All I looked for was whether there was any place any one could be hidden or if there were anything the murderer had left behind him."

"It's blood all right," said Dr. Reilly, rising from his knees. "Is it important?"

Poirot was frowning perplexedly. He flung out his hands with petulance.

"I cannot tell. How can I tell? It may mean nothing at all. I can say, if I like, that the murderer touched her—that there was blood on his hands—very little blood, but still blood—and so he came over here and washed them. Yes, it may have been like that. But I cannot jump to conclusions and say that it *was* so. That stain may be of no importance at all."

"There would have been very little blood," said Dr. Reilly dubiously. "None would have spurted out or anything like that. It would have just oozed a little from the wound. Of course, if he'd probed it at all . . ."

I gave a shiver. A nasty sort of picture came up in my mind. The vision of somebody—perhaps that nice pig-faced photographic boy, striking down that lovely woman and then bending over her probing the wound with his finger in an awful gloating fashion and his face, perhaps, quite different . . . all fierce and mad. . . .

Dr. Reilly noticed my shiver.

"What's the matter, nurse?" he said.

"Nothing—just goose-flesh," I said. "A goose walking over my grave."

Mr. Poirot turned round and looked at me.

"I know what you need," he said. "Presently when we have finished here and I go back with the doctor to Hassanieh we will take you with us. You will give Nurse Leatheran tea, will you not, doctor?"

"Delighted."

"Oh, no, doctor," I protested. "I couldn't think of such a thing."

M. Poirot gave me a little friendly tap on the shoulder. Quite an English tap, not a foreign one.

"You, *ma sœur,* will do as you are told," he said. "Besides, it will be of advantage to me. There is a good deal more that I want to discuss, and I cannot do it here where one must preserve the decencies. The good Dr. Leidner, he worshipped his wife and he is sure—oh, so sure —that everybody else felt the same about her! But that, in my opinion, would not be human nature! No, we want to discuss Mrs. Leidner with—how do you say—the gloves removed? That is settled then. When we have finished here, we take you with us to Hassanieh."

"I suppose," I said doubtfully, "that I ought to be leaving anyway. It's rather awkward."

"Do nothing for a day or two," said Dr. Reilly. "You can't very well go until after the funeral."

"That's all very well," I said. "And supposing I get murdered too, doctor?"

I said it half jokingly and Dr. Reilly took it in the same fashion and would, I think, have made some jocular response.

But M. Poirot, to my astonishment, stood stock still in the middle of the floor and clasped his hands to his head.

"Ah! if that were possible," he murmured. "It is a danger—yes—a great danger—and what can one do? How can one guard against it?"

"Why, M. Poirot," I said, "I was only joking! Who'd want to murder me, I should like to know?"

"You—or another," he said, and I didn't like the way he said it at all. Positively creepy.

"But why?" I persisted.

He looked at me very straight then.

"I joke, mademoiselle," he said, "and I laugh. *But there are some things that are no joke.* There are things that my profession has taught me. And one of these things, the most terrible thing, is this:

"*Murder is a habit . . .*"

XVIII
TEA AT DR. REILLY'S

BEFORE LEAVING, POIROT made a round of the expedition house and the outbuildings. He also asked a few questions of the servants at second hand—that is to say, Dr. Reilly translated the questions and answers from English into Arabic and vice versa.

These questions dealt mainly with the appearance of the stranger Mrs. Leidner and I had seen looking through the window and to whom Father Lavigny had been talking on the following day.

"Do you really think that fellow had anything to do with it?" asked Dr. Reilly when we were bumping along in his car on our way to Hassanieh.

"I like all the information there is," was Poirot's reply.

And really, that described his methods very well. I found later that there wasn't anything—no small scrap of insignificant gossip—in which he wasn't interested. Men aren't usually so gossipy.

I must confess I was glad of my cup of tea when we got to Dr. Reilly's house. M. Poirot, I noticed, put five lumps of sugar in his.

Stirring it carefully with his teaspoon he said:

"And now we can talk, can we not? We can make up our minds who is likely to have committed the crime."

"Lavigny, Mercado, Emmott or Reiter?" asked Dr. Reilly.

"No, no—that was theory number three. I wish to concentrate now on theory number two—leaving aside all question of a mysterious husband or brother-in-law turning up from the past. Let us discuss now quite simply which member of the expedition had the means and opportunity to kill Mrs. Leidner, and who is likely to have done so."

"I thought you didn't think much of that theory."

"Not at all. But I have some natural delicacy," said Poirot reproachfully. "Can I discuss in the presence of Dr. Leidner the motives likely to lead to the murder of his wife by a member of the expedition? That would not have been delicate at all. I had to sustain the fiction that his wife was adorable and that every one adored her!

"But naturally it was not like that at all. Now we can be brutal and impersonal and say what we think. We have no longer to consider people's feelings. And that is where Nurse Leatheran is going to help us. She is, I am sure, a very good observer."

"Oh, I don't know about that," I said.

Dr. Reilly handed me a plate of hot scones—"to fortify yourself," he said. They were very good scones.

"Come now," said M. Poirot in a friendly, chatty way. "You shall tell me, *ma sœur*, exactly what each member of the expedition felt towards Mrs. Leidner."

"I was only there a week, M. Poirot," I said.

"Quite long enough for one of your intelligence. A nurse sums up quickly. She makes her judgments and abides by them. Come, let us make a beginning. Father Lavigny, for instance?"

"Well, there now, I really couldn't say. He and Mrs. Leidner seemed to like talking together. But they usually spoke French and I'm not very good at French myself though I learnt it as a girl at school. I've an idea they talked mainly about books."

"They were, as you might say, companionable together—yes?"

"Well, yes, you might put it that way. But, all the same, I think Father Lavigny was puzzled by her and—well—almost annoyed by being puzzled, if you know what I mean."

And I told him of the conversation I had had with him out on the dig that first day when he had called Mrs. Leidner a "dangerous woman."

"Now that is very interesting," M. Poirot said. "And she—what do you think she thought of him?"

"That's rather difficult to say, too. It wasn't easy to know what Mrs. Leidner thought of people. Sometimes, I fancy, *he* puzzled *her*. I remember her saying to Dr. Leidner that he was unlike any priest she had ever known."

"A length of hemp to be ordered for Father Lavigny," said Dr. Reilly facetiously.

"My dear friend," said Poirot. "Have you not, perhaps, some patients to attend? I would not for the world detain you from your professional duties."

"I've got a whole hospital of them," said Dr. Reilly.

And he got up and said a wink was as good as a nod to a blind horse, and went out laughing.

"That is better," said Poirot. "We will have now an interesting conversation *tête-à-tête*. But you must not forget to eat your tea."

He passed me a plate of sandwiches and suggested my having a second cup of tea. He really had very pleasant, attentive manners.

"And now," he said, "let us continue with your impressions. Who was there who in your opinion did *not* like Mrs. Leidner?"

"Well," I said, "it's only my opinion and I don't want it repeated as coming from me."

"Naturally not."

"But in my opinion little Mrs. Mercado fairly hated her!"

"Ah! And Mr. Mercado?"

"He was a bit soft on her," I said. "I shouldn't think women apart from his wife had ever taken much notice of him. And Mrs. Leidner had a nice kind way of being interested in people and the things they told her. It rather went to the poor man's head, I fancy."

"And Mrs. Mercado—she was not pleased?"

"She was just plain jealous—that's the truth of it. You've got to be very careful when there's a husband and wife about, and that's a fact. I could tell you some surprising things. You've no idea the extraordinary things women get into their heads when it's a question of their husbands."

"I do not doubt the truth of what you say. So Mrs. Mercado was jealous? And she hated Mrs. Leidner?"

"I've seen her look at her as though she'd have liked to kill her—oh, gracious!" I pulled myself up. "Indeed, M. Poirot, I didn't mean to say—I mean that is, not for one moment—"

"No, no. I quite understand. The phrase slipped out. A very convenient one. And Mrs. Leidner, was she worried by this animosity of Mrs. Mercado's?"

"Well," I said, reflecting, "I don't really think she was worried at all. In fact, I don't even know whether she noticed it. I thought once of just giving her a hint—but I didn't like to. Least said soonest mended. That's what I say."

"You are doubtless wise. Can you give me any instances of how Mrs. Mercado showed her feelings?"

I told him about our conversation on the roof.

"So she mentioned Mrs. Leidner's first marriage," said Poirot thoughtfully. "Can you remember—in mentioning it—did she look at you as though she wondered whether you had heard a different version?"

"You think she may have known the truth about it?"

"It is a possibility. She may have written those letters—and engineered a tapping hand and all the rest of it."

"I wondered something of the same kind myself. It seemed the kind of petty revengeful thing she might do."

"Yes. A cruel streak, I should say. But hardly the temperament for cold-blooded brutal murder unless, of course—"

He paused and then said:

"It is odd, that curious thing she said to you. '_I know why you are here._' What did she mean by it?"

"I can't imagine," I said frankly.

"She thought you were there for some ulterior reason apart from the declared one. What reason? And why should she be so concerned in the matter. Odd, too, the way you tell me she stared at you all through tea the day you arrived."

"Well, she's not a lady, M. Poirot," I said primly.

"That, _ma sœur_, is an excuse but not an explanation."

I wasn't quite sure for the minute what he meant. But he went on quickly.

"And the other members of the staff?"

I considered.

"I don't think Miss Johnson liked Mrs. Leidner either very much. But she was quite open and above-board about it. She as good as admitted she was prejudiced. You see, she's very devoted to Dr. Leidner and had worked with him for years. And of course, marriage does change things—there's no denying it."

"Yes," said Poirot. "And from Miss Johnson's point of view it would be an unsuitable marriage. It would have been much more suitable if Dr. Leidner had married _her._"

"It would really," I agreed. "But there, that's a man all over. Not one in a hundred considers suitability. And one can't really blame Dr. Leidner. Miss Johnson, poor soul, isn't so much to look at. Now Mrs. Leidner was really beautiful—not young, of course—but oh! I wish you'd known her. There was something about her. . . . I remember Mr. Coleman saying she was like a thingummyjig that came to lure people into marshes. That wasn't a very good way of putting it but—oh, well—you'll laugh at me but there _was_ something about her that was—well—unearthly."

"She could cast a spell—yes, I understand," said Poirot.

"Then I don't think she and Mr. Carey got on very well either," I went on. "I've an idea _he_ was jealous just like Miss Johnson. He was

always very stiff with her and so was she with him. You know—she
passed him things and was very polite and called him Mr. Carey
rather formally. He was an old friend of her husband's, of course, and
some women can't stand their husband's old friends. They don't like
to think that any one knew them before they did—at least that's rather
a muddled way of putting it—"

"I quite understand. And the three young men? Coleman, you say,
was inclined to be poetic about her."

I couldn't help laughing.

"It was funny, M. Poirot," I said. "He's such a matter-of-fact young
man."

"And the other two?"

"I don't really know about Mr. Emmott. He's always so quiet and
never says much. She was very nice to him always. You know—friendly
—called him David and used to tease him about Miss Reilly and things
like that."

"Ah, really? And did he enjoy that?"

"I don't quite know," I said doubtfully. "He'd just look at her. Rather
funnily. You couldn't tell what he was thinking."

"And Mr. Reiter?"

"She wasn't always very kind to him," I said slowly. "I think he got
on her nerves. She used to say quite sarcastic things to him."

"And did he mind?"

"He used to get very pink, poor boy. Of course, she didn't *mean*
to be unkind."

And then suddenly, from feeling a little sorry for the boy, it came
over me that he was very likely a cold-blooded murderer and had been
playing a part all the time.

"Oh, M. Poirot," I exclaimed. "What do you think *really* happened?"

He shook his head slowly and thoughtfully.

"Tell me," he said. "You are not afraid to go back there to-night?"

"Oh, *no*," I said. "Of course, I remember what you said, but who
would want to murder *me*?"

"I do not think that any one could," he said slowly. "That is partly
why I have been so anxious to hear all you could tell me. No, I think
—I am sure—you are quite safe."

"If any one had told me in Baghdad—" I began and stopped.

"Did you hear any gossip about the Leidners and the expedition before you came here?" he asked.

I told him about Mrs. Leidner's nickname and just a little of what Mrs. Kelsey had said about her.

In the middle of it the door opened and Miss Reilly came in. She had been playing tennis and had her racquet in her hand.

I gathered Poirot had already met her when he arrived in Hassanieh.

She said how do you do to me in her usual off-hand manner and picked up a sandwich.

"Well, M. Poirot," she said. "How are you getting on with our local mystery?"

"Not very fast, mademoiselle."

"I see you've rescued nurse from the wreck."

"Nurse Leatheran has been giving me valuable information about the various members of the expedition. Incidentally I have learnt a good deal—about the victim. And the victim, mademoiselle, is very often the clue to the mystery."

Miss Reilly said:

"That's rather clever of you, M. Poirot. It's certainly true that if ever a woman deserved to be murdered Mrs. Leidner was that woman!"

"Miss Reilly!" I cried, scandalized.

She laughed, a short, nasty laugh.

"Ah!" she said. "I thought you hadn't been hearing quite the truth. Nurse Leatheran, I'm afraid, was quite taken in, like many other people. Do you know, M. Poirot, I rather hope that this case isn't going to be one of your successes. I'd quite like the murderer of Louise Leidner to get away with it. In fact, I wouldn't much have objected to putting her out of the way myself."

I was simply disgusted with the girl. M. Poirot, I must say, didn't turn a hair. He just bowed and said quite pleasantly:

"I hope, then, that you have an alibi for yesterday afternoon?"

There was a moment's silence and Miss Reilly's racquet went clattering down on to the floor. She didn't bother to pick it up. Slack and untidy like all her sort! She said in a rather breathless voice:

"Oh, yes, I was playing tennis at the club. But, seriously, M. Poirot, I wonder if you know anything at all about Mrs. Leidner and the kind of woman she was?"

Again he made a funny little bow and said:

"You shall inform me, mademoiselle."

She hesitated a minute and then spoke with a callousness and lack of decency that really sickened me.

"There's a convention that one doesn't speak ill of the dead. That's stupid, I think. The truth's always the truth. On the whole it's better to keep your mouth shut about living people. You might conceivably injure them. The dead are past that. But the harm they've done lives after them sometimes. Not quite a quotation from Shakespeare but very nearly! Has nurse told you of the queer atmosphere there was at Tell Yarimjah? Has she told you how jumpy they all were? And how they all used to glare at each other like enemies? That was Louise Leidner's doing. When I was a kid out here three years ago they were the happiest, jolliest lot imaginable. Even last year they were pretty well all right. But this year there was a blight over them—and it was *her* doing. She was the kind of woman who won't let anybody else be happy! There *are* women like that and she was one of them! She wanted to break up things always. Just for fun—or for the sense of power—or perhaps just because she was made that way. And she was the kind of woman who had to get hold of every male creature within reach!"

"Miss Reilly," I cried, "I don't think that's true. In fact I *know* it isn't."

She went on without taking the least notice of me.

"It wasn't enough for her to have her husband adore her. She had to make a fool of that long-legged shambling idiot of a Mercado. Then she got hold of Bill. Bill's a sensible cove, but she was getting him all mazed and bewildered. Carl Reiter she just amused herself by tormenting. It was easy. He's a sensitive boy. And she had a jolly good go at David.

"David was better sport to her because he put up a fight. He felt her charm—but he wasn't having any. I think because he'd got sense enough to know that she didn't really care a damn. And that's why I hate her so. She's not sensual. She doesn't *want* affairs. It's just cold-blooded experiment on her part and the fun of stirring people up and setting them against each other. She dabbled in that too. She's the sort of woman who's never had a row with any one in her life—but rows always happen where she is! She *makes* them happen. She's a kind of female Iago. She *must* have drama. But she doesn't want to be involved *herself*. She's always outside pulling strings—looking on—enjoying it. Oh, do you see *at all* what I mean?"

"I see, perhaps, more than you know, mademoiselle," said Poirot.

I couldn't make his voice out. He didn't sound indignant. He sounded—oh, well, I can't explain it.

Sheila Reilly seemed to understand for she flushed all over her face.

"You can think what you choose," she said. "But I'm right about her. She was a clever woman and she was bored and she experimented—with people—like other people experiment with chemicals. She enjoyed working on poor old Johnson's feelings and seeing her bite on the bullet and control herself like the old sport she is. She liked goading little Mercado into a white-hot frenzy. She liked flicking *me* on the raw—and she could do it too, every time! She liked finding out things about people and holding it over them. Oh, I don't mean crude blackmail—I mean just letting them know that she *knew*—and leaving them uncertain what she meant to do about it. My God, though, that woman was an artist! There was nothing crude about *her* methods!"

"And her husband?" asked Poirot.

"She never wanted to hurt him," said Miss Reilly slowly. "I've never known her anything but sweet to him. I suppose she was fond of him. He's a dear—wrapped up in his own world—his digging and his theories. And he worshipped her and thought her perfection. That might have annoyed some women. It didn't annoy her. In a sense he lived in a fool's paradise—and yet it wasn't a fool's paradise because to him she was what he thought her. Though it's hard to reconcile that with—"

She stopped.

"Go on, mademoiselle," said Poirot.

She turned suddenly on me.

"What have you said about Richard Carey?"

"About Mr. Carey?" I asked, astonished.

"About her and Carey?"

"Well," I said, "I've mentioned that they didn't hit it off very well—"

To my surprise she broke into a fit of laughter.

"Didn't hit it off very well! You fool! He's head over ears in love with her. And it's tearing him to pieces—because he worships Leidner too. He's been his friend for years. That would be enough for her, of course. She's made it her business to come between them. But all the same I've fancied—"

"*Eh bien?*"

She was frowning, absorbed in thought.

"I've fancied that she'd gone too far for once—that she was not only bitter but bit! Carey's attractive. He's as attractive as hell. . . .

She was a cold devil—but I believe she could have lost her coldness with him. . . ."

"I think it's just scandalous what you're saying," I cried. "Why, they hardly spoke to each other!"

"Oh, didn't they?" She turned on me. "A hell of a lot you know about it. It was 'Mr. Carey' and 'Mrs. Leidner' in the house, but they used to meet outside. She'd walk down the path to the river. And he'd leave the dig for an hour at a time. They used to meet among the fruit trees.

"I saw him once just leaving her, striding back to the dig, and she was standing looking after him. I was a female cad, I suppose. I had some glasses with me and I took them out and had a good look at her face. If you ask me I believed she cared like hell for Richard Carey. . . ."

She broke off and looked at Poirot.

"Excuse my butting in on your case," she said with a sudden rather twisted grin, "but I thought you'd like to have the local colour correct."

And she marched out of the room.

"M. Poirot," I cried. "I don't believe one word of it all!"

He looked at me and he smiled, and he said (very queerly I thought):

"You can't deny, nurse, that Miss Reilly has shed a certain—illumination on the case."

XIX

A NEW SUSPICION

WE COULDN'T SAY any more just then because Dr. Reilly came in, saying jokingly that he'd killed off the most tiresome of his patients.

He and M. Poirot settled down to a more or less medical discussion of the psychology and mental state of an anonymous letter-writer. The doctor cited cases that he had known professionally, and M. Poirot told various stories from his own experience.

"It is not so simple as it seems," he ended. "There is the desire for power and very often a strong inferiority complex."

Dr. Reilly nodded.

"That's why you often find that the author of anonymous letters is the last person in the place to be suspected. Some quiet inoffensive little soul who apparently can't say Boo to a goose—all sweetness and Christian meekness on the outside—and seething with all the fury of hell underneath!"

Poirot said thoughtfully:

"Should you say Mrs. Leidner had any tendency to an inferiority complex?"

Dr. Reilly scraped out his pipe with a chuckle.

"Last woman on earth I'd describe that way. No repressions about her. Life, life and more life—that's what she wanted—and got, too!"

"Do you consider it a possibility, psychologically speaking, that she wrote those letters?"

"Yes, I do. But if she did, the reason arose out of her instinct to dramatize herself. Mrs. Leidner was a bit of a film star in private life! She *had* to be the centre of things—in the limelight. By the law of opposites she married Leidner who's about the most retiring and modest man I know. He adored her—but adoration by the fireside wasn't enough for her. She had to be the persecuted heroine as well."

"In fact," said Poirot, smiling, "you don't subscribe to his theory that she wrote them and retained no memory of her act?"

"No, I don't. I didn't turn down the idea in front of him. You can't very well say to a man who's just lost a dearly loved wife that

that same wife was a shameless exhibitionist, and that she drove him nearly crazy with anxiety to satisfy her sense of the dramatic. As a matter of fact it wouldn't be safe to tell any man the truth about his wife! Funnily enough, I'd trust most women with the truth about their husbands. Women can accept the fact that a man is a rotter, a swindler, a drug-taker, a confirmed liar, and a general swine without batting an eyelash and without its impairing their affection for the brute in the least! Women are wonderful realists."

"Frankly, Dr. Reilly, what *was* your exact opinion of Mrs. Leidner?"

Dr. Reilly lay back in his chair and puffed slowly at his pipe.

"Frankly—it's hard to say! I didn't know her well enough. She'd got charm—any amount of it. Brains, sympathy. . . . What else? She hadn't any of the ordinary unpleasant vices. She wasn't sensual or lazy or even particularly vain. She was, I've always thought (but I've no proofs of it), a most accomplished liar. What I don't know (and what I'd like to know) is whether she lied to herself or only to other people. I'm rather partial to liars myself. A woman who doesn't lie is a woman without imagination and without sympathy. I don't think she was really a man-hunter—she just liked the sport of bringing them down 'with my bow and arrow.' If you get my daughter on the subject—"

"We have had that pleasure," said Poirot with a slight smile.

"H'm," said Dr. Reilly. "She hasn't wasted much time! Shoved her knife into her pretty thoroughly, I should imagine! The younger generation has no sentiment towards the dead. It's a pity all young people are prigs! They condemn the 'old morality' and then proceed to set up a much more hard and fast code of their own. If Mrs. Leidner had had half a dozen affairs Sheila would probably have approved of her as 'living her life fully'—or 'obeying her blood instincts.' What she doesn't see is that Mrs. Leidner was acting true to type—*her* type. The cat *is* obeying its blood instinct when it plays with the mouse! It's made that way. Men aren't little boys to be shielded and protected. They've got to meet cat women—and faithful spaniel, yours-till-death adoring women, and henpecking nagging bird women—and all the rest of it! Life's a battlefield—not a picnic! I'd like to see Sheila honest enough to come off her high horse and admit that she hated Mrs. Leidner for good old thoroughgoing personal reasons. Sheila's about the only young girl in this place and she naturally assumes that she ought to have it all her own way with the young things in trousers. Naturally it annoys her when a woman, who in her view is middle-aged and who has already two husbands to her credit, comes along and licks her on her own ground. Sheila's a nice child, healthy and reasonably good-looking and attractive to the other sex as she should be. But Mrs. Leidner was something out of the ordinary in that line. She'd got just that sort of calamitous magic that plays the deuce with things—a kind of Belle Dame sans Merci."

I jumped in my chair. What a coincidence his saying that!

"Your daughter—I am not indiscreet—she has perhaps a *tendresse* for one of the young men out there?"

"Oh, I don't suppose so. She's had Emmott and Coleman dancing attendance on her as a matter of course. I don't know that she cares for one more than the other. There are a couple of young Air Force chaps too. I fancy all's fish that comes to her net at present. No, I think it's age daring to defeat youth that annoys her so much! She doesn't know as much of the world as I do. It's when you get to my age that you really appreciate a schoolgirl complexion and a clear eye and a firmly knit young body. But a woman over thirty can listen with rapt attention and throw in a word here and there to show the talker what a fine fellow he is—and few young men can resist that! Sheila's a pretty girl—but Louise Leidner was beautiful. Glorious eyes and that amazing golden fairness. Yes, she was a beautiful woman."

Yes, I thought to myself, he's right. Beauty's a wonderful thing. She *had* been beautiful. It wasn't the kind of looks you were jealous of—you just sat back and admired. I felt that first day I met her that I'd do *anything* for Mrs. Leidner!

All the same, that night as I was being driven back to the Tell Yarimjah (Dr. Reilly made me stay for an early dinner) one or two things came back to my mind and made me rather uncomfortable. At the time I hadn't believed a word of all Sheila Reilly's outpouring. I'd taken it for sheer spite and malice.

But now I suddenly remembered the way Mrs. Leidner had insisted on going for a stroll by herself that afternoon and wouldn't hear of me coming with her. I couldn't help wondering if perhaps, after all, she *had* been going to meet Mr. Carey. . . . And of course, it *was* a little odd, really, the way he and she spoke to each other so formally. Most of the others she called by their Christian names.

He never seemed to look at her, I remembered. That might be because he disliked her—or it might be just the opposite. . . .

I gave myself a little shake. Here I was fancying and imagining all sorts of things—all because of a girl's spiteful outbursts! It just showed how unkind and dangerous it was to go about saying that kind of thing.

Mrs. Leidner *hadn't* been like that at all. . . .

Of course, *she* hadn't liked Sheila Reilly. She'd really been—almost catty about her that day at lunch to Mr. Emmott.

Funny, the way he'd looked at her. The sort of way that you couldn't possibly tell what he was thinking. You never could tell what Mr. Emmott was thinking. He was so quiet. But very nice. A nice dependable person.

Now Mr. Coleman was a foolish young man if there ever was one!

I'd got to that point in my meditations when we arrived. It was just on nine o'clock and the big door was closed and barred.

Ibrahim came running with his great key to let me in.

We all went to bed early at Tell Yarimjah. There weren't any lights showing in the living-room. There was a light in the drawing-office and one in Dr. Leidner's office, but nearly all the other windows were dark. Every one must have gone to bed even earlier than usual.

As I passed the drawing-office to go to my room I looked in. Mr. Carey was in his shirt sleeves working over his big plan.

Terribly ill, he looked, I thought. So strained and worn. It gave me quite a pang. I don't know what there was about Mr. Carey—it wasn't what he *said* because he hardly said anything—and that of the most ordinary nature, and it wasn't what he *did,* for that didn't amount to much either—and yet you just couldn't help noticing him, and everything about him seemed to matter more than it would have about any one else. He just *counted,* if you know what I mean.

He turned his head and saw me. He removed his pipe from his mouth and said:

"Well, nurse, back from Hassanieh?"

"Yes, Mr. Carey. You're up working late. Everybody else seems to have gone to bed."

"I thought I might as well get on with things," he said. "I was a bit behind-hand. And I shall be out on the dig all to-morrow. We're starting digging again."

"Already?" I asked, shocked.

He looked at me rather queerly.

"It's the best thing, I think. I put it up to Leidner. He'll be in Hassanieh most of to-morrow seeing to things. But the rest of us will carry on here. You know it's not too easy all sitting round and look-ing at each other as things are."

He was right there, of course. Especially in the nervy, jumpy state every one was in.

"Well, of course you're right in a way," I said. "It takes one's mind off if one's got something to do."

The funeral, I knew, was to be the day after to-morrow.

He had bent over his plan again. I don't know why, but my heart just ached for him. I felt certain that he wasn't going to get any sleep.

"If you'd like a sleeping draught, Mr. Carey?" I said hesitatingly.

He shook his head with a smile.

"I'll carry on, nurse. Bad habit, sleeping draughts."

"Well, good-night, Mr. Carey," I said. "If there's anything I can do—"

"Don't think so, thank you, nurse. Good-night."

"I'm terribly sorry," I said, rather too impulsively I suppose.

"Sorry?" He looked surprised.

"For—for everybody. It's all so dreadful. But especially for you."

"For me? Why for me?"

"Well, you're such an old friend of them both."

"I'm an old friend of Leidner's. I wasn't a friend of hers particu-larly."

He spoke as though he had actually disliked her. Really, I wished Miss Reilly could have heard him!

"Well, good-night," I said and hurried along to my room.

I fussed around a bit in my room before undressing. Washed out some handkerchiefs and a pair of wash-leather gloves and wrote up my diary. I just looked out of my door again before I really started to get ready for bed. The lights were still on in the drawing-office and in the south building.

I supposed Dr. Leidner was still up and working in his office. I wondered whether I ought to go and say good-night to him. I hesi-tated about it—I didn't want to seem officious. He might be busy and not want to be disturbed. In the end, however, a sort of uneasiness drove me on. After all, it couldn't do any harm. I'd just say good-night, ask if there was anything I could do and come away.

But Dr. Leidner wasn't there. The office itself was lit up but there was no one in it except Miss Johnson. She had her head down on the table and was crying as though her heart would break.

It gave me quite a turn. She was such a quiet, self-controlled woman. It was pitiful to see her.

"Whatever is it, my dear?" I cried. I put my arm round her and patted her. "Now, now, this won't do at all. . . . You mustn't sit here crying all by yourself."

She didn't answer and I felt the dreadful shuddering sobs that were racking her.

"Don't, my dear, don't," I said. "Take a hold on yourself. I'll go and make you a cup of nice hot tea."

She raised her head and said:

"No, no, it's all right, nurse. I'm being a fool."

"What's upset you, my dear?" I asked.

She didn't answer at once, then she said:

"It's all too awful. . . ."

"Now don't start thinking of it," I told her. "What's happened has happened and can't be mended. It's no use fretting."

She sat up straight and began to pat her hair.

"I'm making rather a fool of myself," she said in her gruff voice. "I've been clearing up and tidying the office. Thought it was best to *do* something. And then—it all came over me suddenly—"

"Yes, yes," I said hastily. "I know. A nice strong cup of tea and a hot-water bottle in your bed is what you want," I said.

And she had them too. I didn't listen to any protests.

"Thank you, nurse," she said when I'd settled her in bed, and she was sipping her tea and the hot-water bottle was in. "You're a nice kind sensible woman. It's not often I make such a fool of myself."

"Oh, anybody's liable to do that at a time like this," I said, "what with one thing and another. The strain and the shock and the police here, there and everywhere. Why, I'm quite jumpy myself."

She said slowly in rather a queer voice:

"What you said in there is true. What's happened has happened and can't be mended. . . ."

She was silent for a minute or two and then said—rather oddly, I thought:

"She was never a nice woman!"

Well, I didn't argue the point. I'd always felt it was quite natural for Miss Johnson and Mrs. Leidner not to hit it off.

I wondered if, perhaps, Miss Johnson had secretly had a feeling that she was pleased Mrs. Leidner was dead, and had then been ashamed of herself for the thought.

I said:

"Now you go to sleep and don't worry about anything."

I just picked up a few things and set the room to rights. Stockings over the back of the chair and coat and skirt on a hanger. There was a little ball of crumpled paper on the floor where it must have fallen out of a pocket.

I was just smoothing it out to see whether I could safely throw it away when she quite startled me.

"Give that to me!"

I did so—rather taken aback. She'd called out so peremptorily. She snatched it from me—fairly snatched it—and then held it in the candle flame till it was burnt to ashes.

As I say, I was startled—and I just stared at her.

I hadn't had time to see what the paper was—she'd snatched it so quick. But funnily enough, as it burned it curled over towards me and I just saw that there were words written in ink on the paper.

It wasn't till I was getting into bed that I realized why they'd looked sort of familiar to me.

It was the same handwriting as that of the anonymous letters.

Was *that* why Miss Johnson had given way to a fit of remorse? Had it been her all along who had written those anonymous letters?

XX

MISS JOHNSON, MRS. MERCADO, MR. REITER

I DON'T MIND confessing that the idea came as a complete shock to me. I'd never thought of associating *Miss Johnson* with the letters. Mrs. Mercado, perhaps. But Miss Johnson was a real lady, and so self-controlled and sensible.

But I reflected, remembering the conversation I had listened to that evening between M. Poirot and Dr. Reilly, that that might be just *why*.

If it were Miss Johnson who had written the letters it explained a lot. Mind you, I didn't think for a minute Miss Johnson had had anything to do with the murder. But I *did* see that her dislike of Mrs. Leidner might have made her succumb to the temptation of well—putting the wind up her—to put it vulgarly.

She might have hoped to frighten away Mrs. Leidner from the dig.

But then Mrs. Leidner had been murdered and Miss Johnson had felt terrible pangs of remorse—first for her cruel trick and also, perhaps, because she realized that those letters were acting as a very good shield to the actual murderer. No wonder she had broken down so utterly. She was, I was sure, a decent soul at heart. And it explained, too, why she had caught so eagerly at my consolation of "what's happened's happened and can't be amended."

And then her cryptic remark—her vindication of herself—"She was never a nice woman!"

The question was, what was *I* to do about it?

I tossed and turned for a good while and in the end decided I'd let M. Poirot know about it at the first opportunity.

He came out next day but I didn't get a chance of speaking to him what you might call privately.

We had just a minute alone together and before I could collect myself to know how to begin, he had come close to me and was whispering instructions in my ear.

"Me, I shall talk to Miss Johnson—and others, perhaps, in the living-room. You have the key of Mrs. Leidner's room still?"

"Yes," I said.

"*Très bien*. Go there, shut the door behind you and give a cry—not a scream—a cry. You understand what I mean—it is alarm—surprise that I want you to express—not mad terror. As for the excuse if you are heard—I leave that to you—the stepped toe or what you will."

At that moment Miss Johnson came out into the courtyard and there was no time for more.

I understood well enough what M. Poirot was after. As soon as he and Miss Johnson had gone into the living-room I went across to Mrs. Leidner's room and, unlocking the door, went in and pulled the door to behind me.

I can't say I didn't feel a bit of a fool standing up in an empty room and giving a yelp all for nothing at all. Besides, it wasn't so easy to know just how loud to do it. I gave a pretty loud "Oh" and then tried it a bit higher and a bit lower.

Then I came out again and prepared my excuse of a stepped (stubbed I *suppose* he meant!) toe.

But it soon appeared that no excuse would be needed. Poirot and Miss Johnson were talking together earnestly and there had clearly been no interruption.

"Well," I thought, "that settles that. Either Miss Johnson imagined that cry she heard or else it was something quite different."

I didn't like to go in and interrupt them. There was a deck-chair on the porch so I sat down there. Their voices floated out to me.

"The position is delicate, you understand," Poirot was saying. "Dr. Leidner—obviously he adored his wife—"

"He worshipped her," said Miss Johnson.

"He tells me, naturally, how fond all his staff was of her! As for them, what can they say? Naturally they say the same thing. It is politeness. It is decency. It *may* also be the truth! But also it may *not!* And I am convinced, mademoiselle, that the key to this enigma lies in a complete understanding of Mrs. Leidner's character. If I could get the opinion—the honest opinion—of every member of the staff, I might, from the whole, build up a picture. Frankly, that is why I am here to-day. I knew Dr. Leidner would be in Hassanieh. That makes it easy for me to have an interview with each of you here in turn, and beg your help."

"That's all very well," began Miss Johnson and stopped.

"Do not make me the British *clichés*," Poirot begged. "Do not say it is not the cricket or the football, that to speak anything but well of the dead is not done—that—*enfin*—there is loyalty! Loyalty, it is a pestilential thing in crime. Again and again it obscures the truth."

"I've no particular loyalty to Mrs. Leidner," said Miss Johnson dryly. There was indeed a sharp and acid tone in her voice. "Dr. Leidner's a different matter. And, after all, she was his wife."

"Precisely—precisely. I understand that you would not wish to speak against your chief's wife. But this is not a question of a testimonial. It is a question of sudden and mysterious death. If I am to believe that it is a martyred angel who has been killed it does not add to the easiness of my task."

"I certainly shouldn't call her an angel," said Miss Johnson and the acid tone was even more in evidence.

"Tell me your opinion, frankly, of Mrs. Leidner—as a woman."

"H'm! To begin with, M. Poirot, I'll give you this warning. I'm prejudiced. I am—we all were—devoted to Dr. Leidner. And, I suppose, when Mrs. Leidner came along, we were jealous. We resented the demands she made on his time and attention. The devotion he showed her irritated us. I'm being truthful, M. Poirot, and it isn't very pleasant for me. I resented her presence here—yes, I did, though, of course, I tried never to show it. It made a difference to us, you see."

"Us? You say us?"

"I mean Mr. Carey and myself. We're the two old-timers, you see. And we didn't much care for the new order of things. I suppose that's natural, though perhaps it was rather petty of us. But it *did* make a difference."

"What kind of a difference?"

"Oh! to everything. We used to have such a happy time. A good deal of fun, you know, and rather silly jokes, like people do who work together. Dr. Leidner was quite light-hearted—just like a boy."

"And when Mrs. Leidner came she changed all that?"

"Well, I suppose it wasn't her *fault*. It wasn't so bad last year. And please believe, M. Poirot, that it wasn't anything she *did*. She's always been charming to me—quite charming. That's why I've felt ashamed sometimes. It wasn't her fault that little things she said and did seemed to rub me up the wrong way. Really nobody could be nicer than she was."

"But nevertheless things were changed this season? There was a different atmosphere."

"Oh, entirely. Really, I don't know what it was. Everything seemed to go wrong—not with the work—I mean with us—our tempers and our nerves. All on edge. Almost the sort of feeling you get when there is a thunderstorm coming."

"And you put that down to Mrs. Leidner's influence?"

"Well, it was never like that before she came," said Miss Johnson dryly. "Oh! I'm a cross-grained, complaining old dog. Conservative—liking things always the same. You really mustn't take any notice of me, M. Poirot."

"How would you describe to me Mrs. Leidner's character and temperament?"

Miss Johnson hesitated for a moment. Then she said slowly: "Well, of course, she was temperamental. A lot of ups and downs. Nice to people one day and perhaps wouldn't speak to them the next. She was very kind, I think. And very thoughtful for others. All the same you could see she had been thoroughly spoilt all her life. She took Dr. Leidner's waiting on her hand and foot as perfectly natural. And I don't think she ever really appreciated what a very remarkable—what a really great—man she had married. That used to annoy me sometimes. And of course she was terribly highly strung and nervous. The things she used to imagine and the states she used to get into! I was thankful when Dr. Leidner brought Nurse Leatheran here. It was too much for him having to cope both with his work and with his wife's fears."

"What is your own opinion of these anonymous letters she received?"

I had to do it. I leaned forward in my chair till I could just catch sight of Miss Johnson's profile turned to Poirot in answer to his question.

She was looking perfectly cool and collected.

"I think some one in America had a spite against her and was trying to frighten or annoy her."

"Pas plus serieux que ça?"

"That's my opinion. She was a very handsome woman, you know, and might easily have had enemies. I think those letters were written by some spiteful woman. Mrs. Leidner being of a nervous temperament took them seriously."

"She certainly did that," said Poirot. "But remember—the last of them arrived by hand."

"Well, I suppose that could have been managed if any one had given their minds to it. Women will take a lot of trouble to gratify their spite, M. Poirot."

They will indeed, I thought to myself!

"Perhaps you are right, mademoiselle. As you say, Mrs. Leidner was handsome. By the way, you know Miss Reilly, the doctor's daughter?"

"Sheila Reilly? Yes, of course."

Poirot adopted a very confidential, gossipy tone.

"I have heard a rumour (naturally I do not like to ask the doctor) that there was a *tendresse* between her and one of the members of Dr. Leidner's staff. Is that so, do you know?"

Miss Johnson appeared rather amused.

"Oh, young Coleman and David Emmott were both inclined to dance attendance. I believe there was some rivalry as to who was to be her partner in some event at the club. Both the boys went in on Saturday evenings to the club as a general rule. But I don't know that there was anything in it on her side. She's the only young creature in the place, you know, and so she's by way of being the belle of it. She's got the Air Force dancing attendance on her as well."

"So you think there is nothing in it?"

"Well—I don't know." Miss Johnson became thoughtful. "It is true that she comes out this way fairly often. Up to the dig and all that. In fact, Mrs. Leidner was chaffing David Emmott about it the other day— saying the girl was running after him. Which was rather a catty thing to say, I thought, and I don't think he liked it. . . . Yes, she was here a good deal. I saw her riding towards the dig on that awful afternoon." She nodded her head towards the open window. "But neither David Emmott nor Coleman were on duty that afternoon. Richard Carey was in charge. Yes, perhaps she *is* attracted to one of the boys —but she's such a modern unsentimental young woman that one doesn't know quite how seriously to take her. I'm sure I don't know which of them it is. Bill's a nice boy, and not nearly such a fool as he pretends to be. David Emmott is a dear—and there's a lot to him. He is the deep, quiet kind."

Then she looked quizzically at Poirot and said:

"But has this any bearing on the crime, M. Poirot?"

M. Poirot threw up his hands in a very French fashion.

"You make me blush, mademoiselle," he said. "You expose me as a mere gossip. But what will you, I am interested always in the love affairs of young people."

"Yes," said Miss Johnson with a little sigh. "It's nice when the course of true love runs smooth."

Poirot gave an answering sigh. I wondered if Miss Johnson was thinking of some love affair of her own when she was a girl. And I wondered if M. Poirot had a wife, and if he went on in the way you always hear foreigners do, with mistresses and things like that. He looks so comic I couldn't imagine it.

"Sheila Reilly has a lot of character," said Miss Johnson. "She's young and she's crude, but she's the right sort."

"I take your word for it, mademoiselle," said Poirot.

He got up and said, "Are there any other members of the staff in the house?"

"Marie Mercado is somewhere about. All the men are up on the dig to-day. I think they wanted to get out of the house. I don't blame them. If you'd like to go up to the dig—"

She came out on the verandah and said, smiling to me:

"Nurse Leatheran won't mind taking you, I dare say."

"Oh, certainly, Miss Johnson," I said.

"And you'll come back to lunch, won't you, M. Poirot?"

"Enchanted, mademoiselle."

Miss Johnson went back into the living-room where she was engaged in cataloguing.

"Mrs. Mercado's on the roof," I said. "Do you want to see her first?"

"It would be as well, I think. Let us go up."

As we went up the stairs I said:

"I did what you told me. Did you hear anything?"

"Not a sound."

"That will be a weight off Miss Johnson's mind at any rate," I said. "She's been worrying that she might have done something about it."

Mrs. Mercado was sitting on the parapet, her head bent down, and she was so deep in thought that she never heard us till Poirot halted opposite her and bade her good-morning.

Then she looked up with a start.

She looked ill this morning, I thought, her small face pinched and wizened and great dark circles under her eyes.

"*Encore moi*," said Poirot. "I come to-day with a special object."

And he went on much in the same way as he had done to Miss Johnson, explaining how necessary it was that he should get a true picture of Mrs. Leidner.

Mrs. Mercado, however, wasn't as honest as Miss Johnson had been. She burst into fulsome praise which, I was pretty sure, was quite far removed from her real feelings.

"Dear, *dear* Louise! It's so hard to explain her to some one who didn't know her. She was such an *exotic* creature. Quite different from any one else. You felt that, I'm sure, nurse? A martyr to nerves, of course, and full of fancies, but one put up with things in her one wouldn't from any one else. And she was so *sweet* to us all, wasn't she, nurse? And so *humble* about herself—I mean she didn't know anything about archæology, and she was so eager to learn. Always asking my husband about the chemical processes for treating the metal objects and helping Miss Johnson to mend pottery. Oh, we were all *devoted* to her."

"Then it is not true, madame, what I have heard, that there was a certain tenseness—an uncomfortable atmosphere—here?"

Mrs. Mercado opened her opaque black eyes very wide.

"Oh! who *can* have been telling you that? Nurse? Dr. Leidner? I'm sure *he* would never notice anything, poor man."

And she shot a thoroughly unfriendly glance at me.

Poirot smiled easily.

"I have my spics, madame," he declared gaily. And just for a minute I saw her eyelids quiver and blink.

"Don't you think," asked Mrs. Mercado with an air of great sweetness, "that after an event of this kind, every one always pretends a lot of things that never were? You know—tension, atmosphere, a 'feeling that something was going to happen?' I think people just *make up* these things afterwards."

"There is a lot in what you say, madame," said Poirot.

"And it really *wasn't* true! We were a thoroughly happy family here."

"That woman is one of the most utter liars I've ever known," I said indignantly, when M. Poirot and I were clear of the house and walking along the path to the dig. "I'm sure she simply hated Mrs. Leidner really!"

"She is hardly the type to whom one would go for the truth," Poirot agreed.

"Waste of time talking to her," I snapped.

"Hardly that—hardly that. If a person tells you lies with her lips she is sometimes telling you truth with her eyes. What is she afraid of, little Madame Mercado? I saw fear in her eyes. Yes—decidedly she is afraid of something. It is very interesting."

"I've got something to tell you, M. Poirot," I said.

Then I told him all about my return the night before and my strong belief that Miss Johnson was the writer of the anonymous letters.

"So *she's* a liar too!" I said. "The cool way she answered you this morning about these same letters!"

"Yes," said Poirot. "It was interesting, that. *For she let out the fact that she knew all about those letters.* So far they have not been spoken of in the presence of the staff. Of course, it is quite possible that Dr. Leidner told her about them yesterday. They are old friends, he and she. But if he did not—well—then it is curious and interesting, is it not?"

My respect for him went up. It was clever the way he had tricked her into mentioning the letters.

"Are you going to tackle her about them?" I asked.

Mr. Poirot seemed quite shocked by the idea.

"No, no, indeed. Always it is unwise to parade one's knowledge. Until the last minute I keep everything here." He tapped his forehead. "At the right moment—I make the spring—like the panther—and, *mon Dieu!* the consternation!"

I couldn't help laughing to myself at little M. Poirot in the rôle of a panther.

We had just reached the dig. The first person we saw was Mr. Reiter, who was busy photographing some walling.

It's my opinion that the men who were digging just hacked out walls wherever they wanted them. That's what it looked like anyway. Mr. Carey explained to me that you could feel the difference at once with a pick, and he tried to show me—but I never saw. When the man said *"Libn"*—mud-brick—it was just ordinary dirt and mud as far as I could see.

Mr. Reiter finished his photographs and handed over the camera and the plates to his boy and told him to take them back to the house.

Poirot asked him one or two questions about exposures and film packs and so on which he answered very readily. He seemed pleased to be asked about his work.

He was just tendering his excuses for leaving us when Poirot plunged once more into his set speech. As a matter of fact it wasn't quite a set speech because he varied it a little each time to suit the person he was talking to. But I'm not going to write it all down every time. With sensible people like Miss Johnson he went straight to the point, and with some of the others he had to beat about the bush a bit more. But it came to the same in the end.

"Yes, yes, I see what you mean," said Mr. Reiter. "But indeed, I do not see that I can be much help to you. I am new here this season and I did not speak much with Mrs. Leidner. I regret, but indeed I can tell you nothing."

There was something a little stiff and foreign in the way he spoke, though, of course, he hadn't got any accent—except an American one, I mean.

"You can at least tell me whether you liked or disliked her?" said Poirot with a smile.

Mr. Reiter got quite red and stammered:

"She was a charming person—most charming. And intellectual. She had a very fine brain—yes."

"*Bien!* You liked her. And she liked you?"

Mr. Reiter got redder still.

"Oh, I—I don't know that she noticed me much. And I was unfortunate once or twice. I was always unlucky when I tried to do anything for her. I'm afraid I annoyed her by my clumsiness. It was quite unintentional . . . I would have done *anything*—"

Poirot took pity on his flounderings.

"Perfectly—perfectly. Let us pass to another matter. Was it a happy atmosphere in the house?"

"Please."

"Were you all happy together? Did you laugh and talk?"

"No—no, not exactly that. There was a little—stiffness."

He paused, struggling with himself, and then said:

"You see, I am not very good in company. I am clumsy. I am shy. Dr. Leidner always he has been most kind to me. But—it is stupid —I cannot overcome my shyness. I say always the wrong thing. I upset water jugs. I am unlucky."

He really looked like a large awkward child.

"We all do these things when we are young," said Poirot, smiling. "The poise, the *savoir faire*, it comes later."

Then with a word of farewell we walked on.

He said:

"That, *ma sœur*, is either an extremely simple young man or a very remarkable actor."

I didn't answer. I was caught up once more by the fantastic notion that one of these people was a dangerous and cold-blooded murderer. Somehow, on this beautiful still sunny morning, it seemed impossible.

XXI

MR. MERCADO, RICHARD CAREY

"They work in two separate places, I see," said Poirot, halting.

Mr. Reiter had been doing his photography on an outlying portion of the main excavation. A little distance away from us a second swarm of men were coming and going with baskets.

"That's what they call the deep cut," I explained. "They don't find much there, nothing but rubbishy broken pottery, but Dr. Leidner always says it's very interesting, so I suppose it must be."

"Let us go there."

We walked together slowly for the sun was hot.

Mr. Mercado was in command. We saw him below us talking to the foreman, an old man like a tortoise who wore a tweed coat over his long striped cotton gown.

It was a little difficult to get down to them as there was only a narrow path or stair and basket boys were going up and down it constantly, and they always seemed to be as blind as bats and never to think of getting out of the way.

As I followed Poirot down he said suddenly over his shoulder:

"Is Mr. Mercado right-handed or left-handed?"

Now that was an extraordinary question if you like!

I thought a minute, then:

"Right-handed," I said decisively.

Poirot didn't condescend to explain. He just went on and I followed him.

Mr. Mercado seemed rather pleased to see us.

His long melancholy face lit up.

M. Poirot pretended to an interest in archæology that I'm sure he couldn't have really felt, but Mr. Mercado responded at once.

He explained that they had already cut down through twelve levels of house occupation.

"We are now definitely in the fourth millennium," he said with enthusiasm.

I always thought a millennium was in the future—the time when everything comes right.

Mr. Mercado pointed out belts of ashes (how his hand did shake. I wondered if he might possibly have malaria) and he explained how the pottery changed in character, and about burials—and how they had had one level almost entirely composed of infant burials—poor little things—and about flexed position and orientation which seemed to mean the way the bones were lying.

And then suddenly, just as he was stooping down to pick up a kind of flint knife that was lying with some pots in a corner, he leapt into the air with a wild yell.

He spun round to find me and Poirot staring at him in astonishment. He clapped his hand to his left arm.

"Something stung me—like a red-hot needle."

Immediately Poirot was galvanized into energy.

"Quick, *mon cher*, let us see. Nurse Leatheran!" I came forward. He seized Mr. Mercado's arm and deftly rolled back the sleeve of his khaki shirt to the shoulder.

"There," said Mr. Mercado, pointing.

About three inches below the shoulder there was a minute prick from which the blood was oozing.

"Curious," said Poirot. He peered into the rolled-up sleeve. "I can see nothing. It was an ant, perhaps?"

"Better put on a little iodine," I said.

I always carry an iodine pencil with me, and I whipped it out and applied it. But I was a little absent-minded as I did so, for my attention had been caught by something quite different. Mr. Mercado's arm, all the way up the forearm to the elbow, was marked all over by tiny punctures. I knew well enough what *they* were—*the marks of a hypodermic needle.*

Mr. Mercado rolled down his sleeve again and recommenced his explanations. Mr. Poirot listened, but didn't try to bring the conversation round to the Leidners. In fact he didn't ask Mr. Mercado anything at all.

Presently we said good-bye to Mr. Mercado and climbed up the path again.

"It was neat that, did you not think so?" my companion asked.

"Neat?" I asked.

M. Poirot took something from behind the lapel of his coat and surveyed it affectionately. To my surprise I saw that it was a long sharp darning needle with a blob of sealing wax making it into a pin.

"M. Poirot," I cried, "did *you* do that?"

"I was the stinging insect—yes. And very neatly I did it, too, do you not think so? You did not see me."

That was true enough. *I* never saw him do it. And I'm sure Mr. Mercado hadn't suspected. He must have been quick as lightning.

"But, M. Poirot, why?" I asked.

He answered me by another question.

"Did you notice anything, sister?" he asked.

I nodded my head slowly.

"Hypodermic marks," I said.

"So now we know something about Mr. Mercado," said Poirot. "I suspected—but I did not *know*. It is always necessary to *know*."

"And you don't care how you set about it!" I thought, but didn't say.

Poirot suddenly clapped his hand to his pocket.

"Alas, I have dropped my handkerchief down there. I concealed the pin in it."

"I'll get it for you," I said and hurried back.

I'd got the feeling, you see, by this time, that M. Poirot and I were the doctor and nurse in charge of a case. At least, it was more like an operation and he was the surgeon. Perhaps I oughtn't to say so, but in a queer way I was beginning to enjoy myself.

I remember just after I'd finished my training, I went to a case in a private house and the need for an immediate operation arose, and the patient's husband was cranky about nursing homes. He just wouldn't hear of his wife being taken to one. Said it had to be done in the house.

Well, of course it was just splendid for me! Nobody else to have a look in! I was in charge of everything. Of course, I was terribly nervous—I thought of everything conceivable that doctor could want, but even then I was afraid I might have forgotten something. You never know with doctors. They ask for absolutely anything sometimes! But everything went splendidly! I had each thing ready as he asked for it, and he actually told me I'd done first rate after it was over—and that's a thing most doctors wouldn't bother to do! The G.P. was very nice too. And I ran the whole thing myself!

The patient recovered, too, so everybody was happy.

Well, I felt rather the same now. In a way M. Poirot reminded me of that surgeon. *He* was a little man, too. Ugly little man with a face like a monkey, but a wonderful surgeon. He knew instinctively just where to go. I've seen a lot of surgeons and I know what a lot of difference there is.

Gradually I'd been growing a kind of confidence in M. Poirot. I felt that he, too, knew exactly what he was doing. And I was getting to feel that it was my job to help him—as you might say—to have the forceps and the swabs and all handy just when he wanted them. That's why it seemed just as natural for me to run off and look for his handkerchief as it would have been to pick up a towel that a doctor had thrown on the floor.

When I'd found it and got back I couldn't see him at first. But at last I caught sight of him. He was sitting a little way from the mound talking to Mr. Carey. Mr. Carey's boy was standing near with that great big rod thing with metres marked on it, but just at that moment he said something to the boy and the boy took it away. It seemed he had finished with it for the time being.

I'd like to get this next bit quite clear. You see, I wasn't quite sure what M. Poirot did or didn't want me to do. He might, I mean, have sent me back for that handkerchief *on purpose*. To get me out of the way.

It was just like an operation over again. You've got to be careful to hand the doctor just what he wants and not what he *doesn't* want. I mean, suppose you gave him the artery forceps at the wrong moment, and were late with them at the right moment! Thank goodness I know my work in the theatre well enough. I'm not likely to make mistakes there. But in this business I was really the rawest of raw little probationers. And so I had to be particularly careful not to make any silly mistakes.

Of course, I didn't for one moment imagine that M. Poirot didn't want me to hear what he and Mr. Carey were saying. But he might have thought he'd get Mr. Carey to talk better if I wasn't there.

Now I don't want anybody to get it into their heads that I'm the kind of woman who goes about eavesdropping on private conversations. I wouldn't do such a thing. Not for a moment. Not however much I wanted to.

And what I mean is if it *had* been a private conversation I wouldn't for a moment have done what, as a matter of fact, I actually did do.

As I looked at it I was in a privileged position. After all, you hear many a thing when a patient's coming round after an anæsthetic.

The patient wouldn't want you to hear it—and usually has no idea you *have* heard it—but the fact remains you *do* hear it. I just took it that Mr. Carey was the patient. He'd be none the worse for what he didn't know about. And if you think that I was just curious, well, I'll admit that I *was* curious. I didn't want to miss anything I could help.

All this is just leading up to the fact that I turned aside and went by a round-about way up behind the big dump until I was a foot from where they were, but concealed from them by the corner of the dump. And if any one says it was dishonourable I just beg to disagree. *Nothing* ought to be hidden from the nurse in charge of the case, though, of course, it's the doctor to say what shall be *done*.

I don't know, of course, what M. Poirot's line of approach had been, but by the time I'd got there he was aiming straight for the bull's eye, so to speak.

"Nobody appreciates Dr. Leidner's devotion to his wife more than I do," he was saying. "But it is often the case that one learns more about a person from their enemies than from their friends."

"You suggest that their faults are more important than their virtues?" said Mr. Carey. His tone was dry and ironic.

"Undoubtedly—when it comes to murder. It seems odd that as far as I know nobody has yet been murdered for having too perfect a character! And yet perfection is undoubtedly an irritating thing."

"I'm afraid I'm hardly the right person to help you," said Mr. Carey. "To be perfectly honest, Mrs. Leidner and I didn't hit it off particularly well. I don't mean that we were in any sense of the word enemies, but we were not exactly friends. Mrs. Leidner was, perhaps, a shade jealous of my old friendship with her husband. I, for my part, although I admired her very much and thought she was an extremely attractive woman, was just a shade resentful of her influence over Leidner. As a result we were quite polite to each other, but not intimate."

"Admirably explained," said Poirot.

I could just see their heads, and I saw Mr. Carey's turn sharply as though something in M. Poirot's detached tone struck him disagreeably.

M. Poirot went on:

"Was not Dr. Leidner distressed that you and his wife did not get on together better?"

Carey hesitated a minute before saying:

"Really—I'm not sure. He never said anything. I always hoped he didn't notice it. He was very wrapped up in his work, you know."

"So the truth, according to you, is that you did not really like Mrs. Leidner?"

Carey shrugged his shoulders.

"I should probably have liked her very much if she hadn't been Leidner's wife."

He laughed as though amused by his own statement.

Poirot was arranging a little heap of broken potsherds. He said in a dreamy, far-away voice:

"I talked to Miss Johnson this morning. She admitted that she was prejudiced against Mrs. Leidner and did not like her very much, although she hastened to add that Mrs. Leidner had always been charming to her."

"All quite true, I should say," said Carey.

"So I believed. Then I had a conversation with Mrs. Mercado. She told me at great length how devoted she had been to Mrs. Leidner and how much she had admired her."

Carey made no answer to this, and after waiting a minute or two Poirot went on:

"That—I did not believe! Then I come to you and that which you tell me—well, again—I do not believe. . . ."

Carey stiffened. I could hear the anger—repressed anger—in his voice.

"I really cannot help your beliefs—or your disbeliefs, M. Poirot. You've heard the truth and you can take it or leave it as far as I am concerned."

Poirot did not grow angry. Instead he sounded particularly meek and depressed.

"Is it my fault what I do—or do not believe? I have a sensitive ear, you know. And then—there are always plenty of stories going about —rumours floating in the air. One listens—and perhaps—one learns something! Yes, there *are* stories. . . ."

Carey sprang to his feet. I could see clearly a little pulse that beat in his temple. He looked simply splendid! So lean and so brown—and that wonderful jaw, hard and square. I don't wonder women fell for that man.

"What stories?" he asked savagely.

Poirot looked sideways at him.

"Perhaps you can guess. The usual sort of story—about you and Mrs. Leidner."

"What foul minds people have!"

"*N'est-ce pas?* They are like dogs. However deep you bury an unpleasantness a dog will always root it up again."

"And you believe these stories?"

"I am willing to be convinced—of the truth," said Poirot gravely.

"I doubt if you'd know the truth if you heard it," Carey laughed rudely.

"Try me and see," said Poirot, watching him.

"I will then! You shall have the truth! I hated Louise Leidner—there's the truth for you! I hated her like hell!"

XXII

DAVID EMMOTT, FATHER LAVIGNY
AND A DISCOVERY

Turning abruptly away, Carey strode off with long angry strides. Poirot sat looking after him and presently he murmured:

"Yes—I see. . . ."

Without turning his head he said in a slightly louder voice:

"Do not come round the corner for a minute, nurse. In case he turns his head. Now it is all right. You have my handkerchief? Many thanks. You are most amiable."

He didn't say anything at all about my having been listening—and how he knew I *was* listening I can't think. He'd never once looked in that direction. I was rather relieved he didn't say anything. I mean, I felt all right with *myself* about it, but it might have been a little awkward explaining to him. So it was a good thing he didn't seem to want explanations.

"Do you think he did hate her, M. Poirot?" I asked.

Nodding his head slowly with a curious expression on his face, Poirot answered.

"Yes—I think he did."

Then he got up briskly and began to walk to where the men were working on the top of the mound. I followed him. We couldn't see any one but Arabs at first but we finally found Mr. Emmott lying face downwards blowing dust off a skeleton that had just been uncovered.

He gave his pleasant grave smile when he saw us.

"Have you come to see round?" he asked. "I'll be free in a minute."

He sat up, took his knife and began daintily cutting the earth away from round the bones, stopping every now and then to use either a bellows or his own breath. A very insanitary proceeding the latter, I thought.

"You'll get all sorts of nasty germs in your mouth, Mr. Emmott," I protested.

"Nasty germs are my daily diet, nurse," he said gravely. "Germs can't do anything to an archæologist—they just get naturally discouraged trying."

He scraped a little more away round the thigh bone. Then he spoke to the foreman at his side directing him exactly what he wanted done.

"There," he said, rising to his feet. "That's ready for Reiter to photograph after lunch. Rather nice stuff she had in with her."

He showed us a little verdigrisy copper bowl and some pins. And a lot of gold and blue things that had been her necklace of beads.

The bones and all the objects were brushed and cleaned with a knife and kept in position ready to be photographed.

"Who is she?" asked Poirot.

"First millennium. A lady of some consequence perhaps. Skull looks rather odd—I must get Mercado to look at it. It suggests death by foul play."

"A Mrs. Leidner of two thousand odd years ago?" said Poirot.

"Perhaps," said Mr. Emmott.

Bill Coleman was doing something with a pick to a wall face.

David Emmott called something to him which I didn't catch and then started showing M. Poirot round.

When the short explanatory tour was over Emmott looked at his watch.

"We knock off in ten minutes," he said. "Shall we walk back to the house?"

"That will suit me excellently," said Poirot.

We walked slowly along the well-worn path.

"I expect you are all glad to get back to work again," said Poirot.

Emmott replied gravely:

"Yes, it's much the best thing. It's not been any too easy loafing about the house and making conversation."

"Knowing all the time *that one of you was a murderer*."

Emmott did not answer. He made no gesture of dissent. I knew now that he had had a suspicion of the truth from the very first when he had questioned the house-boys.

After a few minutes he asked quietly:

"Are you getting anywhere, M. Poirot?"

Poirot said gravely:

"Will you help me to get somewhere?"

"Why, naturally."

Watching him closely, Poirot said:

"The hub of the case is Mrs. Leidner. I want to know about Mrs. Leidner."

David Emmott said slowly:

"What do you mean by knowing about her?"

"I do not mean where she came from and what her maiden name was. I do not mean the shape of her face and the colour of her eyes. I mean her—herself."

"You think that counts in the case?"

"I am quite sure of it."

Emmott was silent for a moment or two, then he said:

"Maybe you're right."

"And that is where you can help me. You can tell me what sort of a woman she was."

"Can I? I've often wondered about it myself."

"Didn't you make up your mind on the subject?"

"I think I did in the end."

"*Eh bien?*"

But Mr. Emmott was silent for some minutes, then he said:

"What did nurse think of her? Women are said to sum up other women quickly enough, and a nurse has a wide experience of types."

Poirot didn't give me any chance of speaking even if I had wanted to. He said quickly:

"What I want to know is what a *man* thought of her?"

Emmott smiled a little.

"I expect they'd all be much the same." He paused and said, "She wasn't young, but I think she was about the most beautiful woman I've ever come across."

"That's hardly an answer, Mr. Emmott."

"It's not so far off one, M. Poirot."

He was silent a minute or two and then he went on:

"There used to be a fairy story I read when I was a kid. A Northern fairy story about the Snow Queen and Little Kay. I guess Mrs. Leidner was rather like that—always taking Little Kay for a ride."

"Ah, yes, a tale of Hans Andersen, is it not? And there was a girl in it. Little Gerda, was that her name?"

"Maybe. I don't remember much of it."

"Can't you go a little further, Mr. Emmott?"

David Emmott shook his head.

"I don't even know if I've summed her up correctly. She wasn't easy to read. She'd do a devilish thing one day, and a really fine one the next. But I think you're about right when you say that she's the hub of the case. That's what she always wanted to be—*at the centre of things*. And she liked to get *at* other people—I mean, she wasn't just satisfied with being passed the toast and the peanut butter, she wanted you to turn your mind and soul inside out for her to look at it."

"And if one did not give her that satisfaction?" asked Poirot.

"Then she could turn ugly!"

I saw his lips close resolutely and his jaws set.

"I suppose, Mr. Emmott, you would not care to express a plain unofficial opinion as to who murdered her?"

"I don't know," said Emmott. "I really haven't the slightest idea. I rather think that, if I'd been Carl—Carl Reiter, I mean—I would have had a shot at murdering her. She was a pretty fair devil to him. But, of course, he asks for it by being so darned sensitive. Just invites you to give him a kick in the pants."

"And did Mrs. Leidner give him—a kick in the pants?" inquired Poirot.

Emmott gave a sudden grin.

"No. Pretty little jabs with an embroidery needle—that was her method. He *was* irritating, of course. Just like some blubbering, poor-spirited kid. But a needle's a painful weapon."

I stole a glance at Poirot and thought I detected a slight quiver of his lips.

"But you don't really believe that Carl Reiter killed her?" he asked.

"No. I don't believe you'd kill a woman because she persistently made you look a fool at every meal."

Poirot shook his head thoughtfully.

Of course, Mr. Emmott made Mrs. Leidner sound quite inhuman. There was somthing to be said on the other side too.

There had been something terribly irritating about Mr. Reiter's attitude. He jumped when she spoke to him, and did idiotic things like passing her the marmalade again and again when he knew she never ate it. I'd have felt inclined to snap at him a bit myself.

Men don't understand how their mannerisms can get on women's nerves so that you feel you just have to snap.

I thought I'd just mention that to Mr. Poirot some time.

We had arrived back by now and Mr. Emmott offered Poirot a wash and took him into his room.

I hurried across the courtyard to mine.

I came out again about the same time they did and we were all making for the dining-room when Father Lavigny appeared in the doorway of his room and invited Poirot in.

Mr. Emmott came on round and he and I went into the dining-room together. Miss Johnson and Mrs. Mercado were there already, and after a few minutes Mr. Mercado, Mr. Reiter and Bill Coleman joined us.

We were just sitting down and Mercado had told the Arab boy to tell Father Lavigny lunch was ready when we were all startled by a faint, muffled cry.

I suppose our nerves weren't very good yet, for we all jumped, and Miss Johnson got quite pale and said:

"What was that? What's happened?"

Mrs. Mercado stared at her and said:

"My dear, what is the matter with you? It's some noise outside in the fields."

But at that minute Poirot and Father Lavigny came in.

"We thought some one was hurt," Miss Johnson said.

"A thousand pardons, mademoiselle," cried Poirot. "The fault is mine. Father Lavigny, he explains to me some tablets, and I take one to the window to see better—and, ma foi, not looking where I was going, I steb the toe, and the pain is sharp for the moment and I cry out."

"We thought it was another murder," said Mrs. Mercado, laughing.

"Marie!" said her husband.

His tone was reproachful and she flushed and bit her lip.

Miss Johnson hastily turned the conversation to the dig and what objects of interest had turned up that morning. Conversation all through lunch was sternly archæological.

I think we all felt it was the safest thing.

After we had had coffee we adjourned to the living-room. Then the men, with the exception of Father Lavigny, went off to the dig again.

Father Lavigny took Poirot through into the antika-room and I went with them. I was getting to know the things pretty well by now and I felt a thrill of pride—almost as though it were my own property—when Father Lavigny took down the gold cup and I heard Poirot's exclamation of admiration and pleasure.

"How beautiful! What a work of art!"

Father Lavigny agreed eagerly and began to point out its beauties with real enthusiasm and knowledge.

"No wax on it to-day," I said.

"Wax?" Poirot stared at me.

"Wax?" So did Father Lavigny.

I explained my remark.

"Ah, *je comprends*," said Father Lavigny. "Yes, yes, candle grease." That led direct to the subject of the midnight visitor. Forgetting my presence they both dropped into French and I left them together and went back into the living-room.

Mrs. Mercado was darning her husband's socks and Miss Johnson was reading a book. Rather an unusual thing for her. She usually seemed to have something to work at.

After a while Father Lavigny and Poirot came out, and the former excused himself on the score of work. Poirot sat down with us.

"A most interesting man," he said, and asked how much work there had been for Father Lavigny to do so far.

Miss Johnson explained that tablets had been scarce and that there had been very few inscribed bricks or cylinder seals. Father Lavigny, however, had done his share of work on the dig and was picking up colloquial Arabic very fast.

That led the talk to cylinder seals, and presently Miss Johnson fetched from a cupboard a sheet of impressions made by rolling them out on plasticine.

I realized as we bent over them, admiring the spirited designs, that these must be what she had been working at on that fatal afternoon.

As we talked I noticed that Poirot was rolling and kneading a little ball of plasticine between his fingers.

"You use a lot of plasticine, mademoiselle?" he asked.

"A fair amount. We seem to have got through a lot already this year—though I can't imagine how. But half our supply seems to have gone."

"Where is it kept, mademoiselle?"

"Here—in this cupboard."

As she replaced the sheet of impressions she showed him the shelf with rolls of plasticine, Durofix, photographic paste and other stationery supplies.

Poirot stooped down.

"And this—what is this, mademoiselle?"

He had slipped his hand right to the back and had brought out a curious crumpled object.

As he straightened it out we could see that it was a kind of mask with eyes and mouth crudely painted on in Indian ink and the whole thing roughly smeared with plasticine.

"How perfectly extraordinary," cried Miss Johnson. "I've never seen it before. How did it get there? And what is it?"

"As to how it got there, well, one hiding-place is as good as another, and I presume that this cupboard would not have been turned out till the end of the season. As to what it *is*—that, too, I think, is not difficult to say. *We have here the face that Mrs. Leidner described.* The ghostly face seen in the semi-dusk outside her window—without body attached."

Mrs. Mercado gave a little shriek.

Miss Johnson was white to the lips. She murmured:

"Then it was *not* fancy. It was a trick—a wicked trick! But who played it?"

"Yes," cried Mrs. Mercado. "Who could have done such a wicked, wicked thing?"

Poirot did not attempt a reply. His face was very grim as he went into the next room, returned with an empty cardboard box in his hand and put the crumpled mask into it.

"The police must see this," he explained.

"It's horrible," said Miss Johnson in a low voice. "Horrible!"

"Do you think everything's hidden here somewhere?" cried Mrs. Mercado shrilly. "Do you think perhaps the weapon—the club she was killed with—all covered with blood still, perhaps . . . Oh! I'm frightened—I'm frightened . . ."

Miss Johnson gripped her by the shoulder.

"Be quiet," she said fiercely. "Here's Dr. Leidner. We mustn't upset him."

Indeed, at that very moment the car had driven into the courtyard. Dr. Leidner got out of it and came straight across and in at the living-room door. His face was set in lines of fatigue and he looked twice the age he had three days ago.

He said in a quiet voice:

"The funeral will be at eleven o'clock to-morrow. Major Deane will read the service."

Mrs. Mercado faltered something, then slipped out of the room.

Dr. Leidner said to Miss Johnson:

"You'll come, Anne?"

And she answered:

"Of course, my dear, we'll all come. Naturally."

She didn't say anything else, but her face must have expressed what her tongue was powerless to do, for his face lightened up with affection and a momentary ease.

"Dear Anne," he said. "You are such a wonderful comfort and help to me. My dear old friend."

He laid his hand on her arm and I saw the red colour creep up in her face as she muttered, gruff as ever:

"That's all right."

But I just caught a glimpse of her expression and knew that, for one short moment, Anne Johnson was a perfectly happy woman.

And another idea flashed across my mind. Perhaps soon, in the natural course of things, turning to his old friend for sympathy, a new and happy state of things might come about.

Not that I'm really a matchmaker, and of course it was indecent to think of such a thing before the funeral even. But after all, it *would* be a happy solution. He was very fond of her, and there was no doubt she was absolutely devoted to him and would be perfectly happy devoting the rest of her life to him. That is, if she could bear to hear Louise's perfections sung all the time. But women can put up with a lot when they've got what they want.

Dr. Leidner then greeted Poirot, asking him if he had made any progress.

Miss Johnson was standing behind Dr. Leidner and she looked hard at the box in Poirot's hand and shook her head, and I realized that she was pleading with Poirot not to tell him about the mask. She felt, I was sure, that he had enough to bear for one day.

Poirot fell in with her wish.

"These things march slowly, monsieur," he said.

Then, after a few desultory words, he took his leave.

I accompanied him out to his car.

There were half a dozen things I wanted to ask him, but somehow, when he turned and looked at me, I didn't ask anything after all. I'd as soon have asked a surgeon if he thought he'd made a good job of an operation. I just stood meekly waiting for instructions.

Rather to my surprise he said:

"Take care of yourself, my child."

And then he added:

"I wonder if it is well for you to remain here?"

"I must speak to Dr. Leidner about leaving," I said. "But I thought I'd wait until after the funeral."

He nodded in approval.

"In the meantime," he said, "do not try and find out too much. You understand, I do not want you to be clever!" And he added with a smile, "It is for you to hold the swabs and for me to do the operation."

Wasn't it funny, his actually saying that?

Then he said quite irrelevantly:

"An interesting man, that Father Lavigny."

"A monk being an archæologist seems odd to me," I said.

"Ah, yes, you are a Protestant. Me, I am a good Catholic. I know something of priests and monks."

He frowned, seemed to hesitate, then said:

"Remember, he is quite clever enough to turn you inside out if he likes."

If he was warning me against gossiping I felt that I didn't need any such warning!

It annoyed me and though I didn't like to ask him any of the things I really wanted to know, I didn't see why I shouldn't at any rate say one thing.

"You'll excuse me, M. Poirot," I said. "But it's 'stubbed your toe,' not *stepped* or *stebbed*."

"Ah? Thank you, *ma sœur*."

"Don't mention it. But it's just as well to get a phrase right."

"I will remember," he said—quite meekly for him.

And he got in the car and was driven away, and I went slowly back across the courtyard wondering about a lot of things.

About the hypodermic marks on Mr. Mercado's arm, and what drug it was he took. And about that horrid yellow smeared mask. And how odd it was that Poirot and Miss Johnson hadn't heard my cry in the living-room that morning, whereas we had all heard Poirot perfectly well in the dining-room at lunch time—and yet Father Lavigny's room and Mrs. Leidner's were just the same distance from the living-room and the dining-room respectively.

And then I felt rather pleased that I'd taught *Doctor* Poirot one English phrase correctly!

Even if he *was* a great detective he'd realize he *didn't* know *everything!*

XXIII

I GO PSYCHIC

THE FUNERAL WAS, I thought, a very affecting affair. As well as ourselves, all the English people in Hassanieh attended it. Even Sheila Reilly was there looking quiet and subdued in a dark coat and skirt. I hoped that she was feeling a little remorseful for all the unkind things she had said.

When we got back to the house I followed Dr. Leidner into the office and broached the subject of my departure. He was very nice about it, thanked me for what I had done (Done! I had been worse than useless) and insisted on my accepting an extra week's salary.

I protested because really I felt I'd done nothing to earn it.

"Indeed, Dr. Leidner, I'd rather not have any salary at all. If you'd just refund me my travelling expenses that's all I want."

But he wouldn't hear of that.

"You see," I said, "I don't feel I deserve it, Dr. Leidner. I mean, I've —well, I've failed. She—my coming didn't save her."

"Now don't get that idea into your head, nurse," he said earnestly. "After all, I didn't engage you as a female detective. I never dreamt my wife's life was in danger. I was convinced it was all nerves and that she'd worked herself up into a rather curious mental state. You did all any one could do. She liked and trusted you. And I think in her last days she felt happier and safer because of your being here. There's nothing for you to reproach yourself with."

His voice quivered a little and I knew what he was thinking. *He* was the one to blame for not having taken Mrs. Leidner's fears seriously.

"Dr. Leidner," I said curiously. "Have you ever come to any conclusion about those anonymous letters?"

He said with a sigh:

"I don't know what to believe. Has M. Poirot come to any definite conclusion?"

"He hadn't yesterday," I said, steering rather neatly, I thought, between truth and fiction. After all, he hadn't until I told him about Miss Johnson.

It was on my mind that I'd like to give Dr. Leidner a hint and see if he reacted. In the pleasure of seeing him and Miss Johnson together the day before, and his affection and reliance on her, I'd forgotten all about the letters. Even now I felt it was perhaps rather mean of me to bring it up. Even if she had written them, she had had a bad time after Mrs. Leidner's death. Yet I did want to see whether that particular possibility had ever entered Dr. Leidner's head.

"Anonymous letters are usually the work of a woman," I said. I wanted to see how he'd take it.

"I suppose they are," he said with a sigh. "But you seem to forget, nurse, that these may be genuine. They may actually be written by Frederick Bosner."

"No, I haven't forgotten," I said. "But I can't believe somehow that that's the real explanation."

"I do," he said. "It's all nonsense his being one of the expedition staff. That is just an ingenious theory of M. Poirot's. I believe that the truth is much simpler. The man is a madman, of course. He's been hanging round the place—perhaps in disguise of some kind. And somehow or other he got in on that fatal afternoon. The servants may be lying—they may have been bribed."

"I suppose it's possible," I said doubtfully.

Dr. Leidner went on with a trace of irritability.

"It is all very well for M. Poirot to suspect the members of my expedition. I am perfectly certain *none* of them have anything to do with it! I have worked with them. I *know* them!"

He stopped suddenly, then he said:

"Is that your experience, nurse? That anonymous letters are usually written by women?"

"It isn't always the case," I said. "But there's a certain type of feminine spitefulness that finds relief that way."

"I suppose you are thinking of Mrs. Mercado?" he said.

Then he shook his head.

"Even if she were malicious enough to wish to hurt Louise she would hardly have the necessary knowledge," he said.

I remembered the earlier letters in the attaché-case.

If Mrs. Leidner had left that unlocked and Mrs. Mercado had been alone in the house one day pottering about, she might easily have found them and read them. Men never seem to think of the simplest possibilities!

"And apart from her there is only Miss Johnson," I said, watching him.

"That would be quite ridiculous!"

The little smile with which he said it was quite conclusive. The idea of Miss Johnson being the author of the letters had never entered his head! I hesitated just for a minute—but I didn't say anything. One doesn't like giving away a fellow woman, and besides, I had been a witness of Miss Johnson's genuine and moving remorse. What was done was done. Why expose Dr. Leidner to a fresh disillusion on top of all his other troubles?

It was arranged that I should leave on the following day, and I had arranged through Dr. Reilly to stay for a day or two with the matron of the hospital whilst I made arrangements for returning to England either via Baghdad or direct via Nissibin by car and train.

Dr. Leidner was kind enough to say that he would like me to choose a memento from amongst his wife's things.

"Oh, no, really, Dr. Leidner," I said. "I couldn't. It's much too kind of you."

He insisted.

"But I should like you to have something. And Louise, I am sure, would have wished it."

Then he went on to suggest that I should have her tortoiseshell toilet set!

"Oh, no, Dr. Leidner! Why, that's a most *expensive* set. I couldn't, really."

"She had no sisters, you know—no one who wants these things. There is no one else to have them."

I could quite imagine that he wouldn't want them to fall into Mrs. Mercado's greedy little hands. And I didn't think he'd want to offer them to Miss Johnson.

He went on kindly:

"You just think it over. By the way, here is the key of Louise's jewel case. Perhaps you will find something there you would rather have. And I should be very grateful if you would pack up—all—all her clothes. I dare say Reilly can find a use for them amongst some of the poor Christian families in Hassanieh."

I was very glad to be able to do that for him, and I expressed my willingness.

I set about it at once.

Mrs. Leidner had only had a very simple wardrobe with her and it was soon sorted and packed up into a couple of suitcases. All her papers had been in the small attaché-case. The jewel case contained a few simple trinkets—a pearl ring, a diamond brooch, a small string of pearls, one or two plain gold bar brooches of the safety-pin type, and a string of large amber beads.

Naturally I wasn't going to take the pearls or the diamonds, but I hesitated a bit between the amber beads and the toilet set. In the end, however, I didn't see why I shouldn't take the latter. It was a kindly thought on Dr. Leidner's part, and I was sure there wasn't any patronage about it. I'd take it in the spirit it had been offered without any false pride. After all, I *had* been fond of her.

Well, that was all done and finished with. The suitcases packed, the jewel case locked up again and put separate to give to Dr. Leidner with the photograph of Mrs. Leidner's father and one or two other personal little odds and ends.

The room looked bare and forlorn emptied of all its accoutrements, when I'd finished. There was nothing more for me to do—and yet somehow or other I shrank from leaving the room. It seemed as though there were something still to do there—something I ought to *see*—or something I ought to have *known*.

I'm not superstitious but the idea *did* pop into my head that perhaps Mrs. Leidner's spirit was hanging about the room and trying to get in touch with me.

I remember once at the hospital some of us girls got a planchette and really it wrote some very remarkable things.

Perhaps, although I'd never thought of such a thing, I might be mediumistic.

As I say, one gets all worked up to imagine all sorts of foolishness sometimes.

I prowled round the room uneasily, touching this and that. But, of course, there wasn't anything in the room but bare furniture. There was nothing slipped behind drawers or tucked away. I couldn't hope for anything of that kind.

In the end (it sounds rather batty, but as I say, one gets worked up) I did rather a queer thing.

I went and lay down on the bed and closed my eyes.

I deliberately tried to forget who and what I was. I tried to think myself back to that fatal afternoon. I was Mrs. Leidner lying here resting, peaceful and unsuspicious.

It's extraordinary how you can work yourself up.

I'm a perfectly normal matter-of-fact individual—not the least little bit spooky, but I tell you that after I'd lain there about five minutes I began to *feel* spooky.

I didn't try to resist. I deliberately encouraged the feeling.

I said to myself:

"I'm Mrs. Leidner. I'm Mrs. Leidner. I'm lying here—half asleep. Presently—very soon now—the door's going to open."

I kept on saying that—as though I were hypnotizing myself.

"It's just about half-past one . . . it's just about the time. . . . The door is going to open . . . *the door is going to open.* . . . I shall see who comes in. . . ."

I kept my eyes glued on that door. Presently it was going to open. I should *see* it open. And I should see *the person who opened it.*

I must have been a little over-wrought that afternoon to imagine I could solve the mystery that way.

But I did believe it. A sort of chill passed down my back and settled in my legs. They felt numb—paralyzed.

"You're going into a trance," I said. "And in that trance you'll see . . ."

And once again I repeated monotonously again and again:

"The door is going to open—the door is going to open. . . ."

The cold numbed feeling grew more intense.

And then, slowly, *I saw the door just beginning to open.*

It was horrible.

I've never known anything so horrible before or since.

I was paralyzed—chilled through and through. I couldn't move. For the life of me I couldn't have moved.

And I was terrified. Sick and blind and dumb with terror.

That slowly opening door.

So noiseless.

In a minute I should see . . .

Slowly—slowly—wider and wider.

Bill Coleman came quietly in.

He must have had the shock of his life!

I bounded off the bed with a scream of terror and hurled myself across the room.

He stood stock still, his blunt pink face pinker and his mouth opened wide with surprise.

"Hallo-allo-allo," he said. "What's up, nurse?"

I came back to reality with a crash.

"Goodness, Mr. Coleman," I said. "How you startled me!"

"Sorry," he said with a momentary grin.

I saw then that he was holding a little bunch of scarlet ranunculus in his hand. They were pretty little flowers and they grew wild on the sides of the Tell. Mrs. Leidner had been very fond of them.

He blushed and got rather red as he said:

"One can't get any flowers or things in Hassanieh. Seemed rather rotten not to have any flowers for the grave. I thought I'd just nip in here and put a little posy in that little pot thing she always had flowers in on her table. Sort of show she wasn't forgotten—eh? A bit asinine, I know, but—well—I mean to say—"

I thought it was very nice of him. He was all pink with embarrassment like Englishmen are when they've done anything sentimental. I thought it was a very sweet thought.

"Why, I think that's a very nice idea, Mr. Coleman," I said.

And I picked up the little pot and went and got some water in it and we put the flowers in.

I really thought much more of Mr. Coleman for this idea of his. It showed he had a heart and nice feelings about things.

He didn't ask me again what made me let out such a squeal and I'm thankful he didn't. I should have felt a fool explaining.

"Stick to common sense in future, woman," I said to myself as I settled my cuffs and smoothed my apron. "You're not cut out for this psychic stuff."

I bustled about doing my own packing and kept myself busy for the rest of the day.

Father Lavigny was kind enough to express great distress at my leaving. He said my cheerfulness and common sense had been such a help to everybody. Common sense! I'm glad he didn't know about my idiotic behaviour in Mrs. Leidner's room.

"We have not seen M. Poirot to-day," he remarked.

I told him that Poirot had said he was going to be busy all day sending off telegrams.

Father Lavigny raised his eyebrows.

"Telegrams? To America?"

"I suppose so. He said 'All over the world!' but I think that was rather a foreign exaggeration."

And then I got rather red, remembering that Father Lavigny was a foreigner himself.

He didn't seem offended though, just laughed quite pleasantly and asked me if there were any news of the man with the squint.

I said I didn't know but I hadn't heard of any.

Father Lavigny asked me again about the time Mrs. Leidner and I had noticed the man and how he had seemed to be standing on tip-toe and peering through the window.

"It seems clear the man had some overwhelming interest in Mrs. Leidner," he said thoughtfully. "I have wondered since whether the man could possibly have been a European got up to look like an Iraqi?"

That was a new idea to me and I considered it carefully. I had taken it for granted that the man was a native, but of course, when I came to think of it, I was really going by the cut of his clothes and the yellowness of his skin.

Father Lavigny declared his intention of going round outside the house to the place where Mrs. Leidner and I had seen the man standing.

"You never know, he might have dropped something. In the detective stories the criminal always does."

"I expect in real life criminals are more careful," I said.

I fetched some socks I had just finished darning and put them on the table in the living-room for the men to sort out when they came in, and then, as there was nothing much more to do, I went up on the roof.

Miss Johnson was standing there but she didn't hear me. I got right up to her before she noticed me.

But long before that I'd seen that there was something very wrong.

She was standing in the middle of the roof staring straight in front of her, and there was the most awful look on her face. As though she'd seen something she couldn't possibly believe.

It gave me quite a shock.

Mind you, I'd seen her upset the other evening, but this was quite different.

"My dear," I said, hurrying to her, "whatever's the matter?"

She turned her head at that and stood looking at me—almost as if she didn't see me.

"What is it?" I persisted.

She made a queer sort of grimace—as though she were trying to swallow but her throat were too dry. She said hoarsely:

"I've just seen something."

"What have you seen? Tell me. Whatever can it be? You look all in."

She gave an effort to pull herself together, but she still looked pretty dreadful.

She said, still in that same dreadful choked voice.

"*I've seen how some one could come in from outside—and no one would ever guess.*"

I followed the direction of her eyes but I couldn't see anything.

Mr. Reiter was standing in the door of the photographic room and Father Lavigny was just crossing the courtyard—but there was nothing else.

I turned back puzzled and found her eyes fixed on mine with the strangest expression in them.

"Really," I said, "I don't see what you mean. Won't you explain?"

But she shook her head.

"Not now. Later. We *ought* to have seen. Oh, we ought to have seen!"

"If you'd only tell me—"

But she shook her head.

"I've got to think it out first."

And pushing past me, she went stumbling down the stairs.

I didn't follow her as she obviously didn't want me with her. Instead I sat down on the parapet and tried to puzzle things out. But I didn't get anywhere. There was only the one way into the courtyard —through the big arch. Just outside it I could see the water-boy and his horse and the Indian cook talking to him. Nobody could have passed them and come in without their seeing him.

I shook my head in perplexity and went downstairs again.

XXIV
MURDER IS A HABIT

WE ALL WENT to bed early that night. Miss Johnson had appeared at dinner and had behaved more or less as usual. She had, however, a sort of dazed look, and once or twice quite failed to take in what other people said to her.

It wasn't somehow a very comfortable sort of meal. You'd say, I suppose, that that was natural enough in a house where there'd been a funeral that day. But I know what I mean.

Lately our meals had been hushed and subdued, but for all that there had been a feeling of comradeship. There had been sympathy with Dr. Leidner in his grief and a fellow feeling of being all in the same boat amongst the others.

But to-night I was reminded of my first meal there—when Mrs. Mercado had watched me and there had been that curious feeling as though something might snap any minute.

I'd felt the same thing—only very much intensified—when we'd sat round the dining-room table with Poirot at the head of it.

To-night it was particularly strong. Every one was on edge—jumpy —on tenterhooks. If any one had dropped something I'm sure somebody would have screamed.

As I say, we all separated early afterwards. I went to bed almost at once. The last thing I heard as I was dropping off to sleep was Mrs. Mercado's voice saying good-night to Miss Johnson just outside my door.

I dropped off to sleep at once—tired by my exertions and even more by my silly experience in Mrs. Leidner's room. I slept heavily and dreamlessly for several hours.

I awoke when I did awake with a start and a feeling of impending catastrophe. Some sound had woken me, and as I sat up in bed listening I heard it again.

An awful sort of agonized choking groan.

I had lit my candle and was out of bed in a twinkling. I snatched up a torch, too, in case the candle should blow out. I came out of my door and stood listening. I knew the sound wasn't far away. It came again—from the room immediately next to mine—Miss Johnson's room.

I hurried in. Miss Johnson was lying in bed, her whole body contorted in agony. As I set down the candle and bent over her, her lips moved and she tried to speak—but only an awful hoarse whisper came. I saw that the corners of her mouth and the skin of her chin were burnt a kind of greyish white.

Her eyes went from me to a glass that lay on the floor evidently where it had dropped from her hand. The light rug was stained a bright red where it had fallen. I picked it up and ran a finger over the inside, drawing back my hand with a sharp exclamation. Then I examined the inside of the poor woman's mouth.

There wasn't the least doubt what was the matter. Somehow or other, intentionally or otherwise, she'd swallowed a quantity of corrosive acid—oxalic or hydrochloric, I suspected.

I ran out and called to Dr. Leidner and he woke the others, and we worked over her for all we were worth, but all the time I had an awful feeling it was no good. We tried a strong solution of carbonate of soda—and followed it with olive oil. To ease the pain I gave her a hypodermic of morphine sulphate.

David Emmott had gone off to Hassanieh to fetch Dr. Reilly, but before he came it was over.

I won't dwell on the details. Poisoning by a strong solution of hydrochloric acid (which is what it proved to be) is one of the most painful deaths possible.

It was when I was bending over her to give her the morphia that she made one ghastly effort to speak. It was only a horrible strangled whisper when it came.

"*The window* . . ." she said. "*Nurse . . . the window* . . ."

But that was all—she couldn't go on. She collapsed completely.

I shall never forget that night. The arrival of Dr. Reilly. The arrival of Captain Maitland. And finally with the dawn, Hercule Poirot.

He it was who took me gently by the arm and steered me into the dining-room where he made me sit down and have a cup of good strong tea.

"There, *mon enfant*," he said, "that is better. You are worn out."

Upon that, I burst into tears.

"It's too awful," I sobbed. "It's been like a nightmare. Such awful suffering. And her eyes . . . Oh, M. Poirot—her eyes . . ."

He patted me on the shoulder. A woman couldn't have been kinder.

"Yes, yes—do not think of it. You did all you could."

"It was one of the corrosive acids."

"It was a strong solution of hydrochloric acid."

"The stuff they use on the pots?"

"Yes. Miss Johnson probably drank it off before she was fully awake. That is—unless she took it on purpose."

"Oh, M. Poirot, what an awful idea!"

"It is a possibility, after all. What do you think?"

I considered for a moment and then shook my head decisively.

"I don't believe it. No, I don't believe it for a moment." I hesitated and then said, "I think she found out something yesterday afternoon."

"What is that you say? She found out something?"

I repeated to him the curious conversation we had had together. Poirot gave a low soft whistle.

"*La pauvre femme!*" he said. "She said she wanted to think it over —eh? That is what signed her death warrant. If she had only spoken out—then—at once."

He said:

"Tell me again her exact words?"

I repeated them.

"She saw how some one could have come in from outside without any of you knowing? Come, *ma sœur*, let us go up to the roof and you shall show me just where she was standing."

We went up to the roof together and I showed Poirot the exact spot where Miss Johnson had stood.

"Like this?" said Poirot. "Now what do I see? I see half the court-yard—and the archway—and the doors of the drawing-office and the photographic room and the laboratory. Was there any one in the court-yard?"

"Father Lavigny was just going towards the archway and Mr. Reiter was standing in the door of the photographic room."

"And still I do not see in the least how any one could come in from outside and none of you know about it. . . . But *she* saw . . ."

He gave it up at last, shaking his head.

"*Sacré nom d'un chien—va!* What *did* she see?"

The sun was just rising. The whole eastern sky was a riot of rose and orange and pale, pearly grey.

"What a beautiful sunrise," said Poirot gently.

The river wound away to our left and the Tell stood up outlined in gold colour. To the south were the blossoming trees and the peaceful cultivation. The water-wheel groaned in the distance—a faint unearthly sound. In the north were the slender minarets and the clustering fairy whiteness of Hassanieh.

It was all incredibly beautiful.

And then, close at my elbow, I heard Poirot give a long deep sigh.

"Fool that I have been," he murmured. "When the truth is so clear —so clear."

XXV
SUICIDE OR MURDER?

I HADN'T TIME to ask Poirot what he meant, for Captain Maitland was calling up to us and asking us to come down.

We hurried down the stairs.

"Look here, Poirot," he said. "Here's another complication. The monk fellow is missing."

"Father Lavigny?"

"Yes. Nobody noticed it till just now. Then it dawned on somebody that he was the only one of the party not around, and we went to his room. His bed's not been slept in and there's no sign of him."

The whole thing was like a bad dream. First Miss Johnson's death and then the disappearance of Father Lavigny.

The servants were called and questioned, but they couldn't throw any light on the mystery. He had last been seen at about eight o'clock the night before. Then he had said he was going out for a stroll before going to bed.

Nobody had seen him come back from that stroll.

The big doors had been closed and barred at nine o'clock as usual. Nobody, however, remembered unbarring them in the morning. The two house-boys each thought the other one must have done the unfastening.

Had Father Lavigny ever returned the night before? Had he, in the course of his earlier walk, discovered anything of a suspicious nature, gone out to investigate it later, and perhaps fallen a third victim?

Captain Maitland swung round as Dr. Reilly came up with Mr. Mercado behind him.

"Hallo, Reilly. Got anything?"

"Yes. The stuff came from the laboratory here. I've just been checking up the quantities with Mercado. It's H.C.L. from the lab."

"The laboratory—eh? Was it locked up?"

Mr. Mercado shook his head. His hands were shaking and his face was twitching. He looked a wreck of a man.

"It's never been the custom," he stammered. "You see—just now—we're using it all the time. I—nobody ever dreamt—"

"Is the place locked up at night?"

"Yes—all the rooms are locked. The keys are hung up just inside the living-room."

"So if any one had a key to that they could get the lot."

"Yes."

"And it's a perfectly ordinary key, I suppose?"

"Oh, yes."

"Nothing to show whether she took it herself from the laboratory?" asked Captain Maitland.

"She didn't," I said loudly and positively.

I felt a warning touch on my arm. Poirot was standing close behind me.

And then something rather ghastly happened.

Not ghastly in itself—in fact it was just the incongruousness that made it seem worse than anything else.

A car drove into the courtyard and a little man jumped out. He was wearing a sun helmet and a short thick trench coat.

He came straight to Dr. Leidner, who was standing by Dr. Reilly, and shook him warmly by the hand.

"Vous voilà, mon cher," he cried. "Delighted to see you. I passed this way on Saturday afternoon—en route to the Italians at Fugima. I went to the dig but there wasn't a single European about and alas! I cannot speak Arabic. I had not time to come to the house. This morning I leave Fugima at five—two hours here with you—and then I catch the convoy on. Eh vien, and how is the season going?"

It was ghastly.

The cheery voice, the matter-of-fact manner, all the pleasant sanity of an everyday world now left far behind. He just bustled in, knowing nothing and noticing nothing—full of cheerful bonhomie.

No wonder Dr. Leidner gave an inarticulate gasp and looked in mute appeal at Dr. Reilly.

The doctor rose to the occasion.

He took the little man (he was a French archæologist called Verrier who dug in the Greek islands, I heard later) aside and explained to him what had occurred.

Verrier was horrified. He himself had been staying at an Italian dig right away from civilization for the last few days and had heard nothing.

He was profuse in condolences and apologies, finally striding over to Dr. Leidner and clasping him warmly by both hands.

"What a tragedy! My God, what a tragedy! I have no words. *Mon pauvre collègue.*"

And shaking his head in one last ineffectual effort to express his feelings, the little man climbed into his car and left us.

As I say, that momentary introduction of comic relief into tragedy seemed really more gruesome than anything else that had happened.

"The next thing," said Dr. Reilly firmly, "is breakfast. Yes, I insist. Come, Leidner, you must eat."

Poor Dr. Leidner was almost a complete wreck. He came with us to the dining-room and there a funereal meal was served. I think the hot coffee and fried eggs did us all good, though no one actually felt they wanted to eat. Dr. Leidner drank some coffee and sat twiddling his bread. His face was grey, drawn with pain and bewilderment.

After breakfast, Captain Maitland got down to things.

I explained how I had woken up, heard a queer sound and had gone into Miss Johnson's room.

"You say there was a glass on the floor?"

"Yes. She must have dropped it after drinking."

"Was it broken?"

"No, it had fallen on the rug. (I'm afraid the acid's ruined the rug, by the way.) I picked the glass up and put it back on the table."

"I'm glad you've told us that. There are only two sets of fingerprints on it, and one set is certainly Miss Johnson's own. The other must be yours."

He was silent for a moment, then he said:

"Please go on."

I described carefully what I'd done and the methods I had tried, looking rather anxiously at Dr. Reilly for approval. He gave it with a nod.

"You tried everything that could possibly have done any good," he said. And though I was pretty sure I had done so, it was a relief to have my belief confirmed.

"Did you know exactly what she had taken?" Captain Maitland asked.

"No—but I could see, of course, that it was a corrosive acid."

Captain Maitland asked gravely:

"Is it your opinion, nurse, that Miss Johnson deliberately administered this stuff to herself?"

"Oh, no," I exclaimed. "I never thought of such a thing!"

I don't know why I was so sure. Partly, I think, because of M. Poirot's hints. His "murder is a habit" had impressed itself on my mind. And then one doesn't readily believe that any one's going to commit suicide in such a terribly painful way.

I said as much and Captain Maitland nodded thoughtfully.

"I agree that it isn't what one would choose," he said. "But if any one were in great distress of mind and this stuff were easily available it might be taken for that reason."

"*Was* she in great distress of mind?" I asked doubtfully.

"Mrs. Mercado says so. She says that Miss Johnson was quite unlike herself at dinner last night—that she hardly replied to anything that was said to her. Mrs. Mercado is quite sure that Miss Johnson was in terrible distress over something and that the idea of making away with herself had already occurred to her."

"Well, I don't believe it for a moment," I said bluntly.

Mrs. Mercado indeed! Nasty slinking little cat!

"Then what *do* you think?"

"I think she was murdered," I said bluntly.

He rapped out his next question sharply. I felt rather that I was in the orderly room.

"Any reasons?"

"It seems to me by far and away the most possible solution."

"That's just your private opinion. There was no reason why the lady should be murdered?"

"Excuse me," I said, "there was. She found out something."

"Found out something? What did she find out?"

I repeated our conversation on the roof word for word.

"She refused to tell you what her discovery was?"

"Yes. She said she must have time to think it over."

"But she was very excited by it?"

"Yes."

"*A way of getting in from outside.*" Captain Maitland puzzled over it, his brows knit. "Had you no idea at all of what she was driving at?"

"Not in the least. I puzzled and puzzled over it but I couldn't even get a glimmering."

Captain Maitland said:

"What do you think, M. Poirot?"

Poirot said:

"I think you have there a possible motive."

"For murder?"

"For murder."

Captain Maitland frowned.

"She wasn't able to speak before she died?"

"Yes, she just managed to get out two words."

"What were they?"

"*The window . . .*"

"The window?" repeated Captain Maitland. "Did you understand to what she was referring?"

I shook my head.

"How many windows were there in her bedroom?"

"Just the one."

"Giving on the courtyard?"

"Yes."

"Was it open or shut? Open, I seem to remember. But perhaps one of you opened it?"

"No, it was open all the time. I wondered—"

I stopped.

"Go on, nurse."

"I examined the window, of course, but I couldn't see anything unusual about it. I wondered whether, perhaps, somebody changed the glasses that way."

"Changed the glasses?"

"Yes. You see, Miss Johnson always takes a glass of water to bed with her. I think that glass must have been tampered with and a glass of acid put there in its place."

"What do you say, Reilly?"

"If it's murder, that was probably the way it was done," said Dr. Reilly promptly. "No ordinary moderately observant human being would drink a glass of acid in mistake for one of water—if they were in full possession of their waking faculties. But if any one's accustomed to drinking off a glass of water in the middle of the night, that person might easily stretch out an arm, find the glass in the accustomed place, and still half asleep, toss off enough of the stuff to be fatal before realizing what had happened."

Captain Maitland reflected a minute.

"I'll have to go back and look at that window. How far is it from the head of the bed?"

I thought.

"With a very long stretch you could just reach the little table that stands by the head of the bed."

"The table on which the glass of water was?"

"Yes."

"Was the door locked?"

"No."

"So whoever it was could have come in that way and made the substitution?"

"Oh, yes."

"There would be more risk that way," said Dr. Reilly. "A person who is sleeping quite soundly will often wake up at the sound of a footfall. If the table could be reached from the window it would be the safer way."

"I'm not only thinking of the glass," said Captain Maitland absent-mindedly.

Rousing himself, he addressed me once again.

"It's your opinion that when the poor lady felt she was dying she was anxious to let you know that somebody had substituted acid for water through the open window? Surely the person's *name* would have been more to the point?"

"She mayn't have known the name," I pointed out.

"Or it would have been more to the point if she'd managed to hint what it was that she had discovered the day before?"

Dr. Reilly said:

"When you're dying, Maitland, you haven't always got a sense of proportion. One particular fact very likely obsesses your mind. That a murderous hand had come through the window may have been the principal fact obsessing her at the minute. It may have seemed to her important that she should let people know that. In my opinion she wasn't far wrong either. It *was* important! She probably jumped to the fact that you'd think it was suicide. If she could have used her tongue freely, she'd probably have said 'It wasn't suicide. I didn't take it myself. Somebody else must have put it near my bed *through the window.*'"

Captain Maitland drummed with his fingers for a minute or two without replying. Then he said:

"There are certainly two ways of looking at it. It's either suicide or murder. Which do you think, Dr. Leidner?"

Dr. Leidner was silent for a minute or two, then he said quietly and decisively:

"Murder. Anne Johnson wasn't the sort of woman to kill herself."

"No," allowed Captain Maitland. "Not in the normal run of things. But there might be circumstances in which it would be quite a natural thing to do."

"Such as?"

Captain Maitland stooped to a bundle which I had previously noticed him place by the side of his chair. He swung it on to the table with something of an effort.

"There's something here that none of you know about," he said. "We found it under her bed."

He fumbled with the knot of the covering, then threw it back revealing a heavy great quern or grinder.

That was nothing in itself—there were a dozen or so already found in the course of the excavations.

What riveted our attention on this particular specimen was a dull, dark stain and a fragment of something that looked like hair.

"That'll be your job, Reilly," said Captain Maitland. "But I shouldn't say that there's much doubt about this being the instrument with which Mrs. Leidner was killed!"

XXVI

NEXT IT WILL BE ME!

IT WAS RATHER horrible. Dr. Leidner looked as though he were going to faint and I felt a bit sick myself.

Dr. Reilly examined it with professional gusto.

"No fingerprints, I presume?" he threw out.

"No fingerprints."

Dr. Reilly took out a pair of forceps and investigated delicately.

"H'm—a fragment of human tissue—and hair—fair blonde hair. That's the unofficial verdict. Of course, I'll have to make a proper test, blood group, etc., but there's not much doubt. Found under Miss Johnson's bed? Well, well—so *that's* the big idea. She did the murder, and then, God rest her, remorse came to her and she finished herself off. It's a theory—a pretty theory."

Dr. Leidner could only shake his head helplessly.

"Not Anne—not Anne," he murmured.

"I don't know where she hid this to begin with," said Captain Maitland. "Every room was searched after the first crime."

Something jumped into my mind and I thought, "In the stationery cupboard," but I didn't say anything.

"Wherever it was, she became dissatisfied with its hiding-place and took it into her own room, which had been searched with all the rest. Or perhaps she did that after making up her mind to commit suicide."

"I don't believe it," I said aloud.

And I couldn't somehow believe that kind nice Miss Johnson had battered out Mrs. Leidner's brains. I just couldn't see it happening! And yet it *did* fit in with some things—her fit of weeping that night, for instance. After all, I'd said "remorse" myself—only I'd never thought it was remorse for anything but the smaller more insignificant crime.

"I don't know what to believe," said Captain Maitland. "There's the French Father's disappearance to be cleared up too. My men are out hunting around in case he's been knocked on the head and his body rolled into a convenient irrigation ditch."

"Oh! I remember now—" I began.

Every one looked towards me inquiringly.

"It was yesterday afternoon," I said. "He'd been cross-questioning me about the man with a squint who was looking in at the window that day. He asked me just where he'd stood on the path and then he said he was going out to have a look round. He said in detective stories the criminal always dropped a convenient clue."

"Damned if any of my criminals ever do," said Captain Maitland. "So that's what he was after, was it? By jove, I wonder if he *did* find anything. A bit of a coincidence if both he and Miss Johnson discovered a clue to the identity of the murderer at practically the same time."

He added irritably, "Man with a squint? Man with a squint? There's more in this tale of that fellow with a squint than meets the eye. I don't know why the devil my fellows can't lay hold of him?"

"Probably because he hasn't got a squint," said Poirot quietly.

"Do you mean he faked it? Didn't know you could fake an actual squint."

Poirot merely said:

"A squint can be a very useful thing."

"The devil it can! I'd give a lot to know where that fellow is now, squint or no squint!"

"At a guess," said Poirot, "he has already passed the Syrian frontier."

"We've warned Tell Kotchek and Abu Kemal—all the frontier posts, in fact."

"I should imagine that he took the route through the hills. The route lorries sometimes take when running contraband."

Captain Maitland grunted.

"Then we'd better telegraph Deir ez Zor?"

"I did so yesterday—warning them to look out for a car with two men in it whose passports will be in the most impeccable order."

Captain Maitland favoured him with a stare.

"*You* did, did you? Two men—eh?"

Poirot nodded.

"There are two men in this."

"It strikes me, M. Poirot, that you've been keeping quite a lot of things up your sleeve."

Poirot shook his head.

"No," he said. "Not really. The truth came to me only this morning when I was watching the sun rise. A very beautiful sunrise."

I don't think that any of us had noticed that Mrs. Mercado was in the room. She must have crept in when we were all taken aback by the production of that horrible great blood-stained stone.

But now, without the least warning, she set up a noise like a pig having its throat cut.

"Oh, my God!" she cried. "I see it all. I see it all now. *It was Father Lavigny.* He's mad—religious mania. He thinks women are sinful. *He's killing them all.* First Mrs. Leidner—then Miss Johnson. And next it will be *me.* . . ."

With a scream of frenzy she flung herself across the room and clutched at Dr. Reilly's coat.

"I won't stay here, I tell you! I won't stay here a day longer. There's danger. There's danger all round. He's hiding somewhere—waiting his time. He'll spring out on me!"

Her mouth opened and she began screaming again.

I hurried over to Dr. Reilly, who had caught her by the wrists. I gave her a sharp slap on each cheek and with Dr. Reilly's help, I sat her down in a chair.

"Nobody's going to kill you," I said. "We'll see to that. Sit down and behave yourself."

She didn't scream any more. Her mouth closed and she sat looking at me with startled, stupid eyes.

Then there was another interruption. The door opened and Sheila Reilly came in.

Her face was pale and serious. She came straight to Poirot.

"I was at the post office early, M. Poirot," she said, "and there was a telegram there for you—so I brought it along."

"Thank you, mademoiselle."

He took it from her and tore it open while she watched his face.

It did not change, that face. He read the telegram, smoothed it out, folded it up neatly and put it in his pocket.

Mrs. Mercado was watching him. She said in a choked voice:

"Is that—from America?"

He shook his head.

"No, madame," he said. "It is from Tunis."

She stared at him for a moment as though she did not understand, then with a long sigh, she leant back in her seat.

"Father Lavigny," she said. "I *was* right. I've always thought there was something queer about him. He said things to me once . . . I suppose he's mad. . . ." She paused and then said, "I'll be quiet. But I *must* leave this place. Joseph and I can go in and sleep at the Rest House."

"Patience, madame," said Poirot. "I will explain everything."

Captain Maitland was looking at him curiously.

"Do you consider you've definitely got the hang of this business?" he demanded.

Poirot bowed.

It was a most theatrical bow. I think it rather annoyed Captain Maitland.

"Well," he barked. "Out with it, man."

But that wasn't the way Hercule Poirot did things. I saw perfectly well that he meant to make a song and dance of it. I wondered if he really *did* know the truth, or if he was just showing off.

He turned to Dr. Reilly.

"Will you be so good, Dr. Reilly, as to summon the others?"

Dr. Reilly jumped up and went off obligingly. In a minute or two the other members of the expedition began to file into the room. First Reiter and Emmott. Then Bill Coleman. Then Richard Carey and finally Mr. Mercado.

Poor man, he really looked like death. I suppose he was mortally afraid that he'd get hauled over the coals for carelessness in leaving dangerous chemicals about.

Every one seated themselves round the table very much as we had done on the day M. Poirot arrived. Both Bill Coleman and David Emmott hesitated before they sat down, glancing towards Sheila Reilly. She had her back to them and was standing looking out of the window.

"Chair, Sheila?" said Bill.

David Emmott said in his low pleasant drawl, "Won't you sit down?"

She turned then and stood for a minute looking at them. Each was indicating a chair, pushing it forward. I wondered whose chair she would accept.

In the end she accepted neither.

"I'll sit here," she said brusquely. And she sat down on the edge of a table quite close to the window.

"That is," she added, "if Captain Maitland doesn't mind my staying?"

I'm not quite sure what Captain Maitland would have said. Poirot forestalled him.

"Stay by all means, mademoiselle," he said. "It is, indeed, necessary that you should."

She raised her eyebrows.

"Necessary?"

"That is the word I used, mademoiselle. There are some questions I shall have to ask you."

Again her eyebrows went up but she said nothing further. She turned her face to the window as though determined to ignore what went on in the room behind her.

"And now," said Captain Maitland, "perhaps we shall get at the truth!"

He spoke rather impatiently. He was essentially a man of action. At this very moment I feel sure that he was fretting to be out and doing things—directing the search for Father Lavigny's body, or alternatively sending out parties for his capture and arrest.

He looked at Poirot with something akin to dislike.

"If the beggar's got anything to say, why doesn't he say it?"

I could see the words on the tip of his tongue.

Poirot gave a slow appraising glance at us all, then rose to his feet.

I don't know what I expected him to say—something dramatic certainly. He was that kind of person.

But I certainly didn't expect him to start off with a phrase in Arabic.

Yet that is what happened. He said the words slowly and solemnly— and really quite religiously, if you know what I mean.

"*Bismillahi ar rahman ar rahim.*"

And then he gave the translation in English.

"In the name of Allah, the Merciful, the Compassionate."

XXVII
BEGINNING OF A JOURNEY

"BISMILLAHI AR RAHMAN ar rahim. That is the Arab phrase used before starting out on a journey. *Eh bien,* we too, start on a journey. A journey into the past. A journey into the strange places of the human soul."

I don't think that up till that moment I'd ever felt any of the so-called "glamour of the East." Frankly, what had struck me was the *mess* everywhere. But suddenly, with M. Poirot's words, a queer sort of vision seemed to grow up before my eyes. I thought of words like Samarkand and Ispahan—and of merchants with long beards—and kneeling camels—and staggering porters carrying great bales on their backs held by a rope round the forehead—and women with henna-stained hair and tattooed faces kneeling by the Tigris and washing clothes, and I heard their queer, wailing chants and the far-off groaning of the water-wheel. . . .

They were mostly things I'd seen and heard and thought nothing much of. But now, somehow they seemed *different*—like a piece of fusty old stuff you take into the light and suddenly see the rich colours of an old embroidery. . . .

Then I looked round the room we were sitting in and I got a queer feeling that what M. Poirot said was true—we *were* all starting on a journey. We were here together now, but we were all going our different ways.

And I looked at every one as though, in a sort of way, I were seeing them for the first time—*and* for the last time—which sounds stupid, but it was what I felt all the same.

Mr. Mercado was twisting his fingers nervously—his queer light eyes with their dilated pupils were staring at Poirot. Mrs. Mercado was looking at her husband. She had a strange watchful look like a tigress waiting to spring. Dr. Leidner seemed to have shrunk in some curious fashion. This last blow had just crumpled him up. You might almost say he wasn't in the room at all. He was somewhere far away in a place of his own. Mr. Coleman was looking straight at Poirot. His mouth was slightly open and his eyes protruded. He looked almost idiotic. Mr. Emmott was looking down at his feet and I couldn't see his face properly. Mr. Reiter looked bewildered. His mouth was pushed out in a pout and that made him look more like a nice clean pig than ever. Miss Reilly was looking steadily out of the window. I don't know what she was thinking or feeling. Then I looked at Mr. Carey, and somehow his face hurt me and I looked away. There we were, all of us. And somehow I felt that when M. Poirot had finished we'd all be somewhere quite different. . . .

It was a queer feeling. . . .

Poirot's voice went quietly on. It was like a river running evenly between its banks . . . running to the sea. . . .

"From the very beginning, I have felt that to understand this case one must seek not for external signs or clues, but for the truer clues of the clash of personalities and the secrets of the heart.

"And I may say that though I have now arrived at what I believe to be the true solution of the case, I have no material proof of it. I know it is so, because it must be so, because in no other way can every single fact fit into its ordered and recognized place.

"And that, to my mind, is the most satisfying solution there can be."

He paused and then went on:

"I will start my journey at the moment when I myself was brought into the case—when I had it presented to me as an accomplished happening. Now, every case, in my opinion, has a definite shape and form. The pattern of this case, to my mind, all revolved round the personality of Mrs. Leidner. Until I knew exactly what kind of a woman Mrs. Leidner was I should not be able to know why she was murdered and who murdered her.

"That, then, was my starting point—the personality of Mrs. Leidner.

"There was also one other psychological point of interest—the curious state of tension described as existing amongst the members of the expedition. This was attested to by several different witnesses—some of them outsiders—and I made a note that although hardly a starting point, it should nevertheless be borne in mind during my investigations.

"The accepted idea seemed to be that it was directly the result of Mrs. Leidner's influence on the members of the expedition, but for reasons which I will outline to you later this did not seem to me entirely acceptable.

"To start with, as I say, I concentrated solely and entirely on the personality of Mrs. Leidner. I had various means of assessing that personality. There were the reactions she produced in a number of people, all varying widely in character and temperament, and there was what I could glean by my own observation. The scope of the latter was naturally limited. But I *did* learn certain facts.

"Mrs. Leidner's tastes were simple and even on the austere side. She was clearly not a luxurious woman. On the other hand, some embroidery she had been doing was of an extreme fineness and beauty. That indicated a woman of fastidious and artistic taste. From the observation of the books in her bedroom I formed a further estimate. She had brains, and I also fancied that she was, essentially, an egoist.

"It had been suggested to me that Mrs. Leidner was a woman whose main preoccupation was to attract the opposite sex—that she was, in fact, a sensual woman. This I did not believe to be the case.

"In her bedroom I noticed the following books on a shelf: *Who Were the Greeks? Introduction to Relativity, Life of Lady Hester Stanhope, Back to Methuselah, Linda Condon, Crewe Train.*

"She had, to begin with, an interest in culture and in modern science—that is, a distinct intellectual side. Of the novels *Linda Condon,* and in a lesser degree *Crewe Train,* seemed to show that Mrs. Leidner had a sympathy and interest in the independent woman—unencumbered or entrapped by man. She was also obviously interested by the personality of Lady Hester Stanhope. *Linda Condon* is an exquisite study of the worship of her own beauty by a woman. *Crewe Train* is a study of a passionate individualist. *Back to Methuselah* is in sympathy with the intellectual rather than the emotional attitude to life. I felt that I was beginning to understand the dead woman.

"I next studied the reactions of those who had formed Mrs. Leidner's immediate circle—and my picture of the dead woman grew more and more complete.

"It was quite clear to me from the accounts of Dr. Reilly and others that Mrs. Leidner was one of those women who are endowed by Nature not only with beauty but with the kind of calamitous magic which sometimes accompanies beauty and can, indeed, exist independently of it. Such women usually leave a trail of violent happenings behind them. They bring disaster—sometimes on others—sometimes on themselves.

"I was convinced that Mrs. Leidner was a woman who essentially worshipped *herself* and who enjoyed more than anything else the sense of *power.* Wherever she was, she *must* be the centre of the universe.

And every one round her, man or woman, had got to acknowledge her sway. With some people that was easy. Nurse Leatheran, for instance, a generous-natured woman with a romantic imagination, was captured instantly and gave in ungrudging manner full appreciation. But there was a second way in which Mrs. Leidner exercised her sway —the way of fear. Where conquest was too easy she indulged a more cruel side to her nature—but I wish to reiterate emphatically that it was not what you might call *conscious* cruelty. It was as natural and unthinking as is the conduct of a cat with a mouse. Where consciousness came in, she was essentially kind and would often go out of her way to do kind and thoughtful actions for other people.

"Now of course the first and most important problem to solve was the problem of the anonymous letters. Who had written them and why? I asked myself: Had Mrs. Leidner written them *herself?*

"To answer this problem it was necessary to go back a long way— to go back, in fact, to the date of Mrs. Leidner's first marriage. It is here we start on our journey proper. The journey of Mrs. Leidner's life.

"First of all we must realize that the Louise Leidner of all those years ago is essentially the same Louise Leidner of the present time.

"She was young then, of remarkable beauty—that same haunting beauty that affects a man's spirit and senses as no mere material beauty can—and she was already essentially an egoist.

"Such women naturally revolt from the idea of marriage. They may be attracted by men, but they prefer to belong to themselves. They are truly *La Belle Dame sans Merci* of the legend. Nevertheless Mrs. Leidner *did* marry—and we can assume, I think, that her husband must have been a man of a certain force of character.

"Then the revelation of his traitorous activities occurs and Mrs. Leidner acts in the way she told Nurse Leatheran. She gave information to the Government.

"Now I submit that there was a psychological significance in her action. She told Nurse Leatheran that she was a very patriotic ideal-istic girl and that that feeling was the cause of her action. But it is a well-known fact that we all tend to deceive ourselves as to the motives for our own actions. Instinctively we select the best-sounding motive! Mrs. Leidner may have believed herself that it was patriotism that in-spired her action, but I believe myself that it was really the outcome of an unacknowledged desire to get rid of her husband! She disliked domination—she disliked the feeling of belonging to some one else—in fact she disliked playing second fiddle. She took a patriotic way of regaining her freedom.

"But underneath her consciousness was a gnawing sense of guilt which was to play its part in her future destiny.

"We now come directly to the question of the letters. Mrs. Leidner was highly attractive to the male sex. On several occasions she was attracted by them—but in each case a threatening letter played its part and the affair came to nothing.

"Who wrote those letters? Frederick Bosner or his brother William or *Mrs. Leidner herself?*

"There is a perfectly good case for either theory. It seems clear to me that Mrs. Leidner was one of those women who do inspire devouring devotions in men, the type of devotion which can become an obsession. I find it quite possible to believe in a Frederick Bosner to whom Louise, his wife, mattered more than anything in the world! She had betrayed him once and he dared not approach her openly, but he was determined at least that she should be his or no one's. He preferred her death to her belonging to another man.

"On the other hand, if Mrs. Leidner had, deep down, a dislike of entering into the marriage bond, it is possible that she took this way of extricating herself from difficult positions. She was a huntress who, the prey once attained, had no further use for it! Craving drama in her life, she invented a highly satisfactory drama—a resurrected husband forbidding the banns! It satisfied her deepest instincts. It made her a romantic figure, a tragic heroine, and it enabled her not to marry again.

"This state of affairs continued over a number of years. Every time there was any likelihood of marriage—a threatening letter arrived.

"*But now we come to a really interesting point.* Dr. Leidner came upon the scene—and no forbidding letter arrived! Nothing stood in the way of her becoming Mrs. Leidner. Not until *after* her marriage did a letter arrive.

"At once we ask ourselves—why?

"Let us take each theory in turn.

"*If* Mrs. Leidner wrote the letters herself the problem is easily explained. Mrs. Leidner really *wanted* to marry Dr. Leidner. And so she *did* marry him. But in that case, *why did she write herself a letter afterwards?* Was her craving for drama too strong to be suppressed? And why only those two letters? After that no other letter was received until a year and a half later.

"Now take the other theory, that the letters were written by her first husband, Frederick Bosner (or his brother). Why did the threatening letter arrive *after* the marriage? Presumably Frederick could not have *wanted* her to marry Leidner. Why, then, did he not stop the marriage? He had done so successfully on former occasions. And why, *having waited till the marriage had taken place*, did he then resume his threats?

"The answer, an unsatisfactory one, is that he was somehow or other unable to protest sooner. He may have been in prison or he may have been abroad.

"There is next the attempted gas poisoning to consider. It seems extremely unlikely that it was brought about by an outside agency. The likely persons to have staged it were Dr. and Mrs. Leidner themselves. There seems no conceivable reason why Dr. Leidner should do such a thing, so we are brought to the conclusion that *Mrs.* Leidner planned and carried it out herself.

"Why? More drama?

"After that Dr. and Mrs. Leidner go abroad and for eighteen months they lead a happy, peaceful life with no threats of death to disturb it. They put that down to having successfully covered their traces, but such an explanation is quite absurd. In these days going abroad is quite inadequate for that purpose. And especially was that so in the case of the Leidners. He was the director of a museum expedition. By inquiry at the museum, Frederick Bosner could at once have obtained his correct address. Even granting that he was in too reduced circumstances to pursue the couple himself, there would be no bar to his continuing his threatening letters. And it seems to me that a man with his obsession would certainly have done so.

"Instead nothing is heard of him until nearly two years later when the letters are resumed.

"*Why* were the letters resumed?

"A very difficult question—most easily answered by saying that Mrs. Leidner was bored and wanted more drama. But I was not quite satisfied with that. This particular form of drama seemed to me a shade too vulgar and too crude to accord well with her fastidious personality.

"The only thing to do was to keep an open mind on the question.

"There were three definite possibilities: (1) the letters were written by Mrs. Leidner herself; (2) they were written by Frederick Bosner (or young William Bosner); (3) they might have been written *originally* by either Mrs. Leidner or her first husband, but they were now *forgeries*—that is, they were being written by a *third* person who was aware of the earlier letters.

"I now come to direct consideration of Mrs. Leidner's entourage.

"I examined first the actual opportunities that each member of the staff had had for committing the murder.

"Roughly, on the face of it, *any one* might have committed it (as far as opportunity went), with the exception of three persons.

"Dr. Leidner, by overwhelming testimony, had never left the roof. Mr. Carey was on duty at the mound. Mr. Coleman was in Hassanieh.

"But those alibis, my friends, were not *quite* as good as they looked. I accept Dr. Leidner's. There is absolutely no doubt that he was on the roof all the time and did not come down until quite an hour and a quarter after the murder had happened.

"But was it *quite* certain that Mr. Carey was on the mound all the time?

"And had Mr. Coleman *actually been in Hassanieh* at the time the murder took place?"

Bill Coleman reddened, opened his mouth, shut it and looked round uneasily.

Mr. Carey's expression did not change.

Poirot went on smoothly.

"I also considered one other person who, I satisfied myself, would be perfectly capable of committing murder *if she felt strongly enough.* Miss Reilly has courage and brains and a certain quality of ruthlessness. When Miss Reilly was speaking to me on the subject of the dead woman, I said to her, jokingly, that I hoped she had an alibi. I think Miss Reilly was conscious then that she had had in her heart the desire, at least, to kill. At any rate she immediately uttered a very silly and purposeless lie. She said she had been playing tennis on that afternoon. The next day I learned from a casual conversation with Miss Johnson that far from playing tennis, Miss Reilly *had actually been near this house at the time of the murder.* It occurred to me that Miss Reilly, if not guilty of the crime, might be able to tell me something useful."

He stopped and then said quietly:

"Will you tell us, Miss Reilly, what you *did* see that afternoon?"

The girl did not answer at once. She still looked out of the window without turning her head, and when she spoke it was in a detached and measured voice.

"I rode out to the dig after lunch. It must have been about a quarter to two when I got there."

"Did you find any of your friends on the dig?"

"No, there seemed to be no one there but the Arab foreman."

"You did not see Mr. Carey?"

"No."

"Curious," said Poirot. "No more did M. Verrier when he went there that same afternoon."

He looked invitingly at Carey, but the latter neither moved nor spoke.

"Have you any explanation, Mr. Carey?"

"I went for a walk. There was nothing of interest turning up."

"In which direction did you go for a walk?"

"Down by the river."

"Not back towards the house?"

"No."

"I suppose," said Miss Reilly, "that you were waiting for some one who didn't come."

He looked at her but didn't answer.

Poirot did not press the point. He spoke once more to the girl.

"Did you see anything else, mademoiselle?"

"Yes. I was not far from the expedition house when I noticed the expedition lorry drawn up in a wadi. I thought it was rather queer. Then I saw Mr. Coleman. He was walking along with his head down as though he were searching for something."

"Look here," burst out Mr. Coleman. "I—"

Poirot stopped him with an authoritative gesture.

"Wait. Did you speak to him, Miss Reilly?"

"No, I didn't."

"Why?"

The girl said slowly:

"Because, from time to time, he started and looked round with an extraordinary furtive look. It—gave me an unpleasant feeling. I turned my horse's head and rode away. I don't think he saw me. I was not very near and he was absorbed in what he was doing."

"Look here," Mr. Coleman was not to be hushed any longer. "I've got a perfectly good explanation for what—I admit—looks a bit fishy. As a matter of fact, the day before I had slipped a jolly fine cylinder seal into my coat pocket instead of putting it in the antika-room—forgot all about it. And then I discovered I'd been and lost it out of my pocket—dropped it somewhere. I didn't want to get into a row about it so I decided I'd have a jolly good search on the quiet. I was pretty sure I'd dropped it on the way to or from the dig. I rushed over my business in Hassanieh. Sent a walad to do some of the shopping and got back early. I stuck the bus where it wouldn't show and had a jolly good hunt for over an hour. And didn't find the damned thing at that! Then I got into the bus and drove on to the house. Naturally, every one thought I'd just got back."

"And you did not undeceive them?" asked Poirot sweetly.

"Well, that was pretty natural under the circumstances, don't you think?"

"I hardly agree," said Poirot.

"Oh, come now—don't go looking for trouble—that's *my* motto! But you can't fasten anything on me. I never went into the courtyard, and you can't find any one who'll say I did."

"That, of course, has been the difficulty," said Poirot. "The evidence of the servants that *no one entered the courtyard from outside*. But it occurred to me, upon reflection, that that was really *not* what they had said. They had sworn that *no stranger* had entered the premises. They had not been asked *if a member of the expedition* had done so."

"Well, you ask them," said Coleman. "I'll eat my hat if they saw me or Carey either."

"Ah! but that raises rather an interesting question. They would notice *a stranger* undoubtedly—but would they have even *noticed* a member of the expedition? The members of the staff are passing in and out all day. The servants would hardly notice their going and coming. It is possible, I think, that either Mr. Carey or Mr. Coleman *might* have entered and the servants' minds would have no remembrance of such an event."

"Bunkum!" said Mr. Coleman.

Poirot went on calmly:

"Of the two, I think Mr. Carey was the least likely to be noticed going or coming. Mr. Coleman had started to Hassanieh in the car that morning and he would be expected to return in it. His arrival on foot would therefore be noticeable."

"Of course it would!" said Coleman.

Richard Carey raised his head. His deep-blue eyes looked straight at Poirot.

"Are you accusing me of murder, M. Poirot?" he asked.

His manner was quite quiet but his voice had a dangerous undertone.

Poirot bowed to him.

"As yet I am only taking you all on a journey—my journey towards the truth. I had now established one fact—that all the members of the expedition staff, and also Nurse Leatheran, could in actual *fact* have committed the murder. That there was very little likelihood of some of them having committed it was a secondary matter.

"I had examined *means* and *opportunity*. I next passed to *motive*. I discovered that *one and all of you could be credited with a motive!*"

"Oh! M. Poirot," I cried. "Not *me!* Why, I was a stranger. I'd only just come."

"*Eh bien, ma sœur*, and was not that *just what Mrs. Leidner had been fearing? A stranger* from *outside?*"

"But—but— Why, Dr. Reilly knew all about me! He suggested my coming!"

"How much did he really know about you? *Mostly what you yourself had told him*. Impostors have passed themselves off as hospital nurses before now."

"You can write to St. Christopher's," I began.

"For the moment will you silence yourself. Impossible to proceed while you conduct this argument. I do not say I suspect you *now*. All I say is that, keeping the open mind, you might quite easily be some one other than you pretended to be. There are many successful female impersonators, you know. Young William Bosner might be something of that kind."

I was about to give him a further piece of my mind. Female impersonator indeed! But he raised his voice and hurried on with such an air of determination that I thought better of it.

"I am going now to be frank—brutally so. It is necessary. I am going to lay bare the underlying structure of this place.

"I examined and considered every single soul here. To begin with Dr. Leidner, I soon convinced myself that his love for his wife was the mainspring of his existence. He was a man torn and ravaged with grief. Nurse Leatheran I have already mentioned. If she were a female impersonator she was a most amazingly successful one, and I inclined to the belief that she was exactly what she said she was—a thoroughly competent hospital nurse."

"Thank you for nothing," I interposed.

"My attention was immediately attracted towards Mr. and Mrs. Mercado, who were both of them clearly in a state of great agitation and unrest. I considered first Mrs. Mercado. Was she capable of murder and if so for what reasons?

"Mrs. Mercado's physique was frail. At first sight it did not seem possible that she could have had the physical strength to strike down a woman like Mrs. Leidner with a heavy stone implement. If, however, Mrs. Leidner had been on her knees at the time, the thing would at least be *physically possible*. There are ways in which one woman can induce another to go down on her knees. Oh! not emotional ways! For instance, a woman might be turning up the hem of a skirt and ask another woman to put in the pins for her. The second woman would kneel on the ground quite unsuspectingly.

"But the motive? Nurse Leatheran had told me of the angry glances she had seen Mrs. Mercado direct at Mrs. Leidner. Mr. Mercado had evidently succumbed easily to Mrs. Leidner's spell. But I did not think the solution was to be found in mere jealousy. I was sure Mrs. Leidner was not in the least interested really in Mr. Mercado—and doubtless Mrs. Mercado was aware of the fact. She might be furious with her for the moment, but for *murder* there would have to be greater provocation. But Mrs. Mercado was essentially a fiercely maternal type. From the way she looked at her husband I realized, not only that she loved him, but that she would fight for him tooth and nail—and more than that—*that she envisaged the possibility of having to do so*. She was constantly on her guard and uneasy. The uneasiness was for him—not for herself. And when I studied Mr. Mercado I could make a fairly easy guess at what the trouble was. I took means to assure myself of the truth of my guess. Mr. Mercado was a drug addict—in an advanced stage of the craving.

"Now I need probably not tell you all that the taking of drugs over a long period has the result of considerably blunting the moral sense.

"Under the influence of drugs a man commits actions that he would not have dreamed of committing a few years earlier before he began the practice. In some cases a man has committed murder—and it has been difficult to say whether he was wholly responsible for his actions or not. The law of different countries varies slightly on that point. The chief characteristic of the drug-fiend criminal is overweening confidence in his own cleverness.

"I thought it possible that there was some discreditable incident, perhaps a criminal incident, in Mr. Mercado's past which his wife had somehow or other succeeded in hushing up. Nevertheless his career hung on a thread. If anything of this past incident were bruited about, Mr. Mercado would be ruined. His wife was always on the watch. But there was Mrs. Leidner to be reckoned with. She had a sharp intelligence and a love of power. She might even induce the wretched man to confide in her. It would just have suited her peculiar temperament to feel she knew a secret which she could reveal at any minute with disastrous effects.

"Here, then, was a possible motive for murder on the part of the Mercados. To protect her mate, Mrs. Mercado, I felt sure, would stick at nothing! Both she and her husband had had the opportunity—during that ten minutes when the courtyard was empty."

Mrs. Mercado cried out, "It's not *true!*"

Poirot paid no attention.

"I next considered Miss Johnson. Was *she* capable of murder?

"I thought she was. She was a person of strong will and iron self-control. Such people are constantly repressing themselves—and one day the dam bursts! But if Miss Johnson had committed the crime it could only be for some reason connected with Dr. Leidner. If in any way she felt convinced that Mrs. Leidner was spoiling her husband's life, then the deep unacknowledged jealousy far down in her would leap at the chance of a plausible motive and give itself full rein.

"Yes, Miss Johnson was distinctly a possibility.

"Then there were the three young men.

"First Carl Reiter. If, by any chance, one of the expedition staff was William Bosner, then Reiter was by far the most likely person. But if he *was* William Bosner, then he was certainly a most accomplished actor! If he were merely *himself,* had he any reason for murder?

"Regarded from Mrs. Leidner's point of view, Carl Reiter was far too easy a victim for good sport. He was prepared to fall on his face and worship immediately. Mrs. Leidner despised undiscriminating adoration—and the door-mat attitude nearly always brings out the worst side of a woman. In her treatment of Carl Reiter Mrs. Leidner displayed really deliberate cruelty. She inserted a gibe here—a prick there. She made the poor young man's life a hell to him."

Poirot broke off suddenly and addressed the young man in a personal, highly confidential manner.

"*Mon ami,* let this be a lesson to you. You are a *man.* Behave, then, like a *man!* It is against Nature for a man to grovel. Women and Nature have almost exactly the same reactions! Remember it is better to take the largest plate within reach and fling it at a woman's head than it is to wriggle like a worm whenever she looks at you!"

He dropped his private manner and reverted to his lecture style.

"Could Carl Reiter have been goaded to such a pitch of torment that he turned on his tormentor and killed her? Suffering does queer things to a man. I could not be *sure* that it was *not* so!

"Next, William Coleman. His behavior, as reported by Miss Reilly, is certainly suspicious. If he was the criminal it could only be because his cheerful personality concealed the hidden one of William Bosner. I do not think William Coleman, as William Coleman, has the temperament of a murderer. His faults might lie in another direction. Ah! perhaps Nurse Leatheran can guess what they would be?"

"How *did* the man do it? I'm sure I didn't look as though I was thinking anything at all.

"It's nothing really," I said, hesitating. "Only if it's to be all truth, Mr. Coleman *did* say once himself that he would have made a good forger."

"A good point," said Poirot. "Therefore if he had come across some of the old threatening letters, he could have copied them without difficulty."

"Oy, oy, oy!" called out Mr. Coleman. "This is what they call a frame-up."

Poirot swept on.

"As to his being or not being William Bosner, such a matter is difficult of verification. But Mr. Coleman has spoken of a *guardian*—not of a father—and there is nothing definitely to veto the idea."

"Tommyrot," said Mr. Coleman. "Why all of you listen to this chap beats me."

"Of the three young men there remains Mr. Emmott," went on Poirot. "He again might be a possible shield for the identity of William Bosner. Whatever *personal* reasons he might have for the removal of Mrs. Leidner I soon realized that I should have no means of learning them from him. He could keep his own counsel remarkably well, and there was not the least chance of provoking him nor of tricking him into betraying himself on any point. Of all the expedition he seemed to be the best and most dispassionate judge of Mrs. Leidner's personality. I think that he always knew her for exactly what she was—but what impression her personality made on him I was unable to discover. I fancy that Mrs. Leidner herself must have been provoked and angered by his attitude.

"I may say that all of the expedition, *as far as character and capability were concerned,* Mr. Emmott seemed to me the most fitted to bring a clever and well-timed crime off satisfactorily."

For the first time Mr. Emmott raised his eyes from the toes of his boots.

"Thank you," he said.

There seemed to be just a trace of amusement in his voice.

"The last two people on my list were Richard Carey and Father Lavigny.

"According to the testimony of Nurse Leatheran and others, Mr. Carey and Mrs. Leidner disliked each other. They were both civil with an effort. Another person, Miss Reilly, propounded a totally different theory to account for their attitude of frigid politeness.

"I soon had very little doubt that Miss Reilly's explanation was the correct one. I acquired my certitude by the simple expedient of provoking Mr. Carey into reckless and unguarded speech. It was not difficult. As I soon saw, he was in a state of high nervous tension. In fact he was—and is—very near a complete nervous breakdown. A man who is suffering up to the limit of his capacity can seldom put up much of a fight.

"Mr. Carey's barriers came down almost immediately. He told me, with a sincerity that I did not for a moment doubt, that he hated Mrs. Leidner.

"And he was undoubtedly speaking the truth. He *did* hate Mrs. Leidner. But *why* did he hate her?

"I have spoken of women who have a calamitous magic. But men have that magic too. There are men who are able without the least effort to attract women. What they call in these days *le sex appeal!* Mr. Carey had this quality very strongly. He was to begin with being devoted to his friend and employer, and indifferent to his employer's wife. That did not suit Mrs. Leidner. She *must* dominate—and she set herself out to capture Richard Carey. But here, I believe, something entirely unforeseen took place. She herself, for perhaps the first time in her life, fell a victim to an overmastering passion. She fell in love—really in love—with Richard Carey.

"And he—was unable to resist her. Here is the truth of the terrible state of nervous tension that he has been enduring. He has been a man torn by two opposing passions. He loved Louise Leidner—yes, but he also hated her. He hated her for undermining his loyalty to his friend. There is no hatred so great as that of a man who has been made to love a woman against his will.

"I had here all the motive that I needed. I was convinced that *at certain moments* the most natural thing for Richard Carey to do would have been to strike with all the force of his arm at the beautiful face that had cast a spell over him.

"All along I had felt sure that the murder of Louise Leidner was a *crime passionnel*. In Mr. Carey I had found an ideal murderer for that type of crime.

"There remains one other candidate for the title of murderer—Father Lavigny. My attention was attracted to the good Father straightaway by a certain discrepancy between his description of the strange man who had been seen peering in at the window and the one given by Nurse Leatheran. In all accounts given by different witnesses there is usually *some* discrepancy, but this was absolutely glaring. Moreover, Father Lavigny insisted on a certain characteristic—a squint—which ought to make identification much easier.

"But very soon it became apparent that *while Nurse Leatheran's description was substantially accurate,* Father Lavigny's was *nothing of the kind.* It looked almost as though Father Lavigny was deliberately misleading us—as though he did *not want the man caught.*

"But in that case *he must know something about this curious person.* He had been seen talking to the man but we had only his word for what they had been talking about.

"What had the Iraqi been doing when Nurse Leatheran and Mrs. Leidner saw him? Trying to peer through the window—Mrs. Leidner's window, so they thought, but I realized when I went and stood where they had been, that it might equally have been *the antika-room window.*

"The night after that an alarm was given. Some one was in the antika-room. Nothing proved to have been taken, however. The interesting point to me is that when Dr. Leidner got there he found *Father Lavigny there before him.* Father Lavigny tells his story of seeing a light. *But again we have only his word for it.*

"I begin to get curious about Father Lavigny. The other day when I make the suggestion that Father Lavigny may be Frederick Bosner Dr. Leidner pooh-poohs the suggestion. He says Father Lavigny is a well-known man. I advance the supposition that Frederick Bosner, who has had nearly twenty years to make a career for himself, under a new name, may very possibly *be* a well-known man by this time! All the same, I do not think that he has spent the intervening time in a religious community. A very much simpler solution presents itself.

"Did any one at the expedition know Father Lavigny by sight before he came? Apparently not. Why then should not it be *some one impersonating the good Father?* I found out that a telegram had been sent to Carthage on the sudden illness of Dr. Byrd, who was to have accompanied the expedition. To intercept a telegram, what could be easier? As to the work, there was no other epigraphist attached to the expedition. With a smattering of knowledge a clever man *might* bluff his way through. There had been very few tablets and inscriptions so far, and already I gathered that Father Lavigny's pronouncements had been felt to be somewhat unusual.

"It looked very much as though Father Lavigny were an *impostor*.

"But was he Frederick Bosner?

"Somehow affairs did not seem to be shaping themselves that way. The truth seemed likely to lie in quite a different direction.

"I had a lengthy conversation with Father Lavigny. I am a practising Catholic and I know many priests and members of religious communities. Father Lavigny struck me as not ringing quite true to his rôle. But he struck me, on the other hand, as familiar in quite a different capacity. I *had* met men of his type quite frequently—but they were not members of a religious community. Far from it!

"I began to send off telegrams.

"And then, unwittingly, Nurse Leatheran gave me a valuable clue. We were examining the gold ornaments in the antika-room and she mentioned a trace of wax having been found adhering to a gold cup. Me, I say, 'Wax?' and Father Lavigny, he said 'Wax?' and his tone was enough! I knew in a flash exactly what he was doing here."

Poirot paused and addressed himself directly to Dr. Leidner.

"I regret to tell you, monsieur, that the gold cup in the antika-room, the gold dagger, the hair ornaments and several other things *are not the genuine articles found by you*. They are very clever electrotypes. Father Lavigny, I have just learned by this last answer to my telegrams, is none other than Raoul Menier, one of the cleverest thieves known to the French police. He specializes in thefts from museums of *objects d'art* and such like. Associated with him is Ali Yusuf, a semi-Turk, who is a first-class working jeweller. Our first knowledge of Menier was when certain objects in the Louvre were found not to be genuine—in every case it was discovered that a distinguished archæologist *not known previously by sight to the director* had recently had the handling of the spurious articles when paying a visit to the Louvre. On inquiry all these distinguished gentlemen denied having paid a visit to the Louvre at the times stated!

"I have learned that Menier was in Tunis preparing the way for a theft from the Holy Fathers when your telegram arrived. Father Lavigny, who was in ill-health, was forced to refuse, but Menier managed to get hold of the telegram and substitute one of acceptance. He was quite safe in doing so. Even if the monks should read in some paper (in itself an unlikely thing) that Father Lavigny was in Iraq they would only think that the newspapers had got hold of a half truth as so often happens.

"Menier and his accomplice arrived. The latter is seen when he is reconnoitering the antika-room from outside. The plan is for Father Lavigny to take wax impressions. Ali then makes clever duplicates. There are always certain collectors who are willing to pay a good price for genuine antiques and will ask no embarrassing questions. Father Lavigny will effect the substitution of the fake for the genuine article —preferably at night.

"And that is doubtless what he was doing when Mrs. Leidner heard him and gave the alarm. What can he do? He hurriedly makes up a story of having seen a light in the antika-room.

"That 'went down,' as you say, very well. But Mrs. Leidner was no fool. She may have remembered the trace of wax she had noticed and then put two and two together. And if she did, what will she do then? Would it not be *dans son caractère* to do nothing at once, but to enjoy herself by letting hints slip to the discomfiture of Father Lavigny. She will let him see that she suspects—but not that she *knows*. It is, perhaps, a dangerous game, but she enjoys a dangerous game.

"And perhaps she plays that game too long. Father Lavigny sees the truth, and strikes before she realizes what he means to do.

"Father Lavigny is Raoul Menier—a thief. Is he also—a *murderer?*"

Poirot paced the room. He took out a handkerchief, wiped his forehead and went on:

"That was my position this morning. There were eight distinct possibilities and I did not know which of these possibilities was the right one. I still did not know *who was the murderer*.

"But murder is a habit. The man or woman who kills once will kill again.

"And by the second murder, the murderer was delivered into my hands.

"All along it was ever present in the back of my mind that some one of these people might have knowledge that they had kept back —knowledge incriminating the murderer.

"If so, that person would be in danger.

"My solicitude was mainly on account of Nurse Leatheran. She had an energetic personality and a brisk inquisitive mind. I was terrified of her finding out more than it was safe for her to know.

"As you all know, a second murder did take place. But the victim was not Nurse Leatheran—it was Miss Johnson.

"I like to think that I should have reached the correct solution anyway by pure reasoning, but it is certain that Miss Johnson's murder helped me to it much quicker.

"To begin with, one suspect was eliminated—Miss Johnson herself —for I did not for a moment entertain the theory of suicide.

"Let us examine now the facts of this second murder.

"Fact one: On Sunday evening Nurse Leatheran finds Miss Johnson in tears, and that same evening Miss Johnson burns a fragment of a letter which nurse believes to be in the same handwriting as that of the anonymous letters.

"Fact two: The evening before her death Miss Johnson is found by Nurse Leatheran standing on the roof in a state that nurse describes as one of incredulous horror. When nurse questions her she says, 'I've seen how some one could come in from outside—and no one would ever guess.' She won't say any more. Father Lavigny is crossing the courtyard and Mr. Reiter is at the door of the photographic room.

"Fact three: Miss Johnson is found dying. The only words she can manage to articulate are 'the window—the window—'

"Those are the facts, and these are the problems with which we are faced:

"What is the truth of the letters?

"What did Miss Johnson see from the roof?

"What did she mean by 'the window—the window'?

"*Eh bien*, let us take the second problem first as the easiest of solution. I went up with Nurse Leatheran and I stood where Miss Johnson had stood. From there she could see the courtyard and the archway and the north side of the building and two members of the staff. Had her words anything to do with either Mr. Reiter or Father Lavigny?

"Almost at once a possible explanation leaped to my brain. If a stranger came in from *outside* he could only do so in *disguise*. And there was only *one* person whose general appearance lent itself to such an impersonation. Father Lavigny! With a sun helmet, sun glasses, black beard and a monk's long woollen robe, a stranger could pass in without the servants *realizing* that a stranger had entered.

"Was *that* Miss Johnson's meaning? Or had she gone further? Did she realize that Father Lavigny's whole *personality* was a disguise. That he was some one other than he pretended to be?

"Knowing what I did know about Father Lavigny I was inclined to call the mystery solved. Raoul Menier was the murderer. He had killed Mrs. Leidner to silence her before she could give him away. Now *another person lets him see that she has penetrated his secret*. She, too, must be removed.

"And so everything is explained! The second murder. Father Lavigny's flight—minus robe and beard. (He and his friend are doubtless careering through Syria with excellent passports as two commercial travellers.) His action in placing the blood-stained quern under Miss Johnson's bed.

"As I say, I was almost satisfied—but not quite. For the perfect solution must explain *everything*—and this does not do so.

"It does not explain, for instance, why Miss Johnson should say 'the window—the window,' as she was dying. It does not explain her fit of weeping over the letter. It does not explain her mental attitude on the roof—her incredulous horror and her refusal to tell Nurse Leatheran what it was that *she now suspected or knew*.

"It was a solution that fitted the *outer* facts, but it did not satisfy the *psychological* requirements.

"And then, as I stood on the roof, going over in my mind those three points: the letters, the roof, the window, I *saw*—just as Miss Johnson had seen!

"*And this time what I saw explained everything!*"

XXVIII
JOURNEY'S END

POIROT LOOKED ROUND. Every eye was now fixed upon him. There had been a certain relaxation—a slackening of tension. Now the tension suddenly returned.

There was something coming . . . something . . .

Poirot's voice, quiet and unimpassioned, went on:

"The letters, the roof, 'the window' . . . Yes, everything was explained—everything fell into place.

"I said just now that three men had alibis for the time of the crime. Two of those alibis I have shown to be worthless. I saw now my great —my amazing mistake. The third alibi was worthless too. Not only *could* Dr. Leidner have committed the murder—but I was convinced that he *had* committed it."

There was a silence, a bewildered uncomprehending silence. Dr. Leidner said nothing. He seemed lost in his far-away world still. David Emmott, however, stirred uneasily and spoke.

"I don't know what you mean to imply, M. Poirot. I told you that Dr. Leidner never left the roof until at least a quarter to three. That is the absolute truth. I swear it solemnly. I am not lying. And it would have been quite impossible for him to have done so without my seeing him."

Poirot nodded.

"Oh, I believe you. *Dr. Leidner did not leave the roof.* That is an undisputed fact. But what I saw—and what Miss Johnson had seen— was *that Dr. Leidner could murder his wife from the roof without leaving it.*"

We all stared.

"The *window*," cried Poirot. "*Her* window! That is what I realized —just as Miss Johnson realized it. Her window was directly underneath, on the side away from the courtyard. And Dr. Leidner was alone up there with no one to witness his actions. And those heavy stone querns and grinders were up there all ready to his hand. So simple, so very simple, granted one thing—that *the murderer had the oppor-*

tunity to move the body before any one else saw it. . . . Oh, it is beautiful—of an unbelievable simplicity!

"Listen—it went like this:

"Dr. Leidner is on the roof working with the pottery. He calls you up, Mr. Emmott, and while he holds you in talk he notices that, as usually happens, the small boy takes advantage of your absence to leave his work and go outside the courtyard. He keeps you with him ten minutes, then he let you go and as soon as you are down below shouting to the boy he sets his plan in operation.

"He takes from his pocket the plasticine-smeared mask with which he has already scared his wife on a former occasion and dangles it over the edge of the parapet till it taps on his wife's window.

"That, remember, is the window giving on the countryside facing the opposite direction to the courtyard.

"Mrs. Leidner is lying on her bed half asleep. She is peaceful and happy. Suddenly the mask begins tapping on the window and attracts her attention. But it is not dusk now—it is broad daylight—there is nothing terrifying about it. She recognizes it for what it is—a crude form of trickery! She is not frightened but indignant. She does what any other woman would do in her place. Jumps off the bed, opens the window, passes her head through the bars and turns her face upwards to see who is playing the trick on her.

"Dr. Leidner is waiting. He has in his hands, poised and ready, a heavy quern. At the psychological moment *he drops it.* . . .

"With a faint cry (heard by Miss Johnson) Mrs. Leidner collapses on the rug underneath the window.

"Now there is a hole in this quern, and through that Dr. Leidner had previously passed a cord. He has now only to haul in the cord and bring up the quern. He replaces the latter neatly, blood-stained side down, amongst the other objects of that kind on the roof.

"Then he continues his work for an hour or more till he judges the moment has come for the second act. He descends the stairs, speaks to Mr. Emmott and Nurse Leatheran, crosses the courtyard and enters his wife's room. This is the explanation he himself gives of his movements there.

" 'I saw my wife's body in a heap by the bed. For a moment or two I felt paralyzed as though I couldn't move. Then at last I went and knelt down by her and lifted up her head. I saw she was dead. . . . At last I got up. I felt dazed and as though I were drunk. I managed to get to the door and call out.'

"A perfectly possible account of the actions of a grief-dazed man. Now listen to what I believe to be the truth. Dr. Leidner enters the room, hurries to the window, and having pulled on a pair of gloves, closes and fastens it, then picks up his wife's body and transports it to a position between the bed and the door. Then he notices a slight stain on the window-side rug. He cannot change it with the other rug, they are a different size, but he does the next best thing. He puts the stained rug in front of the wash-stand and the rug from the wash-stand under the window. If the stain is noticed, it will be connected with the *wash-stand*—not with the *window*—a very important point. There must be no suggestion that the window played any part in this business. Then he comes to the door and acts the part of the overcome husband, and that, I imagine, is not difficult. For he *did* love his wife."

"My good man," cried Dr. Reilly impatiently, "if he loved her, why did he kill her? Where's the motive? Can't you speak, Leidner? Tell him he's mad."

Dr. Leidner neither spoke nor moved.

Poirot said:

"Did I not tell you all along that this was a *crime passionnel?* Why did her first husband, Frederick Bosner, threaten to kill her? Because he loved her. . . . And in the end, you see, he made his boast good. . . .

"*Mais oui—mais oui—once I realize that it is Dr. Leidner who did the killing* everything falls into place. . . .

"For the second time I recommence my journey from the beginning—Mrs. Leidner's first marriage—the threatening letters—her second marriage. The letters prevented her marrying any other man—but they did not prevent her marrying Dr. Leidner. How simple that is—*if Dr. Leidner is actually Frederick Bosner.*

"Once more let us start our journey—from the point of view this time of young Frederick Bosner.

"To begin with he loves his wife Louise with an overpowering passion such as only a woman of her kind can evoke. She betrays him. He is sentenced to death. He escapes. He is involved in a railway accident but he manages to emerge with a second personality—*that of a young Swedish archæologist, Eric Leidner,* whose body is badly disfigured and who will be conveniently buried as Frederick Bosner.

"What is the new Eric Leidner's attitude to the woman who was willing to send him to his death? First and most important, *he still loves her.* He sets to work to build up his new life. He is a man of great ability, his profession is congenial to him and he makes a success of it. *But he never forgets the ruling passion of his life.* He keeps himself informed of his wife's movements. Of one thing he is coldbloodedly determined (remember Mrs. Leidner's own description of him to Nurse Leatheran—gentle and kind but ruthless), *she shall belong to no other man.* Whenever he judges it necessary he despatches a letter. He imitates some of the peculiarities of her handwriting in case she should think of taking his letters to the police. Women who write sensational anonymous letters to themselves are such a common phenomenon that the police will be sure to jump to that solution given the likeness of the handwriting. At the same time he leaves her in doubt as to whether he is really alive or not.

"At last, after many years, he judges that the time has arrived; he re-enters her life. All goes well. His wife never dreams of his real identity. He is a well-known man. The upstanding, good-looking young fellow is now a middle-aged man with a beard and stooping shoulders. And so we see history repeating itself. As before, Frederick is able to dominate Louise. For the second time she consents to marry him. *And no letter comes to forbid the banns.*

"But *afterwards* a letter *does* come. Why?

"I think that Dr. Leidner was taking no chances. The intimacy of marriage *might* awaken a memory. He wishes to impress on his wife, once and for all, *that Eric Leidner and Frederick Bosner are two* different people. So much so that a threatening letter comes from the former on account of the latter. The rather puerile gas poisoning business follows—arranged by Dr. Leidner, of course. Still with the same object in view.

"After that he is satisfied. No more letters need come. They can settle down to happy married life together.

"And then, after nearly two years, *the letters recommence.*

"*Why?* Eh bien, I think I know. *Because the threat underlying the letters was always a genuine threat.* (That is why Mrs. Leidner has always been frightened. She *knew* her Frederick's gentle but ruthless nature.) *If she belongs to any other man but him he would kill her. And she has given herself to Richard Carey.*

"And so, having discovered this, cold-bloodedly, calmly, Dr. Leidner prepares the scene for murder.

"You see now the important part played by Nurse Leatheran? Dr. Leidner's rather curious conduct (it puzzled me at the very first) in securing her services for his wife is explained. It was vital that a reliable professional witness should be able to state incontrovertibly that Mrs. Leidner had been dead *over an hour* when her body was found—that is, that she had been killed at a time when *everybody could swear her husband was on the roof.* A suspicion *might* have arisen that he had killed her when he entered the room and found the body—but that was out of the question when a trained hospital nurse would assert positively that she had already been dead an hour.

"Another thing that is explained is the curious state of tension and strain that had come over the expedition this year. I never from the first thought that that could be attributed solely to *Mrs.* Leidner's influence. For several years this particular expedition had had a reputation for happy good-fellowship. In my opinion the state of mind of a community is always directly due to the influence of the man at the top. Dr. Leidner, quiet though he was, was a man of great personality. It was due to his tact, to his judgment, to his sympathetic manipulation of human beings that the atmosphere had always been such a happy one.

"If there was a change, therefore, the change must be due to the man at the top—in other words, to Dr. Leidner. It was *Dr.* Leidner, not Mrs. Leidner, who was responsible for the tension and uneasiness. No wonder the staff felt the change without understanding it. The kindly genial Dr. Leidner, outwardly the same, was only playing the part of himself. The real man was an obsessed fanatic plotting to kill.

"And now we will pass on to the second murder—that of Miss Johnson. In tidying up Dr. Leidner's papers in the office (a job she took on herself unasked, craving for something to do) she must have come on some unfinished draft of one of the anonymous letters.

"It must have been both incomprehensible and extremely upsetting to her! Dr. Leidner has been deliberately terrorizing his wife! She cannot understand it—but it upsets her badly. It is in this mood that Nurse Leatheran discovers her crying.

"I do not think at the moment that she suspected Dr. Leidner of being the murderer, but my experiments with sounds in Mrs. Leidner's and Father Lavigny's rooms are not lost upon her. She realized that if it *was* Mrs. Leidner's cry she heard, *the window in her room must have been open, not shut.* At the moment that conveys nothing vital to her, *but she remembers it.*

"Her mind goes on working—ferreting its way towards the truth. Perhaps she makes some reference to the letters which Dr. Leidner understands and his manner changes. She may see that he is, suddenly, afraid.

"But Dr. Leidner *cannot* have killed his wife! He was on the *roof* all the time.

"And then, one evening, as she herself is on the roof puzzling about it, the truth comes to her in a flash. Mrs. Leidner has been killed from up *here*, through the open window.

"It was at that minute that Nurse Leatheran found her.

"And immediately, her old affection reasserting itself, she puts up a quick camouflage. Nurse Leatheran must not guess the horrifying discovery she has just made.

"She looks deliberately in the opposite direction (towards the courtyard) and makes a remark suggested to her by Father Lavigny's appearance as he crosses the courtyard.

"She refuses to say more. She has got to 'think things out.'

"And Dr. Leidner, who has been watching her anxiously, *realizes that she knows the truth*. She is not the kind of woman to conceal her horror and distress from him.

"It is true that as yet she has not given him away—but how long can he depend upon her?

"Murder is a habit. That night he substitutes a glass of acid for her glass of water. There is just a chance she may be believed to have deliberately poisoned herself. There is even a chance she may be considered to have done the first murder and has now been overcome with remorse. To strengthen the latter idea he takes the quern from the roof and puts it under her bed.

"No wonder that poor Miss Johnson, in her death agony, could only try desperately to impart her hard-won information. Through 'the window,' *that* is how Mrs. Leidner was killed, *not* through the door—through the *window*. . . .

"And so thus, everything is explained, everything falls into place. . . . Psychologically perfect.

"But there is no proof. No proof at all. . . ."

None of us spoke. We were lost in a sea of horror. . . . Yes, and not only horror. Pity, too.

Dr. Leidner had neither moved nor spoken. He sat just as he had done all along. A tired, worn, elderly man.

At last he stirred slightly and looked at Poirot with gentle tired eyes.

"No," he said, "there is no proof. But that does not matter. You knew that I would not deny truth. . . . I have never denied truth . . . I think—really—I am rather glad . . . I'm so tired . . ."

Then he said simply:

"I'm sorry about Anne. That was bad—senseless—it wasn't *me!* And she suffered, too, poor soul. Yes, that wasn't me. It was fear. . . ."

A little smile just hovered on his pain-twisted lips.

"You would have made a good archæologist, M. Poirot. You have the gift of re-creating the past.

"It was all very much as you said.

"I loved Louise and I killed her . . . If you'd known Louise you'd have understood. . . . No, I think you understand anyway. . . ."

XXIX
L'ENVOI

THERE ISN'T REALLY any more to say about things.

They got "Father" Lavigny and the other man just as they were going on board a steamer at Beyrouth.

Sheila Reilly married young Emmott. I think that will be good for her. He's no door-mat—he'll keep her in her place. She'd have ridden roughshod over poor Bill Coleman.

I nursed him, by the way, when he had appendicitis a year ago. I got quite fond of him. His people were sending him out to farm in South Africa.

I've never been out East again. It's funny—sometimes I wish I could. I think of the noise the water-wheel made and the women washing, and that queer haughty look that camels give you—and I get quite a homesick feeling. After all, perhaps dirt isn't really so unhealthy as one is brought up to believe!

Dr. Reilly usually looks me up when he's in England, and as I said, it's he who's got me into this. "Take it or leave it," I said to him. "I know the grammar's all wrong and it's not properly written or anything like that—but there it is."

And he took it. Made no bones about it. It will give me a queer feeling if it's ever printed.

M. Poirot went back to Syria and about a week later he went home on the Orient Express and got himself mixed up in another murder. He was clever, I don't deny it, but I shan't forgive him in a hurry for pulling my leg the way he did. Pretending to think I might be mixed up in the crime and not a real hospital nurse at all!

Doctors are like that sometimes. Will have their joke, some of them will, and never think of *your* feelings!

I've thought and thought about Mrs. Leidner and what she was really like. . . . Sometimes it seems to me she was just a terrible woman—and other times I remember how nice she was to me and how soft her voice was—and her lovely fair hair and everything—and

I feel that perhaps, after all, she was more to be pitied than blamed. . . .

And I can't help but pity Dr. Leidner. I know he was a murderer twice over, but it doesn't seem to make any difference. He was so dreadfully fond of her. It's awful to be fond of any one like that.

Somehow, the more I get older, and the more I see of people and sadness and illness and everything, the sorrier I get for every one. Sometimes, I declare, I don't know what's become of the good strict principles my aunt brought me up with. A very religious woman she was, and most particular. There wasn't one of our neighbours whose faults she didn't know backwards and forwards. . . .

Oh, dear, it's quite true what Dr. Reilly said. How does one stop writing? If I could find a really good telling phrase.

I must ask Dr. Reilly for some Arab one.

Like the one M. Poirot used.

In the name of Allah, the Merciful, the Compassionate . . .

Something like that.